Swords of Riverside

ALSO BY ELLEN KUSHNER

Thomas the Rhymer
The Fall of the Kings (with Delia Sherman)

Swords of Riverside

Swordspoint
The Privilege of the Sword

Ellen Kushner

FANTASY

Published by arrangement with
The Bantam Dell Publishing Group
A Division of Random House, Inc.
1745 Broadway
New York, New York 10019

ISBN-13: 978-0-7394-7336-8

Visit the SFBC online at www.sfbc.com
Visit Bantam Books online at www.bantamdell.com

PRINTED IN THE UNITED STATES OF AMERICA

Swords of Riverside

CONTENTS

Swordspoint

A Melodrama of Manners

FOR MIMI

who was there from the beginning

Man desires that which is Good.

—PLATO

"We all have flaws," he said,
"and mine is being wicked."

—JAMES THURBER,
The Thirteen Clocks

In the end . . . everything will be found
to be true of everybody.

—LAWRENCE DURRELL,
Balthazar

Swordspoint

chapter I

Snow was falling on Riverside, great white feather-puffs that veiled the cracks in the façades of its ruined houses; slowly softening the harsh contours of jagged roof and fallen beam. Eaves were rounded with snow, overlapping, embracing, sliding into each other, capping houses all clustered together like a fairy-tale village. Little slopes of snow nestled in the slats of shutters still cozily latched against the night. It dusted the tops of fantastical chimneys that spiraled up from frosted roofs, and it formed white peaks in the ridges of the old coats of arms carved above the doorways. Only here and there a window, its glass long shattered, gaped like a black mouth with broken teeth, sucking snow into its maw.

Let the fairy tale begin on a winter's morning, then, with one drop of blood new-fallen on the ivory snow: a drop as bright as a clear-cut ruby, red as the single spot of claret on the lace cuff. And it therefore follows that evil lurks behind each broken window, scheming malice and enchantment; while behind the latched shutters the good are sleeping their just sleeps at this early hour in Riverside. Soon they will arise to go about their business; and one, maybe, will be as lovely as the day, armed, as are the good, for a predestined triumph. . . .

But there is no one behind the broken windows; only eddies of snow drift across bare floorboards. The owners of the coats of arms have long since abandoned all claims to the houses they crest, and moved up to the Hill, where they can look down on all the city. No king rules them any more, for good or ill. From the Hill, Riverside is a tiny splotch between two riverbanks, an unsavory quarter in a prosperous city. The people who live there now like to think of themselves as evil, but they're really no worse than anyone else. And already this morning more than one drop of blood has been shed.

The blood lies on the snow of a formal winter garden, now trampled and muddy. A man lies dead, the snow filling in the hollows of his eyes, while another man is twisted up, grunting, sweating frogponds on the frozen earth, waiting for someone to come and help him. The hero of this little tableau has just vaulted the garden wall and is running like mad into the darkness while the darkness lasts.

THE FALLING SNOW MADE IT HARD FOR HIM TO SEE. THE FIGHT hadn't badly winded him, but he was hot and sweaty, and he could feel his heart pounding in his chest. He ignored it, making for Riverside, where no one was likely to follow him.

He could have stayed, if he'd wanted to. The swordfight had been very impressive, and the party guests had been well entertained. The winter garden party and its outcome would be talked about for weeks. But if he stayed, the swordsman knew that he would be offered wine, and rich pastry, and asked boring questions about his technique, and difficult questions about who had arranged the fight. He ran on.

Under his cloak, his shirt was spattered with blood, and the Watch would want to know what he was doing up on the Hill at this hour. It was their right to know; but his profession forbade him to answer, so he dodged around corners and caught his breath in doorways until he'd left the splendors of the Hill behind, working his way down through the city. It was breaking dawn when he came to the river, flowing murky green under the Bridge. No one waited there to challenge him, so he set his foot on the stone, plowing through snowdrifts and the messy trails of other late-night workers who'd come before him, until he'd put the river safely between himself and the rest of the city. He stood now in Riverside, where the Watch never dared to come. People knew him here, and wouldn't bother him.

But when he opened the door to his landlady's, there was a considerable crowd assembled, all wanting to know about the fight. Other Riversiders had been on the Hill too, that night, burgling houses and collecting gossip, and already the rumors had begun. The swordsman answered their questions with as much civility as he could muster, suddenly awash with exhaustion. He gave Marie his shirt to wash, and climbed the stairs to his own rooms.

Less than an hour earlier, Marie the whore and laundress, who also rented out rooms by the week, had lain snoring lightly in the arms of a dear client, unaware of the impending excitement. Her friend was a sailor turned coiner, whose wooden leg leaned handily against the headboard. He was her fifth and last of the night, and she, not as young as she once was, slept through the initial pounding on her shutters. The sailor stirred uneasily, dreaming of storms. When the knock came harder, Marie bolted up with a cry, then shrieked at the cold outside the blanket.

"Marie! Marie!" The voice through the shutter was muffled but insistent. "Open up and tell us all about it!"

Marie sighed. It must be St Vier again: every time the swordsman got up to something they came to her to find out the details. This time, it was annoying to admit, she didn't know—but then, she didn't have to tell *them* that. With the laugh that had always made her popular, Marie got up and unbolted the door to the house.

Her sailor huddled in a corner of the bed while her friends trooped in, taking over the room with the ease of familiarity. It was the right room for socializing, having been the front parlor when the house was a noble's town house. The cherubs painted on the ceiling were flecked with mold; but most of the laurel-leaf molding still framed the walls, and the fireplace was real marble. Marie's friends spread their wet cloaks out on the gilded escritoire, now missing all its drawers, and over the turquoise velvet chair no one could sit on because of the uncertainty of its legs. Lightfinger Lucie coaxed the fire to a blaze, and Sam Bonner produced a jug of something that made the sailor feel much better.

"You know," said Sam ponderously, "your St Vier's gone and killed a duke this time."

Sam Bonner was a former pickpocket with an unhandy taste for the bottle. He'd been repeating the same thing for half an hour now, and his friends were getting tired of correcting him. "Not the *duke*, Sam," one of them tried again. "He's *working* for the duke. He killed two *swordsmen*, see, in the duke's garden."

"No, no, in Lord Horn's garden. *Three* swordsmen, I heard," another asserted, "and from a very reliable source. Two dead, one wounded, and I'm taking odds on whether he'll live till morning!"

"Done!"

Marie sat on the bed with the blankets wrapped around her feet, letting the betting and the squabbling swirl around her. "Who's dead?—Lynch—de Maris—Not a scratch on him—Horn's garden—Hired St Vier?—Not St Vier, Lynch—Wounded—Dying—Who's paying St Vier?—Horn—the duke—the devil—How much?—More'n *you'll* ever see—"

More people trickled in, adding to the clamor. "St Vier's been killed—captured—Five to one—"

They barely noticed when another man came in and silently took a place just inside the door. Sam Bonner was roaring, "Well, *I* say he's the best dam' swordsman in the whole dam' city! No, I'm lying—in the world!"

The young man by the doorway smiled, and said, "Excuse me. Marie?"

He was younger than most of them there; dark-haired, of average height, his face dirty and stubbled.

"Who the hell is that?" Sam Bonner growled.

"The best dam' swordsman in the world," Lightfinger Lucie answered with pardonable malice.

"I'm sorry to bother you," the swordsman said to Marie, "but you know how the stains set." He took off his cloak, revealing a white shirt ugly with blood. He pulled the shirt over his head, and tossed it into a corner. For a moment the iron tang of blood cut through the smells of whisky and wet wool. "I can pay you next week," he said. "I made some money."

"Oh, that's fine with me," Marie said with offhanded airiness, showing off.

He turned to go, but they stopped him with the shouting of his name: "St Vier!"

"St Vier! Who's dead, then?"

"De Maris," he answered curtly. "And maybe Lynch, by now. Excuse me, please."

No one reached out a hand to stop him as he walked through the door.

THE SMELL OF FRYING FISH MADE THE SWORDSMAN'S STOMACH lurch. It was his young gentleman, the University student, wrapped in his scholar's robe, hovering like a black bat over the frying pan in the ornamented fireplace.

"Good morning," St Vier said. "You're up early."

"I'm always up early, Richard." The student didn't turn around.

"You're the one who stays out all night killing people." His voice was its usual cool drawl, taunting in its nonchalance. The accent, with its crisp consonants and long vowels, took Richard back to the Hill: for a moment he was once again crouched amid the topiary of the pleasure garden, hearing the same tones ringing on the air from the party guests. "Who was the poor soul this time?"

"Just a couple of swordsmen. It was supposed to be a duel with Hal Lynch, I thought I told you. Our patrons set it up to take place at this crazy garden party of Lord Horn's. Can you imagine, having a party outdoors in this weather?"

"They would have had furs. And admired the landscaping."

"I suppose." While he spoke, the swordsman was cleaning his sword. It was a light, flexible dueling weapon of a sort only he, with his reputation and his reflexes, could carry around Riverside with authority. "Anyway, Lynch got started, and then de Maris popped out of the shrubbery and started coming at me."

"Whatever for?"

Richard sighed. "Who knows? He's Horn's house swordsman; maybe he thought I was attacking his master. Anyway, Lynch stepped aside, and I killed de Maris. He was out of practice," he added, polishing the blade with a soft cloth. "Lynch was good enough, he always has been. But our patrons wanted it past first blood, so I think I killed him. I *think*. . . ." He scowled. "It was a clumsy stroke. I slipped on some old ice."

The young man poked at the fish. "Do you want some?"

"No, thanks. I'm just going to bed."

"Well, it's revolting cold," the scholar said with satisfaction. "I shall have to eat it all myself."

"Do that."

St Vier passed into the adjoining room, which contained a clothes chest that also held his swords, wrapped in oilcloth, and a large, heavily carved bed. He had bought the bed the last time he had any money; seen it in a Riverside market stall full of odds and ends retrieved from the old houses, and fallen in love with it.

He looked at the bed. It did not appear to have been slept in. Curious, he returned to the front room.

"How was your night?" he asked. He noticed the pair of wet boots standing in the corner.

"Fine," the scholar answered, daintily picking bones out of his fish. "I thought you said you were tired."

"Alec," said Richard. "It really isn't safe for you to be going out alone here after dark. People get wild, and not everyone knows who you are yet."

"No one knows who I am." Alec dreamily laced his long fingers in his hair. His hair was fine and leaf-brown, worn down his back in the long tail that was the defiant emblem of University scholars. He had been in Riverside since autumn, and his clothes and his accent were the only signs of where he had come from. "Look." Alec's eyes, turned to the window, were dark and green, like the water under the Bridge. "It's still snowing. You can die in the snow. You're cold, but it doesn't hurt. They say you get warmer and warmer, and then you fall asleep. . . ."

"We can go out later. If anyone is trying to kill you, I'd better know about it."

"Why?"

"I can't let them," the swordsman said; "it would ruin my reputation." He yawned. "I hope at least you had your knife with you."

"I lost it."

"Again? Well, never mind. I can get you another when the money for the fight comes in." St Vier shook out his arms, and flexed them against the wall. "If I don't go to sleep soon, I'm going to start waking up, and then I'll feel rotten for the rest of the day. 'Night, Alec."

"Good night, Richard." The voice was low and amused; of course, it was morning. But he was much too tired to care. He placed his sword within reach of the bed, as he always did. As he drifted off, he seemed to see a series of white images, scenes carved in snow. Frosty gardens, their branches lush with white roses and crystal thorns; ladies with floating spun-sugar hair escorted by ivory gallants; and, for himself, opponents with long bright swords of clear and gleaming ice.

B Y MIDDAY, MOST OF THE NOBLES ON THE HILL COULD BE counted on to be awake. The Hill sat lordly above the rest of the city, honeycombed with mansions, landscaped lawns, elaborate gates, and private docks on the cleanest part of the river. Its streets had been built expressly wide and smooth enough to accommodate the carriages of nobles, shortly after carriages had been invented. Usually, mornings on the Hill were passed in leisurely exchange of notes written on colored, scented, and folded paper, read and composed in various states of dishabille over cups of rich chocolate and crisp little triangles of toast (all the nourishment that ought to be managed after a night's reveling); but on the morning after the garden duel, with the night's events ripe for comment, no one had the patience to wait for a reply, so the streets were unusually crowded with carriages and pedestrians of rank.

The Duke of Karleigh was gone from the city. From what anyone could discover, the duke had left Lord Horn's party not an hour after the fight, gone home, ordered up his carriage despite the snow, and departed before dawn for his estates in the south without a word to anyone. The first swordsman who had fought St Vier, a man named Lynch, had died at around ten that morning, so there was no asking him whether Karleigh had hired him for the duel, although the duke's abrupt departure upon Lynch's defeat seemed to confirm that he had. St Vier had disappeared back into Riverside, but whoever had hired him was expected to step forward momentarily to claim the stylish and elegant victory over Karleigh. So far, no one had.

Meanwhile, Lord Horn was certainly making enough of a fuss over the use his gardens had been put to, never mind the loss of his house swordsman, the impetuous de Maris; but that, as Lady Halliday remarked to the Duchess Tremontaine, meant precisely what it was supposed to mean. Horn was doubtless trying to coast on the notoriety that the event had given his otherwise unremarkable party for as long as possible. Both ladies had been there, along with most of the city's great aristocracy, many of whom Karleigh was known to have quarreled with at one time or another.

"At least," said the duchess, tilting her elegant head, "it seems to have rid us of my lord of Karleigh for the rest of the winter. I cannot commend his mysterious opponent too heartily for that service. Odious man. Do you know, Mary, how he insulted me last year? Well, it's just as well you don't; but I assure you I shall never forget it."

Mary, Lady Halliday, smiled at her companion. The two women were seated in the sunny morning room of the Halliday town house, drinking tiny cups of bitter chocolate. Both were clothed in billowing yards of soft, exquisite lace, giving them the look of two goddesses rising from the foam. Their heads, one brown and one silver-fair, were perfectly coiffed, their eyebrows finely plucked. The tips of their fingers, round and smooth, peeped continually through the lace like little pink shells.

"So," the duchess concluded, "it's no wonder someone finally got vexed enough to set St Vier on him."

"Not *on him*, precisely," Mary Halliday amended. "The duke was, after all, warned in time to find himself another swordsman to take the challenge."

"Pity," the duchess growled.

Lady Halliday poured out more chocolate, musing, "I wonder what it was all about. If it had been anything clever or amusing, the quarrel would not be kept such a secret—like poor Lynch's last duel, when Lord Godwin's eldest hired him to fight Monteith's champion over whose mistress was prettier. That was nice; but then, it wasn't to the death."

"Duels are to the death only when one of two things is at stake: power or money."

"What about honor?"

"What do you think honor buys?" the duchess asked cynically.

Lady Halliday was a quiet, shy young woman with none of her friend's fashionable talent for clever chatter. Her voice was generally low, her speech soft—just what men always claimed to want in a woman, but were never actually drawn to in the drawing room. However, her marriage to the widowed Basil, Lord Halliday, a popular city aristocrat, was said to have been a love match, so society was prepared to credit her with hidden depths. She was, in fact, by no means stupid, and if she answered the duchess with ponderous slowness it was only that she was, as was her habit, weighing her words against the thoughts behind them. "I think that *honor* is used to mean so many different things that no one can be sure of what it really is. Certainly young Monteith claimed his honor to be satisfied when Lynch won the fight, while privately Basil told me he thought the whole thing a pointless exercise in scandal."

"That is because young Monteith is an idiot, and your husband is a sensible man," the duchess said firmly. "I imagine Lord Halliday is much more pleased with this fight of Karleigh's; at least it accomplished something practical."

"More than that," said Lady Halliday. Her voice had dropped, and she leaned out a little over the furbelows of lace toward her friend. "He is immensely pleased that Karleigh has left town. You know the Council of Lords elects its head again this spring. Basil wishes to be re-elected."

"And quite rightly," Diane said stoutly. "He is the best Crescent Chancellor the city has had in decades—the best, some say, since the fall of the monarchy, which is generous praise indeed. Surely he expects no difficulty in being re-elected?"

"You are kind. Of course the city loves him . . . but . . . ." She leaned even closer, her porcelain cup held out of harm's way. "I must tell you. In fact there is a great deal of difficulty. My lord—Basil—has held the Crescent for three consecutive terms now. But it seems there's a law that no one may hold it for four straight terms."

"Is there?" said the duchess vaguely. "What a shame. Well, I'm sure that won't matter to anyone."

"My lord is hoping to put it to the vote in spring. The entire Council may choose to override the law in the case. But the Duke of Karleigh has been quietly approaching people all winter, reminding them of it, spreading all sorts of nonsense on the danger of too much power in the hands of one nobleman. As though my lord would take that power—as though he *could*, when he expends all his strength just keeping the state together!" Lady Halliday's cup rattled on its saucer; she steadied it and said, "You may see why my lord is pleased that Karleigh's gone, if only for a month or two."

"Yes," the duchess said softly; "I thought he might be."

"But Diane—" Suddenly Lady Halliday seized her hand in an eloquent hissing of lace. "It may not be enough. I am so concerned. He *must* keep the Crescent, he is just beginning to accomplish what he set out to do; to lose it now, even for a term, would be a terrible setback for him and for the city. You hold Tremontaine in your own right, you could vote in Council if you chose. . . ."

"Now, Mary . . ." Smiling, the duchess disengaged her hand. "You know I never meddle in politics. The late duke would not have wished it."

Whatever further entreaty Lady Halliday might have made was forestalled by the announcement of two more guests, the Godwins, who were shown up with the greatest dispatch.

It was unusual for Lady Godwin to be in town in winter; she was fond of the country and, being past that time of life when social duties required her presence in the city, spent most of her time with her husband overseeing the Godwins' great house and estates at Amberleigh. The responsibility of representing the family's interests in the city and on the Council of Lords fell to Lord Godwin's heir, his only son, Michael. Lord Michael's name was surrounded with the pleasing aura of scandal appropriate to a young noble who did not need to be too careful of what was said about him. He was an exceptionally attractive young man, and knew it. His liaisons were many, but always in good taste; they might be said to be his distinguishing social excess, as he eschewed those of gambling, quarreling, and dress.

Now he escorted his mother into the room, every inch the well-groomed, dutiful son. He had attended parties given by the duchess and by the Hallidays, but was not well enough acquainted himself with either lady to have visited her privately.

His mother was greeting her friends with kisses, all three women using each other's first names. He followed her with a proper bow and kiss of the hand, murmuring their titles. Diane of Tremontaine said over his bent head, "How charming to find a young man willing to call upon ladies at a decent hour and in conventional fashion."

"Barely decent," Mary Halliday amended, "with us still in our morning clothes."

"They are so lovely, you ought never change them," Lydia Godwin was saying to her; and to Diane, "Of course: he was very well brought up—and the city hasn't altered his breeding, whatever his father might say. I can trust you, can't I, Michael?"

"Of course, madam." Automatically he answered the tone of her voice. He had heard nothing since the duchess's comment, acid and piquant. He was surprised that a woman of her stature knew enough about his adventures to be able to make such a pointed remark, and was impressed with her audacity in making it in front of the others. The women were talking now, of the season, of his father's grain estates, as he swept his long-lashed gaze over her. She was beautiful, delicate and fair, with the true aristocrat's fragility that all fashionable city ladies strove to affect. He knew she must be closer to his mother's age than to his own. His mother had allowed herself to run to plumpness. It made her look comfortable; this lady looked entrancing. Suddenly Diane was meeting his look. She held it for a moment, unperturbed, before turning back to his mother and saying, "And now, no doubt, you are disgusted with yourself for having missed Horn's winter ball! I nearly had a headache myself at the last minute, but I'd already had the dress made, and where else is one going to wear white at this time of year? Poor Horn! I've heard that someone is saying that it was he himself who hired *both* swordsmen, just to entertain his guests!"

"Not a very kind 'someone,'" put in Lord Michael, "considering how his house swordsman teamed up with Master Lynch against St Vier—"

"Who still contrived to win!" his mother interrupted. "I do wish I'd seen it. I hear it's harder and harder to hire St Vier to fight for anyone." She sighed. "Swordsmen are getting so above themselves these days, from what I hear. When I first came to the city, I remember, there was a man named Stirling—one of the richest men on Teviot Street, with a big house and gardens—*he* was a swordsman, one of the greats, and he was paid accordingly. But no one had to *ask* him who he felt like fighting that particular day; you just sent him the money and he did the job."

"Mother," Michael teased her. "I never knew you had such a passion for swordplay! Shall I hire you St Vier for your birthday?"

"Now, who will he fight at Amberleigh? Don't be silly, my darling," she said fondly, patting his hand.

"Besides," Lady Halliday said, "chances are good that he doesn't *do* birthdays." Her friends looked startled at this pronouncement, coming from her. "Well, you've heard the story haven't you? About Lord Montague and his daughter's wedding?" To her dismay they said they hadn't, and she was obliged to begin: "She was his only daughter, you see, so he didn't mind the expense, he wanted to hire the best swordsman there was to take the part of the guard at the altar. . . . It was only last summer, you *must* have . . . Oh, well—St Vier had fought for Montague before, so he had the man up to his house—well, in his study, I imagine—to ask him properly, so no one would think there was anything shady going on—you know all you need before a wedding's people getting jumpy over swords—so Montague offered him the job, purely ceremonial, he wouldn't even have to *do* anything. And St Vier looked at him, pleasantly enough, Montague told us, and said, 'Thank you, but I don't do weddings any more.' "

Lady Godwin shook her head. "Imagine. Stirling did weddings; he did Julia Hetley's, I remember it. I wanted him to do mine, but he was dead then. I forget who we got instead."

"My lady," said Michael, with that impish grin she had always found irresistible, "shall I take up the sword to please you? I could add to the family fortunes."

"As though they needed adding to," the duchess said dryly. "I suppose you could save yourself the expense of hiring a swordsman to fight your inevitable romantic quarrels, my lord. But aren't you a little old to be able to take it up successfully?"

"*Diane!*" his mother gurgled. This once he was grateful for her quick intercession. He was fighting back a blush, one of the drawbacks of his fair complexion. The lady was too personal, she presumed upon acquaintance with his mother to mock him. . . . He was not used to women who did not care to please him. "Michael, you are a perfect goose even to think of such a thing, and, Diane, you must not encourage him to quarrel, I'm sure his friends are bad enough. Oh, yes, no doubt Lord Godwin would be delighted to hear of his heir taking up the sword like any common street brawler. We saw to it that you had all the training you needed when you were a boy. You carry a pettysword nicely, you can dance without catching your legs in it, and that should be enough for any gentleman."

"There's Lord Arlen," Lady Halliday said. "You can't say *he's* not a gentleman."

"Arlen is an eccentric," Lady Godwin said firmly, "and notably old-fashioned. I'm sure no young man of Michael's set would even consider such a thing."

"Surely not, Lydia," the exquisite duchess was saying consolingly. "And Lord Michael a man of such style, too." To his surprise she smiled at him, warmly and directly. "There are men I know who would go to any lengths to annoy their parents. How fortunate you are, Lydia, in having a son you may trust always to do you credit. I am sure he could never be any more serious about taking up the sword than something equally ridiculous . . . University, for instance."

The talk turned to notorious sons, effectively shutting Michael out from contributing to it. Another time he might have listened avidly and with some amusement as they discussed various of his friends and acquaintances, so that he could store up anecdotes to repeat at card parties. But although no trace of it showed in his pleasant bearing and handsome face, Lord Michael was feeling increasingly sullen, and wondering how he might possibly leave without offending his mother, whom he had promised to accompany on all her calls that day. The company of women, making no effort to include him, made him feel, not so much as if he were a child again—for he had been a very fetching child, and adults had always stopped to notice him—but as though he had wandered into a cluster of foreigners, all chattering with animation in another language; or as though he were a ghost in the room, or a piece of useless and uninteresting furniture. Even the alluring duchess, though clearly not unaware of his interest, failed to be entirely concerned with him. At present, for example, she seemed to be much more taken with a series of stories his mother was telling about one of his lunatic cousins. Perhaps he might see her again soon, in better circumstances—only to renew the acquaintance, of course; his current lover's possessiveness he found exciting, and was not yet ready to give up.

Finally, they returned to the more interesting question of whether Lord Horn had had anything to do with the fighting in his gardens. Michael was able to say sagely, "Well, I hope the suggestion will not get back to Horn's ears. He's liable to become offended and hire himself another swordsman to take care of the rumormongers."

The duchess's fine eyebrows rose in twin arcs. "Oh? Are you intimately acquainted with the gentleman and his habits?"

"No, madam," he answered, covering his discomfort at her challenge with a show of surprise. "But I know him to *be* a gentleman; I do not think he would readily brook the suggestion that he had intentionally set two swordsmen against one, whether in private quarrel or to please his guests."

"Well, you're probably right there," she conceded; "whether he actually did so or not. Horn has been so careful of his reputation these last few years—he'd probably deny stealing honey if his fingers were caught in the jar. He was much more agreeable when he still had something to occupy his time."

"Surely he is as busy now as any nobleman?" Lady Halliday asked, sure she was missing some vital connection. Lydia Godwin said nothing, but scowled at her knuckles.

"Of course," Diane said generously, "you were not yet come to the city then, Mary. Dear, how gossip will trip us up! You will not know that some years past Lord Horn was the reigning beauty. He managed to capture the eyes of Lord Galing, God rest him, who was at the time gaining power in the Council, but didn't quite know what to do with it all. Horn told him. They were a strong combination for a while, Horn with his ambition, and Galing with his talent. I feared—along with my husband, of course—that Galing would be made Chancellor. But Galing died, not a moment too soon, and Horn's influence has faded. I'm sure it galls him. It's probably why he insists on giving such showy parties. His star has definitely fallen: he lacks the coin for further extravagant purchases. Not, of course, that Lord Halliday would wish for any distracting influence!"

Mary Halliday smiled prettily, her color reflecting the rose ribbons on her cap. Lady Godwin looked up and said a trifle brusquely, "Why is it, Diane, that you seem to know the single most unpleasant story about everyone in the city?"

"I suppose," she answered blithely, "because there are so many unpleasant people. How right you are to stay at Amberleigh, my dear."

In despair Michael thought: If they start on about the family again, I shall fall off my chair. He said, "I've been thinking, actually, about Karleigh." The duchess favored him with her attention. Her eyes were the frosty silver of winter clouds. He felt a delicate shiver as they brushed over him.

"You are quite sure, then," she said, in a low, melodious voice, "that it was the duke who hired Lynch?" It was as though she had said something quite different, for his ears alone. His lips were lightly parted; and at last he saw, looking at her, his own beauty reflected there. But before he could answer, his mother cried, "Of course it was Karleigh! Why else would he leave town first thing this morning, making no excuses to anyone—unless he left a note for Horn apologizing for the use his garden was put to . . ."

"Not his style," observed the duchess.

"Then it is clear," Lady Godwin said triumphantly, "that he *had* to get out of the city. His man lost the fight! And St Vier may still be in the pay of his opponent. If Karleigh stayed, he might have to keep hiring other swordsmen to go up against St Vier, until he ran out of money, or talent. And then he'd be up against St Vier himself—and then, you know, he'd surely be dead. The duke doesn't know any more of swordplay than Michael, I'm sure."

"But I am sure," the duchess said, again with that strange double-edged tone, "that Lord Michael would know what to do with it if he did."

Something fluttered at the base of his spine. Resolutely he took control of the conversation. He turned directly to the duchess, speaking assertively, summoning all the confidence of a man used to having his opinions heeded. "As a matter of fact, madam, I am *not* sure that the Duke of Karleigh hired Lynch. I was wondering whether it were not just as likely that he had hired St Vier instead."

"Oh, Michael," said his mother impatiently. "Then why would Karleigh have left town when his man *won?*"

"Because he was still afraid of the person who did hire Lynch."

"Interesting," said the duchess. Her silvery eyes seemed to grow bigger, like a cat's. "And not altogether impossible. Your son, Lydia, would seem to have a far more complex grasp of the situation than any of us."

Her eyes had turned from him, and the mocking disdain was back in her voice. But he had had her for a moment—had her interest, had her seeing him entirely. He wondered what he had done to lose her.

The door to the morning room opened, and a tall, broad-framed man came in unannounced. A sense of exertion and the outdoors hung about him: his dark hair was ruffled all over his head, and his handsome face was high-colored by the wind. Unlike Michael, with his tight-fitting, pastel costume, this man wore loose, dark clothes, with mud-splashed boots up to his thighs.

Mary Halliday's face transformed with brightness when she saw him. Being a good hostess and a well-mannered woman, she stayed seated amongst her guests; but her bright eyes never left her husband.

Basil, Lord Halliday, Crescent Chancellor of the Council of Lords, bowed to his wife's company, a smile creasing his weathered face.

She spoke to him formally. "My lord! We did not expect you back so soon as this."

His smile deepened with mischief and affection. "I know," he answered, coming to kiss both her hands. "I came home directly, before even going to report to Ferris. I should have remembered that you'd have company."

"Company is delighted to see you," said the Duchess Tremontaine, "although I'm sure Lady Halliday is more so. She wouldn't admit it, but I believe the thought of you riding out to Helmsleigh alone to face a cordon of rebellious weavers unsettled her equilibrium."

Halliday laughed. "I was hardly alone. I took a troop of City Guard with me to impress them."

His wife caught his eyes, asking seriously, "How did it go?"

"Well enough," he answered her. "They have some legitimate complaints. Foreign wool has been driving prices down, and the new tax is hard on the smaller communes. I'll have to take it up with my lord Ferris. I'll tell you all about it, but not till afterward, or the Dragon Chancellor will be annoyed for not having been the first to hear."

Lady Halliday frowned. "I still think Ferris should have gone instead. The Exchequer is his concern."

He sent her a brief glance of warning before saying lightly, "Not at all! What is a mere Dragon Chancellor when compared with the head of the entire Council of Lords? This way they were flattered, and felt that enough attention was being paid to them. Now, when I send Chris Nevilleson out to take a full report, they'll be nice to him. I think the matter should be settled soon."

"Well, I should think so!" said Lady Godwin. "Imagine some pack of weavers raising their shuttles against a Council order."

Michael laughed, thinking of his friend riding out to Helmsleigh on one of his fine horses. "Poor Chris! Why do you assign him all the most unpleasant tasks, my lord?"

"He volunteers. I believe he wishes to be of service."

"He adores you, Basil," Lady Halliday said brightly. Michael Godwin raised his eyebrows, and the color rushed into her face. "Oh, no! I mean . . . he admires Lord Halliday . . . his work . . ."

"Anyone would," said the duchess comfortably. "I adore him myself. And if I wished to advance to any political power, I should most certainly station myself at his side." Her friend smiled gratefully at her over the rim of the chocolate cup behind which she had taken refuge. And Michael felt, in consternation, that he had just been measured and found wanting. "In fact," the duchess continued blithely, "I have been grieving over how seldom I see him—or any of you—when not surrounded by other admirers. Let us all dine together privately a few weeks from today. You have heard of Steele's fireworks? He's sending them off over the river to celebrate his birthday. It promises to be quite a show. Of course I told him it was the wrong time of year, but he said he couldn't change his birthday to suit the weather, and he has always been uncommonly fond of fireworks. They will entertain the populace, and give the rest of us something to do. So we're all to dust off our summer barges and go out on the river and enjoy ourselves. Mine will certainly hold us all, and I believe my cook can put together a tolerable picnic; if we all dress up warmly it won't be so bad." She turned her charming smile on Basil Halliday. "I shall invite Lord Ferris, my lord, only if you two promise not to spend the whole evening talking politics . . . and Chris Nevilleson and his sister, I think. Perhaps I had better include a few other young men, to ensure that Lord Michael has someone to talk to."

Michael's flush of embarrassment lasted through the chatter of thanks. He was able to cover it by straightening his hose. A fall of lace cuff brushed his cheek as the duchess stood by his mother saying, "Oh,

Lydia, what a shame, to have to leave town so soon! I hope Lord Michael will be able to represent you at my picnic?" He stopped before he could begin to stammer something out, and simply rose and offered her his seat by his mother. She sank into it with a willow's grace, and looked up at him, smiling. "You will come, will you not, my lord?"

Michael squared his shoulders, sharply aware of the close fit of his jacket, the hang of his sleeves. Her offered hand lay on his like a featherweight, soft, white, and elusively perfumed. He was careful only to brush it with his lips. "Your servant, madam," he murmured, looking straight up into her eyes.

"Such manners." The duchess returned the look. "What a delightful young man. I shall expect you, then."

chapter III

RICHARD ST VIER, THE SWORDSMAN, AWOKE LATER THAT DAY, in the middle of the afternoon. The house was quiet and the room was cold. He got up and dressed quickly, not bothering to light the bedroom fire.

He stepped softly into the other room, knowing which floorboards were likely to creak. He saw the top of Alec's head, nestled into a burlap-covered chaise longue he was fond of because it had griffins' heads carved into the armrests. Alec had built up the fire and drawn the chair up close to it. Richard thought Alec might be asleep; but then he saw Alec's shoulder shift and heard the crackle of paper as he turned the pages of a book.

Richard limbered up against the wall for a while, then took up a blunt-tipped practice sword and began to attack the chipped plaster wall with it, striking up and down an imaginary line with steady, rhythmic precision. There was a counterattack from the other side of the wall: three blows from a heavy fist caused their remaining flakes of paint to tremble.

"*Will you shut that racket up?*" a voice demanded through the wall.

Richard put his sword down in disgust. "Hell," he said, "they're home."

"Why don't you kill them?" the man in the chair asked lazily.

"What for? Marie'd only replace them with some more. She needs the rent money. At least this bunch doesn't have babies."

"True." One long leg and then another swung out from the chaise to plant themselves on the floor. "It's midafternoon. The snow has stopped. Let's go out."

Richard looked at him. "Anywhere special?"

"The Old Market," said Alec, "might be entertaining. If you're still in the mood, after those other two."

Richard got a heavier sword, and buckled it on. Alec's ideas of "entertaining" were violent. His blood began to race, not unpleasantly. People had learned not to bother him; now they must learn the same about Alec. He followed him into the winter air, which was cold and sharp like a hunting morning.

The streets of Riverside were mostly deserted at this time of day, and a thick snow cover muffled what sounds there were. The oldest houses were built so close together that their eaves almost touched across the street, eaves elaborately carved, throwing shadows onto the last flakes of painted coats of arms on the walls below them. No modern carriage could pass between the houses of Riverside; its people walked, and hid in the twisting byways, and the Watch never followed them there. The nobles drove their well-sprung carriages along the broad, sunlit avenues of the upper city, leaving their ancestors' houses to whomever chose to occupy them. Most would be surprised to know how many still held deeds to Riverside houses; and few would be eager to collect the rent.

Alec sniffed the air. "Bread. Someone's baking bread."

"Are you hungry?"

"I'm always hungry." The young man pulled his scholar's robe tighter around him. Alec was tall, and a little too thin, with none of the swordsman's well-sprung grace. With the layers of clothes he had piled on underneath the robe, he looked like a badly wrapped package. "Hungry and cold. It's what I came to Riverside for. I got tired of the luxurious splendor of University life. The magnificent meals, the roaring fires in the comfy lecture halls . . ." A gust of wind whipped powdered snow off a roof and into their faces. Alec cursed with a student's elaborate fluency. "What a stupid place to live! No wonder anyone with any sense left here long ago. The streets are a perfect wind tunnel between the two rivers. It's like asking to be put in cold-storage. . . . I hope they're paying you soon for that idiotic duel, because we're almost out of wood and my fingers are turning blue as it is."

"They're paying me," Richard answered comfortably. "I can pick up the money tomorrow, and buy wood on the way home." Alec had been complaining of the cold since the first ground-frost. He kept their rooms hotter than Richard ever had, and still shivered and wrapped himself in blankets all day. Whatever part of the country he came from, it was probably not the northern mountains, and not the house of a poor man. All evidence so far of Alec's past was circumstantial: things like the fire, and the accent, and his inability to fight, all spoke nobility. But at the same time he had no money, no known people or title, and the University gown hung on his slumped shoulders as though it belonged there. The University was for poor scholars, or clever men hoping to better themselves and acquire posts as secretaries or tutors to the nobility.

Richard said, "Anyway, I thought you won lots of money off Rodge the other night, dicing."

"I did." Alec loosed one edge of his cloak to make sweeping gestures with his right hand. "He won it back from me next night. In fact I owe him money; it's why we're not going to Rosalie's."

"It's all right; he knows I'm good for it."

"He cheats," Alec said. "They all cheat. I don't know how you can cheat with straight dice, but as soon as I find out I'm going to get rich off Rodge and all his smelly little friends."

"Don't," said Richard. "That's for these types, not for you. You don't have to cheat, you're a gentleman."

As soon as it was out he knew it had been the wrong thing to say. He could feel Alec's tension, almost taste the blue coldness of the air between them. But Alec only said, "A gentleman, Richard? What nonsense. I'm just a poor student who was stupid enough to spend time with my books when I could have been out drinking and learning how to load dice."

"Well," St Vier said equably, "you're certainly making up for it now."

"Aren't I just." Alec smiled with grim pleasure.

The Old Market wasn't old, nor was it properly a market. A square of once-elegant houses had been gutted at the ground floor, so that each house opened at the front. The effect was like a series of little boxed stage sets, each containing a fire and a group of Riversiders crowded around it, their hands stuffed under their armpits or held out to the fire, engaged in what could only loosely be termed marketing: a little dicing, a little flirting, drinking, and trying to sell each other stolen objects, shifting from foot to foot in the cold.

In front of one of them Alec suddenly stopped. "Here," he said. "Let's go in here."

There was nothing to distinguish this one from any of the others. Richard followed him to the fire. Alec's movements were languid, with a studied grace that the swordsman's eye recognized as the burden of feverish tension held in check. Other people noticed it too, though what they made of it was hard to say. Riverside was used to odd-looking people with odd moods. The woman nearest Alec moved nervously away, yielding her proximity to the fire. Across it a short man with a rag twisted around his sandy hair looked up from casting dice.

"Well, look who's here," he said in a soft whine. "Master Scholar." A long gleam of metal slid from his side to his hand. "I thought I told you last night I didn't want to see your face again."

"Stupid face," Alec corrected with airy condescension. "You said you didn't want to see my *stupid* face *around* here again." Someone giggled nervously. People had edged away from the dicer with the drawn sword. Without turning his head the man reached his free hand behind him and caught a small, pretty woman's wrist. He reeled her in to his side like a fish on a line, and held her there, fondling one breast. His eyes above her head dared anyone to react.

"That's good," Alec said with lofty sarcasm. "I used to know a man who could name any card you pulled from the deck without looking."

"That's good." The man mimicked his accent. "Is that what they teach you at University, scholar, card tricks?"

The muscles tautened around Alec's mouth. "They don't teach anyone anything at University. I had to learn to recognize people with duckshit for brains all by myself. But I think I'm pretty good at it, don't you?"

The girl squeaked when her captor's arm crushed her bosom. "You're going to be gone," he growled at Alec, "by the time I count three." Spit flecked the corner of his mouth.

Behind them the voices were murmuring, "Six says he's gone by two . . . by three . . . Six says he stays. . . ."

Alec stood where he was, his head cocked back, considering the other down the length of his nose. "One," the man counted. "Two."

"*Move*, you stupid clown!" someone cried. "Brent'll kill you!"

"But I have to stay and help him," Alec said with polite surprise. "You can see he's stuck for the next one. It's 'three,' " he told him kindly. "The one after 'two.' "

Brent flung the girl aside. "Draw," he growled, "if you've got a sword."

The thin man in the scholar's robe raised his eyebrows. "What if I haven't?"

"Well." Brent came slowly around the fire with a swordsman's sure step. "That would be a shame."

He was halfway to the scholar when a bystander spoke up. "My fight," he said clearly, so everyone heard.

Brent looked him over. Another swordsman. Harder to kill, but better for his reputation. "Fine," he purred in his insinuating whine. "I'll take care of you first, and then finish off Mister Scholar, here."

Richard slung his cloak around one arm. A woman near him looked at his face and gasped, "St Vier!" Now the word was out; people were jostling to see; bets were changing. Even as they pressed back to the walls to give the fighters room, the spectators were agitating; a few slipped out to fetch friends to watch the fight. Newcomers crowded across the open house-front.

Richard ignored them all. He was aware of Alec, safe to one side, his eyes wide and bright, his posture negligent.

"There's your third for today," Alec said pleasantly. "Kill him."

Richard began as he usually did, running his opponent through some simple attacks, parrying the counterattack almost absently. It did give the other the chance to assess him as well, but usually that only served to unnerve them. Brent was quick, with a good swordsman's sixth sense for what was coming next; but his defense was seriously weaker on the left, poor fool. Enough practice on some good drills could have got him over that. Richard pretended he hadn't noticed, and played to his right. Aware that he was being tested, Brent tried to turn the fight so that he led the attack. Richard didn't let him. It flustered Brent; trying harder to gain control, he began to rush his counters, as though by coming in fast enough he could surprise St Vier into defense.

The swords were clashing rapidly now. It was the kind of fight spectators liked best: lots of relentless follow-through, without too much deliberation before each new series of moves. The woman Brent had been holding watched, cursing slowly and methodically under her breath, her fingers knotted together. Others were louder, calling encouragement, bets, and enlightened commentary, filling each other in on the background of the fight.

Through his shield of concentration Richard heard the voices, though not the words they spoke. As the fight went on and he absorbed Brent's habits, he began to see not a personality but a set of obstructions to be removed. His fighting became less playful, more single-minded. It was the one thing knowledgeable spectators faulted him for: once he knew a man he seldom played him out in a show of technique, preferring to finish him off straightaway.

Twice Richard passed up the chance to touch Brent's left arm. He wasn't interested in flesh wounds now. Other swordsmen might have made the cut for the advantage it would have given them; but the hallmark of St Vier's reputation was his ability to kill with one clean death wound. Brent knew he was fighting for his life. Even the on-lookers were silent now, listening to the panting men's breath, the scrape of their boots, and the clang of their swords. Over the heavy silence, Alec's voice drawled clearly, "Didn't take long to scare *him*, did it? Told you I could spot them."

Brent froze. Richard beat hard on his blade, to remind him of where he was. Brent's parry was fierce; he nearly touched St Vier's thigh countering, and Richard had to step back. His heel struck rock. He found he was backed against one of the stones surrounding the fire. He hadn't meant to lose that much ground; Alec had distracted him as well. He was already so hot he didn't feel the flames; but he was determined to preserve his boots. He dug in his back heel, and exchanged swordplay with Brent with his arm alone. He applied force, and nearly twisted the sword out of the other man's grasp. Brent paused, preparing another attack, watching him carefully for his. Richard came in blatantly low on the left, and when Brent moved to his defense St Vier came up over his arm and pierced his throat.

There was a flash of blue as the sword was pulled from the wound. Brent had stiffened bolt upright; now he toppled forward, his severed windpipe wheezing with gushing blood and air. Alec's face was pale, without expression. He looked down at the dying man long and hard, as though burning the sight into his eyes.

Amid the excitement of the fight's consummation, Richard stepped outside to clean his sword, whirling it swiftly in the air so that the blood flew off its surface and onto the snow.

One man came up to Alec. "That was some fight," he said friendlily. "You rig it?"

"Yes."

He indicated the swordsman outside. "You going to tell me that young fellow's really St Vier?"

"Yes."

Alec seemed numbed by the fight, the fever that had driven him sated by the death of his opponent, drugged now to a sluggish peace. But when St Vier came back in he spoke in his usual sardonic tones: "Congratulations. I'll pay you when I'm rich."

There was still one more thing to be done, and Richard did it. "Never mind," he said clearly, for those nearby to hear. "They should know to leave you alone."

He crossed to Alec by the fire, but a tiny woman, the one Brent had held, planted herself in front of him. Her eyes were red, her face pale and blotchy. She stared up at the swordsman and began to stutter furiously.

"What is it?" he asked.

"You owe me!" she exploded at last. "Thhh-that man's ddd-dead and where'll I find another?"

"The same place you found him, I expect."

"What'll I do for mm-money?"

Richard looked her up and down, from her painted eyes to her gaudy stockings, and shrugged. She turned her shoulder in toward his chest and blinked up at him. "I'm nice," she squeaked. "I'd work for you."

Alec sneered at the little woman. "I'd trip over you. We'd keep stepping on you in the dark."

"Go away," said Richard. "I'm not a pimp."

She stamped her small foot. "You bastard! Riverside or no, I'll have the Watch on you!"

"You'd never go near the Watch," said Richard, bored. "They'd have you in the Chop before you could open your mouth." He turned back to his friend. "God, I'm thirsty. Let's go."

They got as far as the doorway this time before Richard was stopped by another woman. She was a brilliant redhead of alarming prettiness, her paint expertly applied. Her cloak was of burgundy velvet, artfully draped to hide the worn spot. She placed her fingertips on Richard's arm, standing closer to him than he generally allowed. "That was superb," she said with throaty intimacy. "I was so glad I caught the ending."

"Thank you," he replied courteously. "I appreciate it."

"Very good," she pronounced. "You gave him a fair chance, didn't keep him on the hook too long."

"I've learned some good tricks by letting them show me what they can do first."

She smiled warmly at him. "You're no fool. You've got better every year. There's no stopping you from getting what you want. I could—"

"Excuse me," Alec interrupted from the depths of boundless ennui, "but who is this?"

The woman turned and swept him with her long lashes. "I'm Ginnie Vandall," she said huskily. "And you?"

"My name is Alec." He stared down at the tassels on her hem. "Who pimps for you?"

The carmined lips pressed into a thin line, and the moment for a biting retort came and went. Knowing it was gone, she turned again to Richard, saying solicitously, "My dear, you must be famished."

He shrugged polite disavowal. "Ginnie," he asked her, "is Hugo working now?"

She made a practiced moue and looked into his eyes. "Hugo is always working. He's gone so much I begin to wonder why I stay with him. They adore him on the Hill—too much, I sometimes think."

"Nobody adores Richard," Alec drawled. "They're always trying to get him killed."

"Hugo's a swordsman," Richard told him. "He's very good. Ginnie, when you see him tell him he was perfectly right about Lynch's right cut. It was very helpful last night."

"I wish I could have seen it."

"So do I. Most of them didn't know what was happening till it was over. Alec, don't you want to eat? Let's go." Briskly he steered a way back onto the street, through the blood-flecked snow. Sam Bonner rolled boozily up and past them, forgetting his objective at the sight of the velvet-clad woman standing abandoned in the doorway.

"Ginnie, lass! How's the prettiest ass in Riverside?"

"Cold," Ginnie Vandall snapped, "you stupid sot."

chapter IV

L ord Michael Godwin had never imagined that he would actually be escaping down a drainpipe, but here it was, the stuff of cheap comedy, clutched in his freezing hands. In fact, all of him was freezing: clever, quick-thinking Olivia, with not a moment to spare, had flung all evidence of his presence—which was to say, his clothes—out of the window, and instructed him to follow. He was wearing only his long white shirt, and, ridiculously, his velvet hat, jeweled and feathered, which he had somehow contrived to snatch off the bedpost at the first knock on the chamber door.

He made a point of not looking down. Above him, the stars shone frosty and remote in the clear sky. They wouldn't dare to twinkle at him, not in the position he was in. His hands were freezing on the lead pipe of the Rossillion town house. He'd remembered it as being covered with ivy; but the latest fashion called for severity and purity of line, so the ivy had been stripped last autumn. Just above his hands Olivia's window glowed temptingly golden. Michael sent out a desolate haze of frosty breath, and began letting himself down.

He ought to be grateful for the escape, he knew that, grumbling as he collected his clothes from the frozen ground, resisting the desire to hop from foot to foot. He shoved his feet into his boots, crumpling the doe-soft leather, even as he still hunted for his stockings. His shaking hands made it unusually hard to fasten the various catches and laces of a nobleman's evening dress—I should always remember to bring a bodyservant along on these expeditions, he thought whimsically;

have him waiting right below the appropriate window with a flask of hot wine and gloves!

Olivia's window was still alight, so Bertram was still there, and doubtless would remain for hours yet. Blessed Olivia! Lord Michael finally managed to squeeze out the benison between chattering teeth. Bertram might have tried to kill him if he'd found him there. Bertram was the jealous type, and Michael had been leading him a dance all evening. He had a moment of panic when he discovered that one of his monogrammed embroidered gloves was missing; he imagined the scene the next day, when Bertram found it perched jauntily among the ailanthus branches under the window: *Hello, my angel, what's this doing here? Oh, heavens, I must have dropped it when I was checking the wind direction. . . .* Then he discovered it, stuffed up one of his voluminous sleeves, Lord knew how it had got there.

As dressed as he was going to be, Michael prepared to disappear. Despite all the wool and brocade he was still shivering; he'd managed to work up quite a sweat upstairs, and the sudden plunge into a winter night had turned it to ice on his skin. He damned Bertram roundly, hoping his turn in hell would be one long slide down a perpetual glacier. A sudden shadow fell over Michael as Olivia's curtains were drawn. Now only one slim arrow of light fell across the powdery lawn, where one curtain stood away from the window. Perhaps Bertram had gone—or perhaps he was still there. Michael smiled ruefully at his own folly, but there it was: one way or the other, he had to go back up the pipe and find out what was happening in Olivia's room.

It was much easier climbing with gloves on, and the soles of his soft boots adhered nicely to the pipe. He was even quite warm by the time he reached the tiny balcony outside the window. He rested there, grinning with exertion, trying to breathe quietly. He heard a hum of voices inside, so Bertram hadn't left yet. Michael edged closer to the window, tilted his velvet cap to one side, and one of the voices became distinct:

"—so I asked myself, why do we dream at all? Or isn't there some way of controlling it? Maybe if we got someone *else* to repeat the same thing over and over, as we were falling asleep . . ."

The voice, low and passionate with just the hint of a whine, was Bertram's. A lighter voice made answer, but Michael couldn't catch Olivia's words; she must be facing away from the window. Bertram said, "Don't be ridiculous! Food has nothing to do with it, that's only a scare put about by physicians. Anyway, I know you had a light supper. Did you pass a pleasant evening?" Olivia's reply ended on a rising intonation. "No," said Bertram rather savagely. "No, he wasn't there.

Frankly, I'm disgusted; I wasted hours in a cavernous room that felt like an ice cave and smelt like a barn, because I thought he would be. He *told* me he would be."

Olivia made soothing noises. Michael's chapped lips quirked helplessly into a smile. Poor Bertram! He pressed his dripping nose with the back of his hand. He was probably going to catch a cold from all this, which would not only serve him right, but also provide a convenient excuse for his absence from his usual haunts that night. Prophetically, Bertram was saying, "Of course he'll have some excuse, he always does. Sometimes I wonder whether he isn't off with someone else." More soothing noises. "Well, you *know* his reputation. I don't know why I bother, sometimes. . . ."

Suddenly, Olivia's voice came strikingly clear. "You bother because he's beautiful, and because he appreciates you as none of the others have."

"He's clever," Bertram said gruffly. "I'm not sure it's the same thing. And you, my dear," he said gallantly, both of them near the window now, two long dark silhouettes staining the curtains, "are both beautiful and clever."

"Appreciative," Olivia amended. And then, more softly, so that Michael had to guess at all the words, "and not quite beautiful enough."

Bertram's voice grew at once less distinct and louder; he must have turned away, but was practically shouting, "I won't have you blaming yourself for that! We've been over this before, Olivia; it's not your fault and I don't want to hear you talking like that!"

It had all the marks of an old argument. "Don't tell me that, tell your father!" Her well-bred voice retained its rounded tones, but the pitch was shriller, the tempo faster, carrying through the glass with no difficulty. "He's been waiting six years for an heir! He'd have made you divorce me by now if it wasn't for the dowry!"

"Olivia—"

"Lucy has five children! Five!! Davenant can keep his bedroom full of boys, nobody cares, because he does his duty by her . . . but you—"

"Olivia, stop it!"

"You—where is your heir going to come from? Michael Godwin? Well it's going to have to come from Michael Godwin because we know it isn't going to come from anywhere else!"

Oh, god, thought Michael, hands pressed to his mouth; *And there he is out on the balcony. . . .* He looked longingly at the ground, not at all sure now that he could manipulate the drainpipe again. He was stiff and chilled from crouching there in one position. But he had to get out of there. He didn't want to hear any more of this.

For the third time that night he hooked his legs around the drain-pipe of the Rossillion town house, and began to work his way down it. The pipe seemed slipperier this time, perhaps smoothed from his ear-lier passings. He felt himself losing his grip, imagined falling the ten feet into the shrubbery. . . . His upper lip prickled with sweat as he eased his grip to hunt for surer anchor—and one booted foot swung wildly out, and collided with a window shutter in a desperate rattle and a conclusive thump, shattering the stillness of the winter night.

He thought of shouting, "It's only a rabbit!" His feet hit the ground achingly flat, and he staggered to his knees in the low bushes. A dog was barking frantically inside the house. He wondered if he could make it to the front gate in time to pretend that he had just been pass-ing by and heard the noise . . . but the front gate would already be locked at this hour, his feet remembered, making with all speed for the orchard wall, which Bertram had mentioned needed repairing.

The dog's bark rang crystalline in the cold air. Past the skeletons of pear trees Michael saw a dip in the wall, surmounted by crumbling mortar. It wasn't that high, just about at eye level. He flung himself at it arms first, to pull his body over—and the mortar gave way, crum-bling beneath him as he slipped neatly over it like a salmon over a dam.

The wall was considerably higher on the other side; he had just enough time to wonder when he was going to stop falling before he hit the ground, and rolled the rest of the way down the embankment to the street, where he was nearly run over by a carriage.

The carriage stopped, its horses registering protest. From within a furious voice, male, shouted out fierce expletives and demands to know what was going on. Michael rose to his feet, fishing for a coin to fling at the driver so they could both be on their ways. But the occu-pant of the carriage, too impatient to wait for an answer, chose that moment to step out and investigate.

Michael bowed low, out of politeness and a hopeless desire to hide his face. It was his mother's old friend, Lord Horn, who had kept New Year's with them in the country almost ten years ago, when Michael was only fifteen. Heedless of his driver's sputters of explanation, Horn snapped, "Who's that?"

Over the increasing noise of the barking dog and the men's voices on the other side of the wall, Michael said as clearly as he could, "I'm Michael Godwin. I was walking home, and I fell in the street." He swayed slightly. "Might I—"

"Get in," Horn ordered. On shaking legs he hastened to obey. "I'll take you to my house," said Horn, slamming shut the door, "it's closer. John—drive on!"

The inside of Lord Horn's carriage was dark and close. For a while their breaths still steamed white. Michael watched his own with weird detachment as it emerged in rapid little puffs from his mouth, like a child's drawing of smoke coming out of a chimney. As the chill left him, for some reason he started to shake.

"Not the night to pick for walking home," Horn said. He handed Michael a little flask of brandy from a pocket in the wall. The exercise of opening and drinking from it steadied him a little. The carriage jogged regularly over the cobbled streets; it had good springs, and the horses were good. Michael's eyes grew accustomed to the dark, but still all he could see of the man sitting next to him was a pale profile against the window. He remembered Horn when he'd visited Amberleigh, a handsome blond with lazy blue eyes and pale hands. And there was his adolescent's envy of a green coat of crushed velvet with gold braid. . . .

"I hope your mother is well," said Lord Horn. "I was sorry to miss her on her visit to the city."

"Very well," said Michael. "Thank you." He had stopped shaking. The carriage turned into a drive, and pulled up before a shallow flight of steps. Horn helped him out of the carriage and into the house. He had no chance to glimpse the notorious winter gardens in the back.

A fire was already lit in the library. Michael sat in a heavy upholstered chair, while his host rang for hot drink. The firelight brightened Michael's russet hair to polished copper. His eyes were large, his skin still pale with shock. Lord Horn sat down and pulled a low table up between them. He sat with his back to the fire. Horn's features were in shadow, but Michael could discern a high-bridged nose, wide-set eyes under a broad brow. Hair fair and light as swansdown made an aureole about Horn's head. An ornate clock over the mantel ticked the seconds loudly, as though proud of its place. If you did not immediately notice it for its gilded curves and figurines, you could not miss the noise it made. Michael wondered if it would be appropriate to comment on it.

"You've taken your family's seat in Council, haven't you?" Lord Horn asked.

"Yes." To avert the next question Michael explained, "I'm not often there. It's tiresome. I only go when there's some question directly bearing on Amberleigh."

To his relief, the older man smiled. "I always felt the same. Bore.

All those gentlemen, and not one pack of cards amongst 'em." Michael grinned. "You have other things to do with your time, I think."

The young man stiffened at the insinuation. "Someone's been telling you tales."

"Not at all." Horn spread one jeweled hand on the table between them. "I have eyes."

Michael wondered if he should let Horn believe that he'd been reeling drunk in the street. He'd be a laughingstock if it got round: that sort of behavior was for green boys. "I hope," he said with a convincing and heartfelt sniff, "that I am not getting ill."

"So do I," Horn said smoothly; "but pallor becomes you. I see you have your mother's fine complexion."

With a jolt, Michael realized what Horn had been trying to do for some time now. Now that he knew it, he became aware of the eyes fixed hotly on him from the shadows. They burned a flush of color into his own face.

"I understand," said Horn, "how you might be very busy indeed. But one always finds time for the right things, don't you find?" Mutely, Michael nodded, aware that the betraying firelight was strong on his features. Fortunately Horn slid his hands to the arms of his chair and rose to stand before the fire, his back to Michael. Now, for the first time since his drop from the drainpipe, he let himself think of Olivia.

He'd always felt sorry for Bertram's wife. She was a beautiful woman. Bertram was fool to ignore her as he did. Michael liked Bertram, with his strange ideas and fierce possessiveness. But he didn't think he'd like to be married to him. When Olivia had approached him with her awkward, naive flirtation, Michael had been flattered, for her reputation was chaste. He'd believed then that she had read his sympathy and attraction to her, and was responding in kind. He'd believed, as he was touching her with his expert hands, kissing her white throat and being so careful not to put her in danger, while she made caution almost impossible with her moans and digging fingers, he'd believed that she wanted him.

She hadn't wanted him. His sympathy and desire, all his tenderness, expertise, and charm, were nothing to her, only made her job easier. She hadn't wanted him, she had used him for his sex to get back at her husband and to father an heir.

Horn wanted him: for his youth, his beauty, his ability to please and be pleased. Horn should have him.

He came up behind Lord Horn, sliding his hands onto the man's shoulders. Horn took his hands and seemed to wait. Touched by the formality of their moves, Michael turned him in his arms and kissed his mouth. He tasted spices. The man had been chewing fennel seeds for his breath. The expert tongue flicked eagerly. Michael pressed closer. "Lydia's eldest," Horn murmured. "You *have* grown up." With nothing between them but the costly fabric of their clothes, Michael felt the man's need, twin to his own. Over the roar of blood he heard the ticking of the clock.

A polite knock broke them apart like a nutshell. A roaring breath of mixed lust and annoyance tore through Horn's flared nostrils. "Come in!" he called gruffly. The door opened to a liveried servant carrying a tray with steaming mugs; behind him another bore two branched candelabra, fully lit. Horn stepped forward irritably to hasten their office, and the light caught him full in the face like a mailed fist.

For a moment, Michael could only stare. Slackness had invaded the carefully tended skin, blurring the fineness of Lord Horn's features. Little folds hung like someone else's laundry from the sharp lines of his face. What had been uniform ivory skin was turning sallow, except where blood vessels had broken along his cheeks and the sides of his nose. His blue eyes had faded, and even the luster of his hair was dimmed like old summer grass.

Michael gasped, and choked on his breath. The handsome man in the green velvet coat was gone, swept back to his youth in his mother's garden. Olivia had thrust him into the arms of this revolting stranger. The mug shook so badly in Michael's hands that hot punch spilled over his knuckles onto the carpet. "I'm sorry—terribly sorry."

"Never mind," Horn growled, still annoyed at the interruption, "sit down."

Michael sat, paying close attention to his hands.

"I was with the Duchess Tremontaine," Horn was saying in a loud voice meant for the servants. It would not do to be caught hurrying them. "Charming woman. She extends me such courtesy. Of course I was a close friend of the late duke's. A very close friend. I am to dine with her on her barge next week, when Steele sends up his fireworks."

The liquor, and the effortless inanity of the conversation, were soothing Michael. "Are you?" he replied, and was shocked at the weakness of his voice. "So am I."

The servants finally bowed out. Horn said, "Perhaps we are destined to become better acquainted, then," his voice heavy with innuendo.

Michael sneezed violently. It was timely but unintentional. He found himself genuinely relieved to realize that he really did feel horrible. His head ached, and he was going to sneeze again. "I think," he said, "that I had better go home."

"Oh, surely not," said Horn. "I can offer you hospitality overnight."

"No, really," said Michael, as miserably as he could. "I can see I'm going to be no fit company for anyone tonight." He coughed, praying that Horn's persistence would not outlast his courtesy.

"Pity," said Lord Horn, flicking an invisible bit of thread from his coat into the fire. "Shall I order you up the carriage, then?"

"Oh, please no, don't bother. I'm just a few streets away."

"A torchman, then? It wouldn't do to have you falling again."

"Yes, thank you."

His wet overclothes were brought steaming from the drying fire. At least the water was warm. He walked home, tipped the torchman, and climbed the stairs to his bedroom with a candle, leaving his clothes in piles on the floor for his servants to find. Michael slipped between cold sheets in a heavy bedgown, a handkerchief balled in his fist, and waited for sleep to overcome him.

chapter V

THE NEXT DAY CAME COLD AND SULLEN. LAYERS OF GREY
cloud blanketed the sky. From Riverside the effect was oppres-
sive: the river roiled yellow and grey between the banks,
swirling darkly about the struts of the bridge. Above it stretched the
city's warehouses and commercial buildings, interrupted only by
patches of dirty snow. Richard St Vier got up early and put on his best
clothes: he had an appointment in the city to pick up the second half
of his payment for the Lynch fight. It was a substantial amount, which
only he could be sure of carrying back into Riverside unscathed. He
was to meet someone, probably the servant of the agent of the banker
of the noble who'd hired him, in a neutral place where the money
could be handed over. Both St Vier and his patrons appreciated the
formalities of discretion in these matters.

From the Hill the view was quite another matter. The distant rivers
glittered, and houses sent up cozy trails of smoke. The sky stretched
out forever in rippling layers of silver, pewter, and iron, over the
domes of the Council Hall, the University walls and ancient Cathe-
dral towers, on across the eastern plain and into the tiny hills.

Michael Godwin awoke at noon, having slept a round twelve
hours, feeling remarkably fit. He coughed experimentally, and felt his
throat, but the cold that last night had threatened to overwhelm him
seemed to have vanished.

Just then his manservant came in to rouse him. Michael had forgotten his promise to dine with his friend Tom Berowne that afternoon.

There was just enough time to dress and wash. His dry, clean, nicely pressed clothes felt remarkably luxurious after last night's escapades. He put the memory behind him and went whistling out of the door.

Dinner was predictably excellent. His friend's cook was legendary, and Lord Thomas was full of gossip. Some of it, gratifyingly, was about him. Bertram, Rossillion's son, had lost thirty royals gambling in a popular club last night, and as he left the table had been heard to damn Michael Godwin.

Michael shrugged angelically. "I wasn't even there. Felt a cold coming on, and stayed in all evening with a hot brick. Oh, much better now, thanks. Poor Bertram!"

He was in no hurry to get home. There might be a note waiting from Bertram, or, worse yet, one from Lord Horn. What a lot of trouble from one night! Of course he would run into Bertram sooner or later. Better make it sooner and turn up at the club tonight after supper. He could tell Bertram pretty stories, and take him home with him. Horn, on the other hand . . . hadn't he mentioned the duchess's barge supper next week? It was too bad, but maybe he'd better miss that one. Horn didn't have the air of a man who knew when to give up. But the image of the duchess intruded itself between Michael and his resolves: her silvery eyes, her cool hand . . . and the voice that mocked and possessed and promised. Perdition take Horn. He couldn't refuse her invitation!

To draw out his walk Michael chose the distracting route home, along Lassiter's Row, where elegant merchandise was displayed before each shop to tempt the wealthy pedestrian. But there was little to distract today. Although the snow had been cleared, merchants were leery of setting much out in the cold, and few people were out walking. His thoughts turned again to the duchess. He'd never heard of her taking any lovers; but she was beautiful, a widow . . . he should have asked Tom whether there were any rumors. . . . Michael stopped, half meaning to turn around and return to his friend's, when an odd sight caught his attention.

A man was being ushered out of Felman's Bookshop by old Felman himself with the kind of pomp usually reserved for nobles with enormous libraries. But the man enjoying these favors hardly looked like a book collector. He was young, athletically restless, anxious to depart. No noble of breeding would show such ill ease before servile homage, however gross; and no noble would be caught out in a pair of such undistinguished boots, topped by a brown cloak of old-fashioned cut whose edges verged on the shabby.

Michael let the stranger make his escape before he descended on the bookseller.

Felman nodded and smiled, agreeing that, no, it was not the sort of fellow you'd expect to find in his establishment. "My lord will scarcely credit it to hear who that was. That was the swordsman St Vier, sir, purchasing a volume here."

"Well!" Michael was properly astonished. "What did he buy?"

"What *did* he buy . . . ?" Felman ran pink fingers through the remains of his hair. "I offered him many fine illustrated volumes, sir, such as might be suitable, for I like to think I know how to mate each customer to the appropriate work; well, sir, you will scarcely credit what he *did* buy: a scholarly volume, sir, *On the Causes of Nature*, which is in great demand at the University, being the subject of much discourse these days, I might even say disagreement. I only had the one volume, sir, very handsomely bound indeed; if you would like to order another I can oblige, although the binding will of course take some time. . . ."

"Thank you," Michael said automatically, making his excuses as he headed for the door. Hurried by an impulse he did not quite understand, he went down the street after the swordsman.

Lord Michael caught sight of the swordsman a few streets down, and hailed the brown cloak imperiously: "Sir!"

St Vier looked quickly around, and kept walking. Michael broke into a run. As his footsteps neared, the swordsman was suddenly against the wall with his cloak flung back, hand gripping his sword. It was not the sword a gentleman would wear, but a heavy, undecorated weapon whose stroke would almost surely kill. Michael skidded to a halt in the slush. He was glad no one was there to see this.

"My—Master St Vier," he panted. "I wondered if—if I might speak with you."

The swordsman's eyes were, incongruously, the deep lavender color of spring hyacinths. They raked Michael up and down.

The man hadn't dropped his guard; his hand still held the pommel of his ugly sword. Michael wondered what on earth he was doing with this fellow. Something of his mother's complacent laughter and the duchess's piquant scorn moved him closer to the swordsman. They thought he would have nothing to do with the profession. His mother was sure of it; and something in the duchess seemed to despise him for it.

St Vier seemed satisfied with what he saw; his hand relaxed as he became briskly businesslike. "Do you want to talk out here?"

"Of course not," Michael said. If he wanted to talk to the man, of course he would have to take him somewhere. "Why don't you go along with me to the Blue Parrot for some chocolate?"

Why don't you go along . . . He sounded as though he were talking to an equal. St Vier seemed not to notice. He nodded, and followed Michael back up the street toward the cafe. Michael had to lengthen his stride to match the swordsman's. The man's presence was very *vivid*, at once sensual and aesthetic, like a fine blood-horse. He didn't match Michael's idea of a swordsman: there seemed nothing coarse about him, or surly, or even humorless.

"I'd better say now that my fees are high," St Vier said. "I don't want to put you off, but it usually has to be something pretty serious."

"Yes, I've heard." Michael wondered if he realized just how extensively his fees were discussed on the Hill. "But I don't really want anyone challenged right now."

"No?" St Vier stopped walking abruptly. "If it's not about a job, then what do you want?"

He seemed less curious than annoyed. Quickly Michael said, "Of course, I'm willing to pay you for your time, at your usual rates. I'd like you to . . . I'd like to learn the sword from you."

The swordman's face closed with indifference. Later, Michael realized it was the same bored, impatient look he had been giving Felman. "I don't teach," was all he said.

"Please believe that I'm in earnest." What was he saying? He had never been anything of the kind. But the words came spilling out: "I realize it's an unusual proposition, but I would make sure that you were properly recompensed as befits your skill and reputation."

Barely concealed distaste showed on the swordman's face. "I'm sorry," he said, "I don't have time for this."

"Wait—" Michael stopped him from turning on his heel. "Is there anything I could do to . . ."

For the first time St Vier seemed to soften, looking at Michael as though he saw a person behind the massed signals of breeding and grooming. "Look," he said kindly, "I'm not a teacher. It has nothing to do with you. If you want to learn, there are plenty of others in the city who will teach you. I only do my own work; you can reach me in Riverside if you want me for that."

"Will you . . . ?" Courteously Michael indicated the cafe a few doors down, determined to salvage some dignity.

The swordsman actually smiled at him. There was charm in it, unlooked-for humor and understanding. "Thank you, no. I'm really in a hurry to get home."

"Thank you, then; and good luck." He didn't know if that was the appropriate thing to wish a swordsman, but the man didn't seem to take offense. It occurred to Michael later that St Vier had never asked him his name; and he never found out what the book was for. But he made inquiries that day, and the next, until he finally found himself a teacher.

ALEC WAS MENDING A SOCK. HIS HANDS WERE BATHED WITH the grey light from the window, and his stitches were tiny and careful.

"You should let Marie do that," Richard said, hiding his surprise.

"It's a skill I learned at University. I don't want to lose it. I might need to earn a living some day."

Richard laughed, "As a tailor? Look, get yourself some new socks; get yourself ten pairs, get them in silk. I've just been paid for the Lynch job. We're going to be very comfortable, as long as it lasts."

"Good," Alec grumbled. "We need more candles."

"Beeswax," said Richard giddily, "of course. The best there is. Look, I've been shopping uptown." He took out a brown paper parcel and held it out to Alec. "A present. For you."

"What is it?" Alec made no move to take the package.

"Well, it's a book," Richard said, still holding it. "I thought you might like it."

Alec's eyes widened; then he converted the expression into a raising of the eyebrows. He fussed with the sock. "You idiot," he said softly.

"Well, you've only got the three you brought with you. And they're almost worn out. I thought you might like something new." Feeling a little awkward, he began undoing the brown paper himself. It released the rich smell of leather. The binding alone, Richard thought, was worth the price: burgundy leather with gold tooling, gilt-edged pages; the book was as beautiful as a rug or a painting.

Alec's arm shot out: his hand closed on the book. "Felman's!" he gasped. "You got this at Felman's!"

"Well, yes. He's supposed to be good."

"*Good.* . . ," Alec said in strangled tones. "Richard, it's . . . he's . . . they're wall decorations for noblemen's libraries. He sells them by the inch: 'Do you have Birdbrain in red leather?' 'No, sir, but I have him in green.' 'Oh, no, that won't go with the rug.' 'Well, sir, I do have this lovely work on the mating habits of chickens in red. It's about the same size.' 'Oh, good, I'll take that one.' "

Richard laughed. "Well, it is beautiful."

"Very," Alec said dryly. "You could wear it to Chapel. I don't suppose you know what it's about?"

"Natural philosophy," he responded promptly, "whatever that is. The man said you might like it. He seemed to know what he was talking about. I could have got you *The Wicked Uncle, or, True Love Rewarded* or *The Merry Huntsman's Guide to Autumn Deer Droppings*. But he said this was what everyone was reading now."

"Everyone where?" Alec's voice was stiff, the Hill accent pronounced.

"At University."

Alec went to the window, placing his long palm against the cold glass. "And you thought I would be interested."

"I thought you might be. I told him you went there, to the University."

"But not that I'd left."

"It was none of his business. I had to tell him something: when he thought it was for me he tried to sell me a book of pornographic woodcuts."

"At least they would have been of some use to you," Alec said acidly. "*On the Causes of Nature*—the new translation. They've just lifted the ban on it after fifteen years. Have you any idea—no, of course you haven't."

With a languid motion he turned from the window. The glass was freshly streaked with blood. His palm was scored with the mark of the darning needle.

Richard's breath caught. But he had faced dangerous opponents before. "Come on," he said; "let's go down to Rosalie's and pay off all our debts. I've been drinking on credit for the past six weeks. You can bet gold against Greasepole Mazarene; he'll have hysterics."

"That will be pleasant," Alec remarked, and went to collect his cloak and gloves.

chapter VI

H<small>E'D HAD TUTORS ALL HIS LIFE, M</small>ICHAEL REALIZED; MEN who came to his home and taught him, courteously and slowly, what it was appropriate for him to know. Even when he was eight they were deferential, the University scholars whose best hope for social promotion was as tutors, the masters of their various arts. Suddenly he was glad that St Vier had refused his offer. After a series of discreet inquiries in unusual places, Michael finally lit upon Master Vincent Applethorpe's Academy of Swordsmanship.

For a professional swordsman, the threat of termination is always present. The romantic ideal, of course, is to die fighting, young and still at one's peak. For practical purposes, though, almost any swordsman cherishes the dream that he will live until he first notices his precision slipping, by which time he will have built his reputation high enough to be able to resign gracefully from the active life and be welcomed into the household of some nobleman eager for the prestige his distinguished presence will lend. There he will be required only to do light bodyguarding and to give the occasional lesson to the noble's sons or men-at-arms. The worst thing that can happen—short of being crippled—is to run a school.

Everyone knows that the truly great swordsmen are trained by masters, men who appear out of nowhere, on a country road or in a crowded taproom, to single you out for their exclusive training. Sometimes it is necessary to pursue them from town to town, proving your worthiness until they consent to take you on. Only thugs resort to the schools: common sorts who want an advantage in a street brawl, or to impress a lover; or servants eager to impress an employer for promotion.

The name Vincent Applethorpe was not one that lived in legend.

It should have. Applethorpe had been a brilliant swordsman. In his best days he would have given St Vier a good fight. But his name had been erased from the public lists too early in his career for his last fight to be made a public tragedy. Quite early on, his arm was slashed in a gorgeous, unchancy bit of rapier-and-dagger work. The wound festered, and rather than lose his life he lost his left arm. He very nearly lost both: only the intervention of concerned friends, who carried him to a surgeon's while he was in a drunken stupor of pain and the fear of gangrene, got him under the knife in time to save his life. The choice, for Applethorpe, had not been an easy one. If he had died, he might have been remembered for his early triumphs. Swordsmen appreciate a glorious death. But inglorious examples of what really happens to one whose skill has failed him at the crucial moment, those they prefer to forget.

There has been no great one-armed swordsman since Black Mark of Ariston, who lived two hundred years before Vincent Applethorpe was born. Black Mark's portrait hangs in the halls of Ariston Keep. Sure enough, one sleeve hangs ostentatiously empty. Swordsmen are full of the stories of his exploits. The portrait, however, shows a man of middle age, his hook-beaked face an impressive mass of furrows. And privately they'll admit that you need both arms for balance, sometimes even for the tactical advantage of switching hands. He couldn't have lost that arm until after he'd made his name as a swordsman. But the stories go on getting wilder.

Ironically, Vincent Applethorpe had grown up in the southern hills, within sight of Ariston Keep. He'd never given it much thought, though, until he came home from the city half-dead in the bottom of a wagon. His sister was running the family farm, and he was supposed to be there to help her with it. Instead he took to disappearing frequently on long walks. He went to the Keep, and would stand for hours on a hill above it, watching the people go in and out. He never tried to get into the hall himself, just stood and thought about great one-armed swordsmen. His sister had hoped that he would settle down, marry, and bring another woman into the house. He did wait until after harvest before dashing her hopes and returning to the city.

Enough time had passed, he thought, for his face to have been forgotten. He set up his academy far from swordsmen's haunts, in a large attic above a dry-goods shop. The ceiling sloped in, and it was stifling in summer, but it provided that rare city commodity, a stretch of un-broken space. After a few years there he could afford to move to a large hall built over a stable at the far eastern edge of town. It had been designed as an indoor riding ring, but the flooring was too weak to bear the weight of many horses. He soon hired a couple of assistants, young men he had trained himself who would never be swordsmen, but knew enough to teach. They could supervise the drills that went on the length of the studio, and keep the straw targets with their red patches in repair. Applethorpe was still the Master. He demonstrated the moves for his students, describing what he could not perform. So, ten years after his accident, at a time when he would have had to begin to consider abandoning the active swordsman's life, he was still in command of his career. And in his demonstrations he retained the fire, the precision of motion, the grace that made every move an explication of the swordsman's art, at once both effortless and imperative.

Michael Godwin admired him with a less than scholarly interest. He could not yet appreciate the technical clarity of Applethorpe's movements, but he was thrilled by the Master's vividness—it was almost a glow he projected when he demonstrated a move. Lord Michael wondered if this was what was meant by "flair." He'd always imagined flair to be tied up in dramatic movements of the arms, one of which the Master lacked. As with St Vier, there was a grace and dignity to his carriage that was neither the deliberate languor of the aristocrat nor the choppy energy of the city tradesman. Michael extended his right arm as instructed, trying for a fluidity that looked easy when Applethorpe did it.

"No," the Master said to the line of beginners hopefully strung out before him like birds on a washline. "You cannot hope to get anywhere near it while you stand like that." His voice was remarkably calm, giving off neither impatience nor annoyance—nor any particular kindness. Seeing students doing something badly never upset Vincent Applethorpe. *He* knew the way it ought to be done. He kept explaining, and eventually they would get it, or they wouldn't. He surveyed the entire line and observed dispassionately but accurately, "You look like you are all waiting to be beaten. Your shoulders are afraid to set upright, and your heads crane forward on your necks. So your whole stance is crooked, and your thrust will be crooked, too—except you. You. What's your name?"

"Michael Godwin," said Lord Michael. He hadn't bothered to change it; there were Godwins all over the country, and no one in this place was likely to know him by sight.

Applethorpe nodded. "The Godwins of Amberleigh?" Michael nodded back, amused that the man had come so close in his lineage and region. Maybe it was the hair. "A handsome family," the Master said. "You're lucky. Extend." Michael did so, clumsily. "No, never mind the wrist for now, just show us the arm. Look, all of you, look at that. The carriage of the shoulders, the lift of the head. It gives the whole extension a natural smoothness. Do it."

He always came to this point in his instruction, when the explication of cause and effect came to an end and his instruction was, "Do it." They tried, fingering Michael with the edges of their eyes, trying to shake their shoulders into place without thrusting out their chests, to lift their heads without ruining their sight lines. Michael stopped worrying about his wrist, and fell into a trance of motion as his arm stretched itself out and pulled back in, over and over. He had never before considered his carriage as especially useful. It was an aid to an effect, handy to show off the line of a coat or the turn of a dance step. Now everything fell into place as the steady movement of his arm rolled through his shoulders.

Applethorpe paused in his round of surveillance and correction. "Good," he said. "Godwin. You've got the wrist now."

At home in his large, airy dressing room, with the fire lit against the cold, Michael took off his sweaty practice clothes. His manservant bore away the plain, unstylish garments without comment. Other servants brought up the hot water for his bath. He sank gratefully into the tub, whose steam rose up agreeably scented with clove and rose petals. He had time only for a short soak before he must dress for supper. It was the night of the duchess's party, and he had no desire to be late and miss his place on the barge. Even the prospect of Lord Horn's company was not enough to dampen his excitement. He could not imagine needing to converse with anyone else when Diane was present. He had forgotten how hard she was to talk to, and his estimate of his own powers was back to its accustomed level.

Michael rose naked from the bath, to be confronted with his own form, reflected down from the large mirror over the fireplace. He paused, staring, in the act of reaching for the bath towel. He was accustomed to thinking of his shoulders as frail; he had to pad them out sometimes to meet the demands of fashion. Now they seemed trim and competent. His collar bones followed their line, lithe as birds' wings. A gentleman did not uncover his neck in public, so their delights were reserved for his intimates. But in the room above the stable one grew hot, and adopted the open collar of the workman.

He followed the line they pointed to like an arrow, down his chest. All that the world had counted beautiful could be trained, turned on the lathe of practice to become a dangerous weapon. Looking up, he met his own eyes. The dark lashes that framed them made them seem deeper than they were, the pupil a stone dropped into ripples of color blue-green as the sea. He had the sense of being closely examined by a stranger, of falling into his own beautiful eyes. He didn't know the man in the mirror, but he wanted to. The more he stared, the further from himself he went, asking, *Who are you? What do you want?*

His feet were very cold. The floor was like ice, and his stiff body had begun to shiver. Michael grabbed the towel and rubbed himself briskly. He would have to hurry to dress. The fireworks were due to begin at dark over the river, and the barge must not leave without him.

THE DAY HAD BEEN CLEAR, ALMOST MILD; BUT WITH TWILIGHT a chill had struck that deepened as the dark winter sun began to fall, pulling the temperature with it. It hung low over the city's profile, as red as summer raspberries. The Riverside street was strangely empty, as silent as dawn. The slush of the ground had re-formed into frozen crusts, eerie landscapes-in-miniature of ice and mud. Alec's new boots demolished a fairy castle. He skidded on a patch of ice and righted himself, cursing.

"Are you sure you want to see these fireworks?" Richard asked him.

"I love fireworks," Alec answered glibly. "I value them more than life itself."

"The west bank up by Waterbourne will be crowded," St Vier said, "with carriages and upper city folks and vendors. Too many people live there. Half of Riverside will be over picking pockets. We'd better stay on the east side, it won't be so bad."

"The pickpockets, or the crowds?" said Alec; but he went along with Richard.

They made for the lower bridge, which connected Riverside to the Old City. Some people still lived there, but mainly the east bank was given over to government buildings: the old palace, the castle/fort and barracks. . . . Richard marveled at the foibles of the rich. He had nothing against fireworks. But to require your friends to sit in their barges in the middle of the river late in winter to enjoy them, that seemed eccentric. He felt the cold, the wind cutting across the river, even in his new clothes. He had bought himself a heavy cloak, jacket, and fur-lined gloves. Alec, too, was warmly dressed, and had stopped complaining of the cold. He liked having money to spend, money to waste on food and gambling.

Across the dark breadth of the river the populated section of the city loomed, rising from its banks in steeper and steeper slopes until it became the Hill and blotted out the evening sky. St Vier and Alec had already passed the docks and warehouses, the fort guarding the old river-entrance to the city, and were coming on the Grand Plaza of Jurisdiction, Justice Place, where the Council of Lords had established its hall. Upriver the orange glow of torches from already assembled barges stained the growing darkness. Alec quickened his pace, anxious to catch the first fireworks. Richard had to break into a trot to match his long-legged stride.

Footsteps rang behind them on the frozen stone across the plaza. He heard young men's voices, raised in laughter. One of them called, thin and clear, "Hey! Wait up!" Out of habit St Vier checked out the area. There was no one else they could be calling to. Alec did not look back, nor did he slow his steps.

"Hey!" The callers were insistent. "Wait for us!" Alec kept on walking, but Richard stopped and turned. He saw a small group of boys, all dressed like Alec in black robes, long hair falling down their backs. When he'd chosen this route, he hadn't been thinking how close they'd pass to the University's domains.

Alec's hair streamed out behind him like a comet's tail. Richard ran to catch up. "I can get us out of here if you'd like," he said casually. For reply Alec only looked down at him, and slowed his pace to a deliberate snail's saunter. The swordsman had no trouble matching it; it reminded him of leg exercises.

The students' shoes whispered closer across the stone, until one of them drew abreast of Alec. "Hey," the student said friendlily, "I thought you were locked up with your books."

Alec stared straight ahead, and didn't stop. Richard's hand was on his sword-hilt. The students seemed unarmed, but Alec could be harmed by many things.

"Hey," said the boy, "aren't you—"

Alec looked down at him, and the student stammered in confusion, "Oh—hey—I thought you were—"

"Think again," said Alec harshly in an odd voice, a Riverside voice that troubled St Vier. It was effective, though; the students clustered together and hurried away, and Richard took his hand from the sword.

chapter VII

THE TREMONTAINE BARGE ROCKED WHEN LORD MICHAEL SET his foot on its side; but he had been getting in and out of nobles' barges since he'd come to the city, and had grown proficient at not falling in. A torchman conducted him to the pavilion in the center of the flat-bottomed boat. The hangings were green and gold, the duchess's colors. All of the sides were down while the barge waited at the dock; through the brocade he heard laughter, and the clink of metal. It was one of the most beautiful barges of any noble on the water. He had always wanted to ride in it. But now that he had the chance his mind was scarcely taking it in.

One corner of the brocade was pulled aside for him to enter the pavilion; the people seated at the table inside gasped and shivered at the blast of cold air that entered with him. Diane's guests were already dining off slices of smoked goose, washed down with a strong red wine that took the chill out of the night and the river. Michael slipped into the only empty seat; he had lingered too long choosing a jacket, and paid the price by being the last to arrive. And his clothes weren't even going to matter, he realized now: no one at the table would remove their outer layer of furs, despite the brazier under the table warming their feet. They looked like a country hunting party, swathed in thick greys and browns and blacks that glowed and rippled like living pelts in the candlelight.

The duchess raised her goblet to him. The curve of her wrist was achingly white even against the white fur of her cuff. Michael's throat tightened, but he replied with a courtesy. His cup was filled with wine the color of rubies. The drink, though cool, was warmer than the air outside had been; he seemed to feel it flowing straight into his veins.

They were all there: young Chris Nevilleson and his sister, Lady Helena, whose ringlets Michael could remember pulling at childhood parties; Mary, Lady Halliday, without her lord, the Crescent Chancellor, who had been detained by city business; Anthony Deverin, Lord Ferris, the bright young hope of the Council of Lords, already Dragon Chancellor at the age of thirty-two; and Lord Horn. Horn's fair skin was flushed with warmth. He wore splendid longhaired grey fox. The shadowlight was kind to him, rendering him with a lean, overbred elegance. He wore silver rings, which called attention to his slender hands when he reached for things at table.

He looked at Michael with cool deliberation. It was a look that implied further intimacy, and it made Michael's skin creep. The smile at the edges of his mouth made Michael want to hit him.

The goose and red wine were whisked away, and small bowls of hot almond soup were set down, their contents rocking lightly with the tide. "Oh, dear," said the duchess. "I was afraid of this. We're about to cast off. I hope the river isn't choppy."

"It isn't," said Michael. "The sky is clear, it's perfect fireworks weather."

"Except for the cold." Helena Nevilleson shivered theatrically.

"Pooh," said her brother, "you used to climb out of the window in winter to check on your pony." Lady Helena hit him with her pomander ball.

"My lord," the duchess admonished, "no woman likes to be reminded of her past. Not all of them come as well armed as Lady Helena, though."

"If she's trying to prove what a lady she is now," Horn said primly, "she'd do better to put it away."

"And who," Helena demanded, "will protect me if I do?" The young woman's eyes sparkled with the delight of being the center of attention.

"From what?" asked her brother innocently.

"Why, insult, of course," the duchess defended her.

"With respect, madam Duchess," Lord Christopher answered, "the truth cannot be considered an insult."

"Idealism," murmured Lord Ferris, while Diane responded, "Can it not? That depends on your timing, my lord."

"I had a pony," quiet Lady Halliday spoke up. "It bit me."

"Funny," said Christopher Nevilleson; "Helena's was always afraid *she* would bite *it*."

"Timing?" asked Michael, emerging from a cold draught of stony white wine. He didn't care much about ponies and pomander balls. Diane had barely looked at him since her initial greeting. He was beginning to strain for the cryptic messages she had been sending him the other day. The party felt so normal that it was making him uncomfortable. To find her again he felt he would have to walk a labyrinth of hidden meanings.

Now, at last, her grey eyes were fixed on him. "Is the wine to your taste?" she asked.

"The timing of truth," said Lord Horn with heavy self-importance. "That's a matter for politicians like Ferris, and not mere ornaments like you and me."

The messages, god help him, were coming from Horn. Michael gritted his teeth against the archness of the man.

"The wine for the fish," the duchess continued with relentless, impersonal politeness, "I think is even better."

"Fish?!" Lady Halliday exclaimed. "My dear, I thought you said this was just going to be a picnic."

The duchess made a moue. "It was. But my cook got carried away with the notion of what would be necessary to sustain seven people on the river in midwinter. I don't ever dare to argue with her, or I get creamed chicken for a week."

"Poor Diane," said Lord Ferris, smiling at her. "You let everyone bully you."

T HE SKY OVER THE RIVER LOOKED AS THOUGH IT WERE BURNing.

"Hurry!" Alec said. But as they rounded the corner to Waterbourne they saw that the light came from torches set in the nobles' barges in the middle of the river. Some ten or fifteen of them were clustered in the center of the dark water. They looked like elaborate brooches pinned to black silk shot with ripples of gold.

Alec whistled softly through chapped lips. "The rich," he said, "are looking particularly rich tonight."

"It's impressive," said Richard.

"I hope they aren't too terribly cold," Alec said, implying the opposite.

Richard didn't answer. He was absorbed in the sight of a new barge making its way upriver to join the others. Flames and black smoke spun back from the torches set in its prow, surrounding it with danger and glory. The green and gold pavilion was still closed. But it was the barge itself that intrigued him. He must have made some sound; Alec turned sharply to see what he was looking at.

"But of course," sneered Alec; "no party would be complete without one."

The prow of the barge reared up in the graceful curve of a swan's neck. Its head was crowned with a ducal coronet. In perfect proportion were the wings, fanning back to protect the sides of the boat. Despite the hangings, despite the flat bottom and outsized stern, the barge managed to give the illusion of a giant swan on the river. Its oars dipped and rose, dripping jewels with each stroke, so smoothly that the barge seemed to glide across the surface of the water.

"Who is it?" St Vier asked.

"Tremontaine, of course," Alec answered sharply. "There's the ducal crown all over everything. I should think even you would recognize that getup."

He had thought they were ornamental. "I don't know Tremontaine," he said; "I've never worked for him."

"Her," said Alec sourly. "Can't you detect the woman's touch?"

Richard shrugged. "I can't keep them all straight."

"I'm surprised you've never done a job for her. Diane is such a lady of fashion, and you are fashion's darling—"

"Diane?" Richard groped for and found the connection. "Oh, that one. She's the one who had her husband killed. I remember that. It was before I got fashionable."

"Killed her husband?" Alec drawled. "A nice lady with such a pretty boat? What a terrible thing to say, Richard."

"Maybe she didn't like him."

"It hardly matters. He was crazy anyway. She was made duchess in her own right, and they locked him up. Why kill him?"

"Maybe he ate too much."

"He died of a stroke."

St Vier smiled down at the ground. "Of course he did."

The barges were tilting and rocking as friends tried to get close enough to one another to exchange gossip and pieces of fruit. There were also several competing musical consorts. Their ears were assaulted by a dramatic volley of brass, uncomfortably tangled in the sinews of a harp and flute and the anemic arms of a string quartet.

"Well," said Alec, taking in the chaos down below, "at least we can be fairly sure he didn't die of boredom."

• • •

Iɴ ᴛʜᴇ ʙᴀʀɢᴇs ᴀʟʟ ᴀʀᴏᴜɴᴅ ᴛʜᴇᴍ ᴘᴇᴏᴘʟᴇ ᴡᴇʀᴇ ʜᴜʀʟɪɴɢ ғᴏᴏᴅ and greetings at each other with impartial good cheer. They received a couple of oranges, but in Diane's calm presence the party on the swan boat forbore to join the mêlée, while the swan's wings shielded them from missiles.

Mary Halliday, who, unknown to many, had a good ear for music, winced at the mélange of instruments and tunes. Smiling sympathetically at her, Diane said, "I wonder if we could get them to cooperate on 'Our City of Light'?"

"Not if you love me," said Ferris, the Dragon Chancellor. "I don't know much about music, but I know what I'm sick of hearing. We open every Council season with it."

"But," the duchess grinned at him, "have you ever heard it as a trio for trumpet, harp, and viola d'amore?"

"No; and with any luck I never will. What a pity you didn't bring your portative organ so we could drown them all out with 'God Hath Warmed My Heart.' "

"We would have to set the pipes at the rear, and the image would be unfortunate. If you're cold, my lord; just bite down on a peppercorn."

Suspicion was creeping into Michael's heart. Diane and Lord Ferris seemed terribly familiar. Could they have an intimate connection? Michael tried to tell himself not to be an ass. Lord Horn was boring him and Helena with a complicated story about some state banquet he'd attended, for which it seemed necessary to keep touching Michael's knee for emphasis. If he were a woman, Michael reflected, Horn would never dare to touch his knee. If it were true about Diane and Ferris, perhaps he could contrive to have Ferris killed. Or even— of course, he was still a beginner, but Applethorpe seemed to think he had some promise as a swordsman—he could call the chancellor out himself, without any warning so that Ferris couldn't hire someone else to come up against him. But fighting one's own duels was unknown. Might the duchess find it in poor taste? Or was it the sort of daring originality she looked for in him—

"As I'm sure Lord Michael would agree," Horn finished complacently.

Lord Michael looked up at the sound of his name. "What?" he said inelegantly.

Laughing, Lady Helena tapped his shoulder with her pomander, and Horn's clear grey eye fixed on him. It gave Michael a sudden distaste for the poached whiting he'd been eating.

"Helena," Michael demanded testily of the young lady with the pomander ball, "can't you learn to control your pet?"

The duchess's silvery laughter was all the reward he needed for what he considered a laudable, indeed a magnanimous, rein on his temper.

Iᴛ ᴠᴇxᴇᴅ Aʟᴇᴄ ɴᴏᴛ ᴛᴏ ʙᴇ ᴀʙʟᴇ ᴛᴏ ᴘʀᴏᴠᴏᴋᴇ Sᴛ Vɪᴇʀ ɪɴᴛᴏ ʙᴇᴛting on which barge was going to overturn first. He had the odds all figured out, considering the way those people were carrying on. "Look," he insisted patiently, over his own knowledge that St Vier never bet anyone on anything, "I'll make it very simple for you. If you think of—"

But a sennet of trumpets, well coordinated by the master of the fireworks, drowned Alec out. Amongst the barges servants hastened to put out all their torches at once. The barges rocked wildly as they did so; the musicians, less well bred than their betters, swore. The backwash from the bobbing boats slapped at the shore. Laughter shivered up from the water. Then, abruptly, all was still as the first of the fireworks exploded against the sky.

It burst over them as a blue star, filling the sky with fiery petals for one awesome moment before beginning its lazy disintegration in point by point of blistering fire. On both sides of the river there was a hush as its sparks trickled down into the waiting blackness, leaving a ghostly trail of smoke that vanished even as they stared.

In the pause before the next one, Richard turned to his friend. But Alec's eyes hadn't moved from the empty sky. His face was a mask of blind desire.

Some local people had joined them on the rampart above the river—tradespeople, not scholars. They came in couples, courting, maybe, leaning close together with their arms around each other's waists. Alec never noticed them. Gold and green washed across his face as fiery garlands were hung across the sky.

Now a shrill whistle split the air; some people behind them jumped. Into the silent breach budded a knot of scarlet flame. Slowly it blossomed, and slowly dissolved into a host of tendrils, a floweringtree of a flower, with a golden heart that emerged, pulsing, at its center. For long slow seconds all the landscape was drenched in scarlet. In those red moments Richard heard Alec give one passionate sigh, and saw him raise both his hands to bathe them in the glow.

The boom and snap of the fireworks, echoing from bank to bank, made it hard to catch footsteps. Richard was only aware of the newcomer when he felt the subtle disturbance of cloth at his side. His hand snaked down and caught the intruder's wrist, poised where most gentlemen kept their purses. Without looking down he pinched it savagely between the bones. Then he turned slowly to find out who was making the controlled gurgle of pain.

"Oh," said Nimble Willie, smiling up at him weakly but winningly, "I didn't know it was you."

Richard let go of his arm, and watched him massage the nerve. The little thief was as slight as a child, and his face, though peaky, was guileless. His specialty was housebreaking. Richard was sorry to have hurt his crucial hand, but Willie was philosophical. "You fooled me, Master St Vier," he said, "in those naffy clothes. I thought you were a banker. Never mind, though; it's just as good I've found you. I've got some news you might want to have."

"All right," said Richard. "You may as well get a look at the fireworks while you're here."

Willie lifted his eyes, then shrugged. "What's the point? It's just colored lights."

Richard waited for the thrill of the next to be over before answering, "They're devilish expensive, Willie; they must be good for something."

IT WAS HOPELESS. THE FIREWORKS MUST BE ALMOST OVER, AND Michael saw that he was to be nothing more on the swan boat than one of a party of friends. The duchess treated him no differently than any of the others; if possible, with more distance, since she knew him the least well. Moodily he slung back a draught of burgundy, and picked at his duck. At least she hadn't mocked him as she had Horn, when the fool went on and on about the fireworks he had seen in better days. Horn hadn't the wit to catch the two edges of her meaning. Michael had, but much good it was doing him. He had laughed at her sally, but she turned her eyes then to Lord Ferris.

Why Ferris? Was he better dressed than Michael? He was certainly more powerful; but the duchess wasn't interested in politics. Her money, wit, and beauty were all the power she needed, Michael thought. Ferris was dark where he was fair. Ferris wasn't even whole. He'd lost one eye as a boy, and what was otherwise a handsome face was unbalanced by a stark black eye patch. An affectation: he might at least have had a number of them made to match his clothing. Well, Ferris was not the only one with an attractive eccentricity. Michael himself was already deep enough in the adventures of the sword to cause a minor scandal. Just because he kept it hidden beneath a well-groomed exterior . . . He must find some way to tell her what he had done at her prompting; some way to get her alone, away from these others. . . .

There was a sudden silence. The fireworks seemed to have ended. The others were exclaiming with disappointment, while servants cleared the fifth course away, and lowered the sides of the pavilion again. The duchess gestured to a footman, who nodded and headed for the stern.

"If no one minds," she explained to her guests, "I think we should make our way out of this press before everyone else starts trying to. I know Lord Ferris has somewhere else to go tonight, but the rest of you may want to come into the house to warm up after."

"Oh?" Lord Horn leaned over to the chancellor. "Are you by any chance attending Lord Ormsley's little card party?"

"No." Ferris smiled. "Business, I'm afraid."

The duchess rose, gesturing to her guests not to. "Please, stay comfortable. I'm only going forward for a little air."

Michael's skin tingled. It was as though she had read his mind. He would give her a moment, and then follow.

T HE FINAL VOLLEY OF FIREWORKS WAS A FUGUE OF SOUND AND light. Colors followed upon one another in ecstatic arcs, each higher and more brilliant, until the splendor was almost unbearable.

An awed but hopeful silence followed the last sparks down into the river. But the sky remained empty, a neatly folded blanket of stars on the bed of night. People shivered, then shrugged.

Alec finally turned to Richard. "Do you think," he asked avidly, "that an exploding firework could kill you?"

"It could," Richard answered. "You'd have to be sitting right on top of it, though."

"It would be quick," said Alec, "and splendid, in its way. Unless you kept it from going off." Nimble Willie shifted from foot to foot. "Oh. Hello, Willie. Come to pick—" Richard shook his head, indicating the tradesmen behind them. "—Come to see the fireworks?"

Once more the trumpets sounded, though less enthusiastically than they had at the start. Across the river the crowds were milling apart. The barge torches were being relit, and the string quartet had begun making a squeaky go at jollity. On the swan barge a woman emerged at the prow and stood facing into the wind that ruffled her cloak of fine white fur.

"There," Alec told Richard dryly. "You may admire the owner of your favorite boat. That's the duchess."

"She looks beautiful," Richard said in surprise.

"Anyone would," said Alec tartly, "in a great white boat in the middle of the river. You ought to see her up close."

It was hard to tell what he meant when he talked like that, as though he were making fun of himself for speaking, and you for listening. Richard had heard other nobles use that tone, though not, in general, to him. Nimble Willie, who had never enjoyed any nobleman's conversation, cleared his throat. "Master St Vier . . ."

He beckoned, like a small boy with a robin's nest to show. The two men followed him into a corner of the wall out of the wind and most people's sight.

The little thief brushed away the lock of hair that always seemed to be hanging over his nose. "Ah, now. I just wanted to say, there's been someone asking for St Vier these past two nights at Rosalie's."

"There," Alec said to Richard. "I knew we shouldn't have gone to Martha's"—although it was he himself who had insisted on it.

"And this man," Willie persisted, "has gold, they say."

"In Riverside?" Alec drawled. "He must be mad."

St Vier said, "Why wasn't I told about this before?"

"Ah." Willie nodded sagely. "He's paying, see. Putting out a bit of silver for word to get passed on to you. Two nights running, that's not bad."

"You want us to stay away another night?" the swordsman asked.

"Nah. My luck to find you, but there are probably others out looking, by now."

"Right. Thanks for your trouble." Richard gave the pickpocket some coins. Willie smiled, flexed his nimble fingers, and folded into the darkness.

"How the simple people do love you," said Alec, looking after him. "What happens when you don't have any money?"

"They trust me," said Richard, "to remember when I do."

A MOMENT OF SILENCE FELL WHEN THE DUCHESS LEFT THE PAVILion. All her guests were experienced socializers, but the departure of their hostess demanded a hiatus of reorganization.

In agony Michael listened to Chris and Lady Halliday talking about the weavers' revolt in Helmsleigh. Every second was precious; but he must not hurry out after her. At last he judged enough time to have passed. It being impossible to slip away unnoticed, he yawned extravagantly and stretched his arms as far as he was able in his fitted jacket.

"Not tired already, my dear?" said Horn.

"Tired?" Michael smiled his sweetest smile. Now that he was about to get what he wanted, he could afford to be tolerant. "How could I be tired in such pleasant company?"

"Wine always makes me sleepy," Lady Halliday said in a somber attempt at graciousness. Lady Helena allowed that it did her, too, but she would never dare to admit it before gentlemen. Satisfied that attention was diverted from his movements, Michael began to rise.

Like a filigreed anvil, Lord Horn's hand descended on his shoulder. "Do you know," Horn leaned over to confide in him, "when I first knew Ormsley he barely knew ace from deuce? And now he's giving exclusive card parties in that great big monstrosity his mother left him."

Michael murmured sympathetically, and kept his muscles tensed to rise. "I gather," Horn said, "that you are not engaged tonight?"

"I'm afraid I am." Michael tried to smile, keeping one eye nervously on the doorway. He thought he could just see the white glow of the duchess's fur outside. At least Horn was no longer touching him; but he *was* looking slyly at Michael, as though they shared some understanding. It conveyed roguish charm with a confidence more appropriate to a younger man.

"You certainly are kept busy," sighed Horn, lowering his eyelids alluringly.

"As busy as I can manage," Michael said, with the arrogant glibness that is the opposite of flirtation. He saw Horn's face freeze, and added, "I do try to keep my dignity."

It was needlessly cruel—and hypocritical from a man met climbing out of a window. But Horn must learn sometime that ten years had passed since the days of his glory were even possible—and besides, the duchess had just appeared in the doorway, flushed and beautiful, like some river goddess, crowned with stars. Michael felt his heart knot in a little hard lump that slid down into his stomach.

"It's snowing," the duchess said. "So lovely, and so inconvenient. Fortunately there's plenty to eat if we're slowed by it."

She seated herself in a flurry of fur. The diamonds of snow that spangled her hair and shoulders glittered for a moment in the candlelight before vanishing in the heat. "Now, I am sure you were all too polite to talk about me, so what gems of conversation have I missed?"

Lady Helena tried to match her banter, but fell short at brittle affectation: "Only the delight of Christopher telling us all what a hero he was at Helmsleigh."

"Ah." The duchess gave Lord Christopher a serious look. "The weavers are of some importance."

"To my tailor, anyway," said Horn jovially. "Local wool, he claims, will soon become inordinately priced. He's trying to sell me all of last year's colors at a bargain."

Across the table, Lord Ferris raised the eyebrow not covered by his patch. "Hard to keep your dignity in last year's colors."

Michael bit his lip. He hadn't meant his putdown of Horn to be public, much less to be taken up by others.

Horn inclined his head courteously. "I believe my tailor and I will reach an accord. He has known me for many years, and knows I am not to be trifled with."

The lump in Michael's stomach did a little somersault.

Ferris said to Diane, "I suppose we must call Lord Christopher one of Lord Halliday's circle, if so great a chancellor may be said to have something so small as a circle. But on behalf of my own office I must commend his work at Helmsleigh."

"You're kind," Lord Christopher murmured, assuming the stoic look of those forced to witness their own praise publicly.

"He isn't, really," the duchess told him. "My lord Ferris is horribly ambitious, and the first rule of the ambitious is never to ignore anyone who's been of use."

General laughter at the duchess's wit broke the tension.

There were four more courses in almost an hour of slow rowing before they found themselves once again at the Tremontaine landing. When they arrived they were all a little cold, a little tipsy, and very full.

All Michael wanted was to be off the barge and away from this disastrous group. The duchess had first led him on, and now she was making him feel like a fool—and, worse yet, act like one. But Ferris had no right to take a private comment and use it against Horn, in a way designed to stir up ill feeling. Now Horn was sulking like a child over nothing at all. If Horn himself had been more subtle, Michael would not have been forced to be so overt in his rejection. Horn spent the rest of the trip directing his attention everywhere but to Michael. Michael preferred it to his flirtation. The man was carrying on as though he'd never been turned down before, a situation which Michael considered most unlikely.

Despite his later appointment, Lord Ferris was induced to join the party inside the duchess's mansion for a hot drink. And despite his desire to get away, Michael felt it went against his dignity to leave before Ferris did. He knocked back his punch, and found the warmth of it dissolved some of the lump in his stomach. When Ferris called for his cloak, though, Michael did also. Diane said all the right things about how he really should stay; but there was no special light in her eyes, and he didn't believe her. She did escort both him and Lord Ferris to the door, and there she let Michael kiss her hand again. It was probably the punch that made him tremble as he took it. He looked up into her face, and found a smile so sweet fixed on him that he blinked to clear his eyes.

She said, "My dear young man, you must come again." That was all. But he lingered outside under the portico while the groom patiently held his horse for him, wanting to turn back and ask her whether she meant it, or to hear it again. A pair of missing gloves occurred to him, and he started back to the door. Through it her voice came clear to him, addressing Ferris: "Tony, whatever were you tormenting poor Horn about?"

Ferris chuckled. "You noticed that, did you?"

It was a voice of extreme intimacy. Michael knew the tone well. The door opened and he pressed back into the shadows, to see the duchess's white wrist pressed to Ferris's lips. Then she took a chain from around her neck and drew it across his mouth once before giving it to him.

Before his own reaction could betray him, Michael was out of the shadow of the house and up on horseback. And now he knew something about the duchess that no one else even suspected. And he wished, on the whole, that he were dead, or exceedingly drunk.

Bertram was able to oblige him in the latter. But even while dizzily wrestling in his friend's appreciative grasp, striving for oblivion, Michael was thinking of whether he could hurt her with it—just enough to give him what he wanted.

IT HAD STARTED TO SNOW AGAIN BY THE TIME THEY GOT TO Rosalie's. Soft flakes formed out of the darkness just before their eyes, falling like stars. Alec followed Richard down the steps and into the tavern, ducking under the low lintel. Rosalie's was in the cellar of an old town house. It was reliably cool in summer and warm in winter, always dark and smelling of earth.

The tavern's torchlight dazzled their eyes. Their clothes were steaming in the heat, their noses assaulted by the smells of beer and food and bodies, their ears by the shouts of gamblers and raconteurs.

As soon as Richard was spotted someone shouted, "That's it, everybody! No more free drinks!"

"Aww," they chorused. The serious dicers turned back to business, the serious drinkers reminded each other that life was like that. Certain of the Sisterhood came forward hoping to tease Alec, who would snap their heads off before he let them make him blush.

"Who told you about it this time, Master St Vier?" asked Half-Cocked Rodge, a local businessman. "I've got my money on Willie."

His partner, Lucie, leaned across the table. "Well, you can lay odds it wasn't Ginnie Vandall!"

The laughter this provoked meant something. Richard waited patiently to find out what it was. He had a guess.

Rodge made a place for him at his table. Lucie explained, "It's Hugo, my heart. Ginnie's bonny Hugo is after your job. Must have heard about the silver, and thought of gold. So Hugo walks in here last night, bold as you please, first time he's been here in months, he knows good and well this is your place for work. And he goes right up to this noble, tries to get his interest, but the man's no fool, he isn't having any."

"I'd like to meet this Hugo," said Alec doucely from where he stood behind Richard, leaning against a post.

Rosalie herself brought Richard some beer. "On me, old love," she told him; "you wouldn't believe the business you've brought me the last two nights by not being here!"

"Don't I get any?" Alec inquired.

Rosalie looked him up and down. The tavern mistress was conservative: to her he was still a newcomer. But Richard stood close to him these days, and she'd already seen a few fights fought in his defense; so she called for another mug for him. Then she settled down to argue with Lucie. "It's not a noble," Rosalie said. "I know nobles. They don't come to this place, they send someone else to do the arrangements for them."

"It is so one," Lucie insisted. "He talks like one. You think I don't know nobles? I've had a dozen; ride you up in their carriages on the Hill, put you to bed in velvet sheets and serve you hot breakfast before you go."

Richard, who really had had nobles, smiled; Alec sniggered.

" 'Course it's a noble." Mallie Blackwell had joined the fray, leaning with both palms on the table so that her charms dangled in front of their faces. "He's in disguise. That's how you can tell 'em. When they come down to the Brown Dog to gamble, the nobles always wear their masks. I can tell you, I've had a few."

"It isn't a mask," Rosalie said. "It's an eye patch."

"Same thing."

"Oh, really?" asked Alec with elaborate nonchalance. "Which eye? Does it change from night to night?"

"It's his left," Rosalie attested.

"Oh," said Alec softly. "And is he a dark-haired gentleman with—"

"Hugo!" A joyful roar greeted the newcomer for the benefit of all. "Haven't seen *you* in a boa's age!"

Hugo Seville made a stunning picture standing in the doorway, and he knew it. Hair bright as new-minted gold curled across his manly brow. His chin was square, his teeth white and even, revealed in a smile of confident strength. When he saw who Rodge was sitting with, the smile faltered.

"Hello, Hugo," Richard called, cutting off his retreat. "Come and join us."

To his credit, Hugo came. Richard read the wariness in his body, and was satisfied that he would make no more trouble. Hugo's smile was back in place. "Richard! I see they've found you. Or haven't you heard yet?"

"Oh, I've got the whole story now. Sounds like it has possibilities. I haven't had a really challenging fight since Lynch last month."

"Oh? What about de Maris?"

Richard shrugged. "De Maris was a joke. He'd got fat, living on the Hill." Hugo nodded gravely, keeping his thoughts to himself. De Maris had beaten him once. "Oh, Hugo," St Vier said, "you won't know Alec."

Hugo looked over and slightly up at the tall man standing behind St Vier. He was watching Hugo as if he were an unusual bug that had fallen into his soup.

"I'd heard," Hugo said. "Ginnie told me there was a fight at Old Market."

"Oh, *that* Hugo!" Alec exclaimed, his face animated with innocent curiosity. "The one who pimps for Ginnie Vandall!"

Hugo's hand leapt to his sword. Rodge let out a chuckle, and Lucie a gasp. The buzz of conversation at nearby tables trickled to nothing as all eyes focused on them.

"Hugo's a swordsman," Richard told Alec, unruffled. "Ginnie manages his business for him. Sit down, Hugo, and have a drink."

Alec looked down at Richard, sitting calm and easy, one hand on his mug. Alec's lips parted to say something; then he only licked them and took a drink, his eyes fixed on Hugo over the rim of his mug.

They were green eyes, bright in the angular face, like a cat's. Hugo didn't like cats. He never had.

"I beg your pardon," the young man said, smooth as a nobleman. "I must have been thinking of some other people."

"I can't stay," Hugo said, sitting uncomfortably. "I have to meet someone soon."

"Well, that's all right," Richard said. "Tell me about this man. What did you think of him?"

Hugo could pay for his gaffe with information. It wasn't like him to try to steal Richard's jobs. Richard guessed that he had been unable to resist the money smell.

Hugo made much more money than Richard did. He was in great demand on the Hill for lovers' duels, and as a ceremonial wedding guard. He was dashing and gallant, well dressed, graceful, and fairly well mannered. He had not taken a challenge to the death in years. Hugo was a coward. Richard knew it, and a few others guessed it, but they kept their mouths shut because of Ginnie and the money he was making. Hugo's nerve had broken years ago, at a time when he was still fighting dangerous fights. He could have turned to alcohol to see him through a few more duels before it betrayed him; but Ginnie Vandall had seen the possibilities in Hugo and turned him from that path to a more lucrative one.

Richard appreciated Hugo. Now that St Vier's reputation was flourishing, the nobles were always after him to take dull jobs that challenged nothing except his patience. Richard turned them over to Hugo, and Hugo was glad. Hugo's income was steadier; but when a man was marked for killing, or a point needed to be made in blood, it was St Vier they wanted, and they paid him what he asked.

"Everyone here," Richard prompted, "seems to think he's a lord. Except Mistress Rosalie. What would you say?"

Hugo's flush was just discernible in the dim light. "Hard to tell. He had the manner. But then, he might have been putting it on." He glared in Alec's direction. "Some do, you know."

"Let's face it," said Rodge; "we wouldn't know him if it was Halliday himself. Who's ever seen any of 'em up close?"

"I have," said Alec coolly. Richard held his breath, wondering if his proud companion were going to declare himself.

"Lucky you! Where? Was he handsome?"

"At University," Alec said. "He came and spoke after there'd been a riot over the city's tearing down some student lodgings. He promised to found a scholarship and some new whorehouses. He was very well received: we carried him on our shoulders, and he kicked me in the ear." They laughed appreciatively at that, but Alec seemed unaffected by his new popularity. He said sourly, "Of course you'll never see Halliday here. There are too many important people who want to kill him already; why should he come down here and let just anyone do it for free?" Alec slung his cloak around his shoulders. "Richard, I'm off. Let me know if the eye patch changes eyes."

"Don't you want to stay and see for yourself?"

"No. I do not."

Alec made his way across the tavern with his usual posture: head thrust forward, shoulders slumped, as though he were expecting to run into something. Richard looked curiously after him. After the fight at the Old Market Alec was probably safe enough on the streets, but his mood seemed strange, and Richard wondered what had made him leave so suddenly. He thought he'd go after him, just to ask; just to see what he'd say and listen to him talk in that creamy voice . . . the one-eyed messenger could come again tomorrow night if he really wanted him. Richard excused himself and hurried after Alec, who had stopped in front of the door as it opened inward. A tall man in a black felt hat came in. Alec looked up sharply at him, then brushed past, almost elbowing him aside in his haste to get up the stairs. Richard was about to follow when the man removed his hat, brushing snow off the crown. His left eye was covered with a black patch. He had turned his whole head to look over his shoulder after Alec. Then he slammed the door shut behind him, and turned and saw Richard.

"Dear me," he said wearily, "I hope you're not another unemployed swordsman."

"Well, I am, actually," said Richard.

"I'm afraid my needs are quite specific."

"Yes, I know," he answered. "You wanted St Vier."

"That is correct."

Richard indicated an empty table. "Would you like to sit by the fire?"

The man's mouth froze in the act of opening; then it stretched into a smile, a speaking smile that conveyed understanding. "No," he said courteously, "thank you. If you won't be too cold there, I would prefer a corner where we will not be disturbed."

They found one, between a support-beam and the wall. Richard folded himself neatly into his seat, and the stranger followed, taking care with the placement of his clothes and the end of his sword. It was an old-fashioned, heavy sword with an ornate basket handle. Carrying it exposed him to the danger of a challenge, but not carrying it left him looking more vulnerable than he would wish.

The man's face was long and narrow, with a dark, definite jawline, heavily shadowed. Above it his skin was pale, even for winter. The cord of his eye patch disappeared into hair as dark as a crow's plumage.

Unbidden, Rosalie brought two mugs to the table. The one-eyed gentleman waved them away. "Let us have wine. Have you no sack? Canary?"

The tavern mistress nodded mutely and snatched the beer mugs back. Richard could have told him that Rosalie's wine was sour, her sherry watered; but no one had asked him.

"So you're St Vier," the man said.

"Yes." The stranger's face went opaque as he scrutinized the swordsman. None of them could ever resist doing it. Richard waited politely as the man took in his youth, his uneven good looks, the calm of his hands on the table before him. He was beginning to think this was going to be one of the ones who said, "You're hardly what I expected," and tried to proposition him. But the stranger only nodded curtly. He looked down at his own gloved hands, and back at Richard.

"I can offer you sixty," he said softly.

It was a very nice sum. Richard shrugged. "I'd have to know more about it first."

"One challenge—to the death. Here in the city. I don't think you can quarrel with that."

"I only quarrel on commission," Richard said lightly.

The man's lips thinned out to a smile. "You're an agreeable man. And an efficient one. I saw you fight off two men at Lord Horn's party."

"You were there?" Richard hoped it might be a preface to his identity; but the man only answered, "I had the fortune to witness the fight. It's a mystery to everyone still, what the whole thing was about." His one eye glinted sharply; Richard took the hint, and returned it: "I'm afraid I can't tell you that. Part of my work is to guard my employers' secrets."

"And yet you let them employ you without any contract."

Richard leaned back, entirely at ease. He had a fair idea of where this was going now. "Oh, yes, I insist on that. I don't like having my business down on paper in someone's drawer."

"But you open yourself up to a great deal of danger that way. Should any of your duels be investigated, there is no written proof that you are anything but a casual murderer."

St Vier smiled, and shrugged. "That's why I'm careful who I work for. I give my patrons my word to do the job and to keep quiet about it; they have to be trusted to know what they're doing, and back me up if need be. In the long run, most people find they prefer it that way."

Rosalie returned with two dusty pewter goblets and a flagon of acidic wine. The man waited until she had gone before saying, "I'm glad to hear you say so. I've heard your word is good. That arrangement is suitable."

When he drew off one of his gloves, the expensive scent of ambergris drifted up. His large hand was as creamy and well tended as a woman's. And when he lifted the flagon to pour out the wine, Richard saw the marks of rings still pale on his bare fingers. "I am prepared to pay you thirty in advance."

Richard raised his eyebrows. No point in pretending that half in advance wasn't unusually generous. "You're kind," he said.

"Then you accept?"

"Not without more information."

"Ah." The man leaned back, and drained half his cup. Richard admired the self-control that let him lower it from his lips without an expression of disgust. "Tell me," he asked, "who was that tall man I passed, coming in?"

"I've no idea," Richard lied.

"Why do you refuse my offer?"

Richard said in the comradely tone that had so bemused Lord Montague over his daughter's wedding, "I don't know who you are, and I don't know who the mark is. You can offer me all sixty in advance, I still can't give you my word on it."

The gentleman's eye glared at him with the intensity of two. But he kept the rest of his face blandly civil, contriving even to look a bit bored. "I understand your need for caution," he said. "I think I can set some of your fears to rest." Slowly, almost provocatively, he removed his other glove.

Again the scent of ambergris assailed the air, rich and sensual. It made Richard think of Alec's hair. The man held up his hand. Dangling from it was a long gold chain, with an eight-sided medallion spinning at the end of it so that Richard could not make out its design. The candle between them winked a gold sequin in his eyes. With one finger the man stopped the spinning, and Richard had one sight of the device engraved on the medallion before it disappeared again into the glove.

"Sixty royals," the man said, "half in advance."

Richard took his time as he brought the goblet to his lips, took a sip of the dust-flecked wine, put the cup down, and wiped his mouth. "I don't take money on an unnamed man.—It is a man?" he added abruptly, somewhat spoiling the effect, but wanting to keep things clear. "I don't do women."

The man's lips quirked; he had heard the Montague story. "Oh, yes, it is a man. It is a man of some importance, and I am not going to tell you any more without further indication of interest on your part. Are you at liberty tomorrow night?"

"I may be."

"It would be advantageous. Do you know the Three Keys, on Lower Henley Street?" He did. "Be there at eight. Take a table near the door, and wait." The gentleman reached into his coat and withdrew a little silk purse that clinked when he set it on the table. "This should cover expenses." Richard didn't pick it up. It made a sound like silver.

The gentleman rose, spilling a little shower of copper on the table for the tally, and pulled on his scented glove. "It took a long time to find you," he said. "Are you always so hard to get?"

"You can always leave a message for me here. Just don't make it worth people's while not to deliver it."

"I see." The man smiled wryly. "Your friends are not to be bribed?"

The idea amused St Vier. "Everyone can be bribed," he said. "You just have to know their price. And remember that they're all afraid of steel."

"I will remember." The man sketched him the slightest of bows. "Good night, then."

RICHARD DID NOT BOTHER TO FINISH THE WINE. HE CONSIDERED taking it home for Alec, but it was bad enough to leave. Rosalie did keep a stock of decent vintage, but you had to know how to ask for it. Ignoring the curious looks of his friends, he left the tavern and went home.

The eaves of the house were fanged with icicles. Marie's rooms were quiet; she must still be out. He looked up at his own rooms. The shutters were open, the windows dark. He let himself in by the court-yard stairs, mounting quietly to keep from disturbing Alec.

Despite his care, the floorboards creaked. It was an old house, built of heavy materials with a great care for solidness. At night they heard it settling on its foundations, like an old woman on her doorstep shifting into a comfortable position in the sun.

From the other room Alec called blearily, "Richard?" The bedroom door was open; Alec usually left it that way when he went to bed alone. Richard could see him in the dark, a white figure propped against the heavily carved headboard. "Are you going out again?"

"No." Richard undressed quietly in the dark, laying out his clothes to air on the chest. Alec held the covers back for him—"Hurry up, it's cold." Between the linen sheets Alec's warmth had spread; Richard sank into it like a hot bath.

Alec lay on his back, his hands folded demurely behind his head. "Well," he said, "that didn't take long. Don't tell me it was another wedding."

"No, it's not. It's a real job, looks like it could be interesting. Move your elbow, you've got both pillows."

"I know." Richard could hear the satisfied smile in the dark. "Don't go to sleep. Tell me about it."

"There's not much to tell." Abandoning the pillow, he moved his head into the crook of Alec's arm. "They're playing hard-to-get. I have to show some more interest."

"Who's *they*?"

"You'll laugh."

"Of course I'll laugh. I always do." It was the voice, rich and arrogant and taut with breeding, that always undid him in the dark. He felt for Alec's lips with his fingers, and softly brushed over them.

"It's funny. I think he's a lord, all right, but he seems to be working for another house."

"Working *with* them, more likely." Alec's lips moved against his fingers, the tip of his tongue touching them as he spoke. "I bet you're right, it must be something big. The fate of the state is in your hands—" Alec seized the fingers that were touching him, and Richard's other hand as well, drawing them from what they were doing in a convulsive grip, feeling there for the old ragged scar on Richard's wrist. Richard guided his mouth to it. "So how do you know," Alec murmured into his skin, "that it's two houses?"

Gently Richard freed one hand, and began stroking the length of Alec's back. It pleased him to feel the taut body relax under his touch, straining langorously to be closer to his. "He showed me a medallion with a device," he said.

"Which you didn't recognize and were too embarrassed to ask about . . . ah, that feels nice."

"As a matter of fact, I did recognize it. It was that swan woman's, the duchess."

For all the tricks Alec played with his voice, he had never realized how easy it was for the swordsman to read his body. It stiffened suddenly, although Alec's voice rambled on, "How delightful. Isn't it nice to know, Richard, that you're not the only one to have succumbed to the allure of the swan boat?"

"I haven't succumbed," Richard said comfortably. Alec must have recognized the nobleman. "Although I wouldn't mind a ride on that boat. But they have to name their mark first. If it's a good job, I'll succumb to the money."

"You think so?"

"I think so."

Alec breathed out in a feathery sigh as Richard sought out his pleasure, always careful not to startle him with anything sudden or unexpected. Sometimes finding it was like stalking prey, or coaxing a wild creature to his hand. Alec stopped speaking, let his eyelids fall thin over his bright eyes, and Richard felt his body coursing fluid like water, as though he held the power of a river in his arms.

When they kissed, Alec's arms tightened around his shoulders; then they began to move up and down Richard's body as if looking for something, trying to draw something out of the taut muscles of his back and thighs.

"Ah!" Alec said, contentment mingled with surprise; "you're so beautiful!"

Richard stroked him in answer; felt him shudder, felt the sharp fingers sink into his muscle. Richard teased himself, pulling Alec along with him deeper into no-return with the smoothness of skin against skin, the harshness of breath and bone. Alec was talking now, his voice rapid and full of air—not making any real sense, but a pleasure to have that light voice in his ear, gasped syllables stirring his hair, lips teasing his earlobe, breaking off occasionally to sink sharp teeth there. . . .

"There is no one like you, they never told me there was anyone like you, I had no idea, it amazes me, Richard—Richard—if I had known—if I—"

Alec's hands struck against his throat, and for a moment Richard didn't realize that pain was pain. Then he pulled away, catching the fragile wrists before they could try again whatever mad notion Alec had of attacking him.

"What in hell do you think you're doing?" he demanded, harsher than he'd meant to because his breathing was not yet under control.

Alec's body was rigid, and his eyes were wide, glinting with their own unhealthy light. Richard ran one hand along his face to soothe his terror; but Alec wrenched his head away, gasping, "No, don't!"

"Alec, am I hurting you? Has something happened? What is it?"

"Don't do that, Richard." The long body was trembling with tension and desire. "Don't ask me questions. It would be easy now, wouldn't it? You could ask me anything. And I'd tell you like this, I'd tell you . . . now that you have me like this I'd tell you anything—anything—"

"No," Richard said, gently gathering him into his arms. "No, you won't. You're not going to tell me anything. Because I'm not going to ask." Alec shuddered; some of his hair worked loose across his face. "There's nothing I want to know, Alec, I'm not going to ask you anything. . . ." He started to brush back the hair, soft and brown as an old forest stream; then he changed the gesture and lifted it to his lips. "It's all right, Alec . . . lovely Alec . . ."

"But I'm not," Alec said into his shoulder.

"I wish you wouldn't argue all the time." Richard's fingers luxuriated in the high-bred bones. "You are very lovely."

"You are very . . . foolish. But then, so is Ferris."

"Who's Ferris?"

"Your friend in the tavern. The Mysterious Mr. One-Eye. Also the one and only Dragon Chancellor on the Council of Lords." Alec carefully licked his eyelids, one at a time. "He must be crazy to come down here. Or desperate."

"Maybe he's just having fun."

"Maybe." Alec's long body twisted around him, adding weight to his statements. "Somebody has to."

"Aren't you?"

"Having fun? Is that the idea? I thought we were supposed to be providing material for poets and gossips."

"I kicked them out."

"You skewered them."

"I skewered them. Roast Poet on a Spit."

"Gossip Flambée . . . Richard . . . I think I can see what you mean about having fun."

Richard intercepted the hand poised to tickle him, and turned the motion into quite another one.

"I'm glad. You are lovely."

chapter IX

THERE WAS, AFTER ALL, NO REAL REASON FOR RICHARD NOT to go to the Three Keys the next night. If Ferris took it to mean that Richard accepted the job, that was his mistake. When he knew the name of the mark he would decide whether to take the job or not. He only hoped he would find out now, and not be offered more circumlocutions and little bags of silver.

Richard crossed the Bridge well armed. The poor who lived around the wharves tended to be desperate and unskilled, without pride or reputations to lose. They would jump a friend as readily as they would a stranger, and give no challenge first. The upper city people thought they were a spillover from Riverside. Riversiders sneered at them as graceless incompetents who knew enough not to cross the Bridge.

The Three Keys was admirably suited to mysterious rendezvous. It was set in the middle of nowhere, between warehouses and counting-houses that were vacant at night, silent except for the occasional step of the Watch. People with nowhere else to go went there, seeking anonymity. Some sought oblivion: as Richard approached the tavern he saw the door open, a rectangle of dusky light, and a body come pitching out. The man lay snoring stertorously on the melted snow. St Vier stepped around him and went in.

He had no trouble finding a table near the door. It was a chilly night, with damp fog off the river, and the room's population was clustered at the other end, near the fire. They were mostly men, companionless, nameless. They noticed the newcomer; a few looked at him twice, trying to figure out where they'd seen him before, before going back to what they had been doing.

His contact aroused more interest. It was a woman who appeared poised in the doorway, cloaked and deeply hooded, her shadowed face turned toward the table. Richard wondered if it might not be the duchess herself this time, imitating Ferris's feat of bravado slumming. Whoever it was, she recognized him at once, crossing to his table with a firm stride. Before she could reach him, however, a large red-faced man sauntered up and barred her way, saying in a less than ingratiating growl, "Hello, sweetheart."

Richard started to go to her, then saw her flash of steel. "Clear off." She was holding a long knife to the drunken man's chest.

"Hey, sweetie," the man coaxed, "don't get upset." And he wasn't as drunk as he looked, or else he'd once been a fighter, because suddenly the knife was on the floor. He had her wrist in his hand, and was pulling her in to him when she twisted away, shouting, "Richard!"

St Vier came forward, his knife already out. The man saw and his grip slackened enough for the woman to pull away. "Get out of here," Richard told him, "or find yourself a sword."

A man in a leather apron came hurrying up from the back. "Outside," he said; "you know the rules."

The drunk rubbed his own arms, as though he had been hurt. "Lenny," he said to the tapster, "you know I don't mean anything. What the hell have I got to fight for?"

Richard gestured with his dagger: Back. The man backed off, and faded with Lenny into the rear of the tavern.

With Richard covering her, the woman picked up her own knife and replaced it in her sleeve. She sighed, and shook herself all over. "I can't believe I did that," she said.

"I can." Richard returned to the table. "You've got that hood in your eyes, how do you expect to see anything?"

She laughed and shook the hood away from her face. A mass of fox-colored hair tumbled down with it. "Buy me a drink?" she grinned.

"Just one?" he answered her smile. "Not eight? Or have you lowered your limit these days?"

"I'm not testing it here: this place serves river water, mixed with raw spirits to cut the taste."

"It seems"—he looked back at her assailant—"to do the trick, whatever. Sit here, so I can keep an eye on him."

"Yes." She snuggled down, with her elbows on the table. "They told me you'd look after me. I think you're *awfully* brave. Do you really *kill* people with that thing?"

"Oh, well, only for money." He looked at her blandly. "Is that modest enough for you?"

"It's an improvement. You're the best in the city now."

"I was then, too."

She laughed, exposing brown teeth in a strong pretty face. "That's right. But word's trickled up to the ones who make the judgments. You know the channels as well as I do."

Richard snorted. "Channels! You kill enough people for them, they finally realize you know how to."

Impatiently she said, "Don't start up with that. You're important now, and you know it." She looked stern, her grey eyes opaque and businesslike. "How long do you think that you can keep on playing him out?"

"I don't mean to. I just need more information. Tell me about the other . . . lady."

"What other lady—" Her face began to flush and she dropped her eyes. "I don't think that that has anything to do with this," she said gruffly.

"I'm sorry." Richard reverted to his polite, dealing-with-clients voice. "I thought you were with another household." He had learned a great deal from her discomfort—more than he'd really intended to.

"I'm his chambermaid." She gave him a hard, defiant look across the table. "One of them. We keep the place clean. It's a nice house."

"You look well," he said. Neither of them brought up the name of her master, she by instruction and Richard because he obviously was not supposed to know it. "Life on the Hill agrees with you."

She looked directly at him, cutting through the sociableness. "It agrees with me better than jail. I thought it would be nothing, being whipped; it happened to everyone else, and they just laughed and went back to stealing." She lowered her gaze to her hands, folded on the table. They were well shaped, the rounded fingers in pleasing proportion to the palm. Richard saw that their skin had coarsened from menial work. "But that straw they give you *smells*, and they strip the dress off your back as though it meant nothing, as though you're some actor putting on a good show for the crowd. I saw what it was like, and how it all came out— What happened to Annie?"

It took him a moment to remember who she meant. "She got better. Then she lived like a queen for a while, before they caught her again."

"And then?"

"She died that time."

She nodded. "I'd rather die in private. Or take a nice clean sword thrust, like you did to Jessa—"

"No," Richard said. "You wouldn't."

But she'd left Riverside long ago, and she wasn't afraid any more. The past was a story told, a battle fought. "I really thought you loved her, that one," she said quietly.

"I don't know," Richard said. "It doesn't matter. Why did you get sent down here?"

She shrugged. "He— I work for him. He had to send someone."

"He knew you'd know me."

She looked down at the table, deeply polished and carved from the flow of other people's hands. "He just knows I'm from Riverside. You know the way they lump us all together up there."

She had a right to her privacy. That her noble employer was also her lover seemed sure; how else would Ferris know that her past included St Vier? Nor would the lord be likely to entrust a common servant with such a delicate mission. For Katherine, it was a good thing: Ferris was not unattractive, and his favor could help her stay out of Riverside.

"And you," she asked. "Are you alone now?"

"No." She let out a tiny sigh. He said suddenly, "Katherine. Is he hurting you?"

She looked tired. She shook her head. "No. I don't need anything. Just an answer to bring back."

"You know I can't answer yet," Richard said; "you know the way I work."

"You haven't heard all the question." She was smiling strangely, looking at him out of the corners of her eyes. It was another woman's smile; he didn't know whose, but he knew what it meant.

Richard reached across the table, and covered her hand with his. "It's an idea," he said; "but not yours or mine. Tell him you asked; tell him you plied me with drink, but I was more interested in money. It's actually true," he added lightly. "People get the strangest ideas about swordsmen."

Calmly she repossessed her hand, saying dryly, "I can't imagine where they got them." Then, following his tone with its offer of safe trivialities, "They miss you on the Hill, now you're not young and wild anymore. Who've you finally settled down with, Ginnie Vandall? No one seems to know."

"It's a man," he told her, "a stranger called Alec."

"What's he like?"

He seemed to consider the question carefully. "Nothing else, really. He's not like anything I've ever seen."

"What does he do?"

"He used to be a student, I'm pretty sure of that. Now he tries to get himself killed," he told her with perfect seriousness.

"With what, falling rocks?"

"Falling rocks, knives, people . . . anything that's handy."

She considered the prospect. "A student. Can't fight."

"Total incompetent. It keeps me busy."

"Protecting him."

She let the words hang in the air. She could hurt him now with a name—or try to. *Jessamyn*. A beautiful woman, an accomplished thief, rising con-artist . . . she and the young swordsman together had dazzled Riverside like twin stars. Jessamyn was not incompetent, she knew how to use a knife. Jessamyn had a temper, and one night she had made Richard lose his. There had been no protecting her.

Katherine could try to hurt him with it—but what if nothing happened? Richard had always been likeably sure of himself. But these last few years had cast a glamour over him. There were no more rough edges, no hesitations. He turned a smooth face to the world, making it see him as he saw himself. It pleased her to think that here was someone who didn't care what others thought of him, someone free from the daily struggle for dominance. But it chilled her to think that he believed it himself, that his life was free of all that made human life impossibly painful. She found she did not want to try.

"Really," Richard said, "if you want another drink, you can have it."

"I know," she said. "What's he trying to kill himself for?"

"I don't know. I haven't asked."

"But you don't want him to do it."

St Vier shrugged. "It seems stupid."

Slowly, not to alarm him, she took out her knife to look at it and shook her head. "When I came in here . . . I shouldn't have called for you. I should have stuck that idiot when I had the chance."

"This isn't Riverside. You could have got into trouble."

She kept shaking her bent head, hair dancing along her cheeks like snakes. "No. I just couldn't do it. I missed my chance because I couldn't do it."

"You were cumbered by the hood." She looked up, smiling: "cumbered" was a country word. But he met her eyes gravely: "Anyway, it doesn't matter. You'll never have to go back to Riverside."

She hoped it was true. "Don't tell him I fumbled," she said.

"I won't. I probably won't even see him again."

"I don't know." She pulled a flat, folded piece of paper out of her cloak. It was closed with blank gobs of sealing wax. "It's what you think it is. Open it when you get home. He says he doesn't want to rush you: you've got a week to think about it. If you decide to go ahead with it, be at the Old Bell a week from tonight, same time. Someone will be there with the first half of your payment."

"Half in advance . . . he really meant it. Generous. How will I know the messenger?"

"*He'll* know *you*. By the ring you're wearing."

"What ring?"

This time she handed him a small doeskin pouch. Richard loosened the drawstrings, and glimpsed the heavy glow of an enormous ruby. Hastily he closed it, and tucked the pouch inside his shirt, along with the sealed paper.

"And if I don't go . . . ?"

She smiled at him, a ghost of her old street smile. "Wear it anyway. He didn't say anything about giving it back."

The ring was worth almost as much as the job itself: double payment, the gift that was a bribe. Lord Ferris was no idiot, nor was he heavy-handed.

Katherine stood up, wrapping herself in the cloak. She stood only shoulder-high to St Vier. He dropped one of Ferris's silver pieces on the table for the tally. When she queried with her eyebrows he explained, "It's the smallest he gave me. Maybe he thinks I only drink rare wines."

"Maybe he thought you'd get change for it," she replied. "Get the change, Richard, or there'll be talk."

He got the change, in brass, and pocketed it. Then he stood very close to her and handed over the silver pouch. " 'For expenses' was what he told me. I wouldn't want to be guilty of a cheap evening." Mutely she took what he offered. She could buy a lot with that money; and if he didn't need it, so much the better for him.

As they walked out, the rows of men muttered flatly, "Good night, sweetheart. Take care of yourself, darling."

They left the tavern. Over their heads the three iron keys, with a few flecks of gold still clinging to them, jangled in the wind. They turned up Lower Henley Street, making for the Stooping Eagle Tavern, where one of Ferris's footmen, discreetly attired in buff, waited to escort her back to the Hill.

IT WAS LATE WHEN RICHARD CAME IN, BUT ALEC WAS STILL UP, reading by the light of a candle. Alec looked up out of the circle of light at him, blinking at the darkness across the room.

"Hello, Richard."

"Hello," Richard said amiably. "I'm back."

Slowly St Vier unbuckled his sword. He removed his knives gingerly, as though they were infants, or creatures who might bite, and placed them on the mantel.

"I see you're back," Alec said. "You've missed all the excitement. Marie got into a fight with one of her clients. She chased him three times around the courtyard, throwing socks and using language. He tried to hide behind the well. I threw an onion down at him. I missed, of course, but it scared him. Maybe he thought it was you. Anyway, he finally went away, and then the cats started yowling up on the roof and I didn't have anything left to throw at *them*. Have you?"

"No. I don't think so. I think they've gone away," said Richard, who hadn't heard anything.

"I think we should get a cat of our own. We could train it to fight. It could chase them away. After all, there's no point in sending *you* up on the roof."

"Why not?" Richard asked, going over to the window. He looked up. "I could get up there. Easy." He hoisted himself onto the sill.

"It would be much easier," Alec said, "to get a cat. We could save its life—pull a thorn out of its paw or something—and it would be forever grateful."

Richard swung open the window and leaned out, holding on with one hand. "You are making me giddy," said Alec, "and anyway, all the cats are gone. You said so yourself."

"I'm not going to fall. But it isn't far. You could jump, and probably not break anything, if you had to. Right down to the courtyard."

"Marie would have a fit. You look like an idiot standing in that window. You look like you're expecting to fly away."

Richard laughed, and jumped back down into the room. He landed badly and staggered upright. "There!" he exclaimed. "That's what comes of listening to you."

"I didn't tell you to jump out of the window."

"You're always telling me to get drunk. Well, now I've done it, and I don't like it." He sat down hard on their only chair, assuming the pose of one who didn't intend to get up for a long time.

"Drunk on what?" Alec asked; "the usual blood?"

"No, brandywine. Really horrible brandy. I knew I didn't like getting drunk, and now I can remember why. I keep having to remember where my feet are. I really don't like it at all. I don't see how you can stand it so often."

"Well, I never care where my feet are. Don't tell me you let Ferris feed you horrible brandy!"

"No, I did it myself. All by myself. I thought I might like it. You're always saying I'd like it. Well, I don't like it. You were wrong."

"You've said that," Alec said, "twice. If you think I'm going to apologize because you can't keep track of your own feet, you're mistaken. Let's go out. I'll teach you to dice."

"I'm drunk, not insane. I'm going to bed."

Alec stretched on his chaise longue like a cat, one thumb still in his book. "Richard, *why* did you get drunk? Wasn't Ferris there?"

"Of course he wasn't there. Someone else was there."

"Were they horrible to you? Are you going to kill them?"

"No, and no. God, you're bloodthirsty. I'm not going to kill anybody. I'm going to sleep. Get me anything you want for breakfast, just not fish."

Somehow he must have got himself undressed and into bed, because suddenly there was a hand gripping his shoulder and Alec's voice saying over and over, "Richard, Richard, wake up." He noted crossly how slow his reaction was as he groaned and turned over, saying in a thick voice unlike his own, "What is it?"

He hadn't closed the shutters; a dim bar of silvery moonlight fell across the bed, illuminating Alec's hand tense on the coverlet, crushing Lord Ferris's paper.

"You were snoring," Alec drawled ingenuously; but the whiteness of his knuckles on the paper betrayed him.

"Well, I've stopped." Richard didn't bother to argue. "What do you think of Ferris's message?"

"I think his spelling stinks." With the weight of the seals for ballast, Alec flipped the paper open.

There was no writing on it; only a drawing of a phoenix rising from the flames over a series of heraldic bends.

"It's a coat of arms," Alec said grimly. "Do you know whose?"

"Of course. I've seen it all over the city. On his banners, and carriages, and things."

"It's Basil Halliday," Alec said portentously, as though he hadn't answered.

"It's Basil Halliday," Richard agreed. "You're stealing all the blankets, and you haven't even got into bed yet."

Somewhat frantically, Alec tucked the covers around him, and began to pace the room. "This *is* the man Ferris wants you to kill?"

"Ferris or that duchess does. I haven't quite figured them out yet. He must be protecting her."

"He can't be running errands for her. A man of his rank would no more do that than polish his own boots. Could the drawing mean that Halliday's another patron?"

"No. This is the usual way the smart ones announce a mark. I should burn that paper. Remind me in the morning."

"Don't go to sleep," Alec ordered.

"I don't think I . . ." His jaw cracked in a yawn. But he forced his eyes to stay open. "What's the matter?" he asked. "I've told you everything I know. Can you tell me any more? Is there something I should know?"

It was the wrong thing to say. Alec's face closed like a trap door. "Know?" he repeated, honey and steel. "I know enough to stay out of their way when they're playing these games. You think you're above it all, Richard—but they'll chew you up, and then you won't much care whether they swallow you or spit you out."

Richard wanted to explain that that didn't happen to swordsmen: they took their pay for whatever the job was and went home, leaving the nobles to argue the results out amongst themselves. For the first time he seriously wondered whether Alec knew the Hill at all, not to know that. But all he said was, "I'll be fine—if I take the job at all. I've got time to say no. But the duchess will pay for it, and Ferris will keep me out of trouble. You'll see. Maybe they'll send us up to Tremontaine until it blows over—live in a nice cottage by a stream, go fishing, keep bees . . . how'd you like to go to the country for a while?"

"I detest the country," Alec said icily. "Go back to sleep."

St Vier closed his eyes, and finally it was dark enough. "All right. But only because I'm feeling so agreeable. It's too bad. I'm going to feel awful in the morning."

"Sleep in. You always feel splendid in the afternoon."

And that is just what he did.

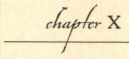

chapter X

I T WAS TOO SOON, LORD FERRIS WAS THINKING AS HE MOUNTED
the street to the Halliday town house; too soon for Basil Halliday
to know what the game was.

Katherine's errand was freshly executed. In a week, if all went well,
Ferris would have the swordsman's answer, and plans for the Crescent
Chancellor's mortal challenge could begin to go forward. Even if
Katherine had contrived a look at the closely sealed paper she carried,
Ferris was certain of her movements for the last day; and he thought
she was not false to him. St Vier was no agent of Halliday's either; of
that Ferris had made sure.

There was no telling what today's invitation from Lord Halliday to
come and "talk privately" meant. It was an informal note in Halliday's
own hand; perhaps his secretary did not even know of it. It put Ferris
on his guard, but the Dragon Chancellor of the Inner Council could
not ignore a summons from its Crescent, however mysterious—and
perhaps it was only a tricky piece of Council business that Halliday
wanted to discuss with him before anyone else heard about it. The informal note might be just that: Halliday's secretaries had been heard
to complain that their master's informalities drove them to distraction. Ferris might have to wait behind whoever else had the official
appointment at this hour.

The Halliday town house stood alone at the top of a steep street;
inconvenient, but possessed of a magnificent view. It was a house
without a gate: all its gardens were at the back, overlooking the river.

Ferris saw a couple of well-built men lingering about the edges of the property. It was not too soon, it seemed, for the Crescent Chancellor to have begun to worry about the danger the election put him in. He was going to be well guarded from now on. It eased Ferris's mind a little: the defense was sufficiently vague to imply that Halliday knew of no specific plan. He was well guarded. St Vier was going to have to be clever. But then, St Vier's reputation said he was. He had just better not be too clever to take the job.

Perhaps, Ferris thought, he should have timed things more tightly, given the swordsman less time to think the offer over. But Ferris had acted on an impression of St Vier at the Riverside Tavern: the swordsman had the self-respect of an artist, the vanity of a lover. Like a lover, he must be wooed; like an artist he must be flattered. Giving him time to think things over was an act of trust and respect that Ferris hoped would clinch the deal. It also wouldn't hurt for St Vier to have made up his mind long before the next set rendezvous, so that he came to it eager, straining at the bit.

Ferris found Basil Halliday in his study, surrounded by papers and half-empty cups of chocolate. Halliday's hair was mussed; he must have been running his fingers through it. There was an ink stain on his forehead to prove it. His smile on seeing Ferris was all the more charming for its preoccupation. Ferris relaxed a shade, and began to wonder what he was expected to be charmed into this time.

"What," Lord Halliday said to Ferris without preamble, "do you think friend Karleigh is up to now?"

"The duke?" Ferris answered. "Sulking out on his estates, I should imagine. Where he should be, after you had St Vier beat his swordsman at Horn's."

"I? I didn't hire him. I know that's what they're saying, but that duel was the first I knew of any challenge."

"It's what Horn's saying." That answered that question. Ferris did not like the implications. Who else but Halliday had the power to frighten Karleigh through a purely formal duel into retreating into the country at this time of year? Someone strong and secret, who wanted no impediment to the Crescent Chancellor's re-election . . . or else Halliday was capable of a dirtier game than he pretended. "I should know not to listen to Horn's opinions."

"You're young," Halliday said cheerily; "it will pass." And it was too bad if it hadn't been Halliday's swordsman: Ferris liked the ironic symmetry of Halliday's chasing Karleigh away, since it would make it easier to fix suspicion on Karleigh if he were out of town.

"So Karleigh is trying to unseat you in absentia, is he?" Ferris helped himself to some lukewarm chocolate.

"My lord duke has gone and put up the money for Blackwell's theater to revive *The King's End* next month—assuming it's stopped snowing by then."

"Oh, it will. It always does. They'll open right on time. You know, Basil, *The King's End* is a really awful play."

"Yes." Halliday grimaced. "I remember it well. It's got a lot of stirring speeches against monarchic tyranny in it: 'Rule by one man is not rule but rape,' that sort of thing. Mary and I will have to sit somewhere obvious and applaud loudly."

Ferris stroked the chair arm. "You could close them down, you know. Blackwell's theater is a thieves' den and a public health hazard."

The older man's eyebrows lifted. "Oh, Tony. And I thought you *liked* the theater. You sound like Karleigh—that's just the tyrannic gesture he's trying to goad me into making. But he gauges everyone else's temper by his own. I won't close the theater—especially because I hear they'll also be reviving one of the old blood-and-revenge tragedies, which I adore. They manage to be rigidly moral, without rubbing your nose in it—unlike *The King's End,* which grinds its point home three times in the first speech. I wonder which actor looks enough like me to play the deposed king?"

"None, I expect; they're all undernourished." Ferris adjusted his eye patch. He must remember not to be so surprised when Halliday showed himself able to see through the machinations of others. And he must resist pushing too hard right now: if it were possible to destroy the Crescent Chancellor through giving him bad advice, Ferris would have contrived to do so long before this, and the forthcoming scene with St Vier would be unnecessary. "I must say you're taking it all pretty calmly. If the city riffraff get turned against you by Karleigh's secondhand agitation, it won't help your re-election in Council any."

"Oh, Mary gets all the temper," her husband smiled; "you get the carefully thought-out plan."

"You have a plan." Ferris walked to the other end of the room, letting amusement mask his relief. Far from uncovering the plot against him, Halliday was about to take him further into his counsels. Well, why not? He had never given the Crescent cause to doubt him. Oh, he disagreed with him in Council from time to time, as a respected opponent. But their true policies lay so far apart that there was no point in even trying to diminish Halliday by orthodox means.

Halliday's policies were built on an uneasy fusion of city and country. He seemed to believe that the nobles no longer provided the link between the two that their control of the land had given them for so many years; that as the city grew more prosperous independent of them, they would lose their influence there, and meanwhile were also losing the land through inattention. Admittedly, the Crescent Chancellor's rapprochements with the Citizens' Council, and his popularity with the general populace, were doing some good; but to Ferris it was a hazy plan for an even hazier future. If Halliday didn't love the city so much, he would have gone back to the country long ago and made a model of his own estates. He was not an inefficient administrator; and Ferris had to admire the way he achieved his ends by disguising them in concepts the Council could accept; but it was all too clear that he was, in the end, a dreamer—and that sooner or later his prized innovations would catch up with him and lose him the support of the nobility. Karleigh, the arch-conservative, had already sniffed out the tone, if not the content, of Halliday's program. The Crescent was dangerously overreaching himself by pressing the election this spring; but then, circumstances left him small choice. And if he won, the support would cement his position, possibly for life. If he lost, his successors might make such an administrative muddle that he could still return in glory.

As for his plan . . . Ferris decided to assume the best. "You honor me with your confidence, my lord."

Halliday smiled. "I have my reasons. *Despite* the fact that you do not make up one of my faction of vocal supporters."

"But neither do I stand up for Karleigh. My reasons for that are evident to everyone with eyes to see it. My lord duke is nothing but a pompous meddler with a touching faith in his own rhetoric."

"Oh, no," Halliday said in smooth surprise. "You mistake him. The Duke of Karleigh is a hero, the last man of integrity with due regard for Council law. Many people have said so, not least himself. We have here a wealthy, and thus powerful, man who now proposes to exercise that power. He gave some marvelous dinners before he found it necessary to leave for the country—at least, I hear they were excellent; I was not invited, though you may have been. Hospitality may obscure pomposity. And his rhetoric has already divided a formerly unified Council. We had an interest, a mutual purpose we had not known in years. Now he is planning to disband it, so that his fantasies of the golden days of Lordly Rule may be given full scope to take us all on the long run off a short dock!"

"You haven't considered," said Ferris gently, "that, technically, he is in the right? The Crescent was a courtesy title; it was never meant to be what you've made of it."

Halliday turned a bleak eye on him. "Wasn't it? Then why do things work better when someone takes central authority, bearing the brunt of complaints by election, rather than by fashionable whimsy? When someone can formally represent us to the Citizens' Council? I have no more power than people and necessity give me. Even Karleigh cannot say I have broken a single procedural rule. Hear me out, Ferris—and then question me. It's not a question I want to see buried and disposed of. But behold Karleigh's vision: where is his candidate to replace me?" Halliday put his chocolate cup down with a little more force than he'd intended. "He hasn't got one. He doesn't care what happens to the Council once he's pulled me down."

"He wants the Crescent for himself, of course," Ferris said. "Several of his forebears held it, back when it meant giving good parties and making sure no one spoke out of turn in meetings. All the dukes are a little crazy about their hereditary rights."

"Which is why, I suppose, he is working so hard to deny me my elective ones! Holding the Crescent will not suddenly bestow greatness on that idiot," Basil Halliday said with rancor. "I should think even *he* would know that by now. His ideas are popular, but *he* isn't. He's quarreled with half the Council over their lands, and with the other half over their wives."

"But not with me," Ferris said quietly.

"Not with you. Not yet." Halliday leaned back in his chair. "Tell me, Tony; what would happen if I set up a puppet to hold the Crescent in my place until I became eligible for the position again?"

"Almost anything. Your man might become too impressed with his own power, and refuse to listen to you. He might try to follow your suggestions and simply be too weak to hold the Council together as you do." And, Ferris was thinking, he would have to be a weakling in the first place even to consider the position.

"Exactly," said Halliday. "A weak man couldn't do it, and a strong man wouldn't want to." Ferris smiled a sour smile at Halliday's insight. "But if the measure to prolong my term is voted down," the Crescent continued, "I shall have to support someone after me. I've given it a lot of thought. I expect you have, too."

Under Halliday's clear gaze, Ferris felt horribly exposed. He thought of the guards outside, and himself in Halliday's house, alone and vulnerable to mortal challenge. But that was not the drift of Halliday's message. Unlike Ferris and the Duchess Tremontaine, Basil Halliday was not given to hiding double meanings behind his words.

Ferris said, "It's all very well for this once. But when I became eligible for re-election, you might not find me so easy to defeat."

"But," Halliday grinned, "it would put me on the same side as Karleigh in this one, if I'm voted down. He'll hate that."

"What a motive!"

"Then you're willing?"

"For the Crescent? I'd be lying if I said I wasn't. To take what you've made of it, to guide a strong Council under the cloak of your support . . ." He told Halliday what he wanted to hear. It wasn't hard to do. But even this surprising act of visionary generosity made him want to laugh. Halliday's eyes were so fixed on the future, he couldn't see what was right in front of him!

"But how is any of this going to solve your problems with Karleigh? I should think you'd want to put your energies into seeing that there's no *need* to support my election!"

Basil Halliday looked surprised. "It's simple. Go and talk to Karleigh."

For once, Ferris was utterly at a loss. "My lord," he said. "That would be fatal. Karleigh can't keep his mouth shut, and I would lose all your supporters in a stroke."

Halliday suppressed an impatient gesture. "Ferris . . . I've watched your careful stratagems to remain neutral in Council. It drives people crazy—they come to me complaining that they can't tell which side you're on. Do you think I don't know how hard it is to build that base? I want to use it, not tear it down. Speak to Karleigh on your own behalf. Say what you need to say. You're not my man; I can't send you to plead my cause, especially not now that I've offered you such a plum if I lose. Just go and confuse him a little—make the issues less clear cut—I know you can do that, Tony." His smiling face hardened. "But mark this: if you play me false, I'll know it. And I'll see that there's no cloak for you to step into."

Ferris said, "You don't like dueling, do you?" Halliday shook his head. "You don't approve of the use of swordsmen in general; perhaps because you've had to preside over the outcomes of too many Duels of Honor. It can make one jaded. But there is a duel on between you and Karleigh. You think adding me will make it a new form of sport?"

"Something like that." The Crescent Chancellor gave an unwilling smile. "Karleigh is so old-fashioned."

"And I am, at heart, a sportsman. But a cautious one. When did you want me to see Karleigh?"

"As soon as you can conveniently make the trip."

"Ah," said Ferris; "that won't be for another week. I have some affairs in hand here that need tying up. But then . . . then, we shall see. It may well be convenient then."

chapter XI

BOTH MICHAEL GODWIN AND LORD HORN WERE TO REMEM-
ber the duchess's barge party, but for different reasons. Michael
had already put the Horn incident out of his mind as one more
unpleasantness in a evening rife with them. To be perfectly correct, he
should have sent Horn a formal apology; but he was young, and arrogant, and very much preoccupied with banishing Diane from his
mind. It required him, in the days that followed, to plunge into a
feverish round of purportedly pleasurable activities: running and riding races, exchanging large sums on their outcomes; going to parties
with people one's mother wouldn't know about, and being fitted for
clothes to wear to them. It was clear that the duchess didn't want him.
She was merely an accomplished flirt. If she was carrying on with Ferris, that was her affair; on reflection Michael realized that to call her
reputation to question publicly would only damage his own. There
were plenty of other distinguished beauties to be had with far less
trouble. He continued to see Bertram Rossillion, and took to flirting
with Helena Nevilleson until her brother told him to stop. He had begun the flirtation to annoy the treacherous Olivia, Bertram's wife; by
the time Chris caught up with him it had done its work: Lady Olivia
was as formal and distant as if she had never stumbled against
Michael's coat to whisper to him the time to come to her room.
Michael was glad of her distance; when he remembered how he had
first encountered Lord Horn, he blamed her for that, too.

It was surprising, with all his other activities, that Michael found time to continue with his sword-fighting lessons. But in fact he found that only in Applethorpe's studio was he entirely free of Diane's image. He was ripe to fall on the day when the Master pushed him.

Standing in front of a group of sweating men, all paired off and glaring at each other after a workout of stroke and counterstroke, Applethorpe had said mildly, "You all want to be the best. Forget about it. The best already exist, and you'll never touch them. Just be good enough to do what you have to do."

The young men had shaken their muscles out and laughed, some at the Master's tendency to lecture, others in shamefaced recognition of their own ambition. Lord Michael stared at him, still panting from the exercise. He felt the blood pounding in his head. Of course he was good enough to do what he had to do. He always had been. For the first time he realized that perhaps not everyone was; that some never would be.

After the lesson, his mouth dry, he went up to the Master and asked, "What did you mean by that, *the best?*"

Applethorpe held out his arm, and one of his assistants removed his glove for him. He said to Michael, "The true swordsmen, of course. Men who must earn their living fighting to the death—and who must win every time. There aren't very many of them, of course; most last only a season or two before they die, or retreat into a cozy guard post on the Hill, or take to easier jobs."

"Where do they come from?"

The Master shrugged both shoulders. "You mean, where did they study? Who knows? I had a teacher; crazy old man, drunk half the time, brilliant when he could see straight. If you need to learn, you do it." He waved his hand as though swatting away gnats. "It's not the sort of thing you come *here* to do. It takes more than two hours a week." The point struck home.

Soon Michael's friends were making up stories to account for his disappearances: he had a low-bred lover on the other side of town; he had discovered a genius tailor living in some garret. . . . someone who saw him near the stables said it was a horse he was training for the spring races. But nothing could be substantiated. Michael was careful. He went to Applethorpe's every day to drill, and took a private lesson weekly.

L ORD HORN'S REACTION TO THE EVENTS OF THE FIREWORKS night was to send a letter to Richard St Vier in Riverside. Alec brought it home from Rosalie's on the day after Richard's meeting with Katherine at the Three Keys. Richard had just got up. He didn't have a headache and he didn't feel sick, but he was moving cautiously in case something should begin. He was terribly thirsty, and was drinking well-water.

Alec waved a large parchment at him. "Letter. For you. It's been at Rosalie's since yesterday. You get more letters than a first-year debutante."

"Let me look at it." Richard examined the large crest that sealed the paper. "Oh, no!" He laughed, recognizing it from the gates of the winter ball. "It's from Lord Horn."

"I know," Alec said demurely. When Richard shook the paper it fell open, and he saw that Alec had already slit the wax away from the paper in one clean piece. "Not bad," he approved; "but didn't they teach you how to seal it up again?"

"I generally don't bother," he answered blithely.

"Well, what does it say?" Richard asked. "Is he trying to hire me, or does he want to take me to court for messing up his shrubberies?"

"I haven't read it yet. I just wanted to know who it was from. The handwriting is really bad—I bet it's his own. No secretary writes like that."

"Clever Horn," Richard observed sarcastically. "Doesn't want his secretary to know he's trying to hire me, but lets everybody in Riverside see his crest. What does it say?" he asked again; but Alec was laughing too hard to tell him.

"Take a deep breath," Richard advised. "I can't understand a word you're saying."

"It's the spelling!" Alec chortled helplessly. "Pompous idiot! He thinks—he wants—"

"I am going to put snow down your back," Richard said. "It's a sure cure for hysterics."

Alec read aloud, " 'As you may be no doubt aware, my servant Master de Maris encountered grave misfortune in his profession last month—' He means you killed him. *Grave misfortune*—I wonder if Horn knows about puns?"

"What is he after, an apology? If he wants a new house swordsman, tell him my rates are twenty—no, make it thirty a day. An hour."

"No, wait, it's not that. '—Happily, this may be turned to your advantage, for I am prepared to offer you employment of the sort which I believe you usually engage in, and will no doubt find acceptable.' "

"No doubt." Richard flipped a knife at the ceiling. "You're right. He's an idiot. Tell him no."

"Oh, come on, Richard," Alec said cheerfully. "Just because he's an idiot doesn't mean his money's no good."

"You'd be surprised," St Vier said, retrieving the knife in one high jump. "I don't like working for stupid people. They can't be trusted. And he doesn't know much, or he'd never have hired de Maris."

"They don't care who they hire. It's only fashion."

"I know," he answered imperturbably. "Who does he want me to kill?"

"*Challenge.* Please. We are gentlemen here, even those who cannot spell. Or read." Alec held the paper at arm's length, squinting at the writing, " 'There is a matter of honor which has touched my honor—' No, that's crossed out—'which has touched my spirit, wounding it with a mighty g-gash that may only be . . .' "

"Steady, Alec."

" '. . . only be healed by the sword! The matter of the injury need not concern you. I am prepared to pay you as much as forty royals as a hiring fee. In return for which sum you will act as my surrogate by means lawful and honorable in the challenge to the death of Lord Michael Godwin of Amberleigh.' "

"Who's that?"

"Who cares? You can off him and be home in time for supper with forty lawful and honorable royals under your belt."

"Can he fight?"

" 'All they know how to do with their swords is poke lapdogs.' I believe I quote you directly. I don't suppose this Godwin rises above the other doggie-prodders."

"Then Hugo can kill him."

"Ah." Alec tapped the letter against his palm. "Shall I tell Lord Horn that?"

"Don't tell Lord Horn anything," Richard said bluntly. He picked up an iron shot and flexed his wrist against it. "I don't do business by letter. If he had any brains he would have found that out first."

"Richard . . ." Alec was swinging his heel over the arm of the chaise longue with an irresponsible air. "How much do you suppose it would be worth to Lord Michael to find out that Horn is **trying to** kill him?"

Richard tried to see his face, but it was hidden by shadow. He asked, "Why? Have you been losing at dice again?"

"No."

The swordsman stood poised on the balls of his feet, the shot balanced between his two hands. "You do understand," he said carefully, "that my reputation rests on people knowing I will keep their secrets."

"Oh, I understand," Alec said blithely. "But it was stupid of Horn to put it in writing, wasn't it?"

"Very. It's why I'm more interested in working with Ferris and his duchess"—he swung the weight in the air—"than with Horn. Burn that letter now, will you?"

WHEN MICHAEL WASN'T DREAMING OF THE DUCHESS'S CHILLY eyes, he was thinking of ways to disengage a man coming at him in perfect form. They knew him at the school, now. A couple of the other serious students, servants training to be guards, wanted him to come drinking with them after, and he was running out of excuses. It wasn't that he disdained their company; in fact, he liked them for being serious about the same thing that he was; but while he was confident of being taken for a commoner through the rigor of lessons, he wasn't sure he could keep it up socially. He was learning to speak more quickly in their company—and had, in fact, recently alarmed his manservant by rapping out the demand that his boots be cleaned "any which way." Michael amused himself around the city by singling out shops he could pretend he worked in; by handling precious stones and imagining he spent his days selecting them for clients instead of for himself . . . but it never could feel real to him.

Michael was not entirely surprised when the Master drew him aside after his lesson to speak with him. He had been asking for an additional weekly lesson, but so far Applethorpe had only nodded absently and said that he would see. Now Michael offered to take him out and buy him some dinner so they could discuss it in comfort.

"No," said the Master, looking off at a tall window at the end of the studio. "I think we can talk in here."

He led the way into a small room originally designed for the old stable's tack. Now it was cluttered with gloves, throwing-knives, pieces of canvas, and other detritus of the academy. They sat down on a couple of targets that gently oozed stuffing.

Applethorpe rubbed his chin with his fist. Then he looked at Michael. "You want to be a swordsman," he said.

"Umm," said Michael—a habit he was supposed to have had trained out of him at an early age. There was no question what the Master was talking about: men who earn their living fighting to the death—and who must win every time.

"You could do it," said Vincent Applethorpe.

A series of inadequate responses flashed through Michael's head: *Oh, really? . . . What makes you say that? . . . May I ask if you're seri-*

ous? . . . He realized he was blinking like a fish. "Oh," he said. "You think?"

Swordsmen were not expected to be masters of drawing-room conversation. Applethorpe answered as though he were making perfect sense, "I think you're suited. And I know you're interested. You should begin at once."

"I should . . ." Michael repeated numbly.

The Master began speaking with the terse excitement he used in the thick of a good lesson: "Of course it's a bit late for you— How old are you, nineteen? Twenty?" He was older than that, but the easy life of a city noble had spared his youth. "You have the feel, though, the movement, that's what's important now," Applethorpe rushed on without waiting for him to answer. "If you're willing to work, you'll have the skills as well, and then you'll be a match for any of them!"

Michael managed, finally, to come up with a complete sentence. "Does it work that way? I thought it took years."

"Of course it does. But some of it you've already got. You had the stance on your first lesson, many of them take months just on that. Still, you'll have to work, every day, for hours on end if you want to be able to take on the others and stand a chance to live. But if you'll take it seriously, if you'll let me teach you, I can give that to you."

Michael stared at him. The Master's one hand was clenched on his knee. Michael was arrested by the sight of the swordsman's body, perfectly poised, tensed for an answer. He thought sadly, Now I have to tell him. I've come to the end of this particular game; I have to tell him who I am. I can't possibly be a swordsman.

Applethorpe studied his face. The tension left the Master, his enthusiasm snuffed out like a candlewick. "Of course, this may not be important to you."

It came to Michael then that he was a fool to think that Applethorpe hadn't known all along who he was.

"Master Applethorpe," he said, "I'm honored. Stunned, but honored."

"Good," said the Master with his customary mildness. "Then let us begin."

chapter XII

S t Vier's answer, when Lord Horn received it, was soon
reduced to a crumpled rag on the floor. In an eccentric handwriting distinguished by strong vertical strokes, it read:

*Thank you for your kind offers. We have enjoyed reading them even
more than you intended. Unfortunately, the job in question does not
really suit our current needs. We wish you luck with it elsewhere.
(Your future letters will be returned unopened.)*

It was signed, "The St Vier Dueling Corporation, serving Riverside
and Gentry of Distinction."

It was enough to make him stop thinking about Michael Godwin
for a while. Wrapped in mute fury, Lord Horn went off to salve his
pride with the prestigious company of the Lords Halliday, Montague,
and other notable gentlemen at a dinner party given by the Dragon
Chancellor.

T omorrow night, Ferris would have his answer. He had
given St Vier enough time to think the job through; enough
time to become eager. Once the swordsman took the advance payment he was committed to the venture, and would wait until he was
instructed to strike. Once St Vier was committed, Ferris was going to
let him wait, as close as he could come to the Council election. It gave

Ferris time to fan the Karleigh/Halliday feud. It gave St Vier time to learn Halliday's routines. There must be no obstacle to the formal challenge being met and Halliday being heroically dispatched: Ferris planned to inherit a martyr's crown. By then some of Halliday's supporters might have learned of his favoring Ferris, so Ferris could take the Crescent before suspicion lit on him. Once he had it, suspicion would light where he willed it to.

Anticipation heightened Ferris's senses, sharpening his appetite for all activities the way that when he was a child the most mundane events of the days before New Year's and its presents had been inexplicably thrilling: the ice breaking on the surface of the washbasin was like a promised revelation; the untying of a shirt savored of unwrapping packages; and every night's blowing out the candle brought the glad day one flame closer. Lord Ferris found some of the same savor in being Dragon Chancellor: something was always about to happen, and every action was invested with meaning. As he sat now at the head of his table, surrounded by wealthy and powerful men and the remains of the dinner they had shared, he cracked a nut between his strong white fingers and smiled to feel the thrill it undeniably gave him.

One by one they departed, for bed, for other engagements, until all that remained were the Lords Halliday and Horn. Ferris knew that Halliday was hoping to talk to him after the last of his guests had gone; what Horn wanted only Horn knew. Perhaps he simply had nowhere else to go, and didn't want to return to his empty house.

The ornate dining room seemed to swallow the three men; even rank cannot stand up to architecture. Lord Ferris suggested that they adjourn to a sitting room to drink hot punch. Ferris was a bachelor, at thirty-two considered one of the prize catches of the city. The sitting room of his town house remained as his mother had decorated it when she first came to the city as a bride, in the bulky, comfortable furniture and deep colors of the previous generation. Although he himself preferred it, Lord Horn had banished the best of his old pieces to his country house, where style mattered less.

A young woman came in to tend to the fire. Ferris smiled when he saw her, inclining his head so that he could encompass all her movements with his one eye. She was broad-hipped, big-breasted, and handled the iron tools deftly; but something about her suggested malnourishment—maybe only her small height, or the tight way she clutched her plain skirts back from the fire. As she curtsied to her master at the door Ferris said, in his lovely speaker's voice that swayed the Council of Lords, "Katherine, stay. We are all a little drunk; we need someone sober to look after the fire."

Her eyes darted nervously to the other two lords and back to him. "I'll get my mending," she said finally.

But Lord Ferris raised one elegant hand. "Indeed you will not," he drawled affably. "You will sit there—there, under the mirror, where the light catches your hair, and I will send for John to bring you a glass of sherry. Unless you'd prefer something else?"

"Sherry will be nice," she said, settling into the chair he had indicated, across the room from the gentlemen; "thank you."

Her voice was flat, the vowels clipped and curt. Lower city. But she moved with assurance, a certain flair to the wrist and the set of the head. It didn't occur to either of the visitors to identify Riverside haughtiness; but then, neither of them had ever been there. They were surprised to see Ferris behaving this way—he must be drunker than he appeared. Bringing a mistress into a bachelor gathering was not unheard of; but it was unlike Ferris, and inappropriate for the company. If she was only a servant, it was unkind to impose their society on her.

Ferris smiled disarmingly at his guests, inviting them to excuse his whimsy. "A touch of feminine beauty," he explained, "is essential to the after-dinner drawing room."

"If we speak of feminine beauty," Lord Horn put in expertly, "it is a shame that Lady Halliday is not with us."

But Lord Halliday resisted being drawn into the conversation. He had had reports of the Helmsleigh weavers that disturbed him; nothing that wouldn't keep until morning, but he would sleep easier knowing that Ferris was worrying about it too. So he kept quiet, in the hope that Horn would be content with center stage long enough to talk himself out and leave. The woman in the chair was now ignored: a momentary whim of Ferris's that he seemed to have forgotten about.

Ferris was enjoying himself immensely. Everyone in the room was now confused except for him. He always took pleasure in Horn's company, for what he knew were ignoble reasons: Horn's dullness, his relentless second-rate innuendo, reinforced Ferris's estimation of his own social cleverness and political subtlety. He could run conversational rings around Horn, make him jump through hoops, bat him across the floor like a cat with its food. It was a private pleasure: the trick was not to let Horn know he was doing it.

Katherine folded her hands in her lap. She knew that Ferris was not so drunk as he was pretending to be. It was nice to sit down and rest, but she was quietly bored, watching the nobles showing off for each other. Lord Horn and her master were avidly discussing swordsmen, although they didn't seem to know much about the subject.

"Bah," Horn was saying. "They have no power. They do what you pay them to, and that's all."

"But," said the younger man, "should they choose not to accept your commission . . . ?"

"Mine?" Horn said sharply; but Ferris's one-eyed countenance was as benign as it could be. He was looking at the girl, smiling.

"Oh, anyone's," Ferris answered. "A figure of speech."

"Starve 'em out," Horn said. "If one won't take your money, another will."

"You don't think it's dangerous, then, to have someone knowing your plans not being in your employ?"

"Dangerous?" Horn repeated, his face flushing with the thought. "Not unless he goes over to the other side. Which isn't likely, knowing the way they work. If he betrays you, he'll never get another job."

Ferris twisted a gold ring on his hand. "That is certainly true."

"It's not so much dangerous—" Horn warmed to the subject, assured now that Ferris knew nothing of his recent disappointment with St Vier, and happy to be able to complain about it all on a theoretical level—"not so much dangerous as it is disgraceful. After all, no one's asking them to think. *They* don't have to rule in the city, they don't have the care of the land in their hands. They've no need to concern themselves with the judgments of their betters. They just take the money, and do the job. Look—my tailor doesn't refuse to make me a riding jacket because he doesn't like horses! It's like that. You let them start thinking they have the right of refusal—"

"But they do have the right." Basil Halliday shifted in his soft chair, unable to keep still any longer. "That at least you must grant them, Asper. They're risking their lives for us, poor fools; it's up to us to make it worth their while, so that they won't refuse the work."

Ferris looked sympathetically at Lord Horn. "Yes, but rejection is never pleasant," he said softly. "No matter who it's from. Asper is right, really: it all comes down to a question of power. Do we have the power, or do they?"

"They have the swords." Lord Halliday smiled down at his hands; "We have everything else. It comes out fairly even, though, with the tip of one pointed at your throat."

"Every man lives at swordspoint," Ferris intoned.

Horn laughed by reflex, scenting an epigram.

"I mean," Lord Ferris elaborated, "the things he cares for. Get them in your grasp, and you have the man—or woman—in your power.

Threaten what they love, and they are absolutely at your mercy: you have a very sharp blade pressed to their throat."

"And so," Lord Halliday picked it up, "you can disarm someone empty-handed. Take honor, for example: if you held mine in your power, I would have to think twice about refusing you anything."

"But honor," Horn broke in, "is a property of nobles, not of common swordsmen—at least, as we understand it. For them, it's a commodity they market along with their swords, and hang on the chimney with them when they go home to their trulls and their drink and their petty quarrels. They live like dogs in Riverside, caring for nothing: they change their women as we change our coats, and waste our money as fast as we can give it to them."

"But you're wrong," Ferris said softly. "There is no man living who cares for nothing." His head was turned to face Horn, but his good eye was on the girl. "All you have to do is to find it."

She downed the last of her sherry in one swift gulp.

"He may not want to admit it—who does?—but even in Riverside human vices bespeak human passions."

"No one's denying that." Basil Halliday spoke calmly. From the tension of the girl across the room, he saw that the exercise in philosophy had ceased to be a game—maybe had never been one. He recognized the impulse in Ferris to play with the power he had been given; it was something one went through at a certain stage. Ferris's end seemed to be domestic. It was not for Halliday to judge another's personal relationships: everyone in the city was strange, if you looked deeply enough. But he saw no need to be a silent accessory.

So Halliday continued, "But Horn is right. Ours is a different kind of honor, because we hold a different power. No lord acts as one man only: he has the power of the state behind him, the power of his birth and wealth. I should say it was beneath our honor to use them in a personal quarrel."

Ferris turned his head to look at him. "That is why swordsmen are so useful, my lord: they represent private enterprise. Indeed, as Horn was saying before, a swordsman's honor extends only so far as he may be trusted."

"And no further?" Halliday asked. "What about what it means to the man himself?"

Ferris smiled his thin-lipped smile. "There's some disagreement on that point. But why not ask Katherine? She's our local expert on swordsmen's honor."

The small woman got up, making for the hearth. But Ferris stopped her. "Sit down, Katherine. The fire is going fine by itself. Tell us about the home life of swordsmen."

She sat stiffly, her spread fingers clenched on her knees. Her eyes on the floor, she said, "It's like what the other gentleman said. Drinking and dicing and fighting."

Ferris sat back, enjoying himself. "I hear they do us a service, pruning out the undesirables of Riverside."

"There's a lot of killing that goes on," she said. "That's why you don't want to go there."

"But their women are safe, surely? There must be something they cherish."

A grim smile spread across her face, as though she'd just got the point of a joke. "I knew a man once who killed his . . . mistress."

"Out of jealousy?"

"No, in a fight."

"A swordsman with a temper."

"Hers was worse, much worse. Nobody blamed him, really; or if they did, there wasn't much they could do about it. We all knew her."

Even Halliday sat transfixed, Riversiders were seldom found as house servants; under her humility a wildness burned, the fear of a trapped animal.

"What about the man," Ferris asked. "Is he dead too?"

"Hardly. He killed two swordsmen in a garden last month."

Horn's breath caught. "Despicable!" he muttered. "First he killed my house swordsman, now he's murdering defenseless women."

"Not the sort of man," Ferris said, "who seems to care for anything. Probably wise of him, considering the position it would put him in otherwise."

"He was well enough cared for himself a few years back, before he got so fussy about commissions," Horn said with sudden rancor. "Of course, I couldn't say whether he took money for it . . . you know how they are when they're fresh from the country: young, and easily impressed."

"Asper," Basil Halliday said quietly. "The woman's a friend of his."

But Katherine was smiling at Lord Horn. "Yes," she said, "those were wonderful times. He used to bring flowers back from the Hill with him. Kind of a shame he ever took up with . . . that woman as he did. But he's turned his back on Riverside *and* the Hill now: got himself a student with no money, and he kills for him for free."

Ferris too turned to smile at Horn. "I suppose vices learned in youth stay with you. He was not in your set, I take it?"

Horn allowed his lip to curl slightly. "I have never approved of chasing after swordsmen. There's no . . . dignity in it."

"You're right," said Ferris.

Katherine got up hastily, bunching her skirts in her fists, and bobbed a curtsy to Lord Ferris. "Will that be all, sir?"

"Yes, thank you." Ferris smiled the melancholy smile his lean face was suited for. "You look tired. Forgive me for keeping you. Yes, that's enough. Good night."

Lord Halliday felt strangely tired himself. The evening had not been pleasant: something was going on between Ferris and Horn, something petty concerning swordsmen—and sex, probably, knowing Horn's proclivities. He had a distaste of staying further in the other men's company. Confessing to himself that Horn had outlasted him, he rose to go. Horn, naturally, followed him. As they waited for their coats, they heard a commotion at the door. The messenger was looking for him, for Lord Halliday, had been to his house already and could brook no delay—

Halliday's guts twisted at the thought of danger in his house; it was almost with relief that he saw the state seal on the paper, and knew that whatever had happened had not happened to his family.

He scanned the letter and looked down at the waiting faces. "It's the Helmsleigh weavers, I'm afraid. They've taken their grievances south into Ferlie, and amassed quite a crowd. They're holding council there, Tony, hard by your estates." Ferris swore. "And they're burning looms and houses."

"Well," said Ferris, his face grim. "Then all those negotiations were for nothing. I'll go at once. Give me a cordon of City Guard, and I can raise my own men on the way to Ferlie. Just give me an hour to settle my affairs—"

"You can't travel tonight. The local bailiffs have already called up some help. If you sleep and start in the morning you'll get there more safely, and far better rested."

There was more clatter in the yard: the arrival of an eyewitness, one of Ferris's own men from Ferlie. He had come with an escort. The men must rest the night; the weavers knew the Lord Chancellor had been sent for, and were still for now.

Lord Ferris's guests left without further ceremony. After seeing to the arrangements of his messengers, the first thing Ferris did was to pen a note to St Vier. The matter could not go forward without his close supervision; he wanted no moves made while he was out of town. For the time being, Halliday was spared.

It was late when he finally sent for Katherine. Clad only in a shirt and dressing gown, he was lying on his bed, not in it, catching a few hours' rest before the dawn. He held the sealed note out to her: "I want you to see that your friend gets this before tomorrow night."

As her eyes widened in protest he said, "Of course you needn't go to Riverside yourself. I've told you I wouldn't send you back there. You have contacts. Use them. I can't send one of my own people, someone might recognize them." She took the letter, still staring at him. "Kathy, you look frightened." He drew her to the bed, and pulled a quilt over them both, undoing her clothes as he continued to speak: "I promise you there won't be much more of this. You'll see him one more time, when I get back, and that will be all." She gripped his shoulders, forcing him to hold her. "I won't let him hurt you, as he did your friend."

"It's not that," she said; "you never thought it was that."

"Well, I'm sorry if I embarrassed you in front of company. There was a point I needed to make."

"Well, you made it. But he won't care what you do to me."

"Ah," he smiled dreamily, "you can't believe that. But even if you do, it doesn't help him any. You see, it works both ways. I can tell how you'd feel if St Vier came on any mischance." He stilled her protests with his thin lips. "Now don't worry. He isn't going to refuse me, and I'm not going to hurt him. But it's nice to know that I can trust you both."

Pressed under him now, she began kissing his chest, his neck, his jaw, as though her fever of nerves could be mistaken for passion and silence his flow of words.

Ferris, breathing hard above her but refusing to be taken in, continued, "Have you seen his scholar lover, by the way?"

"No."

"I have; although it wouldn't have done to say so. I heard all about him in that Riverside place you sent me to. And then he nearly knocked me down coming in the door."

She stopped still, and had to start again. "Oh? What's he like?"

But his hands were on her shoulders now, it didn't matter what she did. "Thin. Ragged. He's very tall."

He leaned his full weight into her.

He slept for a while; when he woke up she was still there, limply curled around a pillow. He said to her, "Incidentally," interrupting her dreams, "incidentally: Asper—that is, Lord Horn—will probably come around asking you for more information about St Vier and his friend. Tell him everything you can, and remember what he says for me. It will amuse me to hear what he's thinking."

She said nothing.

"Horn's a fool," he said; "you can see it yourself. Don't worry so much. I want you to do this for me."

She said, "Yes, my lord."

In the morning, Lord Horn found St Vier's note stuffed in the back of a drawer. He uncrumpled it and looked at the forceful handwriting, trying to spare his eyes its insulting message. What had Ferris said? *Every man lives at swordspoint.* It had been an epigram, after all—and a clever one, too.

chapter XIII

THE NEW NOTE WAS SEALED ON THE OUTSIDE WITH A THUMB-
print, and on the inside with the swan signet. There was only
one word: *Delay.*

"D.E.," explained Alec, chalking it on the hearth with a burnt
twig-end, "that spells *de.* L.A.Y., *lay. Delay.*"

Richard eased the note into the fire, where it burned merrily for a
few seconds.

"Waste of perfectly good paper," Alec protested. "It was hardly
written on!"

"Never mind," Richard said; "when Tremontaine pays me the
thirty advance, I can buy you a sheaf. Is that the same D that's in *Richard*?"

"Ver-ry good!" Alec drawled, diverted. "And in *Diane*. And *duchess*. There is, of course," he added daintily, "no D in *Alec*."

"Of course." Richard picked up a practice sword, nimbly sidestep-
ping the small grey kitten the neighborhood cat-lady had foisted on
them in return for a gift of wood ("Removing the poor thing from evil
influences," Alec had said, accepting). The kitten loved moving
swordpoints.

"You'll have time for Michael Godwin now," Alec said brightly.

"Horn's job? I thought you wrote him a letter."

"I did. But you could change your mind."

"I don't think so." Richard stopped, the tip of his sword just out of
kitten jumping range. "Do you have something against Godwin too?"

"Not yet. But you're always complaining about being poor—"

"*You're* always complaining about being poor. I keep trying to tell you, it's a matter of challenge. You understand about boredom, don't you? Now, Halliday will be well guarded. I may have to fight several of his people before I can even reach him, unless I can plot a way to get him alone—maybe along the roofs and in through a window. . . ."

"You know," Alec said, "you're going to kill that cat one of these days."

"No, I'm not." A barely perceptible turn of his wrist brought the blade out of its reach.

"Neat," said his friend sourly. "They should pay you to do that." He sat silent for a while, watching Richard exercise. The cat stalked the swordsman's right heel in its rhythmic dance across the floor, neither making a sound. Only the wall sent up a steady thud and crack of steel; but either the neighbors were out or they'd grown used to it. When the kitten came close, Alec darted his arm down and scooped it up. It snuggled under his chin; with one finger he absently stroked the length of its spine. He gazed between its ears at the moving swordsman, and said silkily over the exercise, "You've never actually seen the duchess, have you?"

"On the barge," Richard panted. "The fireworks."

"So did a thousand other people. You haven't spoken to her."

The swordsman jumped back, spun on his toe, and came in low. "No."

"Why should she want Halliday killed, do you think?"

Richard paused, wiping sweat out of his eyes. "It's none of my business."

"Then keep it that way."

Richard was silent. He didn't mind Alec being there watching him: Alec never paid real attention to what he was doing. He still couldn't follow a fight intelligently. Richard changed his line of attack and winced as his arm protested: a mistake to let it stiffen in one line. His imaginary opponent parried, and he used all his reach in a complex defensive counter. His imaginary opponents were always so much better than his real ones.

"Richard."

Alec had spoken his name quite softly, but the intensity of the syllables froze him like a scream. Carefully he put the sword down, hearing its clatter loud in the tense, vibrating silence. Alec was sitting very still, with his arms wrapped around himself, but that was good: Richard checked to see that there was no knife near him, no glass he could break. It had happened once before like this, in another time that should have been easy: the sudden change in the air, and then Alec snarling and cursing at him as Richard wrested the steel from his hand, spattered with blood from Alec's ineptly sliced wrist; Alec shouting at him: "Don't you understand? I can't do anything right!" But he hadn't really been trying.

The memory was with Richard clearly now. He stood still, outwardly patient, his senses alert for the sudden movement, the twist of revelation.

"Do you understand what they meant by *Delay?*" Alec's voice was as icy clear as an actor's off the bare walls. "They want you, Richard, and they think they're going to have you." Winter light from the window turned one side of his face to silver. "Are you going to let them?"

"Not let them have me, no." He answered as he had before. "I make bargains, not pacts. They know that."

"Richard," he said with the same intense calm, "they are not pleasant people. I have never liked them."

"Well, I'll tell you something," Richard moved closer to him; "I don't like most of them myself. I don't like very many people, really."

"They like you."

"I'm nice to them, that's why. I have to be nice to them, or . . ."

"Or you'll kill them?"

"Or they'll get upset. I don't like it when they do that; it makes me uncomfortable."

Alec smiled thinly, the first trace of expression on his face since the conversation had begun. "And I make you comfortable?"

"It doesn't matter. You're not boring, like the rest of them."

"I'm a challenge."

"In a way, yes." Richard smiled.

"Well, that's something." Alec uncurled his arms from around his knees. "Nice to know there's one thing I'm good at."

The kitten came back to him then, looking for the warm spot he had made with his legs.

Iᴛ ᴡᴀs ʜɪs ʜᴏᴜsᴇ, ʙᴜᴛ Mɪᴄʜᴀᴇʟ ᴅɪᴅɴ'ᴛ ғᴇᴇʟ ʀɪɢʜᴛ ᴘʀᴀᴄᴛɪᴄɪɴɢ there. The sword study had started out as a joke, an unorthodox skill he might in time present to society as a colorful eccentricity; but now that it was in earnest he felt the need for secrecy. He worked his practice and lesson times at Applethorpe's around his old schedule, being careful to appear when he was expected amongst his peers. He practiced early afternoons with the academy's targets, then changed into fine clothes and made a round of visits, took his dance lessons, or went riding with his friends in the hills above the city. Every other day he dined alone, early and sparsely, and walked to Applethorpe's in the twilight for lessons in the empty studio, before his round of evening entertainments began. As it grew dark they had to light candles; but both he and the Master tacitly preferred this time of day when no one else was there to observe them.

The Master was less patient with him now. The calm detachment he showed in his public lessons was no part of his personality, but a real unconcern for the achievements of his students. None of them were expected to be *swordsmen*: they learned what they could, what they wanted to, that was all. Michael was to master all that his teacher knew. It was a lot; and it was very precise. From his years of teaching, Applethorpe had learned to explain accurately the mechanics of any movement: what rhythms, stresses, and balances were brought into play, and why. And always after these explanations came the bending of his body to specification, and the imprinting of the pattern on his muscles and nerves. Michael would be caught in a frenzy of drill-work, trying to perfect a twist of the wrist that deflected the blade without moving its tip; sweat pouring down his face and breathing a nuisance since it was more hard work; and in his ears, over the roaring of his lungs, a voice like a persistent insect would be shouting, "Balance! Balance! That arm is for balance!"—one more thing to correct without losing what he'd gained. He turned once and shouted back, "Will you leave it? I can only do so much!"

The Master regarded him with a calm, sardonic gaze. "Then you are dead, and we may as well not be bothering."

Flushing, Michael dropped his eyes, following the line of his blade to its tip on the floor. "I'm sorry."

The Master persisted unemotionally, "You're not even facing an opponent yet. When you are, you have to think of where *his* arms are, as well as your own. In fact, you can't be thinking of your own at all: you have to know them. I'll show you." He picked up another blunt sword, and faced off to Michael. "Let's try it. I won't use anything you don't know."

They had drilled together before, but always in predetermined sequences. Facing him, Michael felt a thrill of nerves, excitement—and suddenly wondered whether the Master's missing arm might not be used to throw him off balance if Michael was skillful. . . .

As instructed, he watched his opponent's eyes. Applethorpe's were like mirrors, signaling nothing, only reflecting. Michael thought suddenly of St Vier's at the bookshop, aloof and opaque. He knew that look now.

In that instant the Master struck. Michael's defense grazed the Master's sword on its return from his chest. "You're wounded," Applethorpe said. "Let's go on."

He tried to laugh, or feel admiration, but he was filled with rage. He forgot about eyes, about one-armed men; he silently ordered himself in the Master's voice: *"Feet straight—grip loose—head up. . . ."*

He was retreating, fighting only for defense, sick with the knowledge that Applethorpe wasn't even trying to touch him. He tried at least to anticipate the attack, to have the right move ready for it; he had the feeling he was forgetting something vital he'd learned. . . . Suddenly he found himself advancing, the Master falling back before his attack. He thought of his newest move, the little twist that could give him an opening. . . .

"You just fell on my blade," Applethorpe said, his breathing only slightly ruffled. "Balance."

Michael dusted himself off. "Very nice," the Master said to his surprise, "for starters. Did you enjoy that?"

Michael gasped, getting his breath back. "Yes," he said. He found he was grinning. "Yes, I did."

H E MET THE DUCHESS ONCE, ON AN AFTERNOON RIDE. SHE WAS dressed in grey velvet, and was sitting a nervous grey mare. Her face and hair gleamed above them like snow on a mountain. Her party reined in, and his followed suit. She leaned across to Lord Michael, offering him her hand to kiss, a perilous exercise that he was able to accomplish dextrously while their horses danced underneath them.

"I understand," he said over the general greetings, "that Lord Ferris has gone south to quell the riots."

"Indeed," she said; "the dictates of responsibility. And such dreadful weather for traveling, too." His pulse was beating so hard he was afraid she might see it disturbing the ruffles over his throat. "And how is your new horse?"

He didn't know what she was talking about.

"One hears you are off to the stables a good deal," she elucidated.

Someone was spying on him. Or was it just a rumor to account for his absences? He may have started it himself. Did it mean he'd have to get a horse now? He smiled back at her. "Your ladyship looks quite charming. I hope your lovely mount is not too tiring."

"Not at all."

Her eyes, her silvery eyes like mirrors . . . He knew that look now, and knew how to respond to it. There was her challenge to be met—

met, not fled with backward glances over his shoulder to make sure she was pursuing him. It was she, in a way, who had set him on his current road with her taunting. Someday she might learn of it, and wonder. It did not occur to him yet that in attaching himself to the discipline of the sword he had already met the first part of her challenge.

He steeled his own eyes as well as he could, knowing that, with their sea color, they would never be as immutably hard as he would like. And he smiled at her. "Madam, perhaps I might have the pleasure of calling on you soon."

"Indeed, it may be soon."

The wind blew her words away from him; but that was what he thought she said. Their parties were separating amid laughter and the jingling of harness. In a few days, a week . . . He rode on into the hills, without looking back.

chapter XIV

Two more weeks passed in Riverside without word
from the one-eyed nobleman. Richard and Alec amused
themselves spending the last of the winter garden money. Minor swordsmen whose reputations needed improvement found that
once again St Vier would fight them, if they offended his friend first.
No one had done it so far and lived; it became the kind of wild sport
that fashion imposes on the restlessness of winter's end. Alec seemed
to sense them, before they'd even opened their mouths; it was he as
often as they who led the attack. He said it amused him to give Richard something to do. But he provoked them even when Richard
wasn't there, smelling out the bravos, the ones with violence in their
blood, raising their flow of viciousness like the moon calling the tide.
Sometimes it was only the reputation Richard had built for him that
saved his life. It always made him savage.

Besides self-destruction, his newest obsession was the theater. He
had always loved it; for once he had the money, and someone controversial to be seen with at it. Richard had been to the theater a few times
when he first came to the city, but it was hard for him to understand
the appeal: he found the plays contrived, and the spectacle unconvinc-
ing. Finally, though, to quiet Alec—and take his mind off Horn and
Tremontaine—he agreed to go when the theater opened soon.

"And I have just the play," Alec said happily. "It's called *The
Swordsman's Tragedy*. You'll love it. It's all about people killing each
other."

"Does it have swordplay in it?"

"Actors."

"They can't be very good."

"That's not the point," Alec informed him. "They are excellent *actors*. Blackwell's troupe, who did *Her Other Gown* three years ago. They're better at tragedy, though. Oh, you will enjoy it! It will cause such a stir."

"Why?" he asked, and Alec smiled mysteriously: "Ask Hugo."

He cornered Hugo Seville and Ginnie Vandall in the market that afternoon. "Hugo," he said, "what do you know about *The Swordsman's Tragedy?*"

Lightning swift, Hugo drew his blade. Richard had time to admire Alec's viciousness and to reach for his own weapon when he realized that Hugo had taken out his sword only to spit on it, and was carefully rubbing the spit into the blade with his thumb. With a sigh he resheathed it, never having noticed what St Vier had been about to do.

"Don't," said Hugo, "go messing with the Tragedy."

"Why not?"

Ginnie looked at him closely. "You've been here how long—six years, seven? And no one's told you about the Tragedy?"

"I don't pay much attention to the theater. But it's playing now across the river. Alec wants to go."

Ginnie's eyes narrowed. "Let him go without you."

"I don't think he wants to. Can you tell me about it?"

Ginnie raised her eyebrows in an expressive sigh. She leaned her head against her lover's shoulder and murmured, "Walk off for a while, Hugo. See if Edith has some new rings."

"I'm sorry," said Richard. "I didn't mean to make you uncomfortable."

"Never mind." Ginnie pulled her velvet cloak more tightly around her and walked close to St Vier. She was scented with musk, like a great lady. She spoke softly, as though passing him stolen goods: "Here it is, then. The Tragedy was first played about twenty-five years back. The actor playing the—you know, the lead, was killed in a freak accident onstage. They kept playing it, though, because it was so popular. And everything seemed all right. Then people started to notice. . . . Every swordsman that's gone to see it has lost his next fight," she hissed; then she shrugged, trying to make light of it: "Some badly, some not. We don't go see it, that's all. It's a good thing I told you. If people see you there, they'll think you're unlucky. And *don't* say the name."

Alec was right: it did make the prospect of going to the theater more appealing.

A LEC GREETED RICHARD'S DECISION JUBILANTLY. "WE SHALL SIT in the gallery where we can see everything," he announced, "and get a bag of raisins and almonds to throw at the actors."

"Will people be able to see us, too?" He couldn't imagine that that wasn't the point in going.

"I expect . . ." said Alec evasively. Suddenly he turned to Richard with a dangerous gleam in his eye. "Clothes," he stated. "You must wear something . . . splendid."

"I don't own anything splendid. Not what you're thinking of, anyway."

"Then you must get something."

He did not like the fashionable tailor's. It made him nervous to stand still while the man attacked him with chalk and tape and pins for his measurements, muttering strange formulae under his breath. Alec was perfectly composed; but then, Alec had nothing to do but finger bolts of cloth presented by the goggling staff.

"There," Richard pointed with all he had free, his chin, "that one's good."

"It's brown," Alec said acidly, "just like everything else you own."

"I like brown. What's it made of?"

"Silk velvet," Alec said with satisfaction, "that stuff you said you wouldn't have."

"Well, I don't have any use for it," he said reasonably. "Where would I wear velvet?"

"The same place you wear brown wool."

"All right," he conceded the color. "What about black, then?"

"Black," Alec said in tones of deep disgust. "Black is for grand-mothers. Black is for stage villains."

"Oh, do what you like." Richard's temper was considerably short-ened by the tape and the hovering hands. "So long as it's not gaudy."

"Is burgundy gaudy?" Alec asked with aggressive meekness. "Or blue, perhaps?"

"Not that *peacock* color you liked just now."

"That was an indigo," the tailor observed. "Very fine. Lord Ferris had a coat made in it at the start of the season, sir."

Alec smiled wickedly. "Then by all means, Richard, you must have one too. It matches both your eyes."

St Vier's fingers drummed on his thigh. He pointed to a bolt draped over a chair. "That?"

"A very fine wool, sir, not much like it left this year. It's a russet, known this season as Apples of Delight, or Autumn Glory."

"I don't care what it's called," Richard said over Alec's sniff, "I'll have that."

"It's brown," Alec said. " 'Apples of Delight,' " he further scoffed as they left the establishment. "Peaches of Misery: another brown, like bruised fruit. Pears of Pomposity. Woeful Walnut. Cat's-Vomit Pink."

Richard touched his arm. "Wait. We didn't get you measured for anything. Didn't you want that blue?"

Alec continued down the street. Affluent shoppers moved aside from the tall shabby figure. He said to Richard, not lowering his voice, "It's probably called Hypochondriac's Veins this season. Lady Dysentery ordered a coat for her dog in it."

"Don't you want anything new for spring? I've still got the money."

"There is no point," he said, "in trying to better the bested. Nice clothes only point out my inadequacies. And I slouch: it pulls the shoulders out."

"Green," Richard insisted, having nothing against bright colors provided he didn't have to wear them, "for your eyes. And gold brocade. With a high neck, and a ruffle. You'd look elegant, Alec."

"I'd look like a painted pole at a fair," Alec said, giving his robe a tug. "One Autumn Glory is quite enough."

But on the day of the performance, Richard had his doubts. His new clothes were much more comfortable than he'd expected them to be: the richly colored wool was soft, and moved with him like something he'd had for years. Alec's scholar's robe looked even more frayed by contrast, and it covered most of his new shirt and boots. He hadn't even used the enamel clasp for his hair; it was caught back with an old ribbon.

Richard didn't bother to argue. "Sit down," he ordered. "And stay there." And he disappeared into the bedroom.

From the front room he could hear Alec saying, "What are you doing, trying to change your socks? They're perfectly clean and no one can see them anyway. . . ."

He reappeared with a plain wooden box, the kind used for keeping letters or bills. He opened it so Alec couldn't see in, and brought out its first treasure.

"God," Alec said, and that was all he could manage.

Richard slipped the ring over Alec's finger. It was a massive black pearl, set in heavy silver scrollwork.

Alec stared at his own hand. "That's beautiful," he breathed. "I didn't know you had taste like that."

"It was given to me. A long time ago."

He took out the brooch next, and laid it in Alec's palm: a gold dragon clutching a sapphire. Alec's hand closed on it, hard enough to feel the edges; then he pinned the collar of his shirt closed with it.

"That's very, very old," he said at last.

"It was my mother's. She stole it from her family."

"The banking St Viers?"

"That's right. She didn't like them very much."

He found a small diamond ring that fitted Alec's little finger, and a gold band inlaid with a red-gold rose.

"Clients," he said, smiling down at the rose, "who liked my work. The diamond was a woman's, a nobleman's wife who gave it to me privately because she said I saved her reputation. I've always liked it, it's so fine." He reached into the box again. "This next one I got early on, as partial payment from a man with more jewels than money. I've never known what to do with it; I should have known it was for you." He brought out a square-cut emerald as big as his thumbnail, flanked by citrons and set in gold.

Alec made a peculiar noise in his throat. "Do you know what that's worth?"

"Half a job."

"*You* wear it. What are you giving me these for, anyway?"

"I like the way they look on you. They don't look right on me, and they don't feel right, either."

Entranced despite himself, Alec lifted his hands, now heavy with gold and silver and precious stones.

"That," said Richard, "is the way to dress you."

"You've missed a finger," Alec said, and Richard answered, "So I have," and drew out his newest acquisition, still in its pouch. "Here," he said, "you open this one."

Even in the room's dull light the ruby glowed with liquid color. It was a long red bar that spanned two knuckles, flanked on either side with diamonds set in white gold.

"Where did you get this?" Alec asked, his voice dangerously shaky.

"From another nobleman. It's my latest bribe."

"I think you're lying," Alec said tightly. "I think you got it from a thief."

"No, really," Richard said patiently. "It's from Lord Ferris. He wanted me to wear it to our next meeting."

"Well, wear it, then!" Alec shouted, thrusting the ring at him.

"I'm not comfortable in rings," Richard said quietly, and didn't take it.

"This one in particular," Alec growled. "He had no right to give it to you."

"No problem, then," Richard said, trying to turn things light again: "I give it to you, my lord."

Alec's face, if possible, grew paler and stiffer, his eyes wider. Despite the danger, Richard lifted one jeweled hand and kissed it. "Alec," he said against the cold, heavy fingers, "they are for you. Do what you want with them."

Alec's fingers slowly tightened on his own. When he looked up, Alec was smiling, his eyes sharp and green with wicked pleasure. "All right," Alec drawled, "I will." And he slid the ruby onto his forefinger. It glowed there like a live thing, an icon for the hand that bore it.

They were a noble's hands, now, a foreign prince's, rich and strange. Against the transparent skin, the high-bred bones, Alec's coarse clothing and scuffed boots faded to nothing.

"That's good," Richard said, pleased with the effect. "It's a shame to keep them all in a box. I never wear them; this way I get to look at them."

"They like to be looked at," Alec said. "I can feel them purring with delight, showy little bastards."

"Well, let's take them for a walk—not that anyone will notice them, next to my new clothes."

T HE TWO MEN WERE NOTICED ALL THE WAY THROUGH RIVER-side. The afternoon was golden from the ground up; the snow be-ing gone, their path was covered with mud and winter deposits. Word of what they were planning had got around; people lined up to see them pass like a parade. Richard felt like some hero, going off to war.

He caught sight of Ginnie as they were crossing the Bridge. He called to her before Alec could say something rude, "Hey, Ginnie! What do you think?"

She eyed him up and down, and nodded. "You look good. They'll be impressed." Alec's hand flashed in the sun; she saw the jewels, and her face froze. Without a word she turned and walked past them.

"She doesn't approve," Alec said cheerfully.

"Hugo wouldn't go see this play."

"I imagine Hugo only likes the funny ones."

Even in the city people watched as they went by. Richard kept wanting badly to giggle: all this fuss about two people going to see a play that probably wasn't even going to be very good. "We should have hired horses," he said, "like the Council Lords, so people could see us ride by. My boots are muddy already."

"Look!" Alec cried. "The banners! We're almost there."

"Banners?" But there they were, just like a story-castle's: made of bright cloth, painted with devices that appeared and vanished in the crackling wind: a winged horse, roses, dragons, a crown. . . .

Outside the theater it was like a fair. Grooms were walking horses and clearing the way for carriages while girls walked amongst them, selling bouquets of flowers and herbs, cups of wine, and packets of fruit and nuts. There were printed copies of the play, and scarves, and ribbons the same colors as the banners. Alec looked for Nimble Willie in the crowd but couldn't find him, although one or two of the other melting faces looked familiar. Two unknown swordsmen staged a quarrel and then a swordfight over and over in different corners of the yard. Against the wall someone was declaiming a speech from another tragedy and being drowned out by a blind fiddler with a dancing dog, which some young noblemen were distracting by throwing nuts for it to fetch. The nobles' costumes did indeed make Richard's look somber. Even the middle city people, shopkeepers and craftsmen, were dressed extravagantly, trimmed up with bits of lace and ribbon. They were coming early, to ensure themselves good seats.

"Come on," said Alec, elbowing his way through the crowd, "or we'll find ourselves sitting in some dowager's lap."

The nobles stopped throwing nuts to look at them. A snatch of their conversation carried over: ". . . can't afford him anyway. . . ." A pair of serving-girls, arm in arm, simpered and turned away.

Richard was beginning to be sorry he'd come. The crowd grew tighter as they reached the entryway. Other people's toes and elbows and very breath intruded on him. He kept his hand on the pommel of his sword.

This fascinated a group of small boys, one of whom finally grew bold enough to approach. "Hey, swordsman!" he shouted hoarsely. "Could you kill my brother?"

Richard didn't answer; they always asked that. "Shut up, Harry," another said. "Can't you even see that's St Vier?"

"Hey, are you St Vier? Hey, St Vier, could I see your sword?"

"You can see it up your backside," said Alec, hitting one of them at point-blank range with an almond. Pleased with his aim, he led the way in, and tipped a boy to find them seats.

They got a private box in the upper gallery, directly opposite the stage. Alec was elated. "I've always wanted one of these. It's pure hell

on the benches, with every idiot and his wife trying to sit on your lap."
Richard winced at the thought. They were high above everything
here, with a good view of the stage now bathed in sunlight. People
were craning up to look at them from all corners of the house.

Alec put his feet up on the barrier and ate some of his raisins. There
was a sennet of trumpets from above. "Now you'll see the nobles'
boxes fill," Alec said. "They always come in now."

Set close to the stage, the nobles' boxes, hung with their occupants'
arms, were visible from almost all the rest of the audience.

It was the first time in many years that Richard was able to observe
them all at leisure. He recognized more than he expected to: handsome men who had stalked him at the parties he used to attend; distinguished noblemen and -women whose money and patronage he'd
refused, and others who had reason to be grateful.

He saw Lord Bertram Rossillion with a beautiful dark-haired
woman on his arm, remembered him complaining about pressure to
marry . . . poor lady. Alintyre was there, now Lord Hemmyng. He
wondered if Hemmyng would recognize the emerald on Alec's hand
and smiled, remembering that mad ride through the hills with the
coach just ahead of them, Alintyre's lady love being trundled off to
her aunt's; and her shrieks of laughter as they'd ridden back with her
the way they'd come. He looked harder at the stately lady smiling up
at Hemmyng, and recognized with a start the tilt of the nose. . . .

The man responsible for Alec's rose gold ring was also there, looking young and serene as ever. Of course, it hadn't been so many years
ago. He was talking to an elegant redhead.

"Godwin," said Alec. "One of those delectable confections you're
staring at is a Godwin of Amberleigh, there's the crest."

"The redhead," Richard said. "I've seen him somewhere else before,
I can't think where. . . ."

"How do you know it isn't the other one?"

Richard smiled. "I've seen him before, too; but I remember where."

L ORD THOMAS BEROWNE TURNED BACK TO HIS COMPANION.
"And there it is," he said; "he did come after all."

"Why shouldn't he?" Lord Michael answered. "He's not a coward."

"No, but he's not flashy either. It's a flashy thing to do."

"For a swordsman. Is he superstitious?"

"Doesn't matter. Alban was sure he wouldn't come; he owes Lucius
twenty royals now."

"He can afford it," Michael said absently. His mind wasn't on St

Vier: he was wondering what Vincent Applethorpe would say if he knew Michael was attending *The Swordsman's Tragedy*. "It's just a fairy tale," he said aloud. "No one really believes it."

"Maybe not," said Tom; "but wait for the betting when St Vier's next fight comes up."

"He's stolen Halliday's fire, at any rate," Michael changed the subject. "They were saying that the Crescent was planning to cancel the performance, close down the theater."

"Where have you *been*, Michael?" Berowne asked in mock surprise. "They were talking about *The King's End*, which is a piece of garbage saved only by the presence of one Miss Viola Festin as the king's page. I have already seen it twice, and I can assure you that Lord Halliday was at the last performance. All of it. I came in partway through, when the gentle page—"

"Oh, no," Michael said. "It's Horn. In the box across from us."

"He's probably bet on St Vier. What's the matter?"

"Tell me if he's looking at me."

"He isn't. Poor child, has he been pestering you with his attentions? Or do you owe him money?"

"He makes my skin creep," Michael explained.

"Oh, yes," Berowne said; "I know about that."

T HEY'RE ALL BETTING ON YOU," ALEC SAID CHEERFULLY, PASS-ing him the raisins. "I wish we could get a percentage."

"It comes out of my fees," Richard answered. "When does the play start?"

"Soon, soon; when the music stops."

"What music?"

"There—onstage. You can't hear it, everyone's talking."

"And looking at us," Richard said. It was beginning to seem like a bad idea again.

"They're protecting their investments," Alec said blithely. "I wonder if they'll send you flowers."

Richard groaned. "Flowers. Is Ferris here? What does his crest look like?"

"He's not here. Lord Horn is. No Halliday. No Tremontaine. Nobody serious comes to see us."

L OOK AWAY," SAID LORD THOMAS, "HE'S LOOKING AT YOU."
"Horn?"

"No, St Vier."

"He's probably looking at *you*," Michael said.

"I'm not blushing, he can't be." Berowne looked pointedly away. "Now Horn's looking . . . not at you, at him."

"Who's that with him?"

"With Horn?"

"With St Vier. Thomas, turn around and *look*."

"I can't. I'm blushing. It's the curse of my complexion."

"At least you don't freckle. Send him a note—the swordsman, I mean. Ask him to join us."

"Michael." Lord Thomas looked at his friend. "You offend my pride. Everyone is dying to ask him to join them. I refuse to herd with the common throng. I refuse to be the first to capitulate. And what if he refused?"

I think," Richard said crossly, "that I am not going to like this play. I think it's going to be a silly play. I think we should mess everyone's bets up by leaving now."

"We could do that," Alec said. "But those people who have begun walking around onstage are in fact the actors. Soon they will begin to speak. If you go now you will be walking out in the middle of the first scene, and everyone will stare at you even more. Sit down, Richard. Here comes the duke."

The duke crossed the stage in great panoply, leaving behind some courtiers who wanted to talk about him. It sounded very much like an actual conversation except that all the words were ordered to fit a spoken rhythm. Like music, fragments were passed from speaker to speaker, while the rhythm stayed the same. Sometimes you lost the feel of the beat, but then a strange twist of words brought it back again. The courtiers liked the duke. He was a wise man,

> . . . *more fit to act the part of grace*
> *Than counterfeit a prince's righteous scorn.*

His son and heir, however, had never been known to show any sign of grace. No one liked him much; he threw gloomy parties, and wore black in mourning for his mother, who had died giving birth to his only sister, Gratiana.

The courtiers left the stage. Some curtains at the back opened, and there was a girl with long golden hair talking to a parrot in a cage. She called herself

> . . . unhappy Gratiana—and yet most happy
> In having that which, lacking, many maids
> Must lie in torment on their narrow cots
> Or venture rites under full-mooned skies.

Richard thought it might be a real parrot. She told it:

> You and I, bright captives both
> Of place and person, circumstance and birth
> Must share our burden, you with patient ear
> And I with tongue to tell the cause for tears!

But before she could explain herself, her brother Filio came in, made snide remarks about her maiden virtue and the parrot, and turned to the audience to remark:

> For none dares share my sorrow or my joy
> When I myself can neither either prove.

Richard had been looking forward to seeing the old, virtuous duke; since he was the person everyone was talking about at the beginning, he'd thought the play would be about him. Instead he died suddenly, offstage, and Filio was named duke. A stately minister with a long white beard came to tell Gratiana. His name was Yadso, and he suspected foul play. Later he was warned by his barber, who also shaved a close friend of Filio's, that his life was in danger of mortal challenge if he did not flee the country at once. Yadso took his leave of the girl:

> Not all that is, is as it seems. In knots
> Truth ties up silence; speech undoes us here.
> The game's afoot: Now foot we while we may!

Gratiana cried,

> Flee! Flee! you just and true
> And for your coin take Gratiana's love!

Then, alone, she lamented her treachery to all mankind. Perhaps she was the villain? But no; it turned out she only meant that she had fallen in love with an unsuitable man. The parrot suddenly chose to echo her words: "Love!" it croaked. "Flee love!" Everyone took it in their stride, so it must have been part of the play. Maybe it wasn't a real parrot after all; or maybe it was, but someone was behind the scenes doing its voice.

The new duke kept pestering his sister. Finally he dragged out of her the fact that she was in love with a swordsman. He turned again to the audience and vented his rage in terms uncomplimentary to the profession. Richard caught Alec sneaking looks at him, and grinned. But to his sister, Filio was all sugary sympathy. Virtue, he said, like wine, was no less potent for being poured into unlikely vessels; wine could be drunk as easily from a skull as from a cup of gold. "Oh, dear," Richard muttered. He could see it coming already. Alec shushed him. But Gratiana was comforted, and promised to send her lover to meet her brother. As soon as she left, Filio stomped and shouted and wrung the parrot's neck. So it was either well trained, or a fake one after all. The duke left the stage to try and find a cat to blame it on.

Richard didn't even bother to criticize the swordsman. Maybe, when the play had been written, swordsmen were like that. Of course, in a world where everyone talked in what Alec said was poetry, why should he expect a swordsman to be any different? Duke Filio greeted his prospective brother-in-law warmly. They drank wine out of twin skulls. The swordsman made a weak joke about it, and then toasted the downfall of all the duke's house's enemies. It turned out Filio had a job for the swordsman to do: an enemy had besmirched the honor of the house, and only blood would wash it clean. Obviously flattered at the duke's attentions, the swordsman agreed.

There followed a scene in a madhouse, with much singing and dancing. What it was doing there Richard never did find out; but when it was over the inner curtain was pulled back to reveal an enormous staircase that cleft the center of the stage from top to bottom. The swordsman appeared at the bottom, announced to everyone that it was midnight, and that, after he'd got the duke's little commission out of the way, he trusted to lie in his lover's arms as promised. Richard enjoyed his description of love; it was the most accurate part of the play so far, with its images of hot and cold, pleasure and pain. But at the same time, it made him uncomfortable to hear someone talking about it in front of a great crowd of strangers—even though it was only a play.

At the top of the stairs, a cloaked figure appeared. As the bells began to toll twelve the figure started down the stairs in a pretty flourish of yards of cloak. The swordsman drew his steel, and ran his victim through, crying, "So perish all Filio's enemies!"

"For shame," said Gratiana, falling forward into his arms; "to love my brother more than you love me!"

She was a long time dying, while each of the lovers explained the duke's trick to the other, and promised eternal fidelity. Richard endured it with patience. Finally, the swordsman carried his dead love off the stage, her cloak trailing behind them.

The stage was bare. Then people started clapping. Alec was still staring at the empty stage. His eyes were bright with the same elation he'd had the night of the fireworks.

"That was excellent!" he said. "That was perfect."

Richard decided not to argue; but Alec correctly interpreted the look on his face, and made a face of his own. "Let me guess. The technique was bad. *You* would have killed her so she didn't have time for that speech at the end."

Richard scowled a smile. "It wasn't realistic," he said at last. "No, not the speech, the way it happened. First of all, he was an idiot to take a contract on an unknown mark, especially from that brother, who he didn't trust in the first place."

"But he *needed* the duke's support, that's the point!"

"Yes, but remember when Filio says . . ." To Alec's surprise, his illiterate friend quoted the passage back to him accurately. "*That's* when he should have realized that he had no intention of letting them get away with it."

"Well . . ." said Alec, at a loss. "Well, *we* see that, but he isn't supposed to."

"Then he's supposed to be a stupid man, and I don't see why we should care what happens to him. The brother's the smart one, really."

"Then you can cheer for the brother," Alec said sourly. "But I warn you, he gets killed in the end. Everyone does, in fact."

Richard looked down at the audience, who were milling around buying food and drink and trying to look into their box. "If they want to see people killed, why don't they go to a swordfight?"

"Because your speeches are too short," Alec snapped. "Also," he reflected more leniently, "you're always doing it for money. In the play it's for love, or treachery. Makes it more interesting."

"He should never have bargained with the brother. He lost the moment he let him see his weakness."

"And we could all have gone home early."

There was a scratch at the door of their box. Richard whirled, hand on his hilt. Alec unlocked the door, and accepted the first messenger's offering.

"It's just a rose. No note."

Richard looked across the theater to the nobleman who loved roses; but he was deep in conversation, and didn't look up.

There was plenty of time between the acts for the nobles to social-ize in each other's boxes. Michael relinquished the pleasures of his friend for a talk that Bertram Rossillion seemed bent on having.

"Your friend," Bertram said, "Berowne . . ."

"He's a relation," Michael answered the question. "By marriage. On my mother's side. We've known each other forever."

Bertram's soulful brown gaze slopped itself all over his face, with particular emphasis on the eyes. Michael stepped back, but Bertram came on. Michael said in an undertone, "Tonight is bad for me, my dear. I'll be out late, and too tired when I come in." He was going to Applethorpe's. Tiny creases appeared around Bertram's eyes, and his mouth pinched in the corners. "I've missed you terribly," Michael said, gazing back. "You don't know how. . . ."

"Look!" said Bertram, "the duchess."

She was entering one of the boxes across the way. Already her foot-men were unfurling the Tremontaine banner. Her dark skirts billowed around her, and under a tiny hat crowned with ostrich plumes her fair curls tumbled, each in careful disorder.

"She's late if she's come to see the play," Richard observed. All eyes were off them for the moment.

"She hasn't," Alex answered gruffly. "She's come to make trouble." He stood at the back of the box, huddled into the corner by the door. His hands were tucked in his sleeves, making him look more than ever like a sulky black bird.

Richard looked at the tiny, elegant woman surrounded by her well-built edifice of clothes and manners. "I wonder," he said, "if I should go and see her?"

"You can see her perfectly well from here, she's taken care of that."

"I mean to talk to. Ferris is gone, he doesn't have to know I've done it. You're right, you know; I should find out what she thinks herself."

He'd expected Alec to be pleased; after all, it was his misgivings Richard was trying to allay. But the tall man only shrugged. "She hasn't invited you, Richard. And she's not going to admit to anything."

"If I made it a condition of the job . . . ?"

"Oh, of course," the light voice mocked angrily. "If *you* make con-ditions . . . Why don't you ask her to do your laundry, as well? I'm telling you, stay away—"

A knock interrupted him. He flung open the door, so that it crashed against the wall. A footman in the Tremontaine swan livery filled the doorway. Alec dropped the door latch as though it had burnt him.

"The duchess's compliments," the servant said to St Vier, "and will you join her to take chocolate."

Alec groaned. Richard had to bite his lip to keep from laughing. He glanced at Alec, but the scholar was once again trying to hunch himself into nonentity. "I'll be delighted." He looked around at the accumulated greenery. "Should I take her some flowers?"

"It's an insult," Alec said hollowly, "to the senders. Save them to throw at the actors."

"All right. Are you coming?"

"No. Stay there for the last act, if she'll let you; you'll be close enough to tell if Jasperino really is wearing a wig."

Richard began to follow the footman. "Wait," said Alec. He was twisting the ring on his forefinger.

"Should I wear the ruby?" St Vier asked.

"No." Alec shook his head fiercely.

For a moment Richard broke away from the footman's presence. "What's the matter?" Alec's nervousness was physically palpable to him. Something had undermined Alec's arrogance; he didn't even deny the charge. He retained just enough of his usual air to press his fingers to his brow in mockery of the acting. "I have a headache. I'm going home."

"I'll come with you."

"And leave the duchess waiting? She probably wants to find out who your tailor is. Hurry up, or you'll miss the chocolate. Oh, and if there are any little iced cakes, get me one. Say it's for your parakeet or something. I am uncommonly fond of little iced cakes."

Not long after he left the theater Alec realized that he was probably being followed. At least, the same two men seemed to have been behind him for several turnings now. They were the demonstration swordsmen from outside the theater. They weren't Riversiders, they couldn't be going his way to the Bridge. His heart was clanging like a blacksmith's anvil, but Alec refused to alter his pace. If they wanted the rings, he supposed they could have them. Richard or his friends could probably get them back.

He might still return to the theater; lead them there by another route, and find Richard. He discarded the idea as soon as he'd had it. He wasn't going back. The shops and houses went by like images from another life. Inns and taverns passed, while his mouth grew steadily drier. It was not unlike the effects of poppy juice.

If he got as far as the Bridge, he might see other Riversiders who could help him, or at least tell Richard what had become of him. What *was* going to happen to him? They were letting him get far from the center of the city, into the lonely area you had to cross to reach the Bridge. It would be violent, and extremely painful; all he'd ever imagined, and probably something he'd managed to leave out. He'd been waiting a long time for it, and now it was going to happen.

Now, the ground said, each time his boot sole struck it. *Now.* He tried to vary the rhythm of his walk, to get it to stop. He managed to slow it down to a whisper, and in the shadow of a gateway they caught him.

He had time to say, "You know, your swordplay would make a cat laugh"; and then he found that it was impossible not to struggle.

"THEY ARE ALL JEALOUS," THE DUCHESS SAID, NODDING GRAciously at her peers across the theater, "because they are all cowards."

Richard St Vier and the duchess were alone in the box, with the chaperonage of about five hundred spectators. It didn't bother him; he was intrigued with her portable silver chocolate set. A blue flame heated the water under a little steel-bottomed pot suspended over it on a chain. There was a silver whisk, and china cups with her arms on them.

"They're not as well equipped," he answered her.

"They could have been. Not only cowards, but stupid." It was all said in a pleasant, intimate manner that took the sting out of her words, as though they were not meant so much to denigrate the others as to establish the boundaries of a charmed circle that included only the duchess and himself. Alec did the same thing; much more abrasively, of course, and more sincerely; but the sense it gave Richard of belonging to an elite was the same.

"You might have brought your servant, he would have been welcome. Perhaps I failed to make that clear to Grayson."

He smiled, realizing she meant Alec. "He's not my servant," he said. "I don't have one."

"No?" She frowned delicately. With her postures and careful expressions, she was like a series of china figurines displayed along a chronological shelf. "Then however do you manage those great town houses down there?"

She might be teasing; but he told her anyway about the manors that had been turned into rooming houses, or brothels, or taverns, or those warrens for extended families whose generations moved slowly down floors, with the youngest always at the top.

She was enchanted with it. "That would put you where, now . . ."

looking at him critically ". . . in the upstairs ballroom perhaps, with room to practice—or have they turned that into the nursery?"

He smiled. "I don't have family. Just rooms: an old bedroom and I think a music room, above a . . . laundress."

"She must be very pleased to have such a lodger. I have wanted to tell you for some time now how much I admired your fight with Lynch—and poor de Maris, of course. Although I suppose he deserved what he got, jumping in to challenge you when it was already Lynch's fight. I imagine Master de Maris had tired of Lord Horn's service, and wanted the chance to prove to his party guests how employable he was."

Richard considered the pretty lady with renewed respect. This was exactly his own estimation of de Maris's peculiar behavior in the winter garden. Horn's house swordsman probably thought his lord didn't give him enough chance to show off, and he wasn't really needed as a guard; who would want to kill Horn? By killing St Vier he would have won himself an instant place back at the top of the swordsmen's roster. He should never have tried it.

"My lord Karleigh will be out of the picture for some time, I think."

On the surface, it was a continuation of her compliment, assuming that Karleigh had fled because St Vier killed his champion. It was what everyone thought. But she seemed to be waiting for an answer—something in the posing of her hands, the cup held not quite touching the saucer . . . as though she knew that he could tell her more about the duke. He couldn't, really: he'd taken his payment and that was the end of it for him; but it meant she knew who his patron had been.

"I've never asked," he said evasively, "why the duke and his opponent insisted on such secrecy for themselves, but still chose to have their fight in public. Of course I've honored my patron's wishes."

"It was an important fight," she said; "such are best well witnessed. And the duke is a vain man, as well as a quarrelsome one. He never told you what the fight was about, then?"

She left him little space for an ambiguous answer. "He never told me anything," he said truthfully.

"But now it may be coming clear. A political issue, worth a couple of swordsmen but not their patrons' lives. It put a healthy fear into Karleigh, but that may be wearing off. Lord Ferris will know when he returns from his trip south whether the duke stands in need of another sovereign dose."

Did she want Halliday killed *and* Karleigh out of the way? It meant destroying two opponents, and leaving the field open for a third man . . . Ferris? The duchess hadn't named Halliday; if anything, she seemed to be defending him. Richard gave up: he didn't know enough about the nobles and their schemes this year to figure it out. But one thing still troubled him.

He looked at the duchess directly. "I am already at your service."

"Gallant," the duchess chuckled. "Are you really, now?"

She made him feel young—young, but very secure in the hands of someone who knew what she was about. He said broadly, to be sure, "You know how to find me."

"Do I?" she said with the same amusement.

"Well, your friends do," he amended.

"Ah." She seemed satisfied; and so, for the moment, was he. He hoped Alec would be, too. Trumpets sounded for the play to begin again. "Do stay," said the duchess; "you can get such a good view of the costumes from here. Some of the wigs are beyond belief."

T HE SWORDSMAN WHOSE TRAGEDY IT WAS LASTED UNTIL THE end. His revenge against the evil duke consisted of a series of love letters from an unknown lady with the same initials as Filio's mother, whom the duke fell in love with. The letters demanded that the duke do increasingly odious things to prove his devotion. After a colorful series of rapes, beheadings, and one disinterment, even the most loyal of Duke Filio's courtiers had amassed several reasons to kill him. The only nice person left onstage, a doctor from the singing madhouse, stated the opinion that the prognosis for the duke's mental health was not good.

In the final act, the giant staircase again dominated the stage. The duke, laboring under the promise that the lady of his affections would at last reveal herself to him at midnight, came to the bottommost step. As the bell once again tolled the hour, the figure of his sister, wrapped in her bloody cloak, appeared above him. Too unhinged to be adequately frightened, he muttered,

> Nay, I'll not flee, but mount the tow'r of heaven
> And from your chaste and softly smiling lips
> Suck forth the secret of eternal life!

The duke ran up the staircase, but suddenly the figure flung back its hood. To no one's surprise except the duke's, it was the swordsman:

> Not life, but death's cold secrets will you kiss—
> Now please your mistress, let her give you joy

> *Of her. Come, come, and bid farewell to all*
> *Earth's pleasures in one last ecstatic howl.*

His gleaming sword plunged down from above into Filio's heart (leaving his own front completely unguarded, but affording a fine view of his gory clothes), and the duke screamed, "At last! It is the end!"

It wasn't, of course. The duke had no final speech, but a crowd of courtiers came running on. Finding the duke in the arms of a cloaked figure, presumably his mysterious lover, they shouted, "Vengeance! Vengeance!" and fell upon the pair, hacking to bits the already dead duke, and delivering to the swordsman his mortal wound. It left him strength for one last declamation:

> *Now is the trapper trapped, and in my blood*
> *Steel strikes on steel, and kindles a great flame.*
> *I burn, I rage, and shortly welcome death*
> *That long has been my handmaid, now my spouse.*
> *Are there no tears to put this fire out?*
> *Only my own, and those I will not shed*
> *So long as he regards me with his sanguine orbs.*
> *We'll too soon be two skulls, and jest at grinning then,*
> *But all our plays produce no single laugh*
> *From lungs no sighs will ever fill again.*
> *I hadn't planned on this—but hadn't planned*
> *Beyond it, either. Things were clear enough:*
> *I loved your sister, and I hated you,*
> *Pursued you both and killed you. Now all's one.*
> *Write Nothing on my tomb, that's all . . . I've done.*

The swordsman was by then halfway up the staircase, where he died. While everyone was reacting to this, a nobleman rushed in to announce that a chimney sweep had discovered the duke's secret diary, in which were lovingly detailed all his heinous crimes, beginning with his treatment of his sister. The people agreed that the swordsman was, in fact, a hero, and would be given a hero's funeral, interred next to Gratiana, while the duke would be cast into a bottomless pit. The virtuous and amiable old counselor, Yadso, would be called back from exile to become the next duke of wherever it was. And that was the end.

The audience's applause seemed as much for the happy resolution as for the actors. As they took their bows the duchess observed to St Vier, "In the end, you see, it all comes down to good government.

There can be no state funeral for the hero without a state; and true lovers cannot meet on a staircase that hasn't been properly maintained. I'm sure Yadso will make an excellent duke."

Richard enjoyed the clear path the duchess's footman commanded for them out of the theater. It would be pleasant to live in a world without crowds. At the door of her carriage she stopped and took a basket from her maid, rummaged in it, and handed him a packet wrapped in a linen napkin. Bowing, he heard the swish of her skirts as she was handed up into the carriage. Then he left quickly, before any other of the departing nobles might claim his company. He did note that the Hallidays' phoenix-crested carriage had a door that locked from the inside.

T HE PACKET CONTAINED THE LITTLE ICED CAKES HE HAD FOR-
gotten to ask for. He wondered if they meant something; but determined to save them intact for Alec.

There was no sign of his friend's having been home to their lodgings. Probably off losing his last brass minnow at Rosalie's. Richard hoped he wasn't staking his rings. He decided to go down there and get some dinner.

The cooking fire was high; it was hot as the inferno in the little tavern, though fortunately not so dry. Rosalie wanted to hear all about the play; and because she was an old friend he told her. Lucie wanted to know about the heroine's costume; but he never could remember clothes. News of his visit with the duchess didn't seem to have leaked down yet.

Some men came in and looked at him curiously, as though afraid his bad luck might be fresh enough to rub off on them. They settled down in a corner to eat and play cards. Eventually another man joined them, sporting a kerchief full of stolen goods he was attempting to sell quickly.

"Here," called Rosalie, "let's see those things."

She was admiring an enamel comb, letting Lucie twine it in her hair, when Richard saw the gold ring among the tangle of chains and gew-gaws. Yellow gold, with a red rose.

"Where did you get this?" he asked the man calmly.

"Trade secret." The man laid a finger along the side of his nose. "Do you want it?"

"It's mine."

"Not any more, boy."

"Tell me where you got it," St Vier said, a weary edge to his voice. "It isn't worth fighting over."

The man swore. "Swordsmen." But he gave in. "Some guy passed it on to me, down at the docks. Another swordsman, not Riverside though. Still a sight more civil than you, honey. He just wanted the money for it; I didn't ask any questions. What's the matter, you get robbed when you went out without your sword?"

"I don't get robbed."

Taking a cautious step back, the man mocked, "You're plenty sure of yourself. I bet you're St Vier or something, right?"

"I am St Vier," Richard said quietly. At his side, Rosalie nodded. "When did you get the ring?"

"Not long—hey, look, I'm sorry. I didn't mean—"

"Just tell me when you got it."

"Not long ago. I came straight here. You'll never find him, though, not now."

"I'll find him," Richard said.

URING THE LONG CARRIAGE RIDE LORD HORN HAD THE
leisure to examine his feelings minutely. They were, on the
whole, pleasant feelings. Throughout the play he had barely
paid heed to the stage, so pleased was he with the events unfolding
from his own private gallery. He felt like a playwright, only he had not
had to go to the trouble of inventing his characters: Lord Michael
Godwin, blissfully young and arrogant, all the more lovely because his
days under the sun were now numbered . . . Horn had thought of
sending him a trenchant note; but a distinguished silence had seemed
the most dignified . . . the swordsman St Vier, that fashionable para-
gon . . . in the sunlight, in the great public space, he too had looked
young, his detachment a mere defense. Horn had enjoyed looking at
the dangerous man and thinking how helpless he was about to feel.

The coach pulled up at last at the door of the empty hunting lodge.
There were still some people left who owed him favors. St Vier's
young man should have arrived here over an hour ago. Horn had
stayed for the end of the play. He should find the boy chained in the
empty buttery. Ferris's woman had said he couldn't fight, but these
Riversiders knew all kinds of tricks, and how could you be sure that St
Vier hadn't passed some on to him?

Up here in the hills, the spring was still chilly. Horn kept his cloak
on and went straight to the buttery. A small sliding panel in the door,
some watchman's convenience, had been left open. He could look
through it without being seen, and he did.

The young man was lounging upright in his chains, making them look faintly ridiculous as he leaned against the wall. His hands were lax, long, and useless-looking. They were covered with rings, and there was gold at his throat. His dress was strangely at odds: the jewels, good boots, and shirt, under a jacket with narrow shoulders and too-short sleeves whose cut was a good five seasons old. His breeches, which no longer matched his jacket, had a piece of braid coming off them. And then there was his cascade of hair. In the candlelight he had been left with, it glowed chestnut and sable, heavy and thick as poured cream.

Some black cloth was folded behind his head to keep it from the wall. He was looking abstractedly across at the candle, head slightly tilted, his eyes veiled.

Lord Horn examined the face of St Vier's lover. His nose was long, flat-planed like a ritual painting's. High cheekbones, wide-set so that the eyes above them looked slanted from this angle. The hair pulled back from his high forehead made his face look even longer. Horn's eyes rested on the mouth, almost too wide for the narrow face. Even in repose, the flat lips looked mocking and sensual.

He unlocked the door and stepped inside. At the sound the young man raised his head like a deer scenting the wind. His eyes were vivid green, and open preternaturally wide; they held Lord Horn in frozen fascination, so that his first words were not at all what he'd planned. "Who are you?"

"Your prisoner, I am told." The wide gaze did not falter, but Horn saw that the skin around his eyes was drawn tight with tension. "Are you going to kill me?"

Horn ignored the question, and noted how the face went paler. "Your name?" he demanded.

"It's Alec." The boy wet his lips. "May I have some water?"

"Later. And your surname?"

He shook his head. "I don't have any."

"Your father's name, then."

"Nobody wants me. . . ." The mobile lips turned down mournfully, while above them the wild eyes glittered. "And who are *you?*"

"I am Lord Horn." He forgave the impertinence because it had put him back on the track of his planned opening.

"Oh," said his prisoner. "*You're* Horn, are you?"

"Yes," said Horn. "I am indeed. My—friends tell me you're a scholar. Is that so?"

"No!" The syllable exploded with sudden vehemence.

"But you can write?"

"Of course I can write."

"Fine. I have paper and pen outside. You will write a letter to St Vier telling him that you are in my hands, and that when he has performed the job I have asked him to, you will be sent back to him. Unharmed."

You would expect the fellow to relax. If he'd thought he had been abducted by a mere thug, he knew better now. But his voice was still thin, high and breathy with fear. "Of course. What a tidy plan. And who will you have read it to him?"

"He can read it himself," Horn snapped. He found his hostage's responses unnerving: they walked the knife's edge between frivolity and terror.

"He can't read. I read them for him."

Lord Horn bit his cheek to keep from swearing. The situation seemed to be eluding him. He grasped at his proper authority. "Write it anyway."

"But don't you see," the boy said impatiently, "I *can't!*"

"Are you ill? Have you lost the faculty of your eyes and hands? Or are you just too stupid to realize what predicament you are in?"

The boy went even paler. "What are you going to do to me?"

"Nothing," Horn exploded, "if you'll just stop arguing and do as I tell you!"

St Vier's lover licked his lips. "I don't want to be hurt," he said with soft desperation. "But you have to see how stupid it is to write him a letter."

Horn stepped back, as though his prisoner's insolence were a fire too hot to bear. "Do you hear what you are *saying?*" he demanded. "Are you making *me* conditions?"

"No—no—" the boy said desperately. "I'm just trying to *explain.* Can't you understand anything I'm telling you? Richard St Vier," he continued hurriedly, before Horn could object, "he isn't going to want to let anyone else see a letter with—a letter like that. He doesn't like other people knowing his business. Anyone who reads it to him would know what your demands are, and then if he meets them, they'll know that he gave in to you. He can't have that. It's—it's his honor. So even if I write you the stupid letter, it's no good. You may," here the pale lips flattened in the ghost of a smile, "be stuck with me."

"Oh, I doubt that," the nobleman answered, smiling creamily. The boy must be bluffing, playing for time. Perhaps he expected St Vier to come riding up at the head of a band of cutthroats, storm the house, lift him to the saddlebow, and ride off into the night. . . . "He seems to be very fond of you. I'm sure he is eager to get you back."

The green eyes were staring frankly at him, at his leg. Before he could stop himself, Horn glanced down. His own fingers were curling and uncurling against the fabric. "It must be done quickly," he said, clenching his hand into a fist at his side, and thrusting his face almost into his prisoner's. "I cannot waste time while he looks for you. I want the job done. Then he can have you back, for whatever he wants you for."

"What do you think he wants me for?" The thin voice was taut with desperation. "He can get others for that—whoever he wants. You've made a mistake."

"No mistake," Horn said, certain at last.

"Do you want money?" the boy said breathlessly. "I can get some, if that's what you want."

Lord Horn stepped back, awash in the fumes of power, poignant as pleasure. He would have what he wanted of the swordsman, and the swordsman's lover would provide him with another feast entire. His fear was strong wine, a sop to Horn's pride.

"No money," Horn snarled. "I'll have what St Vier has."

The young man flinched, his hand raised in an oddly virginal gesture of defense. Horn's teeth showed in response. He knew that game from his own pretty-boy days, the titillation and the fear combined. . . .

For a moment, a trick of the light, he saw Lord Michael's features in the young man's face. He wouldn't dare set Godwin of Amberleigh's son in chains . . . but if he could! Michael Godwin would not have the chance to refuse Lord Horn again. Godwin and St Vier, with their blithe rejections! He, himself, Lindley, Lord Horn, had money; he had position; he knew what it was to have the town at his feet, men and women begging for a letter, for a ribbon, for the touch of his mouth. . . .

It occurred to him that if St Vier hadn't written him that letter, that short, insulting note of refusal, then someone else must have. That dark, eccentric hand might belong to the man before him. He would find out shortly.

"Why should I not want what St Vier wants?" he continued. "He will not accept money when it runs counter to his desires. Such is his honor," Horn said dryly. "Why should you expect less of me?"

"I can't help it," Alec said pathetically.

"Write the letter," snapped Horn.

"It won't do any good," Alec answered. His eyes were staring wide as though they would speak for him. His hands strained against their bonds.

Horn saw them, and saw something else. "That ring." It was a ruby, tremendously long and thin, square-cut, set in white gold, flanked at the band with little diamonds. It rode the long hand like a familiar, a fire-beast, large and cold and alive. "Give it to me."

Alec clenched his fist on it, helpless and stubborn. "No."

Horn lifted his bleached and manicured hand, and slammed it hard across the bound man's face.

Alec screamed. The shrill echoes rang in the stone room, hurting Horn's ears. He dropped his hand and jumped back.

The red marks of Horn's hand, rough as a child's tracing, were rising to the surface of the bound man's skin. He stared owlishly at Horn, not blinking away the water in his eyes.

"I'm a coward," Alec said. Horn lifted his hand again, to see the young man flinch. "I'm afraid of being hurt, I told you so. If you hurt me, I'll only scream again."

"Give me the ring."

"You're a thief," Alec said haughtily, his fear pushing him into fury, "as well as a whore. What do you want with it?"

Horn managed to restrain himself from battering the flat mobile mouth into shapelessness.

"You will do as I say, or you and your Richard are going to be very sorry."

At the swordsman's name, the strange young man stiffened. "If you harm me, my lord," he said, "it is you who will be sorry." His chin was up, his long eyes veiled, and his voice dripped breeding and contempt.

"Oho," said Horn. "Trying that trick, are you? And whose little bastard are *you* supposed to be . . . *my lord?*"

The boy flinched again, although Horn hadn't raised a finger. "No one," he mumbled, hanging his head. "I'm no one, I'm nothing at all. And I'm glad of it." He looked suddenly as if he wanted to spit. "I am very, very glad of it, if you are the example I'm meant to follow."

"Insolence!" Horn hissed. Clenching his fist behind his back he said, "And I suggest you learn to control it, my young nobody. Or I will hurt you very much indeed, and no one will hear you scream."

"*You'll* hear," he said, again unable to stop himself.

"I will stuff your mouth with silk," Horn answered smoothly. "I happen to know it's very effective."

"May I have a drink first?" he asked with proper humility.

"Of course you may," said Horn. "I'm not a monster. Behave yourself, do as I say, and we'll see about making you more comfortable."

Horn pulled the ring off the long finger himself, since the chains didn't allow the boy's hands to meet. Horn wasn't stupid. The boy hadn't wanted to give it up: the ruby must mean something to St Vier.

"I shall write the note myself," he said, "and send it with the ring to St Vier at the usual tavern. As soon as the job is done, we'll consider the matter settled."

"Perhaps," Alec inquired, "you will send one of your own rings in earnest?"

Horn looked with pity at the shoddy boy. "I am a gentleman," he explained. "He knows my word is good."

T HEY LET THE MESSENGER GO, AND ST VIER WAS FURIOUS. Rosalie realized that, for all the fights settled under her roof, she had never seen him angry before. His voice wasn't raised, nor his motions unusually abrupt. Those who didn't know him well might not even notice the pallor of his face, or the quiet that hung about him like the silences between thunder. But the pleasant ring of his voice was gone; his speech was flat, without inflection:

"I said anyone. Anyone who came asking for me."

"It was only a messenger," said Sam Bonner again, at his sweetest. He was getting more conciliatory with each repetition; but he was the only one there with the grape-sodden nerve to say anything at all. There was no knowing with men like St Vier when they would decide to put a stop to all explanation. However, the swordsman remained quiet and still—if you liked that sort of stillness. Rodge and Nimble Willie glanced at each other. The little thief stepped forward. He looked up at St Vier with earnest gravity lining his childish face, and tried again.

"We did stop him, see. He was trying just to drop the packet on the table and run, but Rodge here stopped him. But he didn't know any-thing, see, not a thing—rabbit-scared he was, and ticklish with his steel; so we just lifted his purse and let him go. Not much in it."

"You can bet we asked first," Sam asserted; "now you know we would." ("Sam . . ." Rodge cautioned.) "But he didn't know a thing. Got that packet third-hand; third-hand, and didn't know a thing."

Anxiously they watched St Vier break open the wax seal. He flung the paper onto the floor. In his hand was a ruby ring. He stared at it, and they stared too. It was worth a fortune. But it didn't seem to cheer him up. Someone pressed a mug of beer into his free hand; he took it but paid no other notice.

"There's writing on that paper."

It was Ginnie Vandall, who had gone out looking for him in the other direction. "I can read," she said huskily.

Richard picked up the paper, took her elbow, and steered her out into the empty yard.

She peered at the note in the morning light. Fortunately it was full of short words. She read, slowly and carefully:

> *Do the Job for me at once and he will be*
> *returned to you right away unharmed.*

There was no signature.

The seal on the outside had been blank; inside, handsomely stamped in crimson wax, was the crest he'd seen on the other notes, the ones Alec had laughed at.

"Ah," said Ginnie. "That's not so good." He would have to refuse. She knew that. No swordsman could afford to be blackmailed. He had lost his Alec—not that he wouldn't be better off without the unpleasant scholar in the long run. He'd see it himself in a few days, when it had all blown over. She didn't ask whose crest it was. Someone powerful, who had wanted the best swordsman in the city very badly.

She said, "You'll want to lay quiet for a couple days. I'll tell Willie to bring the news round to you at Marie's. If you've got any appointments Hugo can—"

He looked at her as though she weren't there. "What are you talking about?" His eyes were the mute color of drowned hyacinths.

"His lordship won't like it," she explained. "The city's not a good place for you to be."

"Why not? I'm taking the job."

He handed her the full mug and walked away. At the doorway he turned, remembering to say, "Thank you, Ginnie," before he left.

For a moment she stood looking after him; then she spun on her heel and walked slowly back into the tavern.

IT WAS TRUE; HE COULD NOT AFFORD TO BE BLACKMAILED. BUT neither would he let someone under his protection be taken away from him. And that was the more immediate problem, to which Richard St Vier addressed himself.

He had nothing against Lord Michael Godwin, and what he knew of Lord Horn he didn't like: the man was stupid, graceless, and impatient. It meant there was little chance of Richard's finding Alec before Horn gave up on him.

Unfortunately, he couldn't count on Horn being quite stupid enough to have Alec in his town house. It was a shame: Richard was good at breaking into houses. A set of plans like crystalline maps unrolled before him; but they all took time, and the note had said *at once*. There was no one on the Hill who owed him favors: Richard took care to keep himself debt-free both ways. There were people up there who might help him, if he asked, for his own sake; but it was bad enough that most of Riverside now knew about Alec's disappearance—he didn't want the whole city talking about it.

He crumpled the note in his fist. He must remember to burn it. Tonight he would challenge Godwin, take care of him, and hope that the duchess or someone would want St Vier badly enough to protect him from the Godwin family lawyers, should the need arise. He had no faith in Horn's protection. What happened after that, St Vier would have to take care of himself.

chapter XVI

H E LEFT RIVERSIDE WELL BEFORE THE SUN SET, WEARING
his comfortable brown clothes. He knew that most nobles
were at home at that hour, getting dressed up for the evening's activities.

There were very few pedestrians on the Hill; he passed only random servants on last-minute errands. The meat and produce delivery
wagons had departed with the last of their charges hours ago, leaving
the cooks to their own devices; the visiting carriages were being burnished in the yards. The gates and walls of the riverward estates cast
long purple shadows across the wide streets. In the shadows, night's
chill had already set in. He was glad of his long cloak, chosen to hide
the sword he wore. Because of the spring damp, the ruddy clay in the
street was not yet dusty. In the squares of sunlight between houses it
glowed golden, blocked out by shadows in geometric patterns arbitrary and beautiful.

The Godwin town house was not large, but it was set back from the
street, with a conveniently corniced gate. If the lord drove or rode
out, he would certainly come through it. Richard positioned himself
in a shadow against the wall, and waited.

The wait gave him time, unfortunately, to think about Alec and
Lord Horn. He doubted the scholar was curbing his tongue any, and
hoped, despite the note's assurance, that Alec would not be too badly
damaged. These nobles were not like Riversiders: they were used to
acting on their wills, they didn't understand about signs that some-

thing wasn't safe to handle, or instinct that said to let it go for now. That was what had first preserved Alec when he'd entered Riverside alone. People had sensed something not right about him, and had not exacted retribution for his offenses. But Lord Horn wouldn't be thinking that way. And Richard already knew Alec's opinion of Horn. He felt himself smile with the memory.

St Vier shrugged and shivered at the chill that had settled in the folds of his cloak. There was nothing he could do about it now: only wait, and hope Lord Michael was not too heavily attended. So far as he knew he did not have his own bodyguard; if Richard issued the formal challenge to Lord Michael on the street he would have no choice but to fight St Vier then and there. But he was a long time coming out. Richard looked at the sky. He'd give it until sundown before going up to the door to call the noble out. That was a risk, because Godwin might have some servant inside who could take the challenge for him, fight in his stead, and give Lord Michael time to flee the city before Horn could find another challenger. They were a silly bunch of rules, but they made death by duel with a professional seem less like assassination. It was all correct within the boundaries of formal challenge; but Richard doubted that Horn would be pleased, and he needed to keep him happy.

He'd challenged other young lords in his time, and was not looking forward to this. Often they made a great deal of fuss over their clothes, taking off and folding their coats as though they were going to be putting them on again. Even the ones with enough presence to strike a proper stance had hands that shook holding the sword. The only such challenge he'd ever enjoyed was one in which the lady hired him only to scar his mark distinctively.

He heard footsteps suddenly, and looked up. On the other side of the gate a small postern opened, and a man stepped out. When he turned to shut the door Richard recognized him as the red-haired nobleman who'd run after him that winter day at the bookshop, whom he'd pointed out to Alec at the theater. Lord Michael was wearing a sword. He set off down the street, without looking behind him, whistling.

He could easily catch up to him. The space in the street was good, the light not yet failed. And, wonder of wonders, it was an excellent sword from what Richard could see of it: not the nobleman's toy they usually carried. He readied himself to move, and then paused. Where was this noble sauntering off to so purposefully, on foot and without attendance, carrying a real dueling sword? He wanted to know; and he did not really relish butchering the man in front of all his neighbors.

Richard decided it would do no harm to stalk Lord Michael to his destination and satisfy his curiosity. Without undue hurry, he detached himself from the shadows and set off down the Hill after his guide.

Y OU'RE LATE," OBSERVED VINCENT APPLETHORPE, LOOKING UP from the sword he was polishing one-handed, the hilt wedged between his knees.

"Sorry," Michael panted, having run up the stairs. He knew he was being accused, however mildly; and he had learned not to try to bluster his way out. He only explained, "I had some people over, and they wouldn't go away."

Applethorpe smiled slowly, secretly, into the polished blade. "You may find that stops being a problem soon. In a year or so, after you've won your first duel. People become very eager to pick up the slightest of hints from you then."

Michael grinned in return, more broadly than he'd meant to, at the thought of Lord Bertram and Lord Thomas flinching, putting down their chocolate cups, and slinking away at the sign of a yawn. He found it hard to imagine really killing anyone; and if he did someday he certainly hoped none of his friends would find out about it.

Michael stripped down to his shirt and began limbering up. The Master commented, "The Tragedy's in town. Do you know about it?"

"I . . . it's at Blackwell's " he answered noncommitally.

"It's not a good idea to go," the Master said, putting the sword back on the rack. It hadn't really needed polishing, but he liked to keep up contact with his blades, and he didn't like sitting idle waiting for Godwin to come. Now he could pace, watching the young man from every angle, alert to any flaw. "You want to avoid things like that."

"Is there really a curse?"

"I don't know. But it's never done anyone any good."

It satisfied him: practical, like all of Applethorpe's advice.

"Ready?"

Michael caught the practice sword that was tossed to him—possibly Master Applethorpe's only theatrical tendency, but also good for his eye. It meant the Master would be calling out orders, and his student must follow the shifting commands with precision. He hoped tonight Applethorpe would duel with him again. He was getting better at it, learning how to integrate the moves and defenses he'd been taught. It excited him—but not, any more, past skill and reason. He was learning to think and act at the same time.

"Garde!" the Master snapped, and Lord Michael sprang to the first defensive position, already tensed for the rapid command to follow. He waited a beat, two beats, but there was nothing.

"That's strange," the Master said; "there's someone coming up the stairs."

RICHARD COULDN'T THINK WHY THE LORD SHOULD BE WALKING to a common hiring-stable, when he had plenty of horses at home. He watched him go in a side door, and heard the swift tread of feet on wooden stairs. In a judicious few minutes, he followed.

He took it all in at a glance: the clear space, the targets, and the two men, one without an arm, the other still at garde, both staring at him in surprise.

"Excuse me for interrupting," he said. "My name is Richard St Vier. I bear a challenge to Lord Michael Godwin, to fight past first blood, until a conclusion is reached."

"Michael," said Vincent Applethorpe calmly, "light the candles; there won't be enough daylight soon."

Carefully Michael replaced his sword in the rack. He could hear the sound of his own breathing in his ears, but he tried to get it to sound like Applethorpe's voice, steady and even. He was surprised at how well he could control his muscles, despite the racing of his blood: the tinder struck on the first try. He walked around the room, lighting the fat drippy candles, their flames pale and indefinite in the twilight, almost transparent. This was St Vier, the strange man who had bought the book of philosophy from Felman that winter's day. He remembered rather liking him; and his friend Thomas, at the theater, had betrayed a definite interest. *He's watching you....* God, Michael thought, of course he was! He wished he had had the chance to watch St Vier fight, just once. Accidents did happen, and strokes of luck.

While Michael was making his rounds, Applethorpe came forward to greet the swordsman. "I've heard of you," he said, "of course. I'm very glad to meet you." They did not touch hands. St Vier's were inside his cloak, one resting on the pommel of his sword. They faced each other in the dim studio, two men of nearly identical height and build, but for the older man's missing arm. "My name is Vincent Applethorpe," the Master said. It was clear from St Vier's face that he'd never heard the name. "I claim the challenge."

"No!" said Michael without meaning to. He cursed as candle wax dripped onto his hand.

"I wish you wouldn't," Richard answered the Master. "It will make things harder."

"I was told you liked a challenge," Applethorpe said.

Richard compressed his lips in mild annoyance. "Of course it would be a pleasure. But I have obligations. . . ."

"I have the right."

The wax was cooling on Michael's hand. "Master, please—it isn't your fight."

"It will be a very short fight if it is yours," Applethorpe said to him. "You won't learn a thing. It is very much my fight."

"You do have the right," St Vier admitted. "Let's begin."

"Thank you. Michael, get your sword. Now kiss the blade and promise not to interfere."

"I promise not to interfere." The steel was very cold against Michael's lips. At this angle the blade felt heavy; it seemed to pull his hand down. He made his wrist sustain the weight for an extra moment, and then saluted his teacher with it.

"Your honor's good," the Master was saying to St Vier.

"Inconveniently good," Richard sighed. "I won't touch him if you lose. If I lose, please see that word gets back to Riverside; they'll know what to do."

"Then let's begin."

And the master swordsmen began. It was all there as Michael had studied it. But now he saw the strength and grace of Applethorpe's demonstrations compacted into the little space of precious time.

Michael watched with luxurious pleasure the rise and fall of their arms, the turn of their wrists, now that he could follow what was happening. Master Applethorpe was demonstrating again, as fine and precise as at the lessons; but now there was a mirror to him, the polished, focused motions of St Vier. Michael forgot that death was at hand as, indeed, the two swordsmen seemed to have done, leisurely stroking and countering their way across the scrubbed white floor, with the high ceiling catching and returning the ring of their steel.

As the swordplay grew fiercer the sound of their breath became audible, and the nearer candle flames shuddered in their passing. It was almost too fast for Michael to follow now, moves followed up and elaborated on before he could discern them; like trying to follow an argument between two scholars fluent in a foreign language, rich with obscure textual references.

St Vier, who never spoke when fighting, gasped, "Applethorpe—why have I never heard of you?"

Vincent Applethorpe took the occasion to come in high in a corkscrew movement that turned the other swordsman in a half-circle defending himself. St Vier stumbled backward, but turned it to his advantage by crouching into a sideways dodge that Applethorpe had to swerve to avoid.

Subtly, something changed. At first Michael couldn't figure out what it was. Both men were smiling twin wolfish grins, their lips parted as much for air as for delight. Their moves were a little slower, more deliberate, but not the careful demonstration of earlier. They didn't flow into each other. There were pauses between each flurry of strokes and returns, pauses heavy with tension. The air grew thick with it; it seemed to weight their movement. The time of testing, and of playing, was over. This was the final duel for one of them. Now they were fighting for their lives—for the one life that would emerge from this elegant battle. For a moment Michael let himself think of it: that whatever happened here, he would emerge unscathed. Of course there would be things to do, people to notify. . . . He caught his breath as St Vier was forced to lunge back into the wall, between two candles. He could see a crazy grin on the man's face as he held Applethorpe off with elaborate wristwork. For the moment the two were evenly matched, arm against arm. Michael prayed that it would never stop, that there would always be this moment of utter mastery, beautiful and rare, and no conclusion ever be reached. St Vier knocked over a candle; it put itself out rolling on the floor. He kicked aside the table it had been on, extricating himself from the corner, and the action resumed.

Richard knew he was fighting for his life, and he was terribly happy. In most of his fights, even the good ones, he made all the decisions: when to turn serious, whether to fight high or low . . . but already Applethorpe had taken that away from him. He wasn't afraid, but the edge of challenge was sharp under him, and the drop from it irrevocable. The world had narrowed to the strength of his body, the trained agility of his mind in response to his opponent. The universe began and ended within the reach of his senses, the stretch of his four limbs and the gleaming steel. It was too good to lose now, the bright point coming at him always from another angle, the clarity of his mind anticipating and returning it, creating new patterns to play. . . .

He saw the opening and went for it, but Applethorpe countered at the last instant, pivoting clumsily so that what would have been a clean death stroke caught him raggedly across the chest.

The Master stood upright, gripping his rapier too tightly, staring straight ahead. "Michael," he said clearly, "that arm is for balance."

Blood was soaking through the sweat in his shirt, the smell of it like decaying iron overlaying the tang of exertion that still hung thick in the air. Quickly Richard caught him and eased him to the floor, supporting him on his own heaving chest. Applethorpe's breath made a liquid, tearing sound. Michael found his cloak, and spread it over his teacher's legs.

"Step back," St Vier ordered him. He leaned his head down next to Applethorpe's and murmured, "Shall I finish it?"

"No," Applethorpe rasped. "Not yet. Godwin—"

"Don't talk," Michael said.

"Let him," said Richard.

The Master's teeth were gritted, but he tried to untwist his lips to smile. "If you're good enough, this is how it ends."

Michael said, "Are you telling me to give it up?"

"No," St Vier answered over Vincent Applethorpe's hissing breath. "He's talking about the challenge. I'm sorry—you either know it or you don't."

"Shall I get a surgeon?" Michael asked, clutching at the world he was master of.

"He doesn't need one," St Vier said. Again he bent his dark head. "Master—thank you. I do enjoy a challenge."

Vincent Applethorpe laughed in triumph, and the blood spattered everything. The marks of his fingers were still white on St Vier's wrists when he lowered the corpse to the floor.

Richard wiped his hands on the young lord's cloak, and covered the dead man with it. Without quite understanding how they had got there, Michael found himself standing across the room, facing the swordsman's commanding presence.

"You have the right to know," Richard said, "it was Lord Horn set me on. He won't be glad you're still alive, but I've fought your champion and I consider my obligation discharged. He may try again with someone else; I suggest you leave the city for a while." He caught the expected clenching of Michael's fists. "Don't try to kill Horn," he said. "I'm sure you're good enough to do it, but his life is about to become complicated; it would be better if you left." The young man only stared at him, blue-green eyes hot and bright in his white face. "Don't try to kill me either; you're surely not good enough for that."

"I wasn't going to," Michael said.

Calmly, St Vier was collecting his own belongings. "I'll report the death," he said, "and send someone to look after it. Was he married?"

"I . . . don't know."

"Go on." The swordsman put Michael's sword and jacket in his hands. "You shouldn't stay."

The door closed behind him, and there was nowhere to go but down the dark stairs.

Outside it was still early, a warm spring night. The sky was that perfect turquoise that sets off the first scattering of stars. Michael shivered. He had left his cloak upstairs, he was going to be cold without it—but it was no use, was it—he passed his hand over his face in an attempt to clear his thoughts, and felt a hand close around his wrist.

All the violence of the past hour exploded in his body like fireworks. He couldn't really see what he was doing through the red-gold flare, but he felt his fist connect with flesh, his body twisting like a whirlwind, heard a long drawn-out howl like the center of a storm—and then a sharp thumping noise that heralded the most glorious set of fireworks yet, before night fell without stars.

chapter XVII

WHEN HIS VISION CLEARED HE WAS IN A COACH. His hands and feet were tied, and the curtains were drawn. His head ached, and he was thirsty. Considering how soon he would likely be dead it shouldn't matter, but he badly wanted a drink. The jouncing of the carriage over cobblestones was intolerable. Cobblestones—that meant they were somewhere on Hertimer Street, going up towards the Hill.

"Hey!" he shouted. The reverberations in his skull made him wish he hadn't; but at least he could make some trouble for someone. Something terrible had just happened, which was in some way his fault, and shouting might stave it off. "Hey, stop this thing at once!"

The only answer he got—or was like to get—was savage pounding on the roof of the carriage. He felt like a handsomely trussed-up pea rolling around in the center of a drum. He'd meant to eat when he got back from Applethorpe's—

Something in his brain tried to warn his thoughts away, but there was no stopping the flood that broke through. The image struck in his stomach first, so that he thought he was going to spew—but then the pain rose and took over his breathing, knotting the muscles of his throat and face. . . . He would not come before Horn weeping. That at least he could withhold. He had been disarmed by his captors; but there were other ways to kill a man. He'd wrestled, and learned some of them. Never mind what St Vier had said; St Vier hadn't known how soon he would be facing his enemy. Or had he? Michael was amazed at Horn's effrontery: presumably the carriage had been left as a backup in case St Vier failed. Perhaps Horn meant to bed him before setting him up for another challenge. . . . Erotic, violent visions wound through the labyrinth of pain and all the emotions he'd never had to feel before, the pain and grief and fury weaving themselves into a strangely seductively soothing trance. Rapt in it, he only noticed the carriage had stopped when he heard the squeak of the opening gate.

As it clattered into the yard he came fully alert. His breathing was quick, his awareness of his body seemed supernaturally heightened. The pain was there, but also the strength and coordination. When they opened the door he would be ready for them.

But they didn't open the door. The carriage pulled up to what he supposed was the house's main entrance. He could hear his captors getting down, the muffled growl of voices issuing orders. Then there was silence. They weren't going to leave him here all night, were they?

When the carriage door opened it heralded a light so bright that his eyes blinked and watered.

"Dear me," said a woman's voice out of the dazzling nimbus. "Was it necessary to be quite so thorough?"

"Well, your ladyship, he did try to kill me."

"All the same . . . Untie his feet, please, Grayson."

He didn't even look down at the man kneeling over his ankles. The Duchess Tremontaine stood framed by the little doorway, in full evening dress, holding up an inelegant iron lantern.

Finally, he was too bruised to care what she thought of him and his sense of style. "What are you doing here?" he asked hoarsely.

She smiled, her voice like long, cool slopes of snow. "This is my house. My people brought you here. Do you think you can stand up?"

He stood up, and sat down again swiftly.

"Well, I am not a nurse," she said with the same cool sweetness. "Grayson, will you see that Lord Michael is made comfortable indoors? My lord, I will attend you when you are rested."

Then the color, the sweetness, the perfume were gone, and he **was** left to the unpleasant task of imposing his will on his own unruly person.

SEVERAL AGES SEEMED TO PASS AS LORD MICHAEL WORKED HIS way up through strata of dirt, fatigue, hunger, and thirst. Diane's servants had put him in a handsome room with a hot bath and a set table. The room was lit by fire and candlelight. Curtains of heavy red velvet were drawn, so that he could not see which way the room faced. The red hangings, the mellow light, the sense of enclosure, all made him feel unreasonably safe and cared for, like a child wrapped up in a blanket in someone's arms.

The terrible pain of what had happened lay hard and bright at the center of his physical contentment. The memory came and went, like the ebb and flow of waves, but with no predictable pattern. When Michael was a little boy, there was a painting on the wall of his home that he was terrified of: it showed the spirit of a dead woman rising from the tomb, her baby in her arms. He had been afraid even to pass the room where it was. Whether he wanted to or not, he would think of it at the worst moments: in the dark, going up the stairs; so he started making himself think of it all the time, until it became so familiar that he could contemplate it without a tremor. He wasn't quite ready for that yet, not while the confusions and strangeness still enfolded him. Before he went bathing in the events of Applethorpe's death he had to know where the dry land was.

He was sunk in an easy chair before the fire; but at the click of the door latch he jumped like a cat. It was not the door he had come in by. This was a smaller one cut in the red wall.

Diane said, "Please, sit down. May I join you?"

Mutely he indicated a chair. She helped herself to some cherry cordial from the array of decanters, and seated herself across from him. She had changed her clothes: as if to prove that this was indeed her home, she wore a flowing housedress of soft blue silk. Her loose curls tumbled over her shoulders like the crests of waves.

"Please don't be too angry with Asper," she said. "You upset him rather badly the night of my little party. He is a vain man, and proud, and lecherous—you shouldn't find him so hard to understand."

For a moment he made the duchess fear for her personal possessions. But his fingers only left a dent in the pewter flagon at his side. She continued, "You should have come to me, as soon as you suspected he was up to something." Michael still cared enough for her esteem not to want to tell her that he hadn't known. The duchess sighed. "Poor Asper! He isn't very subtle, and he isn't very clever. He was pestering some young woman of Tony's. . . . By the way, Lord Michael, did you kill St Vier?"

"No. He killed my fighting-master."

"I see."

"I am not the swordsman you would have me, madam."

She smiled a bewitching, knowing smile. "Now, why should you say that?"

"I'll never stand a chance against him," he said bitterly, staring not at the beautiful woman, but into the dregs of the fire. "Everyone knew that. Applethorpe was humoring me." Another pain, a little sharp sliver that he'd borne since the challenge and almost forgotten in the weight of the other. "He knew I'd never make a swordsman."

"Once in a generation there comes a swordsman like St Vier. Your teacher never said you were that one." Sunk in his feelings, he did not respond. But her voice was no longer light. "But, for St Vier, there is nothing more. It is all he wants out of life, and probably all he'll ever get. That's not what you want; not all. It just comes closer than most things."

He looked at her, not really seeing her. He felt as though his skin had been peeled back with a scalpel. "What I want . . ."

". . . I can give you," she said softly.

"Fine—if I'm to be Horn!"

He heard the harsh clang of metal, and realized that he was standing up, and that he had thrown the tankard across the room. The duchess hadn't stirred. "Madam," he said stiffly. "You chose to embroil yourself in my affairs. I hope it has given you pleasure. I believe all my desires ceased to be a matter for discussion between us some time ago."

She chuckled richly. He was appalled to find himself thinking of strawberries and cream. "There you are," she said. "I wonder if you men have any idea of how insulting it is to women when you assume that all we can offer is our bodies?"

"I am sorry." He looked up and met her eyes. "It is as insulting as to have it thought that's all we want."

"Don't apologize. I made you think it."

"You made me think a great many things this winter."

"Yes," she said. "Shall I apologize?"

"No."

"Good," she said. "Then I shall go on making you think. I know what you want. You want to be a man of power. I'm going to give you that."

His face unfroze; he was able to smile his charming smile. "Will it take long?"

"Yes," she said. "But it won't seem long."

"I want to be your lover," Michael said.

"Yes," said the duchess, and opened the red silk door to her chamber.

Inside it he paused. "Lord Ferris," he said.

"Ah, Ferris." Her voice was low; it made him shiver to hear it.

"Well; Ferris should have told me he knew Lord Horn was planning to kill you."

H E SEEMED TO FLOAT — AS THOUGH HE NEVER TOUCHED HER body, but was held suspended in some directionless space whose charts only she held. All pride, all fear were gone from him. Even the desire for it not to end was swallowed by the overwhelming present. His vaunted sophistication gave way to something new; and in that infinite space he rose and fell in the same moment into a world's end of fireworks reflected in a bottomless river.

M ICHAEL."
The tip of her finger touched his ear, but all he did was sigh. "Michael, you're going to have to leave the city now. For two weeks, maybe three." He turned over and kissed her mouth, and felt a roaring in his ears. But her lips, while still soft, were not pliant, and he drew back to let her speak. "I would like to send you out of the country. There are some things I would like you to see. The people of Chartil respect a man who can use a sword, especially a nobleman. Will you go?"

His hands refused to leave her flesh, but he said over them, "I will."

"It must be now," she said. "The ship sails in three hours' time with the dawn tide."

It was a shock to him, but he mastered it, stroking her skin for the deliciousness of it, for the memory, without arousing the honeyed longing that would not let him go.

His clothes were set out in the red room. She followed him there, trailing silk and instructions. He should be tired, but his body tingled. It was the feeling he got after lessons— Like a club, the memory struck him hard. Bent over, strapping on his useless sword, he said nothing.

The duchess sat, smiling, swinging one white foot, watching him cover his collarbones. "I have something to give you," she said. He thought of roses, gloves, and handkerchiefs. "You will keep it for me, and no one can take it from you unless you offer it. I am convinced you will not offer it. It is a secret. My secret."

Fully dressed, he kissed her hand formally, the way he had that first afternoon at Lady Halliday's. "Ah," she said; "I was right about you then; and you were right about me. You see, it's true, Michael. Those men who died, Lynch and de Maris, they were not hired by the Duke of Karleigh. *I* hired Lynch—and de Maris got in the way. I needed to teach Karleigh a lesson, to tell him I was serious about a matter he thought I was joking about. He never took me seriously enough. Karleigh hired St Vier. His man won . . . but Karleigh—Karleigh knows he is going to lose in this matter, because I stand against him. If the duke is wise, he will stay in the country this spring."

That was all she was going to tell him, and then trust him to figure the rest out for himself. He didn't feel clever or triumphant, after all. Excited, maybe, and a little frightened.

The duchess reached up and touched his rough cheek. "Good-bye, Michael," she said. "If all goes well, you will come back soon."

There was a private side door, this time, for him to leave Tremontaine House by; and a chilly walk before the dawn, home to give his orders and depart. His sword hung at his side again, a heavy weight, but good protection in the dark.

chapter XVIII

WHEN THE DOOR OPENED RICHARD STAYED WHERE HE was, sitting in the chair opposite. The cat had tolerated his steady stroking of her for almost an hour; but when his lap tensed she jumped off it, and darted over to the man coming in.

"Hello, Richard," said Alec. "What a surprise: you're awake, and it isn't even noon yet."

He looked terrible: clothes wrinkled, face unshaven; eyes within their dark circles a particularly malevolent shade of green. He stood in the middle of the room, refusing to sit down, trying hard not to sway. The door swung shut behind him.

Richard said, "Well, I went to bed early." If Alec didn't want to be touched, he wasn't going to force it. It was enough for him to see that Alec was on his feet, and whole. Alec's face was unmarked, and his tone as light as ever, though his voice was thick with sleeplessness.

Alec said, "I hear you bungled Horn's job."

"Where did you hear that?"

"Straight from the horse's . . . mouth. Godwin's not dead."

"I'm a swordsman, not an assassin. He didn't say to kill Godwin, he said to challenge him. I did. Someone else took the challenge; I killed *him*."

"Naturally."

"I don't see what you're fussing about it for; Horn must have been satisfied, or he wouldn't have— Alec!" Richard stared harder, trying to see beneath the shakily composed exterior. "Did you *escape*?"

But Alec only smiled scornfully. "Escape? Me? I couldn't escape from a haystack. I leave that kind of thing to you. No, he let me go when he found you'd fought the challenge. In the name of honor or something. You understand these people so much better than I do. I think"—Alec yawned—"he didn't like me." He stretched his arms up over his head; high in the air the jewels flashed rainbows over his hands.

Richard's breath caught with a tearing sound.

"Oh." Alec pulled his cuffs back into place. "I'm afraid I've lost one of your rings. The rose. His so-called swordsmen took it. Maybe you can bill him for it. God, these clothes stink! I haven't changed them for three days. I'm going to roll them into a ball and drop them out of the window for Marie. Then I'm going to bed. I kept trying to sleep in the carriage, but it didn't have any springs, and then every time I was about to drop off I thought I smelt civet. I spent most of the trip with my head out of the window. And then they made me *walk* from the bridge! The near bridge, not the far one, at least, but even so . . ."

Everyone in Riverside knew what shackle marks looked like. Richard followed him to bed, and later on he tried to kiss them. But Alec wrenched his wrists away.

"What else did he do?" Richard demanded harshly.

"Nothing! What more do you want?"

"Did he—"

"He didn't do *anything*, Richard, just leave me alone!"

But late that night, when Alec was drunk and excited and no longer cared, Richard kissed the marks again, and thought of Lord Horn.

THE SWORDSMAN'S BUSINESS KEPT HIM OUT LATE THE NEXT DAY. When he came back he expected to find Alec asleep: Alec had been out of bed that morning at dawn, despite his late ordeal. But to his surprise a fire was blazing in the hearth, and Alec was kneeling in front of it. His loose hair, unbraided and unclasped, curtained his face like a temple mystery. With his black robe and long limbs he looked like a child's image of a wizard, peering into the mysteries of the fire. But he was busy doing something: with a shock Richard realized that Alec was tearing pages out of a book, carefully and methodically feeding them to the flames. He did not look up when St Vier shut the door, or when he took a few steps into the room.

Afraid to startle him, Richard said, "Alec. I'm back."

"Are you?" said Alec dreamily. The page he was holding burst into flame; his eyes were fixed on the blaze. His face was lit to flatness like an idol's mask, his eyes two dark slits. "Did you have a nice time?"

"It was all right. What are you burning?"

Alec turned the book's spine around, as though he needed to be reminded of the title. *"On the Causes of Nature,"* he said. "I don't need it any more."

It had been his gift; but Richard didn't give gifts to hold on to them. He stretched out before the fire, glad to be home. "I thought it would take you longer to memorize this one. You haven't even worn the words off the binding yet."

"I don't need it any more," Alec repeated. "I know everything now."

Something in the careful way Alec was taking hold of each page should have alerted him already. St Vier sprang out of his chair and spun Alec around by the shoulder.

"Stop that," Alec said with mild annoyance. "You're hurting me." He didn't resist the fingers prying wide his eyelids. He looked calmly at Richard with eyes that were like two matched emeralds, with only a speck of black to mar each one.

"God!" Richard's grip tightened. "You're sotted on Delight!"

The figured lips curved. "Of course. Am I supposed to be surprised? It's excellent stuff, Richard; you should have some."

St Vier recoiled involuntarily, although his grip held. "No, I shouldn't. I hate what the stuff does. It makes you stupid, and clumsy."

"You're just being stuffy. I have some right here—"

"No. Alec, how—when did you start doing this?"

"At University." The drug intensified the languor of his aristocratic drawl. "Harry and I, doing experiments. Taking notes. You could take notes for me."

"I can't," Richard said.

"No, it's easy. Just write down what I say. . . . We're going to do a book. It will influence generations to come."

Richard held tight to his shoulder. "Tell me where you got it. How much did you take?"

Alec waved his hand vaguely. "Why, would you like some?"

"No, I would not like some. How often do you do this?" It was stupid of him never to have considered it before. He'd thought he knew Alec, knew his habits and his ways, even when he wasn't there. . . .

Alec looked at him complacently. "Not often. Not for a long time. I'm occupied with . . . other things. You look so worried, Richard. I saved you some."

"That's very kind of you," Richard said dryly. "We'll just have to wait it out, then. With other things." He carefully placed his arm around his lover's neck, tasted the sweetness of the drug on his tongue. With his other hand he slipped the book from Alec's fingers, laying it down away from the hearth. Then he led him into the bedroom.

He wasn't much good to talk to, but his body was pliant and sensitive as Richard undressed him.

"Why are you doing that?" Alec asked, more than once, as Richard undid another button, another lace.

"So you won't be cold," Richard answered; and later, "So I can kiss it. There. Like that."

Alec chuckled happily. "I appreciate that. I appreciate *you*."

"Thanks." Richard tickled him gently. "I appreciate you. . . ."

Then Alec stiffened and drew back. "What's that?" he cried.

"Probably me. My heartbeat. Nothing, don't worry. . . ."

"They're watching me, Richard, they're watching me!"

The period of serenity had passed, and the nervousness Richard had hoped to circumvent was upon him. "No one's watching."

But Alec pulled out of his arms and spread himself before the window, his clothes half off him, hanging by ribbons and half-sleeves. He was pressing his palms to the glass, trying to cover it with his spread fingers, while his eyes fixed on the sky above them.

"The stars are watching me," he declared in a voice of terrible pain. "Make them stop!"

"They're not watching. Why should they?"

"God, make them stop. They're watching me!"

Richard interposed himself between Alec and the window, and pulled the shutters closed. "It's all right now. They can't see you."

Alec clung to him, burying his face in Richard's shoulder. "I tried to get away. . . . Stone and Griffin and I, we were so sure . . . we had the calculations, Richard, they were right, I know they were . . . it didn't matter about me, but they needed that stupid degree . . . what's going to happen to Harry's sister?" he cried wildly.

"It's all right . . ."

"No, you don't understand—the chancellors tore it up! I wouldn't believe them, I didn't think they'd do that. . . ."

"The University chancellors?"

"Doctor Pig-Nose."

"And that's why they kicked you out?" He'd always suspected something like this.

"No. Not me. I'm all right. It's *you* I'm worried for. . . ."

"Not me, Alec."

". . . Richard? You have to protect me. I was safe in Rhetoric—do you know what that is?—in History, Geometry, but consider the angle of the sun: the stars describe an arc without a tangent—but they're watching, all the time they're watching me—"

He started violently at the sound of knocking in the hall. Richard held him tighter. Was he trying to destroy himself for that, because the University had rejected his work? He must have put a lot of faith in the place to begin with. If it had been his escape from his nobility, it was understandable. And if he was not noble, the school must have been his last chance. . . .

"You're all right now," Richard repeated mechanically. "That's all over. No one can hurt you now."

"Don't let them find me. You don't know what it's like, knowing they won't touch you, just your friends, and everybody thinking I'm some kind of spy for the nobles—all I wanted was to—"

The knocking was fierce, and it was at their door. A thought came to Richard, and he tucked Alec in the blankets. "Alec," he said carefully, "stay here, don't move. It's all right, there's just someone at the door. I'll be back soon."

He waited until he'd left the bedroom to take up his sword.

Richard flung the door back in one sharp motion, blade already poised. It was a woman standing there, in a velvet cloak.

"Well," said Ginnie Vandall, observing the sword, "you're a little on edge."

"Just being careful."

"You should be. Are you alone?"

"In fact, I'm not. Can it wait 'til morning?"

She took the lowered blade as an invitation to enter, sweeping past him into the middle of the room. "That's up to you, my dear. I'll make it short."

"It can wait, then."

"Look," she said; "I haven't come here alone at this hour to get turned away because you didn't want to put your clothes back on."

He put the sword down. "All right. What is it?"

"It's two men found dead at the bottom of Ganser Steps not an hour ago. The Watch found them, and the stupid bastards can't figure out why they were killed expertly with a sword. Neither can I. It was that neat upper stroke through the heart, and sooner or later someone's going to point out that you're the only one who can do that more than once."

"They're supposed to."

She stared at him angrily. "Those men weren't Riverside. You're not a nobleman, you can't run around the city picking off whoever you want without a contract and expect no one to care. If you're going to commit your little murders, be careful how close to the Bridge you leave the corpses. We don't want the Watch coming in here looking for trouble."

"They won't. And I had to make sure there was no mistake. Are you pretending, or don't you know who those men were?"

Her stare lost some of its hardness. "Oh, Richard," she sighed. "I was hoping you weren't going to say that."

"It's all right," he said. "The lord who set them after Alec isn't going to come forward and demand justice for them. He isn't the type. I really don't see what you're worried about. No one's going to harrow Riverside over a couple of bravos. And I've just made sure that that kind of thing doesn't happen again. Hugo should be glad." He went to the door and held it open for her. "Good night, Ginnie."

"Wait," she said, her hand raised to her throat. "It doesn't have anything to do with Riverside, or with Hugo or any of the others. You've got to be more careful. They can't *let* you go around like that, not outside this district." The hand lowered from her throat, glided down over the velvet. "If it comes to an Inquiry, my dear, you'll hang, no matter what this lord's done to you."

"Thank you. Good night."

She moved closer, not to the door but to him, looking into his face. The shadows picked out the lines etched by her mouth and the corners of her eyes. "I know what I'm doing," she said, her voice as hard as her face. "I've taken care of Hugo, and Hal Lynch, and Tom Cook before him. You don't want to die rich, that's fine with me. You want to take up with people who hate you, that's fine too. Just don't ignore what I say."

"I understand," he said to get rid of her. She wasn't a nervous talker; she had kept her eyes on him, and hadn't noticed the ruined book on the floor, or the mess in the fireplace.

"Richard," said Ginnie, "you don't."

Her arms lifted slowly, and he let her fingers twine through his hair, pressing the back of his skull until his lips were bent to hers.

Richard had never actually kissed Ginnie Vandall before. Even in the heat of her moment she was expert and careful. The softness of her lips and the sharpness of her teeth fluttered down to the base of his spine. He shifted closer to her, catching the heat of her hipbone jutting into his thigh, her breasts flattening against his chest. He pressed his palm into the small of her back, parting his lips to reach her, when she pulled violently away.

The recoil jolted him backwards. He stared at her, still breathing deeply. Ginnie wiped her mouth with the back of her hand. "Fool's Delight," she said in disgust. "That's something new for you. Is that what it takes these days?"

He shook his head. "I don't do that."

She glanced toward the back room, but didn't say Alec's name. Ginnie pulled her cloak around her and shrugged. "Good luck."

He stood for a moment listening to her feet going down the stairs. He heard the sound of another woman's voice: Marie, who must have let her in.

Then a floorboard creaked close behind him. Alec had drifted into the room, unnaturally soft-footed. His shirt still hung loose around his waist.

"I thought I heard something," he explained. He seemed to have forgotten about the stars.

"Someone came to see me," Richard said; but Alec wasn't listening. He stalked the leather-bound book where it lay, just within range of the fire's dying glow, its gold tooling coursing with reflected light.

Alec crouched down. His clever fingers lifted the book from the floor, smoothing the crumpled pages, stroking the grime from its cover. He put the decorated leather to his cheek. The book rested against his face like a beautiful ornament, his eyes large and dark above it. His bare collarbones and shoulders framed its bottom edge.

"You see," he said, "you mustn't give me things."

"Stop it," Richard said, frightened and angry. The pale face looked otherworldly, but he knew it was just the drugs.

"Richard." Alec stared at him without blinking. "Don't tell me what to do. No one tells me what to do." He turned to the fire with the book in his left hand held out behind him like a balance. Alec stretched his right hand toward the embers glowing red in the hearth. It was like watching a magic trick that might succeed. . . . Before his hand could close over the hot coals Richard sprang, pulling him roughly back into his arms, half-sprawling on the floor.

"Ah," Alec sighed, going limp with dead weight on him. "You're such a coward."

"I'm not going to let anything happen to you," Richard said doggedly, as though he were losing an argument.

"It isn't worth it," said Alec dreamily; "you won't always be there. They've got it all worked out now, haven't they? What do you suppose they'll want from you next?"

So he'd figured it out. For once, it had cost Richard something to protect him. But drugs couldn't keep that away forever.

"Don't worry," said Richard. "I'm taking care of that. It won't happen again."

It was hard not to be angry with Ginnie's meddling. Richard owed her too much from the past to lose his temper with her because this once she was wrong. Even Alec knew that she was wrong. The men who had done Lord Horn's work must be found dead at the hands of St Vier.

chapter XIX

IT WAS TOO EARLY IN THE YEAR FOR AN OUTDOOR PARTY, BUT one didn't refuse an invitation from the Duchess Tremontaine. Actually, the whole thing was impromptu and very delightful, as the ladies assured each other, bending over their flamingo mallets to give their wooden urchins a dainty tap: the weather unseasonably warm, the food fresh, the company delightful. Trust Diane to be so whimsically original! The gentlemen, their escorts, were quietly bored. One could flirt, but one couldn't bet—not on other people's wives and sisters, it wasn't decent.

Lord Ferris wondered whether his mistress kept inviting Horn because she thought it would amuse him. Usually it did; but this week he was not eager to be entertained by Horn. His equable settling of the weavers' rebellion had returned Ferris to the city a hero to his peers, and it was important that he circulate amongst them now, visible and accepting praise. The little man and his troubles were of no consequence now. But Horn kept edging up to Ferris, knocking his ball over to where he was standing, even when it was patently obvious that it was doing his game no good.

Diane was, as always, careful not to show any interest in Ferris, although it was the first time she'd seen her lover in weeks. Ferris, too, was careful. He remembered the first time he had been long out of town, near the beginning of their association. On his return he had gone straight to her house, to report to her on his mission, and to peel the silks from her body, inflamed with the memory of her. But he was more experienced now, and more cautious. He had not wanted to provoke comment by coming to see her immediately. He had a dinner engagement later tonight; but perhaps after her party there might be time for them to go to bed.

The glitter of sunlight on water, the merry music, the sparkling laughter and radiant colors of spring wardrobes set free from the confines of winter were giving Lord Ferris a headache. Horn's blue suit was a prime offender. Here it came again. Enthusiastically Ferris turned his back on the approaching nobleman to immerse himself in the nearest pool of gossip.

"We seem to be losing people at a stupendous pace this winter," a sharp-faced noble called Galeno was expounding to a knot of men. "At this rate the town will be empty before the season's officially ended, and there'll be no one left at all to vote in Spring Council."

"Oh?" said Lord Ferris, ignoring Horn's peripheral gesticulations. "Who's missing now?"

"First the Filisands left before New Year because of illness," Galeno elaborated comprehensively, not to be balked of his list; "then Raymond had that falling out with his wife's father; then there was the business with Karleigh and the swords; and now young Godwin's house is shut up, with no word of explanation. No one's seen him for days."

That explained Horn's perturbation. "I hope nothing's happened to him," Ferris said politely.

"Oh, no; the servants said they'd received his personal orders to close up. But no one knows where he's gone, not even young Berowne, who usually can be counted on."

Something must have gone wrong. Too bad for Asper. But Lord Michael had clearly left town, maybe even left the country, and that suited Ferris's purposes. Suddenly he thought, What if Godwin hadn't left at all, what if Diane was hiding him here in her house? But he dismissed the idea as abruptly as it had come. She wouldn't like the bother, or the risk. Her interest in the young man couldn't extend that far already. Godwin had been warned off, and that was all that was necessary.

"Karleigh," said someone with insight. "You didn't see him, Lord Ferris, when you went south? His hospitality's always good, and he must be bored to death out there. Glad of a little company, even from the opposition."

"No, I didn't see him." Let them believe that or not, as they liked. The truth was that he had not gone. He saw no need to let Karleigh feel important, and he'd been in a hurry to get back and settle with St

Vier. He would tell Lord Halliday that Karleigh had seemed docile. It didn't much matter what he told Halliday now. "Karleigh's old news," Lord Ferris told his peers; "midwinter madness. No one with any sense will want to unseat the Crescent next month."

"But the rule—"

"We'll call an emergency and vote it down. There's always an emergency somewhere." Appreciative laughter in reference to the weavers.

"Oh," said old Tielman crustily. "So that's the plan, is it? A sudden emergency that never quite lets up?"

The temperature around the little group dropped suddenly. Tielman was of Karleigh's generation; had been raised, perhaps, on the same stories of evil kings and the sovereign rights of the nobility. Ferris felt attention on him, like a single ray of heat. All across the lawn heads were turning to the knot of men, although no one knew exactly what they were looking for. Ferris had no desire to get himself into a challenge in Halliday's defense; at the same time, it would not hurt for the Crescent's supporters to see him as a benevolent force. "My lord," he fixed his good eye on the old man. "Your words do no one credit."

The Dragon Chancellor had weight and power. He had presence. Tielman backed off. "I pray," he said with dignity, "that my lord will not take offense. But we do not speak of a joking matter."

"Then indeed you must!" a woman's voice chimed. It was the duchess, who, attentive as always to the mood of her company, had attached herself to the fringes of the circle. Now she took Ferris's arm. The wind fluttered the green and silver ribbons that streamed from her hat and dress. "I smell a political discussion: no jokes allowed! But at my party we will be merry, and tell jokes that everyone can laugh at. Such a lovely day, on loan from summer. I don't know why you gentlemen must always be looking out for a chance to quarrel." Her voice rippled on over the last of the dissolving tension. "And if you must quarrel, let it be over women, or something else worthwhile. . . ."

Still talking, she led Ferris across the grass. Those nearest saw her lean her head into him, and caught snatches of her chiding, "Really, my lord, you are just like all the rest of them. . . ."

Not lowering her voice, she said, "Now come, sit where I can keep an eye on you and you won't get into mischief, and tell me all about your trip. I don't suppose you were able to pick up some wool at a reasonable price . . . ?"

He allowed himself to be led to a wide seat under a linden tree. With the spread of her skirts and flounces there was barely room for him to sit down beside her; but he expertly flipped back the hang of his sleeves and poised himself on the edge of the seat.

He was, unfortunately, a sitting target for Lord Horn. To desert one's hostess would be rude; so when the fair nobleman came strolling up to them Ferris determined to stick it out with reinforcement from Diane.

To his dismay, the duchess showed no inclination to assist him in his evasion. "Asper! How splendid you look. You should always wear blue, it is your best color; don't you think so, Tony?"

"Unquestionably." His head was beginning to ache again. "Although I find green always gives him a certain . . . wicked air."

"Indeed?" Horn preened. "And is wickedness something to be cultivated, my lord?"

Oh, god, Ferris groaned inwardly. Desperate, he let his eye stray to the flamingo game. "Madam Duchess! You have no champion. Allow me to take up your cause."

She turned her mouth down mockingly. "Flamingo, my lord? Isn't that a bit tame for you?"

He shrugged. "It's the game of choice. Anyway, I play a poisonous game. I learnt it from my sisters. Even with one eye, I'll bet I can see your ball through to the stake ahead of those field mice."

"How ungallant—for the field mice. I, of course, am flattered. But I'm afraid you can't have my ball, Tony, it's cracked. You'll have to champion someone else."

"Never mind the flamingo," Horn said affably; "come and walk with me, my dear."

"Oh, yes, Tony! You can show Asper the sculpture garden—I don't believe he's seen my additions to my lord the late duke's collection, although I know he saw the originals when dear Charles was alive. Of course I can't leave everyone now, so it will have to be you. I hope you don't mind. . . ."

Defeated and fuming, he bowed. "It will give me the greatest pleasure."

Lord Ferris maintained a frosty silence as he led the other noble across the lawns toward the statuary garden.

"What a wonderful woman," said Horn, complacent now that he'd achieved his desire. Lord Ferris did not answer him, and the two men stepped onto the gravel path bordered by privet. The bushes were just beginning to come into leaf, creating a green-grey screen between them and the party across the lawn.

The first of the sculptures jutted a toe into their line of vision. It belonged to a nymph, innocently bathing her foot in a presumed

stream that ran at about the level of their noses. On the pedestal behind her a leering satyr lurked, preparing to pounce, balked of his desire by an eternity of marble.

They passed it without comment. Horn's light satin shoes crunched
rhythmically on the gravel path, leading deeper into the maze. The
smell of sap and damp earth drifted past the barriers of their perfume.
Under the next statue Horn paused. It was a classic piece depicting a
now-defunct god in his avatar as a ram begetting a future hero on a
virgin priestess who, according to this particular sculptor, was enraptured with her good fortune. For a moment Horn looked vaguely at it,
and then took his carved ivory wand and began tapping the crucial
juncture absently, with the nervous rhythm of someone drumming his
fingernails.

"It didn't work," he said at last.

"Obviously," said Ferris, at no pains to hide his boredom.

"That little bastard Godwin's run off somewhere. God knows what
he told St Vier first. I'll be a laughingstock!"

"You'd better ask the swordsman. Pay him something extra."

Horn swore. "How the devil am I to ask him anything? Getting this
job out of him was bad enough."

"Well, you've still got his friend, haven't you? Just send him—"

Horn's pale eyes protruded further. "Of course not! I sent the fellow
back! It was in the agreement. I couldn't go back on my word. Anyhow, he was a damned bother."

Ferris lowered his hands and walked away.

When Horn caught up with him he stopped. "You realize," Ferris
said, "that now St Vier is going to try to kill you?"

Horn lifted his chin, an arrogant and somehow tantalizing gesture
left over from his days of beauty. "He wouldn't dare. Not on his own.
Not without a contract."

"St Vier doesn't work on contract. You should know that."

"But I sent the fellow back!"

"Well, get him again."

"I can't. The men I used—they're dead. Two days ago. My agent
told me this morning."

Ferris laughed. Birdlike, his one eye glinted at Horn. "Can you
imagine who killed them? Poor clever St Vier; I'm sure he was hoping
you'd have figured it out by now. He doesn't know you; or his faith in
humanity is high."

Lord Horn's face had turned the color of old cheese. His age
showed on it suddenly, lined and hollowed. "Your woman—Katherine—tell her to call him off!"

"I won't have you bothering Katherine; you've been too much with her already."

"I can't leave the city—there'd be talk—"

"Stay, then, and guard yourself."

"He wouldn't dare," Horn hissed. "If he touches me, he'll hang!"

"Yes, if he's caught," Ferris said, and added reasonably, "He's a madman, Asper; all great swordsmen are. It's the devil of a job. But they have their rules, just as we have ours. If you hadn't chosen to act outside them, you wouldn't be having these problems."

He turned to go, eager to rejoin the party; but Horn caught the end of his sleeve, and he was forced to stop lest the fabric be torn.

"You!" Horn spat. "Dragon Chancellor! You're a fine one to talk of rules. Shall I tell them how you encouraged this? You knew all about it from that girl of yours—you sent her to meet me, she told me you wouldn't mind. . . ."

"If by *them* you mean the Council . . ." Ferris tried to repress a slight smile. "All right, I was careless." He had been nothing of the kind. Horn knew only as much as was good for him. But it wouldn't do to have Horn completely against him, in case he got out of this alive. He began to play him out, the cat's paw. "But Asper, I beg you to reconsider. To denounce me before them means exposing your own part in this. I would not have you ruin my career at the expense of your own reputation."

Horn's face was still belligerent, but faintly puzzled. He'd missed the irony, but some of the logic was getting through to him. "There's no crime in setting a swordsman on some young puppy. . . ."

"But they'll want to know why," Ferris said gently. "As you say, there'll be talk. And it *is* a crime to abduct someone, although of course when you've explained your reasons . . ."

Horn swallowed convulsively, the carefully hidden webbing of his throat moving against the cloth. "I can't. . . ."

"No, of course not," the orator's voice soothed. A sudden provocative image of the duchess touched Ferris's mind. He never wanted to go to bed with men, although many people said the excitement and sense of mastery were greater. Ferris liked women, and intelligent ones. For men, he liked the exercise of maneuvering them, not just stupid ones like Horn, but clever ones like Halliday, feeling them hurtle down the slope with him on a sled of his own devising, turning the corners at his chosen rate of speed. . . . it was a pleasure as dense and complex as lovemaking, with effects far more lasting and rewarding.

"Go on," he said kindly to the now humble nobleman. "Increase your guard, get a couple of swordsmen. . . ."

Horn passed a hand over his face. "You don't suppose he would swear out a complaint against me . . . ?" It would be humiliating, but safer.

"And let people know what you did to him? No, I don't think so, Asper. He wants you to sweat; that's why he killed your other men first. I suppose the best thing you can do is to be as carefree as possible. Maybe find someone to challenge him first. It's a bit irregular, but better than being set on yourself some night, don't you think?" They came to another statue, of the ram god enjoying the eternal gratitude of his armorer. "Ah," said Ferris with ruthless good humor; "now this is new. It's by the same sculptor as the nymph; the duke commissioned it just before his death, so of course it's taken the fellow years to deliver. . . ."

But Horn barely had a glance to spare for it. Nervously twisting the ivory wand in his palm, he seemed to be looking about the garden for a means of escape; or perhaps he saw swordsmen lurking in the shrubbery.

Ferris released him, saying, "Go on. Make a few inquiries. Perhaps he's just trying to scare you."

"He killed de Maris. . . ."

"And Lynch. You'd better get three. Good thing you can afford it. Good luck, my dear!"

When Horn had vanished down the path Ferris swore, and kicked the statue's base. He felt silly immediately, but better. Did Diane know about this? St Vier was about to become a difficult man to do business with. If the swordsman was to kill Halliday, he must do it before he murdered Horn and became a wanted man. To his regret, Ferris decided it would be best to leave the party at once, to return home and begin setting things in motion.

I HEAR," ALEC SAID, "THAT YOU'VE BEEN CONDUCTING A FEW small murders."

It was two days since his bout with Delight. Neither he nor Richard had spoken of it since. Today was an unusually warm spring afternoon. On the Hill, the Duchess Tremontaine was giving a garden party.

Richard said, "A few."

"Those two were rotten fighters, even I could see that. Everyone's very excited about it."

"They should be."

"You're a hero. Small children will press bunches of flowers into your hands as you pass by. Old women will fling themselves weeping into your arms. Don't stand too still; pigeons will think you're a commemorative statue and crap on you."

"Ginnie thinks I'm buying trouble."

Alec shrugged. "She just doesn't want you to have a good time. She doesn't understand the fighting spirit. When there's no one left to kill in Riverside, you have to expand."

Richard wanted to touch the hard edges of his lips. But outside of bed, they didn't do that. The swordsman said, "There's always someone to kill in Riverside. That reminds me: I'm going out tonight, as soon as it gets dark."

"Again? Are you going to kill someone?"

"I'm going to the city."

"Not to see Ferris—" Alec demanded.

"No; I still haven't heard from him. Don't worry about that. You'll read me the letter when it comes."

"Who read you the last one, the one from our friend?"

"Ginnie did."

Alec hissed.

"You can go where you like, now," Richard said; "no one's going to give you any trouble. Where will I find you tonight?"

"That depends on how long you're out. Home; Rosalie's; maybe Martha's if there's a game going there. . . ."

"I'll try home first. Don't wait up for me; I'll wake you when I come in."

T HE WOMAN TWISTED IN THE NOBLEMAN'S GRASP, MAKING HIM hurt her with his refusal to let go of her arms. Her hair was in his mouth, and across her eyes; but there was a purpose to her twisting, as he found when her heel hit the back of his knee and he stumbled against the bed.

"Y' little street-fighter!" Lord Ferris grunted, hauling her in half by her hair. "Y've nothing to fear down there!"

"You promised!" she cried, a vanquished wail despite the ferocity of her fighting. "You said I'd never have to go down there again!"

He turned her, so that her naked breasts were crushed against his throat. "Don't be a fool, Katherine. What's the harm in it? I'll buy you a lovely dress, I'm sorry for this one. . . ." The top of it straggled in pieces over her thighs. "Just this once . . ."

She was crying. "Why can't you send a note?"

"You know why. I need someone I can trust, to find him tonight." He eased her onto his lap, nuzzling her throat. "Little whore," he said fondly; "I'll send you down to the kitchens again. . . . I'll have you turned out for stealing. . . ."

"I never—"

"Shh!" Gently, Lord Ferris kissed his mistress. "I don't want your temper now, Kathy. Just do as you're told. . . ."

I N THE DARKEST CORNER OF ROSALIE'S SHE WAITED, A SHAWL covering her head, a dagger naked on the table in front of her to discourage conversation. She had slipped past Marie, but there was no one at home in St Vier's rooms. On the stairs, her heart had thundered like a drum in a too-small space, in the terrible closeness of the limitless dark. She'd listened outside the door, trying to silence her body's noisy breath and pulse of panic. Riverside was a sector of ghosts for her now; everywhere she looked she saw the past. If she opened his door there might be dawn light and a dead woman on the floor, with Richard St Vier looking at her in perplexity saying, "She was screaming at me."

But no one answered her knock. With relief she gave up and went to the tavern, remembering how to hide in a crowd. She didn't want to draw attention to herself by asking if Richard had been there. There were people who would recognize her if she spoke, or if she uncovered her hair. Rosalie's had the same wet smell as ever; it was one of her earliest memories, her mother taking her down there, giving her to some old woman to hold who'd give her a bite of cake if she was good and sometimes braid her hair to make it pretty, while her mother talked with her friends and argued with dealers.

She'd met Richard there, when he was not much more than a new boy come from the country who'd found his way to Riverside because he'd heard the rents were cheap. She'd liked him because of the way he laughed, softly and privately, even then. She watched him fight his early duels, become a fad on the Hill, and finally take up with Jessamyn, a woman who had always scared her a little. But the three of them had sat at one of these tables, laughing together one night until their eyes ran; now she couldn't even remember what it had been about.

She heard echoing laughter across the tavern and lifted her head. The crowded knot of interest looked almost like a fight, but only one man seemed angry; everyone else was laughing. A tall man in black blocked her view. A couple of women were high-talking the tall man, flirting, teasing; and the angry man was turning away from the group in disgust, trying to ignore their mockery. Katherine realized who the tall one must be.

"Alec," she said when she got close enough for him to hear her. He turned sharply; she guessed people didn't use his name much. "I'll buy you a drink," she said.

He asked, "Do you gamble? Max has given up on me—I can think faster than he can cheat."

She drew her breath in softly. She knew the voice. She couldn't place it, but somewhere on the Hill she'd heard it before. She couldn't picture him well dressed, though, hair cut and ruffles ironed. And with his height she'd remember having met him. Still, she knew it, somehow: lazy, cool, and self-assured. Richard said he had tried to kill himself. He must be crazy. He couldn't be stupid: Richard wouldn't like that.

"I'll dice," she said, "if you want."

They had to wait for a table to come free again. "Who sent you?" Alec asked.

"What do you mean, who sent me?"

"Oh," he said after a moment. "You want Richard. Have you got a bribe?"

"I don't need one. He's already doing business with us."

"Oh." He looked her up and down. "I hope you're armed. It's nasty down here."

"I know."

It went beyond aristocracy, his arrogance. Now she wasn't sure she had heard him before. She didn't remember anyone who spoke without care for effect, without courtesy or irony, as though his words were dropping into darkness and it didn't matter who heard them. No wonder Richard wanted him. He wasn't safe.

They found a seat against the wall.

"Are you the one who gave him the ruby?" Alec asked.

"Yes, the ring."

He put his hand flat on the table. The token glittered there on his finger. "Can you accept for him," she asked tartly, "or does he just like to decorate you?"

"Very good," said Alec with lazy amusement. "He just likes to decorate me. Who are you, anyway?"

"My name is Katherine Blount. I work on the Hill."

"For Lord Ferris?"

Nervously she looked around for listeners, then bypassed the question. "If Richard accepts the job, I can give him the money."

"Where is it, sewn into your petticoats?" he inquired politely. "Interesting to watch him get it out."

Despite her annoyance, she laughed. "Tell me where I can find him, and I'll let you watch."

A look of distaste crossed his face. No wonder the whores liked to tease him. It was a striking face, too bony for handsomeness, but beautiful in its way, sharp and fine as the quills of a feather.

He fished in his purse, picking out a few coins of silver that he shifted from hand to hand. "Do you know Tremontaine?" he asked.

He wanted to bribe her for information. She kept her face straight. She wasn't going to refuse the money; not straight off, anyway. "The duchess, you mean?"

"Tremontaine."

"She's a lady."

"God, you *can't* be that stupid!" he said irritatedly.

He had the money; she kept her temper in check. It wasn't his fault he didn't know what he was doing. She imagined Richard liked him that way. "What do you want to know?"

"What does Tremontaine have to do with all this?"

She shrugged. "I couldn't say."

"She didn't give you the ring?"

"No, sir."

He didn't even notice the sudden servility. "Then who did?"

"My master, sir."

He let one coin fall to the table. "Where the hell did *he* get it?"

"I didn't ask," she said tartly, dropping the demureness. "If it's hers, then she gave it to him."

Another coin fell. "Is that likely?"

"Very likely."

He spilled the rest of the coins in front of her, and pressed a fist into his palm; but not before she saw how his hands were shaking. His voice, though, was careless: "Now give me a chance to win them back from you."

"Unless I cheat faster than you can think? You don't know how to cheat, do you, Alec?"

"I don't need to."

"Where can I find Richard?"

"Nowhere. You can't. He doesn't want the job."

"Why don't you want him to take it?"

He looked down at her. "Whatever makes you think I have anything to say about it?"

There it was again, the evasion cloaked in rudeness. She put her chin in her hands, and looked into his haughty, stubborn face. "Your know, he's told me about you," she said, putting into her voice all she knew of them both. "He's not going to kill you, don't pin your hopes on that. He tried it once before, and he didn't like it."

"That's odd," he mused; "he didn't tell me about *you*. I expect he thought I wouldn't be interested."

She stood up. "Tell him I was here," she rapped out, the flat rapid patter of Riverside back in her voice. "Tell him I need to see him."

"Oh?" he said. "Is it a personal matter, then? Or is it just that your master will beat you?"

He would say anything to get a reaction, she told herself; all the same, she found herself leaning over him, saying into his face, "You don't belong here. Richard knows that. You can't keep this up for-ever."

"You belong here," he answered coolly, real pleasure in his voice because at last he had pierced her. "Stay with us. Don't go back to the Hill. They don't let you have any fun there."

She looked at him, and saw in the disdainful face just how badly he wanted to be attacked. And she straightened up, picked up her cloak. "I'll be at the Old Bell tomorrow night with the advance money. Tell him."

Alec sat where he was, watching her leave. Then, since he'd given her all the money he had, he went home.

S HE THOUGHT ABOUT CHECKING A COUPLE OF OTHER HAUNTS. The streets were so terribly dark outside the circle of torchlight that marked the tavern's door. She'd grown unused to not being able to see at night, not knowing what her hand would next encounter, what her feet would find beneath them, what sounds would come lurching out of the hollow silence. Her own fear made her afraid. Peo-ple could tell from how you walked how well you could handle it. Here there was no attempt made to light the entries of houses, no Watch treading the mud and cobbles on their regular route. She stood outside Rosalie's in the circle of torchlight. Richard could be any-where. She wasn't going to search all of Riverside for him, she'd done what she could. For all she knew, he could be on the Hill. She'd deliv-ered her message to his usual place, and that was that.

A child came by, carrying a bundle of torches. Only children and cripples were torchbearers here; no strong man wanted to earn his money guarding those who couldn't take care of themselves.

"Lightcha, lady?"

"Yes. To the Bridge."

"That's extra, to cross it."

"I know that. Hurry up," she said, and drew her cloak around her like a blanket.

chapter XXI

I
T WAS RICHARD'S SECOND NIGHT OF WATCHING HORN'S HOUSE, and already it was paying off. The guards seemed to be concentrated at the front: apparently Horn was expecting a formal challenge, and wanted to be sure of not meeting it himself.

Richard was standing outside the back garden wall, among the leafless branches of an old lilac bush. He would never understand why these people left such good camouflage so near the entrances to their houses, when the whole purpose of walls was to keep people out. Braced halfway up it, between the bush and wall, he'd been able to see all he needed to of the back of the house. When he heard the approach of the guard who occasionally patrolled the back garden, he'd dropped back to the ground. Now he listened to the receding footsteps rounding the far corner of the house. He waited in the darkness listening, for one minute, two, timing by his own breathing to make sure that excitement didn't betray him into moving too soon. A carriage clattered by in the street, the torches of its outriders throwing a streak of shadow against the wall, himself entangled in the lilac branches.

The back of the house was silent. He knew Horn was at home this night, and alone, without visitors. He even had a fair idea now of where to find him: the pattern of lights passing behind the windows had indicated hallways and occupied rooms. Richard took off his heavy cloak, which was fine for waiting out of doors but no good for climbing trees; he wrapped it around the light dueling sword he carried—his pride, a new blade of folded steel, light as a kiss and sharp as a surgeon's tool—and tucked the bundle under his arm. With the help of the bush, climbing the outside wall was no great feat. He remembered the drop on the other side as not too far, and made it. Without the snow, the garden looked a little different; but he had in his head the map the Duke of Karleigh had provided of the formal gardens the night he fought Lynch and de Maris here.

Richard stood still, accustoming his feet to the new ground. The air was very chill; without his cloak he felt it, even through the layers of clothing he wore. He heard the Watch pass on the other side of the wall, making their usual racket. He felt his cold lips curve in a smile. There was almost an acre of ground between him and the house, heavily decorated with topiary. By the faint and steady light of stars he picked his way among the carved bushes, stopping to shelter under a yew shaped like a castle, skirting the outside of the boxwood maze whose paths could be glimpsed through gaps in the hedge.

At last the house loomed above him; just another wall to climb to reach the first-story window he had targeted: a tall window, with a convenient wrought-iron balcony that should hold a man's weight. An immense rose trellis climbed up to it. Very pretty, no doubt, in summer.

He buckled the sword on close to his body, and pinned his cloak at his neck, knotting it into a heavy ball behind him. The rustling of dry branches, the scrape of his toe against stone, sounded loud in his ears; but his world was shrunk to a tiny point where the least sound and movement were mammoth.

The climb warmed him. He tried to make it quickly, since too much deliberation might expose him like a fly on the wall if anyone looked up; but the strong rose stem was obscured by a tangle of creepers and branches, and he had to feel his way. He found toeholds in the joined stone blocks, and was able to rest his hand against the top of the ground-floor window cornice. His own breath rose in front of his face in puffs of vapor. Leather gloves protected his hands, but now and then he felt the piercing of a heavy thorn, and the warm blood flowing down the inside of them.

Finally his hand closed around the metal underside of the balcony. He pulled hard on it. It was firmly bolted to the stone, so he swung himself up onto its ledge.

Richard crouched on the balcony, resting, breathing softly. He took an old knife blade and a bent piece of wire out of his jacket and unhooked the latch; then he slipped inside, closing the window after him.

He had hoped the window led onto a hallway, but from the sound he seemed to be in a small chamber. He pulled back an edge of curtain to let some of the night's silver glow in. He felt his way carefully around the furniture. The carpet was as thick and soft as a pelt.

A sudden flash of movement in the corner of his eye froze him. Across the room from the window, a streak of black had shot across the grey surface. Now it was still. He stared across the room into the darkness at it, looked sideways to catch it again. It resolved itself into a small square of light; another window, maybe guarded. He raised his arm silently to shield his eyes, and a slash of black ran across it again.

It was a mirror. He wasn't used to them. Alec was always complaining that their palm-sized disk of polished steel was not big enough to shave by. Richard supposed he could afford to buy a mirror the size of a window; but he didn't like the idea of it hanging on his wall.

He was glad to find that the bedroom door wasn't locked from the outside. The hallway was lit with tapers, a forest of them in the dark. He ducked back behind the door to give his eyes time to adjust to the light. Then he followed the hall to the room he'd marked.

Lord Horn sat in a heavy chair, reading in a circle of light. He didn't hear the door open, but when a floorboard creaked he snapped, "I said *knock* first, you damned fool." The lord leaned around the side of the chair to look at the intruder. "And why have you left your post on the stairs?"

St Vier unsheathed his sword.

Horn started convulsively, like a man touched by lightning. He knocked the chair back, and his mouth flapped with a frozen scream.

"It's no good calling your guards," Richard lied, "I've already taken care of them."

It was the first time he had come face to face with the man. Horn was younger than he'd expected, although his face was now hagged with shock. There was nothing to admire in him: he had bungled everything, and finally knew it; he had misused his power and now he would pay. It was quite clear that he knew what was happening. Richard was glad of that; he didn't like making speeches.

"Please—" said Horn.

"Please what?" Richard demanded icily. "Please, you'll never meddle with my affairs again? But you already have."

"Money—" the noble gasped.

"I'm not a thief," said Richard. "I leave it all for your heirs."

Lord Horn walked shakily to his desk and picked up a crystal bird. His hand cupped around it protectively, stroking the smooth glass with longing. "You like a challenge," he murmured, almost seductive.

"I've got one," Richard answered softly. "I want to see how long I can make this last."

First he silenced him, and then he took, very slowly, the life from the four corners of his body, being careful not to render him unrecognizable. Richard never spoke, although the man's wild eyes begged him for it while they could.

He had planned it carefully, and he stuck to what he planned, except that, in the end, he didn't deliver his characteristic blow to the heart. It was unnecessary: the precision would label his work, and he didn't want it to look as though he had mutilated an already dead body.

He unlocked the study window and left again through the garden. No swordsman could afford to be blackmailed.

A LEC WAS SLEEPING, DIAGONAL ACROSS THE WHOLE BED AS usual, one arm flung out with fingers loosely curled over his empty palm. The mark the shackles had left on his wrist was a dark streak in the pale light.

Richard meant to go and wash first; but Alec stirred and said sleepily, "What is it?"

"I'm back."

Alec rolled over to look at him. The hollows under his cheeks went taut. "You've killed someone," he said. "You should have told me."

"I had to make sure he was at home first."

Alec's long white arms reached out to him. "Tell me now."

Richard fell onto the bed, letting the tall man gather him in. He wasn't tired at all. "You smell strange," Alec said. "Is that blood?"

"Probably."

Alec's tongue touched his ear, like a hunting cat getting the first taste of its prey. "Who have you gone and killed this time?"

"Lord Horn."

He hadn't been sure how Alec would take it. With wonder he felt Alec's body arc sharply against his, Alec's breath let out in an intense, vicious sigh.

"Then no one knows," he said dreamily in his lovely accent. "Tell me about it. Did he scream?" The pulse was beating hard in the hollow of his throat.

"He wanted to, but he couldn't."

"*Ahhh.*" Alec pulled the swordsman's head to him until Richard's mouth lay close by his ear. His hair was warm across Richard's face.

"He begged," Richard said, to please him. "He offered me money."

Alec laughed. "He hit me," Alec said; "and you killed him."

"I hurt him first." Alec's head tipped back. The cords of his neck stood out like vaulting. "I took his hands, then his arms, and his knees. . . ." The breath hissed through Alec's teeth. "He won't touch you again."

"You hurt him. . . ."

Richard kissed the parted lips. Alec's arms bound him like supple iron.

"Tell me," Alec whispered, mouth touching his face; "tell me about it."

THEY SLEPT TOGETHER UNTIL PAST NOON. THEN ALEC PUT ON some clothes and went downstairs to borrow bread from Marie. In one hand he held a heap of bloody clothes. It was a sunny day, almost as warm as the last one. He found her in the courtyard, skirts hiked up, already begun on the laundry, and held out the clothes to her.

"Burn those," their landlady said.

"Are you out of your mind?" Alec asked. "It'll make a horrible smell."

"It's up to you." She made no move to take the clothes.

"You look awful," Alec said cheerfully. "What's the matter, someone keep you up all night?"

She began a smile, and dropped it. "This morning. You must have been dead not to hear the racket. I tried to keep 'em quiet, not to let 'em upstairs. . . ."

"You should choose your friends more carefully. What's for breakfast?" He sniffed at her pot of boiling laundry.

"*Don't* you go putting your stuff in there," she said automatically; "that blood'll never come out in hot water."

"I know, I know."

"You know . . ." Marie grumbled. She liked Alec; he teased her and made her laugh. But it wasn't any good now. "You know what he's done, then?"

Alec shrugged: *So what?* "Got blood all over his clothes. Don't worry, we'll pay you for it."

"With what?" she said darkly. "You going to turn him in for the price on his head?"

For a moment the long face was still. Then he tilted his chin up, eyebrows cooked audaciously. "*Is* there a price on his head? How much?"

"I don't know. They say there might be."

"How do they know he wasn't working under contract?"

She looked scornful. "Down here, they know. Up there, it may take them a little longer to figure it out. But that wasn't any duel. They say that noble was marked up like a shopkeeper's tally, and not with any dagger."

"Oh, well!" Alec sighed blithely. "I guess we'll have to leave town for a while until it's blown over. Too bad: the country's such a bore, but what can you do? Keep bees, or something."

"I suppose . . ." Marie sounded dubious, but brightened. "After all, everyone else leaves when things get hot. He might as well too. I'll save your rooms, don't you fear."

RICHARD HAD LONG AGO GIVEN UP ARGUING WITH ALEC OVER the use of his left-hand dagger for cutting bread. Alec claimed it was the only knife they had that cut the pieces fine enough for toasting, and that was that.

"I wish you'd told me," Alec said, slicing Marie's loaf, "that we were going to be leaving town. I would have had my boots re-heeled."

"If you're going to toast cheese, look out for the point on that thing."

"It's not your best knife, what do you care? You haven't answered my question."

"I didn't know you'd asked one."

Alec drew a patient breath. "My dear soul, they're already lining up with banners to see you off, and you're not even packed yet."

"I'm not going anywhere."

Alec fumbled with the toasting knife, and swore when he burnt himself. "I see. They've found Horn, you know."

"Have they? Good. Let me have the cheese."

"It's rotten cheese. It tastes like shoe leather. Cheese is much fresher in the country."

"I don't want to leave. I've got another job coming up."

"You could become a highway robber. It'd be fun."

"It's not fun. You lie in the grass and get wet."

"They've found Horn," Alec tried again, "and they're not happy."

Richard smiled. "I didn't expect them to be. I'll have to stay here for a while."

"In the house?"

"In Riverside. They don't trust us down here, so they aren't going to risk sending the Watch, and spies I can handle myself." It wasn't like Alec to worry about his safety. It made Richard feel warm and content. He was going to curl up in the sun today and let other people worry if they wanted to. After last night he felt secure, better than he had in days. The theater, Alec's abduction, the unpleasant notes, the strange young nobleman, and the killing of the sword-master all faded into a past resolved and dispatched. No one was going to try Horn's little trick again or try to force his hand; and no Riversider who'd heard about it would touch Alec now. And from what Marie was saying, they'd all heard about it. Richard laid precisely the right pattern of pieces of cheese on his bread, and set it on the hearth near enough to the fire so that it would melt without getting brown.

In the long shadows of late afternoon they wandered down to Rosalie's for food and drink. Some little girls were skipping rope in the front yard of the old house. They were dressed, like most Riverside children whose parents acknowledged them, in bright eclectic splendor: scraps of velvet and brocade pieced onto old gowns cut down to size, trimmed with ruffles of varying-colored lace culled from a multitude of stolen handkerchiefs. The jumper's plaits bounced as she chanted:

> Mummy told me to have some fun:
> Kick the boys and make them run,

"Charming," said Alec.

> Kick them 'til they run for cover;
> Don't forget my baby brother!
> How many of them did you get?
> One—Two—Three—Four—

One of the twirlers suddenly missed her beat. The jumper caught her feet in the rope and stumbled. "Sylvie, you goon!" But Sylvie ignored her.

"Hullo, old love!" she called to Richard, just like her grandmother, Rosalie.

"Hullo, Sylvie."

"Got any candy?"

"Not on me, stinker."

She stamped her foot. "*Don't* call me stinker! That's for babies."

"Sorry, brat." He tried to walk past her, but she blocked the way to the stairs.

"Gramma says you can't come in."

"Why not?"

"There's people looking for you. Have been all day."

"Are they in there now?"

She nodded. "Sure are."

"Armed?"

"I guess so. You gonna kill 'em?"

"Probably. Don't worry, I'll tell your gramma you told me."

"No." Alec caught his sleeve. "Don't. For god's sake, Richard, let's go home."

"Alec . . ." They couldn't argue out here. Richard nodded at the children. "Do you want to give them a little brass?"

Alec fished in his purse and came up with some coins, which he handed gingerly to Sylvie as though she might bite him.

"Thanks, Richard! Thank you, o my prince!"

A flurry of giggles covered their retreat, mixed with cries of "Sylvie, you goon! I can't believe you did that!"

"What," said Alec, "was *that* all about?"

Richard shrugged. "They've probably made up some story about you. They always do."

"Nasty little objects. I wonder which one made up that rhyme?"

"All little girls say it," said Richard, surprised. "They did it where I grew up."

"Hmph. I don't think *my* sister did. But then, Mother frowned on poetry."

It was perhaps the first time he had mentioned his family. He was tense; the business at Rosalie's had shaken him. Of course, Richard thought: Alec wasn't used to being hunted. And there was no way to reassure him: it could be an unpleasant business, if you let it. It placed constraints on your life that Alec wasn't at all accustomed to. In fact, Alec probably had been right to insist on avoiding Rosalie's once they'd been warned. There was no sense in walking into trouble. But Richard didn't like having to put up with it. Alec, less patient than the swordsman, was going to like the new restrictions even less.

They stopped at Martha's for beer. Unless the informers were working double-time, no one would be looking for him there yet. When they came in there was a stir of movement that subsided into tight-knit groups doing their best to ignore them. It didn't particularly bother St Vier; it was almost welcome relief from the usual fuss they made over him. The two men drank quickly, and left.

"It'll get better come nightfall," Richard told him, walking home. "Everyone's easier then, there's fewer strangers around."

"That's a life for you," said Alec; "just coming out at night, like a mooncrawler."

Richard looked curiously at him. "I don't think it'll come to that."

The rapid patter of footsteps behind them put an end to the discussion.

"Move," said Richard, hand on his sword. "Into that doorway."

For once, Alec did as he was told. Already it was dusk under the lowering eaves of the close-set houses. Their pursuer rounded the corner at too fast a clip to have a prayer of holding ground against the swordsman standing ready.

The small white figure skidded to a halt. "Holy *Lucy!*" Nimble Willie swore. "Master St Vier, for godsakes put that thing away, and come into that doorway."

"Alec's already in there."

"That's all right," the doorway interjected, "we'll have a lovely time. What the hell's the matter with you, Willie," Alec demanded, emerging from it, "coursing like a stoat after rabbits?"

"Sorry," Willie panted. He motioned them off to one side; what he had to say wasn't fit for the middle of the street. "Don't go home that way. Cut through Blind Max's Alley; they're watching Dolphin's Cross."

"How many?"

"Three. City toughs, with swords, out for the reward."

"There's a reward?"

"Not for you yet. It's just the usual; for suspects to be brought in. But these boys think it's you—they might be friends of those other two you killed last week."

Richard sighed wearily. "I'd better kill them."

"No, wait!" cried Willie. "Don't do that."

"Why not?"

"They've already paid me. I figured it'd be easy to give them the slip. But if one gets away, I'll be in for it. . . ."

St Vier sighed, running a hand through his hair. "Willie . . . all right. Only for you. I'll just keep away from Dolphin's Cross."

Alec paid him without having to be reminded.

THE HOUSE SEEMED QUIET. IT WAS SET IN A CUL-DE-SAC WHERE no one in his right mind would want to take on St Vier. Nevertheless, he went first up the stairs, scanning for reckless intruders. There was nobody, not even a neighbor.

"God," Alec huffed, throwing himself down on their old chaise longue. "Hadn't we better check under the beds?"

Richard answered his real question. "I don't think they'll come in here. Even if they can get someone to show them the way, people don't like to attack a swordsman on his own ground."

"I see." Alec sat thoughtfully, turning the rings on his fingers. After a while he got up and found the Nature treatise with the burgundy leather binding and half its pages missing. He flipped through it while Richard limbered up and began practicing. The grey cat came and sat on Alec's lap, trying to interpose her head between his eyes and the page. He scratched her chin, and finally snapped the book shut irritably and replaced it on the mantel, taking instead his worn philosophy text. Finally he gave up all pretense of reading, and watched the swordsman steadily working his body through parrys and extensions and recoils so quick and intricate Alec's eye couldn't make out the discrete elements. All he could do was sense their perfection, a dance made of deadly movements whose goal was not to entertain.

For a while Alec seemed to be drowsing, like the cat on his lap, eyes half-shut watching the swordsman. Only his hand moved, idling along the cat's spine, deep in the lush fur finding the ridges of its bones. The cat was purring; Alec put his fingers on its throat, and left them there.

The frenzy of Richard's movements had slowed to a deliberate pace. It was the cat's favorite stalking game, but Alec's fingers left her too sedated to care. Richard's body obeyed him in his tortuous demands, and Alec watched.

"You know," Alec said conversationally, "they would be so pleased if anything were to happen to you."

"Hh?" It came out a grunt.

"Your friends. They'd finally get their chance at me."

"You'd have to leave." Richard put up his sword and began slowly stretching his muscles out. "They wouldn't follow you out of Riverside."

"If you were dead." Alec finished the thought bluntly.

The anger surprised Richard. "Well, yes."

Alec's voice was low, almost harsh with repressed fury. "It doesn't particularly bother you."

"Well, I'm a swordsman." He shrugged, no easy feat with his head touching the floor. "If I stay active, I can't last much past thirty. There'll be someone better someday."

"You don't care." Alec was still lounging picturesquely, long limbs on display; but the rigidness of his hands clenched on the frayed upholstery betrayed him.

"It's all right," Richard said; "it's what happens."

"Then what," Alec articulated with crystalline clarity, "in hell are you doing all that practicing for?"

Richard picked up his sword. "Because I want to be good." He lifted it over his head and dived at the wall the way he would at an opponent who'd uncovered his front guard.

"So you can give them a really good fight before they kill you?"

Richard twisted and came in high again, his wrist arced like a falcon stooping. "Mm-hm."

"Stop it," Alec said very quietly. "Stop it."

"Not now, Alec, I'm—"

"*I said, stop it!*" Alec rose to his full height, towering and angular in his wrath. His eyes were green as emeralds uncovered in a casket. Richard put the sword down and kicked it into a corner. When he looked up he saw the raised hand, knew Alec was going to hit him, and stayed still as the palm crashed across his face.

"You coward," Alec said coldly. He was breathing heavily and his cheeks were bright. "What are you waiting for?"

"Alec," Richard said. His face stung. "Do you want me to hit you?"

"You don't dare." Alec raised his hand again, but this time Richard caught it, gripping the bony wrist that was so much frailer than his own. Alec twisted the wrong way, making Richard hurt him. "I'm not enough of a challenge," he hissed through gritted teeth, "that's it, isn't it? It would make you *look* bad. You wouldn't enjoy it."

"Enough," Richard said; "it's enough." He knew he was holding Alec too hard; he was afraid to let go.

"No, it isn't enough," the man in his hands was saying. "It's enough for you—it's always enough for you, but not for me. Talk to me, Richard—if you're afraid to use your hands, then talk to me."

"I can't," Richard said. "Not the way you do. Alec, please—you know you don't want this. Stop it."

"*Please*," Alec said, still pulling against his arm as though he were ready to start hitting him again; "that's a new one from you. I think I like it. Say it again."

Richard's own hands sprang open; he flung himself away from the other man. "Look," he shouted, "what do you want from me?"

Alec smiled his feral smile. "You're upset," he said.

Richard could feel himself shaking. Tears of rage were still burning behind his eyes, but at least he could see again, the room was losing its red tinge. "Yes," he managed to say.

"Come here," Alec said. His voice was long and cool like slopes of snow. "Come to me."

He walked across the room. Alec lifted his chin and kissed him. "You're crying, Richard," Alec said. "You're crying."

The tears burned his eyes like acid. They made his face feel raw. Alec lowered him to the floor. At first he was rough, and then he was gentle.

In the end, it was Alec who couldn't cry. "I want to," he said, curled on Richard's chest, fingers digging into him as though he were slipping down a rock face. "I want to, but I can't."

"You don't really want to," Richard said, his hand cupped around Alec's head. "It makes your nose run. It makes your eyes red."

Alec gave a strangled laugh and clutched him tighter. He tried an experimental sniff, and gasped with a sudden convulsion of some emotion: misery, or frustration. "It's no good," he said. "I can't."

"It doesn't matter," Richard said, stroking him. "You'll learn."

"If I'd known you were such an expert I would have made you teach me long ago."

"I offered to teach you the sword. It seemed more useful."

"Not to me," Alec said automatically. "Did you know you were talking just now, too? It sounded like you were reciting poetry."

Richard smiled. "I didn't notice. It might have been."

"I didn't know you knew any poetry."

Richard knew that he ought to be upset. He had just been thoroughly overturned by Alec: had lost his temper, lost his control, behaved in ways he didn't even know he could. But Alec had caught him as he fell, had taken pleasure in it. And now he felt wonderful, as long as he didn't think hard about it. There was no need to think. He never wanted to move again; he never wanted Alec's head to shift from the crook of his shoulder, or the warmth of their legs entwined to dissolve. "I know a lot of poetry," he answered. "My mother used to say it to me. Old things, mainly."

"Something about the wind, and someone's face."

After a while, he began to grow younger.
The years were torn from his face
Like leaves scattered before the wind. . . .
In the end, she made all others seem impossible.

"That's an old one," he explained, "about a man who was taken by the Faery Queen."

"I've never heard it." Alec nestled under his chin, lulled by the words. "Tell it to me."

Richard thought for a minute, reaching back for the beginning, absently stroking Alec's hair:

> *It was never cold under the hill, and never dark.*
> *But the light was not a light for seeing. It deceived.*
> *He tried to remember the sun,*
> *To remember remembering the moon.*
> *He thought—*

Alec's hand was at his lips.

"You've *got* to go!" His voice cracked. "They won't let you walk out of this, they don't dare! I *know them*, Richard!"

Richard tightened his arm around Alec's shoulders, wordlessly trying to comfort, to drain the tension from the anguished spirit.

But the touch was not enough. "Richard, I *know* them—they won't let you live!" He turned his face in to Richard's chest, his body clenched again in a frozen spasm not of weeping but of fury.

At a loss, Richard turned again to the words that still flowed through his mind like water:

> *Day followed day, with never night between:*
> *Feasting and all manner of delight*
> *Hedged him 'round like hounds their quarry's heart—*

"I'm cold," Alec said suddenly.

He knew that arbitrary voice: it was as warm and familiar to him as bread. "Well, we are on the floor," he answered.

"We should get into bed." Alec propped himself on one elbow to observe, "Your clothes are all a mess."

"That can be fixed." Richard stripped his shirt off in an easy motion, and helped Alec to his feet.

"You look as though you've been in a fight," Alec said complacently.

"A lot you know about that. I look," he said, "as though someone's tried to tear my clothes off."

"Someone has."

They were warm that night, never apart long enough to be cold. They talked for hours in the dark; and when words were not enough they were silent. At last they slept, twined helplessly in each other's arms.

Some time in the morning, when the light was still grey, Richard felt Alec slip out of bed beside him. He didn't even open his eyes; just sighed and rolled over, spreading into the spot where Alec's warmth had been.

When Richard came fully awake, it was full daylight. He got up and opened the shutters. Sun streaked the floor in long buttery bars. Richard stretched, feeling the glories of the night in his whole body. Nothing hurt: even the memory of tears and pain produced only a warm glow, the distillation of raw spirits into liquor.

Alec was up and dressed already, his clothes gone from the top of the chest. Richard didn't smell cooking; maybe he was out getting food. Or he might be sitting in the front room, reading. Richard thought, all in all, that it might be a good thing for them to eat and go back to bed.

He heard a noise in the other room, body on upholstery, and pictured Alec sprawled on the chaise longue with a book in his hands, waiting for him to get up. He knew he was smiling senselessly, and didn't care.

He stared at the empty chaise for a moment longer than necessary. The cat leapt down across it, wanting to be petted.

He felt something wrong in the room. There was no presence of intruders. Something was out of place, a space rearranged. . . . He looked again and saw it at once: Alec's books were missing from their corner. Not, he hoped, another bout of self-righteous poverty! Alec was always trying to pawn things, but who would want his books? At least he'd taken his own stuff this time—

But he hadn't. The richest things he owned, the most worth pawning, those he had left behind, in plain sight on the mantelpiece. The rings that Richard had given him, that he'd had so much trouble accepting, lay in a heap together, regardless of their beauty. Richard looked, unwilling to touch them: the pearl, the diamond, the rose, the emerald, the dragon brooch . . . all but the ruby; that he had taken with him.

There was no note. Richard couldn't have read it, and Alec knew this time he would not ask someone else to read it for him. The meaning of the things he'd left behind was clear: he'd taken only what he thought of as his. He wasn't coming back.

It was plain enough what had happened. Alec was fed up with life in Riverside. He'd never really been suited to it. And Horn's killing would make it harder. Alec had been badly shaken yesterday by the first signs of the caution they would have to use for a while. He might be afraid of a manhunt. Maybe he meant to wait it out, come back when the danger was past. . . . Richard closed his mind to the thought, like a key turning a lock. He would not wait for Alec. If Alec chose to return, Richard would be here. If not, life would go on as it had before him.

He couldn't blame Alec, really. Leaving was the sensible thing to do. Most people thought so. Alec had a right to decide for himself. Everyone has their limits, the border between what they can and cannot tolerate. Alec had tried to tell him; but Richard had been too confident, too sure of himself—and, frankly, too used to ignoring Alec's complaints to give any heed to this one. Not that it would have changed anything. Richard had no intention of skulking out of the city just when it needed his presence to remind them all of how dangerous it was to cross him. And he could hardly run from Riverside as though he were afraid of his own peers.

He found himself back in the bedroom, looking in the clothes press. Alec's fur-lined winter cloak was still there, along with two shirts, his old jacket with the braid, odds and ends. He'd left wearing only his scholar's robe over the clothes he'd had on yesterday. Only what he could walk in. It angered Richard; the fool was going to be cold, summer was still a good way off. . . . But of course, he thought, Alec had gone where he didn't need old clothes. He wouldn't just have walked aimlessly out into the street, he was too proud for that. And he wouldn't have gone back to the University, not after what he'd said against it. But he never did speak of his family. That meant something. Of course they must be rich. Of course he was a lord, or a lord's son. They would be furious with him, but they'd have to take him in. His future was secure.

It made Richard feel vastly relieved. Alec was, in essence, back where he belonged. He would never again be cold in winter, or drink inferior wines. He'd marry well, but know where his other desires lay. Last night, in his farewell, he'd proved that.

Richard shut the chest. Mingled with the smell of wool and cedar was the faint aroma of meadowgrass. He'd have to see to giving away the clothes. But not now. A long fine hair was caught on one of his fingers. He untwisted it; it glowed chestnut in the sunlight as it drifted to the floor.

chapter XXII

Lord Basil Halliday put his face in his hands and tried to massage some of the heat out of his eyeballs. When the door opened he sat perfectly still, recognizing the sound and scent of his wife's presence.

Lady Mary looked at the undisturbed bedding still spread invitingly on the couch, pressed her lips together, and said nothing to the man sitting bent over the table littered with crumbs and empty glasses. She drew back the curtains to let in daylight, and snuffed what was left of the candles.

"You just missed Chris Nevilleson." Her husband roused himself to converse. "He ate the last of the seedcakes. We'll have to remember he likes them."

"I'll remember." She stood behind him, her cool hands on his brow. He leaned his head back into the soft satin of her morning-robe.

"I *did* sleep," he said defensively; "I just didn't lie down."

"There are no more seedcakes," she told him, "but there are fresh rolls and eggs. I'll have them brought in, with dark chocolate."

He pulled her head down to kiss. "There are no more like you," he said. "If it's a daughter, we'll name her Mary."

"We will not. It's too confusing, Basil. And we should name her something pretty . . . Belinda?" He laughed and smoothed her hair. "What did Chris have to say?"

With regret he returned to the night's activities. "What I've been sure of all along. It was a swordsman, not a ruffian's murder. Nothing was stolen. And Horn had lately increased his guard. Someone broke into the house expressly to kill him. That looks like a duel, simple enough. But none of our people has been able to ferret out any rumor of a challenge called out against Horn, or any reason for one. He had no debts, his reputation for once was clear. . . . No one much liked Asper, really, but he was harmless. His political importance was over the day his friend the old Crescent died. . . ." He stopped himself and shook his head. "Sorry. Of course you already know that. Well, Chris was there tonight at the examination. There was no question but that it was the work of one skilled sword. A virtuoso job, in fact. As if someone had left a calling card. But who? Chris said Horn's hired swordsmen looked positively green. We're holding them for questioning, but I think it's pointless. They didn't do it. Someone flashy and brilliant and crazy did it, and he's out there walking free in my city right now."

"It might be private justice," Mary said, "such as swordsman practice amongst themselves."

"Against a Council Lord? Utter madness. It *must* have been another noble's challenge, it's the only way anyone would dare. . . . Maybe something new will come to light, maybe someone will declare himself. A swordsman with a grievance against Horn could have sought redress from the civil court, or even from the Council of Lords."

"But with what hope of gaining it?" his wife asked gently. "The nobles have too much power in the city, you say so yourself." He opened his mouth to defend himself, but she silenced him with the pressure of her hand, which said she knew already and agreed. "But even if it was a swordsman working under contract, one doesn't like to think of a man using his skill for such an unclean death."

"St Vier," Halliday said, "always strikes one blow straight to the heart. I have always thought, if I were challenged to the death, I would prefer it be by him."

"Seville, then, perhaps, or Torrion. . . ."

"Yes, you're right." Halliday passed a hand over his unshaven face. "The first thing is to identify the swordsman himself. There are far fewer good ones around than there are men with money who carry grudges. All the major ones will have to make depositions, and lay bond not to leave the city until this matter is settled. The murder of a Council Lord strikes too near the center of our peace. I'm having the roads watched, offering rewards for information. . . .

"Meanwhile, Mary, I've called up some of our own people to

strengthen the house guard. And you—please don't go out alone. Not now."

She pressed his hand to tell him she'd look after her safety as carefully as he would.

He knew he should sleep, or go and tend to business; but even more than he needed rest he needed to offer his thoughts to her. "It's the problem of a system that incorporates swordsmen. They say without them we'd be doing all the work of killing each other ourselves; like the olden days, the streets full of miniature wars, and every house a fortress. . . . But swordsmen are a wild card. They're only useful under the strictest codes. . . ."

Still talking, he let her lead him to the couch. They sat side by side, leaning only slightly against each other, alert for the first sounds of intrusion, the demands of government and housekeeping.

"Basil," she asked when he finally paused, "do you have to do it all yourself? If it's a murder, the city can investigate. Chris can act as liaison."

"I know . . . but it's the slaying of a Council Lord, and with a sword. Which means it still might turn out to be a matter of honor—or something else we don't want to make common knowledge. I'm the head of the Council. I want to go on being the head of the Council— or so everyone keeps telling me. Silly or not, Horn was a member of government. And I have to look after my own. Whoever killed him was a poacher on a very private estate." Despite himself, his eyes kept dropping shut. "Horn . . . I'll have to stop calling him that. There'll be a new Lord Horn now. His grandson, I think. . . ."

She waited until she was sure he was asleep before getting up. One poor dead man, she was thinking, and the whole city threatens to crumble. Mary Halliday pulled the curtains in the study closed again, and let herself quietly out of the door.

A FINE FALL OF RAIN HUNG LIKE A CURTAIN OF MIST OVER THE city, veiling one section from another across the long stretches of sky dividing them. The various greys of the city's stone glittered and glowed with the sheen of the water on them; but that was an effect best admired from indoors, preferably through a pane of window-glass. The Daw's Nest in Riverside didn't have one. It didn't have much, except an interesting clientele and enough for them to drink. There was always something going on there. One section of the earthen floor had been a mumblety-peg arena for as long as anyone could remember.

What really made it attractive was its location: on the south bank of Riverside, far from the Bridge and any encroaching of upper city life. No one who didn't belong in Riverside got this far in. When he didn't have to make himself available for job contracts, Hugo Seville found it a good place to relax.

"Your star is on the rise," a fortune-teller was informing him. "Terrible things are happening in the upper houses. . . ."

"You wouldn't know an upper house from the back of your neck," a failed physician growled at her. "You can't even chart your way home from this place."

She hissed at him.

"Never mind," Ginnie Vandall consoled her; "Ven can't even *see* his way home. Go on, Julia." Ginnie didn't believe in fortune-telling per se, but she understood the techniques involved: a judicious blend of gossip and personal assessment. She did have faith in gossip, and in Hugo's susceptibility to flattery. Ginnie's hair was a new bright red, her bodice purple. She sat on the arm of Hugo's chair enjoying herself.

"The Sword of Justice is lifted high in the northern quardrant, ready to strike. The Sword . . . Do you want to see the cards?"

"No," said the swordsman.

"Hugo," his mistress caressed his golden curls, "why not?"

"They're creepy."

"They're powerful," said Julia, unwrapping them. She handed the deck to Hugo. "Cut them."

"Oh, never mind," said Ginnie Vandall. "I'll do it." The rings on her fingers glowed against the dull backs of the cards. She gave them a professional shuffle and handed them back to Julia, who laid them out in an incomprehensible pattern.

"Money."

One of Ginnie's crew of friends looked on, hanging over her shoulder. "Lucky lady. You know who's worth a lot these days?"

Ginnie said, "He's always been worth a lot. Only this time he hasn't got any choice about it." It was hard to tell whether she was pleased.

"I'm talking about St Vier."

"I know," said Ginnie Vandall.

"He doesn't dare to leave Riverside now. Someone's going to turn him in: what they're paying out for information alone's enough to. . . ."

"No swordsman's going to turn him in," Hugo rumbled. He could be forbidding when he wanted to.

"Well, no," Ginnie's friend simpered; "you've just gone up on the Hill and made your depositories, haven't you?"

"Depositions," Ginnie corrected sharply. "Well, of course. It's crazy not to clear yourself when you can. Sign a piece of paper, give them some money and promise not to leave town. Let them think we want to cooperate—keep them from coming down here and snooping around. . . ."

"Well, that's just what I'm saying," her friend insisted: "When all the swordsmen have gone up to say they didn't do it, it's going to look funny if he's missing, isn't it?"

"That's not proof, though," Ginnie said; "not enough to hang him."

Hugo pulled his pretty Ginnie over to him. "The whole thing's a pain. Nothing funny about it."

"They don't need enough information to hang him yet, they just want something they can arrest him on, or try to. The reward'll be astronomical."

Solemnly, Hugo lifted his cup. "To information."

"Think they'll catch him?"

"Not if he hides."

Hugo said, "His boyfriend's probably turning him in right now. Shifty bastard. Just like in the play."

Ginnie sneered. "Alec? He's not that shifty. He's got butterflies for brains."

"Think it was the Tragedy that did it for him?"

"Did what?" said Ginnie languidly. "Wait and see if the fight kills him first."

Hugo laughed. It caught in his throat when he saw St Vier come through the doorway. He nudged Ginnie but she paid no mind, so he let his laughter continue to its natural end.

Richard ignored the little group in the corner. Ginnie Vandall was draped over Hugo like a carpet claiming its owner. They were laughing over some fortune cards. Ven, the drunken old bonesetter, got up and shuffled over to St Vier.

"You're young," Ven said thickly; "you should live! Don't fart around with these types. Get out of here while you can."

"I like it here," said Richard, and turned away. Ven stumbled forward and clutched at the swordsman's arm. The next second the old man was rolling on the floor. "Don't do that," Richard said, straightening his sleeve. "Next time it'll be steel."

"Hey!" an old woman protested. "He don't mean no harm. What're you pushing people around for?"

The barmaid cautioned her, "Leave him alone, Marty. He's a swordsman, you know how they can get. What's your drink, master?"

The beer was not as good as Rosalie's, but it was better than

Martha's. Alec would have something to say about it. Alec would start a fight. He always seemed to like fights on rainy days.

Richard wandered over to watch the mumblety-peg tournament for a while. He'd been addicted to the game when he first came to Riverside, having finally found some people who were as good with a knife as he was. He was better than any of the ones playing now, though. The players' bodies were close together, not letting anyone in.

He wouldn't come here again; it was not a good idea to establish a recognizable pattern of habits now. Soon the price would be fixed on his head—funny expression, like a hat.

He wasn't interested in Julia's cards. Hugo and Ginnie were laughing again as he went out the door.

A LTHOUGH IT WAS ONLY A SHORT WALK TO THE HALLIDAYS', Lord Christopher ordered up his carriage because of his companion. He was proud of himself; he felt as if he were bringing home a trophy. A liveried footman brought them into the Crescent Chancellor's presence.

"Tell him," Lord Christopher prompted the nervous, overdressed woman. She was small, pretty in a garish way, with painted eyes. "He's the second noble witness we need to make your testimony official, and you can't do much better. We'll record it; then you can go."

"I'll want my mm-money," she said, her clipped Riverside speech marred by a stammer.

"Of course you'll have it," said Basil Halliday. He nodded to his secretary to begin the transcription. "Go ahead."

"Well, the man you want's St Vier. Everyone knows it."

"How do they know it?"

She shrugged. "How do you know anything? People don't mm-make mm-mistakes like that. He mm-must have told someone. But you can ss-see it. Nnn-nobody else that fast, or d-does that good a j-j-job." Chris winced.

"Do you know why he did it?"

"He's a bb-bastard. Probably that scholar told him to."

"What scholar?"

"Some bb-boy he had with him. Who knows? Swordsmen are all crazy. You just pay me, and I'm getting out of this city and hope I never see another one."

She left, and the two noblemen signed the transcript. Halliday swore bitterly. "The one man I was sure of!"

"It's no good," Christopher said sensibly, disturbed to see his mentor so distressed. "They all tell the same story. Unless it's a conspiracy . . ."

"Among thieves?"

"It isn't very likely," Chris continued earnestly. "That leaves us with a handful of consistent testimonies, and the depositions of every other notable sword in town. St Vier must be arrested on suspicion of Horn's death."

"So he must," said Halliday heavily. "Now how do you propose we get him out of Riverside?"

Lord Christopher picked up a pen, opened his mouth, put it down, and shut it.

"Never mind," said Halliday a bit more gently. "I won't have to call in my own land guard. It's very simple, really: we cry the arrest, post the reward, and wait for someone to turn him in."

A FIRE WAS BURNING BRIGHTLY IN THE DUCHESS TREMON-taine's little parlor. The curtains were pulled back, the better for their owner to savor the contrast with the rain outside. She sat curled up in a round chair of velvet, her feet tucked under her, enjoying the comfort and surveying a delightful incongruity.

He stood dripping in her doorway, a lanky figure in tattered black flanked by the gilded cherubs guarding the entrance.

"You're very wet," she observed. "You shouldn't have stayed out in the rain so long."

"I didn't think you'd admit me."

"I have left standing orders to admit you." She lifted her cordial glass; the crystal chimed melodiously off the gold tray. "I suppose you're out of money again?"

"You suppose right." His tone mirrored hers. "But that's not why I came." He released from the folds of his robe the one rich thing about him, glowing on his finger like a heart of fire. "Look what I've brought."

"Goodness!" The duchess raised her fine eyebrows. "Now how did that manage to find its way back to you?"

"It doesn't matter." He scowled. "You really shouldn't let it our of the house."

"You said you didn't want it anymore. The scene is clearly imprinted on my memory: I can see it when I close my eyes." She did so. "I can see it when I open my eyes, too: you were just as badly dressed, although of course you were drier."

"I don't think I have ever been wetter. You should get someone to do something about all that rain."

"Sit down," she said in a friendly tone that did not conceive of disobedience. She patted a cushion at her side. "If you're going to trust me, you'll have to tell me everything."

"I'm not going to trust you."

"Then why did you come, my dear?"

The knuckles of his hand whitened, his fingers storming around the ring. She'd never managed to teach him to hide his thoughts, which had a marked predilection for denying reality—when he was aware of its existence.

At last he sat, arms tightly clasped around his knees, staring rigidly at the fire. "All right," he said. "I'll tell you what I know if you'll do the same."

"I already know what I know," the duchess said sweetly. "Why don't you dry yourself off while I send for some little iced cakes?"

chapter XXIII

IT WAS GETTING HARDER AND HARDER FOR WILLIE TO FIND ST
Vier these days. Which was good, in a way: Master St Vier had always been fair to him, and was a great sword; Willie wished him
well in this adventure. But he resented having to consider leaving
messages for him with Marie: there was nothing and no one Nimble
Willie couldn't find; that was known, and was going to stay known.
Still, as the shadows of the afternoon got longer, it began to look as
though he'd miss his mark entirely, which was bad for his reputation
and his purse—plus it would annoy St Vier to miss a message. Discon-
solately, Willie turned his feet toward Marie's; after all, there was still
the chance St Vier might be home, although it was less likely these
days. His route brought him past Rosalie's tavern. He decided to stop
in for a consoling drink.

He couldn't believe his eyes, so he rubbed them, but there was still
the dark head of the swordsman. No one was sitting near him, but he
seemed unperturbed. He was eating stew.

Willie sidled up to Lucas Tanner. "What's *he* doing here?"

"I don't know," Tanner rumbled, "but I wish to hell he'd leave."

"Trouble?" Willie looked ready to sprint.

Tanner shrugged. "There's a price on him, you know that. I'm not
interested myself, but you never know who is. Makes people edgy;
hard to have a good time."

Willie scanned the room for unreliable strangers. There was a man he didn't know talking to one of the women, but he looked pretty drunk, and harmless.

"I had a price on my head once," Willie said wistfully. "I was pretty young, see, and nervous. It was some old guy with a really nice cane, not much bigger than me. I felt pretty bad after."

"How did they find out it was you?"

"Somebody saw me. It was up on Gatling Street, in the city. They just about got me, too, but I slipped away and got over the Bridge, and didn't I just keep close for a while after that!" Tanner nodded. "I just about starved; no way of getting money for a bit. But nobody turned me in; we don't do things like that down here."

"Maybe. Maybe not. Hard to catch him, anyway, without a troop. But it may come to that."

Willie laughed. "A troop? You're crazy. They'd be ankle-deep in dead cats and rotten eggs before they were halfway down the Loop. Not to mention thrown stones," he added reflectively, his innocent face lit with soft pleasure.

"You want a riot, you can have one. Not but I wouldn't fight if it came to that; but why won't he just leave town! Make everything easier."

Willie nodded over at the man peacefully eating his supper. "*You* tell him."

"I'm no friend of his . . ." Tanner muttered.

"Wouldn't matter," said Willie with cheerful wickedness; "he'd kill you anyway!"

Nevertheless he approached the swordsman carefully. It was the opposite of stalking prey: you definitely wanted him to know you were coming.

Richard saw him, and saw that Willie actually wanted to speak to him, unlike most people these days. "Hello, Willie," he said, and swung a stool out for him. Richard didn't waste time with preliminaries: idle conversation in public places was not what anyone wanted him for. "What's the word?"

"You won't believe who I saw," Willie said chattily, "uptown and dressed like nothing going!"

Richard's heart chose that moment to become athletic; but he managed to match Willie's tone: "Oh? Who?"

"Kathy Blount! Hermia's girl, that was. You remember her."

"Yes, I do." His pulse settled back to its plodding motion.

"She says she'd like to see you again sometime. You've got the luck, haven't you?"

He had put the Tremontaine job out of his mind, being more concerned with the business at hand, and not having heard from them in weeks, not since their "Delay." It might not be a bad idea now: give him something to do, and enough money to see out the summer. He'd have to be more cautious slipping out of Riverside, but he could manage.

"Says she'll be at the Dog tomorrow night, say, if you're free."

"Thanks, Willie."

The swordsman's lack of surprise at his news had not escaped Nimble Willie. Still, he leaned over to Richard, lowering his voice: "Look, I think it's a trap. Sure, the Dog's in Riverside, but only just barely. You don't want to meet anyone anywhere for a while, Master St Vier, not when they know you're coming."

"Maybe." It was true, after all; the Brown Dog tavern stood closest to the Bridge. Its clientele consisted almost solely of city people looking for thrills, and Riversiders eager to fleece them. It was within shouting distance of the Watch. But where else could Katherine meet him safely? He had said he would help her if she was in trouble; it might not even be the job at all. "Was that all the message?" he asked.

"Not quite. She said something funny about a ring."

The ruby was gone, gone with Alec. If they needed it now they'd have to ask him for it. "What about it?"

"She said she knows where it is now. That's all."

Willie saw with nervousness how St Vier's fist clenched on the table. But the swordsman's face remained calm. Willie was glad he only carried the messages.

I N THE END, RICHARD CHOSE TO GO. HE SAID TO MARIE ON HIS way out, "Look, there's a chance I won't be coming back tonight. If you hear anything certain, take what I owe you out of the rosewood chest, and do what you want with the rest of the stuff."

She didn't ask where he was going. These days she liked to be able to tell people who came asking that she didn't know.

He hadn't eaten any supper yet; the best thing about the Dog was its food. When he was new to the city he'd gone there a lot; it was a good place for young people of all professions to pick up work. He and Alec had taken to dropping in every few weeks: Alec liked the food, and liked dicing with the city people because they bet high and they were even clumsier cheaters than he was. But drunken young men were always challenging Richard there to impress their friends; one night one of them had annoyed Alec, and Richard had ended up killing him, putting a strain on St Vier's relationship with the tavern keeper.

No one seemed to be following him as he took the long way round.

The tavern shone like sunrise at the end of the street, its doorway alight with beacons like any uptown establishment. The light showed no one waiting for him by the entrance. Over it hung the brown dog, a large painted wood carving that bore no resemblance to any living breed.

Inside was just as well lit. The place had a carnival atmosphere, fevered and bright. Richard felt as though he'd stepped outside Riverside into another world. Whores were talking animatedly with well-dressed men, completely ignoring the gaudy ones whose hands shuffled and reshuffled decks of cards, who might be their neighbors or brothers. A couple of nobles in half-masks leaned against the wall, trying to look detached and amused, their eyes darting here and there about the room glittering in the mask slits, their naked hands playing on the pommels of the swords they wore for security. Richard thought he would pass unnoticed amongst them, but he saw how the card players deliberately flattened their eyes against seeing him, how the whores turned their backs and raised their volume. Riversiders didn't turn each other in; they just stopped knowing you. That way was easier. It told him he was recognized, though, and warned him that not everyone might be so considerate.

He didn't see Katherine, which further roused his suspicion. His sword hung, a solid weight, at his side. He touched it under his cloak and found the tavern keeper edging up to him.

Harris had his perpetual harried, unctuous expression. "Now, sir, if you will recall an adventure I would not like repeated . . ." He rarely spoke in sentences, but in insinuation; people said he had started as a pimp.

"I'll be careful," Richard promised. "Who's here tonight?"

Harris shrugged. "The usual . . ." he said vaguely. "You understand, I don't want trouble. . . ."

Something made Richard turn around. He was not entirely surprised to see Katherine coming through the doorway. He waited until she saw him, then moved to a table with a good command of the room, brushing past a pretty-boy lolling in the lap of a heavily powdered man who was feeding him whisky in small glasses.

Katherine followed, ridiculously relieved that Richard was here already. He moved through the room with careful assurance, betraying no sign of nervousness, although watchfulness glowed off him like magic. It almost surprised her that the entire room didn't rise up and follow him: Richard at work was more than impressive, he was magnetic. He wanted to be sought after for his skill; but the nobles desired him for his performance.

She couldn't keep her hands from twisting together, so she hid them under the table. Absurdly, Richard said, "Thank you for coming."

She said, "You weren't at the Old Bell last week."

"Was I supposed to be?"

"Not if you didn't know. Of course he didn't tell you."

"Who? Willie?" Her silence made it plain. "Alec."

A young woman cruised by their table, and smiled into Katherine's eyes like an old friend. Richard's hand moved a fraction on the table, ready to take action if she needed it. But Katherine shook her head. "I can't stand it in here," she said fretfully. "Can we go out?"

"Where?" Richard asked. "Shall we go deeper into Riverside? You don't mind?"

"It doesn't matter." There was a dull edge of hysteria to her voice that made his taut nerves quiver.

"Katherine." He would have taken her hand if he could. "Were you sent here, or did you come yourself? If it's business, we'll get it over quickly and you can go."

She glanced quickly behind her. "I came," she said. "On my own."

Anger surged and hardened in him. With a cause to form around, his nerves twisted together into a strong cord of purpose. It was too long since he had had a real fight, too long that he had been sitting, waiting.

"It's bad, then," he said quietly, without any gentleness. "Ferris has done you no good. Never mind. You don't have to tell me about it. I said I would help you and I will."

He couldn't see his own face, set and white with a rage whose coolness his eyes betrayed by being too wide, too blue, too fixed. It was a look she had seen only once before in him, and it froze the life in her bones. "Richard," she whispered, *"please—"*

"It's all right," he said calmly. "We'll leave here, go somewhere else where we can talk. Do you need a place to stay? Don't worry. You should have known I'd come."

"Come, then," she echoed, rising from the table. She was shaking with chill. She wanted to run, to push her way out of the tavern, to flinch from the cold swordsman walking beside her. She took his arm, and together they made a way past the card players and revelers, out of the doorway into the orange light burning a hole in the dark street.

"There," he said; "better?"

She held him tighter as a shadow fell across them. Behind them the door had opened, blocked by dark figures. To the right and to the left, and in front of them the shadows had become men, ringing the aura of light with solid darkness.

"Richard St Vier?"

"Yes?"

"In the name of the Council I charge you to stand—"

He flung her reeling into the darkness, but her weight had held his arm too long, and he drew his sword only as the first of the wooden staves crashed into him.

The impact staggered him back, but he did not fall. The next one drove the breath from his side. He turned blindly in a new direction, where he thought the attack might come. His eyes cleared and he saw the staff descending, glowing like a comet with pain. His cut went wild but so did the staff. The man's guard was down; Richard followed his torch-gold blade true to its mark, and heard the man cry out a moment before the thwack of another blow caught St Vier across the shoulders. His knees hit the ground, but he kept hold of his sword and was on his feet again, just like practice, only he would pay for this later. This time he saw the staff come swinging out of the darkness toward his face. He almost raised his sword to break the blow; but steel would not stand up to oak, so he ducked instead, and missed the one that caught him in the back of his legs.

There certainly were a lot of them. He fell sprawling, scraping his hands along the stone. His sword was gone—he felt for the hilt, somewhere nearby, but the cobbles seemed to be coursing with light. Not light but pain. He was seeing pain flowing like gold, like a basket full of jewels and summer fruit.

He heard roaring in his ears, and a voice he agreed with shrieking, "Stop it! Please stop it, that's enough!"

But they weren't ready to stop until the swordsman had ceased rolling and dodging and lay perfectly still. Then the Watch picked up their prize and carried him over the north Bridge. The prison where he would eventually rest lay on the south side of the river. They'd bring him there by boat, in the daylight.

Nimble Willie waited silent in the shadows of a bridge parapet for the knot of men to pass him. Except for their staves, nothing to attract attention. But he guessed before chance showed him the face of the man they carried.

"Oh, Master St Vier," he murmured to himself in the shadows; "this is a terrible thing."

And Katherine Blount returned to the one who had sent her. She managed to make a clear report; then she asked for brandy, and was given a large decanter without question.

chapter XXIV

LORD MICHAEL GODWIN LAY BACK ON THE EMBROIDERED cushions of his couch, loosened his shirt collar, and tried to encourage himself to be hungry. He thought about early winter mornings after hunting, and about interminable music recitals before dinner. But the expanse of dishes set before him grew no more alluring. He wondered how the small, agile men around him managed. They were cheerfully digging into piles of dyed eggs with unfeigned vigor, cracking the shells in interesting patterns and rolling the eggs in spices; deflowering piles of fruit, cut and arranged like blossoms; spearing little deep-fried objects with the ends of carved picks. He took a grape, for form's sake; it had come from a hothouse, and must be worth its weight in eggshells.

Across the table his compatriot caught his eye and smiled. In the few weeks Michael had been in Chartil, Devin had lost no opportunity to point out to him his deficiencies in local custom. Devin was the second son of a second son; an aristocrat by courtesy, whose lineage came nowhere near Michael's. In the city of his birth Devin felt it sharply; in Chartil he was exalted to the rank of ambassador, and his hospitality was legendary. His saving grace was a sense of humor, which took the sting out of his self-defensive maneuvers. Michael liked Devin; and he thought Devin had decided to like him, in spite of his background.

Above the racket of conversation, the ambassador said to him in their own tongue, "Packet came in today. Lots of gossip from town."

A servant was trying to refill one of Michael's three wine glasses. Michael gave up and let her. Her thigh rubbed against his shoulder. Automatically he turned his chin to nuzzle her waist, but his eye fell on the bangles around her ankles, and his head jerked back. She was a bonded slave. Devin's sardonic eyes glinted at him, reading his thoughts: of course no free woman here, not even a servant, would seek to entice him; that lot fell to those whose bodies and their issue were pledged to an owner. For women, it was a step up from prostitution. He wondered if he had been selected by his host to breed, or to be flattered. Either idea repelled him.

"She likes you," said the ambassador.

Michael hid the color of his face in his widest-brimmed wine cup.

"It's no worse," Devin persisted, "than one who takes your money and wishes you in hell. She'll get paid at the end of her term. More gracious this way."

"Nevertheless . . ." Lord Michael took refuge in an aristocrat's shrug. "What's the gossip?"

"Seems Lord Horn's been killed."

Michael forgot that he was holding a wine cup when his hand opened. He caught it on its way down before it hit the table, but not before its contents had liberally bestowed themselves on their surroundings. The slave mopped at it all with a napkin.

"Friend of yours?" Devin was enjoying himself mightily.

"Hardly. I just didn't think he was ready for death."

"Probably wasn't. They're saying a swordsman did it."

"Oh? Any idea which one?"

"*Swordsman?*" A Chartil noble on his left caught the word, and continued in his own tongue, "That's one of your laborers, isn't it, who dishonors his sword in the service of other men?"

Devin translated the comment for Michael, and chided the speaker, "Now, Eoni, if that were so, it would be dishonor to be a soldier."

"*Ffft.*" Eoni made the usual Chartil comment of disdain. "You know very well what I mean. For the killing of noble enemies, only two things will serve: either the challenge direct, or, saving your courtesy and that of the table, the certain use of poison. None of this pussy-footing around with surrogates. And I've served my time as a soldier and I'm proud of it, so don't think to gall me that way, you small-minded, round-faced foreign excuse for a gentleman!"

" 'Insult, the last refuge of blighted affection. . . .' " Devin quoted sweetly.

Barred by language from the conversation, Michael rolled a grape between his fingers and thought about Horn. Murdered, and he knew by whom. *His life is about to become complicated.* . . . Yes, what was left of it. The clear eyes of the swordsman looked out from his memory, blue as spring hyacinths . . . self-serving little murderer, using his skill with a sword to destroy better men than he'd ever be. . . .

"Excuse me." Michael nodded to his host, and set off in the direction of the urinals. But he didn't stop there; his will took him out onto the street, walking swiftly through the sun-baked alleys of the town. He passed enclosed gardens whose feather-topped trees showed over the walls.

It wasn't that he had any love for Horn. He would have killed Horn himself, if he could. But St Vier couldn't have any quarrel with Horn; no one forced a swordsman to take a job he didn't want. No one had forced him to kill Vincent Applethorpe. . . . Michael stopped for a moment, involuntarily pressing his hand to his mouth. He still dreamed about it, when he wasn't dreaming of wool.

That was what the duchess had wanted—not a swordsman, not a courtier, but someone to look into the direct shipping of wool from her estates to Chartil. She was eliminating the middleman by having the raw wool dyed and woven here into the popular shawls, then shipped back to sell out of her own warehouses. . . . At first he'd thought this tradesman's assignment an elaborate and degrading joke. But on the ship, studying the records and notes she had given him, he came to see how much politics was bound up in business, and how much of his skill the task would require, especially in a place where no one knew him. There were laws, and import taxes to consider. . . . It was the stuff of the Council meetings he always made sure to avoid, the hidden agenda of the grain reports from his father's land, which he glanced over grudgingly each month, whose revenues supported his life in the city.

The wool business had caught Michael up, intrigued him, even made him feel a certain power; but it had not made him forget Applethorpe. He would bear the death to the end of his days. And St Vier, whose skill had lured his Master into the endless night; St Vier, who at the end had seemed to share with his Master a spirit and understanding that Michael could not approach . . . St Vier had walked away and gone to wield his power elsewhere.

Michael looked down. A little man in a dirty headcloth was jabbering at him, asking him something. He shook his head helplessly: *I don't know.* Doggedly, the man repeated the question. Michael caught the words for "lord," and "buy." He shook his head again; but the man blocked his path, not letting him move on. Michael pulled back a fold of his robe, showing the sword he wore to threaten him. The little man grinned excitedly, nodding with great vigor and enthusiasm. He reached inside his own robe and pulled out a little vial; one, two, three of them, all different shapes, thrusting them under Michael's nose, gesticulating with his other hand:

"Four bits! Four times four—" or maybe it was four *and* four—"bits for one! All three, even less!"

Michael had spent time in the market. Still not sure what the product was, but amused despite himself, he employed the bulk of his vocabulary: "Too much."

The man expressed shock. The man expressed dismay. Perhaps the lord did not fully understand the exceptional quality of his stock. He pointed to the vials, pantomimed drinking one, and clutched his throat, emitting realistic choking noises, reeling backwards as though looking for a resting place. He sat down hard on the ground, rolling up his eyes, then grinning happily at Michael.

They were poisons. Poisons for his enemy.

"Five!" the man said. "All three, five each!"

A death no one could stand against, swift and sure. It would not be impossible to arrange it for St Vier. Michael Godwin had friends in the city, and money.

Michael shuddered in the sunlight, remembering the swordsman's animal grace. It was a foul death to offer such a man; a worse death than he had given Applethorpe or Horn. However the Chartils might romanticize expedience, it remained a death without honor, unheralded and unchallenged. *The challenge . . . you either know it or you don't.*

Michael touched the sword he wore. He knew it; and for him it did not lie in feats of arms. He was a nobleman, and nobles did not seek revenge against swordsmen on commission. If anything, he should be plotting against Horn; but the nobleman had gone beyond Michael's revenge. He had no reason to want to avenge Horn, and for Applethorpe no vengeance would ever be enough. It was natural for him to want to hurt the man who had been the instrument of his first adult grief; natural, but not right. He was glad he had not even held one of the vials in his hand.

Michael's face told the little man that the bargaining was over. He drifted back around the corner, and Michael turned back toward Devin and the feast.

It was true, as the duchess had told him, that the Chartils respected a man who could use a sword. The friends he made who practiced with him were intrigued by some of his straight-point technique, and amused at his lack of experience; but one of them said seriously to him, "At least you are a man. Your countryman the feastmaster is a good sort, but . . ."

When he came back in the hall the eating was still going on, and there was a fourth wine cup at everyone's place. He found he was ready for it, and even managed some enthusiasm over almond tarts.

Devin looked at him as he sat down. The ambassador's face was grave, but his eyes glinted with dry mirth: "Get lost?" he said.

"Only temporarily." Michael bit into a cake.

chapter XXV

THE OLD FORT GUARDED THE MOUTH OF THE CHANNEL TO the old city, on the east bank. It was still used as a watchtower, but now its honeycomb passages housed important state prisoners. St Vier had been brought there early this morning, and Lord Ferris had come as soon as the news reached him.

Half an hour in the Fort found Ferris trying hard not to lose his temper. Finally, he sat in the chair he had first been offered, spreading his cloak out not to wrinkle it. It was as comfortable a room as could be made of the heavy stone cells of the old fort. It was the deputy's sitting room, where visitors waited to be escorted to the prisoner of their choice. But it seemed that, in the case of Richard St Vier, they were reticent with the privilege.

When Lord Ferris sat, the deputy sat too, across the table from the nobleman. The deputy was a steady man, but having to match wills with a Council Lord made him uncomfortable and turned his virtues to stubbornness. Doggedly he repeated his information: "You will forgive me, my lord, but the orders I have come from the Crescent himself. St Vier is to be kept closely guarded, and no one is to see him without Lord Halliday's own express permission."

"I understand," Lord Ferris said for perhaps the third time, trying to make it sound freshly compassionate. "But you must realize that, as a member of the Inner Council, I comprise a portion of the Justiciary. All of us will be questioning St Vier as soon as my lord duke of Karleigh arrives in the city."

"In the court you will, yes, my lord. But I have no instructions as to private interviews beforehand."

"Oh, come." Ferris essayed a smile, wilfully misreading him. "Surely the serpent is defanged, and I cannot be harmed now."

"Surely, my lord," the deputy agreed, with the formal tolerance reserved for aggravating superiors. "But *he* might be. We are guarding Master St Vier for his own protection as well as others'. In affairs of this sort, it is not always the swordsman who is the guilty party."

"What?" Ferris exclaimed. "Has he said anything?"

"Not one word, my lord. The gentleman—that is, the young man is most quiet and well behaved. He has not asked to see anyone."

"Interesting," said Ferris, in his role of chancellor, "and possibly indicative of something. But there, I mustn't ask questions of you before the actual Inquiry." He stood up briskly, shaking out the heavy folds of his cloak. "I expect you have also been required to inform Lord Halliday of any who come asking to see St Vier?" The man nodded. "Well, you needn't bother in my case," Ferris said heartily; "I'll go and call on him now myself, inform him of my breach of etiquette, and see if I can't procure that necessary bit of paper for you."

"Very good, my lord," the deputy said—or one of those noncommittal phrases implying measured credulity and the desire to be left in peace by the mighty.

Ferris hurried out of the chill of the Fort and into his waiting carriage, where he put his feet on a hot brick that could have been hotter. He did not drive to Lord Halliday's. He went home. He had no intention of letting Halliday know that he was interested in seeing St Vier. But he very much wanted to see the swordsman before he could tell Basil Halliday about the plan to have him killed.

There was no certainty that St Vier would tell about him, of course. It would not absolve the swordsman of Horn's murder. And, of course, there was not even the certainty that St Vier had ever known the identity of his one-eyed contact. Nothing was certain; but Ferris wanted to control all the odds that he could. He had the best, the surest plan, if only he could implement it: to offer St Vier his protection in the matter of Horn's death, if St Vier would agree to carry through on the Halliday challenge as soon as he was freed. Taking the charge as patron of Horn's disgusting murder would not be good for Ferris, but he could think of some story to explain it, to subtly blacken St Vier's character and add yet another taint to Horn's; and it was convenient that St Vier kill Halliday. The debt would bind the swordsman to Ferris for life, and when he had been elected to the Crescent, Ferris would have much use for him.

As soon as Karleigh came up from his estates to sit on the Justiciary, they would try the swordsman. St Vier would see Ferris on the panel of justiciars, and could recognize him. Ferris didn't dare risk what the swordsman might try to do then to save his life. It was remotely possible that St Vier might think of the double blackmail on his own, but Ferris must find a way to let him know that he would cooperate in it.

But he could not get in to see him now without creating suspicion. He needed a proxy. Katherine had failed him once, when he sent her to Riverside. Now she must serve him again—for the last time, if all went well. Surely they would not deny St Vier's own *wife* permission to see him? It might work—nobody knew what sort of arcane pairings there were in Riverside, and she was a fetching piece.

A servant took Ferris's cloak; another was sent to bring him something hot to drink, and another to summon Katherine Blount.

The hot drink came, but Katherine did not. The footman said, "I sent one of the maids up to her room, my lord. It seems it is empty."

"Empty . . . ? Of what? Of her person, or . . . ?"

"Of her, ah, belongings, my lord. The girl appears to have fled. She was paid two weeks ago for the month. But she seems to be missing since night before last."

"Fled!" Ferris tapped his fingers on the cup rapidly, thinking. "Send Master Johns to me. I shall require some letters sent."

He had not meant to keep her much longer: she was the link that tied him to St Vier, should the matter be investigated. Perhaps he had been too hard on her, and she had simply run away, in which case he didn't care what happened to her. But if she had gone, say, to Halliday . . .

His letters dictated and secretary dismissed, Ferris realized, ruefully, that he must turn to Diane. The duchess's connections were better than his; she might even be able to get him access to St Vier. He would not tell her everything; that would be a great mistake. And a mistake to think that he could simply bend Diane to his will; that had once been tried, and quickly discarded. But he might be persuasive, if she was in the right mood for it . . . even now it was not good to lie to her, but she could be charmed. Once again Ferris called for his carriage to be sent round, and ordered the familiar route to the Duchess Tremontaine's.

He stood in the duchess's front hall, trying to hand his gloves to the footman, but the footman wouldn't take them.

"My lady is not in, my lord."

From upstairs Ferris heard her laughter, and a snatch of song.

"Grayson," he said slowly, "do you know me?"

"Of course he knows you," a new voice drawled from the shadows. "You're a very recognizable figure."

A young man of no more than twenty years was lounging against the side of the staircase, surveying Ferris with an expression that contrived to be both bored and amused at once. He was very beautifully dressed in deep red, and wore a collar of rubies. He held a book in one hand.

"If the duchess told Grayson to tell you she is not in," the young man continued, "it actually means that she doesn't want to see you. Is there a message?" he asked helpfully. "Perhaps I could take it."

He was tall, and fine-boned, theatrically languid in his motions. He turned and drifted partway up the stairs, stopping to look down at the Dragon Chancellor, the hand with the book resting on the rail. Ferris stared up at him, still saying nothing. Was this his replacement? Some young nobody—oh, very young—someone's son fresh from the country? A consolation after her loss of Michael Godwin, an insult to Ferris, a replacement . . . It was not possible that she was throwing him over. She had no cause. Her refusal to see him was some new game, or a trick of this smug young man's who might, after all, be some distant relation of Diane's. . . .

"Is there any message, my lord?" Grayson asked, professionally deaf to the antics around him.

"Yes. Tell my lady I will call again."

"Who knows," the mocking voice drifted after Ferris as he left, his stride so swift that his cloak billowed out, brushing the man who held the door open for him, "she may be in."

And as the door closed behind him Ferris heard the duchess's laughter echoing in the marble hall.

Answers to the letters he had sent were waiting for him when he got home. No one had seen any sign of Katherine; or at least, no one was admitting to it. Perhaps she had gone back to Riverside where, in truth, she belonged.

He stood with his hands on his desk, leaning his weight on his arms. In another minute he would straighten, raise his head, and find another order to give. Before Diane, it had been like this, too often: a sense of his own power blocked; of not being taken seriously; of not being able to choose for himself the strongest course. He was Dragon Chancellor now. People knew him, admired him, looked to him for guidance, for advancement. Basil Halliday confided in him, and would help him if he could. . . . Ferris started, hearing his own sharp laugh. Go to Halliday with his problems, like all the rest of them— tangle himself in that net of compassionate charm, and exchange Diane's dominion for Halliday's . . . that was not the way to the power he sought, cold and uncompromising, the terms his own and his alone. Most people were like Horn: they could be manipulated, rendered agreeable or untroublesome in their actions. Blocks like Halliday could be duped and got rid of. Ferris sighed, shaking his head. If only they all could be ignored. But of course that was unrealistic.

Ferris thought of the day that stretched ahead of him, and decided to emulate the duchess. Turning his back on his study, he ascended to his bedroom, where he wrapped himself in a heavy robe, had a large fire made up, settled next to it with a book and a bowl of nuts, and gave instructions that, to anyone who called, he was not in.

Fᴏʀ Rɪᴄʜᴀʀᴅ Sᴛ Vɪᴇʀ, ɪᴍᴘʀɪsᴏɴᴇᴅ, ᴛʜᴀᴛ ᴅᴀʏ ᴘᴀssᴇᴅ ᴠᴇʀʏ slowly. He had a headache, and there was no one to talk to, and nothing very interesting to think about. Shrugging the day off as a loss, he made himself as comfortable as he could, and retired early to bed with the sun. The next morning brought news of his trial.

The pleasant young nobleman had already explained to Richard all that he needed to know about his coming questioning. The pleasant young nobleman, whose name was Christopher Nevilleson, had been sent expressly from Basil Halliday to do so the day he arrived in the Fort. Richard disliked the young man intensely. He knew there was no good reason for it, but he did. Lord Christopher had had the shackles struck from Richard's wrists and legs, and had expressed official dismay, tinged with personal horror, at the condition the Watch had left him in. But the bruises would heal in time, if there was time left to him. He was horribly stiff, but nothing was cracked or broken.

Halliday's aide was serious and fresh-faced. In him the Hill drawl sounded like a speech defect he had never grown out of. He told Richard that he would be questioned first in private by a collection of important lords, to determine how culpable he was in the killing of Lord Horn. They had to know whether he was working for any patron so they could then decide whether to try him in a Court of Honor or turn him over to the civil authorities as a murderer.

"There are so few laws that really cover the use of swordsmen," he explained. "If you have anything in writing it would be very useful."

Richard stared at him out of one swollen eye. "I don't work on contract," he said frostily. "They should know that by now."

"I . . . yes," Lord Christopher said. He told Richard that he would be required to answer questions under oath, and that depositions had already been sworn against him by witnesses. Richard asked, "Will I see any of these people at the trial?"

Lord Christopher answered, "No, that isn't necessary. They've already signed statements witnessed by two nobles." He kept saying, "You do understand, don't you?" Richard said that he did. Finally, the pleasant young nobleman went away.

Early this morning they had sent someone in to shave and barber him, because the Duke of Karleigh had driven in last night and now the Justiciary was complete. Richard had submitted to the combing fingers and the scissors, but when it came to the sharp-edged razor he asked if he might use it himself, and offered to go unshaven otherwise. In the end they let him shave himself, and stood solemnly around watching to make sure he didn't cut his throat.

It would be interesting to find out what the trial was like. In the past, when he had been hired to kill a lord the noble who hired him had always stood up in the Court of Honor for himself, so that St Vier need not appear at all. Part of his care in choosing his patrons had involved their ability to do so. The Court of Honor was a secret thing, presided over by the Inner Council. Swordsmen who had been called to it were never very clear in their descriptions after: either they had been confused, or they wanted to impress by being mysterious, or both. Richard suspected that the truth was seldom told in the Court of Honor: a noble's ability to manipulate it and his peers seemed to be the key to success there. That was why St Vier took only patrons who seemed to have that knack over men who offered him contracts where his "innocence" would be cast in writing—that, and his own desire for privacy.

He wished now that he had been a little more pleasant with Lord Christopher, and asked a few more questions. But it didn't matter: soon he would find all about the court for himself. He could think about that; could think about the future but not the past. He'd already gone over everything he'd done wrong; once was enough for that sort of thing, to satisfy his mind; any more was useless and unpleasant. If he lived, he could find out who in Riverside had sworn against him. The reason for Katherine's nervousness was clear now. But she wouldn't have done it on her own—somehow, they had made her afraid. He couldn't help her now.

Doggedly he stretched and paced in the small stone room. Whatever happened, there was no point in letting himself get stiffer. His bruised body protested, but he was used to ignoring it. The room was not terrible; there was light, and a bed bolted to the wall. His injuries and the inactivity made him feel tired; but the temptation of the hard bed was resistible.

He paused by the window, leaning on the stone embrasure. It was a privilege, of sorts, not to be thrown in the Chop with the common city criminals. Richard was in one of the upper rooms of the Old Fort, looking out over the mouth of the channel guarding the oldest section of the city.

Far below, the river glittered, grey and bright as the surface of a mirror. His window was an arrow slit, tapering to an opening in the outer wall. The cold stone felt good against his forehead. The tide was running; he watched trade boats passing down to the channel.

Habit made him clap his hand to his side when he heard the door opening behind him. He did not bother trying to convert the gesture when his fingers closed on nothing.

"Master St Vier." The deputy of the Fort stood just within the doorway, backed by a phalanx of guards. "Your escort is here to conduct you to the Council Hall."

He was surprised at the respect they accorded him. He didn't know if it was just the formal good manners extended to all Fort prisoners, or if his being a well-known swordsman outweighed his living in Riverside.

"Is there a crowd?" he asked the deputy.

"A crowd? Where?"

"Outside, in Justice Place," Richard said, "waiting to see us go by." He had assumed that the guards were to keep the curious from pressing in on them on their walk across the plaza. There would be friends there, and enemies; hordes of curious gogglers with nothing better to do than shove and stare.

"Oh, no." The deputy smiled. "We don't go that way." He read St Vier's look. "The guards are for you. My lord would not have you chained, so we need a convoy to prevent your escaping."

Richard laughed. He supposed he could injure the deputy, and maybe capture one of the guards' weapons. He could turn their orderly walk into a slaughter. But the chances were bad, and he had an appointment with the Council.

They came to a stair, and picked up more torches. Their way led downward, underground smelling of stony water and iron earth. It was a passage system under the plaza, connecting the Fort with the hall.

"I never heard of this!" Richard said to the deputy. "How long has it been here?"

"Well before my time," the deputy answered. "I've memorized the passage. It's part of my duties. There are a lot of dead ends and unexplored turns."

"I'll try not to wander off," Richard said.

"Do that." The deputy chuckled. "You're sure of yourself, aren't you?"

Richard shrugged. "Isn't everyone?"

The stairs leading up weren't as long as the ones they had taken down. The guards had to pass single file through the door at the top, with Richard between them. They came into a hall filled with sunlight. Richard's eyes burned, and he felt himself drenched in the fire of day, saturated with the colors of the wood-paneled walls, the marble floors, and the painted ceiling. The sun-baked warmth of the hall, with its high windows, was welcome to them all after the chill of the passage. But the disciplined guards were silent as they marched their prisoner down the corridor.

They came at last to large oak double doors, guarded by liveried men who opened them portentously. Richard was expecting something splendid; instead there was another antechamber, more doors. These, too, were opened, and he and his escort paraded into the Court of Honor.

The room was dim, as though drenched in perpetual afternoon. He had an impression of maybe a dozen men in splendid robes like theater costumes, seated behind a long table facing him. He was given a chair in the middle of the floor, facing Basil Halliday and some others. Halliday wore blue velvet, with a huge ring stitched in gold on the chest: emblem of the Crescent whose chancellorship he held. Richard thought wryly what a wonderful target the circle made. But that job was off for now.

"Master St Vier." The irritatingly nice young man who had briefed him now came forward. "These are the lords justiciar, fully assembled in Inquiry before us. They have already heard all the signed depositions; now they will ask you some questions."

"I do understand," said Richard. "But isn't one missing?"

"I beg your pardon?"

"You said, *fully assembled.* But there are two empty seats: yours and one next to that red-face—next to that man in green."

"Oh." For a moment, Lord Christopher looked flummoxed. He hadn't prepared to answer questions from the accused in front of everyone. But Basil Halliday smiled and nodded to him; so, taking heart, he said, "That is the seat for Tremontaine. Next to my lord duke of Karleigh. Every ducal house has the right to sit on the Court of Honor—"

"But the damned woman won't take her duties seriously!" roared the red-faced man who had been pointed out as the Duke of Karleigh. Although he'd taken the duke's job and his money, Richard had never seen him in person before. Karleigh seemed like the type to require swordsmen frequently: proud and quarrelsome, as well as powerful. "Didn't take long to get *her* the message, I'll warrant! *She* didn't have to come tearing up from the hinterlands on a day's notice for this. . . ."

"Now, my lord." A man with a bird emblem stitched on his chest tried to calm the duke. "That is between the duchess and her honor, not ours." Richard recognized Lord Montague, a man he'd worked for and liked. Montague was Raven Chancellor now, and less given to fights; Richard had been wounded once in his service, and taken into Montague's own house to recover.

When the Duke of Karleigh had been settled, Lord Halliday began the questions. "Master St Vier, we have heard many people swear that you killed Lord Horn. But no one witnessed the event. References are all to your style, your skill, to rumor. If you can summon proof positive that you were elsewhere on the night of his death, we would like to hear of it."

"No," said Richard, "I can't. It *is* my style."

"And is there someone you think might copy that style to get you into trouble?"

"No one I can think of."

"—*my lord*," Karleigh injected. "Damned insolence. *No one I can think of, my lord*—mind how you speak to your betters!"

"And you mind," a quiet voice said lazily, "how you make a shambles of these proceedings, Karleigh." The florid duke fell silent, and Richard could guess why: the speaker was a man of average build, perhaps as old as Karleigh, but with flexible hands that were younger, more capable, and eyes that were much older. ("Lord Arlen," Chris Nevilleson mouthed at him.)

"I'm sorry," Richard said to the Crescent. "I haven't meant to be rude."

He'd noticed that Halliday had been ignoring Karleigh's outbursts; of course, there was trouble between them. Halliday shrugged and said to the Raven Chancellor, "See that that exchange is struck from the notes, my lord?"

Montague jotted something down and motioned to the scribe behind him. "Of course."

"You understand, then," Halliday said to Richard, "that all evidence points to you?"

"I meant it to," Richard said. "That was its purpose."

"You do not deny that you killed Horn?"

"I do not."

Even in the small group, the noise of reaction was loud. Finally, Lord Halliday had to call for silence. "Now," Halliday said to Richard, "we come to the particular business of this court. Can you name a patron in Horn's death?"

"No, I can't. I'm sorry."

"Can you give us any *reason?*" Montague leaned forward to ask.

Richard thought, framing his answer in words they might understand. "It was a matter of honor."

"Well, yes, but *whose?*"

"Mine," Richard said.

Halliday sighed loudly and wiped his forehead. "Master St Vier: your firmness to stand by your word is known and respected in this court. Any patron you select must have complete faith in you, and I'm sure this one does. But if he is too cowardly to reveal himself and stand the judgment of his peers, I want to make it clear to you that your life is at peril here. Without a noble patron, we will have to give you over to a civil authority to try you as a murderer."

"I understand," said Richard. A thought with the voice of Alec whispered silently: My honor isn't worth your attention. But secretly he was relieved. They honestly didn't seem to know why he had had to kill Horn. Since Godwin had escaped his challenge, Horn had not been eager to boast about the blackmailing of St Vier. So far, only Riverside knew anything about that. And Richard would do what he could to see that it stayed that way. He didn't think it would even matter if he did tell them the reason; it probably wouldn't stand up under their contorted rules. The court was turning out to be interesting only in an eerily nasty way: like their rationales for killing each other, there was a separate set of rules that seemed to double back on itself, whose origins they'd long ago forgotten the purpose of.

"Might I ask a question?" said a new voice, faintly familiar. Richard looked at the speaker, and found why: a man with coal-black hair and an eye patch had risen. He, too, was in blue velvet, and there was a nice-looking dragon on his chest. It was Ferris, who'd come from the duchess to ask him to kill Halliday.

"Master St Vier." Lord Ferris courteously introduced himself: "I am the Dragon Chancellor of the Council of Lords. I, too, have heard in many places just how well you may be trusted . . . in many places, sir." He had his head turned so that his good eye was fixed on Richard; his speaking eye. Richard nodded, to show he understood the reference to their meeting.

"Speechmaking, my lord Dragon?" asked the Duke of Karleigh in a low but carrying voice.

Ferris smiled warmly at him. "If you like. It's what comes of being a good boy and waiting my turn." The other nobles laughed, breaking the tension and letting him continue: "And I think, Master St Vier, that in view of your reputation we are perhaps doing you a disservice. For your style bespeaks not only a man of honor, but a man of sense. If you did kill Lord Horn, you did so for a reason. It may be a reason we all wish to hear. The death of a noble concerns all of our honors, whether in formal challenge or no." Down the table, Halliday nodded. "Now, the civil court has been known to use methods less gentle than our own. . . ."

The old-young nobleman asked dryly, "Are you proposing that we torture St Vier, Ferris?"

Lord Ferris turned his head to look at him. "My lord of Arlen," he said pleasantly, "I am not. But, in fact, it's not a bad idea. Something formal, and harmless, to keep his honor intact."

Richard felt as though he were fencing blindfolded. Words were deceiving; one had to move by tone and inference, and by sheer sense of purpose. Remembering Ferris's style in the tavern, Richard thought the lord was saying that he knew what had happened with Horn. If so, he was threatening to reveal it . . . unless what? Unless Richard assured him that he would not reveal the plot against Halliday? But how could he assure him in front of them all?

"Ferris," Halliday interrupted, "Arlen; I must ask you to be serious. Do you really want that proposal put on record?"

"I beg your pardon," Ferris said a little haughtily. "I think it should be considered before we give St Vier over to death at the hands of the civil court. I realize that such a proposal would draw this Inquiry out—longer, perhaps, than some would care to spend on it. But I would like it noted that my own hand is held out to the swordsman as willing to entertain any answer he gives us here. In the privacy of this court, any nobleman's honor is secure, and his reasons may remain his own. I cannot give St Vier that assurance. But I will answer whatever else he asks."

There was the message, as clear as it could be: Whatever they can do to me is nothing compared to what they'll do to you. Use me. But Ferris would not come forward and claim Horn's death himself. He wanted Richard to name him before them all, and destroy the swordsman's own credit with the nobles of the land. If he did it, Richard would be forced to turn to Ferris for patronage. The Halliday job, it seemed, was still on.

Richard sat and thought, and for once no one got up to make a speech. He could hear the scribes' rough scratching. Ferris was promising him immunity, protection, and privacy in the matter of Horn. It was as much as he could hope for. But it was only Horn's game all over again: save Alec's life or save his own; show he couldn't protect what was his or show that he could be bought with the right coin. Still, Ferris had made the offer; his hand was "held out to the swordsman." If Richard refused to take it Ferris might see that the law descended heavily on him, if only to secure his silence. The idea of honorable torture was ingenious—though too sweet and rich, like one of their banquet prodigies, the spun-sugar cage with the marzipan bird inside. Whatever he chose, they had him: there was no more to hope for.

Richard stood up. "The swordsman thanks you," he said. "May I ask the noble court one question?"

"Certainly."

"My noble lords; I would—"

But his words were lost in the sudden commotion from the antechamber. Shouts, the clang of metal, and the scuffle of feet echoed between the two oaken doors. All attention left Richard, as startled birds leave a washline. Halliday nodded to Chris Nevilleson, who unlatched the door to the room.

The guards were holding on to a richly dressed man, trying to keep him from entering. He appeared to want to enter on all fours, since he seemed to be not so much trying to escape them as trying to hit the floor. When the door opened his captors jerked him upright. Green eyes stared across the room at the Crescent Chancellor.

"I've dropped it," the intruder said.

Richard kicked over his heavy chair for a diversion. Sure enough, someone shouted, and in the ruckus he could reach Alec, disarm one of the guards and get them both out of there. . . . Then he realized that Alec hadn't even looked at him. Alec was still talking to Lord Halliday.

"I don't know what you feed them, but they're awfully nervous, aren't they? An excitable job, I suppose."

Two more guards had appeared to right Richard's chair and sit him in it. He craned his neck, enraptured, staring at the young nobleman in the doorway. Alec's hair was cut and washed so that it fell in a soft cap around his head. He wore green brocade and gold, and it looked just as splendid on him as Richard had always known it would. He was even contriving not to slouch, probably because he was so angry that he had gone all stiff and straight and precise.

"If they weren't so eager to turn everyone they meet into rice pudding, I wouldn't have dropped it, and then perhaps we could have avoided all this."

Lord Christopher darted forward and picked up the object in question, a gold medallion on a chain.

"Oh, hello," said Alec. "Nevilleson. I pushed your sister in the fishpond once. How is she?"

Lord Christopher looked up into his face and gasped. "Campion! They—I thought you were dead!"

"Well, I'm not," said Alec. "Not yet, anyway. May I have that, please?"

Halliday nodded, and the guards released him.

"See?" Alec came forward, holding out the medallion. "Tremontaine. It's my signet. And my pass. The duchess sent me. May I sit down?"

The entire room was staring at him as he walked to the empty seat between Lord Arlen and the Duke of Karleigh. He nodded courteously to the scribes, and introduced himself, "Lord David Alexander Tielman (I, E, one L) Campion, of Campion and Tremontaine." He waved one hand airily. "It's all in the heralds' books, you can look it up later."

Even Richard could see the fierce look Lord Ferris was giving the newcomer. He thought, If Ferris recognizes Alec from Riverside, there could be trouble. But Alec only caught the look and smiled at Ferris with a private, malicious joy. Then he addressed the assembled nobles. "I am so sorry to be late. It was very exasperating: no one seemed to be willing to tell me where you were meeting. You really should leave instructions about these things. I've seen more of the Hall of Justice than anyone should have to. It's quite tired me out. I hope it will be lunchtime soon. And now, shall we get down to business, my lords?"

They were all staring at him now, even Basil Halliday. Only Lord Arlen seemed to be amused. Arlen said, "You will want to read the notes first, Lord David. I'm afraid we have started without you."

Alec looked at him with the wind, as they say, momentarily knocked out of his sails. Richard's opinion of the unknown nobleman went up several more notches. He was still too stunned to do much more than take in Alec's performance. So Alec was a relative of the pretty woman with the swan boat after all. The admirable duchess with the wonderful chocolate set had sent her young kinsman to his trial. Maybe *Alec*—or, as it seemed, *Lord David*—was going to claim to be the patron in Horn's death? It wasn't completely wrong. The thought of the elegant young noble with the blistering tongue and terrible manners acting as his patron made Richard feel slightly cold. A lot of Alec's outrageous behavior was due to simple fear and some embarrassment. Whatever he was planning to do here, Richard hoped he could pull it off. He had silenced Ferris for now, anyway.

Alec finished reading the notes, and put them down with a brisk nod. The reading seemed to have given him the time he needed to regain his nerves. "I have several things to add," he said, "and not all of them are suitable to this Inquiry. Tremontaine has been dealt several offenses in this case, and would like to see them brought before the entire Council of Lords. I can't be more specific now without prejudicing the case. Also, as some of you know"—here he looked mildly at Lord Christopher—"I'm interested in old books. Some of them actually contain some useful facts. In one I've found an old legal custom called the threefold challenge. It has never been officially rescinded, although it has fallen out of use. I know observance of the old ways is very much respected by some gentlemen"—and the look he gave Lord Karleigh was less mild—"and hope that by bringing St Vier into the hall before all the assembled lords of the state, we could require his patron to come forward by crying it three times."

"It sounds very dramatic," said Halliday. "Are you sure it will really be effective?"

Alec shrugged. "It will, as you say, be good theater. And you wouldn't want to punish the wrong man."

"But," said Lord Montague gently, "can we summon the entire lordship of the city to a piece of good theater?"

Alec's chin lifted dangerously. "You must be joking. They'd *pay* to see this. Two royals a head, and standing room only. Make 'em vote up the land tax while they're all in there. All card parties will be canceled."

Basil Halliday nearly disgraced his position by chuckling helplessly. "He's right."

"And that," said Karleigh, glad to have something to disagree with at last, "is what you think of the dignity of the Council, my lord?"

But in the end, the vote was passed.

chapter XXVI

TWO DAYS LATER, THE DEPUTY OF THE FORT WAS GETTING tired of being beaten at checkers.

"Beginner's luck," said Richard St Vier. "And anyway, we're not playing for real stakes. Come on, just one more game."

"No," the deputy sighed, "I'd better go and find out who wants to see you this time. Don't these people understand, orders are orders, they don't change from hour to hour. But I'll tell you, I could retire to the country with the bribes I'm offered."

"I'm fashionable," Richard said; "it happens."

The cell was full of flowers, like their box at the theater. The gifts of food and wine had to be refused as possibly poisoned, but the clean shirts, bouquets, and handkerchiefs were checked for secret messages and then gratefully accepted. It might be in poor taste to make a hero of St Vier with Lord Horn barely cold in his grave; but the nobles of the city had always been intrigued by the swordsman. Now popular feeling was that Horn's real killer, Richard's patron, would soon be uncovered at the impending Council. Even Horn's empty house was fashionable; people drove past it several times, looking for the wall St Vier had climbed over and the room where It had happened. And young David Campion, the instigator of the exciting proceedings, was very much sought after at the Duchess Tremontaine's—but he was never in.

• • •

Alec spent much of his days lying on his back in a darkened room, sleeping. The duchess sent up trays of exquisite food at regular hours, which he roused himself to eat. She would not allow him nearly enough wine. At night he prowled the house, haunting the library and reading things at random, scribbling notes and throwing them away. He came across an early copy of the banned *On the Causes of Nature*, and read it through twice without taking in a word it said. The only thing that kept him from dashing back to Riverside was the fact that Richard was not there.

Nor was the duchess at home to Lord Ferris. His letters to her were received, but not answered. Once, he met her in a public place where he knew she would be. She was charming but not flirtatious. Her eyes and words contained none of her usual doubles entendres, and she answered his own blandly. He wanted to scream at her, to beat her, to close his fingers on her flower-stalk neck; but there were people present, he dared not begin a quarrel for no apparent reason. Her delicate features and clear skin drove him to a frenzy he had not known in many months with her. He wanted to stroke the tight satin over her ribcage, to rest his hands in the curve of her waist and pull her featherlight body to him. He felt like a poor man looking through a park gate, helpless and unrelievedly unhappy. *He* knew what he had done to offend her; but he did not see how *she* could possibly have learned of it. Even if she had, he could not continue to live with her begrudging him his independence. He had been her willing apprentice for three years now. She had taught him love, and politics. Through her he had become what he was. And he had served her well, advancing her views in Council while she sat at the center of the city, a delicate hostess everyone adored who everyone knew had no interest in politics. . . .

He couldn't remember how she had cast off the one before him. Her love affairs were discreet. The city was full of her friends; some of them, perhaps, old pupils who had left her more gracefully. He had been so sure that Godwin was targeted to be the next one. It had suited Ferris to assist Horn's little folly, to chase him away. If he had been right about her interest in Godwin, then she might well be angry now—although a lesser woman would be flattered at his jealousy. But how did she *know*? She was playing with him. Should he have come to her with an accusation? Waited to be given his marching orders? It occurred to him now that perhaps he had just been given them: not because of Godwin, but because of this young kinsman of hers, the brash young man with the high cheekbones. He looked Lord David up in the Heralds' List and his eyes widened. The bonds of blood were too close, surely. But nothing was sure with the duchess.

Lord Ferris tried through intermediaries to get word to St Vier; but his agents were all turned away, and finally he had to give up lest his interest become known. For some purpose of her own, Diane was sending in her young kinsman to champion St Vier's cause. He had been sure, at the Inquiry, that St Vier had grasped his meaning, and had been about to answer him affirmatively—but then Tremontaine had interfered. He wished he knew what Diane's game was. The simplest explanation was that she wanted St Vier for herself. But Ferris was not ready to abandon his own purpose. Without Diane's support, his bid for the Crescent would be more difficult, but still not impossible. If St Vier had truly understood him, he would have his chance again in open Council to acquire the swordsman's full cooperation. Why, after all, should St Vier listen to Tremontaine's young emissary, who was obviously using St Vier for his house's own ends? Ferris could promise him freedom, patronage, and work. David Alexander Campion was offering St Vier nothing that Ferris could see.

I N THE COUNCIL CHAMBER, WHICH HAD ONCE BEEN THE HALL of Princes, a festive chaos reigned. Every noble in the city who had the right to sit in Council was sitting today—or standing, or milling, leaning on benches to talk to friends two rows over, or calling their servants to fetch another bag of oranges. The mingled scents of oranges and chocolate overlaid the hall's usual ones of waxed woodwork, ceiling dust, and human vanity. The Council was beginning early this morning, and men unused to going without their breakfast were not about to give it up.

The Lords Halliday, Ferris, Montague, Arlen, and the other members of the Justiciary panel were not partaking of the general merriment, or its sustenance. They sat at a table on a dais at the head of the hall with the paneled wall behind them. The Inner Council chancellors wore their blue robes, and Arlen and the Duke of Karleigh were richly dressed for public viewing. Of Lord David Campion there was as yet no sign.

Halliday looked out over the milling throng. "Do you suppose," he murmured to Ferris, "that we could get them to pass an act or two while they're all here?"

"No," Ferris answered flatly. "But you're welcome to try."

"Where's Tremontaine got to?"

"You don't imagine," Montague said, "that he's got lost again?"

"Probably." Halliday glanced out at the crowd of nobles. "Better get started anyway, before they begin having orange fights." He leaned across to his aide. "Chris, tell the heralds to call for silence, and then go and tell the deputy we're ready for St Vier."

Richard and the deputy of the Fort were waiting patiently in an overcrowded antechamber stuffed with guards.

"I'm telling you," the deputy was saying to his charge, "you never saw a set of knives like that foreigner had, each one long as your forearm, and balanced like God's judgment—"

Then the huge double doors swung open like shutters on the confining chamber, revealing a world of immense magnificence: a hall whose ceiling reached up to four times a man's height, studded with tall windows letting in sunlight that gilded the expanse of carved wood above and tilework below. The deputy dusted off his knees, and Richard straightened his jacket before they passed through those portals.

Closer up, Richard had a dazzling impression of ancient oak and freshly gilded scrollwork; and of a vertical sea of faces, bobbing and roaring just like real waves, but multi-colored, as though struck to rainbows by the sunlight. He sorted it out into three banks of seats, filled with nobles, and on the fourth side a raised table behind which were seated the men from the Inquiry. Alec was missing. But Alec would be there; must be there. Richard wondered if he would be wearing the green and gold again. Now that he was allied with the Duchess Tremontaine, it was fitting that he look the part. Richard pictured the clever duchess giving Alec the kind of look she had given *him* at the theater, long and appraising and amused, perhaps saying in her aristocratic purr, "So, you're seeing sense and giving up on poverty at last. How convenient. I have a use for you. . . ." But just what that use was, Richard couldn't begin to fathom. Perhaps she was simply confirming Alec's return to the fold in sending him to Council. Obviously, there'd been some rift with Ferris; maybe she'd decided not to kill Basil Halliday after all, and sent Alec to stop it. Richard assumed that, with the duchess behind him, Alec could save his life as efficiently as Ferris could, and at less cost to himself. He didn't think that Alec would want to hurt him.

They gave Richard a chair facing the panel of justiciars. Their interest was all on him: Halliday's look gravely considering; Ferris's cool; the Duke of Karleigh frankly staring. Lord Montague raised his eyebrows at Richard, grinned, and mouthed the words, "Nice shirt." Behind Richard the stands were noisy with comment. He really didn't like having his back to so many strangers. But he watched the faces of his judges like mirrors for what was going on behind him. Halliday's betrayed irritation; he gestured, and heralds began pounding for silence.

Slowly the ruckus died with a hissing of "Shhh!" and one clear, "They're getting started!" At last the room was as quiet as one so full of living souls could be. Feet shifted, benches creaked, cloth rustled, but human voices were stilled to a soothing murmur. And in that silence one pair of footsteps rang on the tiles.

From the far end of the hall a tall figure in black made its way across the expanse of floor. As it drew nearer, Richard's breath caught in his throat. Alec's customary black was all of velvet this time. His buttons glittered jet. The snowy edges of his shirt were trimmed with silver lace. And, to Richard's utter amazement, a diamond glittered in one ear.

Alec's face was pale, as though he hadn't slept. As he passed Richard's chair he did not look at him. He went up to the dais, and took his seat among the justiciars.

The duchess had advised her kinsman of the precise time to arrive. He had badly wanted not to be approached before the Council began, and not to have to talk to any of the other justiciars when he sat at the table. His seat was between Lord Arlen and the Duke of Karleigh, on the other side of the Crescent Chancellor from Lord Ferris.

The muttering in the stands was rumbling its way to thunder again. Quickly the heralds called for silence, and the questioning began.

Reading from notes, Lord Halliday repeated his questions from the other day, and Richard repeated his answers. At one point someone from the stands called out, "Louder! We can't all hear!"

"I'm not an actor," Richard said. He was snappish because they were making him feel like one. He almost expected Alec to make a crack about throwing flowers; but it was Halliday who told him,

"Move your chair back a few paces; the sound will spread."

He did it, and felt the high ceiling somehow picking up and projecting his words through the chamber. These people thought of everything.

Finally, Lord Halliday addressed the Council: "My noble lords: you have heard the Justiciary question the swordsman Richard, called St Vier, in the matter of the death of Asper Lindley, late Lord Horn. That he did conspire in that death and succeed in it is now beyond question. But the honor of a noble house is a fine matter, and not touched on lightly. We thank you all for your attendance in this hall today, and charge you silence in the attendant threefold question."

He looked over to Lord Arlen, who leaned back in his high-backed chair. Through the relaxation of Arlen's gesture a terrible focus burned; and the hall, feeling it, was still. Arlen lifted his head, and the deep gaze of his old-young eyes seemed to touch all the sides of the chamber, from the solemn men in front to the young men wrangling excitedly in a corner where they thought they would not be noticed.

Arlen's voice was dry and clear. It carried to the ears of everyone. "By the authority of this Council, and of the Justiciary that presides for it, and by the honor of every man here, I charge any man bearing title of the land, whose father bore it and who wishes his sons to bear it, to stand forth now and proclaim himself if his honor or the honor of his house was touched to the death by Asper Lindley, late Lord Horn."

The first time he heard the question Richard felt a chill down his spine. There was not a sound to be heard in the hall, and the world on the other side of the windows had ceased to exist. When Arlen repeated the question, Richard heard shuffling, as though people were preparing to rise, though no one did. Arlen waited for silence before repeating it a third time. Richard closed his eyes, and his hands closed on the arms of his chair to keep himself from answering the challenge. It was not his honor these people were concerned about. And in the doom-filled silence, no one stood forth.

"Master St Vier." Richard opened his eyes. Basil Halliday was speaking to him in a quiet orator's voice that everyone could hear. "Let me ask you one last time. Do you lay claim to any patron in the death of Lord Horn?"

Richard looked over at Lord Ferris. Ferris was looking at him in mute urgency, the lines of his face rigid with veiled frustration. It was a stifled command, and Richard didn't like it. He turned his eyes to Alec. Alec was gazing out over his head with an expression of abstract boredom.

"I do not," Richard answered.

"Very well." Halliday's voice broke Arlen's spell, decisive and normal. "Has anyone anything further to add?"

As if on cue, Alec stood up. "I do, of course."

A long sigh seemed to issue from the corporate mouth. Alec raised his hand. "With your permission," he said to the others; and when they nodded, he went down the steps to Richard.

As the figure in black approached, Richard saw Alec's hand reach into the breast of his jacket. He saw the flash of metal, and saw his own death at the end of the fine blade wielded by the man in black velvet. His hand shot up to turn the knife.

"Jumpy," said Alec, "aren't we?" He held out the gold Tremontaine medallion, and, still a few feet away, tossed it to Richard. "Tell me," Alec drawled; "and while you're at it, say it loud enough for everyone to hear, have you seen this particular object before?"

Richard turned it over. It had been in Ferris's hand, in Riverside, the night they'd spoken at Rosalie's. Ferris had shown it to him to dispel his doubts about going along with the unnamed job. The job which had proved to be the killing of Halliday. The job Alec hadn't wanted him to take. To identify the medallion and its purpose now meant pointing the finger at Tremontaine, in front of Halliday himself.

"Are you sure—" he began; but Alec's voice overrode his: "My dear soul; I've heard a lot of scandalous things about you, but no one ever told me you were deaf."

Or it meant pointing the finger at Ferris. Tremontaine and Ferris had fallen out. Tremontaine would deny all complicity in the Halliday job. Or perhaps . . . perhaps there had never been any in the first place.

"Yes," Richard said. "I've seen it."

"You amaze me. Where?"

The tone of Alec's voice, the showiness of his antagonism, were hopelessly reminiscent of the first time they'd met. Then, his foolish daring and bitter wit had attracted Richard. He knew Alec better now, well enough to recognize his fear and desperation. Alec had come close enough for Richard to smell the steely smell of freshly ironed linen, the citron he'd been barbered with, and, under them, the sharpness of his sweat. Its familiarity made him feel suddenly dizzy; and to his dismay it streaked his senses with desire for the nobleman in black. He dared to look up into Alec's eyes; but, as ever, Alec looked past him.

"I was shown this—the Tremontaine medallion—a few months ago, in Riverside. By someone . . . by an agent of Tremontaine." Richard did not look at Ferris.

"An agent of Tremontaine?" Alec repeated. "Re-ally? Are you sure it wasn't just someone trying to sell you stolen goods?"

He thought, Re-ally, Alec! But that was probably what the nobles believed Riverside was like. "He came about a job for me," Richard answered.

"Was he a regular agent, one you recognized?"

"No. I'd never seen him before."

"Would you know him if you saw him again?"

"Not necessarily," Richard said blandly. "I only saw him the once. And he seemed to be in disguise."

"Oh, did he? A disguise?" He could hear the pleasure in Alec's voice. It felt as if they were fighting a demonstration match, the kind the crowds liked, with lots of feint and flash. "What kind of disguise? A mask?" They both knew what was coming, and it forged the first bond of complicity between them that day.

"An eye patch," Richard said. "Over his left eye."

"An eye patch," Alec repeated loudly. "Tremontaine's agent had an eye patch."

"But then," Richard added sweetly, "so many people do."

"Yes," Alec agreed, "they do. It's hardly enough to convict anyone of falsely claiming to represent Tremontaine in a matter of honor, is it, my lords?" He turned to the Justiciary. "Nevertheless, let's try. May I have the Justiciary's permission to call as witness Anthony Deverin, Lord Ferris and Dragon Chancellor of the realm?"

No one had any trouble hearing Alec. But the hall remained desperately quiet this time.

Ferris rose smoothly and slowly, like oiled machinery. He came down the stairs and stood next to Alec, in front of Richard. "Well, Master St Vier," he said; just that. "Well?"

He was trying to make Richard afraid. Richard felt something mad about the chancellor, even more intense and furious than Alec at his worst. It was as though Lord Ferris did not yet believe he had been beaten, and at the same time believed it so much that he was willing to do anything to deny it.

"My lord," Richard said gently to Alec—and this time Alec could not make him take back the title—"you must ask me what you want to ask me."

Alec said, "Is this the man you spoke to in Riverside?"

"Yes," Richard answered.

Alec turned to Ferris. Alec's body was so stiff with tension that he couldn't tremble. His voice had changed: formal, dreamy, as though he were caught himself in the ritual of accusation and justice. "My lord Ferris, Tremontaine charges you with falseness. Do you deny it?"

Ferris's good eye was turned to look at the young man. "False to Tremontaine?" His mouth thinned in a sour smile. "I do not deny it. I do not deny meeting the honorable St Vier in Riverside. I do not deny showing him the Tremontaine signet. But surely, my lords," he said, his voice growing stronger with assurance as he faced the line of his peers, "any of you can think of another reason for me to have done so."

Richard's mouth opened, and then closed. Ferris meant that he had come to him to have Diane killed.

Alec said it for him: "St Vier doesn't *do* weddings."

The familiar phrase broke some of the tension in the room: "No weddings, no women, no demonstration fights. . . ." Montague rehearsed ruefully.

"Very well," Alec said directly to Ferris, his voice ringing with restrained excitement. "And if he refused the job, which he surely did, why then did you twice send your servant, Katherine Blount, to negotiate with him?"

Ferris's breath hissed sharply through his nose. So that was where she'd gone—to Diane, her rival in his bed. The slut had no pride. But that must be it—how else would Tremontaine know about her meetings with St Vier? Knew it, then; but couldn't prove that *he* knew it.

"My servant." Ferris forced himself to sound surprised. "I see. Then I fear Tremontaine has been misled. Mistress Katherine is herself Riverside-born. I took her into my service to keep her out of prison. I had no idea she was holding to her old ways, her old friends. . . ."

"Just a minute," said Richard St Vier. "If you mean she is my lover, she is not. You should know that very well, my lord."

"Whatever she is," Ferris said coldly, "does not concern me. Unless you intend to produce my servant here before this Council to testify that she was running messages from me, I'm afraid we'll have to let the matter rest."

"What about the ruby?" Alec spoke to Ferris so quietly that even Richard could barely hear him. But the old note of mockery was back in his voice.

"Ah," Ferris began, in stentorian tones for the public. "Yes. The stolen—"

"It's mine," Alec murmured. With an actor's grace and timing he opened his hand, holding it low between his body and Ferris's. The ruby ring blazed on his finger. "Always has been, always will be. I recognized it at once when Richard brought it home." Ferris was staring into his face. "Yes," Alec continued in an insinuating purr, "you're awfully dim, aren't you? I even wore black especially so you'd make the connection. But I suppose you can't really be expected to see things as clearly as the rest of us. . . ."

The insult struck home; Ferris clenched his fist. Richard wondered how he was supposed to keep Ferris from killing Alec here in Council.

"My lord . . . ?" Basil Halliday's voice tried to recall the drama to the public sphere; but Ferris stood frozen by the sudden double vision

of the young man before him as he had been the night of the fireworks, dashing up the Riverside tavern stairs.

*They say he's got a tongue on him to peel the paint off a wall. Richard
says he used to be a scholar.*

Thank you, Katherine. *I've seen him. He's very tall.*

Tall, and much more handsome than he'd been with hair straggling
in his face—dressed in black, to be sure: the black rags of a student,
then. Ferris remembered asking about the swordsman and being told
by a chortling taverner, "Oh, it's St Vier's scholar you'll want to apply
to, sir. He's the one knows where he is these days." And Ferris had
watched Alec go past him out of the door, noted the bones . . . but he
never would have connected that ragged man with the honey-and-
acid creature who'd insulted him at Diane's house.

It was not Katherine who had informed the duchess, then, but her
own kinsman. With his information Diane would have pieced together everything Ferris had done, and intended to do. Ferris wanted
to laugh at his own stupidity. He had been watching her right hand
these last few days, the hand that held his affections, wondering like a
jealous husband why she was casting him off; while all the time it was
her left hand that held the key to his future, his plots, and his mind.

Diane had discovered his treachery, and from her lover and student
it was unacceptable. Basil Halliday was her darling, the cherished
heart of her political hopes for the city. She had already hired the
swordsman Lynch to fight one of Karleigh's in Halliday's defense, and
succeeded in scaring Karleigh off. She would not forgive Ferris for trying to dispose of his political rival. For Ferris to have pretended that
the orders were coming from her was doubly damnable.

He hadn't meant to do it. He'd thought he could convince St Vier
to work for him on his own merits. But when the swordsman had
proved recalcitrant, Ferris had remembered the Tremontaine signet
resting in his pocket, lent by the duchess that night for an entirely different purpose. It had seemed the height of cleverness to show it to St
Vier. He remembered thinking that if, someday, St Vier was called to
trial for the killing of Halliday, the evidence would point back to Tremontaine, and the duchess, finally, would be forced to set foot in the
Council Hall herself to defend her house before Ferris, the new Crescent Chancellor. . . .

Once he'd begun the charade with the signet, giving St Vier the
Tremontaine ruby as well had seemed too good an opportunity to
miss. Diane had tossed it to him one day with a joke about pawning it;
she didn't seem to expect it back. It was Ferris's passion for detail, his

love of dupes and of complexity, and his belief in his own power to control everyone, that had tripped him up.

Now he was caught on the gilded curlicues of his own plots. If he had left Godwin alone, if he had left Horn alone, St Vier might never have come before the Council; and Alec might never have returned to the Hill for help for his lover. . . .

Well, he could still take the blame for Horn's death—it was just that he do so, after all. That would be what they wanted, the duchess and her boy. Lord David wanted to save his lover's life. And Diane wanted her lover ruined. She possessed the means to do it. The duchess had seen to it that a considerable crowd was assembled to watch: every lord in the city was there today. If Ferris refused to act to save St Vier, Tremontaine would reveal the Halliday plot before them all.

W ELL, MY LORD?" TREMONTAINE'S VOICE SPOKE CLEARLY FOR all to hear. "And shall we have to let the matter rest? For you are quite right; I am not holding your servant up my sleeve, waiting to testify against you."

There came to Ferris then one of the moments he treasured. He felt himself standing at the pinnacle of the past and future, knowing his actions would rule them both. And it seemed quite clear to him then that he must take control, and how. He would ruin himself by his own will, his own power, in front of the eyes all perfectly focused on him.

Lord Ferris turned, so that his back was neither to the Justiciary, nor to the mass of men who waited on his words. He addressed Tremontaine, but his words were for all of them, delivered in that carrying orator's voice which had so often swayed the Council. "My lord, you need pull nothing from your sleeve. You shame me, sir, as I hoped never to be shamed in my life; and yet, for the sake of justice I must speak. You may say that I am willing to sell my honor to keep my honor; but to trade honor for justice, that I can never do."

"Interesting," said Alec conversationally, "though it follows no rules of rhetoric known to man. Do go on."

Correctly assuming that no one else had heard that little commentary, Ferris proceeded. "My lords; let the justice be yours, and let the honor be Master St Vier's." Richard felt himself redden with embarrassment. For Lord Ferris to make a show of himself was his business; but Richard had no taste for theatrics. "Before you all, I here freely confess that I did falsely represent myself to St Vier in Tremontaine's name, and it was through my agency that Horn met his death."

And that, Ferris thought complacently, was not even a lie.

Basil Halliday was staring at him in disbelief. All of the justiciars were frozen, silent, calculating, looking at the one from their midst who had stepped onto the floor and broken himself. But the stands were another matter. The nobles of the land were shouting, arguing, comparing notes and comments.

Over the cover of their noise, Halliday said to him, "Tony, what are you doing!"

And, riding the crest of his pure manipulation, Ferris found the delicious nerve to look him gravely in the eye and say, "I wish it weren't true; I wish it with all my heart." He meant it.

"Call for silence, Basil," said Lord Arlen, "or there'll be no stopping them." The heralds pounded and shouted, and eventually some order was attained.

"My lord Ferris," said Halliday heavily. "You take responsibility for the challenge of Lord Horn. It is a matter for the Court of Honor, and may be dealt with there."

But that would not serve Ferris, although the duchess might be pleased to have him swept away under the rug. For his purposes his downfall must be spectacular; something to be remembered with awe . . . something to be returned from in glory. So Ferris held up his hand, a deprecating gesture that made his palm burn as though he held their living spirits in it. Of course they would all listen to him. He had been their prodigy, the bright young man of courage and charm. He had seen to it that they were ready to follow him: he could have had the Crescent for the asking. It would take longer now; but by his very act of abnegation he was already working his way back into their hearts.

"My lords," he addressed the hall. "The council of my peers, the noble lords of this land, is court of honor enough to me. I freely grant that I deserve chastisement at your hands, and do not shrink from the weight of their justice. But I believe that which fated my ill deeds to be revealed before you all has also fated me with the small gift of letting you hear my reasons, the 'cause of honor' that impelled me to the deed, here, from my own lips." The gallery stirred with interest. This was what they had come for, after all: the drama, the passion, the violence; the making and unmaking of reputations in one morning. Almost as an aside, but pitched for all to hear, Ferris pointed out, "In matters of honor, the wise man fears his friends' censure far less than he does their conjecture." There was a ripple of approving laughter at the epigram.

The justiciars muttered amongst themselves, deciding whether to concede the unusual request. Only Alec was worried: Richard knew that look of utter disdain and what it signified. Apparently a speech by Ferris was not on Tremontaine's agenda. But there was not much Alec could do about it, only stand there letting haughtiness mask his nerves. Richard couldn't take his eyes from him, slender and brittle and poised. All that which, in Riverside, coming from a shabby, long-haired academic reject, had inspired men to homicidal rage, was fit and meet in this elegant creature's world—refined almost to a parody, but still within the range of normal. The nobles wouldn't love him for it, but they would accept him in their midst. It was where he belonged, after all. Richard tried to picture Alec as he was now, back in their rooms in Riverside—and felt his stomach clench with an emotion he thought best to disregard. He pulled his eyes away from the secrets of Alec's comportment and back to Lord Ferris.

The chancellor had bowed his sleek head; but his squared shoulders spoke gallantry and a noble determination. Whether from his posture or the pure curiosity his plea invoked, Ferris got what he wanted. In the pause in proceedings while the Justiciary made its decision to let him speak, Ferris had been working out the details of his story; now he launched into it in a new key, not humble but fierce with the desperation of a man given one last chance to clear his name of calumny; yet tinged with the resignation of one who knows he's done wrong.

"My lords," he began again, striding into the center of the floor. "As you know, in matters of honor some explanation is owed amongst ourselves. I give it to you all now, tardily and with some shame. The clear-eyed among you will already have guessed the reason: I called for the death of Asper Lindley, and then hid that fact, to prevent a surge of rumor in which the innocent might suffer. I pray that you will regard it now as I did then—as rumor only; as the malice, maybe, of an aging—" His voice rising, Ferris stopped and passed a hand over his face. "Forgive me. This is not the place to re-fight the challenge. Suffice it to say that I had come to believe that Lord Horn attempted to dishonor a kinsman of my mother's. In his cups, Asper spoke disrespectfully of my kinsman's wife, and even began to claim that the man's son resembled him more than he did his own father. The boy—the young man, I should say, since he was almost twenty-five—was in the city at the time, and I feared . . . what every man fears in such a case. The truth is, he *did* resemble Asper, in looks and . . . other ways."

Ferris paused, as though collecting himself. The hall was stone silent. But he knew each man was going over the roster of slender, fair young men recently in the city. He might have been too obvious already; surely he had provided enough detail to label Michael Godwin as Horn's bastard, forever, in some people's minds. For all he knew, it might even be true. And there it was, his parting gift to Diane; a taint set deep on the man she had dared consider to replace him. Let her work her delicate strategems on that!

Lord David, oddly enough, was smiling as though amused. Ferris looked at him out of the corner of his eye, and was suddenly pierced with the awful thought that he'd got it wrong—that Tremontaine was not really who he said he was; she had deceived him one last time and was taking this awkward beauty to her bed—but it was too late to change his story now. He reined his fancy in sharply. It was his misfortune to be a jealous man. He must not let it get in the way of his next step, the performance he still had to give.

He turned to face the Justiciary, giving his left shoulder to the young man, not to see his face. "My lords," he said in a low but carrying voice, one of his specialties, "I hope that the honor of the court will be satisfied with this. If—"

"Honor may be satisfied," Lord David drawled in interruption, "but Tremontaine is not. If we could dispense with honeyed rhetoric for a moment, I would like to point out that you lied to St Vier, and have tried to defame your servant's name in court to hide it."

Ferris smiled to himself. A young egalitarian. This court didn't care how he used his servants; the boy had been in Riverside too long. If he was Diane's latest choice, she would have a job teaching him patience in statecraft; anyone could see that he *cared* about things too much. St Vier, on the other hand, sat like calm itself, betraying only an intelligent interest. Ferris was sorry to lose him. He had such perfect balance.

"I beg Tremontaine's pardon," Ferris said gravely. "I am not unaware that I have acted shamefully. Other restitution is for the Justiciary to require. As for the rest . . ." A gasp went round when they saw what he was doing. The blue velvet robe, richly embroidered with the chancellor's dragon of the Inner Council, hung loose now on his shoulders. With careful formality he undid the last buttons, and slid the robe of office from his body. Lord Ferris folded it carefully, keeping it from the floor. He stood before them all dressed in stockings, breeches, and a white shirt whose full sleeves and high neck covered as much as the robe had, but to much less effect. Alec had the effrontery to stare.

In a cold and terrible way, Ferris was enjoying himself. It was all politics, after all. With every act of poignant humility, he drew his public closer to him. When he was down so low that he had nowhere else to go, they would be merciful. And of their mercy he would build his fortune.

Deeply he thanked them for permission to resign his office. Courteously he signed the depositions of his testimony. And humbly he stood in the shadow of the Justiciary dais from which he had fallen, while his recent colleagues recessed to decide his fate.

The nobles in the stands were all moving amongst themselves. They were sending out for oranges again. No one came near Ferris and St Vier, marooned in the center of the floor. At last Ferris motioned to a clerk to fetch him a chair. St Vier was paying no attention. His friend had departed with the other justiciars.

It hardly mattered whether they believed Ferris's story or not. They were none of them anxious to punish St Vier, only to fix the blame for Horn's death. With a noble patron standing up in court, all blame shifted from St Vier's shoulders—he emerged a hero, true to his patron's faith even unto death. Of course all swordsmen were crazy. People liked them that way. It had been risky for Ferris to insist on being heard in open Council: someone might easily have brought up the mauling of Horn. But they had respected his humility, or been distracted by it, and no one did.

Expectant murmurs in the stands told Ferris that the Justiciary was returning through the double doors. He waited a long moment before turning his head to look at them. One by one the men took their seats again, their solemn faces telling him nothing. Would they still make an example of him? Had they somehow seen through his pretense? Or were they only suffering from the trauma of his divestiture? Ferris's fingers dug into his palm; he concentrated on keeping them still. His last image must be of meeting his fate with grace.

It was Arlen who spoke, not Halliday. Ferris kept his gaze averted from the still pool of the other man's eyes: he had known them to make men blush before. Arlen spoke of financial restitution to Horn's estate, published apology to Tremontaine. . . . Ferris tried to fight the growing lightness of his heart. Could it be all? Could he still hold Halliday's love and trust? The fool, he thought, the fool . . . and set his face in lines of deep concern. It was a physical effort to keep it so when Arlen finished; as hard, in its way, as lifting rocks or climbing stairs not to break out in a grin of relief.

Before the silence attending Arlen's sentence could be broken, Lord Halliday said, "This is the restitution the Council of Honor sees fit to demand. Let it be so noted. I speak now for the Council of Lords, of whose Inner Council you are late a member. We do not forget the services you have rendered there, or your skill in despatching them.

Although your current position now makes it impossible for you to continue to serve there, it would please the Council to accept your service to the realm in another sphere. To that end we propose your appointment as Ambassador Plenipotentiary to the free nation of Arkenvelt."

Ferris had to bite his lip to keep from laughing aloud—not, this time, in relief. But hysterical laughter was not the correct public response to crushing defeat. Arkenvelt! The journey was six weeks by sea, or three months overland; he would be far from the borders of his realm. The news would be two months' stale, his work useless and dull.

It was banishment, then, and they knew him at last. Banishment to a frozen desert of tribal anarchists who happened to control half the world's wealth in silver and fur. The port city, seat of all major commerce, was a giant international fishing village whose houses were carved into the very earth. He would sleep on a pile of priceless furs, and wake to chip a hunk of frozen bear meat from the carcass by the door. His work would be interceding between commercial interests, helping lost captains find their way home . . . counseling the policies of merchants and of miners. The most he could hope for was to line his pockets with local riches while he waited to be recalled. He could not know when that would be.

"My lord of Ferris, do you accept the position?"

What more could they do to him? What more could *she* do to him? He knew the law; he had Diane to thank for that. But then he had Diane to thank for everything.

He heard his own voice, as if at the end of a tunnel, rattling off the right phrases of gratitude. It was not an ungenerous offer: the chance to redeem himself in a position of responsibility which would, in time, lead to others. If he behaved himself, it would not be long. And they would forget, in time. . . . So Ferris told himself. But it was hard not to give way to laughter, or shouting, to tell them what he thought of them all as they watched his dignified bow and straight back, all those eyes following his slow walk across the echoing floor and out of the door of the chamber of the Council of Lords.

chapter XXVII

IT SEEMED THAT THE NOBLES OF THE CITY WANTED TO CONGRAT-
ulate Richard St Vier. They wanted to apologize to him. They
wanted him to admire their clothes, they wanted to take him to
lunch. He was going to hit someone, he knew he was going to hit
someone if they didn't back off, stop clustering so close around him
trying to touch him, get his attention.

The deputy of the Fort appeared at his elbow. Richard followed the
path his men cleared out of the chamber, into the little waiting room.
There a voice he knew said, "Surely you didn't think they'd just let
you walk away?"

He was thirsty, and every bruise in his body ached. He said, "Why
not?"

"They adore you," said Alec, sounding horribly like himself. "They
want you to have sex with their daughters. But you have a previous
engagement with Tremontaine."

"I want to go home."

"Tremontaine wishes to express its gratitude. There's a carriage
waiting outside. I've just spent a fortune in bribes to secure the path.
Come on."

It was the same painted carriage he remembered handing the duchess into, that day at the theater. The inside was cushioned in cream-
colored velvet that felt like it had a layer of goose down under it.
Richard leaned back and shut his eyes. There was a gentle jolt as the
carriage began to move. It was going to be a long trip; the Council

buildings were far south and across the river from the Hill. They couldn't be planning to drop him off in Riverside, the streets wouldn't accommodate a carriage this size.

He heard a rustle of paper. Alec was offering him his pick of a squashed parcel of sticky buns. "They're all I could get." Richard ate one, and then he ate another. And another somehow disappeared, although he didn't remember taking it, but he did feel less hungry. Alec was still poking around in the creases of the paper looking for dropped bits of icing. Despite the splendor of his black velvet he didn't seem to have a handkerchief, and Richard had lost his somewhere in prison.

"There'll be champagne up at the house," Alec said. "But I'm not sure I dare. I haven't been drunk in days; I think I've lost my head for it."

Richard leaned his head back and shut his eyes again, hoping to go to sleep. He must have dozed, because he didn't have any coherent thoughts, and sooner than he expected they had stopped and a footman was opening the door.

"Tremontaine House," said Alec, stepping down after him. "Excuse me, please, I"—he glanced warily at an upper window—"I have a pressing engagement."

It had, apparently, all been foreseen and arranged. Richard was led, alone, to the kind of room he remembered from his own days of playing on the Hill. There was a very hot bath, which he stayed in for less time than he'd have wished, because he didn't like the servants hovering around him. They left him to dress himself. He put on a heavy white shirt, and fell asleep across the dream-soft covers of the bed.

The door opening woke him. It was a tray of cold supper, which he was privileged to eat alone. He set the tray on a little table by the window, overlooking the landscaped grounds and lawns rolling down to the water's edge. The sun struck the river to burnished brass; it was late afternoon. He was almost free to go.

Servants always made him uncomfortable, especially the well-trained ones. They seemed to be trying to act not like people but like self-effacing automatons that just happened to breathe and have speech. Everyone was always very polite to them, but the nobles were adept at ignoring their presence, and he never could do that. He was always aware of the other person there, the unpredictable body and the curious mind.

The Duchess Tremontaine's people were among the best. They treated him with courteous deference, as though they'd been told that he was someone powerful and important. Keeping just far enough in front of him, they escorted him down halls and staircases to his inter-view with his benefactor.

He didn't know what he should expect, so he tried very hard to ex-pect nothing. He couldn't help wondering if Alec would be there. He thought he would like to see Alec again, one last time, now that his head was clearer. He wanted to tell him that he liked the new clothes. In the duchess's house it seemed less surprising that Alec was a Tre-montaine, as he walked through the ornate corridors whose overcare-ful display seemed to mock their own opulence.

The duchess's sitting room was so ornate that it confused the eye. It was cluttered with intriguing possessions of diverse shapes and colors, all caught up and reflected in the enormous convex mirror hung over the fireplace. On a chair in front of the fire, a woman sat sewing.

Richard saw the fox-colored hair, and turned to leave. But the door had been shut behind him. Katherine Blount stumbled to her feet, dropping her sewing. "My lady—" she said softly, her throat con-stricted with fear, "my lady should be here—"

"Never mind," Richard said, still standing by the door. "I expect I was brought to the wrong room."

"Richard," she said, nervously rushing her words, "you must under-stand—I was told you wouldn't be hurt."

"You can't disarm a swordsman without hurting him," he said calmly. "But I'm fine now. Can I open the door myself, or am I sup-posed to knock and let a servant do it?"

"You're supposed to sit down," she snapped; "sit down and *look* at me!"

"Why?" he asked politely.

She gripped the back of the chair for strength. "Don't you even care?" she demanded. "Don't you even want to know how it hap-pened?"

"Not anymore," he said. "I don't think it matters."

"It matters," she said fiercely. "It matters that Lord Ferris pushed me too far—that I came here to my lady—that *she* sent me down after you. I didn't want to, but I trust my lady. She's been better to me than Lord Ferris ever was. She didn't want to hurt me, and she didn't want to hurt you. But Ferris wanted you to kill Lord Halliday. If you'd done it it would have bound you to him. We *had* to get you out of Riverside, to stand trial before the Council so that my lady could clear you and set Ferris up to be punished in your stead."

"What did she have against Ferris? And does she expect me to work for her now?"

Katherine stared at the overly self-possessed man standing across the room. "Don't you know? Alec is here."

"Oh, I know he's here. He was at the trial." He looked at her. "You should be careful of how you let yourself be used, Kath. Once you let them start, they'll go on doing it."

"It's not like that—"

"Why not? Because she's nice to you, makes it worth your while? Look, I'm all right—but I wish you hadn't done it."

"Oh, shut up, Richard!" He realized with dismay that she was crying. "I thought I'd never have to see you again!"

"Kathy . . ." he said helplessly, but made no move to comfort her. Her nose was red, and she was dabbing her eyes with the backs of her wrists. "I don't owe you anything," she sniffled. "Except an apology—well, you have that. I'm sorry I can't be a tough little Riversider. I'm sorry I let people use me. I'm sorry you got beaten up and it was my fault—now will you please go away and leave me alone!"

He did turn to the door, but it opened and a woman in grey silk came in.

"Katherine, dearest!" said the Duchess Tremontaine. "You made my dear Kathy cry," she scolded Richard, sweeping past him to take the woman in her arms and let her tears stain the silk. The duchess offered her a snow-white square of lawn to use. "Never mind it," the lady said soothingly to them both. "It's all right now."

He realized that the duchess had meant for them to meet this way. Richard stared at the elegant lady busily comforting his friend, and kept his frank gaze on her even when she looked up at him.

"Master St Vier," she said, as though nothing had happened, while Katherine continued to sob on her breast; "welcome. And thank you. I know what you had to do to save—Alec's—life from Horn, and what it must have cost you. And I know you cannot be altogether pleased with my letting Lord Ferris take the credit. You have compromised your position twice to my benefit. I cannot think of any repayment for all this that would be less than ingratitude."

If she was expecting him to thank her in return, she would have to wait for it. Katherine blew her nose on the pristine handkerchief.

"But," the duchess said, "I would like you to have something. A memento only." From between her breasts she drew a chain. On it hung a ruby ring.

"That's Alec's," he said aloud.

She smiled. "No. This one is set in yellow gold, you see? His is white. They are a matched set of twelve, culled from the disbanded ducal coronet. Valuable, and highly recognizable. It would be hard to sell; but it makes a pretty toy, don't you think?" She dangled the chain, setting the jewel spinning.

"You're very generous." He made no move to take it. "Would you be good enough to give it to Lord David as a"—what was the word she'd used?—"memento from me? I think he'll have more use for it."

The duchess nodded, and slipped the chain back into her bodice. "Gallant." She smiled. "What a noble you would make. It's a pity your father was . . . but no one knows who your father was, do they?"

"My mother always claimed not to remember what she called insignificant details." It was an old story; it had made the rounds on the Hill once already.

"Well, then, Master St Vier, I will not keep you any more. I wish you godspeed," she said with quaint, old-fashioned grace, "in all your endeavors."

Richard bowed to both ladies. He followed the servants out of the room and down the corridors he had already memorized coming in.

It was blue dusk in the city. He had his sword back, and a bundle of his old clothes, washed and pressed for him by Diane's staff. The new suit he was wearing, he realized now, was peacock blue—Hypochondriac's Veins, Alec had called it. It fit Richard perfectly; but then, Alec knew the tailor who had his measurements. The cloth didn't look so gaudy out of doors. Now that he was popular with the lords again, he could wear it to their parties. He quickened his step, breathing in deep draughts of freedom in the evening air.

A LEC FOUND THE TWO WOMEN STILL SITTING TOGETHER IN THE duchess's parlor. He burst in without knocking, announcing, "He's not in his room. The servants said he might be with you."

"Oh," said the duchess sweetly, her calm only mildly disturbed. "I'm so sorry. I didn't know you wanted me to keep him particularly for you to see, so I let him leave."

"Leave?" The young man stared at her as though she were speaking gibberish. "How could he have left?"

"I believe he wanted to go home, dear. It is getting dark, and it's a long walk down."

For the first time, Katherine felt sorry for Alec. She'd never seen his face with that raw and defenseless look, and hoped she never would again. "Oh," he said finally. His face closed like a cabinet drawer. "Is that it. I see."

"It's for the best," Diane said. "Your father's getting old. He'll need help with the estate soon."

"He wouldn't notice if the sows started farrowing two-headed calfs," Alec said conversationally. "And don't say my mother needs someone to wind yarn for her, either. She is in the prime of domination." Katherine hiccuped a helpless giggle. Alec's eye fixed on her. "What's the matter with her?" he demanded. "Why are her eyes red? She's been crying— You let her see Richard, didn't you? You promised she wouldn't have to, and then you—"

"David, please," the duchess said wearily. "I was delayed upstairs, and he came too early."

Alec stared at her, his face white with anger. "There was no point to that," he said to her. "None. You did it to amuse yourself."

Katherine's flesh prickled. In Riverside, there would have been a fight. But the duchess turned, still smiling. "You're a fine one to talk, my dear. Don't you do most things to amuse yourself?"

Alec flinched. "It amused you to go to University," she went on pleasantly, "because it gave your parents hysterics. You liked that, you told me so."

"But that's not why—"

"Oh, you could have thought of something else well enough. But that served."

"You sent me the money. I wasn't of age; I hadn't any of my own." Alec's flat voice tried vainly to match her insouciance. "I didn't know which you wanted more—for me to spy on the University people for you, or just to upset my mother."

"Well, you refused to spy for me, so I suppose it must have been to upset your mother. I don't like her very much. I told her she was throwing herself away on Raymond Campion, but she wouldn't listen to me. She thought she was getting a hero, but she ended up with an aging cartographer with no dinner conversation. It has made her very unpleasant. I always could get a rise out of her through you. It's not as if I couldn't *afford* to support you. And there wasn't much she could do if I wanted to let her eldest study and drug himself with a lot of cowherds."

"They weren't—" Alec carefully unclenched his hands.

The duchess made a dismissive gesture. "There's no need to justify any of it: they amused you, and that's quite enough. You see, already you know more about the perquisites of power than most who have it; and when the time comes you'll be able to use your knowledge. They amused you: and when they ceased to do so you abandoned them for other . . . pleasures."

He must have done the same thing to other people hundreds of times: but here he was walking right into her trap, his emotions utterly engaged; reacting with the pain and fury of a man who's been kicked in his soft spot, no longer aiming his blows or planning his strategy.

"You're wrong," Alec said, his voice gruffly musical like an angry cat's. "They were kicked out—for having ideas no one else had, no one else could even understand—all stripped of their robes but me. The school didn't ask me to leave. I suppose no one wanted to *offend* you. I suppose it *amused* you to keep me there."

"You amused yourself, my dear. It wouldn't have been much fun for you to go home to mother, and you wouldn't come up here to me. So you chose to stay; because there were still the drugs, and the people who didn't know who you really were to argue with."

"Can't you shut up about the drugs? They're on the Hill too, you know. But we *did* something with them, we made notes—"

"Was that your dangerous research?" she laughed. "The revelations of drugged sixteen-year-olds? No wonder no one took you seriously!"

"The stars!" he shouted. "Light! Did you know light moves? The stars, the planets are a measurable distance away. They're fixed, they don't move; *we* move. It's provable mathematically—"

"David," she said softly, "you're shouting. Lord," she sighed, "I really don't see what the fuss is all about. It makes no difference to me what the stars do with themselves."

"Politics," he said flatly. "Just like here. It went contrary to the ranking professors' findings, and they couldn't have that."

The duchess nodded approval. "Politics. You should have stayed there. You would have learned a lot."

"I didn't *want* to learn that!"

His voice rang in the gilded reaches of the cornices. The duchess shrugged her shoulders as though shaking off a gossamer scarf. "Oh, David, David . . . use some sense. You already have. What do you think you've been playing at in Riverside? Politics of the crudest nature: the politics of force. And you enjoy it, my dear. But you're capable of more. What about Lord Ferris? You convicted him admirably."

"It wasn't . . . fun."

"Mmm," she nodded. "More amusing when you get to watch them die when you're through with them."

He picked up a green glass paperweight, tossed it from palm to palm. "That disgusts you, does it?"

"Not at all. It's just the kind of charming eccentricity society looks for in a duke. Put down that paperweight, David, I don't want you breaking it."

"You're mad," he said. The edges of his lips were white. "I'm not even your heir."

"I'm about to name my heir," the duchess replied with a hint of steel; "and I'm not mad. I know you, and what you're capable of. I know it to a hair's fineness. I must parcel out the power that will succeed me; no one person can hold it all. You should be pleased; your part is one of the easiest, and you'll get all the money."

"I am not going to be duke," he said stiffly. "Even if you died tomorrow. Or right now," he added; "that would be fine with me."

"Don't be so quick to reject the dukedom, Davey. Wouldn't you like some real power, for once? You could build a library, even found your own University, independent of the city's. You could hire Richard St Vier to protect you."

He turned as though he would have hit her if he'd ever learned how to. His eyes were hot, like molten emeralds, in his white face. "Halliday," he managed to say; "your hope for the city. Make *him* your heir."

"No, no. He has his place already." She rose on a burst of angry energy, strode across the room in a hissing of skirts. "Oh, David, *look* at yourself! You were born to be a prince—you were a prince in Riverside, you shall be so again! I've seen you do it. Just look at the men who love and follow Halliday—and look at the one who loved and followed you."

"And then there's Ferris," Alec said acidly, "who loved you and followed Halliday, with a detour to Arkenvelt."

"Very clever," she answered. "Very nicely reasoned. You should be this clever all the time. It would have spared your Richard a good deal of trouble if you'd been clever enough to tell Horn who you really were when he was stupid enough to abduct you."

"Maybe," said Alec. "But I was hoping to avoid something like this."

"Avoid it?" she said, scorn showing on her face. "Is that all you want—to avoid things? Do you think the world exists to provide a playground for your whimsies?"

He looked blandly at her. "Well, doesn't it? I thought you'd just been telling me to amuse myself."

The duchess's knowing smile was strained. "Ah, so that's what you want to hear, my young idealist. Power for the good of the people; power to effect change; great responsibility and great burdens, which must be shouldered by those with the brains and the skill to use them. I thought you knew all that, and didn't want to hear it."

"I don't," said Alec. "I've told you what I think. I don't want any part in it. I don't know why you think I'm a liar. Even Richard doesn't think I'm a liar. Richard doesn't like to be used, and neither do I."

"And I, too," the duchess said icily, all warmth gone from her, "do not like to be used. You came to me because I could be helpful. You never could have saved him on your own. But my dear child, you can't just turn around and go back now. Surely you knew the risk when you took it. You've lost him. You let Tremontaine use him for its purposes today. He's a proud man, and a clever one. He knows what you did."

He was trying to see past the net she was folding him in, and failing, by the pallor of his face and the dullness of his eyes. But even in his weakness, he had managed to anger her past the point where she should be. And because she was a mistress of men's weakness, of frailty, of uncertainty, she twisted truth around him like a decoy.

"I was going to spare you this," she said stiffly. "I don't want to hurt you—I thought you'd see reason on your own. But come here."

Drawn by compulsion to the scent of danger, he came. She drew out the second ruby from her bodice. "Do you see this? I offered it to him with my thanks. But he threw it back in my face. He knows exactly how we used him, you and I. He didn't want it. He told me to give it to you—as a parting gift. He's through with you, David—*Alec*. So you see, there's no way out."

"Oh, don't be silly," said Alec. "There's always a way out."

He turned from her and walked to the full-length window; and when his hand shattered the glass he kept on walking a few steps more, then stopped. He stood at the center of a storm of broken glass. Shivers of it lay across his shoulders, rising and falling and winking in the light of his slow, ragged breath. His outstretched arm was flowing with blood. He was looking clinically at it.

The Duchess Tremontaine stood, too, watching the wreck of a man through the wreck of her picture window. Then she said, "Katherine. Please see that Lord David does not die before he leaves here."

She turned, and the grey silk whispered that the duchess was leaving, leaving to tend to some other piece of business that required her attention in the house, the city, the world.

She left Lord David Alexander Tielman Campion alone with his bleeding arm and a servingwoman who was ferociously and methodically tearing her petticoat to strips for him.

Finally the blood's flow abated. The cuts had been many, but not deep. "The funny thing is," Alec told Katherine conversationally, "I can't feel anything."

"You will later," she said to him. "When you get home, soak all the glass out. He did give the ring back, but he still wants you. I'm sorry I waited so long to tell you. It's going to hurt plenty, believe me."

"You're upset," he said. "It's a good thing you left Riverside. Don't ever go back."

"I won't," she said.

"And *do* remember to let grandmama bully you. She's perfectly charming as long as you let her."

"Yes—Alec, leave now, before she comes back."

"I will," he said, and pocketed some silver ornaments.

B Y THE TIME RICHARD GOT BACK TO RIVERSIDE, WORD OF HIS release had spread through the district. Already a few of his possessions had been returned; he found them lying piled like offerings in front of his door: a small rug, the dragon candlesticks, and the rosewood box with a few coins in it. He stuck his candle stub in one of the sticks and went inside. The rooms were not much disturbed: some furniture had been shoved around, and a cushion he'd never liked was gone. He wandered the rooms, bathing in the familiarity of shape and shadow. He lifted clothes out of the chest, folded and put them back; puffed up pillows and rearranged his knives. There was very little of Alec left in the house, and he was glad. His circuit ended on the chaise longue. It had been almost a year since he'd sat on it regularly. He stretched out, with his ankles over the edge, and fell asleep.

When he awoke, Richard thought he was dreaming. A tall man in elegant clothes was shutting the door behind him.

"Hello," said Alec. "I've brought us some fish."

T HE WARM SPRING NIGHT CURLS ITSELF SILENTLY AROUND Riverside like a sleepy cat. One by one the stars come out in the clear sky, twinkling cheerily over whatever mischief is brewing below them in the twists of streets and houses there tonight. Under their gaze the chimneys rise up in jagged argument, cold and still and picturesque.

From the celestial heights the arbitrary acts of life seem patterned like a fairy-tale landscape, populated by charming and eccentric figures. The glittering observers require vital doses of joy and pain, sudden reversals of fortune, dire portents, and untimely deaths. Life itself proceeds in its unpredictable infinite patterns—so unlike the measured dance of stars—until, for the satisfaction of their entertainment, the watchers choose a point at which to stop.

ACKNOWLEDGMENTS

This novel would not exist in its present form without the help of more people than I can name on one page. However, I would like particularly to thank

Isabel Davidson Swift for listening and ironing;

Linda Post, Caroline Stevermer, and the rest of You Guys for believing I could do it before I did (or putting on a convincing act);

The Kushner "Medici" Foundation for Assistance to Struggling Artists;

David G. Hartwell for waiting till I came 'round again;

Tom Canty for the jeweled box;

. . . and Mimi Panitch for unplugging the telephone and inventing Writer's Stew.

Ellen Kushner
New York City
1989

Oh, the follies of the young! Elegant and cryptic, yes, but so inadequate is the above. It may take more than one page, but let me also acknowledge the great gifts that *Swordspoint* received in its nativity from my agent, the inimitable Julie Fallowfield of MacIntosh & Otis, who loved the book and believed in it and me when nobody else dared to . . . from Joy Chute, my college writing teacher, who first took me on because, she said, she liked the way I rewrote, and nearly ten years later was kind enough read this in manuscript and assure me that it wasn't ridiculous to take so long to write such a book.

Jim Frenkel was the one who first explained to me that all those short stories I was writing actually wanted to be a novel, and Joan Vinge encouraged me to try it. Eve Sweetser and Alex Madonik patiently awaited installments. Fred Smoler paced up and down his cramped living room, waving a cigarette while expounding on the politics of villains for me. Tappan King said it might be radical, but do it anyway. David Fielder and Jane Johnson shepherded me into the glorious company of Unwin authors, publishing the book first in Britain. David Hartwell was the only editor in America with the nerve to take it on, and has been its fervent champion ever since.

My editor at Bantam, Anne Groell, has been immensely patient as I insist, like James Thurber with *The Thirteen Clocks*, on "tinkering with clocks and running up and down secret stairs" until the last possible minute; and my current agent, Christopher Schelling, has been a friend and advocate of Richard & Alec's for more years than either of us can quite believe. Finally, *Swordspoint* has encountered many kind friends over the years—bookstore people, reviewers, readers of many lands—but none more wise and understanding than Delia Sherman, who long ago bought a first edition, and now walks freely in the City, sharing the author's fortunes there and everywhere that fact and fancy take us.

Ellen Kushner
Boston
2002

AFTERWORD

to the Second Edition

I resolved never to write a sequel to *Swordspoint*.

Right after this book first appeared in 1987 and readers began asking "What happens next?" my standard answer was, "Oh, there's a diptheria epidemic the following year, wipes out half the city. They're all dead. The End."

Silly me. I was afraid of a lot then, especially of What People Might Think. Would I look like I was repeating myself? Or copying other writers or trying to be too commercial . . . ?

I missed them, though. I missed my city, which was, after all, made up of my favorite bits and pieces of every other city I'd walked in or read about: Shakespeare's London, Georgette Heyer's Paris, Damon Runyon's New York, for starters—and the New York I was living in then, where former students could still live in cheap apartments of decayed splendor near Columbia University, sharing a block with criminals and artists and immigrants and scholars.

And I missed my mad, bad boys. *Just once,* I thought, *won't do any harm.* . . . I'll write about them right after the novel's end, but I won't be repeating myself because I'll take on issues that the novel doesn't touch: Richard and Alec's failure to deal with the unpleasant role of women in their society, and a little bit of Alec's family history. I wrote "The Swordsman Whose Name Was Not Death," and it was published in the *Magazine of Fantasy & Science Fiction* in 1991.

I did try to write other short stories, but these characters don't fit comfortably into that format—or I don't. "Red-Cloak" was the very first thing I ever wrote about Richard and Alec (and the very first piece I ever sold! It was published in 1982 by Stuart David Schiff in the Stephen King issue of his magazine *Whispers*). My first novel went through many false starts as I slavishly tried to copy the style of "Red-Cloak" and work in elements of other short-story fragments . . . before finally heading off in a different direction altogether, to produce the novel you hold in your hands.

By 1992 I was hooked; I had started a new novel that begins some fifteen years after this one with the Mad Duke Tremontaine deciding to train his niece Katherine as a swordsman. Shortly thereafter, my public radio career took over my life, as I became host of a national series called *Sound & Spirit*, so I put that book on the back burner. Meanwhile, I'd gotten together with Delia Sherman, another novelist, who admitted to having read *Swordspoint* more than once. We started to play "What happens next?" if only to amuse ourselves on long car trips—but, both being writers, we decided it would be fun to get it all down, so together we wrote the novella "The Fall of the Kings" for Nicola Griffith and Stephen Pagel's 1997 anthology *Bending the Landscape: Fantasy*. That novella became the seed of our 2002 novel, *The Fall of the Kings*. It takes place some sixty years after this book, but many of the people from *Swordspoint* appear in cameo as ghosts or elders or legends to their descendants. Its protagonists are an idealistic University scholar and a troubled young nobleman with interesting relatives. As a writer of historical fiction, Delia was particularly interested in plumbing the country's history to see what sort of past would have evolved into *Swordspoint*'s present, and, as a self-described "recovering academic," she was interested in slamming the University. But no matter how much she begged and argued, I still refused to name the city.

The short story "The Death of the Duke" came to me as a sort of fantasia, a meditation on the ending of one set of lives and the beginning of the next. "Holy smokes!" (or words to that effect) exulted the editor, Patrick Nielsen Hayden; "I've got the Missing Link!" It appeared in his 1998 anthology *Starlight 2*.

I watch myself changing as I get older. I watch the world changing around me, too. Neither of us should be surprised, but sometimes we are anyway. I've stopped worrying about repeating myself. I am eager to explore these transformations—and what better laboratory than an imagined city that already comes complete with its own past and possible future?

So I give up. I love this place, I love these people, and I want to find out what happens next.

Ellen Kushner
Boston, Massachusetts
2002

To justify her passion for interconnected fiction, Kushner and friends have founded the Young Trollopes literary movement (named for the novelist Anthony Trollope), a branch of Interstitial Fiction dedicated to character-based writing, to generosity of spirit, and to genuine affection for both characters and readers. More information at: www.endicott-studio.com.

The Swordsman Whose
Name Was Not Death

AFTER THE FIGHT, RICHARD WAS THIRSTY. HE DECIDED TO leave the parrots alone for now. Parrots were supposed to be unlucky for swordsmen. In this case the curse seemed to have fallen on his opponent. Curious, he had asked the wounded man, "Did you slam into me on purpose?" People did sometimes, to provoke a fight with Richard St Vier, the master swordsman who wouldn't take challenges from just anyone. But the wounded man only pressed his white lips together. The rest of him looked green. Some people just couldn't take the sight of their own blood.

Richard realized he'd seen him before, in a Riverside bar. He was a tough named Jim—or Tim—Something. Not much of a swordsman; the sort of man who made his way in the lawless Riverside district on bravado, and earned his living in the city doing cheapjack sword jobs for merchants aping the nobility in their hiring of swordsmen.

A man with a wreath of fresias hanging precariously over one ear came stumbling up. "Oh, Tim," he said mournfully. "Oh, Tim, I told you that fancy claret was too much for you." He caught hold of the wounded man's arm, began hauling him to his feet. As a matched set, Richard recognized them: they'd been the ritual guards in the wedding procession he'd seen passing through the market square earlier that afternoon.

"Sorry," the flower-decked drunk said to St Vier. "Tim didn't mean to give you trouble, you understand?" Tim groaned. "He's not used to claret, see."

"Don't worry about it," Richard said charitably. No wonder Tim's swordplay had been less than linear.

Over their heads the caged parrots started squawking again. The parrot lady climbed down from the box where she'd escaped to get a better view of the fight. With St Vier there to back her up, she shook her apron at the two ruffians to shoo them as if they were chickens escaped from the yard. The children who'd surrounded them, first to see if the quiet man was going to buy a parrot so they could see one taken down, and then to watch the fight, laughed and shrieked and made chicken noises after the disappearing toughs.

But people made way for Richard St Vier as he headed in the direction of a stall selling drinks. The parrot lady collared one of the street kids, saying, "See that? You can tell your grandchildren you saw St Vier fight right here." Oh, honestly, Richard thought, it hadn't been much of a fight; more like bumping into someone on the street.

He leaned on the wooden counter, trying to decide what he wanted.

"Hey," said a young voice at his elbow. "I'll buy you a drink."

He thought it was a woman, from the voice. Women sometimes tried to pick him up after fights. But he glanced down and saw a pug-faced boy looking at him through slitted eyes, the way kids do when they're trying to look older than they are. This one wasn't very old. "That was real good, the way you did that," the boy said. "I mean the quick double feint and all."

"Thank you," the swordsman answered courteously. His mother had raised him with good manners, and some old habits cling, even in the big city. Sometimes he could almost hear her say, *Just because you can kill people whenever you want to doesn't mean you have a license to be rude to anyone.* He let the boy buy them both some fancy drink made with raspberries. They drank silently, the boy peering over the rim of his cup. It was good; Richard ordered them both another.

"Yeah," the kid said. "I think you're the best there is, you know?"

"Thanks," said the swordsman. He put some coins on the counter.

"Yeah." The kid self-consciously fingered the sword at his own side. "I fight too. I had this idea, see—if you needed a servant or something."

"I don't," the swordsman said.

"Well, you know," the boy went on anyway. "I could, like, make up the fire in the morning. Carry water. Cook you stuff. Maybe when you practice, I could be—if you need somebody to help you out a little—"

"No," said St Vier. "Thank you. There are plenty of schools for you to learn in."

"Yeah, but they're not . . ."

"I know. But that's the way it is."

He walked away from the bar, not wanting to hear any more argument. Behind him the kid started to follow, then fell back.

Across the square he met his friend Alec. "You've been in a fight," Alec said. "I missed it," he added, faintly accusing.

"Someone slammed into me by the parrot cages. It was funny." Richard smiled now at the memory. "I didn't see him coming, and for a moment I thought it was an earthquake! Swords were out before he could apologize—if he meant to apologize. He was drunk."

"You didn't kill him," Alec said, as if he'd heard the story already.

"Not in this part of town. That doesn't go down too well with the Watch here."

"I hope you weren't thinking of getting a parrot again."

Richard grinned, falling into step beside his tall friend. It was a familiar argument. "They're so decorative, Alec. And you could teach it to talk."

"Let some bird steal all my best lines? Anyhow, they eat worms. *I'm* not getting up to catch worms."

"They eat bread and fruit. I asked this time."

"Too expensive."

They were passing through the nice section of the city, headed down to the wharves. On the other side of the river was the district called Riverside, where the swordsman lived with sharpsters and criminals, beyond reach of the law. It would not have been a safe place for a man like Alec, who barely knew one end of a knife from another, but the swordsman St Vier had made it clear what would happen to anyone who touched his friend. Riverside tolerated eccentrics. The tall scholar, with his student slouch and aristocratic accent, was becoming a known quantity along with the master swordsman.

"If you're feeling like throwing your money around," Alec persisted, "why don't you get us a servant? You need someone to polish your boots."

"I take good care of my boots," Richard said, stung in an area of competence. "*You're* the one who needs it."

"Yes," Alec happily agreed. "I do. Someone to go to the market for us, and keep visitors away, and start the fire in winter, and bring us breakfast in bed . . ."

"Decadent," St Vier said. "You can go to the market yourself. And I keep 'visitors' away just fine. I don't understand why you think it would be fun to have some stranger living with us. If you wanted that sort of life, you should have—" He stopped before he could say the unforgivable. But Alec, in one of his sudden shifts of attitude, which veered like the wind over a small pond, finished cheerfully for him, "I should have stayed on the Hill with my rich relatives. But they never kill people—not out in the open where we can all enjoy it, anyway. You're so much more entertaining. . . ."

Richard's lips quirked downward, unsuccessfully hiding a smile. "Loved only for my sword," he said.

Alec said carefully, "If I were the sort of person who makes crude jokes, you would be very embarrassed now."

Richard, who was never embarrassed, said, "What a good thing you're not. What do you want for dinner?"

T HEY WENT TO ROSALIE'S, WHERE THEY ATE STEW IN THE COOL underground tavern and talked business with their friends. It was the usual hodgepodge of fact and rumor. A new swordsman had appeared across town claiming to be a foreign champion, but someone's cousin in service had recognized him as Lord Averil's old valet, with fencing lessons and a dyed mustache. . . . Hugo Seville had finally gotten so low as to take a job offing some noble's wife . . . or maybe he'd only been offered it, or someone wished he had.

Nobles with jobs for St Vier sent their messages to Rosalie's. But today there was nothing. "Just some nervous jerk looking for an heiress."

"Aren't we all!"

"Sorry, Reg, this one's taken; run off with some swordsman."

"Anyone we know?"

"Naw . . . fairy-tale swordsman—they say all girls have run off with one, when it's really their father's clerk."

Big Missy, who worked the mattress trade at Glinley's put her arm around Richard. "I could run off with a swordsman." Seated, he came up only to her bosom, which he leaned back into, smiling across to Alec, eyebrows raised a little provocatively.

Alec took the bait: "Careful," the tall scholar told her; "he bites."

"Oh?" Missy leered becomingly at him. "Don't *you*, pretty baby?"

Alec tried to hide a flush of pure delight. No one had ever called him "pretty baby" before, especially not women other people paid to get into.

"Of course I do," he said with all the brittle superciliousness he was master of. "Hard."

Missy released St Vier, advancing on his tall young friend. "Oh *good*. . . ," she breathed huskily. "I like 'em rough." Her huge arms pointed like weather vanes into the rising wind. "Come to me, lover."

The old-time crowd at Rosalie's was ecstatic. "Missy, don't leave me for that bag of bones!" "So long, then, Alec; let us know how it comes out!" "Try it, boy; you just might like it!"

Alec looked like he wanted to sink into the floor. He held his ground, but his hauteur, already badly applied, was slipping treacherously.

At the last minute, Richard took pity on him. "I saw a wedding today," he said to the room at large.

"Oh, yeah," said Lucie; "we heard you killed one of the guards. Finally made them earn their pay, huh?"

"Thought you didn't *do* weddings. Master St Vier." Sam Bonner looked around for approval of his wit. Everyone knew that St Vier disdained guard work.

"I don't," Richard said. "This was after. And I didn't kill him. Tim Somebody."

"No lie! Tim Porker? Half-grown mustache, big ears? Said he hurt himself falling down some stairs. Dirty liar."

"No weddings for Richard," Alec said. He'd regained his aplomb, but was still eyeing Missy warily from across the room. "He is morally opposed to the buying and selling of heiresses."

"No, I'm not. It's just not interesting work, being a wedding guard. It doesn't mean anything anymore, just rich people showing they can afford swordsmen to make their procession look pretty. It's no—"

"Challenge," Alec finished for him. "You know, we could set that to music, you say it so often, and hawk it on the street as a ballad. What a good thing for the rich that other swordsmen aren't too proud to take their money, or we'd never see an heiress safely bedded down. What's the reward offered for the runaway? Is there one? Or is she damaged goods already?"

"There's a reward for information. But you have to go Uptown to get it."

"I'm not above going Uptown," said Lucie haughtily; "I've been there before. But I don't know as I'd turn in a girl that's run away for love. . . ."

"Ohh," bawled Rosalie across the tavern; "is that what you call it?"

"Speaking of money," Alec said, rattling the dicebox, "is anyone interested in a small bet on whether I can roll multiples of three three times running?"

Richard got up to go. When Alec had drunk enough to become interested in mathematical odds, the evening's entertainment was over for him. St Vier was not a gambling man.

The Riverside streets were dark, but St Vier knew his way between the close-set houses, past the place where the broken gutter over-flowed, around the potholes of pried-up cobbles, through the back alleys, and home. His own lodgings were in a cul-de-sac off the main street; part of an old town house, a discarded veteran of grander days. Richard lived on the second story, in what had once been the music rooms.

On the ground floor, Marie's rooms were dark. He stopped before the front door: in the recessed entryway, there was a flash of white. Cautiously St Vier drew his sword and advanced.

A small woman practically flung herself onto his blade. "Oh, help!" she cried shrilly. "You must help me!"

"Back off," said St Vier. It was too dark to see much but her shape. She was wearing a heavy cloak, and something about her was very young. "What's the matter?"

"I am desperate," she gasped. "I am in terrible danger. Only you can help me! My enemies are everywhere. You must hide me."

"You're drunk," said Richard, although her accent wasn't Riverside. "Go away before you get hurt."

The woman fell back against the door. "No, please. It means my life."

"You had better go home," Richard said. To speed her on her way, he said, "Do you need me to escort you somewhere? Or shall I hire you a torch?"

"No!" It sounded more annoyed than desperate, but quickly turned back to pleading: "I dare not go home. Please listen to me. I am—a Lady of Quality. My parents want to marry me to a man I hate—an old miser with bad breath and groping hands."

"That's too bad," Richard said politely, amused in spite of the inconvenience. "What do you want me to do about it? Do you want him killed?"

"Oh! Oh. No. Thank you. That is, I just need a place to stay. Until they stop looking for me."

Richard said, "Did you know there's a reward out for you?"

"There *is?*" she squeaked. "But—oh. How gratifying. How . . . like them."

"Come upstairs." St Vier held the door open. "Mind the third step; it's broken. When Marie gets back, you can stay with her. She's a, she takes in customers, but I think propriety says you're better off with her than with me."

"But I'd *rather* stay with you, sir!"

In the pitch-black of the stairs, Richard halted. The girl almost stumbled into him. "No," St Vier said. "If you're going to start that, you're not coming any farther."

"I didn't—" she squeaked, and began again: "That's not what I meant at all. Honestly."

Upstairs, he pushed open the door and lit a few candles. "Oh!" the girl gasped. "Is this—is this where you—"

"I practice in this room," he said. "The walls are wrecked. You can sit on that chaise, if you want—it's not as rickety as it looks." But the girl went over to the wall, touching the pockmarks where his practice sword had chipped holes in the old plaster. Her fingertips were gentle, almost reverent.

It was an old room, with traces of its former grandeur clinging about the edges in the form of gilded laurel-leaf molding and occasional pieces of cherub. The person who had last seen fresh paint there had long since turned to dust. The only efforts that its present occupants had made to decorate it were an expensive tapestry hung over the fireplace, and a couple of very detailed silver candlesticks, a few leather-bound books, and an enamel vase, scattered about the room in no discernible order.

"I'd offer you the bed," said Richard, "but it would annoy Alec. Just make yourself comfortable in here."

With the pleasantly light feeling of well-earned tiredness, the swordsman drifted into the room that held his big carven bed and his chests for clothes and swords, undoing the accoutrements of his trade: unbuckling the straps of his sword belt, slipping the knife sheath out of his vest. He paced the room, laying them down, unlacing and unpeeling his clothes, and got into bed. He was just falling asleep when he heard Alec's voice in the other room:

"Richard! You've found us a servant after all—how enterprising of you!"

"No—" he started to explain, and then thought he'd better get up to do it.

The girl was hunched up at the back of the chaise longue, looking awed and defenseless, her cloak still wrapped tight around her. Alec loomed over her, his usual untoward clutter of unruly limbs. Sometimes drinking made him graceful, but not tonight.

"Well," the girl was offering hopefully, "I can cook. Make up the fire. Carry water."

Richard thought, That's the second time I've heard that today. He started to say, "We couldn't ask a Lady of Quality—"

"Can you do boots?" Alec asked with interest.

"No," Richard stated firmly before she could say yes. "No servants."

"Well," Alec asked peevishly, "then what's she doing here? Not the obvious, I hope."

"Alec. Since when am I obvious?"

"Oh, never mind." Alec turned clumsily on his heel. "I'm going to bed. Have fun. See that there's hot shaving water in the morning."

Richard shrugged apologetically at the girl, who was staring after them in fascination. It was a shrug meaning *Don't pay any attention to him;* but he couldn't help wondering if there would be hot water to shave with. Meanwhile, he meant to pay attention to Alec himself.

A LEC WOKE UP UNABLE TO TELL WHERE HIS LIMBS LEFT OFF AND Richard's began. He heard Richard say, "This is embarrassing. Don't move, Alec, all right?"

A third person was in the room with them, standing over the bed with a drawn sword. "How did you get in here?" Richard asked.

The pug-faced boy said, "It was easy. Don't you recognize me? My enemies are everywhere. I think I should, you know, get some kind of prize for that, don't you? I mean, I tricked you, didn't I?"

St. Vier eased himself onto his elbows. "Which are you, an heiress disguised as a snotty brat, or a brat disguised as an heiress?"

"Or," Alec couldn't resist adding, "a boy disguised as a girl disguised as a boy?"

"It doesn't matter," St Vier said. "Your grip is too tight."

"Oh—sorry." Still keeping the sword's point on target, the kid eased his grip. "Sorry—I'll work on it. I knew I'd never get in like this. And girls are safe with you; everyone knows you don't like girls."

"Oh, no," Richard protested, surprised. "I like girls very much."

"Richard," drawled Alec, whose left leg was beginning to cramp, "you're breaking my heart."

"But you like *him* better."

"Well, yes, I do."

"Jealous?" Alec snarled sweetly. "Please die and go away. I'm going to have the world's worst hangover if I don't get back to sleep soon."

Richard said, "I don't teach. I can't explain how I do what I do."

"Please," said the boy with the sword. "Can't you just take a look at me? Tell me if I'm any good. If you say I'm good, I'll know."

"What if I say you're not?"

"I'm good," the kid said stiffly. "I've got to be."

Richard slid out of bed, in one fluid motion regathering his limbs to himself. Alec admired that—like watching a chess expert solve a check in one simple move. Richard was naked, polished as a sculpture in the moonlight. In his hand was the sword that had been there from the start.

"Defend yourself," St Vier said, and the boy fell back in cautious *garde*.

"If you kill him," said Alec, hands comfortably behind his head, "try not to make it one of the messy ones."

"I'm *not*—going to *kill*—him." With what was, for him, atypical flashiness, Richard punctuated each word with a blow of steel on steel. At his words the boy rallied, and returned the strokes. "Again," snapped the swordsman, still attacking. There was no kindness in his voice. "We're going to repeat the whole sequence, if you can remember it. Parry all my thrusts this time."

Sometimes the boy caught the quick-darting strokes, and sometimes his eye or his memory failed, and the blade stopped an inch from his heart, death suspended by the swordsman's will.

"New sequence," Richard rapped out. "Learn it."

They repeated the moves. Alec thought the boy was getting better, more assured. Then the swordsman struck hard on the boy's blade, and the sword flew out of his pupil's hand, clanging on the floor, rolled into a corner. "I told you your grip was too tight. Go get it."

The boy retrieved his sword, and the lesson resumed. Alec began to be bored by the endless repetition. "Your arm's getting tired," St Vier observed. "Don't you practice with weights?"

"Don't have—any weights."

"Get some. No, don't stop. In a real fight, you can't stop."

"A real fight—wouldn't go on this long."

"How do you know? Been in any?"

"Yes. One.—*Two*."

"You won both," Richard said coldly, his arm never resting, his feet never still. "Makes you think you're a hero of the field. *Pay attention*." He rapped sharply on the blade. "Keep going." The boy countered with a fancy double riposte, changing the line of attack with the lightest pressure of his fingers. Richard St Vier deflected the other's point, and brought his own clean past the boy's defenses.

The boy cried out at the light kiss of steel. But the swordsman did not stop the movements of the play. "It's a nick," he said. "Never mind the blood."

"Oh. But—"

"You wanted a lesson. Take it. All right, fine, you're scared now. You can't let it make a difference."

But it did make a difference. The boy's defense turned fierce, began to take on the air of desperate attack. Richard let it. They were fighting silently now, and really fighting, although the swordsman kept himself always from doing real damage. He began to play with the boy, leaving tiny openings just long enough to see if he would take advantage of them. The boy took about half—either his eye missed the others, or his body was too slow to act on them. Whatever he did, Richard parried his attacks, and kept him on the defensive.

"Now—" the swordsman said harshly—"Do you want to kill me, or just take me out?"

"I—don't know—"

"For death"—Richard's blade flew in—"straight to the heart. Always the heart."

The boy froze. His death was cold against his burning skin. Richard St Vier dropped the point, raised it to resume the fight. The boy was sweating, panting, from fear as much as exertion. "A good touch— can be anywhere. As light as you like—or as deep."

The pug-nosed boy stood still. His nose was running. He still held his sword, while blood welled onto his skin and clothing from five different places.

"You're good," Richard St Vier said, "but you can be better. Now get out of here."

"Richard, he's bleeding," Alec said quietly.

"I know he's bleeding. People do when they fight."

"It's night," Alec said, "in Riverside. People are out. You said you didn't want to kill him."

"Hand me that sheet." Sweat was cooling on Richard's body; he wrapped the linen around himself.

"There's brandy," Alec said. "I'll get it."

"I'm sorry I'm bleeding on your floor," the boy said. He wiped his nose with his sleeve. "I'm crying from shock, that's all. Not really crying."

He did not examine his own wounds. Alec did it for him, dabbing them with brandy. "You're remarkable," he told the boy. "I've been trying to get Richard to lose his temper forever." He handed the flask to St Vier. "You can drink the rest."

Alec undid what the sword had left of the boy's jacket, and began pulling out the shirt. "It's a girl," he said abruptly, unsuspecting midwife to unnatural birth.

The girl said something rude. She'd stopped crying.

"So are you," Alec retorted. His hand darted into her breast pocket, pulled out the small book that had rested there, its soft leather cover warm and sweaty. He flipped it open, snapped it shut.

"Don't you know how to read?" the girl asked nastily.

"I don't read this kind of trash. *The Swordsman Whose Name Was Not Death.* My sister had it; they all do. It's about some noble girl who comes home from a ball and finds a swordsman waiting in her room for her. He doesn't kill her; he fucks her instead. She loves it. The End."

"No—" she said, her face flushed—"You've got it wrong. You're stupid. You don't know anything about it."

"Hey," said Alec, "you're cute with your nose running, sweetheart—you know that?"

"You're stupid!" she said again fiercely. *"Stupid bastard."* Harsh and precise, as though the words were new in her mouth. "What do you know about anything?"

"I know more than you think. I may not have your exceptional skill with steel, but I know about your other tricks. I know what works for you."

"Oh," she flared, "so it's come down to *that.*" Furious, she was starting to cry again, against her will, furious about that, too. "The sword doesn't matter to you; the book doesn't matter—*that's* all you can understand. You don't know anything—anything at all!"

"Oh, don't I?" Alec breathed. His eyes were bright, a spot of color high on each cheek. "You think I don't know all about it? With my sister, it was horses—both real and imaginary." He mastered himself enough to assume his usual sneer, passionless and obnoxious. "Mares in the stable, golden stallions in the orchard. She told me their names. I used to eat the apples she picked for them, to make it seem more real. I know about it," he said bitterly. "My sister's magic horses were powerful; she rode them across sea and land; she loved them and gave them names. But in the end they failed her, didn't they? In the end they took her nowhere, brought her nothing at all."

Richard sat on the edge of the bed, brandy forgotten in his hand. Alec never spoke of his family. Richard didn't know he had a sister. He listened.

"My sister was married—to a man chosen for her, a man she didn't like, a man she was afraid of. Those goddamned horses waited for her in the orchard, waited all night for her to come to them. They would have borne her anywhere, for love of her—but she never came . . . and then it was her wedding day." Alec lifted the book high, slammed it against the far wall. "I know all about it."

The girl was looking at Alec, not at her broken book. "And where were you?" she said. "Where were you when this forced marriage took place—waiting in the orchard with them? Oh, I know, too—you took them and you escaped." Holding herself stiffly against her cuts, she bent over, picked up the book, smoothed it back into shape. "You don't know. You don't know at all. And you don't want to. Either of you."

"Alec," Richard said, "come to bed."

"Thank you for the lesson," she said to the swordsman. "I'll remember."

"It wouldn't have made a difference," he told her. "You'll have to find someone else. That's the way it is. Be careful, though."

"Thank you," she said again. "I will be careful, now that there's something to be careful for. You meant what you said, didn't you?"

"Yes," Richard said. "I don't usually get that angry. I meant it."

"Good." She turned in the doorway, asked in the same flat, cold tone, "What's your sister's name?"

Alec was still where he'd been when he threw the book, standing stiff and pale. Richard knew that his reaction, when it hit, would be violent.

"I said, what's her name?"

Alec told her.

"Good. I'm going to find her. I'll give her this"—the book, now fingerprinted with dried blood—"and your love."

She stopped again, opened the book, and read: " 'I was a girl until tonight. I am a woman now.' That's how it ends. But you never read it, so you'll never know what comes in between." She smiled a steel-biting smile. "I have, and I do. I'll be all right out there, won't I?"

"Come to bed, Alec," Richard said again; "you're shaking."

Red-Cloak

I T WAS RAINING. THEY THOUGHT THEY MIGHT GO OUT DRINK-
ing to relieve the tedium, but Alec didn't like getting wet, and
said so. Richard shrugged, and executed a quick series of moves
against the battered wall of their lodgings with the end of a long, well-
polished rapier.

Alec recrossed his legs. "How long are you going to do that?" he said.

The swordsman stopped, to keep from marring the rhythm of his
thrusts. "Until the neighbors get home."

Alec sneered. "Since when have you cared about the neighbors'
complaints?"

"I don't," the swordsman answered. "But they're noisy. I can't concentrate then. When they arrive, I'm going out. You can come if you
like."

Alec sneered again. "And in the meantime, I derive unbounded
pleasure from watching you practice?"

"You could go to sleep," Richard said reasonably. "You could go out.
Or you could watch. You might learn something."

"I've watched you before," the other man answered smugly. "It
doesn't help."

Richard stopped again and looked at him. "I could teach you, you
know. You really ought to learn, now that you're living in Riverside,
abandoned by God and the City Watch. Your books and scholarship
are no help to you here, and I won't always be around. You wouldn't
be that bad, if only you'd practice."

Alec laid both feet firmly on the floor. "Well, I am that bad, and I won't practice. Look, it's stopped raining. Let's go out."

It hadn't stopped raining, but they went out anyway.

T HE HOODS OF THEIR CLOAKS MUFFLE THEIR FACES AS THEY stalk through the dripping streets. One figure is especially tall; his long limbs seem to amble casually, but a practiced eye will note the tension in their swing. He slouches, indicating that he is not the master swordsman of the two: that is the other, a man just tall of short, lithe, and compactly muscled. The one who resembles a cat is the tall one, Alec, because in this part of the City cats are scraggly and lean. Richard cannot be compared to any animal, even the well-fed sleek cats on the Hill: he is a breed of his own, the City Man, who knows his way through every twisted street, and past most of the people in them.

"It's quiet," said Alec.

"It's early," said his companion.

"Where are we going?"

"I thought to Martha's. It's not too crowded."

"It will be once they hear you're there. Everyone will be trying to buy you a drink." The former scholar grimaced wryly at his friend. "It's a good thing, too; I haven't any money."

"So naturally you assume I haven't either. As it happens, I didn't gamble it all away this afternoon, so I'm flush."

"Don't let on; they'll expect you to treat them all."

"No, they won't," the swordsman said. "I never treat anyone, and they know it."

"And still they love you," Alec mocked. "How do you manage it?"

"They don't love me. They respect me."

"They're afraid of you. I'm not. You'll buy me a drink, won't you?"

"I always do."

And so they pass under a low doorway, into the light and the damp smelly warmth of Martha's little tavern, which is to be distinguished from all other such Riverside establishments only by the names of the owner and the regular clientele.

A LTHOUGH HE VERY MUCH WISHED THEY WOULDN'T, AS SOON as Richard pushed his sodden hood back from his face every eye in the tavern fixed on him, then fleeted away, while their mouths were busy working: "St Vier . . . St Vier . . ." Perhaps he should have gone somewhere closer to home, where people had learned the courtesy of merely nodding and looking away. Alec smiled broadly, affably on the assembled company. Richard felt for his sword hilt.

"Good evening, all," said Alec. How he managed to make the words sound like a variant of an ever-popular gesture of contempt was a mystery no one could fathom but everyone responded to. Richard's hand closed on the hilt; but there was no one here he really felt like fighting with, so with his free hand he guided his friend to a table in a corner, out of the way of the crowd.

Alec stretched his long legs out under the table. "No one here," he remarked loudly. "As an educated man, I must deplore the lack of stimulating company. Their deficiencies in your line of competence are all too clear, alas for them."

Richard St Vier stifled a smile. "We came for the drink, not the company," he said. "I seem to recall your saying you were dry."

"Dry? What utter nonsense," Alec returned, "it's pouring rain. Must have been someone else."

They drank beer, this being the only drink at Martha's worth the act. Through half-lidded eyes, Alec watched Riverside at work. A youth was divested of his dagger by one of the light-fingered brethren; the women plied their trade, emptying the tavern, early tonight, because of the rain. . . . The usual crowd of people one knew as a genre; no need to pick out individuals. The new arrivals only added to the dampness and intensified the smell of wet wool. When the stranger did appear, he was so quiet that it took a moment before every head in the place turned, and every eye widened.

It took the tongue of Alec to break the awesome silence. "My, my," he said, still reclining in the corner. "Look at the stuff of that cloak. Five groats an ell, easy, that, and three of them must have gone to the dyer. I do admire a man who can dress."

The stranger whirled at the voice from the shadows, his blood-red cloak swirling behind him. Alec waved one long white hand, but didn't get up. The stranger bowed to him, and the taverners caught the glint of gold at his belt, and the dark shine of his boots.

"Lovely," drawled Alec. "A bit outlandish, though. Or have the fashions changed since I was last on the Hill?"

The crowd, turned observers, laughed at that, not imagining that the lanky, shabby young man ever had been there.

"I do not come from the Hill."

The stranger's first words silenced the laughter as an arrow stops a bird in flight. His voice was a thin harsh whisper that carried throughout the room.

"That's all right," Alec consoled; "you're in good company."

Again the crowd laughed. Richard smiled: it was unlike Alec to have a crowd on his side; he hoped he was enjoying it.

"I come," growled the stranger huskily, "from fa-arther than that."

"Indeed," said the young man. "Then you must sit here—shove over, Richard—sit here and tell us all about it. I may not look it, but I am a man of learning, and I admire the well-traveled."

"I may not sit," hissed the stranger.

"Then you'd better be off, sir." Martha spoke up for the first time, anxious to be rid of this peculiar non-customer.

The stranger ignored her. "I have traveled far," he continued in a throat-grating growl. "I may not rest until I find what I seek."

"Poor man," muttered Alec audibly. At last he set his feet on the floor, and ambled over to the standing stranger. Richard, who had always kept both feet firmly where they could be used, leaned forward. "Confidentially," said Alec, "I doubt you'll find it here." He made to put an arm on the red-cloaked shoulder, but the stranger drew away. "In fact," he continued, "there's very little of any worth here at all, excluding my companion and myself."

The crowd wasn't laughing now. My God, thought Richard St Vier, am I going to have to fight them all besides?

"No," said the stranger, "there is not."

Hmm. Richard calculated the odds. If he's with us now that makes three . . . three to fifteen—well, fifteen and two, actually, unless Martha hefts a tankard, or Alec strangles someone. . . .

"But with the swordsman your companion, I would be glad to hold conference."

"It's St Vier," Alec said blithely. "He doesn't work on contract, and I don't take bribes. But what's the pay? He's expensive, you know."

"Danger," hissed the man. "Perils and horrors such as you may not imagine. Should you survive, you may have your choice of riches and power beyond the dreams of mortal man."

"I doubt it," said Alec. "I am a very expert dreamer. Cash in advance, I'm afraid, though—it *is* St Vier," he added apologetically. "And we've been stumbling around in the dark without candles for three nights, now; you can't imagine the peril and horror of it. Really."

"I know you," hissed the stranger.

"I doubt it," smiled Alec—and flashed one hand out to pull the clasp from the stranger's cloak.

The strange man was all in black, relieved only by the dull glow of gold at waist and neck. His sword was long, and bright as a mirror in the tavern light. Richard wondered fleetingly where Alec's vaunted subtlety had gone; then he was only aware that his friend was safely out of the way of his sword before it met the stranger's.

Riverside fights, even between master swordsmen, are usually played to an accompaniment of shouts, bets, and private tussles from the onlookers. But the only sounds to be heard in the crowded tavern that night were the bump and rustle of the fighters' feet on the packed dirt floor, their irregular breaths—the black man's soft, hissing; Richard's quick gasps—and the swords: talking, quarreling in a furious steel whisper that clashed and rang its way to a shout, and then was silent as the swordsmen circled one another, measuring and feinting, until the swords cried out again. From the circle of rapt onlookers came only the occasional creak of boots or rustle of skirt as someone shifted in place. Once, the fighters came too close to the edge of the ring; a woman shrieked and jumped back, the breeze from Richard's outflung arm fanning her spitcurls.

Even in the cold, hard trial of the fight, the swords never came near where Alec stood, gnawing one knuckle in a show of abstract interest. But the young man's eyes were fixed on Richard, across the room. It was a glorious fight, a rare challenge for the master swordsman; here was the kind of opponent he complained he never could find. And Alec saw the paleness of St Vier's lips, parted, unsmiling.

Even the crowd's rustling stopped when the black man began to fall back before Richard's sword; then they realized what was happening, and a small sigh like the wind ran round the circle. The fighters were too good to finish in the closed space. Smoothly giving ground, the stranger was allowing St Vier to push him toward the door. The circle broke before them: no one wanted to precede the black man out into the rainy darkness.

The swordsmen passed through the doorway without touching it. The red cloak still lay like a pool of blood in the middle of Martha's floor; Alec considered picking it up, and did not. He looked up to see the crowd frozen in the doorway. Muttering a curse, Alec began to elbow his way through them, when a flare of lightning threw the world into blue relief, and a roar of thunder drowned all sound. In its ringing echoes they heard St Vier cry out.

Alec was first to the door. He nearly collided with Richard coming back in. "Did you kill him?"

"Of course."

"Hurt?"

"Not a scratch. God, it's wet out there."

Martha managed to find an entire cup and some beer to fill it with.

St Vier downed it, and sat on the edge of a fallen bench. An onlooker rushed back in from the rain. "Gone!" he gasped. "He's gone!"

"So's his cloak," Richard observed. "Nimble Willy must have slipped it. And someone must have dragged the body off to a nice dry spot, to pilfer the gold. Good work, here in Riverside."

"They're out of beer," said Alec, "let's go home."

HOME WAS BLESSEDLY FREE FROM DRIPS, AND THEY BURNED their last candle.

"You're not saying," said Alec, "what happened when the lightning struck."

"Nothing happened," said Richard. "First I hit, and then it flashed."

"Oh. I thought so. You wouldn't claim another man's victory, much less God's."

"No, it was my touch. Then all I saw was his form, blacker than night against the glare."

Alec looked at him narrowly. "And then he was gone. Was that when you shouted?"

"No," Richard said absently. "Did I shout? I simply came back in."

"You did shout," Alec insisted.

"All right, I shouted. Does it matter? What's bothering you?"

"I touched his cloak," said Alec, "when he first came in. That street's too narrow for a carriage, but he was bone dry."

Richard smiled. "I wondered what had gotten into you. You're losing your head for Martha's brew, Alec."

"I'm not losing my head. And there were flames in his eyes."

"Reflections." The swordsman shook out his arms. "I like that— risking my life for your drunken fancies. Pure quarrelsomeness I can abide, but dry cloaks and flaming eyes are a bit much. Can't you just say you didn't like him?"

"I didn't," said Alec, and they went to bed.

The Privilege of the Sword

*T*his book is
for Delia
and always was

Small pow'r the word has,
And can afford us
Not half so much privilege as
The sword does.

—Anon., "The Dominion of the Sword" (1658)

If the old fantastical Duke of dark corners
had been at home, he had lived. . . .
The Duke yet would have dark deeds darkly answered.

—Shakespeare, *Measure for Measure*, IV.iii; III.ii

All the same, he had no manners then, and he has no manners now, and
he never will have any manners.

—Rudyard Kipling, "How the Rhinoceros Got His Skin"

What a gruesome way to treat one's niece.

—James Thurber, *The Thirteen Clocks*

the PRIVILEGE of the SWORD

Part I

TREMONTAINE

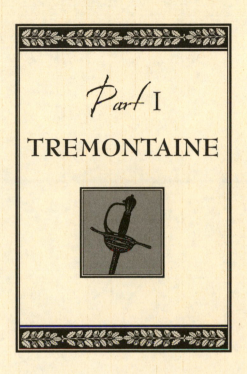

chapter I

NO ONE SENDS FOR A NIECE THEY'VE NEVER SEEN BEFORE
just to annoy her family and ruin her life. That, at least, is
what I thought. This was before I had ever been to the city.
I had never been in a duel, or held a sword myself. I had never kissed
anyone, or had anyone try to kill me, or worn a velvet cloak. I had certainly never met my uncle the Mad Duke. Once I met him, much was
explained.

ON THE DAY WE RECEIVED MY UNCLE'S LETTER, I WAS IN THE
pantry counting our stock of silverware. Laden with lists, I
joined my mother in the sunny parlor over the gardens where she was
hemming kerchiefs. We did these things ourselves these days. Outside, I could hear the crows cawing in the hills, and the sheep bleating
over them. I wasn't looking at her; my eyes were on the papers before
me, and I was worrying about the spoons, which needed polishing, but
we might have to sell them, so why bother now?

"Three hundred and thirteen spoons," I said, consulting the lists.
"We're short three spoons from last time, Mother."

She did not reply. I looked up. My mother was staring out the window and gnawing on one end of her silky hair. I wish I had hair like
that; mine curls, in all the wrong ways. "Do you think," she said at
last, "that we should have that tree taken down?"

"We're doing silver inventory," I said sternly, "and we're short."

"Are you sure you have the right list? When did we count them last?"

"Gregory's Coming-of-Age party, I think. My hands smelt of polish all through dinner. And he never even thanked me for it, the pig."

"Oh, Katherine."

My mother has a way of saying my name as though it were an entire speech. This one included *When will you* and *How silly* and *I couldn't do without you* all at once. But I wasn't in the mood to hear it. While it must be done and there is no sense shirking, counting silver is not my favorite chore, although it ranks above fine needlework and making jam.

"I bet no one likes Greg there in the city, either, unless he's learned to be nicer to people."

There was a sudden jerky movement as she set her sewing down. I waited to be chastised. The silence became frightening. I looked to see that her hands were clutching the work down in her lap, regardless of what that was doing to the linen. She was holding her head very high, which was a mistake, because the moment I looked I knew from the set of her mouth and the wideness of her eyes that she was trying not to cry. Softly I put down my papers and knelt at her side, nestling in her skirts where I felt safe. "I'm sorry, Mama," I said, stroking the fabric. "I didn't mean it."

My mother twisted her finger in a lock of my hair. "Katie . . ." She breathed a long sigh. "I've had a letter from my brother."

My breath caught. "Oh, no! Is it the lawsuit? Are we ruined?"

"Quite the contrary." But she didn't smile. The line that had appeared between her brows last year only got deeper. "No, it's an invitation. To Tremontaine House."

My uncle the Mad Duke had never invited us to visit him. It wouldn't be decent. Everyone knew how he lived. But that wasn't the point. The point was that almost since I was born, he had been out to ruin us. It was utterly ridiculous: when he had just inherited vast riches from their grandmother, the Duchess Tremontaine, along with the title, he started dickering over the bit of land my mother had gotten from their parents for her dowry—or rather, his lawyers did. The points were all so obscure that only the lawyers seemed to understand them, and no one my father hired could ever get the better of them. We didn't lose the land; we just kept having to sink more and more money into lawyers, while the land my uncle was contesting went into a trust that made it unavailable to us, along with its revenues, which made it even harder to pay the lawyers. . . .

I was quite small, but I remember how awful it always was when the letters came, heavy with their alarming seals. There would be an hour or two of perfect, dreadful stillness, and then everything would explode. My father would shout all sorts of things at my mother about her mad family, and why couldn't she control them all, he might as well have married the goosegirl for all the good she did him! And she would cry it wasn't her fault her brother was mad, and why didn't he ask her parents what was wrong with the contract instead of badgering her, and hadn't she done her duty by him? I heard quite a lot of this because when the shouting started she would clutch me to her, and when it was over she and I would often sneak off to the pantry and steal a pot of jam and eat it under the stairs. At the dinner table my father would quarrel with my older brothers about the cost of Greg's horses or Seb's tutors, or what they should plant in the south reach, or what to do about tenants poaching rabbits. I was glad I was too young for him to pay much attention to; only sometimes he would take my face in his big hands and look at me hard, as if he were trying to find out which side of the family I favored. "You're a sensible girl," he'd say hopefully. "You're a help to your mother, aren't you?" Well, I tried to be.

Father died suddenly when I was eleven. Things got much quieter then. And just as suddenly, the lawsuits stopped as well. It was as if the Mad Duke Tremontaine had forgotten all about us.

Then, about a year ago, just when we had begun to stop counting every copper, the letters started coming again, with their heavy seals. It seemed the lawsuit was back.

My brother Sebastian begged to be allowed to go to the city to study law at University, but Seb was needed at home; he was much too clever about land and farming and things. Instead Gregory, who was Lord Talbert now, went to the city to find us new lawyers, and take his place on the Council of Lords. It was expensive having him there, and we were once again without the revenue from my mother's portion. If we didn't sell the spoons, we were going to have to sell some of my father's land, and everyone knows once you start chipping away at your estate, you're pretty much done for.

And now here was the Mad Duke, actually inviting us to the city to be his guests at Tremontaine House. My mother looked troubled, but I knew such an invitation could mean only one thing: an end to the horrible lawsuits, the awful letters. Surely all was forgiven and forgotten. We would go to town and take our place amongst the nobility there at last, with parties and dancing and music and jewels and clothes—I threw my arms around my mother's waist, and hugged her warmly. "Oh, Mama! I knew no one could stay angry with you forever. I am so happy for you!"

But she pulled away from me. "Don't be. The entire thing is ridiculous. It's out of the question."

"But—don't you wish to see your brother again? If I hadn't seen Greg or Seb for twenty years, I'd at least be curious."

"I know what Davey's like." She twisted the handkerchief in her hand. "He hasn't changed a bit. He fought with our parents all the time . . ." She stroked my hair. "You don't know how lucky you are, Kitty, to have such a kind and loving family. I know Papa was sometimes harsh, but he did care for all of us. And you and I have always been the best of friends, haven't we?"

I nodded.

"Davey and I were like that. Friends. Good friends, together against the world. We made up games, and protected each other. But people grow up, don't they? You can't stay a child forever. When my parents chose a husband for me, we were—he was—well, Davey just didn't understand that things must change."

"He hated Papa, didn't he?"

"He was only a boy; what did he know? Charles was a neighbor, not some stranger. My parents trusted him and knew he'd take good care of me. Of course I shed a few tears; I was a young girl, afraid to leave my home for the first time. My brother, though—well, he simply could not understand that, in the end, one has a duty to one's family. He never did, and he never will."

She was going to ruin that cloth, but I didn't want to stop her flow of words. A lot had happened in our family that no one had ever explained to me.

"And now it's the same thing all over again!" she cried, ripping the hem without seeing it. "Just when we thought things were about to get better, he went and made them worse, much worse, to please himself and hurt the rest of us. Just the same as now."

She started stabbing at the kerchief with her needle. "How?" I breathed, hoping to still her hands, hoping to keep the words coming. "How is it the same?"

"The duchess," my mother said, her lips tight. She wasn't even seeing me, I could tell; her eyes were on an invisible past when everything had gone wrong before I was born. "Our grandmother, the noble Duchess Tremontaine. Who didn't even come to my wedding; she still wasn't speaking to our mother. But she invited my brother to the city, to stay with her at Tremontaine House. It was his big chance—

our big chance—to reconcile with her, to make something of himself. And what did he do? He ran away."

"Where?"

"To University." She bit a thread in half. "Right there in the city, right under the duchess's very nose. Mother was beside herself. Gregory had just been born, and I had to leave him here all alone with your father and the servants to go and tend to her. You know what she was like." I nodded; Grandmother Campion had been terrifying. "Next we heard, he'd run away from University as well, gone to live in some city slum. We were sure he was dead. But he wasn't dead. He was bringing more shame on us by carrying on with a notorious swordsman. It all came out when the duchess found him. I suppose he amused her, because a few years later she died, naming him her heir! Mother wrote him a long letter, and sent him some things, but he never replied."

"Go and see him," I urged her poetically. "Who knows but that he may yet relent, and remember the days of his youth, when you were the best of friends?"

"Katherine Samantha." She looked away from the past, and directly at me. "You have not been listening to what I've been telling you. It's you he wishes to see."

"Me! But—but— Why?"

She shook her head. "Oh, it's too ridiculous even to contemplate."

"Mother." I took both her hands in mine. "You cannot say that and expect me to go on counting silver as if nothing had happened. It is impossible. What does he want to see me about?"

"He says he wants to make a swordsman of you."

I laughed—well, I snorted, actually. If I'd had anything in my mouth, it would have flown across the room. That sort of laugh.

"Just so," she said. "You go live with him and study the sword, and in return he'll not only drop the lawsuits, he'll pay off all our debts, and—well, he's prepared to be very generous."

I began to see, or thought I did. "He wants me to come to the city. To Tremontaine House," I breathed. "To make our fortune."

She said, "Of course, the thing is impossible."

"But Mother," I said, "what about my duty to my family?"

chapter II

Y OU HAVE NO USE FOR GIRLS. YOU TOLD ME SO YOURSELF."
In a fine room in the Mad Duke Tremontaine's house, a fat
and messy young woman sprawled on a velvet chaise longue,
one hand buried in a bowl of summer strawberries. Across the room,
the Mad Duke examined the back of his chimneypiece for cracks.
"Utter incompetents," he grumbled. "They wouldn't know wood-bore
from a tick on their dog's ass."

She stuck to the subject. "Neither would girls."

"I *do* have no use for girls. Not that way; not with ones I'm related
to, anyway." He popped out of the fireplace to leer briefly, but getting
no response went back and continued, "You should be grateful. Or, as
the only respectable female of my acquaintance, you are the one I
would have to impose upon to escort my niece to dances and things
when she gets here."

The homely woman, whose name was Flavia, but whom everyone
thought of as That Ugly Girl of the Duke's, put a large berry in her
mouth, wiped her fingers on the velvet of the chaise and talked
around it. "Any titled lady whose husband owes you money would be
delighted to take your niece in hand, if only to show you how it's done
properly and try to instill some gratitude in you." She licked juice off
her lips. "You know, I've been meaning to ask you: why do you talk so
much, when half of what you say is utter crap?"

"To keep you on your toes," he answered promptly. "How would you like it if everything I said suddenly started making sense? It would only confuse you."

Unfolding his long body from the guts of the fireplace, the duke thrust his ruffled cuffs under his fat friend's nose for inspection. "Would you say these are dirty?"

"*Dirty* is not the word I would use." She stared at the lace. "That implies that somewhere under the carbon there exists white linen in its original state. But I think an alchemical transformation has been effected here."

"At last!" He lunged for the bellpull. "I shall have to document it." His fingers left black smudges on the embroidered fabric. "You will be amazed to learn that I, too, have read Fayerweather. You have, as usual, completely bollixed his concept of Original State: it has nothing to do with alchemy."

"Did I quote Fayerweather?"

"No. You eviscerated him, and threw his carcass to the geese."

The duke's summons was answered by a stocky boy. Everything about him was middling: his height, weight, color and curl of hair, skin, ears, even his deportment, caught as it was in the middle between a boy's awkwardness and a young man's strength. His arms were a little long, but that was all.

"Isn't he wonderful?" the duke asked fondly.

The Ugly Girl threw a strawberry at the boy, which he failed to catch; nor did he run after it to pick it up when it rolled into a corner. "Dear one," she said to the duke, "you could surround yourself with much prettier company than those present."

"I do," he replied. "But they have a tendency to think too highly of themselves. So I get rid of them. Over and over and over and over," he sighed. "Marcus," he told the boy, "get me a clean shirt."

"Yes, my lord."

The duke pulled the one he was wearing over his head. "And have this one examined—the cuffs—for alchemical transformation."

"Yes, my—" The boy's face bent and broke into a laugh. "Do you mean it?"

The duke tilted his head to one side. "Hmm. Do I? I'm not sure. It was *her* idea. *Do* I mean it?"

The Ugly Girl rolled onto her back, gazing nearsightedly at the elaborate blur of the sculpted ceiling above her. "You never mean anything."

When the boy had left the room, she said approvingly, "He's got brains. It's funny how you can always tell."

"Like calling to like." It was as close to a compliment as the duke ever came; she wisely ignored it. "Well, as you pointed out, I hardly chose him for his beauty."

"I'm surprised you chose him at all. He lacks the aura of great wickedness, or great innocence. You like extremes."

"I do." The duke helped himself to the strawberries; they were his, after all. He ate them one at a time, in the manner of one who is not used to plenty.

Making sure that her fingers were well licked and dried, the Ugly Girl went to take a book from the pile on the mantelpiece. She sat by the window reading her treatise on mathematics, ignoring the duke as he received and donned his new shirt, received and interviewed an informant (who was not offered strawberries), received and made fun of a small but very ugly lamp meant as a bribe and finally went back to his fireplace excavations.

Then she lifted her head and announced, "I have thought of and discarded many conceivable reasons for you to have sent for your niece. It therefore remains that your reason is inconceivable."

"To any but me, of course."

She waited an appreciable amount of time before giving in and asking, "May one hear it?"

"I intend to make a swordsman of her."

The Ugly Girl slammed the book shut. "That tears it. That is idiotic. Possibly the stupidest thing that I have ever heard you say."

"Not at all." The duke could appear quite elegant when he chose to. He did so now, lounging in his wide shirtsleeves against the ornate mantel. "I must have protection. Someone I can trust. Of course I have a lot of hired guards—but I am paying them. And I do not like the constant company of strangers."

"You could hire handsome ones. They need not be strangers long."

"I do not think," drawled the duke at his most stickily aristocratic, "that that is very appealing. And yet—I must constantly be protected from the sudden sword-thrust, the irrevocable challenge. There are so many people around who imagine their lives would be miraculously improved by my removal. So: who better to fulfill the protective function than family?"

"Surely you have nephews?"

"Whole flotillas of them. So what?"

Not being the sort to throw a book, she pounded her fist on her cushion. "So *what*, indeed! Not content to find freaks, you must create them as well?"

The duke did not try, ever, to hide his contented smile. "I do not make the rules," he said creamily. "This annoys me, and so I comfort myself by breaking them. She is my favorite sister's—my only sister's—youngest child. I shall ensure that she has a distinctive and useful trade to follow, should the family fortunes fail. Or should the Good Marriage that is every noble's daughter's ambition prove elusive or less than satisfactory. A distinctive and a useful trade . . . it is, alas, too late for her older brothers to learn anything, really. And, anyway, I think one sword in the family is enough, don't you?"

"Crap," she said. "Utter crap. You must really hate your sister a lot."

I HAD ALWAYS KNOWN I MUST GO TO THE CITY, BECAUSE THAT IS where one goes to make one's fortune these days. Men go there to take their seat on the Council of Lords and meet influential people; girls go to make a brilliant match with a man of property and excellent family. We had scraped together the funds to send my eldest brother, but apart from writing the occasional letter complaining about the food, the streets, the weather and the people, Gregory didn't seem to be doing much. I wasn't surprised. Greg always lacked dash.

I, on the other hand, while not quite pretty, look very nice when I get dressed up, and neighbors at parties have been known to admire my dancing. I always remember the steps, and never tread on toes or bump into others. Before my uncle's letter came, I had often tried to encourage my mother to send me to town to try my luck at finding a good match. But no matter how I begged and reasoned, it always ended with her saying, "Kitty, you're too young," which was ridiculous, since she was married herself at fifteen. If I explained that a dazzling City Season was completely different from one's mother picking a convenient neighbor, she'd say, "Well, but what man would have you with your portion tied up in a lawsuit?"

"A very rich one, of course, who cares nothing for my sad estate! I will enchant him. He will love me for my winning ways. And for my connections. I'm very well connected, aren't I? Your brother's still a duke, even if he is mad and dissolute. That counts, you said."

"But think how much more enchanting you will be when you have reached your full height, and gotten all willowy and elegant, dressed up in long gowns with real lace—"

"And a train! I must have a train, for staircases, mustn't I, Mother? And a peacock feather fan, and shoes with glittery buckles and a velvet cape." I knew that was all I needed to break anyone's heart. Let me appear on the right staircase just once in a velvet cape, and I was a made woman.

Now I was headed for one of the most glorious houses in the city, at the invitation of Duke Tremontaine himself. The lawsuit would be withdrawn, my dowry restored, if not, indeed, doubled. I was sure he had a staircase.

So there I was in the carriage, hurtling toward the city, my expectations high. The letter had included all sorts of bizarre rules I was to follow once I got there, like not writing or receiving any letters from family for six months, but that wasn't forever. I had no doubt that I was doing the right thing, and that all would be well. My uncle might have quarreled with the rest of the family, but he'd never met me. Of course I would have to prove myself to him at first; that's why he had set up the rules. I was going to be tested for courage, for endurance, for loyalty and other virtues. Once I had demonstrated my worthiness, I would be revealed to the world in my true guise and reap the rewards. The masked ball would turn to wedding feast, the silly comedy to glorious romance with myself as heroine. First disguise, then revelation. That was how it worked. What else could the story possibly be?

It was not at all the way I had ever planned to go to the city, but at least I was going. If my mad uncle wanted me to learn to use a sword, fine, as long as I would also attend balls and meet eligible men. The important thing was, he was inviting me to join his household. The Duke Tremontaine wanted me by his side, and the world was open to me.

chapter III

A YOUNG GIRL STEPS OUT OF A TRAVELING CARRIAGE INTO A courtyard already in shadow. But all above her, the house's high windows glitter with the last golden rays of the sun.

She is wrapped in a simple grey wool traveling cloak. As she looks up at the house's glorious facade of honey-colored stone and many-paned glass, she furls a corner of the cloak like a ballgown, and slowly pivots in place.

M Y UNCLE THE MAD DUKE LOOKED ME UP AND DOWN.
"You aren't very tall," he said.

Beyond his face I could see his back reflected in the convex mirror over the fireplace, so that he swallowed up the room.

"No, sir."

It was a delicious room, painted blue and white with touches of gold; very modern, very airy, filled with pictures on the walls and curios scattered on little tables that seemed to have no other purpose but to hold them. Tall glass doors opened onto gardens overlooking the river.

He said, "This is Tremontaine House. It is very elegant. I inherited it from my grandmother, the last duchess." When he mentioned her, the planes of his face hardened in distaste. I recognized the expression from many family dinners of our own. My uncle's face kept turning familiar, as though I'd known him all my life. A tilt of the head, a flick of the eye—I knew him—and then it was gone, and I was confronting a fearsome stranger. He had my mother's long brown hair, which looked very odd. I thought only students had long hair. He'd been a student once, but surely that was long ago.

"But you need not dress for dinner," the duke said. "Nor for much of anything, really." He drifted off, his attention caught by a china statuette on a little table. I had never been so effortlessly ignored; it was as if I'd disappeared, as if his attention could only hold one thing at a time. He picked the china up, and brought it close to his eye to examine its gilded curlicues in the light.

"I did bring nice dresses," I said. He'd almost beggared us, but he needn't think I could not dress for dinner.

"Did you?" my uncle asked idly. "Why?"

"Why?" I repeated. "To—well, to wear." His attention returned to the statue in his hands. The duke had very long, graceful hands; just the sort I've always wanted, only bigger, and studded with jeweled rings: a whole fortune, riding on one hand. This ill-mannered, well-dressed man, the monster of the family stories, was like nothing I'd ever seen before. I had no idea what he was going to do next—and, I reminded myself, I mustn't anger him. The family fortunes were at stake. But how to make him like me? I should try being more modest, and display maidenly virtue.

"I'm sure they're not in style," I said humbly, "but I could make my dresses over, if someone will show me. I do know how to sew, although I'm not very accomplished."

He finally turned his head and looked at me. "Oh, I wouldn't worry about that. Dresses. You won't be needing any."

Finally! I thought. I'd been right about one thing: the duke was going to dip into his coffers to provide me with a whole new wardrobe. I remembered my manners and said, "Thank you. That's very generous of you."

His long mouth quirked in a half-smile. "We'll see about that. Anyhow, I've arranged for your training to begin tomorrow. You will be living here at Tremontaine House for a while. I don't like it here. I'll be at the Riverside house. Unless I change my mind. I've got you a ladies' maid, and a teacher . . . and there are books and things. You won't be bored." He paused, and added coolly, "And if anyone tries to bother you—just tell them I've said not to."

I was gone again; I could see it on his face. He subsided into an arm-chair. How was I going to charm him with my winning ways if he wouldn't even look at me? Of no use now, the pretty speeches I'd planned in the carriage mile after mile. I stared at the elegant figure. It didn't seem rude, since by his lights I wasn't there at all. The duke had ivory-pale skin, long brown hair and long, thinly-lidded eyes and a long, rather pointed nose. He was perfectly real: I could see the fine lines in the corners of his eyes and mouth, hear him breathe, feel him shift his weight when he moved. But he was still like something in a dream. My uncle the Mad Duke.

He looked up, surprised to find me still there. "I should think," he said, in a slow, drawling purr, "that you would want to go to your room now . . ." It was one of the most unpleasant things an adult had ever said to me, awash in surprised scorn: " . . . after the carriage ride, and having to talk to me."

I risked a smile, in case he was joking. But he did not smile back.

"I don't know where it is," I finally said.

He waved one arm through the air. "Neither do I. Looking over the river, I think: it might smell a bit in summer, but the view is better." He reached out and found a bellpull. "What was your name, again?"

If he hadn't seemed simply not to care, I might have lost my temper. Still: "Campion," I said icily. "Like yours. It's Katherine Samantha Campion Talbert, in full."

He was seeing me again. The duke leaned toward me. His eyes were green, fringed with dark lashes. For the first time, his face was edged with humor. "I have been the Duke Tremontaine for something like fifteen years now," my uncle said. I didn't see what he found funny about that. "Do you know what my real name is?"

It seemed important to know it. As if, by knowing it, I might prove to him that I was real. Put all his names together, and I might come to some understanding that would tell me what he wanted.

I stared back at him. As if we were mirrors of each other, I felt curiosity, and fear, and excitement—and did not know whether those feelings were his, or my own.

"I know two of them," I said. *Campion*, and the one my mother had called him. "Three, if you count Tremontaine. I can ask my mother for the rest."

"No, you can't. Not for six months, anyway." The duke swung himself round in the chair, hooking his long legs over one arm in the graceless sprawl of a child settling down with a book. "Don't you read your contracts before you sign them?"

"I couldn't sign. I'm not of age."

"Ah, of course. Your family took care of all that for you." He swung back around to face me, with an expression on his face that made me feel cold all over. "Do you understand the terms?" he demanded. "Did she even tell you? Or did they just send you here like some sacrificial goat to buy me off?"

I met his fierce gaze, although I hated doing it. "I know about the swords," I told him, "and the six months. I have to do what you say, and wear the clothes you give me. Of course they told me. I'm not a goat."

"Good." He swung away, satisfied.

A very handsome man with short blond curls and a snub nose came into the room. He walked right past me without a glance, and leaned over my uncle's chair. He leaned down farther and farther, and my uncle reached up one arm and put it behind the man's head, and pulled him down farther still.

There was no mistaking the meaning of that kiss. This was one, just one of the many reasons my uncle the Mad Duke was not considered fit to know. I could not stop looking.

And I saw the beautiful man as he came up for air cast me a triumphant glance.

He murmured to the duke so I could hear, "Having truck with serving girls, this time?" I tugged at my dress to smooth it. It was not cheap cloth by any means, even if it was plain.

The duke hauled himself up in the chair to a level nearer dignity. "I am dismayed, Alcuin," he said in that unpleasantly smooth voice, "that you do not immediately note the resemblance. This is my niece, my only sister's youngest and dearest child. She will be staying here awhile, so you had better keep a civil tongue around her, or you will not be."

"I *beg* your pardon," said the beautiful Alcuin. "I see it now, of course—a certain, ah, cruelty about the mouth. . . ."

It took all my self-control to keep from wiping my mouth. The duke said, "Alcuin, you're not very bright. You're just nice to look at. I suggest you play your strongest suit."

The beautiful man dropped his eyes like a maiden. "Certainly, sir, if it pleases you. Will you be my master at cards, as in other things?"

"Always," said the duke dryly; "and I'm doing you a favor." Then they started kissing again.

I went and yanked the bellpull myself. Whatever it produced next, it could not be worse than Alcuin.

A boy slipped into the room like a shadow. He nodded at me, but addressed the busy duke: "My lord. Fleming asked me to remind you that your guests will begin arriving in two hours' time, and do you really want to wear the blue velvet tonight when it's this warm?"

My uncle disentangled himself from Alcuin. "Guests? What guests?"

"I knew Your Grace would say that," the boy answered with perfect equanimity. I wanted to laugh, and I thought he did, too. "You invited the poet Almaviva to read his new work here tonight. And you've invited a great many people who don't like poetry, and a sprinkle of ones who do. It's not really a fair fight."

"Oh." My uncle turned to me. "Do you like poetry, Lady Katherine?"

"Some," I managed to answer.

"Then you must swell the ranks of the believers. Can you drink?"

"*What?*"

"Can you drink a great deal of wine without behaving like an idiot?"

"Certainly," I lied.

"Good. Then go have a bath and all that. Don't rush: it'll be hours before they all get here so we can eat. Marcus, tell me, did Betty ever show up?" he asked the boy.

"Oh, yes: she's in the kitchen, practicing her curtsey."

"Well, she can practice it up here. I expect," my uncle said to me, "your room will be wherever they've put your bags. Someone will know."

B ETTY PRACTICING HER CURTSEY WAS A TERRIBLE SIGHT TO SEE. She had each separate move in the right sequence, but getting them to flow together seemed beyond her skill. She tugged her skirts out to each side of her. She crooked her knees. She came perilously near the ground. Then she did it again. And again; but it was never very convincing. Short and fat with middle age and scarlet with embarrassment, she resembled a quaking beet-pudding about to collapse in on itself.

"My lady," she stammered, "forgive me—there's a right way to do these things, I know—and I'll begin as I mean to go on, just the way you like it . . ."

"Thank you," I said, in an agony of impatience; "yes, thank you."

But she kept right on going: "You'll get satisfaction from me this time, my lady, and no messing about with the master, not this time, not this one, bless his boots—"

Finally I gave up and just said it: "Please, could you show me my room?"

"Of course," she panted, nearly worn out with curtseys; "that's what I'm here for, isn't it?" I handed her my cloak, in hopes it would steady her. "Of course," she said. "Of course, my lady."

She didn't look as if she could balance much more than the traveling cloak. I picked up my other small things myself. "My room," I repeated. "Please."

"Yes, well, it's a great big house, this one, isn't it? So many doors you don't know where you are—not like the Riverside house, well, that one's big too, but different; here everything looks the same . . ."

My heart misgave me as I followed her up the sweeping staircase (it was, in fact, the Perfect Staircase of my dreams, but I was too busy handling Betty to notice. Poor woman, I thought; trying to make a good impression and not quite equipped for it! I had considerable sympathy for her, after what I'd just been through).

"Now I know it's this way," she repeated as we rounded the same corridor a third time. But at last the door stood open to the right place.

There were my trunks in the corner, looking especially shabby in the glory that was my room at Tremontaine House. A huge bed with gauzy curtains, just right for the time of year; a painted wardrobe set off perfectly against the pale butter-yellow of the walls; prettily framed pictures and vases of flowers . . . and the whole reflected in the curly gilded mirror that hung over the marble fireplace.

Betty looked at the room, looked at me, attempted another curtsey and fell flat on her bum. When I leaned over to help her up, I found that my sympathy had been misplaced. Her breath smelt like a drover's on payday.

It was too much. My rich uncle had hired me a drunkard, a slovenly woman from who knows where, to serve as my first very-own lady's maid!

I looked at her red, babbling face, at my bags, at all of it reflected in the mirror (including my own shocked face and travel-frizzled hair) and burst into miserable tears.

"There now, my lady." And the creature had her arms around me. "There now." I let her hold me while I sobbed my heart out on the drunkard's warm breast.

M Y ROOM DID INDEED LOOK OUT ONTO THE RIVER, AND INTO the hills beyond, where the sun was finally setting. That morning it had found me waking in a strange inn on the road, surrounded by strangers. What a long day it had been! I leaned as far as I could over the balcony—*my* balcony—drinking in the sight. For natural beauty, the view from my room was not a patch on the rolling hills of home, the long vistas and sudden curves. No one could get lost in *these* hills, or tired walking along that river. But still they seemed far more exciting. And below me stretched a shadowy garden, suggestive of hedges and statues and paths one could, perhaps, get lost in. I watched as it all went blue and cold, and stars began to come out in the distance.

My huge white bed seemed to glow with its own light. I lay on its downy luxury, just for a moment—and woke to pitch darkness, and a thud against my bedroom door, and footsteps in the hall, and laughter.

Wide awake, I pulled an overdress on over my wrinkled chemise, and peeked out into the hall. A candle on a stand flared in the draft from my door. A man and a woman, whispering and laughing, were running down the hall toward its light, their inky shadows smeared out along the carpet behind them. I turned the other way, toward the stairs, where most of the noise was coming from. There were laughter and shouts, and the strains of string music flowed remarkably placid under the revelers. The party was in full cry.

I had no idea where Betty was, or how to get her to help me dress. I struck light to a candle, and picked out a green overdress that had covered deficiencies in the past; unplaited and combed out my hair, and knotted it up with a couple of pins, and clasped my coral necklace around my neck. My dove-grey slippers were nowhere in evidence, so I had to wear the apple-green, even though they did not match the dress. But I have noticed that, in large crowds, no one looks at anyone else's feet. I'd be all right if I could just get down the staircase unseen.

I paused at the top of the stairs to examine the scene below. People were spread out across the great hall; they looked like badly arranged pieces on its gameboard squares of black and white marble. They seemed to be just the spillover from the crowded receiving rooms beyond the double-doors.

I did my best to drift inobtrusively down the stairs. I was terribly hungry; there might be food beyond the doors. The people all looked very grand—*gaudy*, my mother would have said—in rich fabrics and jewels and lace and ruffles. Bobbing amongst them was a dyed ostrich feather, elegantly curled over a sleek, dark head, almost like a little hat. The head turned to me, and suddenly I was looking right into the eyes of a girl my own age. She darted forward, and seized my hands in hers.

"Isn't this *fun?*" she said. Her cheeks were pink, her blue eyes sparkled, and she wore a very good pair of pearl earrings.

"I've only just arrived. I came today, from the country."

"And already you're invited to all the wickedest parties! But I can tell that you are very, very good; I can always tell about people—aren't you just a little bit terrified, being *here?*" She gave a theatrical shudder. "Of course, the old duchess had exquisite taste; that's really why I wanted to come, to see the house, you know. Although the duke's parties are events all their own—the ones at Tremontaine House—not the Other Place—we wouldn't go *there*, of course." My new friend flashed a smile at the whole room. "Isn't it *grand?*"

I could not really see much for all the people. I noticed a cunning little pair of diamond buckles flashing by on someone's feet—or maybe they were paste, I couldn't tell. I wished I had a pair.

"Oh, yes!" I breathed.

She put her arm around my waist. "I just know we are going to be the best of friends. Where is your escort? I came with my brother Robert—the truth is," she pulled me a little closer in; "I made him bring me. He didn't want to. He said it wasn't any place for me. But I said if he did not I would tell our parents the true reason he needed the advance on his allowance. *He* told them he'd given the money to a poor friend who needed it—they encourage us to be generous—but I knew it was really because he'd spent it all on a duel over Lavinia Perry, which is silly, because she's almost a cousin. I wouldn't fall in love with a cousin, would you?"

"Oh, no!"

I had been in the city only a few hours, and already I had a friend—someone whose brother hired swordsmen, and who admired me for getting into dangerous parties. I felt very happy as she circled my waist with her arm. My new friend was shorter than I; the feather tickled my cheek.

"So . . . you're just up from the country. This must all seem very strange to you—although one wouldn't know it, you have such natural grace. And of course you will be at all the dances. I'm sure to see you there—we will have such fun, searching out beaux together!" She was leading me out of the press, to a corner where we could be fully absorbed in each other.

"Do you know, I've already received flowers from—an admirer!"

I clutched her arm. "Oh, *who?* Is he here?"

"No, not here; this isn't the sort of place he would be seen at. I shall get a dreadful scolding from him if he hears about it." She tossed her

head, looking pleased. "But next week . . . Will you be at the Godwins' ball?"

"I—don't know. I don't believe we've been invited yet."

My elegant friend said, "But I feel sure that Lydia Godwin would
dote on you, if only she knew you as I do! I shall speak to her. She is
such a dear friend of mine. Perhaps you could come in our party, with
your brother. Or was it your cousin?"

"Cousin?"

"With your escort—the one who brought you here."

"Oh. It's my—uncle."

"Oh." She frowned briefly but prettily. "Not one of those boring old
married men who only comes to parties to play cards?"

"No, I—don't think he's married. I mean, he isn't. He's very elegant."

"Perhaps you'll introduce us." She pulled away for a moment, to
fish in her beaded reticule for a little engraved card. "You must call on
me tomorrow." She laughed happily, indicating the throng of revelers:
"Not too early, of course!" I had no idea what time it really was. Close
to midnight, surely. No one at this party would be up early tomorrow.

I pocketed the card. "I will come, if it's not being a bother," I said
shyly, picturing a disaster, with no one home. But she squeezed my
hand in hers. "Yes, yes, you must! Then you can meet my brother
Robert in decent circumstances—maybe even turn his head away
from the Perry chit!"

Was that all it took to get beaux—just meeting friends' brothers?
This was going to be easier than I'd thought! I said, "I have no card,
not yet—we don't need them at home, everyone knows everyone else.
But let me introduce myself—"

"No, let me. It's much more decent," a voice announced from
above. "This is my niece, the Lady Katherine Samantha Campion
Talbert." My friend was staring, rather pale, over my head, at the tall
duke dressed in black. He turned all the pink and silver and powder
blue and turquoise in the room to sugar candy. Even my friend's delicious feather looked addled. He said, "And you're a Fitz-Levi. I can
tell by the nose."

She sank down in a very lovely curtsey, with her head bowed to
hide her flaming cheeks. "My Lord Duke."

My uncle looked down at the feather. "Fitz-Levi . . . hmmm . . . I
don't remember inviting you. Marcus will know—" His eyes scanned
the room, presumably for the boy Marcus. From what I had seen this
afternoon, the duke didn't remember having invited anyone. But I
could hardly tell her so at this moment. She flashed me a haunted

look, pressed my hand once more and fled. By the time my uncle looked down again, she was gone.

He looked curiously at me, as though I had performed a conjuring trick.

"What happened?"

"You frightened her," I told him.

He shrugged. "Well. At least you're still here. Let's get something to eat. Are you hungry?"

I was ravenous. "Yes, please. But—why did you say that, about her nose?"

"What about her nose?"

"You said she was ugly."

"Did I?" He considered for a moment. "I suppose I did. I'd better make her an apology, then. I'll have Marcus send her some flowers."

"Don't!" I exclaimed quickly. "You'll get her in trouble."

He looked at me again with great curiosity. "What do you care?"

All the while he had been maneuvering us out of the hall and off to a side room where tables were spread with food and drink.

"By the way," he said absently, "those shoes don't match that gown."

He handed me a plate piled with strawberries, bonbons, smoked fish and asparagus.

"Ah!" he said. "Finally. Someone to talk to."

The duke was looking with great delight at a large, ugly woman coming toward us across the room. Her complexion was muddy; her hair was chopped like badly mown hay, and of the same rough color and texture. It was hard to tell how old she was; older than I, and younger than Tremontaine, I would guess. Under her shapeless dress, her big body looked thick and without contours. She couldn't be a serving maid; any of them would take pains to present a better appearance. He had terrified my friend with the lovely feather, but was smiling warmly at this troll-like apparition. The corners of his eyes crinkled, which is how you can tell whether someone is really smiling, or just curving their lips.

The ugly woman stumped up to us. "Is this the niece?"

"This is Lady Katherine. She's not very tall, but I think she'll grow."

"How do you do?" I said to her, trying to restore myself to my rightful place in the situation.

"Hello," she said to me. She nodded to the room. "What do you think?"

It was not a question I, or anyone else, could answer. She didn't seem to realize it. I reached for the safety of the commonplace: "It's very nice."

"Oh." The ugly woman nodded, as if that told her all she needed to know about me. She seized a bonbon from my plate and bit it in half. "*Ig*," she objected. "Peppermint." She began to drop the other half back onto my plate, realized what she was doing just in time before she did it and cast about for somewhere else to bestow the offending morsel.

My uncle the Mad Duke was watching her, vastly diverted, and not offering to help. I realized I was watching her with the same fascination. It was not right. "How was the poetry?" I asked.

"Brilliant." "Awful," they said at the same time.

"It depends on your perspective."

"It depends on your brains."

"The most discerning brain could find nothing to catch and hold on to in those babblings."

"What—the articulation of the *soul* holds no interest for you?"

"As a matter of fact, it doesn't."

I wished I had not missed the poetry. I had thought a great deal about my soul in the past year.

"One wonders, then," the duke said to her, "why you are here at all, since you don't like poetry, and you don't know how to dress for a party."

"I come, of course, for the food. Here." She held out her hand, with the squashed and sticky half a bonbon. I could actually watch him making up his mind whether or not to take it. From his sleeve the duke pulled out a clean handkerchief. He pincered the candy in its folds, and turned to a passing gentleman who, at the touch of the duke's hand on his arm, stopped with a pleased expression.

"Furnival," the duke said engagingly, "I was wondering if you could take care of this for me?"

He didn't even watch to see what the man did with it.

"Have you seen Marcus?" he asked his ugly friend.

"Yes, he was stopping some people in the Violet Room from climbing the curtains."

"What for?"

"They were not professionals."

"Oh."

I could see my uncle the Mad Duke eyeing the asparagus on my plate. To forestall them making any further inroads on my supper, I picked up a green spear myself, and ate it as best I could without a fork. It suddenly occurred to me that asparagus was not in season.

I ate another. I realized that my nerves were partly hunger. I couldn't remember the last thing I'd eaten; maybe some bread on the road. I had a vision of it always being like this: a house without rules, without regular meals, one that came alive only when it was full of guests, a house whose inmates had to inhabit the party world just to get something to eat. Impossible—or so I hoped. But it was even harder to imagine the mundane, us sitting down to dinner together and discussing the events of the day: what lands needed grazing, what room airing out and what servants correcting— I was suddenly brutally homesick. As if I'd eaten something tainted, I would gladly have sicked up this whole new life to get back the old. *Stop it*, I told myself sternly. I would not cry. Not here, not now—not at all. This was the world I'd wanted: the city, the parties, the glitter and gallants, fine clothes and rare company.

It would be better in the morning.

The Mad Duke had drifted off to make someone else's life miserable. The ugly woman was gone in his wake like a seagull following a ship to scoop up what amusement he let fall.

I filled another plate, made myself small in the folds of a curtain, ate resolutely, and then found myself so tired there was nothing to do but wend my way back up the impressive stairs. My new friend was nowhere in sight; she'd probably gotten her brother Robert to take her home. I felt the little square of cardboard in my pocket, reassuring like a talisman. By some miracle, I found the door to my own room. The noises of the party roared around me like the sea.

chapter IV

IN THE MORNING, THERE WAS CHOCOLATE.
   Betty seemed recovered from the previous day's excesses. She
must not have been working the party. The tray barely rattled as
she set it down by the bed, and a heavenly rich scent filled the room.

I got up at once to engage with the little pot of bitter chocolate, set
out with an entire jug of hot cream, as much sugar as I should care to
put into it and, oh, the loveliest china cup to mix it in! I wished my
mother were there to share it with me. I poured slowly, watching the
cream swirl in the cup. It made the confusions and indignities of last
night seem a little more worth it; I felt even better when Betty said,
"And your new clothes have come, too."

The chocolate was marvelous, but I gulped it down, assuring myself, There will be more again tomorrow, and tomorrow, and again the
day after that. I was eager to get to the brown paper parcels piled at
the foot of the bed. I unknotted the string myself, being careful to put
it by to be used again. Fine white linen, some heavier blue; a little
lace, good . . . no silk, no velvet, but maybe I would be fitted for ball-
gowns later. I shook out the blue: it was a tight, short linen jacket. Not
a fashion I'd seen before; maybe a riding coat? It had a skirt to
match—no, it was breeches. Breeches that buttoned up on either side,
with a flap in the front.

I frowned. "Betty, are you sure these are for me?"

"Oh, yes, my lady. The duke sent them."

"But they're men's clothes. I can't put these on."

"Oh, don't worry about that." She chuckled. "I've helped a few fellows in and out of those, to be sure. I can dress you up all right and tight."

"But—but I can't wear these!"

"Why not, dearie?"

"They're not—they've got—"

She unrolled stockings, white neck-cloths still in need of ironing, vests and jackets with heavy buttons and shirts with loose sleeves.

"See? They're made specially to your measure sent beforehand, my dear; they'll fit a treat."

I could hardly bear to touch them. It wasn't that I'd never handled men's things before; I've mended my brothers' often enough. But these were for me. I was to dress myself in what men wear. Stockings, neck-cloths, vests and jackets, with heavy buttons and loose sleeves— they were all wrong.

I said as calmly as I could, "They're very nice things. But I will not wear them today. Please take out my blue flowered gown, and the yellow petticoat—"

"Oh, no, my lady. You're to put these on right away, and go to your lesson."

"Lesson?" I said sharply, remembering things like sketching and arithmetic, the lessons I'd had at home until we had to let my governess go, but doubting that was what she meant.

"Yes, that's right; a proper swordmaster coming all the way to Tremontaine House, just to teach you."

I felt my bargain closing in on me, tighter than neck-cloths and hard-buttoned jackets.

"Not today—surely not today, not yet—"

But of course it was today. He had told me it was. The duke owned me now, and I had agreed to it, weeks ago.

"I shall wear them in the house," I said firmly, "if it pleases him. For my lessons." But that, I secretly promised myself, was all.

So I let her pull the shirt over my head— clean, crisp linen that would have made the loveliest chemise!—and then the breeches— the buttons pulling closed flaps that were all that stood between me and the world, and nothing to hide my legs from anyone's eyes but the short hang of the jacket and the coarse stockings that revealed in outline everything they covered. The jacket buttoned tightly; it was well tailored, flattening my breasts and clinging around my arms. Men's clothing gripped me in places I did not want, showed me in ways I could not like, claimed me with strange bindings and unbindings.

I stood trembling, like a young horse being broken to saddle, as

Betty's fingers did the final buttons up. I would not look in the mirror. I couldn't bear to see myself transformed into something neither boy nor girl. Was this what my uncle wanted? I hoped he would be satisfied, then!

Betty drew out a blue velvet ribbon, smiling conspiratorially as if it were a sugar cake. It was for my hair, to tie it back in a queue. I let her do it: wearing my hair unbound was not going to change me back.

"Now you're all ready for your lesson. I'll show you the practice-room, and by the time you're done, I'll have all these nice things tidied up and put away."

I had left my last night's party gown spread out upon the chair. Before she could collect it, I snatched from its pocket the pasteboard card my friend had given me, and stowed it well away in my jacket, a little piece of comfort nestling there.

When I moved, no swing of petticoats surrounded me. I had lost the protection of full skirts, the support of boned bodice. There was nothing for my hands to hide in. I felt the air on my legs as I moved. Cloth covered my skin, but still I was naked, exposed. Anyone could look at me, and see almost all of me!

A plum-colored cape peeked out of the brown paper; in desperation, I seized it and wrapped it around myself. At least it covered my knees.

"No, no, my lady, you won't need to be going out of doors, His Grace has had a whole room made over, just for your practice."

But I clutched the cape tight around myself. And so we ventured through the halls of Tremontaine House, Betty uncertain, as always, of where we were going, and I doing all I could to keep from looking in mirrors. It wasn't easy. Frames were all over the gilded corridors, startling on walls and sudden turns; sometimes the frames contained still, painted pictures, and sometimes glass reflecting a window, a staircase or my own pale face. But even when I didn't look, I knew. I was dressed as a man. I was wearing men's clothes. They were like men's eyes looking at me; like men's eyes touching me. The cape came to just below my knees; if I'd let go of it, it would have swirled very nicely; it was well cut and full. But I held it tightly, like a blanket wrapped against the cold.

Betty kept up a frantic babble which I barely took in: she was grateful to the duke, unworthy of the position, knew a thing or two about ladies and never would mess with their husbands now, no, not if you forced her at swordspoint—

"Here." At last she stopped. "It's the double-doors with the wet rabbits on them." Well, it was a reasonable description of the artfully painted woodland storm scene. Before she could fling them open, I knocked.

"Yes!" a man shouted. "Hurry up!"

He was standing in the middle of the huge, sunlit room. A thickset, muscled man, half-clothed, wearing only breeches and an open-collared shirt. He had a full black beard and bristling mustaches, like nothing I'd ever seen.

"How? How?" he demanded. "You are cold, you wear your bed-blanket?"

My fingers unclenched from the folds of the cloak. I let it fall to the floor. The man nodded curtly at me, and then at a rack of real swords.

"Pick one up. And I will show you how you do it wrong."

His voice was so strange; I could barely recognize the words, the way they trilled and sang high and low in unexpected ways. "Come! Come! Venturus does not like to keep him waiting. Venturus have many many students are beg him for instruction. He must tell them, 'No, no, I am not for you, I must be for the Mad Duke whose little boy does not even know to pick up the sword!'"

"I'm not a boy," I said.

He shot me a look. "No? You are a rabbit? You have furry paws? Then pick me a sword!"

I grabbed the closest one.

He stood to one side, hands on his hips. "Good." He nodded. "Oh, very good." I began to feel a little less cold. "Very good—*if you are chopping up chicken!*" he thundered. "How you think you are defend yourself when you are need to change lines, eh?"

I had no idea what he was talking about. And I was too afraid to tell him that this was not the way you hold a knife to chop up chickens.

"Lines, change lines—shift the tip by you shift the wrist!"

I tried to, but the sword's weight pulled against me until I turned the hilt in my hand; then I could move my fingers to direct the point better. He wouldn't like that. I stared at the tip, refusing to look at him.

"Yes," Venturus said. "Now you are see. You see—but you do not see!" With a sword in his hand, he suddenly struck my own blade so hard that my hand stung. My sword went flying.

"Ha!" he shouted triumphantly. I didn't see that disarming a beginner was such a triumph. "Don't grip so tight like you mama's tit. Hold gentle, gentle—like you are hold a baby child, or a dog that bite."

I tried not to laugh at the picture. When I held the sword more loosely, it flexed in my hand. "Ye-e-es," he hissed contentedly. "Now you see."

I smiled and, feeling not quite foolish, struck a swordsman's pose.

Venturus screamed as if he had been lashed. "*Wha-a-at* you think you do with you legs? You arms? Do I give you permission to do that thing? I would not. I could not! No student of Venturus ever look like *this*." His imitation of my pose looked like a rag doll strung with wires.

In a small voice I said, "I'm sorry." I hate being made fun of.

"You know you sorry! Stupid duke-boy! Now you practice: practice holding, only holding. You like you kill someone now—maybe you kill Venturus, yes—but first, you hold! Ha!"

The weird foreigner flung a cloak around his shoulders.

"Where are you going?" I asked.

"I go see other students, students know how to listen to Venturus. You study to hold. Maybe tomorrow, I show how not to stand. Ha!"

And with a swirl of his cloak, he was gone.

I held the sword. Even after the door closed, I was not at all sure Master Venturus would not suddenly reappear through it, his mustaches bristling.

In my hand the sword looked solid and workmanlike, like a rolling pin, or the handle of a hoe. Then I looked down the entire length of it and saw how narrow the steel was, how shiny. It had no purpose but distance and death.

I wondered what my mother would say, and found no answer. For the first time in my life, I wished I could be holding a sewing needle instead; suddenly that instrument of torture seemed small and comfortable and harmless. My arm ached, no matter how I turned the sword. I decided to put it away, and go back to my room and change into the sort of girl who might ask a housekeeper if she needed help with the mending.

In the wardrobe, my new clothes were neatly hung and folded. I looked behind them for my old gowns, and found nothing. Nothing in the chest, nothing hung out to air; nothing remained of all my skirts and bodices and petticoats and stockings, carefully chosen and mended and packed a few days before.

I did not bother trying to find Betty. I knew what had happened. I knew, and I was not having it. This was one contest the Mad Duke would not win.

The card in my pocket read: ARTEMISIA FITZ-LEVI, BLACKBURN HOUSE. I would be seen on the street in these ridiculous clothes once only. Grimly clutching my cloak around me, I set out through the gates of Tremontaine House to find my friend.

IT WAS NOT LONG BEFORE LADY ARTEMISIA FITZ-LEVI BEGAN TO tire of the antics of her new pet. The parrot was a bit too clever— she had expected a sort of colorful talking doll, not something with a mind of its own. The parrot preferred fruit to cakes, earlobes to fingers and velvet to the bottom of its cage. It liked women better than men; when her cousin Lucius Perry came to call, it flew at him, and she had to get her maid to take it downstairs, where, no doubt, it would amuse the house staff far more than it did her, though it had not been acquired for that purpose.

"You look decorative," she approved her cousin Lucius. Artemisia thought that the right amount of lace always complimented a man's appearance. Of course, with his slender build, dark hair and blue eyes, Lucius had good material to work with.

"And you look exhausted." Lord Lucius Perry, lounging in her windowseat, gazed longingly at the fragile cinnamon wafers that lay just at the edge of his reach on an equally fragile painted table. "Out dancing your slippers to ribbons again, coz? What gallant has caught your eye this time?"

In strictest confidence she was perishing to tell him about the duke's party last night, but he went on without waiting for an answer, "And where is your reprobate brother? Robert promised me a bout of tennis today; is he out already paying court to his last night's conquests, or still sleeping them off?"

Artemisia smiled patiently at him. He was a cousin, so not worth much more, and a younger son at that. "Do I look awful, Lucius? Have I got rings under my eyes? I bathed them in cucumber water, but I'm not sure it's done any good—and I particularly don't want Mama to know what I've been doing," she hinted broadly.

Lucius did not even pretend to be interested. "Nothing awful, I hope. You don't want to get yourself talked about, Artemisia, not when your prospects are so good this year."

"Of course nothing awful! What do you take me for? You're a fine one to lecture me, Lucius, indeed you are. I understand you were once up to all sorts of mischief Mama won't even tell me about."

"That's just it," he drawled; "I've reformed."

"Well, it's made you uncommon dull."

"Do you think so?" He smiled just a little; his eyelashes fluttered over his cheeks as he extended one languid finger toward the plate— but his cousin was impervious to that particular sort of innuendo.

"Honestly, Lucius, you are the laziest man I ever met! Lean over and take your own biscuit, don't expect me to get up and pass them to you when you're this close to the table!"

Lucius Perry leaned back, instead, bathing his fine-boned face in a slanting patch of sun. All he could see through his eyelids was a rich, comforting red; if his cousin stopped talking for a minute, he might fall asleep.

No, he wouldn't: a knocking on the front door and a flurry of feet below heralded the approach of another visitor. "Artemisia," he said, not bothering to open his eyes, "you want to be careful. You're pretty, the family's good, your father's generous and you've got a nice voice. I wouldn't be surprised if someone offered for you before the year turns. Just don't compete with Robert in daring: city ballrooms are not exactly the same as climbing trees and jumping out of haylofts back home."

She drew herself up proudly. "Thank you for the advice, cousin. As if I don't know how to behave in town! I like it here, a great deal better than in the country. As far as I'm concerned, I'd be happy to call this home for the rest of my life, and I hope I marry a man who thinks so, too: someone with style and a bit of dash like Robert, not a dullard like you, who thinks an exciting day is playing tennis and calling on relatives, and an exciting evening is staying home and reading a book or whatever it is you do with yourself—anyhow, I didn't see *you* at Tremontaine House last night!"

"Tremontaine House?" Lucius Perry abandoned his lassitude. "You don't want anything to do with those people, cousin."

She tossed her head, and her curls bounced. "And why not, pray? I am not the Country Filly you seem to think me, cousin. I know how to handle myself in Society."

"Do you?" He was leaning forward, his blue eyes dark and full on her.

She squelched the humiliating recollection of her host putting her to flight. "Certainly. There's nothing so terrifying at Tremontaine House"—she laughed brightly—"except perhaps for the Mad Duke himself, of course. He's quite rude, isn't he? I don't know what all those people see in him, really."

"No, you wouldn't. That is why he's dangerous." His smile was now consciously charming. "Of course you understand Society, cousin: you are one of its brightest ornaments. But the Duke Tremontaine is outside Society. Even he agrees that that is where he belongs. And he encourages others—not, of course, that you could be so encouraged—but those around him, to, ah, to explore those outposts as well."

"Well, they all seemed perfectly normal to me: the usual sort of Ball and Salon types, just both in one place, that's all. It's hardly—"

Her curls splashed her neck as she turned her head toward the commotion downstairs: a clatter in the marble hall of booted feet, a shrill cry.

"Perhaps it's Robert," Lucius drawled, "with a new conquest."

Someone was running upstairs—two someones. The first was the footman, who opened the door to the sitting room just wide enough to announce breathlessly, "A—female, my lady, who will see you, she says, though I did—"

"From the party," a girl's voice insisted shrilly. "Tell her Katherine, Lady Katherine Talbert—only I don't have a card—from Tremontaine House."

Lucius dealt his cousin a jaded look.

The footman threw open the door. "Lady Katherine."

There stood the oddest figure Lady Artemisia had ever seen outside the theatre; worse than the theatre, really, because there the actresses in boys' roles at least made some attempt to trim their hair, hide their figures and adopt a manly bearing. This was so clearly a girl, small and round, her long hair messily escaping from a ribbon in frizzy tendrils. Only her clothes were a perfect copy of a man's, in every detail.

Artemisia Fitz-Levi put a hand over her mouth. She knew it was rude, but she couldn't help it, the laughter just came squeezing out. The girl stared at her. Her face went pale, then red.

"From Tremontaine House," said Lucius smugly. "Well: you see my point."

Katherine Talbert spun on the heel of her ridiculous boots, and ran clattering out the hall and down the stairs.

N O ONE WOULD HAVE LOOKED TWICE AT THE BOY IF HE HAD not been running frantically through a very sedate section of the Hill, where running generally meant some kind of trouble.

"Hey, there!" A hand shot out, bringing the figure to a skittering stop. Philibert, Lord Davenant, was not an observing sort of man; he saw a boy's face because he expected to see a boy's face, and the estimable Lord Davenant was one who liked the world to be compassed by order and decorum. This boy's long hair, therefore, meant University, and few scholars belonged on the Hill. Furthermore, the boy had been crying and seemed terrified at being apprehended.

"Aha," said Lord Davenant. "What's your hurry? Something in

your pockets, maybe?" He thrust a hand into one of them, keeping a grip on the boy's wrist.

"Help!" shrilled the boy. "Let go of me!" He tried to wriggle out of the older man's grasp. "How dare you?"

"Little rat!" Davenant surveyed him, half-amused. "Shall I call the Watch, or just thrash you myself?"

The boy wiped his nose with his free arm. "If you were a gentleman," he said suddenly, "you would escort me back to Tremontaine House."

"Oh." Abruptly Lord Davenant dropped the wrist as if afraid of contagion. "So you're that kind of rat, are you?"

"What do you mean?"

"Go on, get off with you." Davenant's views on Tremontaine were well known in Council. The last thing he wanted was to be seen accosting one of the Mad Duke's fancy boys on the open street. "There's your direction, go on."

The boy drew himself up and walked away shakily.

I HAD FORGOTTEN THE WAY AND HAD ONLY A DIM RECOLLECTION of what Tremontaine House looked like from the street. All the walls of all the great houses looked the same, and all their black and gold-tipped gates. I tried to walk as if I knew where I was going.

"Hello, Lady Katherine."

Standing before me was a boy about my age. He was plainly dressed, with a plain, ordinary face. It took me a moment to recognize the duke's servant, the valuable Marcus, the boy who knew where everything was. He said, "I'm heading back to Tremontaine House, if you'd like to come with me."

I followed him in silence. He had never introduced himself, and he didn't do so now, just talked to me as if we had always known each other.

"It's a nice day, isn't it? Betty thought you'd run away, but I guessed you might just have gone for a walk; you wouldn't want to get her in trouble by disappearing or something. You should try exploring the House gardens," he chatted amicably, "they're very interesting. Paths, and statues and fountains and things, though I think they've turned the fountains off for the season. The gardeners dig up the flowers all the time and put new ones in. They grow them in a big glass house. It's quite a production. You can have flowers put in your room, if you like. Want me to order them for you?"

The front hall of Tremontaine House was cool and white and empty. Gone the bustle and striving of last night; in their place was a spooky sweet serenity.

"Where is the duke?" I asked.

"Gone. Everyone's gone to the Riverside house."

"Everyone? But I—"

"Oh, not you. You're staying here."

"Alone?" Panic sharpened my voice.

"Not really. There's a whole staff lives here. He comes and goes, you see. He likes to have things ready for him always, here. They'll take care of you. Just tell Betty what you need."

"Are—are you staying here?" I hated myself for wanting a particular answer, but at least he was a friendly face.

"No. I go where he goes."

"When will you—will he—be back?"

"Whenever he feels like it. The Riverside house is warmer in winter; this one's better in summer. In between, like now . . ." Marcus shrugged.

"Is it far out in the country?"

"Is what far?"

"Riverside."

The boy laughed, as if I'd told him a joke on purpose. Then he shook his head. "Riverside? It's right here in the city. The other end of the city, the old bit, near the docks. Riverside's an island in the river. It's nothing special, really. I wouldn't live there. But he likes it."

"Is it a nice house?"

"It's an odd house." Again, the shrug. "He likes it."

"Well," I said, and something struck me. "Then, while he is there, I am the mistress of this house?"

"Why would you be?"

I'd never met such a rude servant. But then, this wasn't a normal household. I explained carefully to him, "Well, most houses have a master and a mistress. If the lord is unmarried, it's a sister, or a daughter, most often, who takes over the duty. So it stands to reason—" Marcus continued to look at me patiently, waiting for me to begin making sense. It put me off. "It stands to reason that, as the duke's niece, I would— In his absence I would be—"

"He left no instructions about that," Marcus told me gravely. "I could ask him, if you like, but . . ."

He didn't have to complete the thought. I had had quite enough of the Mad Duke's notice already. "Well, then," I said airily, looking around the huge front hall, "with no duties, I shall be a lady of leisure."

"If you're all right," he said, "I'd better be getting back."

Marcus did not bow as he left me. Only after he was gone did I realize that he had not seemed to notice the strangeness of my clothing, and that, while I was with him, neither had I.

I N MY BEAUTIFUL ROOM OVER THE RIVER, I SAT IN A DELICATE armchair working out just how miserable I could be. My visit to Artemisia's had been a disappointment. But then, probably she hadn't recognized me without my gown, and that terrible man with her had started being snide before I could explain. I'd just have to watch and wait for another chance. Artemisia had spoken last night of eternal friendship. Surely, once she knew what my uncle had done to me, my friend would help me to find some decent clothes and make sure I met decent people. I could not escape Tremontaine House entirely. I must do what I had to do to please the duke; after all, my family's fortune depended on it. But surely I wasn't meant to be a prisoner here!

I took a deep breath, and comforted myself opening a pretty box that contained beautifully ironed handkerchiefs. It wasn't going to be so bad, was it? Alone in one of the loveliest houses in the city, with no Mad Duke popping out from behind doors to torment me. No onerous duties, no housework whatsoever, as far as I could tell. Stupid clothes and pointless lessons, of course. But Master Venturus hadn't said anything about my killing people; he seemed to just want me to look nice with a sword. Like dance lessons; I could do that.

I looked in the charming gilded writing desk to see if it contained notepaper. There was none. I would have to tell Betty to get me some so that I could write to Artemisia, and to my mother. No, wait, that was in the bargain, too: no family letters for six months, and no visits, either. My brother Gregory had lodgings somewhere in the city, but he was not permitted anywhere near me. It was probably just as well. Gregory is very earnest, like our father; although he had been in the city for several months, the Mad Duke had never invited him to visit, and I could see why, now. Gregory believes in rules, so he would probably not try to sneak around and find me, even though my mother probably wished he would. I could write to her, anyway . . . but the thought of page after page of letters piling up unread over the weeks just made me feel worse.

How was she getting on without me? I worried. She was probably doing everything wrong, even though I'd left her a list—forgetting to air the winter linens, not keeping the tables waxed, letting the kitchen maids fight over the boot boy. . . . And who was going to comb her hair out so it didn't hurt, and match her embroidery silks, and remind her to take her tonic?

The house was doubtless going to wrack and ruin in my absence, and here I was, a useless creature being asked to take up useless skills I wasn't even any good at and never would be! And all for some mad whim of my mad uncle, who couldn't even be bothered to say good-bye to me when he left me alone in a strange house.

My boots made a satisfying thump as I stomped downstairs to look for a library where there might be paper. Or maybe I could find a genealogy that would tell me all of my stupid uncle's mysterious names, so I could impress him if ever I saw him again. At last I found it, a grand room laced floor to ceiling with more books than I'd ever seen in my life. They looked very dull: *On the Causes of Nature*, *The Tyrant's Dialogue*, that sort of thing. Most of the bindings were chased and stamped with gold, making the outsides far more appealing than the insides. Lost in the wealth of volumes, at last I found a lavish book called *Geographical Exotica* and settled into a window seat to examine pictures and descriptions of distant places I only half-believed existed. In the margin of a page about the island of Kyros, someone had written, *Where the honey comes from!* The book said it was an island of thyme, in which the bees sang all day.

I N A WARM AND RICHLY FURNISHED ROOM IN RIVERSIDE, THE smell of candles and food and bodies and wine wove a net of security and comfort around a group of men who usually settled for less. They were as happy as they were ever likely to be, with bellies nearly full, and no brakes upon the conversation.

"Pass Soliman the meat," the Duke Tremontaine commanded. "He can't discuss our animal nature until he becomes one with it!"

With his plate well stacked, the philosopher started up again. "All I was saying, with Dorimund's permission, is that training is the antithesis of nature. It must be. If shunning what is called vice were natural, as shunning cold or the pain of a fire is, then we would not need to be counseled against it!"

Taking a drink, an older, bearded man said, "I see you have no children, Sol. You must pull their hands back from the fire a hundred times, or risk losing them to it."

"Experience," another asserted. "Experience is the teacher there. 'The burnt hand shuns the fire' and all that. There is a difference between experience and training."

"Abstract thinking is what we're talking about. The fruits of vice are not immediately apparent, as the pain of fire is."

The duke leaned forward across the table. Like the scholars he was dressed in black, only his was studded with jet and dark embroidery. "The 'fruits of vice,'" he said, "are open to debate. They are not em-

pirical, like a burnt finger. They may be abstract, Dorimund, but—"
He stopped when the boy Marcus appeared at his side. "Yes, what?"

"A woman," Marcus murmured, "has come to the West door."

"Bugger the woman," the duke snarled. "Make her wait."

His servant showed him a ring. "She said you gave her this."

The duke's eyes widened slightly. "And so I did. I didn't think she'd
show. I had better—" He pulled himself up from the table, bowing to
his guests. "Gentlemen. I'll catch the rest of this later, or when Soliman publishes his controversial theories to the disgust of all right-
thinking people, an effort I will be delighted to finance. Sol, stop eating, you look all round and rosy and harmless; people will feel silly
hissing someone on the street who looks like a cradle doll."

To the laughter of his guests he left the table, ducking between
hanging cloths, following Marcus through an arched door and down
two small flights of steps, each one a different width, one turning to
the left and another to the right.

T HE CLOAKED WOMAN STARTED WHEN HE ENTERED. SHE HAD
not expected a door behind the paneling. The duke shrugged.
"It's quicker. I didn't want you to wait. I was afraid you'd lose your
nerve."

Her voice was only a little breathy. "It's quite steeled, thank you."

Abruptly he caught her hand in his. "But you're cold."

"Chilly. I often am before a performance."

"I'm not a demanding audience."

"I've heard otherwise."

His smile was slow and personal, oddly charming. "And you the
celebrated Black Rose. Well, I am honored."

"The honor is mine, my Lord of Tremontaine." She took a strand of
his long hair between her fingers, put it to her lips.

The duke closed his eyes for a moment. Then he twined thumb and
forefinger about her wrist. "Not just yet," he said. "There is the matter
of your intriguing friend, first."

She stood quite still. "He's not all that intriguing."

"I find him so."

"You don't have to sleep with him."

"Neither do you, really, but you choose to do so." She drew breath
to speak, but he put his fingers lightly on her lips. "Lord Davenant is
becoming an important man, closely allied to the new Crescent
Chancellor. Prestige, money, adventure . . . It's your game; I won't tell

you how to play it. I'm just delighted you're going to play it with me, too."

She raised her own hand to his to caress the backs of his fingers on her lips. Abruptly he turned away, businesslike. "I asked you for evidence of his latest clever scheme. Now, let's see it. Even flat on my back—or yours—I can tell a real document from a fake one."

The actress reached into the folds of her cloak. He stepped back a pace, because it might always be a dagger. But she produced a real document, hung with seals and ribbons, very official.

"Nice," the duke said, examining it. "Very nice. This will more than do. Marcus—" Without looking behind him, he handed it to his servant. "Arthur knows what to do with this. Tell him to make two copies and return the original"—he looked the woman in the eyes— "how soon, do you think?"

"Soon. I'll be missed if I'm not back tonight."

"Can't you tell him your rehearsal ran late?"

"I already have."

The actress was trembling. The duke drew her into the crook of his arm, and slipped his ring back onto her finger. "Keep it."

"I'll probably sell it."

"That's all right." The man in black pulled her against his chest. "I don't give things away with an eye on their future."

The Black Rose turned in his arms, a tall woman who still came only to his chin. Her mouth sought his skin above the embroidered collar. "You're very generous."

"Am I? You don't have to sleep with me, either, but if it—"

"Prestige," she murmured into his throat, "money, adventure."

"—if it makes it any easier, I can give you—"

She kissed him, and he was silent.

They left through the door he had come in. Like a young man squiring a debutante through crowded seats at a ball, the Mad Duke escorted her through the mad halls of his house, from the secret room to a bedroom hung with red curtains, already warmed by a fire.

B UT THAT WAS NOT WHERE MARCUS FOUND HIM TWO HOURS later—more than two hours, for it took him a while to locate his master, after the woman had been shown the door. The Duke Tremontaine was alone in a room empty of furniture. He was hunched over a dying paper fire in an elaborately carved fireplace. His unbound hair swept the ashes. The room was cold and dark, but for the red glow of the last of the embers.

Marcus knew which floorboard creaked.

"I need more wood," the duke said without turning around. "I'm cold."

"There's a fire in your bedroom."

A shudder passed through Tremontaine. "No. I won't go back there."

"Shall I get blankets for you?"

"Yes. No—I can't sleep in this room. Not here."

"If you'd let me move a bed in, or even a couch . . ."

Tremontaine wore nothing but a velvet robe. It twisted around his long limbs when he turned to look up at his servant. "No, Marcus. There will not be any bed in here ever again."

"All right. What if I make a fire in the library? You could have some blankets in there, and read for the rest of the night."

"Where are my guests, my scholars?"

"They've all gone to bed, or gone home. Shall I wake one up for you?"

The duke shook his head, and noticed his hair. He tucked most of it into his collar. "No, you go to bed. I'll . . . I'll be along."

"I think you'll like the library," coaxed Marcus doggedly. "There are cushions, and rugs, and nice heavy curtains. And plenty of books."

"I know what's in the library," the duke snarled, sounding a bit more like himself.

Marcus held out his hands, and the tall man took them; together, they pulled him to his feet.

chapter VI

I T WAS ALL RIGHT DURING THE DAY. BUT AT NIGHT, STRIPPED down to my boy's shirt, tucked in the great bed in the empty house in a city of strangers, I wanted my mother! We always shared our woes and tried to help each other. I wished she knew how brave I was being, but there was no way to tell her about any of it, and what could she do, anyway? I cried very quietly, not liking to hear myself.

In the morning, I let the chocolate console me, and let Betty do up all my clothes with her able fingers. She didn't smell of drink—yet. I left half the chocolate for her.

My new clothes were not so hard to move in today. They seemed looser, more welcoming, less restrictive.

Master Venturus was waiting for me in the wet rabbit room. He was practicing against a wall, and didn't seem to see me when I came in.

"Good morning!" I said, to show I wasn't afraid this time.

"Yes," he said, still crouching and springing with sword in hand. "Why aren't you practice?"

"I will if you like."

"You get up, you practice. You eat, you practice. You go to bed, you practice—first." He turned at last to face me. "Otherwise, no good. No point." He looked me over. "No blanket today? Not so cold? Very good. Now you show Venturus you hold."

I held. Then I stood—wrong, of course, at first, and then right, so perfectly, I was told, that I must not move, and did not, and thought I was going to die of the ache in my arm holding the sword and my legs holding the stance, a gradual ache that became pain that sharpened to agony.

"Strike!" Venturus shouted suddenly.

I sprang forward, heedless of form, just to release the pain—and nearly fell over. My sword clanged from my hand to the floor.

"Not so good." My master's exaggerated sympathy failed to cover his smugness. "Not so good, ha? You practice, practice, practice, then no pain, no hurt, you strike—strike like snake. Ha! Now pick up sword." He hissed. "Tsss! No thumb on blade! Stupid. Rust, dust, all kinds of blick. You polish, make good."

It was worse than polishing silver. The blade's shiny metal darkened the moment my finger touched it. And those edges could be sharp, too, though the tip was blunted. Venturus gave me lime powder and oil and a soft leather cloth. For once, I was glad of my breeches; it would have been hard to do in skirts.

Venturus waited 'til I was done. Then he said, "I go. What you do now?"

I looked out to the garden. It was raining. "I practice," I said.

"Good." To my surprise, he added, "Not too long, first day. Then make bath, good soak with—tss!—how you call, good salts—then wine. After." On his way out the door, he paused and whirled back to me: "No-wine-no-sword!"

"I beg your pardon?"

"You no drink with sword! Drink is ruin sword."

With a swirl of his cloak, he was gone.

⌒

THE MORE TIME I SPENT IN TREMONTAINE HOUSE, THE MORE beautiful I found it. I couldn't understand why my uncle the Mad Duke didn't like it here. Maybe it was just too good for him and he knew it. Everything about the house was perfect: the colors carefully chosen, the furniture balanced in form and size to every room; even the views out the tall windows were as lovely as pictures. I would find myself just looking at the way the lines of a room's molding met the ceiling. Sometimes they joined in carven leaves, edged with just a little gold; sometimes faces peered amongst them; sometimes there were patterned jags, hard edges that almost made blocks of letters, like words you couldn't quite read.

Each room was filled with treasures. I made myself choose a favorite in each one: the game was that I could save only one thing from each room, and what would it be? In one it was a tiny ivory carving of balls within balls, each one moving separately but never touching. In another I was hard put to choose between a painted fan mounted on a stand and a little china calf with the most winning expression! I was surprised at how many of the things I found were ladies' things. I remembered the duke my uncle saying with some distaste, "It's very elegant. I inherited it from my grandmother." His grandmother had been Duchess Tremontaine before him; that much I knew. Perhaps it was her very own armchair that I loved to sit in, in my room above the river, my feet tucked up under me as I watched the colors change over the hills.

I liked to visit the dining room with the long windows and mirrors, even though I never ate in there. At the center of the enormous table, there was a serving epergne as large as a baby's cradle, made out of silver. Branches twisted around it, ending in oak leaves on which sweets might be placed; the middle was a large dish supported by silver deer that grazed or glanced up around it, amongst life-sized silver walnuts that were half as big as the deer were. Sometimes I patted or stroked the deer, although I knew it would make the silver tarnish faster. But it was folly to leave silver out like that in the air, anyway. A girl came in once a week to polish it; I came upon her one day and offered to help, but she would not let me. If the servants found me odd, they didn't say so. They were very polite and always called me Lady Katherine. Of course, they must be accustomed to behavior far odder than mine. And you couldn't know where they themselves had come from—though, as my mother had taught me, it would be the height of rudeness to ask. It's different in the country, where we know everybody for miles around. It seemed like a waste to keep on polishing the thing, but I was not invited to give advice on housekeeping. I began to realize just how much money my uncle the duke had at his disposal, and was fascinated by what he chose and did not choose to spend it on. I wondered whether the Riverside house were as richly furnished, or even more so.

And I wondered what was in my uncle's private rooms, here in Tremontaine House. I knew which ones they were: at the other end of the house from mine, a large suite that overlooked both the river and the courtyard. He could watch the sunset, and he could see visitors arriving. Once I stood outside the door, wondering if it was locked, and what I would do if it wasn't. He'd never know if I looked in, would he? But what would I see if I did? Next time he makes me really angry, I promised myself, I'll sneak in and look at everything, no matter what. Behind me, the portrait of a sad young woman gazed mournfully at me, as if to warn me of the perils of intrusion.

Portraits spattered the walls of Tremontaine House: large and small, square and round, dark and bright. In our house in the country there were portraits, too, but they were all my father's forebears. This was my mother's family. I tried to figure out which of the painted people looked familiar, and who was related to whom. When I couldn't guess, I'd make it up. The young man with the sour face and riding crop in the upstairs narrow hall was pining for the stiff young woman holding a rose in the little salon. But she was betrothed from birth to a red-faced bedroom man with a goblet. I could tell they would never be happy. I considered having the young man break his neck in a riding accident just to make sure everyone was good and miserable. I even wrote a poem for the young lady beginning Ah, *never shall I see thy shining face once more*, but all I could think of for next was *When I stand looking out the garden door*, and even though it did rhyme I knew it wasn't really poetry.

But the pictures also discomfited me: after looking at them long enough I would begin to wonder who these people truly were, and what order they had come in. Was the old man the son of the pretty young girl, or her father, or her husband? Or had he died before she was born? My painted forebears could not speak to answer, and no one in Tremontaine House could tell me who they were.

In the mirrored salon was one portrait that always pleased me. The painting was vivid and bright, not so old-fashioned as the rest: a woman in a pretty dress, with curls so fair as to be almost silver. It was a wonderful, lively painting. She was looking just past my shoulder as if someone was coming in the door behind me and she was sharing a joke with them, laughing as if she wanted a secret teased out of her. Her eyes glistened, and the pale grey satin of her dress did, too; even her jewels looked real, until you got close enough to see that it was only bits of paint: streaks of white over rose swirling to red, and such. Behind her, I was almost sure I recognized the lawn of Tremontaine House itself, sweeping down to the river. People were playing flamingo on the grass. I decided we had nearly the same nose. I wondered if, when I had the right gown, I might get the same artist to paint my portrait, too, and if I might look even half as lovely as the lady in grey.

A RTEMISIA FITZ-LEVI'S MOTHER DID NOT THINK MUCH OF HER choice of gowns for the evening's festivities, and was busy telling her so. "A supper-party, my dear, is not a ball," she said. "Even if there is dancing after, you want something a little more . . . restrained."

"But Mama," Artemisia argued, "the green silk was most particularly admired by the Duke of Hartsholt at the Hetleys'! And you said his taste is impeccable."

"So it is, my dear—and don't think he won't notice if you wear it again! Do you want to look as if you are courting his favor? And Hartsholt a married man . . . no, no, it would never do."

Artemisia pouted. "Don't be ridiculous, Mama. No one would think that. Besides, I wanted to wear the tourmalines Papa gave me, and they suit it perfectly."

"So they do, my love, and you shall wear them at the next possible occasion. But not the green, not so soon after you've worn it once. Do you want people to think you don't have enough gowns?"

That worked, where nothing else had. "What about the yellow?" Artemisia asked hopefully. The yellow dress was the result of an argument her mother had lost, with a bodice cut down to there, and enough flounces to trim a cake.

"Don't you think it might hurt Lydia's feelings, since it is her party and she looks so peaky in yellow?"

"Mama, you are an angel of kindness!" Artemisia flung her arms around her mother's neck. "How could I be so unfeeling? I know—I shall write to my dear Lydia." Artemisia settled in a ruffle of dressing gown at her escritoire. "I'll see what she's wearing. If it's white or cream or ecru, I'll wear mine, too."

"Now why," her mother said dryly, "did we not think of that before?"

And Lady Fitz-Levi went to scribble off a note to Lydia's mother, so that Dorrie could take them both at once, and return with the correct response.

M ASTER VENTURUS CONTINUED COMING EVERY DAY. EVERY day Betty laid out my sturdy practice clothes, and every day I dutifully put them on and went to the practice room to meet him. And every day after he'd left I'd practice for an hour or more. What else was there for me to do with my time? I could hold the sword without my arms aching for quite a while now, and my legs could hold their position without trembling, at least until Venturus was gone. I learned how to hold, how to stand, even how to strike—if aiming at a spot in the air can be accounted striking. It was all a bit dull, really, this training to be a swordsman. Venturus talked, and I repeated drills for him, and he talked some more, and finally he left and I did them again and again, until it was time for my bath.

I didn't even notice the morning I woke up with no ache in my muscles at all. Betty did, though; *sprightly*, she called me, and I went down to my lesson feeling very pleased with myself for being sprightly instead of sluggish and dull. Venturus retaliated with a whole new set of moves for me to learn: parries and ripostes, with no particular purpose that I could see except to make me turn my wrist in funny ways and feel like even more of a useless idiot. He would never even show me how to do them properly, just talked talked talked until I got it right, it seemed, only to stop his voice. I began to wonder if he was ever going to teach me to fight for real.

So it was a great startlement to me, the day he stood waiting for me stripped to his breeches and shirt, holding a powerful sword with an intricately woven basket. It was not a practice sword. It had an edge, a real one.

I drew in a deep breath. Guard, feint, parry, riposte . . . I could do this. I would have to, to keep that evil blade from me. Venturus had thrown his jacket over the rack of practice swords. He smelt sweaty, as if he'd been drilling already. But when I went to pick up a weapon, he stopped me. "No. You no sword. You stand."

His sharp steel tip directed me to the center of the room. I stood there at the guard, miming a sword in my hand.

"No guard!" my strange teacher corrected. "You standing stand."

I stood still, my arms at my sides. He raised the sword in one swift motion. I flinched.

"Stand."

I said carefully, "I think that you are going to hurt me. I can't just stand here without—"

"Good. Good you think. No laughing sword. Laughing sword is death sword." He smiled, showing large yellow teeth. "But Venturus not to hurt. No hurt if stand, no move. No-o-o move." I didn't move. Slowly, but perfectly steadily, the sword was swinging in a great arc towards me. I watched it come. I thought as hard as I could about how much practice it must have taken for Venturus to be able to keep it at that steady rate, without wavering.

The blade stopped at the cloth of my shirtsleeve.

"No-o-o move."

I did not move. He swung it suddenly to my knee, and I would have jumped except that I was afraid he'd hit me by accident then.

Venturus stepped back a pace. "Good."

So quickly I had no time to be frightened, he had the tip at my neck. Without appearing to change his stance, Venturus extended his arm a crucial fraction simply by tightening his muscles, and the metal pressed into my skin. I knew it did not break through, although I felt it all the way down to the small of my back. I did not swallow until he'd taken it away.

"Yess," he said in his satisfied hiss. He was not even winded. "Now you see."

"See what?" I demanded hotly. When I lose my temper, I'm afraid it's gone. "See you are the biggest show-off in the world, or see you nearly scared me out of a year's growth?"

He lowered his blade and twirled it at his side in a very show-offy way. "Hmm," he observed to the air around him, "little scared duke-boy gets anger."

"Yes, I get angry when I'm scared—what do you want me to do, cry?"

"Anger," Venturus said, "is enemy to sword. Many angry men killed by sword."

"Is that so?"

Venturus made a tour of the room, working the sword in flashy patterns so that I had to keep well away. "Fear," he observed to the air, "is enemy to sword. And fear to sword is friend. You see now?"

"No."

"No? Why not? You have eyes, but you no see. I teach and teach, but you no learn. Why you no learn, silly duke-boy?"

I took a deep breath. "I see one thing," I said, "and that's that I'll never be any good at this. And you know what? That's just fine with me, because it was never my idea in the first place, remember? So why don't you just go ahead and tell my uncle that I have too bad a temper and I'm too scared and stupid ever to be a decent swordsman, and then we can all go home!"

He turned to me with real hardness in his eyes. The sword was down at his side, but for the first time, the man truly frightened me. "Do not sharpen your tongue on Venturus," he growled. "Do not command like to some servant." His nostrils flared as he breathed deeply. "I go now, yes? This no day for sword."

I stood very still as he put on his shirt and jacket, picked up his sword-belt and weapon and left. *"Do you ever even take a bath?"* I shouted to the door once it had closed behind him.

As the cloudless sky above the river faded from blue to grey to green before settling into another deeper, darker blue that set off the evening star to perfection, the curtains of Godwin House were drawn against the night chill and the vapors of the river.

Scented candles were lit in the music room, which turned warm, hazy and dreamlike amongst their fumes, the vases of flowers and the perfumed men and women in their whispering satin.

The young Lady Lydia Godwin had assembled a group of friends for a dinner—or, rather, her mother had assembled them for her from a slightly longer list of Lydia's. Since her first ball, Lydia was now allowed a certain number of small gatherings, carefully monitored and chaperoned.

After a dinner of eleven dishes and much innuendo, all Lydia wanted to do was to disappear into a corner with her closest friends to discuss the preceding events: looks and comments, dresses and ornaments, jokes and compliments. Instead, she must play the hostess and restrict herself to the occasional glance across the room at Artemisia Fitz-Levi when anything particularly struck her.

It wasn't so easy to catch Lady Artemisia's eye. Her attention was occupied by a nobleman in mulberry silk who seemed always to be speaking earnestly to her.

Artemisia could not be certain of whether Lord Terence Monteith was a bore or not. He had good clothes and good jewels, and a very pleasant face. The Godwins had invited him and he was unmarried, so clearly he had prospects. But nothing he was saying interested her. Which was odd, because he was not, as is usual with men, demanding that she listen to him. He was asking her opinion of things, and hanging on her every word. It was just that she had no opinion on the things he asked her. She hadn't spent a lot of time thinking about whether musicians who played on the street should be required to have licenses, or livestock entering the city be inspected for disease. It was, of course, flattering that he wanted to know. "Really?" he kept saying. "Do you think so? And what about . . . ?" until she was taxed for invention. In fact, it was beginning to feel a bit too much like a lesson she hadn't prepared for, which made her cross. She was not, after all, in the schoolroom any longer. Artemisia tossed her curls. "Lord Terence," she said, "how charming to find a man who thinks a woman knows more than just fashion and poetry!" hoping that at least he'd want to ask her about those.

His eyes never left her face. "What perfect teeth you have," Lord Terence said, confirming her suspicion that he was, in fact, a bore and, having no conversation of his own, had simply been asking her to provide it while he stared at her.

Lydia's parents came in then with a handful of their own friends who had been dining elsewhere. Artemisia had to restrain herself from dropping a schoolgirl's curtsey to Michael, Lord Godwin, and his lady, now that she was a young lady herself.

The eddy of newcomers should have been enough to detach her from Lord Terence, but the young nobleman was nothing if not persistent. In a moment he would ask if he might call on her, and she would have to say yes, or she would hear about it from her mother. She looked desperately for Lydia to signal for aid, but the daughter of the house was being dutiful with one of her parents' guests: a tall, dark-haired man with a distinguished air.

"Old people," Artemisia murmured daringly to Terence, no longer caring what he thought of her, "why must they insinuate themselves and spoil the party?"

Sure enough, her suitor drew back a little shocked. "That is Lord Ferris," he said, "the new Crescent Chancellor himself! Really, I wonder that Lady Godwin will have him here, now that he has taken her husband's place as head of the Council of Lords; but I suppose they are used to these ups and downs in politics. I have already taken my seat in Council, of course, but I've spoken only once or twice, on minor matters. . . ."

"About cattle?" she asked piquantly, "or fish?"

Lord Terence missed the mockery completely, and was about to tell her which, when suddenly Artemisia made the mistake of catching Lydia's eye, and burst into helpless laughter.

Lord Ferris turned his whole head to look at her. His left eye was covered with a black velvet patch. "Hmm," he said to Lydia. "Possibly the first person ever to find Terence Monteith at all amusing. Pray introduce me to your friend."

"Do you mean *Artemisia?*" Lydia could have bitten her own tongue for sounding like a schoolgirl. But the Crescent Chancellor smiled at her in such a way as to indicate a complete understanding of what a complicated task it was for a young woman to play hostess at her own dinner party; indeed, he made her feel, just for a moment, as though running a party of eligible young people and running the Council of Lords were not such entirely different tasks.

"With pleasure," Lydia said smoothly. Lord Ferris must be older than her father, but unlike her father, he took the trouble to treat a young girl like a proper lady, not someone who still ate in the nursery with her little brothers. His hair was very black, with just a little silver, and his hands were finely shaped, ornamented with heavy, tasteful gold rings. The eyepatch only gave him an air of mystery. She felt tremendously grown-up when he offered her his arm and guided her across the floor to where Artemisia Fitz-Levi stood, with Terence Monteith gawking beside her.

Lord Ferris was, after all, a widower; and if Terence had had the sort of mind that observed the world around him, he would have known to exactly what purpose Lady Godwin had invited the Crescent Chancellor to stop in at her daughter's party.

Having said I would not cry, I was honor bound not to. After Venturus left, though, I was ready to cry or spit.

I stalked down to the library. It was a soothing room, quiet and well proportioned, with cozy chairs and an excellent view. But to my annoyance, the duke's librarian was there. He was a dreamy man who hardly seemed to exist, and usually he did not notice that I did. He catalogued and rearranged, making faces at things no one else knew the meanings of, like flakes on the outside of books and notes on the inside of them. He saw me come in, this time, and said, "Good day, Lady Katherine. Can I help you with your studies? Or are you looking for some more, ah, feminine diversion?" To this day, I don't think he noticed I never wore a dress.

"Yes," I said poisonously; "what have you got that's really feminine in here?"

The librarian's face took on a worried look, as though if he couldn't find the right thing, he'd have to kill himself forthwith. "Ah, nature," he said nervously, "I believe is suitable for young ladies. The late duchess had many rare volumes of plants and animals—and though the classification of birds as animals is still in dispute by Doctors Milton and Melrose, I have put the bird books over here."

I settled myself in a cushioned window seat with a big illustrated volume. The pictures were bigger than live birds are, and you could see all the details. But it was hard to concentrate after my fight with Venturus, with the librarian there muttering to himself. I looked up and saw him pry a little worn leather volume out from between two grand tomes on a shelf. He flipped it open, then dropped the little book on a table as though it had a contagious disease, making disapproving noises all the while. When he left to wash his hands, I pounced on it.

"*The Swordsman Whose Name Was Not Death,* by a Lady of Quality." Opposite the title page was a woodcut of a man in old-fashioned clothes bowing to a lady, one hand on the sword at his side.

I opened to the first page. Many hours later, when the sun went down and I couldn't see the words, I had only gotten to the part where Lady Stella discovers she is with child, and runs away to her cousin in the country so that Fabian does not know it is his, which would ruin his concentration as he prepares for his duel against his great enemy in the University clock tower—although I was fairly certain even then that he would win it, but Mangrove would get away somehow, which he did.

I wrapped the book in my handkerchief and took it to my room. It wasn't stealing, because the duke's book was still in the duke's house, and it had looked to me like the librarian was just going to throw it out anyway.

I wasn't sure how Fabian got to be such a great swordsman when he never seemed to practice, but I admired the way he could fight up and down stairs, and how he lived by the swordsman's code but still was so clever about not killing Lady Stella although he was bound to. He took money for his work, but no one could make him do a thing that he despised, or harm the innocent. His word and his sword were his honor, everyone knew it, and they all respected him, even Mangrove, who hated him.

I tucked the book under my pillow, determined not to open it again 'til morning. But after supper I put a fresh candle in the holder, and settled down to find out who won the fight in the clock tower, and what became of Stella's baby. I cried so hard I had to get up and hunt for a fresh handkerchief. Even when I'd snuffed the candle I lay with my eyes open, thinking of swordsmen in dark cloaks, their perfect form, their steady hands and clear, unwavering eyes.

The next day I finished the book and immediately started it over again.

When the librarian appeared I asked him if there were any more books about swordsmen. He gave me *Lives of the Heroic Swordsmen*, which didn't mention Fabian or Mangrove, but did have some interesting people in it, like Black Mark of Ariston, who had fought one-armed after his great battle; and Harling Ober, who never refused a challenge, and had carried the sword at the wedding of my great-grandmother, Diane, Duchess Tremontaine. Ober had learned his art by sneaking up to a dangerous rooftop and peeking down at the great swordsman Rampiere, who had refused to teach him. I supposed that I was lucky to have Master Venturus. But my teacher failed to show for my next lesson. Perhaps he had quit, insulted. Perhaps he was staying away just to try and teach me respect. And perhaps he was preparing more mockery about a little scared duke-boy who could not learn the sword. I was all dressed for practice, so I practiced by myself. I wondered how I would fare if I were set upon by king's guards (if we still had a king), or had to fight with one foot on water, the other on the shore. I thought that I would like a cloak as black as night, and a jeweled pin to bind up my hair.

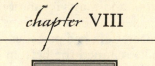

chapter VIII

HAVING SOWN DISSENT AT A MEETING OF THE COUNCIL OF Lords that morning, and being in the process of acquiring a new coat that afternoon, the Duke Tremontaine was in excellent spirits. He stood in a sun-washed room in his Riverside house, permitting one of his secretaries to read him the latest set of letters received and logged, while he simultaneously dictated responses, tried to hold still for the tailor and entertained a friend.

The duke's chief secretary, a balding young man named Arthur Ghent, removed the tapes from another roll of papers and shook them out. "These are the ones addressed to 'the Duke of Riverside,'" he explained. "I've passed the requests for money on to Teddy; he'll work from your list and include it in the month's report for you to approve. What's left are from people I've never heard of that maybe you have: the usual litany of complaints and suggestions." He shook out a ragtag batch of correspondence written on anything that could hold a sentence, from the backs of old bills to leaves torn from books. "Hmm . . ." He observed the writing on note after note. "Same hand, same hand, same hand . . . popular scribe. I wonder who it is?"

"Here, let me see." The duke stretched out his hand for the papers, opening up the seam the tailor had just carefully pinned. "Yes . . . I know him. Another University man—like you, Arthur, but not so fortunate as to have secured an important secretarial post. First he tried verse, then plays, then drink, which brought him to scribing letters for the less fortunate in Riverside. Let's see . . . what is on the mind of the less fortunate these days?" The duke scanned a few lines of one, then another. "They don't like the tearing down of ruins—too bad. They like the new gutters—I should think so. Sam Bonner fell in one of them and twisted his foot and wants reparation. Bonner . . . is he still alive? He was already pickled when I was a boy." He held the letter out to his secretary. "No reparation, bad precedent. No, wait—where's he writing from?" The duke scanned the bottom of the sheet. " 'At Old Madge's off Parmeter Street.' God, he's living in a cellar. Send him something; send him some wine. But no money." Ghent made a note on the back of Bonner's letter.

"It's a joke, you know." The Ugly Girl was sitting in the corner, watching the sun move across the patterned carpet. "This 'Duke of Riverside' business. It isn't your real title. You derive no income from Riverside; it's just your toy."

"That's what you think." The duke eased his long arms out of the coat for the tailor.

"You're wasting your time on all this. The world will always be full of drunks and liars and people down on their luck who never had any to begin with."

"Stick to your field, and let me amuse myself with my particular corner of it. Not so tight," he told the tailor, who nodded, his mouth full of pins. "I must have my hobbies. I don't ride, I don't dance, I don't race, and I don't collect objects of virtue."

She snorted at that. "I still say it's a waste of time. You'd do better to apply yourself to your mathematics."

Because he was in a good mood, he did not attack her. "But I am so useful. I am useful all the time. Today I managed to scuttle an appalling suggestion from an appalling nobleman who thinks he knows something about how this state should be run, and has managed to convince far too many people that he is right. It's just the beginning, of course: Davenant won't stop there; oh, no. He and his very good friend the Crescent Chancellor have a bright new tax plan in mind. One doesn't go after the Crescent like that, so I have started a rumor campaign against Davenant on the street, and called his allies into question with a plethora of minutiae in Council. It will take them days to get over it, by which time I have every reason to believe his mistress will be abandoning him for one of his supporters, which will make him do something stupid." The duke preened. "It is so nice to have work to do that is both useful and amusing."

The Ugly Girl grinned. "All right. I take it back. You are an ornament to society."

"I will be when this jacket gets done. You," he told the tailor, as he eased the duke back into it, "are nothing short of brilliant. I shall be the only man in the city able both to move his arms above his head and look well composed. I'll have another in blue—a different blue, I mean. Lighter. Silk. For when it's hot."

The tailor said, "I will have cloth samples sent for my lord to choose from." He nodded at his assistant, who stood against the wall trying to be invisible, to make invisible note of the duke's request.

"Ahem," said Arthur Ghent. "You said you'd decide today about the Talbert money. For your sister."

"Did I? I thought we'd set the whole thing in motion the day my niece arrived."

"You said not to. You said to wait."

"Did I?" the duke said again. "Well, I suppose I was worried that she'd bolt. She hasn't bolted, has she?"

"No, my lord," said Ghent's assistant. "Still at Tremontaine House, studying with Venturus."

"Well, then. Send the family the big sum, everything they asked for, as a loan against releasing their entire disputed property at the end of the six months."

"How complicated," Flavia said.

"It wasn't my idea; it's what I have lawyers for."

Arthur Ghent finished his notes and picked up another sheaf of papers, on better paper, some of it scented. "These are this week's invitations. Marlowe wants you to listen to his new soprano—"

"No. It's his mistress. She howls."

"Lord Fitz-Levi wants you for cards Wednesday—"

"On the Hill? No."

"Right. But you've turned him down twice now."

"Invite him to the next thing he can be invited to. Not the wife, though, just him."

"Right." He made a note. "Private theatricals at the, ah," he took a deep breath and said it: "the Gentlemen's League of Self-Pleasure."

The duke crowed. "Never! Tell them I am decadent, not desperate." The secretary's hand wavered above the inkwell. "Never mind," his master said mercifully. "Don't answer."

"Thank you, sir. Now, this is a grateful letter from the Orphans' Asylum, thanking you for the beds and the new roof and inviting you to their Harvest Pageant, where the children will sing, dance and recite."

"Regrets." The duke grimaced. "Just regrets. Ignore the other nonsense."

The Ugly Girl swung her foot under her. "You founded the place. Why don't you want to go?"

"I don't like children," the duke replied.

"Then why put out all that money to preserve them?"

"Because it is wrong to let them die." The duke shook the foam of lace at his cuffs, each flower and petal and leaf twisted thread upon thread by the fingers of an artist. "I did nothing to deserve this. I got it all because I had a grandmother with lots of money who left it to me. Before that I lived in two rooms in Riverside. I saw what happened to the products of a moment's pleasure. Other people do not deserve to starve or to be fucked before they know what the word means, just because they have no one."

The beautiful Alcuin had wandered in to hear his final words. He placed a proprietary hand on Tremontaine's silk-covered shoulder. "No one? Then you must get them someone."

"Sometimes," the duke drawled without looking up, "I am almost sure I do not deserve *you*."

Alcuin fiddled with the fall of lace on Tremontaine's collar. "I wish you would not speak that way."

The duke's secretary glanced over at the Ugly Girl. She caught his look and smirked back.

"The nobility of this city have no right to live the way they do," the Duke Tremontaine returned to his observations. "When they undid the monarchy, they revoked the traditional magical rights, not just of kings, but of themselves. They thus have no real right to rule, nor to hold land and profit by others' labors on it. It's odd that nobody's realized that. Though I suppose if anyone tried to say so, he'd be challenged or locked away somewhere, depending on his rank and his lucidity. The Court of Honor, you see, exists not just to legalize noble assassinations but to ensure that only a court of nobles ever has the right to judge a noble's deeds. A neat system, although I believe the privilege of the sword, as they call it, is beginning to show signs of fraying and wear."

"Is that so?" Flavia asked, drawing him out, amused—he did love to lecture—and he obliged:

"Most challenges are fought as pure entertainment. Your swordsman gets a scratch, or *his* does, and you're done for the day. The two nobles who called challenge on each other know what the fight was about, and usually their friends do as well, and everyone respects the outcome. Nobody asks swordsmen to die anymore just to prove a point of honor. Accidents or infection happen, of course, but as long as your man doesn't expire on the spot, nobody's bothered.

"But the darker side still exists, the practical origin of those little skirmishes. A noble can still hire a swordsman to challenge a nobleman without giving him time to find a professional proxy for himself. Even with all the protocols of formal challenge, at the end of the fight, unless he's amazingly lucky, you've got one dead nobleman. Does privilege of the sword extend to the swordsman who did it? Certainly, as long as he can prove he was in a noble's employ. The privilege belongs to them, after all. But to determine this, the matter is brought before the Court of Honor. That's where the real fun begins. The rules of the Court of Honor are arcane, the judgments colorful and highly personal . . . it's a perfect charade. I've been through it"— he shuddered— "I know. There's more honesty in Riverside, where all the privilege is about who's stronger and madder and meaner."

"What about your noble *women*? What's their privilege?"

He held up his arm to test the stretch of the sleeve again. The tailor nodded. "A woman's honor is still the property of her male relatives, according to the Court."

"Naturally."

"Noblewomen have been known to hire swordsmen when they felt a point needed to be made. But it's considered unladylike these days, as I understand it."

"And your niece?"

"What about her?"

"Will she, as a noblewoman, be fighting her own battles on her own behalf, or will she have to hire a man to do it?"

The duke smiled. "Well, that is the question, isn't it? She seems like a peaceable enough child. We'll just have to wait and see."

Cautiously, the tailor eased the duke out of his new jacket, and handed it to the assistant to fold. The duke watched with interest. "I think you fold things better than my valet," he said. "How would you like a new job?" The assistant turned bright red with the inability to answer. "You should seize your moments," the duke told him; "they may not come again. This is why it's so hard for tradesmen to advance in this city," he explained to the room at large: "timidity, lack of initiative; that, and the refusal of nobles to let them marry their daughters. You see," he told Flavia, as if their conversation had never been interrupted, "the nobles are going nowhere. The people who've actually done something to get the comforts they enjoy are the ones who are worth something: the merchants and craftsmen—not to mention the farmers, though you can't get rich off little patches of land, you have to have lots of it, and get others to work it for you— You didn't know that, I suppose?"

"I'm not a historian, or an agrarianist. Go on, though; I'm fascinated."

"If the nobles had any sense, they'd marry into families who knew how to fold things properly, instead of working so hard to marry back into each other."

"The trouble with you," the Ugly Girl said, "is that you think you know just what everyone should do, don't you?"

The Mad Duke smiled at her. His face was bright and sharp, smooth and glittering. "Yes," he said, "I do."

"And what," she said, "if you're wrong?"

"And what," he said, "if I'm not?"

WHEN MY NEXT LESSON CAME, I WAS READY. "MASTER VENTU-rus," I told him, "I deeply regret any unpleasantness between us." I'd never said anything like that before; I'd copied it from a speech of Mangrove's, the lying villain, because although he was at core a rotten being, no one could fault him for style. (I did, however, leave out the bit about passion overwhelming, because it did not suit.) "I hope you will forgive me, and consent to teach me as before."

The foreigner frowned. "Venturus is here, no? Why else here but to teach? You think he come to drink chocolate and pass the biscuit?"

So that was all right. We did the standing-still exercise with his serious blade again. But this time I remembered that, however weird he was, Venturus was a master swordsman. He wouldn't hurt me unless he wanted to. I admired his form. He was in perfect control of his body, the sword an extension of it; he could repeat the same move precisely, and he did, without wavering. Once I'd realized that, I started to enjoy the illusion of danger, the way his blade hissed past my cheek, tickled my sleeve.

"Good!" he said. "Because this time, you know no angry. You know no fear. You trust Venturus. But you not always fight Venturus. So you learn you trust you skin. Know where man's sword is all times. Know how close, how far."

This time the sword came from above. My whole scalp prickled with the sensation as it came at me. I felt the blade in my hair, like a leaf that had fallen, or a bug.

I knew when it was gone, before I even looked to see. It was not only that I no longer felt it, or that I saw him move. Or, I suppose, it was both of those things, and another I can't quite explain. Anyway, the sword was gone, and nothing in my body or Venturus's said it was coming at me. It was the oddest thing. I unclenched the hand at my side.

"Now you try," he said, standing perfectly still.

I retrieved a practice sword, harmless and dull; but before I could swing he was out of my reach, his sword up and guarding against me.

"You no say 'No move,'" he taunted, like a child. I felt a slow flush of anger. "Venturus always move," he grinned, "no matter you say." But then he turned to display a bulky figure behind him, swathed in a cloak. Theatrically, he whipped the cloak off to reveal a straw man. "So *here* this your partner to practice. He no listen, but he no move!"

I swung my blade at the straw figure, and was proud when I stopped the sword just short of it without wavering much. I targeted another point on it, and again I made it. I'd almost forgotten my teacher was there, when he said, "How? How? This you practice you chopping down trees? No!" But I did not fear his roaring. In fact, I thought he sounded amused. "Is practice now. Once again with the guard, the feint, the parry—but this time, when you strike—hit home!"

In guard, I glared at the straw man. If he tried a direct cut I would do—thus—and counter with—thus—feinting so that he changed his line—and I plunged the sword home into his heart! The tip went in so deep it was almost out the other side. I looked at it half in shame, half in satisfaction.

"How?" Venturus roared again. "What trickery is this? These are not patterns Venturus teach you, this mummery-flummery dancing about! Venturus is no dance-master. You think you partner is some girl-doll to play with, you make up you move? Why you laugh?"

The very last doll I loved was a china-faced lady with painted blue eyes. I used to dress Fifi in stylish gowns made from my mother's old dress scraps.

"Again," he said. "You show you move, just like I teach."

What sort of costume would I dress this huge straw doll in? Perhaps Betty would help me make a sweeping cloak as black as night. Using the patterns of attack and defense that he had taught me, in just the right order I had practiced many times, I stabbed Huge Fifi right through the heart.

Venturus nodded. "See, now, when you follow Venturus teaching, see how sweet she is?" He almost sounded coaxing. "See, how swift and clean is the stroke? The pure attack? The sureness of the thing that there is?"

I grinned at him. It did work, after all. "Good!" he cried. "I go now.

You follow teaching, is good. No follow, no practice, you hear me?" I nodded. "Bad habits ruin sword. Practice practice practice . . . now!"

I waited 'til he was gone; then I stared hard at Fifi. The straw head was just a featureless orb. Could I find somewhere a wig with inky curls? "You," I said, "may live to regret this day. Or, if not this day, the day that you met me. They are much the same. For two entered by that window, but only one of us shall leave by it. Have at you!"

I T WAS AN AWFUL, AWFUL DAY. ARTEMISIA COULDN'T SAY WHY, but it was. Her new dress had been delivered, and when she tried it on, she was convinced that the blue, so becoming in the shop, made her look like a frump, or an old lady. She actually cried over that, until Dorrie, her maid, in despair went and fetched her mother, who swore that it became her better than Lady Hetley's rose taffeta, which she had so much admired at Jane's barge party. Artemisia sniffled and allowed Dorrie to pin some ecru lace to the collar, and thought perhaps that did help. As she stared at herself in the mirror, she realized she had a spot coming out on her chin. Her gasp of horror was interrupted by her brother Robert storming into the room, calling, "Mother! Mother, I've been all over the house looking for you. Kirk says I cannot have the carriage, because Artemisia wants it to pay calls."

"Indeed she does," Lady Fitz-Levi said, "and doesn't she look like a picture?"

Her brother bit back a nasty comment about what kind of picture his sister made. "It is intolerable, Mother. I told you two days ago I needed the carriage to go out to the races today."

"Why don't you ride there, dear?"

"Mother, no one rides to the races! Where is Artie going, anyway, just across the street or something? Why can't she walk?"

"Oh, it's all right for *me* to get splashed with mud, is it?" Artemisia cried. "You pig, Robert! Well, it hardly matters, does it, since I have nothing to wear and I'm the ugliest thing in creation. Take your carriage, then—I just won't go. I'm never going anywhere again. And get out of my room, you pig."

Lady Fitz-Levi motioned Robert to follow her out into the hall.

"What on earth has gotten into her? She used to like going to parties."

"You must be patient," their mother explained. "She is a bit under the weather today. She did not receive an invitation to the Galings' musical luncheon, and she particularly wanted one, because a certain—ah, gentleman said he would be there."

"Oh really? Who?"

"Never you mind." His mother put a finger to her cheek. "The less said on that front, the better."

"Come on, Mother, maybe I know him."

"I'm not sure you do—he is a rather plodding young man, not for your set at all."

"If he's plodding, what does she see in him?"

"My concern is what he sees in her. He was starstruck, moonstruck, and paid her all sorts of compliments at the Montague ball. Trust Helena Montague to invite half the city, even ineligibles. I made the mistake of telling Mia not to take him seriously, so of course now she is making a meal of it. I would have done better to keep my mouth shut. Don't *ever* have a daughter."

Robert laughed. "I shall have several, and send them to you for advice. But maybe a dull, plodding sort of fellow is just what Artie needs to settle down and be happy with."

"Don't be patronizing, Robert. Dull is not what your sister needs. And most particularly, not dull and poor with romantic connections." Robert raised his eyebrows. His mother nodded. "Gregory Talbert. Yes. The most unmarriageable young noble in the city."

"*And* Tremontaine's oldest nephew. Who's to say there's not a duchy in his future?"

"Tremontaine, for one. There's a feud between the families. The duke has the privilege of naming his heir, and I doubt it will be any of his sister's children."

"What about the daughter, that girl he had brought here?"

His mother pressed her lips together. "You don't see her at any of the parties for the young ladies, do you?" She did not mention, even to Robert, that she had already intercepted one letter from the Lady Katherine to Artemisia, frantic and flowery and badly spelt, hinting at dire fates and desperate measures. She profoundly hoped that there would be no others. "Whatever the duke means to do with her, it can't be anything decent."

"The brother seems a solid enough fellow. . . . Don't worry, Mama, when I see him I'll try to warn him off."

"Thank you, Robbie. I know I can trust both my children to do the right thing. Anything you can do to help your sister right now . . . you see, you cannot underestimate the importance of her always being in her best looks and spirits at this particular time."

"Oh, she's always a huge hit. I don't see what the fuss is about."

"Robbie." His mother sighed. "Darling. May I speak to you as an adult?" He drew himself up. "All right. Listen. What happens to Artemisia this Season or the next will determine the course of her entire life from now on. She is on display, everything about her: her clothes, her hair, her teeth, her laugh, her voice . . . so that some gentleman can choose whether he wants to make her the mistress of his household and the mother of his heirs. Think of it as—oh, I don't know, as a horse that has only one race to win. If she marries well, she will be comfortable and happy. If she makes a poor choice, or fails to attract a worthy man, the rest of her life will be a misery. I know you young people think that, ah, physical attraction is enough. But when you're forty and the parent of a brood, if your spouse is poor or poor of judgment, believe me, there is no romance there."

She leaned forward confidentially. "Now, you and I know what a tremendous success Artemisia is, once she gets out there. You know no one has anything but good to say about our darling—and you'd tell me if they did, wouldn't you, Robbie, dear? But a woman alone, in her boudoir, well, she suffers certain anxieties. So you see, we all need to be very kind and helpful to her, right now. You understand that, darling, don't you?"

"If it will help get her married and out of the house, I shall do everything in my power," her brother said devoutly. And though his mother said he didn't mean it, and that there was no friend like a sister to see you through life's ups and down, he rather thought he did, and left, nearly colliding with the footman coming up the stairs with flowers for his sister.

Dorrie brought them in to her, hoping her mistress would be cheered by them. And indeed, Artemisia's face brightened when she saw the fine bouquet of roses and freesias. If a Certain Person had sent them, it would make up for everything, and she might hope again. With trembling hands (and with her mother standing by), she unfurled the note from the center of the bouquet. She could imagine already the soft words from one whose eye had caught hers, whose hand had gently caressed hers, and whose heart, perhaps, might someday win her.

"Oh no!" she shrieked. The note was signed *Terence Monteith*.

She cast herself upon the bed, sobbing, "I *hate* Terence Monteith! I hate everyone! It's all a disaster! Everybody hates me. Oh, leave me alone!"

In the end, they had to put her to bed with tea and a little brandy.

Had Robert only been a little more patient, he might have had the carriage, after all.

Artemisia curled up with her favorite book, and cried, and wondered whether any man would ever love her enough to risk his soul's honor for her sake, and why swordsmen were so *boring* these days.

chapter IX

My uncle's servant Marcus had been right: the gardens of Tremontaine House were beautiful, and beautifully tended, delightful and various. There were well-kempt paths and carefully clipped bushes punctuated by classical sculptures. Some of their stories I knew; other figures were quite obscure, but seemed to be involved in unlikely couplings. Perhaps they were a joke, or came from books only my brothers were allowed to read. There were also arcs and swirls of flowers and leafy plants of different heights and colors, set throughout with benches and bowers, though no one ever was sitting in them. And long grassy alleys ran down to the river. The more I practiced my sword, the more I felt like running down them, especially as the last of summer began to take on the bite of autumn.

In my boy's clothes I could hurtle along the banks and slopes without pausing to think about my skirts. Stone walls were easy to get over. I never had to go around, and even falling down never meant a torn hem or ruffle. I did tear a sleeve once, but that was a piece of foolishness, stretching my arms out over my head and rolling all the way down the grass to the river landing. The duke's barge floated there, wrapped in canvas. I wondered when I'd get to ride in it. I mended the sleeve myself as best I could, but it showed. When Betty took it away from me I thought she was angry and might tell the duke, but she only had it mended by a real tailor, good as new.

If my family had had the money for lessons, I might have learned to sketch and paint well enough to portray the gardens. If Artemisia had been a true friend to me, I might have invited her by now to do just that, for I was sure she had all the accomplishments. If ever I saw my uncle the Mad Duke again, perhaps I would ask him why I could not have a drawing master, in addition to Master Venturus? I could not spend every minute on swordplay. Why should he mind if I learned watercolors or something nice in my spare time?

Certainly I was not failing in my lessons. Venturus watched carefully as I strove against my straw doll, Fifi. He gave me pointers, and I began to realize that despite the bluster, his advice was always solid. I couldn't help giving Fifi a personality and clever countermoves to go with it—one day, when Venturus was being unpleasant about a failed move of mine, I said, "But what else am I to do when Fif—when my opponent comes at me with a high disarm?"

"Here." The swordmaster took a weapon from the rack. "I show." He came at me with a high disarm, which I failed to disengage and pass under until he showed me how. And, so simply, that was how we started sparring together.

I came to know the bright blade, first as something like a dance-partner as we rehearsed our patterned strokes and counters, parries and ripostes, and then as an unexpected visitor, to be anticipated in a half-breath, and turned as brusquely away.

The hardest part was looking in my teacher's eyes as I fought, but this he said I must do, although it felt horribly bold and immodest.

"No watch sword," he rasped, "watch man. Man is mind of sword."

As often as we sparred, my teacher grumbled that I was a waste of his time. "I fall asleep practicing you, duke-boy. Other students of Venturus learn on each other. You all alone with straw man and me, too much alone. Lucky have great teacher, very lucky he be practicing you. Why you crazy father make you live alone?"

"He's not my father," I said automatically for what was surely the hundredth time. "I'm not a boy."

"Venturus not fight with no girls." He raised his sword high, and pointed it downwards to signal a pause in the bout, so he could attack me with his temper. "You got no respect for teacher, you! Other students beg Venturus for lessons. You *argue* him. Ha!"

In the end, always we went back to practice, all morning now. I liked the feel of my teacher giving way on the floor before me, even if it was only an exercise. But I thought I deserved a chance at watercolors, too.

THE DUKE'S LOVER SAID, "I WISH YOU WOULD MAKE UP YOUR mind."

He shivered as the duke ran a cold finger down his back. "My mind is quite made up. The problem is, you don't like the way it's gone."

"I want to stay here in Riverside."

"And so do I. But not tonight. My poet must have dignity. He'll have more standing on the Hill."

"The whole city knows what you are. Which house you do it in hardly makes a difference."

The duke said, "You don't like my ideas, you don't like my choices . . . the truth is, you don't like me very much, Alcuin, do you?"

"Of course I do, I love you."

"It's all right. I don't like you much, either."

"Why do you keep me, then?"

"Who said anything about keeping you?"

Alcuin bent his beautiful head over the duke's manicured hand, sweeping it with his lips. "Please . . ." And Tremontaine did not push him away.

When the duke slept, though, Alcuin dressed, and scribbled a little note and propped it on the duke's dressing table, and ordered up a carriage to take him to the Hill. In the duke's bedroom, the curtains were always drawn; his lover was almost surprised to find that outside it was daylight.

They knew him at Tremontaine House, and he still wore their master's ring. They let him in, and nobody followed him through the corridors to the duke's apartments. There he looked for papers, any papers that might serve his needs and embarrass his lover, but he could not find what he wanted there, any more than he had in Riverside. He proceeded to the library and opened the likeliest books, but all that they contained were words. He had expected the room to be empty, and started violently when he heard the crackle of paper.

It was only a boy, pretty and well dressed, with astonishingly long hair—a student, then—sitting in the window seat with a book. As he prided himself on his ability to deal with any situation, Alcuin bowed to him. It was not, after all, as though he had been doing anything but looking at books. That was what one did in a library. He'd just have to wait for privacy for the desk to divulge its contents.

The boy got up hurriedly, shoving the book under a cushion. "Oh!" he said. "Is my uncle back?"

Alcuin stared. "And who is your uncle?"

"The duke, I mean," the boy stammered. "You're—you're Alcuin, aren't you?"

The man smiled, not unflattered to be known. "You've come early for the party, child." He moved in a little closer. Yes, you could see the family resemblance if you looked hard, though it was mostly in the tone of the skin, the setting of the eyes.

"Were you looking for something in here? Perhaps I could help you." This boy's lineaments were soft and round where the duke's were sharp-cut. In fact—

"No!" Alcuin snapped. "You keep out of my affairs." He should have recognized her sooner. Those silly clothes confused him.

The duke's niece boldly faced him, looking at him with a direct gaze he found disconcerting.

"There is no call to be so angry," she said. "When will my uncle be back?"

"I—" But he could not say he did not know. "Soon. In time for his party. Will you be performing the comic theatricals?"

He had the satisfaction of seeing her blush. But she stood her ground, and so the library was closed to him for now.

He returned to the duke's own chambers upstairs, which he found now occupied by their master in a snarling foul humor, attended by his boy, Marcus.

He was preparing to leave them when the duke said, "Stay out of the way tonight, Alcuin."

"Why? Are you afraid I'll draw attention from your precious poet?"

"I'm afraid you'll bore them to death. Nobody wants to hear your opinion on meter and verse. It is all too painfully obvious that you start thinking of these things only after other people have begun to talk about them."

"You're screwing your poet, too, aren't you?"

"If I am, you'll still have nothing interesting to say."

Alcuin went off to kick his valet, who surely had arrived by now.

"And stay out of my papers," Tremontaine said to the closed door behind him.

I HAD NOT ACTUALLY BEEN INVITED TO THE DUKE'S PARTY, BUT I was sure that was an oversight. I lived here, after all. And it would be a literary party, the servants said, not some debauched revelry, so there was no reason for me not to attend.

Except for one thing. My clothes.

"You have perfectly nice clothes, my lady," Betty said grumpily, "lovely ones the duke had made for you special." She was grumpy because the house staff were all busy getting ready for the influx of guests, and no one was listening to her stories of past mistakes. She'd gotten into the wine already, and it was making her stubborn. No matter how hard I explained to her that it was out of the question for me to appear before my fellow nobles dressed so outlandishly, she refused to listen. Clearly nothing short of a direct order from the duke himself would persuade her to retrieve even my meanest old gown out of wherever she'd hidden them all. I decided to go get that order from him myself.

I knew where the duke's room was. I marched right up to it and readied myself to knock.

The door opened, and a boy slipped out. It was Marcus, the servant about my age. He stood between me and the door, his back tightly to it, as if shielding it from me, or me from it.

"I just wanted to—" I began, but he held up his hand and looked concerned. "I wouldn't," he said. "Not right now."

"But it's—"

He shook his head. "Honestly. Trust me. Later. There's about to be an explosion." The door shuddered behind him. "And I have to go and get egg whites. Later." He fled down the hall one way, and I went back the other, sighing. So much for the party, then.

With the kitchen in chaos, it was easy to sneak in and supply myself with provender. I shut myself in my room to wait the evening out. I heard carriages arriving, names being called, people laughing. There was a long silence as they left the main hall for dinner; not a huge party, then. I ate apples and biscuits, watching the ever-glorious sunset over the river. As I lit a candle, I heard servants passing in the main hall below, lighting the many candelabra. It occurred to me, then, that I might easily watch undetected from the shadows at the top of the stairs.

It was just like when I was a child, sneaking out to the banisters to watch the grownups at my parents' parties. People had begun to mill about the hall's great gameboard, few enough at first that I could discern individual voices, fragments of conversation:

". . . Godwin doing here? I thought . . ."

". . . well, in poetry, if nothing else . . ."

". . . not if you held a candle to my feet!"

"Bernhard! Never knew you liked poetry."

"I don't. Wait and see."

". . . I knew he was pretty, but my god!"

"I doubt he'll last much longer. But consider, my dear . . ."

As I got to the top of the stairs, the horrible Alcuin came stagger-ing up them from the hall. Even I could see that he was very drunk, his eyes and feet unsteady, his lovely face slack with incomprehen-sion. He was without his coat, and his shirt was loose. His hair was weirdly spiky, as if he'd gotten egg whites in it.

I stepped aside. He seemed to be reaching for the banister, but he grabbed my wrist instead, leaning hard, as if he would have fallen with-out me. He did not look happy to see me. "Tremontaine," he slurred. "Another one." The weight of his grip was pulling me down. I couldn't shake him off. There were people downstairs in the hall just below us; I could get help if I needed it. But I would rather not let them know I was there. "Another Bitch Duchess."

Stupidly, I laughed. "I'm not anyone."

He pulled me to him. Amazing, how someone so beautifully made could be so loathsome. He began calling me names. I protested, "I haven't done anything to you. Stop it. Leave me alone." It was as though he couldn't hear me. If I screamed, everyone would come run-ning, but it would be so embarrassing. I brought my heel down, hard, on his foot.

Alcuin howled, but no one heard it because of the uproar that be-gan downstairs: ladies' shrieks mingled with cries of delight; more laughter, and shouts to come look. Alcuin staggered down the hall to throw up, and I raced to the railing to see.

Two men were standing in the middle of the hall with drawn swords. Crouched, they began to circle each other, taking each other's measure. There were no tips on their blades. The sharp steel was pointed at each other's faces. This was it, then: real swordsmen, my first swordfight! I clutched the railing, looking down, half afraid of be-ing seen, but more afraid to miss it.

Right under me, people were edged against the wall to watch. Their voices drifted up: "Not a chance . . . The dark one's got the reach."

"But look at that arm."

"Fifty on the dark one—what's his name? Anyone know his name?"

"You know who it *isn't*."

"Fifty, done."

Both swordsmen looked decent to me. One dark, one fair, and the fair one seemed edgy. *Fear hurts sword*. But was he really nervous, or just cautious? He seemed alert to everything, every possible move.

That could be to his advantage. The dark one had a lot of force. He might overspend that, though.

"Who else is game? Hurry up, before they're through."

There was a clash of weapons. Were they trying each other's mettle, or just making noise to get attention? Steel on steel rang out like a pure bell, long and long in the Great Hall.

"Nice form, there. Good job."

"And twenty more!"

I saw my uncle the duke, his arm around the shoulders of a rather pale young man who was clutching a bundle of papers. In the ringing silence the young man squeaked, "This is ridiculous. I am sure there was no insult intended."

The fighters began circling again.

"But a moment ago, you were sure there was," the duke said.

"I should not have said so."

The dark one made a feint, which the other backed off from.

"In real life, my sweet poet," the duke said as the swordsmen circled, "words can never be undone."

"But these men—to fight over such a thing—it's ridiculous."

"You are my guest," the duke said smoothly. "Your poetry was challenged in my house. It's lucky there were swordsmen here to take up the matter. Look out for Finch, the blond one; he's defending your verse's virtue."

A guest shouted, "All right, boys, let's go, let's see some action!"

The dark man's point was steady, pointed at Finch's chest.

"Let's have it!" a man's voice cried. "I've got money on this, let's go!"

Finch pressed suddenly forward, too quickly. It was a flashy move designed to startle your opponent and go right through his defenses, but it only works if you make them think you're doing something else, and he didn't take the time. Finch's opponent had no trouble blocking the blow. He parried and thrust home.

"Blood!" a guest called, and others took it up: *Blood! First blood!*

Finch staggered back. A dark stain spread on his white shirt. His opponent stood very still, his sword lowered. There was silence in the hall.

The duke said to the poet, "You've lost. Or, rather, Finch has lost in your person. It comes to the same thing. Unless you want them to go past First Blood to the Death? There's still a chance—"

"No," said the poet.

Finch dropped his sword then, and pressed the free hand to his side. The winning swordsman bowed to the duke.

I gripped the stair rail. I wanted to make them do it over again, do it right this time; but it wasn't an exercise. I wasn't sure what it was.

Finch sat down and put his head between his knees. Servants passed through the circle with bandages and water for him.

"Well, that's it, then," the duke announced loudly, and, just as loudly to the poet, "I'm afraid you will have to leave."

"But—why?"

"Your poetry turns out to be awful. I wouldn't have thought it, but there it is. Finch is bleeding."

The poet laughed uncertainly. "I see. Very amusing. But it's not real; you can't take it seriously."

The duke just looked at him. "My dear. Here on the Hill, I'm afraid we take it very seriously. A nobleman of the city brought your poetry's virtue into question—'Duller than a rainy Tuesday and twice as long' was the way you put it, Bernhard, I believe? A challenge was issued. There was a duel, and the swordsman defending the honor of your verse was defeated."

"But—one man sticking another with a sword cannot change my poetry from good to bad just like that."

"The duel is the ultimate arbiter of truth. Where men's judgment may be called into question, the opinion of the sword always holds fast." Half the room was listening to him, amused; the rest were settling debts or debating the fight. If these people didn't stop laughing and gambling soon, I wasn't going to be able to stand it. "If you stayed—well, you could stay. If you like. But it gives license for people to be very rude to you. I don't think you would enjoy it. No, really, you had better go."

They brought the poet his cloak and hat. My uncle saw him to the door himself; as they passed beneath the stairs, I saw his ringed hands pass the poet a small heavy purse.

I wondered if the poet would think it had been worth it.

"Bernhard!" the tall duke turned and shouted into the crowd. "That was not very nice."

"You are ungracious." A large well-dressed man detached himself from the throng. "I thought you would enjoy a good fight better than whining poetry."

"You . . . thought?" An invisible wind had blown the duke from hot to cold. The room itself felt chilly, and the guests were still. "Let me ask you, Bernhard: do you think the Lords Justiciar would be pleased to hear that you called formal challenge on some poor scribbling fool who, as far as they are concerned, has no honor to defend?"

Lord Bernhard had the sort of heavy face that turns red with any emotion. "Hardly a matter for the Court of Honor, I would have thought."

"Or did you mean the challenge for me, here in my own house?"

"I had not known you for such a traditionalist, Tremontaine," Bernhard said, earning a laugh from some of them. "Although," he went on, "I suppose the purity of swordsmen is a passion of yours, isn't it, my lord?"

The laughter stopped. The duke spoke quietly, but I had no trouble hearing him. "Bernhard. Let me do a little thinking for you. You are in my house. Finch is not my only sword. If I call challenge on you this very moment, who will come forward to fight on your behalf?"

Bernhard forced a laugh.

A nice-looking man in blue said, "Tremontaine, really; you know the world. The Court doesn't attend to such trivia. And I am sure Bernhard meant no insult to you or to your house."

I would have done whatever he suggested; even the duke shrugged mildly. "I am not insulted, Godwin. When I am, Bernhard, I'll send you formal notice. I just wanted to point out that this fight was not strictly legal. And since Tremontaine sits on the Court of Honor (when I have a mind to), I could invoke the Lords Justiciar to attend to such 'trivia.'" He turned to the room, holding up his hands as if he were in a play: "Good heavens; if I, a known scoffer and reprobate, am the only one left willing to uphold the ancient forms, what hope is there for any of us? Who else are we planning to extend the privilege of the sword to?"

There was an embarrassed silence. My uncle let it last a long time before he said cheerfully, "Oh, well. Now that you have taken our original entertainment from us, Bernhard, I'm afraid I must ask you to supply the lack. What can you do?"

"I?" The man was bright red.

"Can you fight? Well, of course not. You do breed dogs, but nobody wants to watch that—not unless they're a member of your Gentlemen's Self-Pleasure League." I heard a woman shriek with embarrassed laughter. "Heavens, Bernhard, what *can* you do? Surely you can . . . read. Yes, I think you had better read to us. Something of my lady," he bowed to a serious-looking woman, "my lady Evaine's choosing. If you will follow me to the library, we'll find many excellent volumes there. You can regale us with . . . poetry, I think, don't you, my lady?"

And so, one by one, the party and its guests passed out of my sight. Of the two swordsmen no sign remained. Not even a smear of blood marked the black-and-white patterned floor of the hall of Tremontaine House. Instead there were fragments of flowers, a dropped fan, half a pastry, several buttons, a comb and a broken glass.

I took off my clothes and got into bed. I felt the hard lump of the book under my pillow, *The Swordsman Whose Name Was Not Death*. How could I sleep with that thing sticking into my head? There was not a grain of truth in it, none. Swordplay was two fools hacking at each other with razors until one of them was hurt. I took the book out and hurled it across the room.

chapter X

TREMONTAINE HOUSE WAS QUIET THE NEXT MORNING, NOT because it was uninhabited, but because its occupants were mostly asleep. Everything wet or edible had already been cleared away; everything valuable had been cleaned.

Only one large, high-ceilinged room had its curtains pulled back to let in the long cheerful ribbons of morning sunlight. Outside the tall windows, a garden beckoned. But the muscular black-bearded man stood with his back to it. Occasionally he would spin around as if to challenge the view, stamping one foot on the floor to make the decorated ceiling ring, then turn again towards the door. Once he sprang from a crouch and leapt almost the length of the room. He hummed disapproval into his mustache. He inspected the rack of glittering swords, first overall, then blade by blade, looking for rust spots or fingerprints. As he found none, he permitted himself a smile.

Because he heard the door open, and saw who it was reflected in a blade, he did not turn around to look at the girl dressed in sober blue-grey linen. When she had shut the door behind her, then he turned, and let her see the smile.

"Clean blades," he said. "Very good."

"Thank you."

"Well? You are a statue? Pick up sword!"

The girl fixed on his face the steady gaze that he had taught her. "I will not fight today."

"How, not fight? You will not fight? Maybe we will play at dice, then, ah? Or learn the dance? *Booger,* you will not fight!"

She did not smile. "No. I will not be going on with these lessons."

"What lessons, then?" He thrust a finger in her face like a dagger. "You have some other lessons? Your mad father think you are too good now for Venturus, that you will learn more better from some street-puke swordsboy indeed? Ha!"

"Ha," she repeated tonelessly. "Do you know, Master, you sound like a jealous lover?"

"Do you know . . ." he mimicked. He took a step back, with a little bow. "But who have we here? Is it not some fine-aired lady, indeed? This lady I do not know, though she wear the britches."

"I will be sure that you are properly paid," she went on. "I am certain that there is money here for that. And your other students will no doubt be glad of your time."

"But this is grave." He stopped his posturing and met her gaze with one of his own. "This is no girlish humor, I think."

She dropped her eyes. "No. It is not."

"Why you no wish fight?"

She turned away. "You wouldn't understand."

"Ha. Girlish humor after all. You are in love?"

She spun in quick riposte. "Certainly not! Love? I shall never be in love, if people always think it makes you stupid! No, I'll tell you what it is—" And it was her turn to lean in to him, her face closer to his than a swordsman would normally allow— "I've seen them. Real ones. Last night, at the party here. Two swordsmen. A duel. It was disgusting."

"Blood. A mess. Now you are afraid—"

"I am *not* afraid. I see twice as much blood every month. It was the duel— I told you you wouldn't understand."

"I am not paid to understand you humors." He'd pulled a blade from the rack and began circling her with it. "You not afraid, ha?"

"No, I'm not. But I will *not* be made a show of."

"A show, ha?" He jabbed at her with the padded tip, feinted and jabbed again. "Just a show?"

"That's all any of it is, a show for people to laugh at. It was a *game* to them, that's all, just some stupid game! They place *bets*—stop that."

"Bets?" He was forcing her back a pace, two paces, now that she had begun to take notice of his blade.

"Bets on the outcome—two perfectly good— Ouch!" Her back was to the rack; he'd jabbed her in the shoulder. "Perfectly good swordsmen, nothing wrong with them, but they were doing it for—"

"Money? You think men should not fight for money, little girl?" He backed off, making midgelike circles with the tip of his blade. "Men without nice dukes should beg they money in streets, before fight they for pay?"

"He's not paying *me*," she said tightly. "I don't know what *your* fee is, but he's not paying me. I'm supposed to do it for free, to make a show of myself to amuse—to amuse—" The swordmaster feinted high, low, elaborate little spirals of disengage and riposte up and down his target, annoying as summer flies. "I said, stop that."

"What for? No peoples looking here. Just us, little boy duchess."

The sword was in her hand, and she attacked. Venturus fell back before her. She tried to kill him, despite the blunted tips, and he fought with a grin splitting his beard. She went for the eyes, the throat, but he was quick in his defense. Around and around the room they went, and he let her tire herself out with every trick she knew. He waited until she began to slow, and then Venturus stepped in with one perfect thrust.

She flung her blade into the corner. It rattled and clanged.

"Not too sad a fight," said Master Venturus. "Now we will stop for awhile. Good day, Lady Katherine."

And she was alone, sweating, in the practice room with the wet rabbits on the door.

I WAS AWAKENED EARLY THE NEXT MORNING IN THE COLD GREY light. The fire had not yet warmed the room any. Betty was bustling about, folding clothes and putting them in a trunk. "Come," said Betty, "hurry up, dear. My lord says you're to travel. The carriage waits."

There was no point in arguing with her. If he said travel, travel I must. I let her button me into my chilly traveling clothes topped with long boots, hat, heavy cloak. A mist was on the river.

Into the carriage with bread, a hot flask and blankets. Betty waving to me; a cluck of the coachman, a creaking of gates and Tremontaine House was behind me. The city passed away like a series of pictures; then, for the first time in many weeks, I was in the open country. The sun was coming up, a golden haze of warmth. Wrapped in the blankets, I dozed, woke to a stop for the horses, stretched my legs and sat the rest of the afternoon, watching as unfamiliar countrysides of fields of golden wheat gave way to streams and cows and orchards. When the shadows started to stretch across the road, they stopped the coach to consult with me.

"Shall we push on to Highcombe tonight, my lady? It will be dark. But there's a nice little inn not far along, if you'd rather stop for the night."

It was all one to me. But I knew when I was being suggested to. We stopped at the nice little inn, and I got a good dinner and a reasonable bed. I did not ask the coachman or the groom what Highcombe was, could not think of a way to do it that would not betray the fact that I had no idea what was going on. Until they had named our destination, I had dared to think that perhaps I was going home—a failure, maybe, but going home, still. A trunk of my belongings was lashed up behind us; wherever I was being sent, it was not for a brief visit.

The next morning we rose again early, and by the time the sun shone watery above in a cloudy midmorning, the carriage was rolling through the gates of a lodge and down a graveled alley lined with tall trees. I caught glimpses of a great stone house, three times the size of my old one. But instead of rounding the drive to its front steps, we suddenly went off the path and began bumping over the grass to the other side of the house. We pulled up before a little cottage tacked onto the wall, with its own wooden door painted a cozy blue.

I stood in the damp grass and smelt earth and apples crossing with hay and horses. It wasn't quite the smell of home, but it wasn't city, either. Stretching away from the blue door across from the lawn (now beribboned with the silver marks of our carriage wheels) was an apple orchard in one direction and fields in another. A stream cut through them both. The fields were silvery with long, wet grass; it had rained here in the night, and clouds still lingered. Coming across the fields I saw a man with a staff, his head uncovered.

"There he is," said the coachman, and hailed him: "Master!"

Fine drops of mist ornamented the man's dark hair. He raised his head and leapt the stream, and came to us.

The footman spoke. "The duke's greetings, Master. He presents his niece, the Lady Katherine. She will be studying with you, he says. And we've brought you some things from the city."

"Thank you," said the man. "You can put them inside."

The blue door was not locked. I stood looking at my new tutor and wondered what I would be studying. He had the earth-caked hands of a gardener, well-shaped fingers squared off at the tips. His face was unshaven but not yet bearded. He did not seem to mind my staring, though his own gaze was less direct. I felt he was looking past me.

"Are you Janine's daughter?" he asked.

"You know my mother!"

"No. But Alec's spoken of her."

"Who's Alec?"

The man smiled. "The duke."

Another name. "You're his friend? Is this Highcombe?"

"Yes, it's his house. One of them. I live here."

The men had finished their deliveries. Even my trunk was stowed inside. "Will that be all, sir? Will you need anything else?"

"Thank you. Nothing else, if you've brought everything I asked for."

"All in the chest, according to my list. The spoons are wrapped in the linen. We can wait if you like, but our orders are to return to town as soon as convenient."

"That's all right, then. Thank you; good-bye."

I did not feel melancholy or afraid as the Tremontaine carriage pulled away, leaving me in a strange place with a strange man. Indeed, I could hardly wait for them to go, so I could find out what would happen next.

Part II

HIGHCOMBE

chapter I

W HAT HAPPENED NEXT WAS THAT HE ATTACKED ME. HIS
staff swung up and I ducked, my hands over my head.
The staff hovered in midair, brushing the edge of my
cloak.

"You haven't been studying long," he said.

"Not very," I agreed, adding, "You aren't supposed to do that. You
didn't call for my guard, or issue a challenge, or anything!"

"Sword against staff is tricky," he observed. "But you didn't even
reach for your blade."

"I'm not wearing one."

"Even then. You aren't in the habit, and that's dangerous. Go put
one on right now, and then we can get you fed and rested."

None of my baggage was long enough to contain a sword. I followed him through the blue door, into the little cottage.

"Climb that narrow flight of stairs," my host said. "At the top, in
the corner of the room, left of the window, you'll find a chest with
blades wrapped in oilcloth."

I had to open the shutters before I could see anything. It was a very
plain bedroom. The chest was plain as well, but what was inside it
made my breath catch. From the protective cloth I unwrapped long
gleaming blades of extraordinary beauty, with hilts both plain and intricate. I'd never seen anything like them. Everything about them was
sharp, including the tips. One, with a dragon's head on the pommel,

looked just like the sort of thing Fabian would carry, or someone in *Lives of the Heroic Swordsmen.*

I called downstairs, "May I choose any one I want?"

"No." His voice was firm but amused. "Try the twisted basket hilt; it's probably closest to the right weight for you."

I stood at the top of the stairs. They were horribly steep, not much more than a pitched ladder, really. If I slipped or stumbled, the sharp edges in my hand could turn against me.

"Had I better find a scabbard?" I asked nervously.

"Bottom of the same chest. Leather, and not too gaudy, youngling."

Getting the long sword into the soft scabbard was a bit like getting a bootie onto a baby's foot: neither was very interested in helping, though in the end they fit together just fine. I came carefully down the steep stairs.

"Don't I need something to stick it in? I've got a belt, but there's a hanging thing, too, isn't there?"

"Oh, dear," the man sighed. "He wasn't thinking, was he?"

Whether he meant the duke or Venturus was all one to me; I was just glad he didn't think it was my fault. Reaching for his staff, the man rose suddenly, and I jumped, clutching the sword to myself. To my surprise, "I'm sorry," the man said. "I'll try to move more slowly, until you learn me better. I was just going to get you a hanger."

He stood closer to me than Venturus ever had, fitting the sword's hanger on my belt, and the sword in with it. His fingers were steady and sure, like a stableman's harnessing a horse; he didn't even have to look, and I felt his breath warm across my hair. When he moved away, there was a part attached to me that had not been there before. It moved when I moved, like a cat's tail—though without any of its grace!

He put a loaf of bread on the table, and a block of yellow cheese. When I sat on the bench I had to move the sword out of the way to keep from sitting on it, which wasn't as easy as you'd think. I looked to see if the man was laughing at me, but he was cutting bread. It was good bread, and the cheese was good, too.

"What about a knife?" he asked. "Did he give you a knife, at least?"

"I—I have a penknife." It had been a New Year's gift from my brother.

"No sword, no knife . . . Use this." He handed me his. It was well worn and rather ugly, with a plain wooden handle, but the blade very bright and thin with repeated grinding.

"I couldn't take your knife," I began to demur politely, but he interrupted, "I've got more. One with a dragon's head, one like a falcon . . .

I won't miss this one. Don't lose it, though; wear it on your belt." He caught my moment of hesitation as if it were a ball I'd thrown. "—In a sheath, of course. Oh, dear."

When he got up from the table I jumped and fumbled for my sword, which took the bench up and over with it. This time, he did laugh. He sounded so helpless, as if I'd just crippled him by telling a brilliant joke very well, that I laughed, too.

"Never mind," he said when he could speak again. "You're just going to give yourself a stomachache. Learn to walk with it, first, and then we'll see about defending yourself."

I was so horribly grateful that I had to stand up for my pride. "I can fight. I fought Master Venturus."

"Did you? Who won?"

"He did," I mumbled.

"Good. Then it was a real fight." He put the bread and cheese back in the cupboard. I swept up the crumbs. "There's milk in a pitcher in the stream," he said, "and sometimes beer, when they remember. Well water's in the courtyard—it's a bit of a haul, so I keep a bucket by the door. Don't drink from the stream; the cows step in it. It's all right for washing. You can go off exploring now if you'd like; you must be cramped from the ride. Just don't go in the field with the bull. Oh, and I'd stay clear of the village; I don't think they're ready for you."

I concluded regretfully that he was right, which was a shame, since they could probably tell me all about him. But I knew our own villagers. They would not warmly receive a girl dressed as a tumbler, and I bet the Highcombe folk wouldn't either. So I followed the stream into the woods instead, and found a little waterfall and a blackberry thicket with plenty of berries left, and an empty bird's nest floating in the water.

I came back as the shadows were long across the fields, my favorite time of day. The man was standing in front of the cottage, wearing nothing but a shirt over his breeches, sword in hand. I waved, but he didn't wave back; instead he turned and did something like a dance that wasn't, because the sword was flashing about in a determined manner, and when he stopped, you had the impression that he had won. I took a deep breath and went forward.

"Are you ready?" the swordsman asked.

"Wait—" I fumbled, and wrestled my sword out of its sheath. I was on guard, and so was he. And then things were happening very fast. He'd move, and I'd find his blade within my guard, and I'd think of the parry I should have made if only I'd seen him coming in time, but by then he'd struck again somewhere else. After a bit of this, at least I was ready to do *something* when he moved, even if half the time it was something that left me poking into thin air while he came at me again. Of course I never came anywhere within his guard; I only had to think about it for him to be right where I wanted to attack. As if he were weaving a fence around himself with his steel.

At last he stepped back and put up his blade, and I saw it just in time to keep from making a fool of myself by trying to skewer him.

"I take it," he said, "you've never killed anyone."

"Oh, dear no!"

"Just checking." He turned and went in the house. He wasn't even panting. I went and washed my face in the stream. And then went in to supper, which was vegetables boiling on the hearth. And bread and cheese.

But on the plain wooden table were a pair of candlesticks, silver dragons supporting the candles with their mouths. At each of our places was a wineglass flecked with gold, whose stem was a twisting dolphin.

"How beautiful!" The words escaped me. He held his glass by the stem, stroking the fragile curves familiarly. I could almost feel the cool, smooth glass just by watching him.

The vegetables needed seasoning, but I was hungry enough not to care. When I finished eating, suddenly I was so tired I could have put my head right in my empty plate.

"Sleep upstairs," he said. "I'll help you carry your things."

I wrestled myself and my gear gingerly up the narrow stairs, holding the candle.

"Don't worry," he said. "There's a pot under the bed; you don't have to risk breaking your neck in the dark."

I grinned, then considered that since there seemed to be no house servants I'd have to empty the thing myself. Not down the ladder-stairs, please! Maybe out the window. There were two: a large one with shutters, and a little round one over the bed. It glowed red with sunset, like stained glass.

He reached out and shuttered the window. As with everything else he did, his movements were economical and practiced. Suddenly my heart started to beat very hard. This was his bedroom. Did he know I was not a boy? He did know, didn't he? I could sleep in my clothes. I had a knife, but I'd better not try it. I remembered his hands on my belt, his breath in my hair, the sharp tip of his blade dancing around me. Maybe it would be all right. He was so quiet.

"Take the belt off," he said, "sword and dagger all at once, and try not to drop them. Hang the whole thing on that hook, then you can put it right on in the morning."

With cold fingers I complied. Of course I dropped the whole kit on the floor: the sword pulled one way, the dagger another, slipping along the belt. It was hopeless.

"Never mind." He smiled. "Good night."

He was on the stairs before I had the wit or the breath to object politely, "But where will you sleep?"

"I've got a pallet by the fire. It's fine. I get up during the night; this way I won't disturb you."

I heard an owl cry once, and then I was asleep.

———

D RESSING THE NEXT MORNING, I FOUND A TINY RIP IN THE sleeve of my jacket, as if it had caught on something sharp like a nail. Betty hadn't packed me any needle and thread; it was my turn to mutter, "Oh, dear." The swordsman apologized. "That was me, I'm afraid." He seemed annoyed. "I'm sorry; I didn't mean to touch you at all."

He had caught my jacket once in the entire bout with naked blades. I didn't think Master Venturus could do that well. Maybe he could. Fabian certainly could; he could even put out a candle flame. Maybe everyone could but me, even those showmen dueling at the duke's party.

"Let's go find some practice weapons," the man suggested. "I don't want to tip my good steel, and you're bound to knock it about some at first."

That was when I found out there was another door to the house. It was next to the hearth, and I hadn't even noticed: a piece of the wall with a handle and hinges. We passed from the modest cottage into the marble grandeur of the great house at Highcombe, like moving from one dream to another. A great hall with ceilings twice as high as the entire cottage. Useless, decorative space, and everywhere there was furniture shrouded in sheets, tall windows shuttered.

"Does he come here ever?" I wondered aloud.

"Oh, sometimes. He doesn't like the country much."

We found the old armory, full of antique weapons and country things like boar spears. My teacher picked us out some old, blunt practice swords, and we started back through the hall.

Suddenly, he grinned at me. "Hey!" he cried. "On your guard!"

I raised my sword, and he retreated before me. "Don't worry," he called, "I'll keep falling back—just come on!"

And so I advanced on him, all the way down the long gallery, driving the master swordsman back with my clumsy tipped blade, sweeping past the portraits and landscapes, the swathes of sheeting, the covered mirrors, over the polished parquet.

He fetched up against a door, his face bright with laughter, and spread his arms open to me. I sighted my spot, to the left of his breastbone, and lunged—but he deflected the point with the tiniest of motions and my sword jarred in my hand.

"You want to relax your grip," he said, "but that was good: a nice, clean attack." He was laughing, looking back down the length of the hall. "God, I've wanted to do that ever since I got here! Thank you."

As the doorlatch behind him clicked, he spun, weapon raised. The woman coming through the doorway screamed and dropped her tray. He jumped back, and I chased after the rolling silver goblets while he said, "I'm so sorry," and she gasped, "Oh, sir! Oh, sir!"

It was awkward having no apron to collect them in. Boys don't need aprons, do they?

"This is my new student," he said, and to me, "Marita is the housekeeper." I was grateful to him for not revealing me as the duke's niece; it would have been all over the countryside by nightfall. As it was, she just looked hard at me, registered my sex and decided not to do anything about it. Then she took her silver and curtseyed. "I'm sorry to disturb you, sir," she said, for all the world as though he were some nobleman, and not the tenant of a tacked-on two-room cottage. "Is everything in order?"

"Yes—no, wait, we need, what was it? Needle and thread."

She curtseyed again.

I suppose being able to kill people was enough to make them very polite to you, but I couldn't help wondering. "Are you a lord?" I asked when she was gone.

"Me?" His smile flashed white. "Hardly."

And that was all. He dressed very plainly, he wore no rings. He did not speak like a countryman. But neither did he sound educated, and there were no books where he lived. Nothing but swords, and precious things.

"I expect you have killed a great many people," I said at dinner in my best grown-up conversation voice.

"Yes, I have."

"Is it hard?"

He looked out past me. His eyes were unusual: blue, almost violet, like the heart of a candleflame. "Killing them instantly is hard. You want a blow to the heart, which is tricky, or through the windpipe, or through the eye to the brain, but people don't like to see that." I began to be sorry I asked. I put down my food. "Disabling them is easiest; they may die later, from infection or loss of blood. It's less satisfying. But it takes a lot of force to kill with one blow. You'd be surprised. I'm not sure you've got the strength yet. Even to pierce a lung . . . I could give you some exercises. Did you mean dueling, or street fighting?"

"Neither," I whispered. "I don't want to kill anyone."

"Then put your sword away," he said mildly, "or you will be killed." I shot a look up at him, but he merely looked interested.

"I don't want it," I blurted. "I never wanted any of this!"

"Really?" He considered me with his head tilted. "Then what do you want?"

I thought of gowns and balls, and of sewing and housekeeping, and of swordsmen and towers. . . . Nowhere could I see myself. "Nothing! I wish I was dead!"

He did not mean to laugh, but I could hear the stifled breath. "How old are you?"

"Fifteen. And a bit."

"Hmm. When I was sixteen I left home and went to the city. I didn't know what I wanted, either. But things kept happening to me. It was interesting, and I found I could manage."

"That's different. You're a man. And you could fight."

"So you're a woman. And you will be able to fight. Are you sure you wouldn't like to reconsider?"

"Reconsider what?" I said rudely, deep in my own misery. "It's not as though I have a choice."

"Well," he said, "I suppose that's true. Do you have any idea why he's doing this?"

"None," I said. "Because of my father. He hates us."

"I think he hated his own parents more. I think he thinks that if your mother had known how to fight, they couldn't have forced her to marry if she didn't want to."

I stared at the man across from me. "Did he tell you that?"

"No. I figured it out."

"They didn't force her. She wanted to get married. No one's going to want to marry me."

"So what? You can have lovers."

I nearly yelped with shock. What did he think I was? "I'll clean up," I said instead.

Before going to bed, I opened his sword chest. The weapons were so finely crafted, they looked like settings for jewels. I touched the tip of one, gently, so that it did not break the skin. The oil from my finger's tip would be enough to darken and corrode the steel. I pictured the shining metal covered with blood. Keeping cloth between my hands and the blade, I examined the dragon's head sword. Near the hilt, a fleck of red. I rubbed at it. Rust. I should clean it, or tell him it was still there. Carefully, I wiped away the bit that I had touched.

H E WAS GONE WHEN I GOT UP THE NEXT MORNING. HE'D LEFT plates and crumbs on the table and walked away. I helped myself to breakfast, then began to rearrange things—not on purpose, but piece by piece, as I got ideas on where they would look nice. I set the dolphin glasses to catch the sun, made the jam and oil and honey pots line up in order of size and even angled the benches so we'd each have more room to sit. I did it all wearing my sword, too. Nothing had been moved in a long time; there were marks everywhere on floor and shelf, and so I swept and dusted as well. When I finished, it looked quite nice: a tidy room, glowing in the autumn sun.

I was drinking cold tea when the swordsman came in. His face was bright, his cloak thrown back, as if he'd been for a good long walk.

"Hello," I said politely. "Would you like some tea?"

"Yes." He smiled. He didn't say anything about the room. He walked forward and smashed into the bench, landing hard on the table, and sent my cup flying. I shouted, "Are you all right?"

"Yes." The swordsman got up slowly. "I just didn't see it. Have you moved things?" I'm afraid all I could do was stand and gape. "Because it would be better if you didn't."

He could see, I knew he could! I remembered the way he'd shown me around, the sure way he cut the bread and dished things up. . . . My skin crawled when I thought of our duel with the bare-tipped swords, and his annoyance at having grazed my sleeve just once.

"I'm sorry," I managed to whisper. "I won't anymore."

He brushed himself off, found the bench and righted it and walked around the table, touching it, seeming to see it with the edges of his eyes.

I glanced over at the glasses, the pots.

"Shall I show you the rest?"

"No, I'll find them. I just wasn't expecting it."

"I'm sorry. I could move things back—"

"No, I'll take care of it."

I had to know, and was afraid to ask. I watched him touch things and look at them. He never held them up in front of his face, but somewhere to the side, or even above. Sometimes he'd find them and touch them first, and never seem to see them at all. It was as if his hands and his eyes were not connected: one knew the world one way, the other another one, and to make them speak to each other was an act of deliberation.

"Lady Katherine." He did not like being watched. "You might take this time to practice. We will duel this afternoon."

I should have been quiet, obeyed the dismissal in his voice, been a good child, kept the unspoken agreement between us that neither would ask anything uninvited, or come too close. But I was frightened now. Nothing was as I'd thought. I had power over him, to move things and make him crash into them, to hurt him by shifting a bench, and he had power over my every breath and I didn't even know who he was—

"Are you blind?" I demanded.

"Almost."

"But then how . . . ?"

"Hold your hands up in front of your eyes. No, a little further than that. Now, can you see?"

"Yes— No—I can see around them, but not . . ."

"That's exactly it. It takes some getting used to."

"What happened to you?"

"Nothing. It just came on me."

"Were you a swordsman?"

"I am a swordsman if I am anything."

"But if you can't see—"

"I can see what I have to."

"Did you work for the duke? Were you his swordsman?"

Surprisingly, the man smiled. "I suppose you could say I was his. And I certainly am working for him now: I've never been anyone's tutor before. It will be interesting to see what you can learn."

This time, I took his unspoken direction. "I'd better go practice, then."

Outside, I closed my eyes and hurled myself against the weight of the sword, the quickness of my own breathing, the slowness of my feet, the brightness of the day.

chapter II

As the Duke Tremontaine had predicted, there was chaos in the Council of Lords, and some of it could be laid at his door. The apportioning of new land taxes had been all but decided upon, and penalties for noncompliance laid out strictly but fairly. The unfortunate lack of rain in the south did not excuse a poor harvest; the nobles whose lands were the country's breadbasket would just have to extend themselves in some other way—lumber, perhaps. It was unfair that the northern nobles were expected to provide more than their share of wood for shipbuilding, at a time when trade was so profitable and the river so low that in places you could barely bring the northern lumber down at all. But foreign grain was cheap this year, and shipping lucrative. And if the river was impassable, roads could be widened and improved—roads that happened to pass through the lands of the ambitious Philibert, Lord Davenant, and his political affiliates. They were powerful men; they served their country well, as had their fathers before them. What harm in a little profit for their faithful service, when the benefit to all was so clear to any but the most pig-headed of councilors?

But when copies of a certain document—a private agreement between Davenant and a foreign shipper, misleadingly worded so as possibly to be mistaken for a treaty between two countries—began to circulate, it threw the motives of all his associates, these noble councilors, into question. The original of the document was never found, of course, and no one could ascertain where the copies had come from; but it was enough to throw the coalition into disorder, their opponents into a rash of aggressive realignments and their tax proposals into brightly fluttering shreds. If that wasn't enough, that same Lord Davenant was suddenly burdened with a faithless actress mistress, an angry well-placed wife and a chief lieutenant who'd acquired one and, some said, the other, as well.

While no one could say exactly how or why, many of the coalition thought their troubles stemmed once again from indiscretions on the part of the Mad Duke, who always seemed to know more about the city than anyone could remember having told him. Nor did he scruple to disseminate his knowledge where a true gentleman would have kept his mouth shut. There was no use challenging him again; his swordsmen were as likely to win as not. The sword loved Alec Campion, it seemed, and always had.

The Crescent Chancellor, leader of the Council of Lords and head of the Inner Council, decided to go and speak to the Duke Tremontaine. Anthony Deverin, Lord Ferris, had not visited the Riverside district in many years—not since his days as Dragon Chancellor, when the future duke had been a callow and obnoxious boy known only as Alec, and Deverin, already Lord Ferris, a rising star. Diane, Duchess Tremontaine, had taken Ferris under her wing and tutored him in statecraft. When he tried to outsmart her in that shadowy arena, she smoothly engineered his downfall, sending her young kinsman to Council to do the deed. Everyone knew, after all, that the beautiful duchess never meddled in politics.

His punishment, an ambassadorship to the icy and barbaric lands of Arkenvelt, wasn't a death sentence, though, and Ferris liked to think Diane had retained enough feeling for him to send him where he might succeed if he had the nerve and the brains, not to mention the endurance. The rewards of frozen Arkenvelt did include access to some of the world's finest fur trading, and when his exile was over Ferris returned home with enough wealth in his pockets to reestablish himself in style. He frequented the right gatherings, married the right woman with the right connections, who died leaving him a small country estate and a good house in the city. He resumed his family seat on the Council of Lords, and there combined sense with statecraft in such perfect accord that, a mere ten years after his return, he was elected head of that august body of noblemen. It was in that capacity, now, that he paid a visit to Diane's heir and successor, whom he disliked as much as ever.

At the time of his last visit to the little island between the river's banks, Riverside had been no one's domain: a warren of criminals and swordsmen living in abandoned houses. But the Mad Duke in his fancy now occupied it, in more ways than one. Ferris was aware that once he crossed the Bridge, he trod the duke's territory. The City Watch still gave wide berth to the unsavory district, but it was honeycombed with Tremontaine's people. So the Crescent Chancellor traveled in semi-state, with both guards and swordsmen, that no one there might mistake his person.

Lord Ferris had never been invited to Tremontaine's Riverside house, and knew he was not welcome. Nevertheless his horses were stabled, his escort refreshed with courteous efficiency, and he was ushered into the ducal presence in very little time. It was not a house he himself would have chosen to live in: old-fashioned small rooms, dark paneling, heavy curtains . . . nothing shocking, though. Ferris felt almost disappointed. If there were indeed the pornographic frescos, instruments of torture, naked serving girls and other items popular opinion had decorated the duke's house with, they were not on public view.

The duke himself was sitting in an upholstered chair eating crackers and cheese and slices of apple. He was wearing a brocade robe, and possibly not much else. His hair was tousled, imperfectly caught back in a black velvet ribbon.

He bit a cracker and shrugged. "Sorry. I get hungry."

Lord Ferris refused the offer of any refreshment. If he'd roused the duke from carnal pleasures so be it, but he would be heard. "Tremontaine," he said, "I'll not take much of your time. I come from the Council on my own initiative, to ask you to reconsider your stand on the new tax laws."

"Stand? I have no stand."

"Of course not," Lord Ferris said with mild irony. "You never do. Like your grandmother, the late duchess, you have no interest in politics."

The duke smiled. "Exactly like." One of the late duchess's secret protégés, Lord Ferris knew the worth of that statement better than most. "It's a family tradition."

"And it is by pure accident that you have managed to bring down a coalition that was months a-building to make some honest change—"

"Honest change? Honest? Has someone altered the definition of the word while my back was turned, or have you recently developed a sense of humor?"

Lord Ferris pressed his lips together tightly. He endured these little sallies in the open Council Hall, as His Lordship of Tremontaine sporadically descended upon their proceedings. But there was no audience here to snicker appreciatively.

"Oh, Campion," Ferris sighed. "Your grandmother was no friend to chaos. I wonder what she was thinking of when she made you her heir."

"Perhaps," the duke said around a mouthful of apple, "she thought I would reform."

Ferris flashed him a look. In these, his later years, he had even less patience with people pretending to be stupid. But he only said, "I do not think it."

"Nor do I," the younger man said frankly. "Perhaps she did not care what happened to the state, once she was dead. Maybe she wanted to bring it down after her."

From a low, polished table, Ferris bent to pick up one of the little glass birds she had collected. He held it gently. "Oh, no, not she."

"Or she thought you and Godwin and all her other fancy boys would rise to the occasion. As indeed you do. She trained you well. The Council bears her stamp, I bear her title and everyone is happy."

Carefully, Ferris put the bird down. "There is something else I thought . . ." his drawl had become almost as long as the duke's, a relic of both their youths ". . . when I heard you had inherited after all. I wondered if she had not intended all along for your exquisite swordsman, St Vier, to direct the duchy. One so admired his balance. And you did seem inseparable, back then." He looked lazily at a spot over the duke's head. "Yet you did separate. Perhaps that was the flaw in her reasoning."

The duke scrutinized his pearl-handled fruit knife as though he had forgotten just what it was for. Finally, he applied it carefully to the skin of his apple.

"It is interesting how one idolizes the departed," the duke mused. "You admire the late duchess now, but I remember you calling her some very ugly names when she had you exiled to Arkenvelt over the matter of your misuse of my exquisite swordsman. I did think then, my lord, that you had learned that St Vier cannot be used against Tremontaine."

Ferris heard the message and noted it for further study. He had been wondering if the swordsman was still alive. It appeared he might be. *Alive, but not in play.* He chose to ignore the dig at his own past disgrace; it was, after all, Tremontaine who had brought him to the political exile he had spent years and a small fortune to return from, and there was no reason for either of them to have forgotten it. "I remember," the Crescent Chancellor added, "how very much in demand he was in his heyday, your swordsman. He killed with one blow to the heart."

"If he liked you. As you may also remember, he was not always so merciful." The duke gathered the folds of his poisonous green-and-black robe around him. "And now, if you will excuse me, there's someone waiting for me."

Lord Ferris did not bow, but said tightly, "We must all excuse you. Constantly. I trust we will see you no more this season in Council?"

The duke cocked his head. "Now, why should you think that?"

Lord Ferris opened his mouth to make a double-edged rejoinder, and closed it again, suddenly sick of the whole thing, and not at all sure of keeping his temper—another provocation he very much resented from the duke. "You disappoint me," Ferris said heavily. "You could be more, much more."

"I don't think the city would take much more of me."

"It would if you put your position to good use!" This was the speech Ferris had come planning to make, but it came pouring out of him untempered. "You have opinions, everyone knows you do; why will you not come and debate them in open Council with the rest of us? Statecraft and policy take time. They take patience and forethought and, yes, even compromise. They are not toys—we are not toys—to be picked up and put down at your whim, because you cannot stay the long course that it would take to effect real change. You are not stupid, you must surely know that. You find no one worthy of your vision, you do not wish to be a reliable ally? Fine. But at least be a reliable opponent, instead of shifting like a weathercock, blown by the wind of your fancy."

The duke paused and looked at him with real surprise. "Ferris," he said, "I am not a boy any longer. I don't particularly care if I disappoint you or not. Save your pompous sermonizing for the young fools who want to impress you and run the country into the ground with self-serving tax schemes."

Many years ago, Lord Ferris had lost his left eye. He turned the patch to the duke, a black velvet gaze that often unnerved people. "Someday," he said, "you will regret the loss of that swordsman."

Which was not at all what he had intended to say. Before his temper could drive him to further indiscretion, Lord Ferris turned and left the room. His own swordsmen and guards stood ranked to escort him; and in the shadows of the corridors of the Riverside house, he fancied he saw the shapes of others, watching.

THE DUKE TREMONTAINE THREW HIS FRUIT KNIFE AT THE WALL, where its point stuck, quivering, due to luck or the fury of the blow.

Then he went into the adjoining room, where the Ugly Girl was sitting on his bed reading, fully dressed.

"God, you're a pig when you wake up," she observed.

"He should not have come so early."

"Early!" she snorted. "It's after noon. Though you'd never know it; in your room, it is eternal twilight." She reached for one of the red velvet curtains, but he barked, "Stop. I like it this way."

"Come down to the library," she suggested, "where there's plenty of light, and quit hoarding books in your room. What else have you got in that pile?"

"Poetry," he said sweetly. "And pornography. Nothing to please your maiden eyes."

"Crap. You've got Merle's *Antithesis*, and after you swore you'd let me read it first."

"I will let you read it first. I was saving it to give to you on a special occasion."

"Like when you've been really annoying?"

"Just so. Where else are you going to get a copy of a banned book?"

She extended herself across the bed and snatched it from the pile. "For a noble and a libertine, you're not so bad. Want to go downstairs and work on Coverley's Last Theorem?"

"No," he drawled; "I want to stay here and smoke something."

The fat woman shrugged. "Suit yourself. But when I solve it without you, don't expect any credit for helping."

"I am going to have visions."

"Some people," she said, "have no idea how to enjoy themselves."

But the duke opened a cabinet by his bed, and began sorting through his collection of little vials. "*You're* all right," he said to the door closing behind her. "Without poetry or pornography, it's unlikely that anyone will ever strike you through the heart."

Soon he began to feel better.

chapter III

I LEARNED THE SWORD FROM HIM, BUT I LEARNED MORE. I learned to be quiet in the wood, and how to breathe so no deer could hear me. I learned how to gut a fresh-caught fish, and how to rob a beehive of its honeycomb. I learned to know where my feet were at all times, and how to make the sword I wore a part of myself, so that when my teacher took a sudden swipe at me, my hand was no longer empty, and I was not defenseless.

I rediscovered skills I'd had as a child: climbing trees, knocking down nuts, skipping stones across a pond.

And I learned him well enough that it became harder for him to surprise me with a sudden attack. I could sense the stillness of his impending motion, and I was ready.

I raided the great house's kitchen gardens for herbs, and made a little plot by our door so that I would not have to go so far to make our food taste like something. As the harvest came in, the house staff left us baskets of good ripe squash and tomatoes and leeks and chard. I was going to miss the sweet green peas I ate by the handful that were already gone by. I dried bunches of thyme and sage, and brought indoors a little pot of rosemary I hoped would last out the winter.

There was always enough butter and cream and cheese, since there were more than enough cows. And suddenly, as the night air turned cold and the day sky burned a bright and gallant blue, the world was full of apples. The air smelt of them, sharp and crisp, then underlaid with the sweet rot of groundfall. One day the orchard was infested with children, filling their baskets with them for cider. The next week, pigs were rootling for what was left.

On one of the last warmish nights of autumn we sat by the stream, grilling trout stuffed with fennel over a fire of apple wood. The stars were thick as spilled salt above us.

He pulled his cloak around him and poked the fire with his staff. "There were apple trees where I grew up. I used to collect fallen wood for my mother. And steal the lord's apples, with his sons."

"Were you caught?"

"Chased, not caught. He was a nice man. He understood boys get hungry. He liked my mother; used to lend her books and things."

"Did your father die?"

"I never had one, not in the usual way of things. My mother ran away with him when she was young, but she decided she didn't like him after all. By then she was stuck with me, but I guess she didn't mind. She used to show me bat skeletons and teach me the names of plants."

My mother seemed so far away she hardly seemed worth mentioning. And mine never had any bat skeletons. "She sounds a bit . . . unusual."

"Yes, I figured that out later."

"Did she teach you to fight?"

"Oh, no. I learnt from a swordsman. No, she couldn't do anything practical, really."

We'd eaten all we wanted to eat, but were in no mood to leave the fire.

"It's too bad neither of us can sing," my teacher said. "The nights are getting longer. Can you recite anything?"

Poetry? I thought in panic. "Just schoolroom things: 'The Maid Forlorn,' 'The King's Run,' that sort of thing."

"Can I hear them?"

He was always amazing me by not knowing the most common things. "Well, if you like."

But he stopped me halfway through "The Maid Forlorn." "Do you think that could really happen?"

I sucked fish off my fingers. "A girl believing everything a man tells her? Probably. Some people are very gullible."

I heard him smile. "True. But—are you supposed to admire her as well as feel sorry for her? Or just to think, *I'll never do anything that stupid?*"

I'd never considered it. "You know," I said, "I think the point is she's in love with him, even though she isn't supposed to be. That's what makes her stupid, really. It's not to say she isn't clever with other things. She might have been very good at sums or geography or something, beforehand."

"So they made you learn this as a lesson not to fall in love with unsuitable men?"

I drew myself up. I did not like having my upbringing criticized, even by him. "I learnt this," I said, "because it is *poetry*. Girls are supposed to know poetry. It is the inner beauty of the soul made art."

"I take it she dies at the end."

"She wants to die. She's been betrayed. She's lost her *honor*." He made a dismissive noise. "Well, what do you want her to *do?*" I demanded. "Go off somewhere and open a *shop?*"

"Well, why not?"

"Because then it wouldn't be *poetry*."

"How's 'The King's Run'?"

"It's heroic. The young king dies, but it's for the land."

"I thought nobles hated the kings."

"We overthrew the bad ones," I explained, drawing on my schoolroom lessons of a lifetime ago. "There used to be better ones, before, in the really olden days. Those are the poetry ones."

He leaned forward. "Look, I've been wondering about that. People have written books of history, haven't they? We might find a few in the library here."

"I could read to you."

"Yes, I'd like that."

I thought, and then said, "Your mother, she never taught you to read, did she?"

"It didn't seem important, then. You know how it is."

Well, I did know. Learning things was hard, and people were always trying to teach you things you didn't want to know. If I had a daughter, I'd never make her sew or cook if she didn't want to. But she'd have to learn to read and keep accounts. "History books?" I asked. I suspected they'd be dull. But maybe I'd find other books in the Highcombe library, good ones, like travel or adventure. "Could we send for more from the city?"

"I'll tell them, next time someone comes. Do you know how long you'll be staying?"

It was the first time he had asked.

"I don't know. I don't think anyone does. Maybe he has forgotten about me."

"I don't think so. He'll forget you for a few days, ignore you for a month, but he won't forget forever."

I had stopped thinking that the duke might send for me and drag me off to yet another life. I did not want to go.

I smothered the fire, while my master waited under the stars. He wouldn't let me touch him to guide him in, but walked straight over the field, his staff before him to intercept surprises.

In the dark, my teacher saw almost nothing. But he liked the night. He would go out for walks, and return at dawn to sleep. Sometimes I'd wake to hear him practicing, stomps and shuffles and whipcracks of steel, broken rhythms in the night. The first time it happened I crept, frightened, to the top of the stairs with a candle. My master was below, in the dark empty room. He was nearly naked, sweating, spinning and dodging with blade in hand, like someone battling a nightmare. My little flame flung his shadow wild against the wall.

If he heard me he did nothing, just kept on with the attack, high and low, behind and before. I watched him do things I did not know a swordsman could do. I began to see the design, the opponent's moves that his were counter to. I could never give him a fight like that. Neither, I was sure now, could the swordsmen I'd seen at the duke's party.

I knew when the death came, a blow straight through the heart. In the pale rays of my candleflame, finally he turned to look up to where I sat. "I'm sorry," he said. "I wasn't thinking about you. I'll try to be more quiet when you're asleep."

"Can you see in the dark?"

"Not at all. But night sounds completely different."

He was quiet and I was quiet, listening. There was no birdsong, only the distant calls of hunting owls, and skitterings of small things in the brush. I almost felt I could hear the daytime creatures breathing their slow sleep in the night.

"May I practice with you?"

"I have the advantage."

"I know. But you do anyway. It would be interesting."

He wiped his chest with a towel. "Not tonight, I think. Another time, without a candle, yes."

And I did that, once the days grew so short there was no light left after supper; standing so still, in the shadowed dark, waiting for him to move out of shadow or for one of the shadows to become him. We practiced with sticks. I never felt him move until he struck. Over and over, until I wanted to cry. My every attack beat off by one of his.

"Listen," he'd say. "Be still."

I closed my eyes. I stood still until my arms and legs ached. Then I heard him move.

I cracked him right in the head, and then I had to be sorry and get a cold cloth to put on it.

"Next time," he grinned, "you'll find the target. Although . . . in a street fight you'd be fine."

"No one," I said, "stands like a block of ice in the middle of the street after dark."

"You'll be surprised, when you get to the city, just what people will do."

"Tell me about the city, then."

The master shrugged. "It's crowded. It smells. There are lots of things to buy."

I snorted. "I've been there," I said. "I know all that." But I didn't know the city, not really. I'd only passed through in a carriage, and spent my days in the duke's house on the Hill. "Did you like it?" I asked.

"It was interesting." He always said that about things another person would have strong feelings about. I knew there was a long story in him about the city and that he was hiding it from me.

"I expect I will have a house there someday," I said breezily. "Perhaps you will come visit."

"No. I would not like to go there now." But his calm, sure voice was quiet; he sounded as though perhaps he would.

I repented of my relentlessness. "Does your head hurt very much?"

"Not very much. Help me roll out the bedding."

The master staggered as he bent over to pull the pallet out. I had to make him sit down. "Oof!" he said, as I spread his bed on the floor. "It wasn't such a bad knock. It's funny; I was always sure I'd never live to be twenty-five. This all comes as a surprise, this business of after."

I had lit a candle, being unable to find things in the dark as he could. In the rich light he looked pale, fine-drawn, neither young nor old. I wanted to give him a strong dose of poppy and make him tell me things before he fell asleep.

I heated some wine on the hearth instead. Twenty-five seemed terrifically old to me. I couldn't imagine the time it would take to get there, let alone get past it. When I was twenty-five, my whole life would be decided. I'd probably be married, with children; at least, I hoped so. Unless I was killed by a sword, the way he had planned to be.

I put the wine into his hands. He drank it all, but did not ask for more. He wasn't going to tell me anything. I should have known.

chapter IV

I<small>T WAS ONLY A LIGHT FEVER.</small> A<small>RTEMISIA</small> F<small>ITZ-</small>L<small>EVI HAD MAN-</small>aged to hide it from her family and was now on her way to the Halliday ball, dressed and decorated and dazzling. In the chill of the winter carriage, it was a positive benefit that she felt so hot. The Hallidays were important, their ball was always one of the best of the season, and she was not going to miss it.

When she emerged into the ballroom, her eyes glittering, her face flushed, heads turned to admire her. Young men asked her to dance, asked if they could fetch her a cooling drink. She laughed and flirted with her fan, feeling her head floating high above them all, knowing that she could keep going forever, since if she stopped or sat down for a moment she would collapse. She accepted the dances, accepted the drinks, accepted the compliments and the jealous or inquiring looks of the other nobles' daughters who were also there to attract a husband of worth.

Seeing that she needed no coaching, Artemisia's mother had already gone off to find the card tables, her father to find a convivial crew to drink with and observe the gathered beauties. Her particular friend, Lydia Godwin, was traversing the floor with the scion of the house of Lindley, and seemed to be enchanted by the boy. Artemisia looked around for the next arm to take, the next eye to catch. She was relieved not to see the Mad Duke's nephew, Greg Talbert, anywhere; he had turned out to be a bore after all, despite his ardent admiration and exotic connections. She knew better, now; weeks of experience had taught her that flowery phrases and passionate glances were a minnow a handful. Every man was full of them; it was what came next that mattered. Her eyes darted anxiously. If no one approached her again soon, she would have to make for the haven of Lydia, Lindley or no Lindley; it was beyond impossible for her to stand in the middle of the floor looking as if she had no one to talk to. She bent her head down, carefully adjusted a curl by winding her dark tress around and around her jeweled finger. When she looked up, she was surprised to find her cousin Lucius bearing down on her.

"Cousin!" Lucius Perry kissed her cheek. "My friend Dav has begged for an introduction to the beauty of the evening."

She thought dear Lucius had had more than a little to drink; that accounted for the rose of his cheeks as well as the fulsomeness of his speech. But young Lord Petrus Davenant was a likely-looking man, with a jaunty eye and nice hair.

"Must all your friends beg you for favors, Lucius?" she teased. "You should be more generous!"

"You note," her cousin said to Lord Petrus, "she does not demur at being called a beauty!"

"That is because I know how free men are with their compliments, when they cost them nothing."

"Philosophy." She felt a strange shiver when the back of Davenant's hand swept her wrist as if by accident. She was wearing demi-sleeves, whose lace fell to just halfway down her forearm. The ruffles of his cuff had fallen back, exposing a broad hand tufted with wiry hair. "You did not tell me your cousin was one of those learned ladies, Perry."

"Oh, I assure you, my lord, I never pick up a book except to throw it at my maid!"

Lord Petrus said, "A learned man is merely a bore, a learned woman an abomination."

She tapped his sleeve with her fan. "You must not be cruel to learned ladies, for I fear they are so because they lack the power to charm and to delight."

"Only the fair are free to know nothing, then," observed Lucius Perry, and, bowing, "You will excuse me?"

His place was taken by Lord Terence Monteith, a man who managed to bore without being learned; but he seemed content to stare at her charms while Davenant attempted to delight her with his conversation.

The flashing jewels and fluttering fan, the rippling laughter and high-flung head were attracting other men. Artemisia Fitz-Levi found herself at the heart of a clutch of eligibles, saying anything that came into her head because it all elicited laughter and compliments from well-dressed, well-tended, well-jeweled men.

"The country!" she cried in response to Davenant's friend Galing. "Don't speak to me of the country! It is well enough for those who live to be milked two times a day!"

There was an edge to the laughter that surprised her; she must have said something really clever without realizing.

"I know some who do!" said Davenant.

"Well, don't we all?"

"What does any of us know, compared to the wit and wisdom of this most excellent lady?" a voice said warmly.

The young men's hilarity flattened out, and they turned like flowers in the sun in the direction of the speaker.

It was the older nobleman from the Godwin dinner who had so admired her spirit and told her so. Lord Ferris, the Crescent Chancellor of the Council of Lords, tall, commanding, still dark-haired despite his years, and dressed with elegant simplicity.

All the men were looking at Lord Ferris, but he was looking at her.

Artemisia felt her cheeks burning. She smiled brilliantly at him, tried to think of something to say that was clever and high-hearted, but her invulnerable feeling of a moment ago was suddenly gone. Her giddiness resolved into dizziness, and she reached out one arm. The crowd parted, and Ferris was miraculously at her side, giving her the support she needed.

"A breath of air, perhaps, my lady?"

"Oh, no—no, thank you. If I might just sit down for a moment. . . ."

"Of course." He kept up a stream of easy chatter as he guided her off the floor, past people and through them, keeping her on his right side, where he might see her with his good eye: "These endless parties are exhausting—not any given one, to be sure, for all must be equally delightful, but in the aggregate they are enough to send anyone reeling."

"Oh, but I love parties!" Artemisia rallied.

"Because you are such an ornament to them," he said smoothly, "as the jewel must love its setting, or the, ah, the pearls in your ear must love the place that shows them off to such advantage."

His voice was low and silky in her ear. She wondered if he should be speaking to her so; but he was a great nobleman, and more than old enough to know how things should be conducted properly in society.

She tried to say something pertinent. "What can jewels know of love?"

"Indeed." Lord Ferris seated her in an alcove. "They are love's servants, and not the thing itself. A wise lady, to know the difference." He seized a drink from a passing footman and offered it to her. "So you do not love the country, Lady Artemisia?"

"I had rather live in this city than anywhere else on earth."

"Not everyone agrees with you. But I do. No, I cannot see you buried in the country, raising herbs and children, and waiting for your husband or your eldest son to come home from Council with bolts of cloth and news of how new taxes will affect the estate. . . ."

She shuddered.

"Just so. You must adorn our ballrooms here for many years to come, I think."

Artemisia smiled. "Thank you, my lord."

She wanted to hear more, only her head was pounding so. He must have noticed something. "Will you permit me to fetch your shawl?" he asked, and she answered, "Oh, no, it is so very warm. I promised Lord Terence a dance, but I do not think that I could bear it now."

"You must be protected," the Crescent Chancellor said, "from such as Lord Terence, to be sure. Ah! Here is your mother. Lady Fitz-Levi is your surest bulwark. Madam, your daughter has given so much of her charm and beauty for the delight of the company, I fear she has little strength left to sustain herself."

"Curious," said her mother; "dear Artemisia is so seldom tired or weak. I assure you, my lord, she has never given us a moment's worry."

I N THE CARRIAGE, HER MOTHER HUGGED HER AND THEN SHOOK her. "What do you mean, languishing in front of Lord Ferris like that? Do you want to get a reputation as a vaporish miss? No man wants a sickly wife!"

"No, Mama," she said, too tired and ill to try to explain how well the rest of the evening had gone. Her mother would surely hear of it from the other girls' mothers. "But he said I was a jewel and an ornament, Mama."

"He is a man of very good address," said Lady Fitz-Levi. "He married late, but Ferris has always had a way with women."

"I did not know that he was married, Mama."

"She died, poor thing, and his heir with her. Sickly, both of them. So you see where that gets you, miss!"

But her mama was pleased enough when the flowers began to arrive the next morning: lilies from Petrus Davenant, chrysanthemums from an anonymous admirer, more mums from Terence Monteith, even a bunch of carnations from her cousin Lucius. And from Lord Ferris, a great bunch of white roses.

THE COLD ENCLOSED AND ENFOLDED US. DAYS WERE SHORT; when they were fair the sun was sharp and clear, the earth hard and sparkly with frost, and I dressed in layers of clothes and set out across the fields, to race back again before early sunset stained the sky violet. I dredged up old nursery games and riddles to amuse us by the fire, and we burned a wealth of beeswax candles keeping up with our reading. Highcombe was well endowed with history books. Some of them weren't bad. I learned a lot about the habits and practices of my noble ancestors that no one had seen fit to teach me before. There was a lot more to history than dates: you had taxes and alliances and trade and secrets, and the wicked ways of certain kings. My teacher was particularly fascinated with battles. We spent hours and stacks of twigs, pebbles and candle-ends setting up and replaying the Battle of Pommerey. I was more interested in travel, though, and so we also learned about the wonders and marvels of foreign lands.

"It's never cold in Chartil," I suggested, "even in the winter, and all the noblemen are swordsmen, too. Let's go there."

"It would be summer by the time we got there," he said. "I understand, their summers, you can cook an egg on a rooftop."

"Well, how about one of the Cycladian Islands? Here's one, Kyros: 'the climate temperate, and so too its handsome inhabitants, who take their industry and pleasant mien from the humming of the bees that do perpetually labor and sing in the great banks of thyme and olive orchards to make that honey which is renowned throughout the world, as its sands are for whiteness.'"

"Promising. But it sounds a bit like poetry; not reliable. How about the place with the two-headed beasts that uproot trees with their tusks?"

"And red flowers big as cottages? You think that's reliable?"

"There's only one way to find out."

But we didn't really want to go far from the fire.

We practiced, of course. I practiced my footwork up and down the house's long gallery, but my favorite drill was a kind of game where we'd sit at either end of the cottage hearth, using nothing but our arms, working out flashy and subtle wristwork. There was a pile of nuts in the middle. Every touch was one nut to the victor, and every flinch, start or attempt to use the legs was a forfeit of two. I was lucky if I had any by the end of a bout. He could sometimes be tricked into moving too soon; I kept the first one I ever won off of him by feinting.

The tiny staff that kept Highcombe in order for its owner kept us well supplied with food and comforts. But if before I had secretly envied the grandeur of its halls and chambers, wishing we might occupy them ourselves, now I was reluctant to venture into those icy caverns.

As the winter dragged on, night and day alike seemed grey and steely and unwelcoming. I missed the snow we had back home. Around Highcombe it never got deep enough to be much fun.

I couldn't stay indoors all the time, though. And I liked looking at the patterns the bare branches made against the sky, the cracks of ice on the path, the dried grass frozen in the field. Sometimes just before nightfall the sky would clear. There was that one night I caught the most glorious sunset at the top of the rise, and ran all the way back to the cottage against the shadows. The smoke from our chimney was heavy. When I came indoors, I found him sitting by a fire going so strong that the room was really hot.

The master's face was golden. "Put more logs on," he said; "really pile them high. It's Year's End tonight."

"Is it?" I thought of the famous city Last Night parties I would be missing. The notion of all that glitter and noise made my head ache. Sparks shot up as I dumped the new logs on the blaze. "I should have baked a cake, or something."

"No; I think a fire is just right to celebrate the Sun's return. When I was a boy, we built bonfires and threw all sorts of things on them."

"Oh! They did that down in our village, but we were never allowed to go." I pitched another log on in remembrance. It was so hot, we had to move away from the hearth, and I stripped down to jacket and shirt. "We had a big fire at home, and threw our naughtiness and re-grets onto it."

The master smiled into his past. "Yes, bonfires, and people got very drunk and danced; that's probably why you weren't allowed."

I watched and let the flames dance for me. Year's End, and another year begun. In spring, I would dig out some beds. Maybe when the roads cleared, I would ride out to see my mother, and get some seeds from home. We could have little baby carrots in July.

"Listen!"

Carriage wheels rumbled on the drive. I grasped the leg of his chair without meaning to. Oh, please, I thought, oh please don't let it be anyone coming here. Please don't let them find us. The carriage swept on up the drive toward the main house. We both sat very still, listening.

"Maybe it's someone come to pay a Last Night call on the duke," I offered.

"They'd know he's not in residence."

"Maybe—maybe he told them he would be."

The master smiled, slowly, to himself. He knew my uncle. "Maybe he did."

Over the crackle of the fire we heard shouts and whoops of laughter, then doors slamming, and then nothing at all.

"In the main house."

"What if it's thieves?" I gasped.

"I doubt it, making that racket. Still . . ." He took up his sword. But nothing happened. No more sounds from the house.

"Should we go look?" I said.

He said, "Just wait."

My teacher slipped his jacket off, and sat with his sword in his shirt-sleeves before the blazing hearth.

Next to the hearth, the doorlatch clicked. It was someone from the house who had a key. The swordsman's hand tightened on the hilt; then I saw him sit back.

"Hello," said the man in the doorway. "I've brought us some fish." He had a large basket on either arm. "And some very good wine, and cakes, and smoked goose, and candied fruit and anise wafers. I hope you're hungry. I am."

"Hello." The master was smiling at my uncle as though the sun had risen early. "Come in. Sit down. Have something to eat."

My uncle the Mad Duke edged his way in, cumbered with baskets and parcels. He dumped everything onto the table. His eyes were on the master; but he never came near him, as though the man were a fire that burned too hot for him to approach.

I couldn't believe it. Of all the people who had to come here on this night of all nights, why did it have to be him? Why didn't he warn us he was coming? Why didn't he ask me how I was? I'd almost rather it were burglars after all. I busied myself unwrapping things, opening jars and unfolding layers of paper. The duke said nothing 'til I took out my knife to cut a knotted string.

"Here," he said, "I've brought you something."

He reached into his coat, produced a slender bundle. "Happy New Year. A little early."

Oh, no. Should I have been stitching him some slippers or something? I hadn't made anything for anyone, hadn't even thought about them. Well, it was too late now. I unwrapped the duke's present.

It was a dagger in a glorious sheath of chased leather. The grip was twisted to look like vines, and the blade, when I pulled it, was bright and damascened, chased with a pattern of leaves.

"She likes it," the duke said to my master.

"She does."

"What have you been teaching her, then; useful things?"

"Very. She'll do all right."

The duke and my teacher seemed to know one another so well, they could leave half the words out and still have perfect understanding. I had to pretend not to hear them. Everything they said was for each other. I busied myself with putting the new knife on my belt. They were talking about me, though; that was something. I rather hoped the master would praise my progress at swordplay, but he did not, or not that I could hear.

The duke shook out his long hair, and cast aside scarves and overcoat. "It's hot in here. Good. It was cold on the road."

"A sudden whim?"

"Just so. My friends were bored, and decided they wanted a country party."

"Friends? What friends?"

"Oh, Davenant, Hetley, young Galing . . . They've taken to following me around. Their lives are so dull. I said I was coming here for Year's End, and they insisted on coming too. I don't know; I think they must have been drunk or something."

"Oh, Alec." The swordsman sounded very amused. "What have you done now?"

"Well, they *would* come. But I seem to have lost them."

"Lost them?"

"Somewhere in the Great Hall. It was so dark in there."

"You left them in the hall. In the dark. My dear, did you forget to tell them that the staff always goes home for the White Days? Or did you just forget?"

"Is that why it was so cold?" My teacher made a noise. "Oh, well, they'll find wood. And somewhere to sleep—God knows there's plenty of rooms in this pile."

He really *was* mad, I thought. But my teacher was laughing.

"Here." The duke had gotten a bottle of wine open. He found the dolphin glasses, and a cup for me. "Don't drink too much; wait 'til it warms up a bit, it tastes better." But already Tremontaine's wine exhaled the tang of summer raspberries, and the savor of sun on apple wood.

He busied himself with plates and spoons like any footman. "Cherries? No, you don't like them—good, more for me—try the cheese, it's got something odd in it; oh damn, the fish is squashed, but here, have a bite. . . ."

I had forgotten food could taste this good, with layers of flavor and texture. The lovely wine washed it all down with waves of richness, and then there was sweet wine for the wafers and the fruit and the cakes, which were not squashed but retained the shapes of flowers, with sugar leaves and marzipan bees and another wine for them, as well.

"And how is your honey?" I heard the duke ask.

"If you think I can eat any honey after all this—"

"No, no, I was just being polite. About your bees."

"I'll tell them you asked after them, next time I see them."

That thought of the master conveying the duke's compliments to his bees made me giggle, which made me cough, so I drank more wine. I don't always like wine, but this was wonderful stuff, what the duke gave me.

"Let's see, you've got your bees, and what—do you garden now? Or fish?"

"Oh, now, fishing . . . where's the challenge in that?"

I let out a whoop at the picture: the master would be holding the one sword, and a bright gold fish the other, and they'd bow to each other and then they'd . . . I thought I would never stop laughing. It would be better to go outside and get a breath of fresh air, but the only door I could find was right next to the fire, and that was no good. The other side of that door was grey and cold, nowhere to travel on such a night.

The hearth was heaped with red and golden coals, now, like a pile of roses. I wondered what it would be like to lie down in it. What kind of creature would I have to be, to lie in the fire and not feel it? I began to see little beings, flickering white hot in the spaces between embers. They winked and danced and sometimes seemed to sing. I watched them for a long time, as the fire grew darker and they slept, or departed for hotter fires.

The men were talking, ignoring me; they didn't see what I saw. Stories that burned themselves into my eyes, that faded away as the fire died and the year ended. I turned to tell them, and found that the room was spinning.

The room was spinning. I lay down on the master's pallet, because I was too dizzy to make it all the way up the stairs. It was very quiet, lying down, and dark. I must have slept; then voices began weaving their way into my dreams, words that were about to have meanings, but then they changed before I could follow them. Voices I knew, but sounding all wrong. I knew where I was, safe at Highcombe, but it didn't make any sense because my uncle the Mad Duke was here.

"What about *her*?" I dreamed them saying it.

"She's asleep."

I opened my eyes to show I was not asleep, but all I could see was red fire; I was still in the heart of the fire.

"Why did you come?"

"Do you wish I hadn't?"

"No, of course not."

"Come to me," my mad uncle purred.

"Like this?"

"No. In the dark." The hiss of silk. The fire went black. "Perfectly in the dark. Come to me now. . . ."

Silence. Long silence, and I was asleep again, only someone was being hurt, I heard them crying out; I struggled, but I could not free myself from the blankets to help them.

Then the crash of a log falling, and a whisper: "I love you."

"Liar! If you did, then you'd come back."

The swordsman's voice was low but clear, the voice I knew from hours of practice: "You know I would if I could."

"You can. You *must*!"

"I can't, Alec. Not like this."

"It wouldn't matter. I could make it not matter—"

"No, you could not. Not even you, my lord."

If I had had a sword, I could have stopped the voices, and the noise; but I had left it outside in the snow, the blade was turning to diamonds.

"You only stay here to feel sorry for yourself."

"Is that so?"

A muffled sound, then, "Don't, you're hurting me."

"I know." The swordsman, cool and detached. "If I kept on, I could kill you."

"But you'd miss me then."

"I miss you now. You aren't happy, you know."

"I would be, if you were there."

"No."

"Your pride, that's all that's holding you, just pride—"

"If you like."

"But I can undo that with my hands alone. . . ."

"Your hands. Your voice. You can, my lord. You do." A hissing of fire. "But only because there is something left of me to be undone. Be sensible, Alec. Just for a moment. What is there for me to do there, now, in the city?"

"What do you do here?"

"Here. Here . . . before you sent me this little diversion . . . I walk. I practice. It's quiet. Trees. Nobody bothers me."

"It's the people, then."

"Why do you stay there yourself? They only make you crazy. I saw what it was doing to you."

"I hate the country."

"Because you can't shock it. Or annoy it. Oh, Alec . . ." he sighed.

"What?"

"I don't know. I love you."

"I do not think so. Do you even think of me, when I am not right here pressed against you?"

"I think of you. I try not to."

"And is that difficult? Or is it easy here, not to think of me?" A hiss of breath, a cry of pain. "Is that what the country is for? So you can forget me? I give you a house to live in and safety, all so you can never think of me? Well, I think of you. I think of you a lot. Almost always, in fact. Do you know what my days are really like, Richard? My days, and my nights. Shall I tell you?"

"Shh, I know. Don't you think I know? I can feel it, feel it all over you. There, and there, and there— They are making you one of them after all. All that excess to no purpose."

"Shut up. You're never there, what do you know?"

"I know you. Be still, Alec, don't . . ."

"You've done this to me. I wish I could kill you, but I'm already dead. I'm dead, and everyone else is a ghost. I sleep with everyone I can find—I plunge myself into flesh like buckets of cream, and I am always starving. My mouth is open, but nothing gets in. You are the only one that's real. How do you do that, Richard? If you killed me, would I be real, too?"

"If I really killed you, you would be really dead. Please don't start that."

"Ah," said the duke coldly. "*Please*. Yes. Let's have you do some pleading for once. Because I'm tired of it. I'm sick of begging. I am not supposed to beg, certainly not to beg you. Do you know who I am? Sometimes I wonder if you understand how different things are now. I am not a ragged student who needs to be protected from tavern bullies. I am Tremontaine. I hold the power, the lands, the money. I hold Riverside, for one, and more of the city. I hold them, and I would burn them to the ground for you, Richard, I would kill them all and leave nothing—"

"So we could walk in a ruined city?"

"If that's what you want."

"Oh, my dear idiot. Then stay. Just stay here, with me. There's nothing to ruin, here."

"No, there isn't." The duke's voice, thin and flat, mud gone to ice. "Is that it? Have you simply lost your edge?"

A sigh. "Do you think I have?"

"You don't want challenge. How could you take one up, as you are?"

"I don't need that sort of challenge now."

"They would be looking at you there." The voice was honed like cold iron. "Looking at you, and you not know it. That's the challenge you can't take up. It's not their swords that vex you, it's their eyes. Isn't it? Not that they might kill you—you'd probably welcome that. But they might see you first, and know."

"Does it give you pleasure, my lord, to think that?"

"It is, believe me, one of my more comfortable theories. What else is there? That it bores you, our city where we were together? That you don't mind if I drop in from time to time, but really I bore you, too?"

"That is not so."

"Oh, then it's yes, you love me, yes, you want me, but not all that much? Not enough to risk being seen first, unknowing? Yes, you still love me, but in the end I'm not worth it to you. You'd kill for me, but you wouldn't give up an ounce of your pride. I'm not worth that to you, in the end, am I?"

"Hush, Alec, hush."

"Leave me alone. I want brandy."

"That's not what you want. Come here."

"I'm not your lackey. I don't come and go at your command."

"Please, then. Please come to me."

"I hate this." The low voice shook the room with misery. "I can't stand it."

"Come to me. That's better. Yes. You smell of smoke—ash—you've been in a tavern. Your hair—ah!—you washed it at home. Chypre. Something else—citron—barber—fish on your hands, your finger-tips—walnuts—bitter—"

And I was dreaming of all those things and more, dreaming them thrown onto a fire that consumed but did not consume them, that fed but was never satisfied. The old sun was devoured by the new, and gave its strength to light a new year, in the course of a long night whose dawn seemed never to come.

My uncle shook me awake. "Get your things. We're going."

He stood a long way above me. I saw him filmed with grey, as though the whole air of the cottage were thick with the ash of last night's bonfire.

I tried to find my feet, but they were tangled in the blankets. I raised myself on my arms. They shook under me.

"She's ill."

"She's just hung over." He pulled my arm. "Come on."

I was standing up. The master put a cup of water in my hands, and lifted them to my mouth. I drank. My throat hurt.

"Alec," he said. "You drugged her."

"I didn't poison her. I just didn't want her bothering us. If she's sick, I'll take her to a doctor back in town. Come on."

I could see where my feet went if I thought about it.

"What about your guests?"

"They'll find their own way home. They can walk into Highcombe village."

The master laughed. "You're leaving them, are you? I wonder if they've made a bonfire of your furniture."

"There's plenty of furniture." The duke gripped my arm. "Come on."

"You're leaving? Now?"

"We're leaving. Come on."

The carriage was cold. The drowsy footmen piled us with rugs. My uncle chewed on his thumb and said nothing. We bumped across the frozen rutted drive. The further we went, the more I shivered. He took out a flask of brandy, placed it against my teeth. I was crying, I think. I drank. I slept.

I woke up coughing. The carriage was swimming with sweet, heavy fumes. But I was warm. My uncle held me in his cloak. I watched the pipe rise to his lips, and felt his breath expand and collapse against me. Again, and again, like a cradle rocking.

His breaths were forming curls around me. "Richard," he said. "Richard."

Part III

RIVERSIDE

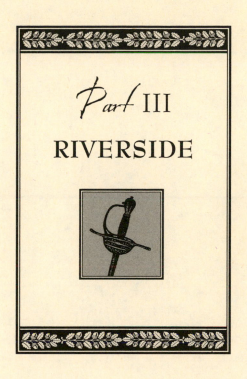

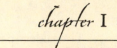

I LAY IN A CAVE OF DEEPEST BLUE, STAR-SPANGLED WITH SILVER crowns. I was explaining to Betty that I must not sleep in Tremontaine's bed; I could sleep on the floor next to the master. But every time I tried to explain something especially important, she'd make me drink a bitter potion. It was annoying, because it made it impossible for me to get up and practice, and at one point I was quite sure that the villainous Mangrove was coming to Highcombe, and if I didn't defeat him he would set it on fire. I was very hot and very cold and my eyes ached. I was very tired, too. Eventually I slept without trying to explain anything.

When I woke up I was thirsty, but my starry cave had become only curtains: silk velvet with silver embroidery, hung around a heavy, old-fashioned bed of dark wood. I pulled back a velvet corner.

Sunlight sifted in through the narrow windows of the room. The walls were paneled with dark wood, hung with old tapestries. I heard a chair scrape; a boy appeared in the gap in the bedcurtains, one finger in a book.

"You stir," he said. "I was told to give you this if you stirred." He handed me a cool goblet. I drank; it was not bitter.

"I'm Marcus," he said. "I work for the duke."

I remembered him from my first days in the city; a boy about my age, with brown hair and brown eyes. His voice was deeper than I remembered.

"You took ill on the road," Marcus said. "But your fever's broken. Now, I expect you'll be bored."

"I'm tired," I said. "How did you get here?"

"Where?"

"Isn't this Highcombe?"

"No. You're back in the city. The oldest part of the city, actually; you're in the Riverside house."

"Oh." I realized that the ride in the smoky carriage had been real, and the feast at Year's End, too, all those dreams were real—which meant that my master was gone, and Highcombe was gone, and even if I could find my way back there, nothing would be as it had been.

I didn't even have the strength to care if I cried or not. Marcus kindly dropped the bedcurtains closed so I could do it in private.

B EING SURROUNDED BY FLOWERS IN ARTEMISIA'S ROOM SHOULD have been enough for the two girls, but it was only the prelude to the important task of passing judgment on their senders. The man who was under discussion now would have been horrified to hear that his considerable bouquet was being subjected to a very knowing scrutiny. But then, the girls had been reading aloud to each other while they sewed—so that their mamas would not say they did nothing but waste time together—and it had affected their outlook, not to mention their speech patterns.

"Armand Lindley," Lydia Godwin sighed. "I like him very much, but in all honesty, he isn't a bit like Fabian."

"That's all right," said her friend; "you aren't a bit like Stella."

Lydia looked crossly at Artemisia Fitz-Levi. No one likes being told that they do not resemble the heroine of their favorite novel, and while it was true that Lydia was unlikely to become pregnant by a swordsman of dubious reputation, like any young girl she liked to think that she could attract one to commit folly for her sake.

But Artemisia was smiling cheerfully, and offering her more of her favorite biscuits, which both of them knew were bad for their complexions, so Lydia decided not to take offense.

"He does have melting eyes." Lydia returned to her current obsession. "Like Fabian's trusted Tyrian, now I think on it."

"I wonder if he is as steady."

"I begin to doubt it." Lydia tossed her head. Artemisia greatly admired her pearl drops. The earrings were Godwin heirlooms, and perhaps should not have been worn on an afternoon visit, but Lydia was so proud of them that she wore them whenever she could. "Oh, Mi, what shall I do? I was sure, when he sent those flowers the next morning, that he had enjoyed the dance as much as I did! He pressed my hand, as well."

"Many men send flowers; but when they press your hand, what else are you to think? No, he loves you, it's sure."

"But then why did he not call yesterday? I made certain he knew I would be at home! No, no man who sends flowers and then fails to call can be said to be in love."

"What kind of flowers were they?"

"Roses, I told you."

"Roses . . . all roses, or mixed?"

"Roses with carnations. White and red."

"Mixed, that's bad. Though white and red is good. It could mean your complexion, or even heart and soul. Was there a note?"

"Of course." Lydia slipped it from her reticule. "Here, see what you think."

"'To the most adorable of all the Godwins,'" her friend read. "'With the fond admiration of her devoted Armand Lindley.'"

Lydia shrieked and fell back on the sofa cushions. "*Fond! Devoted!* Oh, Artemisia, I shall perish! How dare he so trifle with my heart?"

"What I wonder about is *adorable*," the other girl considered. "*Fond* and *devoted* are well enough, true, but is *adorable* what a lover says? It sounds—forgive me, Lydia—rather *papa*-ish for a lover."

Lydia fished a handkerchief from the reticule as she began to sniffle. "Oh, no. I cannot bear for him to mean it so."

"Of course, it might mean something else entirely, my sweet."

"I do think it must. After all, he is not old enough for a papa. And," she twinkled, "I do not feel at all daughterly when Armand leads me onto the dance floor. In fact, it makes me feel quite like Stella. After the ball."

"'I was a girl before tonight,'" Artemisia quoted with half-closed eyes; "'I am a woman now.'"

"Yes," Lydia breathed. "I fear I must have him or die. But how can I let him know, when he does not come to see me?"

"I expect he is delayed on business, or ill. Only think, there may be a letter waiting for you at home right now."

Lydia jumped up. "Oh, do you think?"

Artemisia patted her hand and pulled her friend to her on the window seat. "Very likely. You must tell me the moment you hear from him!"

"Oh, yes! But—what if Papa does not let me answer him?"

"Why should he not? If you may receive Lindley's flowers and visits . . ."

"Well, a letter is more serious, you know. Of course I show all mine to Papa and Mama—"

"*All* of them, Lydie?" her friend teased.

"Well . . ." she admitted, "yes."

"Even the ones that might be, say, hidden in a bunch of flowers?" Artemisia wriggled with pleasure. "Those are the very best."

"My maid is instructed to shake them out before she gives them to me. It is because of Papa's position. Now that he is to assume the post of Raven Chancellor and be back in the Inner Council, we must be very careful again."

"What a good girl you are, to be sure. We should all strive to imitate you. But what possible objection to your suitor can Lord Godwin have? Armand Lindley will most likely inherit the estate and become Lord Horn after his uncle's death. I think it a very good match indeed."

"Of course it is. But I have heard Papa say that all the Horns have evil tempers and goatish dispositions. . . ."

"He cannot mean Lord Armand! He is thinking of someone else. Have you told him how you feel?"

Lydia blushed. "I dare not tell Papa. He has a very poor opinion of all young men. Why, just the other day he said at breakfast to Mama, quite loudly, so I could hear, 'The thought of any of them coming near our Lydia chills my blood. I know what they're made of. Perhaps we'd better'—oh, Mi, it was so awful—'Perhaps we'd better lock her in a tower until she is old and ugly!'"

Artemisia shrieked and hugged her. "He cannot mean it! What did your mama say?"

"She just gave him a look and sighed, 'Oh, Michael,' the way she does. Perhaps they had one of their little talks together; they left the table shortly thereafter, and I did not see them again until past noon, when he was much better-tempered."

"I am sure she will set him right. Your mama is such an angel."

"As are you, dear Artemisia."

DAYS PASSED. I ATE AND DRANK AND SLEPT. I CRIED A LOT, AND my head ached and I missed my mother; kind and careful as she was, Betty did not have the cool hands and sweet voice I loved when

I was ill. I tried not to think about it, and I tried not to cry when Betty was there. It wasn't her fault, any of it.

As soon as I could stand up by myself, I went to the window to look out. The window was made up of little squares. The glass was thick and greenish; the little square panes had circles in them. The murky view was of snow and the corner of a roof. I didn't think much of Riverside so far.

When Betty saw that I was well enough to get up by myself, she made me try on all my clothes so she could have them altered. I had gotten taller, thinner in some places and thicker in others. There were new clothes for me in the wardrobe, town suits for winter: one bottle-green fustian with gold piping, one a deep blue wool with threads woven into it that made it almost crimson in the light. I supposed the new clothes meant the duke was pleased with me. But I didn't believe they meant I would be going back to Highcombe any time soon. So I didn't much care.

At first I was only well enough to sit up and walk about for a few hours each day. The rest of the time I was amazingly tired, and, as there was nothing to keep me from sleeping, I slept. Betty sat with me and told me servants' gossip about the household: Cook was a dear, but the steward down here, Master Osborne, thought altogether too highly of himself! If she had been drinking before she came in, she never drank while she was with me. As I thought I was doing her good, I tried to keep her by me. I heard all about Riverside, too, and so I found out at last who my master at Highcombe really was.

Of course I should have known. Even I had heard of St Vier, the greatest swordsman of our time, some said of any.

Everyone knew that he had dueled in the streets of Riverside and killed men in taverns and alleys to protect and amuse a mysterious runaway student, who later became the Duke Tremontaine.

"You wanted to watch out," Betty reminisced, "when those two were around. Riverside then wasn't like Riverside now: you had to be clever to live here, or stupid, or brave. We lived by our wits in those days, and took our luck where we could find it."

"Did you know them then?"

"Not know them like you'd *know* them, exactly," she slurred. I waited for her to untangle herself. "But I saw the pair of them, along with everyone else. Hard to miss. *Him* towering like a raggedy scare-crow in that flapping black scholar's gown, and the sword always quiet next to him, sweet as honey, and poison with it. Taverns would quiet when those two came in. Where would the fight be, and how would it start? Sometimes there wasn't a fight at all, and sometimes the night ended in blood. Real blood, not like now. But that was Riverside in those days. You didn't care so much how you died, as long as you did it well."

No one knew where St Vier had gone, not even Betty; some said he'd been killed in a fight—or poisoned, because he couldn't be killed by steel. Some said he'd found another lover, far away, where even the duke couldn't touch him, unless it was that the duke had killed him when he'd learned of it. Betty had also heard that St Vier had been wooed away by the Empress of Cham, to rule at her side in her palace over the sea. But she didn't believe that.

The man at Highcombe had not seemed like a legend to me, not while I was there with him. It was hard to imagine my teacher here, in this house, in the city, doing the things Betty said he had done. But back when it was different? When Riverside was the forest he'd stalked through, and he a young man who thought he would not live to be twenty-five?

At least it explained why I could never even come close to winning a fight with him.

T HE ONE THING BETTY COULD NOT DO WAS READ TO ME; LIKE the swordsman, she had never learned how. The duke's Riverside house boasted a large library, but it seemed to be heavily stocked with modern, scholarly works.

"Ask the boy," Betty said. "That Marcus. He goes where he likes, goes back and forth. Does what he likes, too. Yesterday Cook caught him eating cream from the pot, bold as you please. Complained to His Grace, but duke said he's a growing boy, let him alone. You're growing, too, but you don't take liberties. Better brought-up, you are."

I wasn't sure how I felt about being compared, even favorably, to a Riverside servant. But I only said, "He's the duke's man, not mine. Why should he do anything for me?"

"If you didn't still look like something the cat dragged in, my lady, I'd say he'd taken a fancy to you, always hanging around here when he should be off keeping His Grace from jumping off roofs and his other fool nonsense. Not that I'm complaining; working for Tremontaine is being in Seventh Heaven next to . . . but never mind about that. Just tell that boy what you need; you'll see."

So I asked Marcus to send to the Hill for picture books and lighter matter.

He brought them to me himself: a book of birds, and one of poisonous plants, some poetry, an illustrated geography called *Customs of Many Lands*, and, tucked in amongst them, a surprisingly familiar little worn volume of soft leather.

I did not thank him for it, nor ask him how he had found it, just slipped it directly under my pillow to examine when I was alone.

It was my very own copy of *The Swordsman Whose Name Was Not Death.* I recognized the stain on the third page, where I had dripped apricot juice. I opened the book at random, expecting now to find it silly stuff. But it opened to Stella's escape from the city, right after she's lost the child and thinks Fabian's betrayed her, with Mangrove hot on her heels. No one could find that silly.

Stella wants to despair, but Tyrian won't let her. *You have done tonight,* he says, *what ten thousand men could not. Now show your great enemies what one woman alone can do.*

I am not alone, she says, and is about to make Tyrian very happy indeed when the hunting cats appear on the rooftops.

I did not read the book straight through. I read my favorite parts, and then the bits between them. Fabian still never practiced. Stella still nearly ruined everything by keeping secrets from those she should have trusted. But it didn't seem to matter. If anything, I knew now that people were even stranger and more unpredictable than that, and that when we don't know the truth about someone, we will make it up ourselves.

A FEW DAYS LATER, MARCUS BROUGHT ME THE SWORD.
"From one of the country estates," he said, "for you, along with a big bag of fresh game, which is a good thing, I can tell you: I am getting awfully tired of fish."

It was the basket-hilted sword I had practiced with at Highcombe. One of his, one of my master's swords, mine now. I slipped it on a belt, along with the twisted dagger the duke had given me. The weight settled comfortably on my hips, one balancing the other.

"I'm going out," I told Marcus. He looked me over and nodded.

I was lightheaded in the bright day, and did not go far. Snow crumbled under my feet—I was glad my boots were of the best—and wind cut through from both sides of the river. Everything in Riverside was timber and stone and plaster: old houses with crumbling fronts, some missing windows, some set with coats of arms, their stone worn away like melting butter over the centuries. The houses were clustered up against one another as if they were afraid to let in too much sky, as if to be sure nothing would grow there. Still, there were weeds frozen in the cracks between the cobbles of those streets so narrow no carriage could pass through.

I felt someone following me. I'm not sure how, but I had learned the feel of a stalk now. I looked for the nearest tree, found the corner of a house, stepped behind it and drew the untipped sword.

It was a boy, younger than me—or at least smaller. He had no sword, no coat either. "Pal," he rasped, looking past the blade right at me. "Hey, pal, you got any money?"

I would have given him some if I had any. But I was not carrying a purse. I shook my head. The rake of his eyes up and down, from my thick boots to fur collar and hat, showed what he thought of that.

"Help me out," he whined; "I won't hurt ya."

I shook my head again, helpless, but I started to sheathe my sword. He fumbled in his shirt and pulled out a knife, flat-bladed and worn.

"Give me what you've got."

"No." *For death, you want the heart, the throat, the eye. . . .* I was not going to kill this boy. I would not. This was awful; there was no challenge here, no rules, no purpose but survival. I moved, he yelped, there was blood on the snow. I was fairly sure I'd only touched his hand. But he was gone before I could really see.

"Nice work." It was a woman's voice. She stepped out from the shadows of the house across from me, holding the edges of a tatty green velvet cloak heavily lined. Her red hair was dyed so bright she looked like a holly bush. "You really know how to use your blade. How about a drink for you?"

I felt so tired I couldn't answer. I nodded, followed her. "You new here?" Her voice was a pleasant purr. She moved through the streets with confidence, barely even looking to avoid ruts and puddles. "You a foreigner? Can't you speak? A drink, definitely, and then you can tell me all about yourself."

I realized, suddenly, what she wanted of me, what she thought was going on. I stopped in the grey patch of light between the darker shadows of the houses. "I'm a girl," I said. "I'm the Duke Tremontaine's niece."

"Is that a fact?" She squinted into my face, and shook her head. "He gets crazier every year." The red-haired woman shrugged. "Well, you tell him Ginnie says hello. Ginnie; he'll know who you mean."

I was going to tell him nothing of the kind. So far, I had not seen my uncle, and I was just as glad to keep it that way.

"Well, good-bye," I said, "and thank you for the—for the offer—"

"You should buy *me* one, young Tremontaine."

"When I have money, I will," I said lamely.

"Doesn't he give you any, your rich uncle?" Ginnie snorted. "You make him pay you what you're worth. He can afford it."

OUTSIDE TREMONTAINE'S RIVERSIDE HOUSE THE SNOW WAS WET and trampled with horse and cart tracks. It wasn't really one house; it was a twisting series of them, distinguished from the others around it by well-kept facades: the stone pointed, the shutters painted, the slate roofs and the gutters in perfect trim. I had made the mistake, when I left, of not looking behind me to note which door I'd come out of. Now I had to choose one at random, or rather, apply to one, for the doors of the duke's Riverside house were gated and guarded. Luckily, they had orders to admit me.

I passed into a stone hall hung with tapestry, a huge fireplace and dark stairs carpeted in red. It looked like the right one; I remembered the tapestry. Up the stairs and down a hallway with windows that seemed a bit narrower than mine. I had decided that I was in fact lost when I heard voices: lots of people laughing, like a party. I knocked. Getting no answer, I opened the door.

The room was full of naked people.

"Shut the door, it's cold!"

My uncle the Mad Duke strode amongst them in a very beautiful dressing gown. He saw me.

"Ah! You're up. Good."

He had a bottle of brandy in one hand, and began tipping it down the throat of an upside down man with his knees hooked around the bedpost. There wasn't a stitch on him; if I had ever wondered how accurate the classical statues in the gardens of Tremontaine house were, I certainly knew now.

I started to back out.

"Don't you want a drink?" drawled the duke. "Everyone else does."

I heard my own voice, quiet and still. "I am not like everyone else."

The upside down people wriggled and laughed, reaching for him and for each other. I was terrified that they would soon reach for me.

"Bravo." He swigged on the bottle, just out of their reach. "Bravo, Lady Katherine."

There was no one between me and the door. "Oh, by the way," I told Tremontaine, doubtful of just how much longer he'd still be standing to hear anything, "Ginnie says hello."

"Does she indeed?" The duke looked hard at me, swaying. "She always wants what's mine. Miserable cow. You tell Ginnie Vandall the moment she touches you, her pension's gone; I don't pay her to meddle in my affairs—"

That was all I heard before my hand closed on the safety of the doorlatch. I didn't understand, and I didn't want to.

chapter II

IT WOULD HAVE BEEN CHURLISH, WHEN LYDIA GODWIN RE-
ceived an offer of marriage from Lord Armand Lindley, for her
dear friend Artemisia to be anything but delighted at her friend's
good fortune. With the Godwin and Lindley families' glowing approval, they were quickly betrothed and a wedding date set for the
spring. But Lady Artemisia had always believed she herself would be
the first to capture a husband, and she had to be careful not to think
of that while congratulating Lydia and listening to her endless plans
for the future. Of course, Lydia vowed a hundred times a day that even
marriage to the sweetest man alive would never alter her eternal bond
with her dearest Mi.

So said Lydia as they sat together in Artemisia's window seat, dark
and fair curls bent over the scraps of ribbon she had brought so that
her friend could help her decide what colors she should trim the table
with for her betrothal dinner. But the young lady was sensitive
enough to note when her friend began to tire of the details of her up-
coming nuptials, and she leaned back in the window seat and said encouragingly, "Now come, tell me about your suitors."

Artemisia crunched a biscuit. "What suitors?" If she could not be a
blushing betrothed, it would be best to take on the air of someone
much wearied with the follies of courtship. "It is all very tedious. I go
to dances, I receive flowers, but there is no one who touches my
heart."

"But surely there must be *one*—what about Greg Talbert? He is poor, but of ancient lineage and utterly mad for you."

"Oh, him." Artemisia rolled her eyes in what she trusted was a jaded way. "Last week's news, my dear. All talk, no action."

Her friend hissed in delighted horror. "You don't mean that!"

Artemisia lowered her eyelids. She had seen Lady Hetley doing that, and thought it looked very sophisticated. "Do I not?"

"Well, then, what about Lord Ferris? He's certainly been paying you marked attention."

Artemisia shrieked. "As a *lover*? But he is so *old*!" She recollected her sophistication and smiled wryly. "He has polish, I'll give him that. And he's sent the most adorable roses—here, smell."

"Mmm, lovely." Lydia buried her face in the blossoms. "Expensive, too. Well, then—Terence Monteith?"

"Snowdrops." Her friend gestured.

"Even so . . . it's clear he's vastly taken with you."

She yawned. "Oh, he's pretty enough, but a terrible bore. Besides, what are the Monteiths? He is only a second son; what can he offer a wife? He'll be back to the country as soon as he's found one, to manage his brother's estate. I want a city life, and jewels, and gowns. How I envy you your Lindley, dearest!"

Lydia blushed. "Hardly mine. But I would not care were Armand as poor as a goatherd. I think I could live with him anywhere, if I could just feel his strong arm around me, and look into his eyes and know he loves me."

"There." Artemisia sighed. "That is true love. I believe it has made a woman of you already, Lydia, indeed I do. Your eyes—yes, there is a grave beauty in them that was never there before." She took her friend's face in her hands. "How I envy you!"

"Oh, dearest Mi."

Lady Artemisia's maid interrupted these girlish confidences with the news that her father required her immediate presence in the morning room. And so the friends were forced to part, with mutual assurance of future consultations.

T HE MORNING ROOM CONTAINED BOTH FITZ-LEVI PARENTS. Artemisia made her curtseys, and wondered frantically what she might have done wrong this time. They could not possibly have found out about the parrot. If they had, she'd kill her maid, truly she would.

"Daughter," her papa said, "there's very good news for you." Not the parrot, then. Maybe her dress bill had been lower than she thought, or the shoemaker had lost her receipts. "Anthony Deverin, Lord Ferris, Crescent Chancellor of the Council of Lords, has asked our permission to pay his addresses to you, and if you agree, we'll begin the thing at once."

Artemisia felt the room grow exceedingly hot, and the next thing she knew, she was sitting on the couch, smelling spirits of hartshorne.

"There, Fitz," her mother said, "I knew you'd make a botch of it." Lady Fitz-Levi took her hand. "Listen, child, one of the most important nobles in the city wants to make you the mother of his heirs and mistress of his establishment. There's not a girl in town but will be sick with envy. (Nor a mother, neither, I'll warrant!) You let him pay his court to you, and we'll make certain Lord Ferris makes a very decent settlement and allowance on you: all the dresses you want, shoes, jewels, gloves—and the houses, of course, furnished to your liking. Your dowry is nothing to sneeze at, and we mean you to live properly. You'll be one of the first ladies of the city, right after Lady Godwin, what do you think of that?" Artemisia managed to smile. "Lording it even over your friend Lydia and the rest of that family, how's that, then?"

Artemisia drew in what felt like her first full breath of air. "Yes, Mama. Thank you, Mama."

Her father leaned over the back of the couch. "How about a kiss for your dear papa, then? Pretty chit, I don't know how he could resist you— Of course, he couldn't, could he? Ha ha!"

Her father smelt of whiskey and barber's scent. Lord Ferris, she thought, was possibly even older. But contrary to her father's cozy sloppiness, Ferris was lean and fastidious; elegant, even. He was always dressed to the fashion, and knew exactly what to say.

Her mother picked up a flat box from the sideboard and brandished it in front of her. "He left you a gift, miss, and not only flowers this time."

Artemisia took the box and opened it.

A necklace nestled in the velvet folds: a delicate collar, designed just right for a young girl's daily wear, in the very latest style. But the twisted web was gold, the dangling jewels sapphires.

For the most exquisite woman in the city, the note with it said, *with the heart of Anthony Deverin, Lord Ferris.*

Artemisia breathed in her gilded fate. She wondered what Lydia would say.

chapter III

Even when I was healthy again, my uncle's manservant still came to see me. Marcus liked to read, it seemed. He brought me a book of poems and wondered if we might discuss them.

"It's a new movement," he said. "The scholars are all mad for it; they think it mixes sentiment with science."

I did try. The new poetry seemed to have a lot to do with spheres: the motions of the heavens and the motions of the heart. But I'd never learned much about the motions of the heavens, except by observation. I thought of the glittering night skies at Highcombe, the keen air and the silence by the fire. I looked at the words on the page, and felt too defeated to keep at it.

Nothing was said about sword lessons, so I practiced on my own. The hall outside my room was long and no one much seemed to come there; after a while, Betty got used to checking before she turned the corner. I began not only to drill, but to construct opponents in my mind and fight my shadow self. Sometimes their style was like the master's, as he was the best I knew. I wondered what it would be like to fight Venturus now. Sometimes I played that game, and then I always won.

I went out a lot, wrapped in coat and scarf and hat. Most people made Ginnie's mistake, calling me "sir" because they could see nothing of me but clothes and sword. I did not have cause to draw it again; with the duke's men so thick about the place, Riverside was not what it had been in the master's day. There were guards and footmen and messengers in livery, but not all the duke's people wore the Tremontaine silver and green. On the streets I recognized men I had seen in the house, and knew they were about Tremontaine's business. Just what that business was I only got inklings of from Betty; it was all a lot of names I didn't recognize, and money, and veiled threats, and threats enforced. When I mentioned Ginnie to her, Betty said, "Poor thing. You stay away from that Ginnie Vandall. She knows how to make herself useful, but not to you." I didn't ask her any more; none of it made sense, anyway. It was all my uncle the duke's business, not mine.

M ARCUS BROUGHT ME A GOLD-CHASED CLASP.
"What's this?"

"It's for your hair. If you're going to go around with hair like a student, you should at least do what they do, and tie it back."

It was too rich to be a gift from Marcus. "Is it one of *his*?"

"He won't miss it."

"I don't want it."

Marcus grinned. "I thought you might say that." He fished a bit of crumpled black ribbon from his pocket. "Here. Try this."

Without looking in a mirror, I pulled the hair back from my face and tied it.

"Where are you going, anyway, Kate?"

"I don't know. Out."

"You could get lost down here."

"I've been out. I always find my way back. It's not as though everyone doesn't know where this place is."

"True." He went over to the windows, started scraping patterns in the frost with his fingernail. "Last year, the river froze solid and we skated under the bridge."

"I can skate. We skate on the duck pond, at home."

"That's right, you're from the country. I've only been once. Hated it."

"Why?"

He frowned. "Too noisy."

I had to laugh. "Riverside's not noisy?"

"Well . . ." Marcus scraped spirals around spirals. "But the noise here is—it's only people. You know where you are."

I said, "They never sleep. I hear them at all hours of the night. I woke up, went to my window last night, and there were men staggering by with torches."

Marcus shrugged. "The duke gives parties. It's different, here, from on the Hill. Especially in winter. The rooms here are smaller. Do you want to see?"

"Explore the house? I thought— I thought I was supposed to keep out of his way."

"Did you?" He turned his plain face and brown, open gaze to me. "I don't have any orders."

He did it a little too well. I thought suddenly, Oh, you do too have orders. The duke's personal servant wouldn't be spending free time with me because he wanted to. I wondered, was he supposed to find out if I was mad or vengeful? To keep me distracted? To cheer me up?

"Show me your room," I commanded. "You've been in mine. Now show me yours."

A hundred years ago, when I was a girl at home, I would never have invaded a servant's privacy. But in the Mad Duke's house, who Marcus was and what I was were not so clearly delineated. And if Marcus was spying on me, I wanted some parity.

"If you like." My rudeness did not seem to bother him. But he was used to my uncle's whimsies.

Some of the halls were white and new; others were strings of little old chambers, paneled in worm-eaten wood. As we passed from house to house what was under our feet changed, too: some floors were stone, some wood, some tile. There were steps and doorways to mark the passages, but you had to watch for the sudden shifts. The sounds of the street were muffled here, and there were closed doors everywhere. Once, though, we burst into the light of a gallery which ran the length of a courtyard in which people were drawing water from an old stone well.

I was fairly certain that Marcus was taking me the long way round to his quarters. I couldn't blame him.

In a hall with diamond-paned windows, he stopped at a tall dark door.

"Here."

I had expected a small room under the eaves, or at least at the top of the simplest of stairs, whitewashed and minimally furnished. Marcus's room was larger than mine. The walls were polished oak, hung with contemporary landscapes and a couple of maps. There was a row of books, and a jet-and-ivory shesh set on a table by the window seat.

The bed was new, as well, with good woolen hangings and a huge feather quilt, puffed almost to perfect symmetry at the corners.

I couldn't say any of the things I was thinking.

There were thick cushions on the window seat. Marcus plopped himself down on one, utterly comfortable. The richness of the room did not embarrass him, nor my conjectures about his special status with the duke. Which could, of course, be wrong—

"Do you play shesh?" he asked.

"Only a little. I know the moves, but I'm not very good."

"Sit down," he said. "You'll get better if you play more."

I sat. He put a black and a white peon in either fist, and I picked for color and first move, and then we started to play. He watched me carefully, like a swordsman. It made me nervous, but I pretended to ignore it.

A blow on heavy wood made the sheshmen shiver. Through thickness of wall I heard a scream. I'd missed the other door to the room— bad observation, always dangerous, my master reminded me. Marcus just sat there, swinging his foot. He wasn't pretending not to hear, but his only response was a little smile. There was a shout, and yet another crash on the other side of the door.

"I've got the room next to his," he explained.

"Really?"

"In case he needs anything."

It sounded as though someone had just dropped a sheet of glass. I put my hand on my knife, I couldn't help it. "Do you think he might—need anything now?"

Marcus shook his head. "Naw. It's just Raffaela. She gets mad when he lies on the floor and laughs at her. Then she starts throwing things, and then *he* does." I jumped as another one hit. "I wish he wouldn't. He's always sorry afterward. He doesn't really like things to get broken."

You wouldn't guess from the sound of it. "I thought he didn't like women," I ventured.

Marcus righted a shesh piece that had fallen over. "At this point, I'm not sure he can really tell the difference."

"Oh." They were making a lot of noise. "Doesn't he ever *stop?*"

"Not since you came back. He's been taking a lot of stuff, smoke and all, plus drinking. I have the feeling," Marcus said, carefully positioning a piece in the exact middle of its square, "that he did not really have a very nice time at Highcombe."

Now I understood. That was why he was sticking so close to me. Marcus wanted to know what had happened to the duke.

"I don't know," I said truthfully. "I was asleep through most of it. And I got sick."

Marcus nodded. "So did you know he'd brought young Davenant and two friends down with him for Year's End? Brought them, and abandoned them there in the Great Hall. Dark and freezing. No fire, no food, no beds, no light. They had to find their own way back to town." He shrugged. "Of course, they should have known better than to go with him. Probably they did. That seems to be what draws them. Now Davenant's father has sent him a nasty letter, and Galing's lawyer is requesting damages. Which is very stupid; it'll be all over town how the duke made fools of them. People do talk."

Something was beginning to make sense to me. "Is that why he does it?" I asked slowly. "Because no matter how badly he behaves, no matter what he does, he always gets other people to be worse? Or to feel as if they were?"

Marcus looked at me as though I were suddenly more interesting than the sheshmen. "I think so. But something at Highcombe made *him* feel bad. I didn't think it was Petrus Davenant."

I thought of the duke's face, lit by a tentative wonder and by the Year's End fire.

"No. I don't think it was."

"*Marcus!*" It was the duke shouting. "Marcus—show the lady out!"

"Oh, no." Marcus shook himself. "Not me. Last time I took hold of that one, she got me. She scratches. I'm calling the guards; they're dressed for it."

I sat alone in the middle of the sun-drenched room. Pointless to try to ignore what I could hear clearly enough: the woman screaming, "*Bastard! Bastard! I hate you!*" and the old wall shuddering as something struck it. I stood by the door, wondering how tiny a crack I could make opening it, but not quite willing to do it for fear of what I would see. "*I'm not some nobody, you know! Who's good enough for you, bastard, if I'm not?*"

I closed my eyes, listening in the dark as my master had taught me. The duke tripped over something, fell hard and cursed.

I thought suddenly, I'm training to be his guard. Should I rush in there? Would I be expected to stand watch over these—proceedings, someday? I snorted. What could I do with his discarded mistresses, skewer them from a standing thrust?

Then Marcus arrived with real guards, and I heard how it went. Definitely a job for someone else.

At last the next room was quiet, and Marcus sat back down on the window seat.

"Is she beautiful?" I asked.

"She's a singer. Famous, I think. Anyway, he heard her at a party, and next thing you know . . . !"

"What happened to Alcuin?"

"Who? Oh, him. Gone. Right after you, actually. He was a piece of work."

Marcus took a pear from a bowl, and handed me another. We ate in silence, then I said, "Let's go out."

Marcus shook his head. "Can't. He might need me."

I looked around at the luxurious room with its many diversions. "Do you want me to stay?" I tried not to let my reluctance show. "We could finish the game."

But to my boundless relief, he said, "No, better not. There'll be a lot of cleaning up to do."

"Don't the chambermaids . . . ?"

"That's not what I meant. You go on, Kate. Have you tried the pies at Martha's yet?"

I felt myself dismissed, but was not sad to go.

———

Lady Artemisia Fitz-Levi, intended bride of Anthony Deverin, Lord Ferris, sat alone in her window seat with papers spread all over her lap, drawing up lists for her betrothal party. Her mother had tried to help her, and she had chased her mother out, certain she could do a better job herself. But it was harder than it looked, these questions of seating and decorating and precedence.

She was relieved when Dorrie told her Lucius Perry was at the door, and she admitted her cousin at once. He leaned over to kiss her cheek. "Congratulations, my lady! You've taken the prize, and no mistake. Everyone is pleased as the devil." He looked at her strained face. "But how are you?"

"Taxed," she said. "Lucius, I used to think all our friends were so agreeable, but here's Petrus Davenant and Albright Galing barely speaking to each other."

"Betrothal has sobered you up, I see." He sank gracefully into the chair by the window. "How sweet of you to be worrying about two unattached young men."

"Well, they used to be attached to each other, everyone knows that. And I wanted to invite them both to my betrothal party, as they're so amusing, but now if one of them is in the room, the other leaves it."

"Oh." Lucius Perry fiddled with his cuff. "That."

"Are you going to tell me, or are you just going to work at that buttonhole until you ruin it?"

"It doesn't matter," he said. "If you invite only one it must be Petrus Davenant, because his father is an associate of Lord Ferris, and if you invite Alb Galing, old Davenant won't come."

"I know that, goose. I just want to know why."

"Because Dav's father is going around telling everyone Alb corrupted his son."

"The hypocrite!"

"Not because they were 'attached,' but because the attachment led Dav to everyone's favorite opponent of all that is good and decent, the Mad Duke Tremontaine."

"Oh."

"Yes, oh. It all came to a head when the Mad Duke dumped them both in the country at Year's End, leaving them to get home by themselves."

"My mother would say it served them right. I should think Dav's father would be pleased."

"My dear Artemisia, try to see the full picture. It's political as well as personal: Lord Davenant and the duke are adversaries in Council, and Petrus Davenant knew it perfectly well when he took up with him." Artemisia gave him what she hoped was a knowing eye, but Lucius Perry was looking out the window. "It's the old story: boy comes to city, boy disobliges family, family hears about it, ructions ensue. Dav was lucky to have someone else to blame."

"Dear me!" Artemisia leaned forward in a rustle of striped taffeta, her papers forgotten. "I imagine Albright Galing doesn't think so. Is this politics? I suppose I am going to have to learn all about it, if I am to run Lord Ferris's household, and throw parties and all. Now . . . explain to me again just who hates who, and why?"

As the winter went on, Marcus and I worked on our shesh. I was never going to beat him, but at least we could have a good game, now. If letting someone else get ahead is cheating, he cheated: sometimes I'd feel him watching me as I went move after move in the direction I'd planned, and just when I was congratulating myself, he'd swoop down with something that confounded all my strategies. I didn't mind, though. It was only a game. I had a real dueling partner, now: a sober young swordsman named Phillip Drake, who turned out also to have studied with Venturus.

Phillip demanded that I practice even more. He showed me no mercy in our bouts, and was always very happy to point out what I'd done wrong and what I might do to improve on it. When I did well, he only asked for more. As there was little else for me to do with my time, I practiced hard between lessons. I grew less and less tired at the end of our grueling bouts, and Phillip Drake had less and less to criticize. He said I had a long way to go, still, before he'd be happy contemplating me actually dueling a real opponent—"You're not as good as all that yet," he'd say; "but every once in a while, you do something . . ."

I did not tell him St Vier had been my other teacher, but he usually knew when I was departing from the ways of Venturus. When I broke through his guard, he'd stop, whistle, shake his head and say, "Well, it works, I guess. It isn't stylish, but it works."

B ECAUSE I WAS OFTEN WITH MARCUS I DID SEE MORE OF THE duke, who required him to be close by where he could find him. And so I saw my uncle drunk and otherwise incapacitated, and I also saw him doing very normal things like going over accounts and dictating letters and approving dinner menus and ordering new curtains. He never spoke to me of Highcombe, or of swordplay, or much else. He tended to treat me like some friend of Marcus's who had dropped in for a visit and might as well make herself useful while she was there. I helped Marcus to run errands, and began to learn my way around the house and around the city. I also took his lead on when to disappear; there were certain moments in Tremontaine's life, and certain visitors to the Riverside house, that no one was invited to witness.

We were sitting in the hallway outside a very splendid room hung in shades of azure and violet silk. That room always gave the impression of dusk, like twilight over a mountainside. We sat out in a sunlit embrasure, waiting for Marcus to be called for, and played knucklebones; Marcus didn't seem to know it was only a game for girls and was quite good at it.

A slightly built man with sleek black hair and fashionable clothes brushed softly past us on his way to the twilit room. Despite his finery, he moved like someone who knew how not to be noticed; he looked like a very stylish otter, swimming through the halls. So I looked hard at him, seeing the nice rings, the soft shoes, the very fine velvet and very wrinkled linen and the hair a little long, clearly tended to stay just that way. Hands that he held very still, even while he waited at the door to be admitted. I looked, and it occurred to me that I had seen him somewhere else, if only I could remember where.

"Who's that?" I whispered to Marcus.

"Who do you think?" When the young man had safely closed the door behind him, Marcus elaborated, "It's one of his fancy-boys. From Glinley's."

"Glinley's what?"

Marcus cleaned dirt from under his fingernail, saying casually, "Glinley's Establishment of Try-and-Guess. . . . Well, why would you know, a nice girl like you? It's the finest brothel in Riverside. That fellow comes here once a week to pay a little visit. They won't be long." I stared at the door. "I like the way he looks harmless, don't you? But my dear, he is riddled with vice. He takes money for engaging in sexual congress with strangers. Are you shocked? Say you are shocked, Katie."

"Shut up, Marcus," I said automatically; but then, because I really did want to hear more, "I *am* shocked, I guess. But not because of that. I don't think he's really a—one of those brothel people. He's a nobleman. I've seen him before."

"Re-eally? Where?"

His drawl made me giggle. "You can't imagine who you sound like."

"What do you mean?"

But I did not have to answer him, because the door opened and the young man stepped out, his linen a little less disheveled. His back to us, his hand on the doorframe, he bowed into the room and said one word: "Tremontaine."

Then I knew where I'd seen him.

I clutched Marcus's sleeve, but said nothing because the man was turning towards us as he closed the door. I lowered my head and busied myself picking up knucklebones so he would not see and recognize me. He had laughed at me at my friend Artemisia's, when I went to her for help. Maybe it was his fault she'd never answered my letter. Maybe he was her brother, or one of her beaux. If so, she had no idea what he truly was.

It was Marcus who spoke up, bold as brass. In the duke's house, he feared nothing. "Do you need help, sir, finding the way out?"

"I know the way," he said mildly.

"Can I summon you a chair?"

The man's voice smiled. "I'll walk, thank you."

He turned down the hall away from us. As soon as he turned a corner, *"What's his name?"* I hissed in my friend's ear.

"I don't know it. Shall we ask the duke?"

"No! I'm going to follow him."

"You're *what?* Why? Katie, whatever is the matter with you? Why
are we whispering?"

"I'll tell you later."

I noted which corridor the man turned down, and left the house by
another door where I could see him leave and catch his direction.
Marcus was right behind me. I gave him a *Go back!* glare, but he just
grinned.

Our man crossed the Bridge into the lower city. It was a warm day
for winter and the city stank. But dipping and dodging the people and
puddles behind the mysterious man sent me back to the stalks with
the master, the green green fields and trees, the silver sky, the cool
wind's breathing and the musky deer waiting. It was strange to be in
both at the same time. We left the docks behind, heading for the
newer part of the city. The wider streets, more light, more air, made it
harder to stay in the shadows, but there were more people and distrac-
tions to hide amongst.

Our young man went quickly. He seemed used to walking, and he
knew his route well. He never checked behind him, and he did not
stop to look at anything or to shop. Marcus stayed just behind me,
only sometimes reaching out a hand to caution when I started to
move forward too fast. It was hard not to be distracted by the shops
with their displays and tantalizing smells; here was a part of the city
I'd never seen before, and I liked it very much. We seemed to be heading toward the Hill, though; perhaps he was leading us to his noble
family's house, and then what? Maybe even back to Artemisia's . . . ?
But, no. He turned down a side street full of pretty little houses and
gardens.

Marcus and I fell back on the quiet street, and sank into a doorway
when our quarry stopped suddenly before a little gate. He had the key.
We watched him slide it from inside his jacket, look up and down the
street, then turn it in the lock, and slip like an afterthought through
the gate and into the house.

We shot down an alley around the back. There was a garden wall,
with a fruit tree limb hanging tantalizingly overhead. "Boost me up. I
think I can—" But the tree branch wouldn't hold me, and I tumbled
ingloriously back to earth, smudged with whitewash from the wall.

"You have to go over the *top*," Marcus said, uncharacteristically dancing with impatience. "Country girl, climbing trees. Anyone can see you've never tried to break into a house before."

"Don't come all Riverside with me," I growled. "You never have either, and I've skinned my palm." He produced a clean handkerchief. "Do you want to try again?"

"Not now," he said. "Maybe at night would be more . . ."

"Discreet?"

"Just so."

We noted the house, and started back downhill.

"That was fun," said Marcus, brushing whitewash off his knees. "Now are you going to tell me why we did it?"

"Marcus . . . do you remember that day, my first day on the Hill when you found me all lost and took me back home? I'd gone to see a girl I met at the duke's party, a girl my age who was there on a dare or something. When I went to visit her, *that man* was there, sitting in her day room. He said something nasty about Tremontaine House, I remember now."

"Did he? What a nerve. He's been coming there since last year, at least. And I don't see signs of him finding it especially nasty."

"Perhaps we ought to warn her. If he's a relative, or he's even courting her . . . don't you think she'd need to know he's doing this?"

"Living in a house near the Hill? It's not an outrage, that."

"First of all, we aren't sure he lives here, he's just got a key. Second, you know that's not what I meant. If I were betrothed to someone who worked at Glinley's, I'd want to know it!"

He said, "Oh, I'm sure it won't come to that. Your uncle's weird, but he's not that weird." I ignored this. "Is your friend betrothed to him?"

"She's *something* to him, or he wouldn't have been with her that day. Maybe he's her brother, I don't know. But I think it's important. You're sure," I demanded, "about Glinley's?"

"Oh, yes."

"But are you sure about what he does there? Maybe he just does—other business."

"There is no other business at Glinley's." Marcus was smug. "I'm sure."

"But why would he work there if he didn't have to?"

"Maybe he does have to. Or maybe he's just bored," Marcus said airily, sounding more like the duke than ever, "and too lazy to relieve it any other way."

"Lazy? You think that's lazy?"

"Of course. Or he would take the trouble to learn something new. As we have. Everyone already knows how to copulate."

We had to be quiet while some people passed us: other servants, carrying baskets and looking harried.

"Well, why would he go all the way down to Riverside to do it?" I persisted.

"Glinley's," Marcus explained importantly, "is a very particular establishment. It is expensive, and caters to specialized tastes."

I did not know what he meant, but I wasn't going to tell him that. "Then I'm surprised the duke doesn't live there," I said tartly.

"He doesn't need to. He's part owner. Our man was bringing him his share of the take."

I drew breath hissing in between my teeth. "That's disgusting." We were passing into the part of the city with all the lovely shops in it. "Marcus," I said suddenly, "do you have any money on you?"

"A little. Why?"

"Could we go in somewhere and eat cakes? And drink chocolate?"

"We could."

"Well, I want to."

He said, "People are going to take you for an actress."

I looked down at my legs, encased in breeches and high boots. "As long as they let actresses drink chocolate, I don't mind."

We found a place called the Blue Parrot where they served us excellent cakes. When we'd eaten and drunk all we could afford, we went to the Ramble by the river and watched children running races with hobbyhorses. Then we were hungry again, and bought gingerbread with some coins I found in the bottom of my jacket pocket. We watched a trained dog jump through hoops, and heard a fiddler playing "Maiden's Fancy," and whistled it all the way home.

The duke met us on the stairs of the Riverside house. He looked sober and displeased. "Do you have any idea what time it is? No, I suppose you were off courting murder and mayhem, and couldn't be bothered to wonder whether any was occurring at home."

"We went out for gingerbread." I offered him the bag. He took a piece and ate it.

"Well, I've been calling all over for you," he said, licking powdered cinnamon off his fingers. "I can't find my—" For the first time, he looked fully at Marcus. "Why is there dirt on your knees?"

Marcus looked down. "I dropped my money. When we were buying the gingerbread. I had to pick it up."

"Oh? And did Lady Katherine drop hers, too?"

My own breeches had a smear of whitewash from the wall we'd climbed, plus mud from where I fell. "I was helping."

"Nice try." The duke was smiling with the pleasure undoing a knotty problem gave him. "But a couple more questions, asked of you independently, and your whole story would unravel. You see—" he crouched down so he wasn't towering over us—"it's not street dirt, for one thing; it's whitewash and garden mud. Your palms are scratched. And this is Robertson gingerbread, with the cinnamon, and that is not sold on the street."

I felt at once very annoyed, and thrilled with the sort of challenge that a good swordfight gave me. "Some boys knocked us down and ran off."

Amused, the duke's eyes glowed green deep behind his crinkled features. "The gingerbread bag was closed at the time? And where did they push you down?"

"On the West Bank," Marcus said, "by the river."

The duke unfolded himself back up to his full height. "It is very annoying, I know," he drawled, "to have to account for all your time to someone older than you are. Very annoying. But I take care to be an annoying person."

"I give you my word," I said earnestly, as I had heard my brothers do when they'd been caught out, "we didn't do anything—"

"Gingerbread," Marcus overrode me coolly. "Katie told you."

Tremontaine's hand flashed out and gripped his shoulder. The sudden movement had sent my hand to my swordhilt; I admired my friend's ability not to flinch. "Marcus," he said, "I had a visitor this afternoon. You offered to fetch him a chair, and then you disappeared."

"He didn't want the chair. If you heard me asking, you heard what he said back."

"Katherine, please take your hand from your sword. It's a bad habit to get into; it makes people think you're about to start a fight."

I saw Marcus press his lips against the sharp grip on his shoulder. But I took my hand from my hilt; I did, indeed, know better than that.

"Do you know this man's name?"

"No," I said, and the duke lessened his grip on Marcus and turned to me.

"Then why did you follow him?"

I looked at Marcus; Marcus looked at me.

"You were seen," the duke said, "leaving the house after him."

I shrugged. "We lost him in the city."

"I'm going to ask you again. Why did you follow him?"

I drew in my breath, opened my mouth to ask him the questions only he could answer—and then I shut it again. He had plenty of his own secrets already. This one was ours. "For a test," I said. "I'm learning to be a swordsman. This is part of it."

"Did Master Drake assign you this test?"

"No." I stared him in the eyes, telling him where I had learned it, and from whom.

The duke looked away. "Well, then," he said. "If you lost him so easily, you'd better practice harder. Just not on my guests, that's all."

We started to turn away, but the duke's voice stopped us, hard and serious. "Understand this, both of you, about people who come to this house. Their business is my business. Their secrets are my secrets. Stalk whom you like, but not my guests. Like just about everyone in the city but you, it seems, that man is not supposed to be here. It would go very ill for him if anyone outside this house learned of his presence here. Do you understand?"

Marcus looked down at the floor. "We're sorry." I nodded in agreement, looking penitent as a good niece should.

"Where's the rest of that gingerbread?" my uncle asked.

We shared it out, and then went down to the kitchen together looking for more cake. The pastry cook was creating little icing flowers to decorate something. The duke appropriated the flowers and bore them and us off to the library, where we saw the sun down playing a complicated gambling game using them as tokens, joined by a couple of resident scholars. Winners got to eat their own sweets; Marcus occasionally was sent down for more plates of flowers to keep the game going. No one wanted any supper—instead, the scholars started quizzing each other on points so obscure that the joking guesses Marcus and I threw out were sometimes right. Candles were lit. The duke scrambled up and down ladders fetching volumes to adjudicate between them.

The night went on, the candles burned down and we sent for more, and the kitchen started sending up jellies and syllabubs, along with cakes decorated with the little flowers. The duke's homely friend Flavia came in, looking for a book, but she refused to play. She picked a few flowers off the cakes, listened for a bit, and then said, "I didn't know it was possible to get drunk on sugar, but I think you've managed it," and went off grumbling. She may have been right, though. One moment I was screaming with laughter, and the next it was all I could do to keep from falling asleep on the window seat.

"The untroubled dreams of youth," one scholar said, and the duke asked me, "Where did you learn so much about the Battle of Pommerey?" and Marcus said, "Bedtime, Katie."

I felt faintly sick, and altogether happy. Before he shut the library door behind me, I got the chance to whisper to Marcus, "There's something going on! He doesn't want us to know. I'm going to find out—are you with me?"

"I'm with you," he said softly, and shut the door.

A RTEMISIA FITZ-LEVI HAD NOT YET BEEN ALONE WITH HER betrothed. She did not mind; it made everything they did together seem like a play, performed for an appreciative audience of ever-changing watchers. She was always well dressed and the sets were beautiful. Lord Ferris also was well dressed and knew his part to perfection. The Crescent Chancellor gallantly handed her into her carriage under the eyes of dinner or ball guests; he courteously escorted her and her mother to shops, and even to the theater, while other girls looked on in envy; he monopolized her at balls, and said very nice things about her where everyone could hear. She appeared at parties decked out in jewels that he had sent her, and he was always sure to tell her how well they became her. They were to be married in the spring, before people left town for their country estates. Sometimes Artemisia wished this engagement could go on forever.

More of her other friends had now been spoken for. They drank chocolate together, a very worldly-wise group of young ladies, casting knowing glances at the less fortunate and freely dispensing advice. Whatever their fortunes, though, Lady Artemisia knew, as did they all, that she had taken the prize. Ferris was rich and he was powerful; he was still fairly handsome, and clearly he adored her to distraction. When she was with him, she felt witty and beautiful, drunk on the same fevered wine she had known the night of the Halliday ball.

Tonight, though, she was conscious of a vague unease. Oh, the room glittered, the people glittered, and the jewels round her neck and on her fingers, all gifts of her betrothed or lent her by her mother against her inheritance. Nothing pleased her, though, not the rare sweets and drinks or the swirling patterns of costumed dancers. . . . It seemed to her that the envious looks were fewer, that the handsome young men looked only once at her, saw her as taken and did not look again, no matter how rich her jewels or how low-cut her gown. Lord Ferris had arrived late, pressed by business of the Council, and though he apologized handsomely and thenceforth never left her side, she found herself wishing he had never come at all.

She made him fetch and carry for her, changed her mind a dozen times about her shawl, her drinks, whether she would dance or no. It gave her less pleasure than she'd expected, knowing she could command one of the chief nobles of the city, the head of the Council of Lords. It changed nothing, really: they were still the same drinks, the same dances.

Lord Ferris kept his temper admirably. She knew he was doing it, and even that made her cross. For his part, he tried flirting with her, praising her, until finally he realized that only direct address would work. And so he took her aside and said, "My dear. Tell me what's wrong. Has someone insulted you? Or injured you in any way?"

To her own amazement, Artemisia burst into tears.

"Dear me," Ferris sighed. "It's not your mother again, is it?"

She giggled through her tears. Her handkerchief was soaked; not surprising, since it was a tiny piece of paper-thin fabric surrounded by waves of useless lace. Lord Ferris handed her his: a reasonable linen square, lightly scented with something agreeable, some fine, expensive scent twined with something else she could not name. She held it to her nose, praying it was not getting too red. He reached a hand up to hers, as if he would take the kerchief from her, then he touched the tip of her nose, instead. The tip of her nose, and then her ear.

"It's the waiting, isn't it?" he murmured. "It's hard on your nerves. I had thought best to give you time to enjoy your Season and enjoy lording it over the other girls . . . but there is too much of a good thing. Perhaps we might move up the date?"

His breath was warm on her face. The other scent on the handkerchief was Lord Ferris himself. He was so close that she could see the pinpricks of beard that made up the shadow of his cheek.

"What say you, pretty lady? Shall we be married right away?"

"No!" she cried, but it came out a whimper. "No, I cannot—"

"Nerves," he breathed, "that's all. All this fuss . . ."

She drew a deep breath and exclaimed passionately, "I wish I were not getting married at all!"

Her father would have laughed, her mother *tut-tutted*, but her intended did neither of those things. She felt the chill as he backed away. "No? Be careful what you say, my dear. It is certainly within your power to break off the engagement if you choose."

"I—" The wet handkerchief was tight in her hand.

"But if you so choose, you must give good reasons. Neither of us wants to look like a fool."

"I don't—I didn't—"

He smiled at her, the fond lover once again. "Of course you didn't. Nerves. It will all be over soon."

She sniffled into the kerchief. Of course he was right. She didn't know where she was these days, with everything changing so.

"I'll find a maid to help you wash your face."

"Don't let Mama know—"

"Certainly not. This is between the two of us." But secretly he resolved to give her fewer gifts and more attention.

T HE DUKE NEVER CAME TO WATCH ME PRACTICE, AND AS A rule, Marcus didn't either. He wasn't interested in swordsmen. When he showed up in the middle of one of my lessons, I knew it had to be important. Master Drake and I were running through a complicated sequence of attacks and counters that had defeated me twice already—like the worst kind of patterned country dance, where if you fall out of step you have everyone piled up on top of you—and I hated to stop just when I felt I was getting the flow of it set in my bones. Besides, I wanted my friend to see me carry off something really hard, so I just edged my back closer to Marcus and asked, "What?"

"Our man's back," he muttered. "Headed out the West door."

"Go follow him!"

"Can't. I'm waiting on Tremontaine. Just came to tell you—"

"Can't, now! Dammit, Marcus, you made me miss my stroke!"

My swordmaster laughed. "Avoid distracting onlookers. Very important, Lady K. First rule of dueling. No, no, keep going, don't stop. That's it, come at me in four, from the passe, and . . . *now!* Good, very good. . . ."

I picked up the rhythm again, and moved across the room after Phillip Drake, my concentration suddenly perfect with Marcus watching. I wasn't even counting under my breath. It was as if I had become the sword and knew just what to do without thinking. I finished triumphantly, my point at Master Drake's chest. Both of us were breathing heavily. I heard Marcus give a low *whew!* of approval. He said, "I didn't know you could do that."

I felt very much like Fabian at that moment. "There's a lot," I said, just for the pleasure of saying it, "you don't know about me."

Master Drake rapped on my blade. "Enough," he said. "Remember the rule: in any given fight, the weaker sword can win through luck or sheer accident. Let's do it once more, to prove it wasn't accident."

It certainly wasn't that, but it took me three more trials before I fell back into the unthinking rhythms of the match. By the time I emerged from practice, dripping and happy, I had forgotten all about the mysterious nobleman, and he was long gone.

A YOUNG GIRL ABOUT TO MAKE A GOOD MARRIAGE IS AT THE center of her world, and may perhaps be forgiven for thinking she is more important than she actually is, or wiser. Since crossing her often leads to a spasm of pre-bridal nerves, older relatives may choose to indulge her until the wedding. Relatives closer to her own age, however, are less inclined to make allowances. Already Artemisia's brother Robert had thrown a shoe at her. Her cousin Lucius Perry, who had dropped by to find Robert gone, soon wished he hadn't.

"Lucius, where *were* you last night? I particularly wanted you for my little supper party, to sit next to Lydia's cousin Harriett who is just in from the country and knows no one yet."

"How delightful for me." Lucius yawned. "I sent a note; something came up."

"I don't believe you. You're always late these days, or tired, or missing. Are you up to something?"

"If I were," he said, "do you think I'd tell you?"

There was an edge to his voice she wasn't accustomed to. "Now, now." She cocked her head to one side in a charming and feminine fashion. "I think I know what the problem is. You need to settle down, that's all. Find a nice young lady who will care for you and all will be well."

He snorted rudely. "Someone like Lady Lydia's country cousin? You must not think much of her, to want to fob her off on the younger son of a younger son with no money and no prospects."

"My dear," she said gravely, "do you think that is all that marriage is about?"

"And it's not as if the Perrys are depending on me to carry on the name. Both sides of my family breed like rabbits already—a fact surely not lost on your prospective bridegroom."

"Lucius Perry! How can you say such things? Rabbits, indeed. Marriage is a sacred bond of two loving hearts."

He looked hard at her. "Oh, it is, is it? And do you love Lord Ferris?"

"I—well, I don't know yet. I hardly know him, do I? But he admires me to distraction. I admire him, too, of course."

"You hardly know him."

"That will change. I feel sure we will be blissful together. Oh, Lucius, you must not be hard on yourself. I feel certain that the right woman—"

He gritted his teeth. "Artemisia. Come back in a year and lecture me on the joys of the married state. Right now, stop preaching about things you know nothing about."

"And what is that supposed to mean, pray?"

"Nothing, nothing at all."

"No, Lucius, I want to know what you mean."

"Nothing. I'm sure your parents have taken every precaution to ensure that your bridegroom is all he should be. Your dowry's substantial, everyone knows it, and the lawyers will have drawn up an excellent contract. As long as you produce a son for him quickly, Lord Ferris should never give you a moment's unease."

Artemisia gasped in shock. "That is vulgar talk, Lucius Perry," she managed to say. "If you mean to imply that Lord Ferris is—is *buying* me, somehow—"

He shook his head and turned away. "Nothing. I'm not implying anything. I'm sorry, Mia; I—I lost a bet earlier; something I can't afford to lose, and I'm out of sorts, that's all. I'll try to be more enthusiastic."

Lucius Perry never spoke about himself if he could help it. Even a month ago she would have accepted the peace offering for what it was. But he had unnerved her, and she attacked. "You have no right to walk in here and criticize Lord Ferris!" she shrilled. "He is the Crescent Chancellor. Everyone approves of him! He's an important man! Who are you, anyway? A nobody—you said so yourself."

"Right." He stood up. "Fine. I'm nobody, he's everything, and it's nothing to me whether you go into this marriage with your eyes open or squinnied tight shut."

Artemisia lifted her chin. "What are you babbling about, Lucius?"

"You don't know him very well, that's all. Ask him, sometime, about the balls and parties you're not invited to."

She raised her chin even higher. "There are no balls I'm not invited to."

"Yes, there are. Ask him."

"All right, then, I will."

He saw the haughty terror on her face, and thought of another woman he knew who had been this young, once, and faced the same choices with even less to go on. "No, don't," he said gently. "Look, I spoke out of turn, and I'm sorry. I should not have said anything."

"No, you should not."

"But, coz—" He took her hand in his; not the light touch of the ballroom, but tight and earnest. "Artemisia. You do understand, don't you? The difference between a man's world and a woman's world?"

Tears trembled in her eyes. "What do you mean?"

"You know what I mean. There are parts of a man's life—any man's life—that you're expected to ignore. Men have secrets, and it's best to let them keep them."

"Do you have secrets, Lucius?"

"Oh, many," he said. "If you were my wife, it would be particularly important that you knew nothing about them, or pretended, anyway. But we get along, don't we? I'm sure Lord Ferris is no better or worse than any other man you could have chosen. I'm sure he'll make a fine husband."

"I know he will." She dabbed her eye before a tear could fall. "Lucius," she said in a small voice, "you mustn't bet or gamble again if losing makes you so unkind. Promise me you won't."

He kissed her hand, and patted her head, but promised nothing.

ONE DAY MY UNCLE SAID TO ME, "SABINA IS PLANNING A Rogues' Ball. I think you should come. It will be instructive." Wouldn't you know it? My first real city ball, and it was something roguish. Still, "Shall I wear a ballgown?" I asked.

"Not for this."

The last thing on earth I wanted was to make my city debut dressed like a boy. "Can I go masked?"

"You won't need to go masked. No one you know will be there. No one, that is, that you could admit to knowing to the sort of people you would go masked against. It is, after all, a Rogues' Ball." He flicked the invitation's stiff paper between his long fingers, then glanced at it again more closely: "Or, *Rouges'* Ball, as she's put it. If the woman can't spell—and believe me, she can't—she should get someone else to do her writing for her. She's invited half of Riverside, and everyone on the Hill who still finds her amusing. I wouldn't miss it for anything. We have a bet on how long it will take a fight to start. Dress for action, and don't carry a purse with any money: I can guarantee those will be the first to go, with all the cutpurses in attendance."

I knew who Sabina was by now: a professional mistress. She seemed to know my uncle well. She sent him chatty letters from her house in the Old City, which he sometimes read aloud to me and Marcus.

Sabina claimed always to be bored, bored, bored—bored by the lovers, bored by the duels, bored by the gold and the silk. But she kept at it nonetheless; the letters were full of her conquests and extravagances. I confess I was shocked by them: what she paid for a bracelet would have put a new roof on my mother's house; what she paid for bed-hangings would have bought the woman a small farm. It seemed to me that if only Sabina could be bothered to put some aside, she could retire very nicely from the conquests and find something that did not bore her.

Now she was hiring a guildhall to have room for all her inviteds, along with the inevitable drop-ins. The duke said to me, "Come armed."

There was no question in my mind but that I would take my master's sword. For form's sake I consulted with Phillip Drake, and to my surprise he was against it. "Old-fashioned," he said. "Look at the hilt."

"It's perfectly balanced."

"I'm not saying it's not a good sword; nice, flexible steel and all, but plain, lady, plain." He smiled. "I think we could persuade the duke to part with some funds to make a good showing at your first ball."

I shook my head, though I was tempted for a moment. "There's my New Year's knife for pretty. Although . . . a new scabbard would be nice. I don't think anyone would notice the hilt," I wheedled, "if it were tucked in a green leather scabbard worked with gold and scarlet, do you?"

Phillip Drake said, "I'll tell you what: you break my guard three times with the new double-pass I taught you, and I'll see to it you get any scabbard you like."

In any given fight, the weaker sword can prevail through sheer accident. But not in a drill, not three times in a row. I did it, though, and got my scabbard. So that was all right.

T HE NEXT TIME THEY MET, AT A CARD PARTY, LORD FERRIS WAS determined to let Lady Artemisia feel her consequence.

"You will be pleased to know," he said, "that half the young men of the town aren't speaking to me, because I have carried off the jewel that might have been in one of their caps."

Knowing her friends were looking, Artemisia could not resist tapping the Chancellor's arm with her fan.

"Really, sir?" she said frostily. "Then how is it that you find yourself invited to so many *fascinating* parties without me?"

He said, "No party is fascinating without you, sweet. And, as you well know, no one would dare to invite me anywhere without my intended."

Artemisia felt herself blushing. At first she was inclined to mind, but then she remembered that to see a blushing woman in a courting couple was expected. She raised her fan to her face to be sure that it was seen.

"I hear," she murmured behind it, "there is a ball to which I have not been invited."

"Really?" the Crescent Chancellor drawled. "Then I expect that I have not been, either."

"Oh, but I think you have, sir. Or what is that letter in your pocket, which you were not eager to let me see?"

And, indeed, the Crescent Chancellor's ringed hand flew to his inner pocket, but only for a moment. "Oh, that. Do you think it is from some woman?" he said loudly. "God love the puss, she's jealous already." He looked around the table for confirmation; the men guffawed, and Artemisia blushed in truth.

But she got it out of him in the end, when they were nearly alone, with her maid a discreet distance away. It was a ball, a ball comprised of rogues, the invitation said, but a ball nonetheless, and was she not an ornament at any ball? Her star shone too brightly for such low company—very well, then, she would cover it with a mask. She'd heard of married ladies who went to such places for a lark, suitably disguised, and were she and my lord not to be married so soon as made no never mind? As for rough company, well, it was soon to be his life's job to protect her, and what better place to test it than at a roguish ball? Ferris laughed at that, and allowed that if he could not protect her, no one could. But this would require more discretion than he feared she was mistress of, to quit the house without even her maid's knowledge. And what would her parents think of him if they found out?

Pooh, she said, her parents thought he'd hung the moon. If he wouldn't take her, she'd find another who would. There's Terence Monteith, quite mad for her, everyone knew he'd been drooping like a willow ever since she'd put on Ferris's engagement jewel . . . or her cousin Lucius Perry, he'd do anything for her.

Well, said His Lordship, we can't have you imposing on discarded lovers or worse yet, relatives. I see it is my duty to escort you safely there and back, for one last little girlish adventure. . . . If she could contrive to be at her own garden gate when the clock struck nine that night, he would be waiting, cloak in hand.

When he left, Artemisia was breathless with excitement. Such a victory, to bend such a man to her will! She would not mind being married to him at all, if this was a taste of things to come.

On the night of the Rogues' Ball, Betty laid out my nicest suit, the blue shot with crimson, and a new shirt with ruffles and a little gold edging, and low boots neatly cuffed. Just because I had no ballgown, I need not go looking like the dog's offal! I was going to the ball, and I was going as the Mad Duke's niece who studied the swordsman's art and wore a swordsman's clothes. What was the point of trying to hide it? Sooner or later it would all come out. It might as well be now. And if I found a mask to wear, he would only tear it off. I did have my new scabbard, though.

Marcus was delighted. He had retired to his room with a book of essays and a bowl of apples, with instructions to me to enjoy myself because he hated these things and not to let the duke do anything really stupid.

I waited in the front hall for some time, trying not to fidget with my sword. Nothing looks stupider than a swordsman who can't keep his hand off his tool, the master had said, and although Phillip Drake had laughed uproariously when I repeated that to him, I planned to stand by it. Finally I gave up and went and knocked on the door of the duke's chamber. Although the sun was nearly setting, the world bathed in its last colors, my uncle's rooms were shadowy and candlelit, the heavy curtains drawn. He still sat before the glass, his long hair falling all about him, sleek and new-brushed. His eyes looked very large, their color bright, gazing into the glass in which he saw me behind him. There was something about him of the enchanted prince, in the pallor of his skin or the brightness of his eyes, the surprising fineness of his hair and the etched bones of his face. He wore only plain black linen, over a very white shirt whose edges reported crisply at neck and wrists.

"Nothing too gaudy," he said to me in the mirror, "for a Rogues' Ball." But his right hand dazzled with rings. His valet combed the hair back from the duke's face and bound it with a velvet ribbon.

My uncle rose, and looked down at my head, and further down to my toes. He nodded; I was all right. "Stay close to me," he said. He wore not even a dagger. The gold rings, I supposed, were his weapon. And the plain black linen was exquisitely tailored; when he turned, I saw all the tiny folds and tucks stitched up and down the front.

He stumbled into a stool, and flung his hand out to the bedpost for support, and steadied himself there. "Stay close to me," he said again. "Things aren't quite where they should be."

"My lord," said his valet, "do you wish a draught of something steadying?"

"No," said the duke; "what for?"

I followed him down the stairs, where he was wrapped in a heavy cloak. At the door, a palanquin was waiting. He got through the curtains and into his seat very slowly, and lay back with his eyes closed. "Is it summer?" he said. "It's very warm."

I didn't answer; he wasn't listening to me anyway. When we were over the old bridge, a carriage attended. It took us slowly along the river. Now I could see all the other people going our way, mostly on foot—Riversiders, all decked out in their tasteless best, like painted poles at a Spring fair. Some impudent rascal rapped at the side of our door, demanding a lift—our footman beat him off, but the duke put a restraining hand on my arm, although I hadn't moved but to look. "Easy," he said. "Not yet."

The guildhall was so brightly lit inside that from the outside its tall windows shone like beaten gold. I was not the duke's only guard; other of our men had ridden outside the carriage, and it took the entire escort to clear a path to the guildhall steps. But they left us at the door. The duke put a hand on my shoulder, balancing. A huge footman in a livery all of ribbons came forward. He looked at my uncle. My uncle looked at him. Clearly something was supposed to be happening but wasn't. I wondered just how awful things would get if the footman tried to throw us out.

"We were invited," I said nervously, but nobody even looked at me.

My uncle spoke, finally, to the footman. "What a getup. You look," he said slowly but clearly, "like a booth at a fair."

"Ah," said the footman. "You've got that right. Shall I announce you, sir?"

"Why bother? Everyone knows who I am."

And so we entered the Rogues' Ball.

I recognized Sabina only because I didn't think our hostess would allow any other woman at her ball to be reclining in a nest of red velvet at the heart of a huge golden shell. Anyone, I suppose, was free to wear pink gauze and a necklace of the biggest pearls I'd ever seen. The shell was on a platform at the center of the room; all the activity swirled around her. The duke was staring hard at it and blinking. She caught sight of us and called "Alec!" and waved a napkin in our direction. As we drew nearer she shrieked, "Black! You wore *black* to my party!"

"Get me a drink," my uncle muttered, but he wouldn't let go of my shoulder.

By now, of course, everyone was staring at us. "Is *this* your new *boyfriend?*" Sabina demanded. We were now at the foot of the shell. It was raised above the throng, supported by carved horses with fishes' tails rising from the waves. It reminded me a lot of a serving platter for a banquet table, and I'm not sure she didn't mean it to.

"No, dear," he replied; "this is one you'd find very hard to steal from me. Unless you *like* unnatural blondes?" he asked me; but, not waiting for an answer, told her, "This one *guards* my body, instead of trying to rob it of my vital fluids."

Sabina threw back her head. She did have a glorious neck. "Brilliant. We all wondered when you were going to think of that. Well, then, I won't worry about your getting snuffed at my party. You're so considerate, you plan for everything."

"Shove over," he told her; "I want to sit down."

The pink gauze shifted in our direction. "No. You'll ruin my effect."

"Shove over, I said; you've got the best view."

"I will not."

She was getting mad, and I wasn't Marcus. But I tried. "My lord duke," I said, "don't you want to go see who's here?"

"Oh, good god," said Sabina. "This isn't a boy at all. It's the baby chick poor Ginnie was telling me about. Send her home, Alec, what's wrong with you?"

"I can fight," I said staunchly, to my surprise.

"Well," she replied, "keep your uncle out of trouble, or you're going to have to."

"I am staying out of trouble." He arranged himself on the steps to the shell. "How's that? And don't say you won't get a huge bang out of having the Duke Tremontaine sitting tamely at your feet. People will talk for days."

"No, no, no!" She smacked him with her fan. "Not only are you ruining the effect, but people always *want* things from you. I am not having my lovely seashell turned into a queuing for petitions for better drains on Tulliver Street."

"I'll stand guard," I said. It seemed like the safest place to be.

"I'm sure you will, angel," she purred, "but I want you to have a good time. Both of you. Alec, dearest darling, do go enjoy yourself and pick up some pretty man, and then you can tell me all about it tomorrow. I'll let you be the very first one to call on me, I promise, and we'll thrash the whole thing out together first thing. Will you do that for me? Please? Oh my goodness, who's this dashing blade?" This last was addressed, not to us, but to a masked young man in very tight breeches and an open collar. He was awfully good-looking, and he was leaning over us to kiss her hand.

"Oh god," my uncle groaned, "dinner is served. Get me out of here."

I took his cold hand, and led him into the throng.

⌒

Lady Artemisia Fitz-Levi was afraid that her mask was slipping. Nervously she tugged at the ribbons that held it in back. If only she hadn't had to sneak out without her maid's help; Dorrie would have been able to pin it more tightly into her hair. Unlike every other party she'd ever been to, here there was no room to retire to with ladies' maids standing by to mend tears and turn up stray locks of hair. She was on her own.

"Don't worry," her escort breathed in her ear, "they'll all think you are my ladybird, isn't that the point? Put your head up, dearest, and laugh. Look like you're having a good time, or they'll know you're not."

"But I'm afraid it will come loose—"

"My dear." Her intended ran his finger carefully along the place where the bottom of the mask ended and her cheek began. She felt a chill at the base of her spine: excitement, or fear, or that thing the older girls talked about? "If I see any sign of it coming loose, I will be the first to help you hide your face. Do you think I want the world to know my wife was at this affair? No, my little madcap puss," and his arm was around her back now, holding her to him, his hand cradling her hip through the heavy layers of her skirt, "this will just be our little secret, our first adventure together. Isn't that what you wanted?" and she had to say, "Yes, of course it is."

The room was aswirl with people. It was like being in a pool of water, in a river that moved against her. Someone knocked into her and Artemisia gasped reflexively, "Oh! Excuse me!"

But her escort squeezed her waist and chuckled, "That's no way to go about it. Not here, not with these types. The next time that happens, you jab out with your elbow and say, 'Watch it, jackass!'"

She giggled nervously. "I can't!"

"Yes you can . . . try it." Without warning, he swung her around so she ran into a short man whose hands were full of pie. "Watch it, sister!" the man sputtered through a mouthful of pie, and she said, "Watch it, yourself," and though she spoiled the effect by giggling, he told her she had done well.

Aband struck up in one corner of the room. It was the kind of music you could hear in any Riverside tavern, fiddles and ratchety pipes and drums, and everyone loved it. The Riversiders and University students knew the tunes and the steps that went with them and threw themselves into the dance, right at home. The nobles, some dressed in rags and some in ball regalia, but all easily distinguished by their cleanliness, started casting about for likely looking girls to dance with. I was glad my clothes ensured that no one could take me for one. I passed behind, the dark duke's bright shadow, as he drifted looking for amusement.

His eye was caught by a group of men dressed in brightly fluttering tatters. They had braided ribbons into their hair, twined them through the careful rents in their shirts and sleeves and breeches. Some had tied in little bells; you couldn't hear them above the noise, but they looked nice.

"What ho!" one of them cried, roguishly, I guess, to the crowd. "We are the Companions of the King! Come join us in our devilish revelry!" They seemed to be trying to arrange people into a pyramid against the wall behind them. A red-haired man had a food-stained tablecloth laid out on the floor and was drawing on it with a burnt stick.

The duke moved towards them as if their colors were flame on a cold night. One spotted us and shouted, "Oh, joy! It's darkest Night—"

"Or Nightmare," said the redhead, "allied with Temptation. Just what we need to complete the tableau. Do join us, please, and we'll make you immortal."

"I am already immortal," the duke said, a little thickly. "Have you discovered a new method?"

"Art, sir, art is the medium! As it ever was. Art renders immortality through the medium of allegory. Twin art with morality, and there is nothing to offend anyone, yet something for all tastes."

We looked up at the artists' tableau. It was a complicated twist of people arranged reaching for fruit, for wine, or for each other. "It doesn't look very moral to me," my uncle said.

"Exactly."

"What my friend means, severe and beautiful one, is that in the interest of revealing virtue, we mask it in vice."

"Didn't Placid say that?" asked the other.

"No, I said it," snapped the red-haired artist. "It is a grand concept.

A masked ball of virtue, the obverse of roguery, disguised as the very thing it seeks to cast down."

The duke actually smiled. "Very apt." He gestured to the pyramid. "And this represents . . . ?"

"Man's heedless quest for Pleasure, of appetites temporal and carnal. See how in their striving each man treads upon the other? And how the Pleasures reach out mindlessly to tempt us?"

I certainly did. One of the Pleasures, a man all tucked up behind another one, untwisted his arm, encased in peacock blue silk, to wave it languidly at the duke. I had seen his sleek head before, and this time I knew where.

It was Artemisia's friend, and the Mad Duke's as well. I was dying to say something clever to my uncle about that particular beauty being one of the pleasures he'd already enjoyed—but if I hoped to find out more about the mysterious young man who visited nice young girls on the Hill and also worked at Glinley's, I would have to be chary. I would discover his name tonight; that would be my quest, and if I was very lucky, my uncle would not know of it.

"So in the interest of illuminating virtue," the artist was saying, "it is possible, indeed necessary, to show vice in all its manifestations. It will be a tremendous crowd-pleaser."

"Right," said the duke. "Well then, get out your sketchbooks and get started, because I want to be at the top, and I probably won't last long."

As he handed me his empty glass, I recalled my duty. "Oh, no. I really don't think you should—"

"You are my swordsman, not my governess," the duke said sternly. "If someone attacks me with anything sharp and pointed, you kill them. Otherwise, leave me alone."

There was no use arguing with him. If he broke his leg, someone could probably set it.

The duke set one finely shod foot on the thigh of a crouching earth spirit and began his ascent. I'd climbed some trees in my time, and clearly so had he. But the trees didn't usually shudder and giggle underfoot. The red-haired artist wasn't really helping, rushing in and patting people who were falling out of pose back into place. He nearly got kicked in the teeth by a ticklish Temperance. A couple of the others began sketching madly. It looked like roiling clouds of form all over their paper, not like people at all, but I saw they were drawing a sort of map of the scene. I'd never seen anything like it, and I was so fascinated that I missed the downfall of the allegory. I heard my uncle shout, "*You!* You—" and then the voices became indecipherable, and it was all a mess of arms and legs and skirts and hair and ribbons and shrieks and laughter.

The duke crawled out from underneath the heaving throng. He pointed into it. "Kill him," he said. "He bit me."

"I don't think I—"

"My lord, I beg your pardon." A bright head with rosy cheeks emerged from the sprawl. "I mistook you for a most delicious fruit."

"An easy mistake for anyone to make," the duke said smoothly. "Do I know you?"

I knew him. It was the horrible Alcuin.

A
RTEMISIA HAD A STITCH IN HER SIDE. SHE REACHED ACROSS the dancers for Lord Ferris, but his hand seemed to slip away from hers as if pulled by the awful music, the straining strings. A stranger with garlic breath had his arm around her waist, and she was close to tears. The dance was not one she knew. There were no steps, it was just leaping back and forth in time to the music, with your partner swinging you this way and that and handing you off to someone else at a signal, but she did not know what it was. All sorts of men had had their hands all over her, and it was too much, really too much, but every time Lord Ferris came in view he smiled brightly at her and said, "Enjoying yourself, sweetheart?" It was all that kept her from tearing herself out of the crowds and running for home. . . . The garlic went away and she smelt a familiar scent, looked up and realized it was Lord Ferris with his arms around her, and she leaned into his chest and whimpered up at him, "I'm thirsty."

"Poor kitten," he said. "Of course you are. What a treat you were there, a jewel ornamenting the arms of some of the roughest men in town." He was holding her as close as some of them had, closer than he had ever held her before. But at least they were off the dance floor, headed for a quiet corner away from the worst of the brawl. "What shall I feed you now, my sweet pet, wine? Or maybe beer, in the spirit of the evening."

"Water," she said, "or a fruit coolant."

But he went on as if she had not spoken, "I'm not sure she's serving wine tonight; they'd guzzle it like rough ale, these types, and there would be chaos. But don't worry; I've brought this." He drew a flask from his jacket, and raised it to his lips. When he lowered it, a little moisture clung to them. "Taste?" he whispered.

"What?" Artemisia was baffled.

He leaned his face down to hers, so that his wet lips were nearly touching hers. "Put out your tongue," he said, "and taste."

No one knew where she was. No one here would care what he asked her to do. They were in a corner where no one could see them. Closing her eyes, she slowly put out her tongue and tasted burning brandy and the skin of his lips.

"Ah!" His sudden hot breath shot right into her lungs; she gasped and tried to pull back, but his arms were tight around her.

"Ah," he said again, and his mouth was all over her, her lips, her chin, her ears, her neck, her chest where the gown was cut as low as she had dared.

"My wicked girl," he said, "how I adore you." Artemisia knew she should be pleased, but she was frightened. His hands were everywhere, too, rumpling her skirts, pushing at her bodice, pinning back her hands while he kissed her.

"Please," she breathed, "I—"

"Oh, do you?" he growled. "Do you? Of course you do, of course you do, so do I—"

"No!"

She said it, she heard herself say it, but he did not seem to. He did not seem to hear anything except his own hot breath, which was terribly loud in her ear while he did things to her skirts until there was nothing at all between him and her, really nothing whatsoever, and although she wailed in distress it only seemed to make him hotter and he forced her up against the wall and rammed himself into her over and over and she had to stop thinking because there was nothing else to do until he let out a revolting noise and draped himself over her all sweaty and said, "Couldn't wait, could you?"

She was shivering as if her whole body would shake to pieces.

"My dearest love," he said, and pulled a lock of hair back from her cheek, "are you cold?"

"Please," she said, "I want to go home."

"Come home with me," he murmured. "We've the whole night ahead of us."

He wrapped his arms tight round her, and she tasted sick in the back of her throat. She swallowed hard and tried to match his tone, but her voice came out all squeaky. "How can you say that? How can you say that to me?"

"But why not, sweetheart?" Lord Ferris murmured in her hair.

"How dare you suggest that I—that I—"

"That you are the sort of young lady who would go off unchaperoned with a man to a strange place with no protection? That you'd allow him liberties with you there?" Something caught in her throat and she made a kind of barking noise. "Now, now," he said, "don't cry. Can't you see I love you all the better for it, you wanton little sweet sweet slut?"

She was sobbing so hard she could scarcely breathe, and she heard herself making awful retching noises. She reached out blindly for someone, for something, but only his hands were there to catch hers, and "Oh, come on," he said; "it's not that bad. Stop howling like a kitchen maid. Maybe I was a little quick for your first time, but can you blame me? Overcome as I was by the rapture of your beauty—I've been overcome for weeks, now, and you damn well know it, you hot little piece. You lead me on, and then expect me to control myself? There, there, stop crying; I promise I'll be good and slow and patient when we're married. You'll like it fine, you'll see."

"Married?" she gasped. "Married? To *you?*"

As she spoke the words, she realized what it meant. Married to Lord Ferris. There would be all the gowns and the jewels, the wedding ceremony and the guests and the banquet, and then she would go home with him to his house, and she would belong to him forever and he could do this to her whenever he liked, without asking. That was what it meant.

"Well, yes, married to me," he said reasonably, and chuckled. "Were you thinking of doing this, and then marrying someone else? That's not how it works, you sweet little slut, and you know it."

Artemisia tried to catch her breath—once, twice, and she found the air she needed to say, "Never. I will never marry you."

"Oh, yes, you will," he said comfortably. "Think of it this way: at least we know now we'll suit between the sheets. Not bad, that. Now pull yourself together; you're a bit of a mess. I'll find you something nice to drink, and when I come back we'll have a little dance, shall we?" She shook her head in protest. "Don't worry," he said, "I won't make you dance with any of those buffoons. I admit I enjoyed seeing them holding you there—but you're mine now, and I won't let you out of my hands ever again."

M Y UNCLE LOOKED ALCUIN UP AND DOWN. "OH. YOU. I thought I got rid of you ages ago. What were you doing lurking in allegories biting me?"

"Old habits die hard?" suggested the beautiful Alcuin.

"It is a habit," the duke said, "that I would endeavor to correct if I were you."

"Oh, really?" Alcuin lowered his eyelids and looked up through long lashes. "And are you going to help correct me?"

As if entranced, the duke slowly moved one hand toward the handsome man's face—but at the last moment, Alcuin turned his face away. "Leave me alone," he said sharply. "You had your chance."

I didn't like this. Other people were getting interested. I looked around for the sleek man from Glinley's, but he had slipped away from the crowd. The artists may not have known who my uncle was, but various Riversiders did, and I heard the whispering behind us: *Tremontaine . . .*

My uncle looked his former lover in the eye. "You shoe-scraping," he said. "You worthless piece of trash."

Alcuin's face turned pale, and then dark. "Not so worthless," he said. "I've got something you don't have. Something I happen to know you want."

He raised his chin and made a little moue with his rosy lips. A well-built dark-haired man came to his side, a sword slung low at his hips.

"Is someone," the swordsman said to his friend, "offering you trouble?"

The duke's face stiffened with distaste. Ignoring the swordsman, he said to Alcuin, "You can't challenge me, you monkey's turd. Only a noble can do that, and you're not exactly noble; the Court of Honor would never hear your case. A civil court would sentence you to death, even if you won."

"No one would dream of challenging you, sir." Alcuin did not budge. "But my swordsman has every right to challenge your . . . your *thing.*"

My hand was on my sword. I heard the duke say, "It appears, Lady Katherine, that my old sweetheart here would like some of our blood."

I didn't care. I was more than ready for him.

And I did not like being called a *thing.*

Alcuin's swordsman was much bigger than I was, and much stronger, too. He looked me up and down. "Do you really think this is even worth it?"

"Just do it," Alcuin told him through gritted teeth.

"But—no offense, dear—but it's a *girl,* right?" Like Alcuin, he wasn't very bright.

"I don't care if it's a spotted baboon! She's got a sword, and she offends me. So if you want to get any tonight, or ever again for that matter, you'll draw your steel right now and teach her some respect!"

"She is a noble," the duke drawled, "and you are not. The privilege of the sword extends only to—"

"I accept the challenge," I said quickly. "On my own behalf, sword to sword, I accept."

"Well, then," my uncle said.

I looked around at the considerable crowd. "Where do we—"

"Fall back." The duke and some others started clearing people back to form a circle. I had the sudden fierce wish that Marcus could be there, not to help me, but to see me doing it for real at last.

"Five on the girl." The betting had begun. "Twenty on Rippington." So that was his name. What a stupid name. Rippington.

Rippington and I faced each other across the circle. "Oh, lord," he said, and sighed. As the challenger, he had the right to begin the match, but as the challenged, I could call the terms.

"First blood," I said. My hand was closed around the pommel of the master's sword. I was glad I had not let Phillip Drake talk me out of bringing it tonight. I thought, Well, at least *you've* done this before. I breathed deep, felt the balance in my feet. Balance is everything.

"Ready?" he asked formally.

I nodded. He drew, and I drew, and we stood at guard. Then Rippington advanced and tapped my blade gently. I didn't move. Don't waste your moves, and don't show your strengths until you have to. Make them wait, and make them guess, and make them show you theirs.

Rippington fought like a training lesson. He pulled back and executed a perfect lunge, hoping to get it over with quickly, I guess, but I saw it coming a mile away and stepped gently aside to let him pass, which he did, nearly falling on his face.

"Dammit!" he said, and I heard, "Twenty on the girl."

I turned around and attacked him in a high line to see if he'd go for it, and of course he did, opening his entire front for just long enough for me to have killed him if I had wanted to. He parried this time, and I replied a bit show-offishly with a fancy riposte, just to see if he'd follow the move. God, he was slow! I realized later he must have been drinking to be so slow and precise; he fenced as if he was doing lessons, as if he was always trying to be sure his feet were in exactly the right position. Wine is enemy to sword. But at the time, I thought that he was making fun of me, refusing to take me seriously, so I got a little flashy and began speeding things up.

Mistake. Drunk or not, his sword was still perfectly long and deathly sharp, and when we closed at close quarters I realized that he could wrench the blade from my hand simply by applying enough force. Spooked, I backed off, nearly crashing into the ring of onlookers. There were jeers; I tried not to hear them, but I knew what they meant. I looked like a fool, and I felt like one. This was not a lesson. Rippington's blade was not tipped, and he would not pull back if he came too close. When he lunged, I felt the steel sweep past my face, and knew it *was* steel. He hadn't been making an effort because he thought I wasn't worth it. Now he wasn't so nice. Now he was working harder, testing me, trying to draw me out. I kept my moves small, trying to give little away, but it was hard not to bring out my fiercest defensive moves. Save them, a voice inside me said. Save them for when you need them. Watch him and see what he does.

I watched, and I responded. The crowd was quieter now. This was the way it was supposed to be, a conversation between equals, an argument of steel. I wasn't going to die. The worst that I could do was lose the bout, but I wasn't going to lose if I could help it. Because at last I found the move that my opponent loved best: a nice, flashy double-riposte. I found it, and I found that I could make him do it every time. High parry, low parry, wherever I came in didn't matter, I could count on him coming back with that double-riposte. Like making a cat jump to a piece of string. It probably worked better with a taller opponent; with me he didn't have to reach quite so far as he was used to. He kept doing it out of habit, and because he looked good in the pose, but the difference between us made it just a little off-balance for him. That's the problem with having one favorite move. I enticed him into it one more time, and then I came in right where I was supposed to, in a clean line straight to the—

Straight to the heart, it would have been, and I don't know whether he could have defended himself in time, but at the last minute I realized what I was doing, and turned my wrist just a fraction so that instead the point slashed messily across his arm, tearing his shirt and the skin under it.

"Blood!" The cry went up. I fell back, gasping; I hadn't realized I was working so hard. "First blood to—what's your name, dearie?"

"Uh, Katherine," I said. "Katherine Talbert."

My uncle was gazing delightedly at me. "This," he began, "is my—"

"Shut up!" I told him. "Just shut up, don't say it, all right? Just for once."

So then he was laughing so hard the red-haired artist had to hold him up. I had a feeling the red-haired artist who loved allegory was in for an interesting night.

"Alec!" Sabina had arrived; I guess it took her a long time to get down from the seashell. "Alec, *when* did I tell you there would be *fighting* at my party?"

I looked for Rippington. Alcuin was binding up his wounds surrounded by a coterie of friends. They shot me some truly dirty looks. It had never occurred to me that not everyone loved you after you'd won a fight. It wasn't in the books. Even Richard St Vier hadn't mentioned it.

Not that people weren't all around me saying some very nice things, trying to get my attention. But I had no stomach for answering questions just then. I was thirsty, and I just wanted to be alone for a bit.

"Here, you." Someone put a cup in my hands. It was the woman I'd met my first day out in Riverside, the colorful Ginnie Vandall. I drank. Water had never tasted so good. She put her arm around my waist, and I let her lead me out of the crowd. But she wanted something from me, too. "Where is he?" she murmured low and urgent in my ear. "I know those moves. Where is he?"

I broke away from her, and ran.

I ran to the furthest corner I could find, but it was already occupied, by a dark-haired woman in a truly beautiful lavender gown, a color I cannot wear. Her back was to me, but then she turned around and I recognized Artemisia Fitz-Levi, of all people.

"Oh!" she said brightly. "It's you! Are you here, too? Are you having a good time?"

It was perfectly obvious that she'd been crying her eyes out. And her hair was a mess.

"What happened?" I asked because clearly something had, and it was not good, whatever it was.

"Oh, nothing. I'm just fine. How are you?"

Her hands were shaking. I took them in mine. They were icy cold. I said, "I'm fine. I just almost killed someone. I'm here as the duke's bodyguard, but I think you need one more."

She looked at me with terror. "Is my hair really awful?"

"A rat's nest."

Her face melted and crumpled, and she started to cry. She put her hands up over her face, as if she could hide it, and she shook her head when I tried to touch her, but I did for her what I sometimes did for my mother, and just put my arms around her until she naturally laid her head on my shoulder and clung to me, and she sobbed there for a good long while. When she got a little quieter, I disengaged enough to dig out my handkerchief and offer it to her.

"Look," I said, "can you tell me what happened? Maybe I can do something."

"You can't do anything," she sniffled. "No one can. It's all my fault and there's nothing I can do, but I'll never marry him, never!"

"Marry who?"

"Lord F-Ferris. My intended. I made him bring me here, and then he—he—"

I stepped back a pace. "A nobleman brought you here? To this? What is he, an idiot?"

"He's the Crescent Chancellor, you dolt!" Well, she was upset. "I'm supposed to marry him, but I can't, now. I can't marry anyone, never, ever. I'm ruined!" she wailed.

"Ruined how?"

She hiccupped and looked me in the eye. "Ruined. Exactly like in the books. That kind of ruined."

"And your Lord Ferris stood by and let someone—"

"No. He did it himself." I seized her sticky hand, and she gripped mine, hard. "He says I'll learn to enjoy it. But I won't. I won't. I won't marry him. I'll never let him touch me again."

I said, "Certainly not. Look, you'd better go home."

"Will you take me?" she asked piteously.

"I—I'll have to ask my uncle."

"No! You mustn't tell anyone! Above all, not him!"

"I won't tell him, I'll just . . ." Just what? Then I thought of something. "Look," I said, "do you remember that day I came to see you? And you were visiting with that pretty young man?"

"Pretty enough, I suppose," she sniffed. "That's my cousin Lucius. Lucius Perry."

"Your cousin! Perfect. Because he's here, Artemisia, I saw him not long ago. I'm going to go find him, and he will take you home."

She clutched my sleeve. "Oh, no! Don't leave me! Lord Ferris might come back at any moment."

"Then you must hide. Hurry, the time is short." We found her a niche outside the main hall and she huddled into it, pale in the moonlight and the shadows from the hall.

"Be strong," I said to her; "be brave, Artemisia. I'll find this Lucius, and all may yet be well."

Her eyes got a little wide, and then I watched her face change subtly. Some of the pain went out of it, to be replaced by a soft determination. "All will be well," she said, and I knew she was thinking of the same chapter I was, "with you at my side."

I turned back to the ballroom then, which was good because I was blushing. Although I'd thought about it a lot on my own, no one had ever compared me to Fabian before.

The place was a madhouse, with people dancing and kissing and who knows what. I was never going to find her cousin Lucius without some kind of a plan. *Lucius Perry, Lucius Perry . . .* He was a nobleman, and a Perry at that. Even I had heard of the Perrys, a large and prosperous family. No wonder the duke didn't want us to know who his visitor really was. The duke was encouraging Artemisia's cousin Lucius in a life of vice, and taking his share out of the profits, too. Maybe the duke was blackmailing young Perry. Did Tremontaine blackmail people, or did he draw the line at that? He had some strange notions about honor, did my uncle the Mad Duke.

"Out of my way, boy!" A big man in red brocade bumped into me, and I jumped about a foot. Was this Artemisia's betrothed, that evil man? I didn't know what the Crescent Chancellor looked like, but I wanted to be sure he didn't find her again tonight. Now I really wished Marcus were here. But he wasn't. That might be for the best, though. I would definitely tell him about Lucius Perry; Perry was ours. But what had happened to Artemisia Fitz-Levi, that was something I must keep to myself.

If you were a nobleman leading a double life who had decided to attend a Rogues' Ball where half the people knew you as one sort of person, and the other as another, where would you be? Masked, I thought, if you had any sense. But had he? He had been in the allegory bare-faced. My master said that there were swordsmen who courted the dangerous opponent and the sudden move. He must be like that, her cousin Lucius.

"I'm writing a song." The voice was so close I thought it was directed at me, but the speakers were off to one side, above my head. "'The Maid with the Blade.' It will sell like mad on the street."

"Dirty or clean?"

"Oh, romantic, I think. With lots of verses; maybe I'll even run to two sides. . . ."

It was about me, and it wasn't, but I couldn't worry about that now. I moved slowly onwards, looking.

Lucius Perry was masked, so it's a good thing I recognized his smooth dark hair, that and his sleeve, which was of an unusual cut in that glorious peacock blue. When you've mended as many clothes as I have, you sort of memorize fabrics without realizing it. He stood off to one side, leaning against the wall with a drink in his hand, watching everyone.

"Come quickly!" I said, without wasting time. "Artemisia is here, and she needs you!"

He lifted the soft velvet mask off his eyes. "Who—oh, you're the—Wait a minute. What's happened?"

I grabbed his wrist. "Just come!"

I had thought she would fall into his arms weeping, but when she saw her cousin, Artemisia simply held out her trembling hands. "Lucius," she whispered, "take me home."

"I will." But first he took off his mask, and tied it securely over her face. "Come," he said; "come with me, and don't speak a word."

He put an arm around her waist, and she leaned on him, very shaky. "Don't worry," I said encouragingly, and tried to think of something better to say. "Tonight's deed will not go unpunished."

She turned and smiled at me, and then she and Lucius Perry disappeared into the crowd.

Pinking Alcuin's bullyblade Rippington had been nothing, just swordplay and acrobatics. But at least now I knew that I could win a fight against a full-grown man. What Lord Ferris had done to my friend was unspeakable, disgusting. When she told her family, they would probably kill him. But if they didn't, I would.

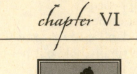

I WOKE UP WITH KITTENS ALL OVER MY FACE. I RAISED A HAND to brush them off, but they turned out not to have any legs or tails. My uncle the mad duke was sweeping swathes of velvet over me, cheerfully urging, "Get up, get up—have some tea and tell me which one you like best."

I pulled the blankets up around my neck. The swathes were attached to several large bolts of fabric, which a nervous shop assistant was holding while the duke tried them against my face. I looked around for Marcus, but he, thank god, was not there to see; only Betty stood by, patiently holding a cup of tea. I seized it from her and drank, and said, "My sword!" I had put it away dirty last night. Blick, blick, blick, as Venturus would say. I'd be ages getting the rust out.

"Never mind that," my uncle said. "Just tell me which one you like best."

"I like them all," I said, playing for time while I tried to wake up. There was a fire in the hearth, and the sun coming through the thick old windows was mid-afternoonish. I remembered coming home in the thin light of dawn, my uncle a dead weight in the sedan chair beside me. He'd had his fill of the red-haired artist and a number of other stimulants, besides. There'd been no moving him without two hefty footmen. I'd tumbled into bed without a thought for anything other than how soft it was.

"Well, you're not having them all, just one."

"One what? You shouldn't be here," I groused. "I'm not even dressed."

"Don't be prudish. You can defend yourself perfectly well. You proved that last night. I am very, very pleased. Also relieved. I'm making you a present: a lovely velvet cloak. Made to your measure, with room to grow. Now, which do you like best?"

I clutched at the nearest velvet, and to my shame I started to cry. It was unbelievable. I had almost killed a man last night, and now I was going to have the cloak of my dreams. And my friend Artemisia had been forced in a crowded ballroom, in her beautiful lavender gown.

I t's not to be borne." Lady Fitz-Levi put her hands on her breast. "Really, Fitz, it is intolerable."

"Agreed." Her husband shifted his chair closer to the fire, and picked a spot of egg off his vest.

"Something must be done."

"Indeed."

"I can hardly bear it."

"Terrible." Her husband shook his head in annoyance. "What on earth was she thinking of, running off like that? A young lady betrothed, and to such a place. It's a wonder she wasn't set upon by rogues of the vilest kind." His lady nodded. "Of course, Ferris had no business taking her there. A grown man like that, helping her in a schoolgirl prank. I thought he had more sense."

"It was she, my dear, who lacked sense. I'm sure she just twisted Ferris round her little finger, as she always does. She got in over her head, and now she's sorry and wants to call off the wedding. Well, I'm not having it. She'll take the consequences of her folly and make us proud in the end, and that is that."

"I saw those flowers he sent this morning; man's besotted."

"He surely must be. She's a lucky girl and doesn't even know it. Refusing her food like that. I've tried all morning, but I cannot talk sense into her."

"Well, girls have their humors. We cannot *force* her to eat."

"Do you think so?" Nervously his wife twisted her lace fichu in her ringed fingers. "They always forced *me* to eat. Boiled carrots. I hated them."

"I think she's a bit old for boiled carrots," said her husband. "But you're welcome to try."

"She's a bit old to be carrying on like a baby! Maybe boiled carrots is what she deserves."

"Why don't you make her something she particularly likes? A nice cake, or something."

"She refused her toast and chocolate; am I to treat her like an invalid? No, indeed. She must know that I am very displeased. All she will say is that she wants you to challenge Lord Ferris."

Lord Fitz-Levi snorted. "Why would I want to do that? Ruin the wedding and ruin her name at the same time? And ruin our highest ally in the Council of Lords? I'm counting on him to help Robbie to a good post this year. What a lot of fuss over nothing."

"That's what I told her. Do you know, I think we should move the wedding up? They'll have to work harder on the gown, but it will be worth it. Oh, she'll make a lovely bride!"

T HE DUKE TREMONTAINE PERSONALLY SIGNED THE ORDER FOR his niece's new garment, all three yards of it, silk lining and tassels and all. He signed it with a flourish, and picked up his next piece of business, ignoring the opening of the study door, since he knew perfectly well who it was.

"Are you happy now?" the Ugly Girl said. "Your niece is the talk of the town."

"How would you know?" the duke asked, amused. "You don't get out much."

She held up a cheap sheet of paper, as cheaply printed. It was a rude cartoon of a tall, thin, unhappy-looking man and a bosomy girl with a sword pointed upwards; the words underneath were: "*Oh, no! My Tool is useless, I must find a Girl to do the Work for me!*"

He took the page from her, and held it up to a candle. "Don't let her see it. And if she does, don't explain it to her."

"What about you? Don't you mind?"

The duke singed the edges of the page so that they were evenly crisped all round. "About this one more than any of the others? Why should I? I'm a popular figure. They like doing my nose." He turned it around again; the lowest letters, which named the printer and engraver, blackened away. "Alcuin's not the first of my discards to try something like this: nasty drawings, imprecations on my manhood. Horrible, isn't it?" he said cheerfully. "Do you think I should have him killed, or what?"

"You've already subjected your pretty friend to a fate worse than death, haven't you?" she said peevishly. "Let's leave it at that. What I want to know is, are you through with the girl, or just beginning?"

"I didn't know you were so fond of her," the duke said.

"I'm not. It's a theoretical question. I'm interested in the way your mind works—or doesn't work, depending."

"Do you mean: she's done her trick, now I should find some nice nobleman and marry her off? In that case, no, I'm not done with her. Besides, she's company for Marcus. He needs more friends his own age."

THE FIRST LETTER REACHED ME THE NEXT MORNING. IT WAS ADdressed to the Lady Katherine at Tremontaine House, and had clearly passed through several hands, not all of them clean. The sealing wax was scented, and the loopy handwriting was in violet ink. But there were spots on the paper where tears had made the ink run, and the letters sloped downward across the page.

> *Dearest Friend, it read. I am beset. I am without hope. My parents Know All, but my woe means nothing to them. They are monsters and tyrants. They want me to marry him, still. I will die, first. You understand. You are the only one who does. I will never forget your kindness to me. Do not try to visit me. I am a prisoner here. But if you can contrive to send a line or two of simple hope to me in my wretched misery, it will speak more than volumes of insincere verse from less noble souls than yours. I hope this letter finds you well. I will bribe the underhousemaid with my last year's silk stockings to bring it to you from your own—*
>
> Stella

I stuffed it in my pocket when Marcus came in. Of course he noticed.

"From your mother?" he said.

"No. You know that's not allowed."

"I don't care." He studied his nails. "I'm your friend. I'll help you, if you like."

"I don't need help, thanks."

My friend took a step backwards. "I guess not. After that swordfight, and all. The duke's pleased, anyway. Do whatever you want; you could fill your room with apes and parrots, and he'd only ask if you wanted to feed them oranges."

"I don't want parrots," I said. He did not look happy. "Do you want to play shesh?" I asked, partly to make him feel better, and partly to distract him from the letter.

"Not really."

"Well, then . . . do you want to hear about my swordfight?"

"Dying to tell me, are you?"

"Well, who else am I going to tell?" I was dying to tell someone, after all. It was my first real fight, and I had won! I almost wished that Venturus were still around, so I could tell him. Marcus lacked expertise and enthusiasm, but at least he would listen. I decided to ignore his mood and continued ruefully, "Betty will only start going on about how I should have seen St Vier in his heyday or something; besides, I want to get it all clear in my head before I have to run through it for Phillip Drake so he can tell me everything I did wrong."

Marcus wasn't interested in the subtleties of my swordplay, but he was very enthusiastic about the results. He'd disliked Alcuin more than most, and utterly approved of his public humiliation at the Rogues' Ball. "You've got a real future, Katie," he concluded approvingly, "in hitting irritating people where it hurts. No wonder the duke is pleased with you."

He didn't ask again about my letter, but then, it wasn't the only one I got. Sabina actually wrote to thank me for providing such wonderful entertainment at her party, and did I want to do it again for a private event? Two people offered me jobs as a guard, and a theatre asked if I would be interested in entertaining crowds between shows. The duke's private secretary, Arthur Ghent, offered to open all my letters and take care of the crazy ones for me. But I didn't want him to see what was coming to me, because I was expecting another one soon from Artemisia.

I had written her back saying:

> *Stella—*
>   *To live is to hope, and while we breathe, we hope and live.* (That was from the book.) *Though I serve another, I am yours to command.* (So was that; it was a line of Tyrian's, but I liked him sometimes better than Fabian. He had sense.) *Be brave, be strong, and know that you are ever in the thoughts of your faithful—*
>   *KT*

Getting it delivered to the Hill without any of my friends on the duke's staff knowing about it would be tricky. In the end, I went out on the streets of Riverside and picked the hungriest kid I could find.

"Watch it, pal," he said, and I said, "You!" because it was the one who had tried to rob me that first day in the snow. He had nerve, even if he didn't have much sense. His name was Kevin, and I gave him two coppers to carry my letter to Artemisia's maid, with the promise of five more if he came back with a ribbon to prove it had gotten there.

It was a lavender ribbon. I tied it around my wrist under my shirt, as a token not to forget.

Aᴛᴛᴇʀ ᴀ ꜰᴇᴡ ᴅᴀʏꜱ, Aʀᴛᴇᴍɪꜱɪᴀ'ꜱ ᴘᴀʀᴇɴᴛꜱ ᴡᴇʀᴇ ᴀᴛ ᴛʜᴇɪʀ ᴡɪᴛꜱ' end.

"I am at wits' end, Fitz," his lady said to him for the third time that hour. "She's showing no sense whatsoever."

"Seems simple enough," her husband repeated. "Easy for her, really. She's already agreed once to this marriage. She just has to do it again. Simple."

"It's not as if we forced her into it, is it? We let her choose for herself, and she chose Lord F."

"Certainly she did." Lord Fitz-Levi examined his neckcloth in the mirror. It had held up remarkably well under the morning's stresses. "All this fuss over a little cuddle in the dark."

"They were, after all, betrothed."

He gave a final tug to put it in place. "She'll settle down once she's married, god love her."

But their daughter seemed to have suffered a sea change. She spoke wildly, most unlike herself. She had no wish to go out, she said, lest she encounter *him*. She refused even the most tempting food, and would not try on her wedding dress, although it was magnificent. There was talk of a physician, or a trip to the country, and they put it about that she was down with the grippe. No one but her maid noticed the purple inkstain on her middle finger.

Gentle Friend,

Do not believe anything they say of me. Not even if you hear the wedding is going forward. If it does, it is without my consent. They say I am to blame. I do not understand how that could be. Men are supposed to protect women. And when they do insult them, their fathers and brothers are supposed to rush to their defense, not call them horrible names and laugh at their distress.

How I envy you. Your uncle may be mad, but at least he lets you fight back.

The anguished,

Stella

I replied to her at once:

Lady Stella,

I am not so gentle a friend that I am not filled with righteous wrath on your account. By no means hearken to the voices of those who say it was your fault, because it wasn't. Any more than it is my fault that I have to learn the sword and wear funny clothes. They are bigger than we are, and older and have more money and can make us do things we don't want to. Remember when we met at my uncle's ball? I thought you were so brave and elegant and daring, and you were, too. I wished I could be like you.

I have a new cloak now. It is moss green figured velvet with gold tassels and a silk lining called moth's wing. I wish you could see it.

Your family is wrong, that's all. Don't get married to him, whatever you do.

I looked at our two letters, sitting side by side. *He lets you fight back.* What would I do in her place? Well, that was the wrong question, because I would never be in her place. Thanks to the duke, no one like Lord Ferris was ever going to want to marry me. Did that mean my uncle was protecting me? If someone violated me, would he have them killed without question? I bet he would. But did that mean he cared, or just that he was crazy and bloody-minded? How could Artemisia's parents love her and not believe her now?

Oh, it was hopeless. I wasn't Artemisia, and she wasn't me.

I liked the way Artemisia saw me as a heroic swordsman. Was St Vier heroic? He was, in his way, as much a legend as *The Swordsman Whose Name Was Not Death.* What would he say about Artemisia? He'd probably say she shouldn't have been there in the first place without knowing how to defend herself, and he was probably right. But what did he know about it? He'd always been able to defend himself. He'd probably never been to a ball in his life, and if he had, he didn't know what it was like to hope you were pretty, and that people would like your dress and ask you to dance. . . . What did he know? What did any of them know?

Of course her father and brother were hopeless. They didn't know, either.

I did.

I picked up my pen again.

The insult is not to be borne, I wrote. *If neither father nor brother will rise to your defense, then the lot must fall to one who, however unworthy of the position, is eager to stand as your champion. Not only for your own sake, but for that of all ladies misprised. What, after all, am I doing here, anyway? To what end my skills, if not for this? I wear your ribbon, and will avenge your wrong. And woe to he who stands in my way!*

Your loving friend and staunch defender,

KT

But don't worry, I added in postscript. *I'm not telling anyone.*

I sealed it with candlewax and went looking for Kevin to deliver it. He was eager for the work. "So am I, like, your new guard or something?" he asked. "I'd make a good guard."

"You are my private messenger," I said. "It's very confidential."

"Huh?"

"Secret. Go and return within the hour, and I will have another task for you. Now, make it snappy!"

Then I went and found Arthur Ghent and asked the secretary a lot of intelligent questions about the Council of Lords and its officers: the Crescent Chancellor, the Raven and the Dragon, and all the rest. He was pleased that I was taking such an interest in government. "Would you like to visit the Council Hall someday?" he asked. "His Grace's attendance is, ah, spotty, but I usually know when he's going to take his seat. You could accompany him, and watch it all in action."

"Thanks," I said.

But I wasn't going to wait that long. It was a bright, clear day. I dressed warmly, and strapped on my good sword and dagger, and waited for Kevin to come and take me to where the Council of Lords met across the river.

I had never crossed to the East Bank before. It was in the oldest part of the city, the part built by the old kings and queens that had ruled before the Council of Lords deposed them. Kevin didn't know anything about that; his sense of the place was based entirely on where he had or had not gotten into food or into trouble. The docks and warehouses were especially fertile grounds for these reminiscences, but as we came up upon the Old Fort and finally to Justice Place, he ran out of narrative.

He wasn't stupid, he just didn't know about anything. I decided to instruct him, since it distracted me from being nervous and might do him some good. "These are very historic buildings," I told him. "The Council Hall was once the Hall of the Kings—see those heads carved all along it? They're carvings of the old kings."

"I hate kings. We always kill the king on Harvest Night—throw him in the fire, and he burns up like this—blam!! If I saw a king, I'd kill him dead. What are you doing here, anyway? You gonna kill someone?"

"Stick around and find out. But make yourself scarce for now, so nobody sees you. I'll pay you when we get back to Riverside."

Kevin faded back into the buildings' shadows, and I was alone watching the great doors of the Council Hall remain resolutely closed. My fingers were cold. I bought some hot chestnuts from one of the vendors that scattered the plaza, and that helped some, although they turned dusty in my dry mouth. At last a bell rang, as I knew it must. Servants and secretaries started coming out the door, and then carriages began pulling up along one side of the plaza, to carry their masters home.

And there he was on the steps. It wasn't hard to recognize Lord Ferris from the secretary's description. There might be more than one tall, handsome middle-aged man with black hair streaked with silver, but there was only one with an eyepatch. Arthur Ghent had neglected to mention that his mouth was cruel. At least, I thought so. He was talking to another noble, waiting for the carriages to come round. I took a deep breath, and walked boldly up to them.

"Lord Ferris?" I asked, and he nodded. "Um, Anthony Deverin, Lord Ferris, Crescent Chancellor of the Council of Lords of this city and this land, I challenge you."

He looked down his long nose at me. "Whatever for?"

"I'm not sure you want your friend to hear."

The other man blinked and laughed. "Good lord! It's that chit of Tremontaine's! My valet told me about it. Were you at that famous ball, too, Ferris?"

"Ask your valet," Ferris retorted.

"What can you have done to offend Tremontaine this time?"

"What can one do not to offend him?" Ferris drawled. His friend laughed, but the Crescent's look on me was fierce for a moment. "Come, young lady," he said with smooth civility, "let us discuss this matter out of the cold." I followed him back up the shallow steps of the Council Hall. At his nod, the guards drew aside. Lord Ferris led me into a small room, wood-paneled like the Riverside house, with a small fire just dying in the hearth. "Now then," he said, "what is this nonsense?"

"It's not nonsense. I challenge you."

"My dear." Lord Ferris unpeeled his gloves from his hands and held them to the fire. "Please tell your uncle that this descends well below the annoying to the merely pathetic. If Tremontaine has a quarrel with me, let him say so himself, and not send a girl to do his business for him."

"It's not his quarrel. It's on behalf of someone else." Ferris tilted his head inquiringly. I did not like looking at him, knowing what he'd done. I found it hard to speak the crime out loud or say her name. "A friend of mine. You forced her. Against her will."

"You know nothing about it." But he didn't sound so smooth now.

"I know that honor has been violated. I know you did it, and that it has gone unpunished. On behalf of Artemisia Fitz-Levi, I demand satisfaction. I challenge you to combat in the place and time of your choosing, with what champion you will, until honor is washed clean with blood."

Ferris laughed, and I hated him. "The girl is not without family. She has a father. She has a brother. If honor has been violated, as you so quaintly put it, it is their business, indeed their duty, to call challenge on me."

"But it isn't their honor, sir. It's hers."

He went on as if I hadn't spoken, "And have they come after me with swordsmen? They have not. Indeed, I hope to be married soon. So you just run along."

I was so angry I wanted to cry. I swallowed my tears. "It's hers. Her honor, not theirs."

"You don't seem to understand," Lord Ferris said. "It is not the duke's business to interfere in this. Whatever strange notions he holds about women—and if your situation is an example of them, I hope you will not take it as an insult when I say that they are very strange indeed—" He lifted a hand against my interruption. "Stop just a moment and think. You're an intelligent girl. I mean you no harm. Why should I? Your uncle, the Duke Tremontaine, is a dreamer and a lunatic. His treatment of you should tell you that, if nothing else. My dear, I know you're in a difficult situation. A poor relation, he's got you where he wants you, and no fault of yours. . . ." I let the insults go by. A good swordsman doesn't pay attention to words in a fight. Lord Ferris turned his head to look me full in the face with his one good eye. "But I am here to tell you that if you persist in this, you'll only make fools of the lot of us."

"The challenge stands," I told him. "Artemisia's the only one who can call it off now, and I bet she won't. You could, I suppose, try going down on your knees and begging her forgiveness. I'm not sure it would work, but you could try. Otherwise, name the time and the place, and look to your honor and your sword."

He said, "How quaintly old-fashioned. No, my dear, it is you who will withdraw the challenge. There will be no time and no place, and we will not speak of this again." He did not wait for my answer, simply pulled on his gloves and opened the door to the little room, saying with the practiced heartiness of someone who is always telling people what to do, "Now, you are going to walk out of this building and back to Riverside and tell your uncle what I said. And there will be no more of this nonsense."

The sun was very bright. I walked stiffly across the expanse of Justice Place, not looking behind me. It was my guide who caught up to me.

"You didn't kill him," he accused. "I was sure you were gonna kill him."

I said, "I wish I had."

L ORD FERRIS STROLLED WITHOUT HASTE TO WHERE A KNOT OF noblemen awaited carriages to take them home to a hot dinner. "Trouble, Tony?" Philibert Davenant asked. "I heard there was something like a challenge."

"Something like." Ferris smiled. "Only a joke, that's all. Just more madness from poor Tremontaine."

His friends nodded. In recent years few of them had not been touched by some slight or folly of the duke's.

"Someone should do something," grumbled old Karleigh, and Ferris said, "Perhaps someone should."

I TOOK KEVIN DOWN TO THE KITCHENS WITH ME TO SEE WHETHER anyone would feed him or give him a real job. If he ever learned to shut up, I thought he'd make a good guard or footman or something.

"Bread and cheese," the undercook told me, "that's all you're getting at this hour, with a host of starving scholars coming tonight that always expect the best, with hardly any warning, and woe betide us if they don't get it, too! He's more particular about his scholars than about his ladies and gentlemen."

At the other end of the long kitchen table, behind a stack of cabbages, beets and half-plucked fowl, someone made a choking noise. It was Marcus, coughing on a crumb from a large meat pie, or possibly his bowl of soup. I grabbed his soup bowl and offered it to Kevin.

"Hey!" Marcus protested.

"You don't need it."

"I do need it. I'm growing. I need my strength. Arthur Ghent says so, and he's got five brothers, he should know."

He was growing, it was true. "Marcus," I asked, "what about you? Do you have any brothers?"

"All thinking men are my brothers," Marcus said loftily.

Kevin lowered the soup bowl from his face for a moment. "I ain't your brother, pal."

"You can say that again." Marcus examined him. "Where'd you pick this one up?"

"Same place as you," Kevin cheeked him, and called him a name.

Marcus shoved back his bench. He rose towering above the scrawny Kevin. "Give me my soup back."

"Make me."

It looked as if he would, too. I could not believe it. "We are not starting a brawl in this kitchen!" I hissed at them both.

Marcus shrugged and drew back. "Have you checked your pockets, Katie? I would if I were you."

Kevin put down his soup and raised his hands. "I never did! You think I'm stupid or what? Not with the duke's own, never, I swear."

"Oh, honestly!" I huffed. "He was helping me, Marcus, to keep me from getting lost, that's all." I didn't like lying to him, even indirectly. But I wasn't ready to tell anyone about the challenge to Lord Ferris, not even Marcus. It was Artemisia's secret.

"I'm sure he was. But what do you think he does for a living, when he's not helping you cross the street?"

I stared hard at my friend. He reminded me of a farm dog when someone's on his territory. "I can guess," I said. "But it's none of my business."

"You think he's only a pickpocket? Not likely. Guess again."

"It's none of my business," I repeated doggedly. "And it's not very polite to talk about him in front of him like that, as if he weren't really there."

"Yeah," Kevin jeered. "Where was you raised, fella, in a ditch?"

Marcus grabbed his collar. "Out," he said. "Now."

"You kids are *all* outta here, right now!" The senior cook descended on us like the wrath of the storm god. "You think this is a schoolyard, or what? Out—or do I need to call Master Osborne?" Master Osborne was the steward. He had a lot of time for Marcus, who made his life so much easier by explaining what the duke really wanted, but you wouldn't want to risk getting on his bad side. Master Osborne was the one who decided how often your sheets got changed and how much firewood was in your room. "There's work going on here; someone's gonna chop you up instead of an onion, you don't yield space this minute!"

While Marcus was busy placating the cooks and I was busy avoiding him, Kevin disappeared with the soup bowl and a handful of beets.

So that was why Marcus still wasn't speaking to me. I didn't have much to say to him, either. Around the duke and his people, Marcus was always very poised and subtle; I'd never seen him downright rude before. To be fair, he'd lived in this house a long time, and he wasn't going to learn manners from my uncle. But I saw no reason for him to be so mean to some poor starving Riverside kid. He'd been edgy ever since my fight at the Rogues' Ball. Had he guessed that I was keeping secrets from him? If he was my friend he would ask me himself, not take it out on a boy I was trying to help, wouldn't he?

I don't know how long this would have gone on if Lucius Perry hadn't made one of his regular visits to the Riverside house.

I got out of the way just in time. One of the servants was guiding him down the hall to my uncle's bedroom, and I was coming the other way, and I realized that meeting Perry here after the events of the Rogues' Ball would be more awkward than I could bear. So I grabbed the nearest doorknob and ducked inside, which was not very swordsmanly of me, but swordsmanship is not made for awkward social situations.

I turned, and there was Marcus, sitting at his shesh board, wrapped in a quilted silk robe. "You should knock first," he said snarkily. "Where were you raised, anyhow?"

"Look, I'm sorry," I babbled, "but it's him and I forgot to tell you but I know who he is now!"

He put the piece he was holding carefully down on the board. "How intriguing."

"I'm going to kill you," I snapped. "I know how, and all."

"One blow, straight to the heart . . . if I have to hear it one more time, I'm going to kill *myself,* don't bother. Who's in the hallway?"

I inclined my head toward the duke's bedroom.

"Alcuin?"

I couldn't resist a smile. "Lucius Perry."

"Who the hell is Lucius Perry?"

I told him.

Before I had even finished, Marcus was dressing to go out. "Rope," he said. "This time, we're going to get over that wall."

"What on earth for? We already know who he is."

"Maybe. Maybe not. I thought you were worried about your friend and him."

"It turns out he's her *cousin,* that's all, I already told you. What he does with his spare time is his own business."

"Or ours."

"Or the duke's," I said primly, remembering my uncle's admonitions.

"It's the duke's business only if we want it to be. But we don't. What do you bet His Lordship doesn't even know about that little house?"

"So what? It's just a regular house, Marcus. If we were going to follow Lucius Perry to Glinley's House of You-Know-What, that would be something."

"Next time," Marcus said, pulling on his boots, almost breathless with excitement. "Oh, Katie, can't you see it? Your Perry is a nobleman who lives all these different lives, and nobody knows about all of them, not even Tremontaine. We're the only ones; we'll be the only ones who'll have all the pieces."

"I don't want to hurt him," I cautioned. After what I'd witnessed in the kitchen, I wasn't sure I knew Marcus as well as I thought. "I mean, if you were thinking of extortion or something. . . ."

"Don't be silly." Marcus pulled his boots snug. "I just want to know. Don't you?"

WE WERE NEITHER OF US VERY BIG, BUT SOMEHOW THESE PAST weeks Marcus had gotten taller than I. He was walking so quickly that I had to break into an undignified trot to keep up. "What's the hurry?" I panted as we toiled up the sloping street across the river.

"Are you sure you remember the house? I want to get there before him. I want to see him come in, see what he does."

We had a brief dispute about which alley it was, and then we recognized the cherry tree limb sticking out over the back wall of the house—it was definitely cherry, I could tell, now that it was showing signs of budding—so we knew we were in the right place. We did clever things with the rope and the branches, and then it was really pretty easy for us to skimble up and over the wall with hardly any whitewash on our legs.

It was a smallish garden, nicely laid out with little stone paths running between bushes and herbs that had been cut back for the winter, and patches covered with straw that would probably be flowers or strawberries. The back room of the house had tall windows that looked onto the garden. The tall bushes against the wall gave us a perfect spot for hiding, and a perfect view of the room and its occupant.

It was a woman close to my mother's age, with a strong face and auburn hair that looked like it had been carefully dressed in braided coils and a chignon that morning, but turned into a bird's nest by the succession of pens and paintbrushes she was pushing in and out of it. Her eyes were very wide set, and her lower lip was so full that it looked as though someone had taken a dessert spoon and scooped a little out from under it. She was not plump, but she was large, somehow, like a heroic stone sculpture. And even under the loose smock she wore, I could see she had quite a bosom.

The woman sat at a long table, staring intently at a bowl of fruit. Then she pulled a paintbrush out of her hair, licked the tip, dipped it into some paint and drew a few lines on the outside of a white bowl.

"What on earth is she doing?" Marcus hissed in my frozen ear.

"Painting china."

"Is she a painter, then? Is that all he's doing here, getting his portrait done?"

"This is different. It's very stylish; everyone wants painted china. Even ladies do it sometimes."

We watched her work on the bowl. It was turning into the petals of a flower.

"Is she a lady, then? She doesn't look like one. She's got paint on her smock, and her hands are dirty."

"Maybe it's his sister. Let's go," I whispered to Marcus; "I'm cold."

"Put your hood up," he murmured. "Wait 'til he comes."

I shifted uncomfortably. The shrub was scratching my neck. The woman looked up, and I was sure she'd heard me, but it was the maid coming into the room, and after her came Lucius Perry.

As soon as the maid had left with his cloak, Lucius Perry leaned over the woman and kissed her. He drew the pens and brushes out of her hair one by one, and he put his fingers into it and pulled it way out over her shoulders. It was very thick and lush, the woman's hair. You could tell from the way he was holding it that it weighed a lot. He kissed her again, and started to draw her toward the couch by the window.

"That's enough," I said, trying not to sound nervous. "I'm going."

"Shh!" said Marcus. "Do you think we can get closer? I want to hear what they're saying."

"They're not saying *anything*, Marcus. Just *Ooh, ahh, my darling* or something like that."

"They're talking," he said. "She's annoyed with him."

"Maybe she's just found out about Glinley's."

"Not that annoyed."

"So what is she saying?"

S HE WAS SAYING, "I'VE GOT TO GET THAT LAYER DONE BEFORE IT dries, Lucius. Really."

"Paint it over." Lucius Perry was untying her smock with one hand, and feeling underneath it for her bodice with the other. "Later. I'll help you."

"Goodness. Such enthusiasm." Pulling herself up on one elbow (and pulling her chemise back over her shoulder), she ran a finger along his lips. She felt his hands loosen, his mouth part a little, and she smiled. "What have you been up to, to be so inspired?"

"Paying the duke his fee."

"I should have known. You always like that."

He lay back in blissful reflective surrender, and in a flash she'd leapt off the couch and over to her work table.

"Teresa!" Lucius Perry leaned precariously off the edge of the daybed, reaching across the studio to her. "Don't leave me like this!"

"Go to bed, Lucius," she said, and picked up a brush. "I mean, to real bed. I'll come to you there when I'm done."

"When?" he asked plaintively, lying back and staring at the ceiling.

"What does it matter, when? You'll go right to sleep, I know you. You've been up all night at the one place and half the day at the duke's already." She saw him arranging himself in an attractive position, left arm flung carelessly over his head, right-hand fingers curled against his thigh. He stretched like a cat in the weak winter sun, so that everything he had to offer was clearly defined.

Teresa took a sip of tisane that had gotten good and cold. "Now, listen," she said. "This afternoon Helena Montague is coming to take chocolate. She's one of the few still speaking to me; I cannot disappoint her. And she's asked me for six matching bowls." She curled her brush around the rim of this one, making an azure border. "I showed her my work last time she came, and very admiring of it she was. Claimed it was quite the prettiest she'd ever seen, and wanted a complete set, if I wasn't too busy." Teresa smiled dryly. "I assured her I was not. I can't imagine what she'll do with them; give them to her hatmaker or something, I suppose, but she's going to pay me good money, and that's what matters."

"Good money?" Lucius said dreamily. His body had gone slack, as if he were talking in his sleep, which he practically was. "I've got money."

"I'm sure you've got plenty. Buy yourself a new hat."

He closed his eyes at last. His face was suddenly as still and holy as a king's on a tomb. "Marry me."

"Not this year," she said. "Maybe next. Come on, wake up," she said without looking at him, still working on her bowl. "Don't you want to be able to marry a respectable woman? If Helena Montague finds you lolling on my daybed looking like a model for the Oak God's lover, whatever is left of my name will go up in smoke like bonfire wishes."

"Marry. . ."

"Mmm-hmm. Well, at least they dry quickly. Though I suppose I'll just have to keep giving her more cakes until they do, so she can see. I should have started these last week, but I got a new idea for my first act. I do wish writing paid as reliably as painted china; it's so much more entertaining. But the public is fickle, and the theatre such a quagmire. . . . I'm sure Sterling is cheating me on the gate. I wish I could do something original. I wish I could do comedy, but I'm just not—*Lucius!*" She said it so loudly that the two listening in the garden heard her voice bounce off the walls. "Wake up and go to bed. And send Nancy in to do my hair; it's come all undone."

WE WATCHED LUCIUS PERRY GET UP AND DRAG HIMSELF OUT of the room. "It's sooo exhausting," Marcus whispered, "working for the duke."

I giggled. "Now what?" I said.

"Back over the wall, Katie, quick! We have to see if he goes out the front."

"If he does, we'll follow him, right? Maybe he's got another girl somewhere else."

"Two girls! And don't forget the pony. . . ."

We barely made it over the wall, and when we had watched the front of the house for long enough (in a not-very-good hiding place next to a house down the street—"Bring knucklebones next time," said Marcus; "we'll need to look like we're playing, like we belong here."), we went back and wrestled the rope out of the tree. No one set any dogs or guards on us, so we must have been quiet and stealthy enough, though we were so charged up with the thrill of our triumph, I was sure we'd be caught.

Flushed and sweaty and grinning, we stowed the rope away. "And so?"

"Gingerbread," said Marcus. "It's traditional."

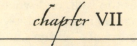

chapter VII

T HEY TRIED FORCING HER TO EAT, AND THEY TRIED DENYING
her food. It made no difference; Artemisia remained obdu-
rate. They tried promising her treats, offering to buy her pets
and jewels, even a trip to the races, for which she'd been agitating for
months, but to no effect. Her mother considered threatening to cut
off her hair—that had worked once—but it would spoil the wedding.
Lord Ferris sent flowers, and daily notes inquiring after her health,
which, after what she did to the first one they showed her, they kept
to themselves.

When her good friend Lydia Godwin came to inquire after her,
they very nearly turned her away. But Lydia was glowing with joy at
her recent engagement to Armand Lindley, and perhaps, thought
Lady Fitz, the girl could talk some sense into her.

When she saw Lydia's sweet face come through the door to her
room, Artemisia melted altogether. She flung herself into her friend's
arms, and wept there without a word. Strongly moved, Lydia wept,
too. It was not until they both stopped to look for handkerchiefs that
Lydia asked, "My dearest Mi, whatever is the matter?"

Artemisia seized her friend's hand. "Your father," she said tremu-
lously, "Lord Godwin, he knows the law, does he not? Might you—
might you ask him for me whether a girl is compelled to marry if her
parents wish it, even if she does not? Even if she has given her word in
betrothal—but now, she does not wish to?"

"Of course I will ask him, sweetest one. But surely your parents will not force you against your will? Even they cannot be so hopelessly old-fashioned."

"They will, I know they will—they are at me every day, and no one understands!"

"Dearest Mi, whatever has happened to you? What has Lord Ferris done, for you to take him so violently in dislike?"

For a moment, Artemisia considered telling her friend everything. But she knew that her dearest Lydia was a very conduit of news about all their friends' doings. And so she knew that, despite their great love, it would be next to impossible for Lydia to keep the sensational news of her ruin to herself. Artemisia wisely contented herself with crying out, "I cannot marry him! I would rather die!"

Lydia did her best to explain that, from her experience, true love and mutual understanding, such as she shared with her gentle Armand, were enough to conquer all impediments. But her words had little effect. Artemisia pressed her hands to her mouth and would not look at her.

Lydia sat and gently stroked her friend's hair. It was worse than she had thought. She'd seen Artemisia in a passion before, especially when she was trying to scare her parents. But never before had she refused to open her heart to her dearest friend—and never before had her eyes been quite so red, her face so taut, her breath so ragged. Lydia thought best how to divert her, that she might regain some comfort and composure.

"Mi," she said, "do you remember when we went to the theatre to see *The Empress*, and you had nightmares after?"

Artemisia shuddered. "That terrible woman, putting all those men to death. Why, is it playing again? I declare I would love to see it now, indeed I would. I understand her perfectly, now."

"It's not playing again, no; but the same splendid actress who was so proud and fierce in the role of the Empress, the actress they call the Black Rose . . . what will you think when I tell you that her company has commissioned a new play, for her to play the part of Stella!"

"You mean—" Artemisia caught her breath at the thought. "They are going to perform *The Swordsman Whose Name Was Not Death*—in a *theatre*?"

"It's already been played! Lavinia Perry and Jane Hetley both have seen it, for Jane's birthday."

"And?"

"Lavinia says that Henry Sterling as Fabian is a pale and feeble joke, though Jane says she'd marry him in an instant. But Lavinia has hardly a good word to say for the piece; she's vexed that they've left out the entire bit about the hunting cats, though I can hardly see how they'd play that onstage. Jane says it doesn't matter, because Mangrove's repentance at the end is even more affecting than it is in the book. But Lavinia thinks it is not true to the spirit of the novel."

"I never thought he was truly penitent. It's all a ruse, to confuse Stella to the last."

"That's what Jane says, too. She says you want to kill him yourself, he is so very wicked. Deliciously, she says."

"What about Tyrian? Is he handsome?"

"Oh, as for that, it hardly signifies. They've got a girl playing Tyrian."

"A girl? The same one who played the hero's friend in *The King's Wizard*? I bet it is. My brother Robbie was greatly taken with her. Still, a girl playing Tyrian . . ."

"They say her swordplay is very dashing."

"Does she kiss Stella, though?"

"They didn't say."

"What, after all that time we all spent practicing kissing with Lavinia, she didn't say? Rubbish."

"Well, we must go, then," Lydia said cheerfully, "and see it together and find out for ourselves."

Artemisia drew back. "I cannot."

"You cannot stay locked up in here forever!"

"I won't go out; I can't go out until I am free of this marriage."

"I'll tell you what, then!" Lydie tended to bounce when pleased, and she did so now. "We can sneak you out in secret. You can go masked—"

"No! No! No!" Artemisia's hands were over her ears. Lydie drew back in alarm, but then she chided herself for a false friend. She approached Artemisia cautiously. "Dearest darling, can't you tell me what is wrong?"

"I cannot marry him," Artemisia repeated. "I shall never marry anyone. It is too horrible to contemplate."

"Mi," Lydia said delicately, "has your mama perhaps said something to you about the married state that, perhaps, might frighten you or strike you as distasteful?"

Artemisia looked wonderingly at her. Was this the same Lydia who had helped her hide *The Couch of Eros* under her last year's hats? But she only said, "Mama speaks much of gowns and jewels and houses in the country. And," she added meanly, "of how marrying Lord Ferris means I should take precedence over you, no matter who you marry."

Lydia drew back. "Does she?"

"I hate her!" Artemisia exploded. "I hate her, I hate you all!"

To her eternal credit, Lydia Godwin weathered the storm. Indeed, she brought her friend nearly all the handkerchiefs in her box, one by one, saying cheerfully, "I shall have to speak to Dorrie about keeping your box well filled."

"Robbie says I am a watering-pot. I hate him, too."

"Robbie is often hateful. But I hope you know I would never do anything to injure you, my darling."

More tears, then, and vows of eternal friendship. And in that sweet moment, Artemisia thought of something. "Lydia," she said, "do you remember when Stella is in the country and Mangrove's minions are all around her and she doesn't know who to trust? And she needs to get a message to Fabian that would kill him if it goes awry? Well, there is a letter I need you to carry for me—just carry it out of the house, no more, and give it to someone to deliver."

Lydia's eyes opened wide. "Artemisia Fitz-Levi," she said, "do you have a *lover?*"

"Don't be disgusting, Lydia. What would I do with a lover? No, it's just a friend. But don't you understand? I'm a prisoner here. They guard me from all visitors but you, my darling, and of course they read my mail. I'm running out of things to bribe Dorrie with—I need you to do this!"

"I see. . . ." Lydia twisted the handkerchief in her hands. "Give me the letter."

"Here." Artemisia lifted up one corner of her pink-flowered rug. "The maids only sweep under it once a week, lazy things."

It was addressed to *KT, Riverside House.* Lydia tucked it in her apron pocket, and Artemisia gripped both her hands, staring into her face with a desperate fury not unlike that of the Empress when ordering her favorite to the sword. "Now swear!" she said. "Swear by your precious love for Lindley that you will tell no one. Not your mama, not your papa, not even him who your soul adores. No one. If you will do this for me, Lydia, then someday I will dance at your wedding, though I can never hope myself for such joy as you possess."

S OMETIMES AT BREAKFAST, IF SHE KEPT QUIET ENOUGH, LYDIA'S parents would forget that she was there. It was one reason she did not often breakfast in her room. She ate her toast very slowly, and listened to her mother telling her father, "Tremontaine is at it again. Dora Nevilleson told me her husband told her his valet saw him at the

Rogues' Ball. Of course you know Nevilleson was there himself and just won't own up to it. The number of valets who were there, it must have been a convocation of nothing but gentlemen with clothes brushes, to hear the husbands tell of it."

"Funny." Lydia's father, Michael, Lord Godwin, buttered a piece of toast and sat watching the butter melt into the crispy bread. He was very particular about his toast. "My own valet did not attend. Or if he did, he's not saying."

"Good," said his wife. "Then you know nothing about this putative niece? The girl with the sword, who fought Todd Rippington there?"

"Of course I've heard about the niece, Rosamund, what do you take me for? I'm the Raven Chancellor. If the Duke Tremontaine has trained up some girl with a sword, and she's a relative, and she's begun to fight duels, it's going to come up before the Council of Honor sooner or later. It's our business to know. We don't want to look too alarmed when it does."

"Why should that alarm you?"

"The privilege of the sword is one of the rights of the nobility. The privilege only, and not the sword itself. That, we leave to professionals."

She touched his hand. "I know one noble who did things differently, once."

From the way Godwin returned his lady's look, Lydia was afraid her parents were going to head right upstairs for one of their little talks, leaving breakfast unfinished and her curiosity unsatisfied. But Michael Godwin just said, "That man took up both blade and privilege only once, and for a very worthy prize."

Was this the notorious duel her father had fought over her mother? She held her breath, waiting for details. But even her silence was too loud. Her mother returned to the debate.

"So," Rosamund persisted, "a young noblewoman with a blade who could fight for herself if she chose is very different from that young man?"

"Possibly." Lord Godwin sighed. "You have no idea what a muddle the rules and traditions of the Court of Honor is. Does the privilege even extend to women, or does it merely derive from their male relatives? There are precedents for one, and for the other, case by case and year by year, as the members change by fate and election. The dukes and Arlen have the only permanent seats, which is supposed to give it all some stability—and you'll know what that means when I remind you that the Duke Tremontaine is one of them!" His lady nodded wryly. "'Honor' appears to be a maze of unwritten rules and fiercely defended traditions. In the end, what is this girl? What's her legal status, and even her social one? Does she pass back and forth from noble to sword at a whim? And if so, whose whim?"

"Her uncle's, I imagine. Unless she kills him first."

"She can't kill him. Not in honorable challenge, anyway; the Court permits no one to profit from challenge within their own family. If she kills, she does it on his behalf."

"Or her own."

"It's all pretty alarming."

"I see. And what will you noble lords do about it now?"

"We watch and wait."

"I cannot like it, Michael. If this truly is his sister Talbert's child, then it's disgraceful for the duke to be encouraging her to run wild like that. A noble's daughter should be gently raised and properly cared for. Someone should do something."

"Tremontaine is the head of the family, and the family has not complained—not in Council, anyway, where it might do some good. I hear Greg Talbert's locked himself up with a serious head cold rather than answer any questions."

"She's only a girl, they say, no older than Lydia here."

"Well, sometimes I do wonder," Michael Godwin said, "if I should not have taught Lydia the sword. I won't always be around, you know, and if that goatish Lindley tries anything once they're wed . . ."

"Oh, Papa!" It hadn't been funny the first time, and had grown less so with every repetition since.

Her mother rushed in to the rescue, asking "How is your friend Artemisia, Lydie? I heard she was ill. Did you visit her yesterday?"

Her mother was so sensible and kind, not at all like Lady Fitz-Levi. It wouldn't be breaking her word to her friend to tell her mother how unhappy Mia was. "She's not so much ill as heartsick, Mama. She does not want to marry Lord Ferris at all, and they are going to *force* her. She weeps and weeps and will not eat, and is truly pitiful. Oh, is there nothing we can do?"

Her mother, who had ample experience of young Lady Artemisia's temperament, said cautiously, "Do you know what made her change her mind about her intended, dearest?"

"She will not say. But she is wretched, Mama. I've never seen her so distraught—well, almost never. Not for so long, anyway."

Her father gave her mother a look across the table. "My word on it," he said, "she's found out about the Black Rose."

"Michael," Lady Godwin warned, "perhaps this is not the time. . . ."

"Rosamund, I think it is very much the time, with Lydie about to be married herself and launched into the world. I've been meaning to speak to her about it, in fact." He turned to his only daughter. "Lydia, dearest, what do you know about women who . . . Lydia. Let me begin again." Lady Godwin sighed audibly, but did not offer her husband assistance. "Men, as you know, have certain interests in life, and these interests sometimes lead them to do foolish things. Things their wives would not approve of. And I hope that if you see your husband doing anything foolish, you will not stand by without calling him to account for it."

Lydia tried to look very adult and trustworthy. "You need have no fears on that account, Papa. Armand and I have vowed always to tell each other everything."

"Just so," said Lord Godwin. "Of course, unmarried men are allowed to be a little foolish sometimes. It gives them something to improve upon, and their wives as well. So I hope you will not be altogether surprised if you learn, someday, that one of your friends' young husbands before his marriage was, ah, friendly with certain women of the town, hostesses and actresses and such, and became their protector. Most men, in fact, have such a past."

"But never their wives?"

"Oh, never the wives." Eyes downcast, her mother smiled. "Women have no past, just a grand and glorious future."

Lydia kept her face schooled to look as if all this was news to her. "The Black Rose is an actress," she said helpfully. "Is Lord Ferris her protector?"

"Was," said Michael Godwin. "She's a magnificent piece, just the sort of high-ticket, high-profile item Ferris goes for, and he went for her. It wasn't easy, either. The Rose is very picky. Easily bored, she says, and considering how many 'protectors' she's turned away, it must be true. But he likes a bit of a challenge, does our Crescent."

"Michael." His wife's voice carried a hint of steel.

"Just common knowledge," he added doucely. "It didn't last long, though. They had a bit of a row."

"A bit?" her mother said with relish. "I heard he had her thrown out of his house in the middle of the night like a common thing, with only the shift on her back."

Lydia gasped. "If Artemisia did something he disliked, would he have her thrown out in the snow, too? No wonder she doesn't want to marry him!"

"Certainly not, darling. No nobleman would dare to treat his wife that way. It would get back to her parents and her brother, and he would pay dearly for it. No, don't worry, it's surely not anything like that."

"Think about it, Lydie," her father said. "Your friend has a great deal of pride. She heard about the affair, and she wants to make him sorry. You must admit, she always does like to have the upper hand."

Lydia knit her brow in thought. It was true that Mia had been most interested when the Black Rose's name came up. And, to be fair, Mia had never liked being upstaged by anyone. "But if Lord Ferris has already left his mistress, then why should Mia mind so?"

"Because," her mother explained crisply, "it all happened around MidWinter. He was courting them both at the same time, that's why." Lydia let out a low whistle. "There!" Lady Godwin accused her husband. "That's what all this vulgar talk leads to. Lydia, no whistling in public, you know better."

"If you knew about Lord Ferris and the Black Rose, then surely her parents did as well. Why didn't anyone say anything?"

Lord Godwin said, "Artemisia's father is, ah, a man of the town. Even if he did know about Lord Ferris's affair with an actress, he surely knew it would blow over. He wouldn't let it interfere with a good marriage contract."

Lydia sat slowly digesting all this knowledge. Artemisia had never really loved Lord Ferris, she knew that. Maybe she was right not to marry him. Her parents could not force her, surely. This matter would prove to be just another long contest of wills, such as were not unknown in the Fitz-Levi family. She vowed to visit Mia again soon with a box of her favorite chocolates and some diversion.

"The Black Rose is in a new play," Lydia said, "and all my friends have seen it. May I go?"

"Oh, dear," sighed her mother, "it's that awful piece of trash about the swordsman lover, isn't it? My friends were mad for that book when we were young."

"It's not trash," her daughter said. "It is full of great and noble truths of the heart. And swordfights."

"I'll have to read it," her father said brightly, but no one paid him any attention.

"I so want Mia to see the play," Lydia said. "If I can assure her that Lord Ferris will not be there—"

"He won't," her mother chuckled. "The Black Rose denied him entry to the theatre the morning after, and he hasn't been back since."

"Well, there you have it," Michael Godwin said to his daughter. "Actresses are spiteful creatures. You be sure you tell your Armand that he should be very cautious when he chooses a mistress."

A year ago, Lydia might still have giggled when he talked like that. But love had turned her serious, at least where love was concerned. "Oh, Papa," she said. "You know Armand never would."

"Of course not," her father said. "He knows I've got my eye on him."

Just knowing about Lucius Perry and his ladylove made life more enjoyable. Whenever the duke got highhanded with us, implying that we were young and what did we know? we had to bite the inside of our cheeks to keep from laughing over the things we knew now that he did not.

Marcus and I speculated endlessly on what we had witnessed. I thought the lady was very wise, knowing Perry's proclivities, to refuse to yield to his advances, since clearly he'd lose interest the moment she did. Marcus, though, claimed she must be ignorant of his other lives, or she'd never let him in the door. His colorful theories included the possibility that the woman was really Perry's sister, so a little kissing was all she would allow. "He's steeped in vice," he said; "why shouldn't it run in the family?"

I pointed out stiffly that these things did not always run in families.

We should have been trying to find out who owned her house. It would have been fairly easy to go up to the door with a misdelivered message and use that as an excuse to grill the maid, or the neighbors' maids. . . . We talked about it, but we never did anything. That wasn't the game, really. It was more of a challenge to try and catch both Lucius and his lady out together, see what they would betray to our inquisitiveness. What did they mean to each other? What were they hiding, and why? We wanted the secrets of their hearts, something no one else had, something they would be reluctant to yield to anyone else. We would hold it for them, and keep it safe, our treasure, whole and unique. Besides, the maid had a walleye.

It is possible, though, that lurking in late winter gardens was bad for the health. A few days later, Marcus caught a serious cold. While Marcus was in bed, my uncle sent for me. The duke was in his study with his friend Flavia, the unmercifully homely woman he kept around so they could make fun of people and do mathematical puzzles or something—at least, that's what they always seemed to be doing when I saw them together. Today they were constructing some kind of a model—a tower, or maybe a clock, I couldn't quite tell, and I didn't want to ask and be lectured. I was wearing my splendid new cloak, because the day was finally warm enough that I could sling it back by the tassel and not have to worry about puddles.

Flavia looked up at me when I came in and said, "I've got it: You could have a career on the stage."

"As what?" my uncle asked. "She can't memorize anything, none of us can. Dates of crowns and battles leave her hapless."

"I know poetry," I said, but they ignored me.

"Well," Flavia told him, "in case you haven't noticed, the demand for female swordfighters is pretty much limited to Tremontaine House and the theatre, where they are enjoying a certain vogue."

"They can't really fight," he said crossly. "They just know a few moves, and they leap about showing their legs. Whereas Katherine is an excellent duelist—and always very modestly dressed," he added primly.

"Three yards of silk velvet isn't what I'd call modest," she said, but I knew he meant I didn't flash my legs around.

"Look," said my uncle, "speaking of theatre, how would you like to see a play?"

"Me?" I squeaked.

"Why not? I've got a box at the Hart, you may as well use it. They're playing this afternoon. You should go. Enjoy yourself." I waited. As a benevolent uncle, he wasn't very convincing. "And when it's done, you might like to go backstage and meet one of the actresses."

"The swordfighter?" Did he want me to give her a few tips? I'd die.

"No, the romantic lead. She's called the Black Rose. I've got something I'd like you to give her." He handed me a brocade pouch with something heavy slinking inside it. "It's a gold chain," he said, "and I'm trusting you not to run off with it. Just give it to her. She'll know who it's from, and what it means. But if anyone asks, it's a tribute from you to her, in admiration of her fine performance."

"Is she really that good?"

My uncle smiled creamily. "The best."

"Dear one, cease the salacious thoughts and hand me that piece—no, the little one. Butterfingers."

"Butterfingers, yourself."

S O THAT WAS HOW I WENT TO THE THEATRE FOR THE FIRST TIME. I would have thought it was a temple, with its painted columns and bright facade, but the banners proclaimed it the LEAPING HART THEATRE, HENRY STERLING, ACTOR/MANAGER. At the last minute the duke had realized that if the chain was not to be seen coming from him, I shouldn't sit in his box. So he gave me money for a good seat in the stalls across from the stage, and money to tip the seatman, and more for snacks and incidentals. A girl in a lowcut bodice was selling nuts; I bought some but forgot to eat them, I was so excited to be there.

I felt a bit like an actress myself, in my gorgeous cloak and a new hat with a plume that Betty had produced at the last minute. The ticket-taker called me "sir," and I didn't bother to correct him; why not pass for a boy and enjoy the freedom of one? All things were permitted here, it seemed. I couldn't wait to see the actress with the sword.

Candles were lit on the stage, although it was still broad daylight. There was a bed on it, a big one with curtains. There were also curtains at the windows at the back of the stage, which were very tall, and a dressing table and a carpet. It looked like a lady's bedroom.

To the side of the stage, a consort started to play, and the audience quieted. Then a woman entered. There was a little sigh, because she was so very beautiful, deep bosomed and dark haired, gorgeously dressed in a rose-colored gown with many flounces, but her white throat was decked with simple pearls.

"No, thank you," she said to someone we couldn't see offstage, her maid, I guess. "I will put myself to bed." Somebody chuckled and was shushed. The woman unclasped her cloak and laid it on a chair. She did it with such an air of sweet weariness that you somehow knew that she had been out late, and enjoyed herself, too, but was more than ready for the day to be over. Languidly she reached up to her hair, and pulled two pins out. A fall of dark tresses released itself down her back, like an animal let loose. She reached for the clasp at her throat. It was then, when we were admiring her private moment of grace and release, thinking it was only for us, that a man stepped out from behind one of her long bedroom curtains. He was devastatingly handsome and carried a sword. His voice, when he spoke, was warm and rich like poured chocolate—but it was not that which made me catch my breath.

"Lady Stella," he said. "Allow me."

I had to dig my nails into my palms to keep from squeaking out loud. As it was, I began moving my lips along with the lines. I knew them all, from the opening chapter of my favorite book.

Fabian snuffed the candles, one by one. On the dusky stage he drew Stella to him, and they disappeared together within the bedcurtains. A woman behind me squeaked happily. The curtains didn't stir, but the consort began to play a slow and lovely air. When it was done, her maid came in and pulled back the draperies, first the high ones at the window, and then the bedcurtains.

Stella was revealed alone in the bed, her dark hair falling over her white ruffled nightdress. She rose and went to the window, and we saw that it was open a little, as though someone had left without quite closing it behind him. She turned and looked out over the audience, one hand stroking her hair.

"I was a girl before tonight. I am a woman now."

It was the oddest feeling in the world, seeing something that had belonged so utterly to me alone being made to happen up on the stage with living people doing it, and others watching it. (I'd lent Marcus the book once. When I finally asked for it back he never said anything, so either he hadn't liked it or he hadn't bothered to read it.)

When they got to the fight in the clocktower between Mangrove and Fabian, the swords finally came out in earnest. Henry Sterling's swordplay was not bad—he certainly had the flair and the spirit of Fabian—but whoever played Mangrove really knew what he was doing with his wrist. It was almost a surprise when he dropped his sword and fled in confusion.

Mangrove was all wrong, of course—too short, for one thing, because he's supposed to be much taller than Fabian, and Henry Sterling was a truly magnificent Fabian, especially when he tells Stella (wrongly) that he's glad it's Tyrian's child because Mangrove is right and his own seed is cursed—but it must have been hard to find an actor taller than Sterling. And Mangrove should have had a mustache, because in the scene where he kisses Stella, she is repelled by it, but of course they left that out. The gorgeous actress playing Stella, who surely the Black Rose, did a wonderful job of looking repelled just the same: she did a little thing with curling her fingers behind her back that meant she was filled with disgust, you could tell.

Tyrian. I wasn't sure how I felt about Tyrian. You could tell it was a woman, if you looked hard and thought about it. But everyone on-stage referred to her as "he" and treated her like a man, so you sort of had to go along with it. She did take big swaggering steps like a man, and held her head a certain way, and she had cut all her hair right off, so that it stood in fair little curls all over her head. Even in the book there is a certain softness to Tyrian, a gentleness that makes you like him and think it would not be so bad if Stella chose him over his friend. The actress was very good at that, the way she looked at Stella when Stella wasn't looking, and the way she stepped back when Stella was thinking and all. Maybe they just couldn't find a man to play Tyrian that well. She did look very dashing with her sword at her side; I could hardly wait to see her use it later.

Tyrian made his vow to Fabian, and the two of them left, and everyone applauded. I waited eagerly, but nothing happened. The stage was empty, the consort was playing, and the audience started talking and getting up. I worried that something had gone wrong, but no one else seemed concerned. Vendors came back selling bags of nuts and bunches of flowers. Some had little black silk rosettes and tiny silver swords for people to pin in their hats or on their sleeves as tokens of the two lead actresses to show which they liked best. The actress playing Tyrian was called Viola Fine. Her little sword appealed to me, but I thought I should buy a rose if I was going to see the Black Rose. In the end I did neither, but I did get a printed picture of the actor Henry Sterling in the role of Fabian, his arm raised to his brow in an attitude of anguish. They had colored ones, too, for more money, but I thought I could color it myself when I got home. I would ask my uncle to give me watercolors.

Then they blew trumpets, and we all found our seats again.

The second half wasn't as good as the first, because they had to cut too much out, like Stella's horse race and the terror of the hunting cats. Instead the actors made long speeches about love which were never in the book, and weren't as good. I watched Tyrian more closely. Viola Fine was supposed to be an actual man, not a woman swords-man, but if you thought about it realistically, that's what she was. Like me. Only not for real: my uncle was right, her swordplay was just for show. That huge disengage of hers would get her killed in a real fight. I wondered if she liked playing a man. When Viola Fine first went on the stage, had she *chosen* roles where she could stride about, her cloak swirling around her, or had she really been hoping to play Stella or someone with gorgeous gowns and luxurious curls and jewels that couldn't have been real but glittered fantastically, and men saying they would die for her?

I was not the only person in the audience holding her breath when Tyrian approached Stella for the kiss. "You have done tonight," she said, "what ten thousand men could not."

"Now," the Black Rose murmured low, but we could all hear it, somehow, "let me show you what one woman alone can do."

She leaned towards Viola. Viola's eyes closed languidly. The Black Rose came closer—and then her eyes opened wide, following the entrance of Mangrove's minions on the roof (instead of the hunting cats).

It might be nice to be an actress, after all. I was a better swordsman than Viola Fine already, wasn't I? Maybe someone would write a play just for me, one where a real woman could fight with her sword, and had many fine adventures and changes of costume. Maybe Henry Sterling would play a man who loves me madly but thinks I love only the sword, while really I am smoldering with passion for him. Or maybe Viola could play the hero, and I could play a woman who disguises herself as a man in order to get close to her and—what? We could have a terrific fight at the end, maybe, and kill each other, and the audience would be sobbing, the way they do at the end of the play when Tyrian cradles Stella's head in his arms, rocking her and letting her think he's Fabian, who's already taken the potion, but Stella doesn't know it.

I can make myself cry just thinking of it. And the way Viola rose to her feet, looking for someone to fight but there is no one left—there was such a look of desolation there. I wondered if she was lonely, too.

All around me, people were jumping to their feet and clapping and yelling and throwing things—flowers, nuts, handkerchiefs stained with kisses—and wiping their eyes, as well. A girl behind me said to her friend, "I've seen it eleven times now, and I always say I won't cry, and then I do."

"I know," her friend said. "I keep wanting it to end differently, but it never does. Oh, there she is!"

The Black Rose swept back onstage, glowing with a tragic dignity. Her magnificent bosom swelled as she took a deep breath and bowed low to the crowd. The girl behind me started gasping, "I'll die, I'll die . . . Oh, just hold me! Isn't she *fine*? I've written her a dozen letters, but she never answers."

I thought smugly of the chain in my pocket that would gain me access to her dressing room.

But it turned out not to be that simple. There was a porter guarding the back door to the stage, and quite a few other people who were trying to get in, as well. Most of them had brought bunches of flowers, some very nice indeed. A couple of the biggest were carried by liveried servants, whose masters waited behind in their carriages, watching through the doors to see what transpired.

It was too late to go back for flowers, I thought; best get this over with. I shoved myself to the front of the crowd, right up against a woman with a necklace of silver swords strung around a turban on her head. She pulled away as though I had bitten her. "How dare you, fellow!"

"I'm sorry," I stammered, horribly flustered, for if I had been a man it would of course have been unspeakable for me to brush up against a woman like that. "I'm not— It's all right, really it is. I'm a lady—like Tyrian, I mean Viola."

"Rea-ally?" She looked me up and down. "Is it a new fad?"

"I wish I had the legs for it," said the well-dressed older woman next to her, who wore a black velvet neck ribbon with a silver sword depending from it. "What's your name, sweetheart?"

"Katherine."

"Is that a real sword you've got?"

"Do you like swords, Katherine?"

The people behind us were pushing forward, so that the ladies were very nearly on top of me. They smelled of powder and expensive perfume. Their only blades may have been finger-length, but I fell back before them as if they carried real ones, and I defenseless.

I stepped on the porter's toe. "Oi!" he said. "None of that here. What do you think you're doing?"

I turned around and looked up into his solid face. "My name is Katherine Talbert. I'm here to see the Black Rose."

"You and half the city," he grumbled. "Listen, kiddo, nice try, but the part of Tyrian is already booked. You want to act, you come back another time. Master Sterling don't see new actresses but on Tuesday mornings."

"Oh, please," I said. "I'll only be a moment. I've just got to give her this—" and I held up the chain in its sack, letting him hear the chink of metal.

"Nice for her," he said gruffly. An aggressive servant shoved a huge hothouse bouquet in his face—as the porter tried to defend against it, I reached for his hand, stuck a coin in it, and, with the slippery little sideways wriggle that always worked when I needed to grab something from the kitchen table when the cooks were all busy, slipped past him and through the back door of the theatre.

It was a different world: quiet and frantic, real and imaginary, all at once. It smelt of oil and wax and sweat and fresh wood shavings. There were raw beams and intricately painted canvases, yards of dusty air overhead and people appearing and disappearing below.

"I'm sick to death of it!" One of Fabian's friends strode past me with another, still wearing the top half of his costume. "He does it every time, on purpose, just to make me look cheap."

"Of course he does, my dear; you threaten him."

Against the wall I recognized props from scenes in the play: Stella's bedroom candelabra, Mangrove's velvet chair, the trunk from the sea voyage and halberds from the guards. A workman held one in his hand, shouting, "You're mad if you think I can make another horse before tomorrow! What do I look like, a brood mare? Just nail the damned thing back together, and tell him I'm working on it!"

"Excuse me." I tugged at his sleeve. "I've come to see the Black Rose."

He nodded at a door across the way. "In there." He raised the halberd again. "And tell them to be *careful* next time! It's *not a real horse!*"

The door was not fully closed. I stood for a moment, trying to breathe normally, to get the feel for where I was and what I was doing.

I heard a woman's voice inside. "God, you are the biggest tease in the world. I'll have that kiss now, Rose, if you please."

There was a low, throaty chuckle. I recognized it from Stella's ball scene. "Why not? You worked hard for it."

Stiff cloth rustled. Someone hummed. Then the voice that was not Rose's spoke a line from the play, mockingly, romantically: "*I was a girl before tonight.*"

I put my head very carefully inside the door. A black head and a fair one with short, close-cropped curls were pressed together.

It was the missing kiss from *The Swordsman Whose Name Was Not Death*, the kiss Tyrian wanted but never got. Stella was giving it to Tyrian now, at last, as I watched them. I lifted my fingers to my own mouth, barely breathing. Viola was still wearing her costume; the Black Rose had changed into a loose gown over her chemise. Viola's fingers were pressed into the Rose's hair, pulling her head even closer. She moaned softly, and I think I did, too.

I felt a strange glowing in my body, right at the fork of my breeches. It was like nothing on earth I'd ever felt before, and it was right there where a man keeps his tool. Oh, dear god. Heat and cold touched me all at once. Was all this dressing up and swordfighting turning me into a man? Had it happened to the actress already, with her sword and her breeches and her cropped hair? No one had warned me. What could I do? I would die, I would die if I was growing one. Slowly, cautiously, I put my hand down there to see. I didn't feel anything through my breeches that hadn't been there before. I squeezed a little harder to be sure, and caught my breath at the sense that shot through me. It was indescribably, undeniably good. Suddenly it didn't seem to matter what was down there. So what if I was growing one? Men never complained of it, did they? In fact, if this was the pleasure they were always crowing about, I wasn't sure I didn't want one after all. I thought of Marcus. He had one, too, didn't he? He could show me how to use it. I wouldn't mind if he did. I squeezed a little harder.

My eyes were closed. I saw Tyrian kissing the Black Rose, and Viola kissing Stella. I thought about curling up in bed with my curtains drawn and reading the book again, but this time seeing the two of them kissing, kissing, kissing after the play was over and the real story began.

I squeezed harder still, and then I didn't think anything at all except how I wished what was happening wouldn't stop, only it did, rather suddenly, and I had to put my hand on the doorpost. The kiss had finished; they were looking into each other's eyes.

"You're a girl still," the Black Rose told her. "Don't let that sword deceive you."

Viola laughed huskily. "Thanks for nothing. I know exactly what it's good for."

"Be careful," Rose said. "Don't let it go to your head. They come on strong, but they can leave you with nothing."

"Speak for yourself, sweetness." Viola straightened her jacket. "I know how to handle them."

Rose shook her head. "You really don't mind, do you?"

"Mind what?"

"The way they want you to be *him* for them."

"Why not? I love acting. Don't you?"

"In a well-crafted play, of course. But I don't do private theatricals."

"You don't know what you're missing." As she turned to the door, I gathered myself together and knocked. "Adoring Public, Rose!" Viola cried jauntily as she passed me.

My face was still flushed, my breathing shallow. "Come in!" the Black Rose sang out melodiously, but when she saw me in my boy's clothes she said, "Oh, dear."

"It's not what you think," I said. "I'm real."

She said, "Oh," and then she said, "Oh," again, in a different tone. "I know. You're the duke's girl."

"He sent you this." I fumbled the brocade pouch out of my pocket with my sweaty hand, and held it out to her. I couldn't meet her eyes.

The Black Rose was very tall. She looked at me, and then she went and closed the door, and came back and sat down. She took the chain out. It was heavy, made of several links braided together, and very long.

"That's worth a lot," she said. She bent her neck and pulled her hair up out of the way. "Would you like to put it on me?"

She must have known my face would be in her hair. She smelled like nothing else on earth. I kissed her hair, and put my hand on her white hand that held it above her neck. She turned, and tilted her head up to me, and I kissed her on the lips.

Her lips were very soft and warm and full. I felt them curve in a smile under mine. I couldn't help smiling back.

"I see," she said. She lowered her hair and turned around, and reached up and kissed me again, a mother's kiss. "What's your name, sweetness?"

"Katherine. Katherine Talbert."

"Well, Katherine Talbert, thank you for the gift."

"It's from my—"

"That wasn't what I meant."

"Oh." I felt my face color up, but I stood my ground. She must have liked the kiss, after all. I was sure I'd done it all wrong.

She weighed a length of chain in her hand. "He's a kind man, your uncle. Thoughtful. Please tell him—since we are alone here—please tell him that I will have something for him soon."

I said, "He likes other men, you know."

"So do I." The Black Rose smiled. She reached up her hand again and pushed back my hair. "You're a pretty girl, Katherine. Did you like the play?"

"Yes. Very much."

"Come again, then. I'll do better next time on the 'I am a woman' speech. I don't think I quite nailed it tonight. Though the bit with Mangrove on the stairs went rather well, I thought. . . ." There was a sharp knock on the door. "My dresser," she told me. "You'd better go before the hordes descend."

I went out the door. I felt as if I had no body, I was so light. It was not an entirely pleasant feeling; I had gotten used to knowing exactly where I was. I leaned against the wall and watched as the dresser opened the door to some well-dressed men with flowers. I heard the actress crowing, "My dear! It's been ages! What hole have you been hiding in?"

I left the theatre. I walked for a long time, and not home to Riverside. When I stopped, I was standing in front of the house of the china painter, Lucius Perry's mistress. The last time we were there, I had wanted to leave when they started kissing on the couch. But now I wished that I could see it, very much. I wanted to bang on her door until she came out with brushes in her hair, and make her invite me in for tea so I could ask her whether she really liked it, and if she'd done it with anyone besides Lucius Perry, if she even had, and why? But I didn't dare. I was wearing my best clothes; I could not go up over the wall, either. And if I did, all I'd probably see was her painting china, anyway.

T ERESA LAY ON THE COUCH IN HER STUDIO, AND CRIED AND cried. She was pretty much done when Lucius came in, pink and disheveled from a quick nap in her room and a long night before that. He blinked at her and said, "I have to go. I'm expected at my cousins' for a card party, and I've cried off too many times before."

"Off you go, then," Teresa said, but her voice sounded strange, even to her. She jammed the letter into her pocket.

"What's that?" he asked.

"Oh, nothing. Another bill, that's all."

"You've been crying."

"Rubbing my eyes, that's all. I got paint in them or something."

"Do you need money?" He sat on the couch, on a shawl still damp and wrinkled from her weeping, and held out his hand to her, asking, "What is it, what's the matter?"

She stared at the hand as if it might bite her. But she answered him. "It's Roddy—my husband's family, I mean. They send me these horrible letters. I shouldn't read them, really, they're always the same. It all comes down to the same stupid thing: they won't return my dowry, what remains of it, anyway, because I left him. That's all."

There was a table between them, cluttered with art supplies. Still, he went down on his knees, self-consciously theatrical, and held out his arms to her.

"Marry me," he said. "I know I'm not much of a prize, but I can offer you the protection of my name, and all the true devotion you can stand."

She stared at him. "Oh, Lucius." She was laughing, but the tears refused to stop. "Oh, Lucius, no. I can't."

"Am I too loose for you? I could reform, you know."

"I don't want you to reform. You're even worse than I am. I like that."

"Then marry me, and we'll be bad together all the time."

"I can't." He looked so silly down there. She was laughing; the tears were just left over, that's all.

"Come on, Teresa, please?"

"I just can't, that's all. Even if I wanted to, I couldn't marry you."

"Why not?"

"Because my husband's still alive."

He dropped his arms. From his knees, he looked up at her. "Your husband is dead."

"No, he isn't. I wish he were, but he is not."

"You told me he was dead."

"I never said so. I just let you think it."

"And you think I didn't inquire elsewhere? No one's seen Roderick Trevelyn for years."

She jammed her hand in her pocket. "Then how is he writing me letters?"

Her lover took the paper from her. She let him unfold it and watched him scan the words, his face wrinkling in disgust. "This is insane," Lucius said. "It's revolting. He doesn't—this is insane."

"Yes. They've got him nicely locked away, but he still writes."

"Who lets him send them?"

"His family, of course. They won't give me a divorce. They want me back."

"For landsake, *why?*"

She wiped her eyes, took a breath. "To punish me, I suppose. I didn't give them what they wanted. It got worse, after I left, they tell me. They say if I came back, he would get better."

"No one who writes like this is going to get better. Why didn't you try to divorce him before you left? There would have been witnesses, you could have—"

She seized the paper back from him. "Do you think I wanted witnesses?" she flared. "Do you think I wanted the world to know what he was doing to me? I had no family, no money of my own—do you think anyone would even have believed me if I'd taken my stories to court against my husband and all his family?"

He watched her blaze across the room, back and forth like a comet in its course.

"I'm sorry," he said. She flew at him as if she would attack him, but he stood his ground, arms at his side, and she flung hers around him and clung to Lucius Perry for dear life.

IT WAS COLD IN THE SHADOW OF THE HOUSES. I FELT LIGHT-headed; it was hours since I'd eaten anything. I reached in my pocket for the nuts I'd bought at the theatre, and ate them, and felt a little better. I unfolded the paper they came in. It was a playbill from the theatre.

THE SWORDSMAN WHOSE NAME WAS NOT DEATH,
A New Drama
by a Lady of Quality
NOW PLAYING
at the Leaping Hart Theatre on West Bank,
Henry Sterling, Actor & Manager
With the additional talents of
the incomparable Black Rose,
the fierce Master Pincus Fury,
and introducing
the bold & dashing young Mistress Viola Fine and
Diverse other Talents
Certain to Enrapture & Entertain
A NEW DRAMA never before played before the Public!
Unlimited Engagement open to the Vagaries of Public Taste.
If you Appear, we will Play!

"By a Lady of Quality." Was it the same one who had written the novel? Maybe it was someone younger, someone who had read the book as a girl and loved it and wanted to see it on the stage. "A Lady of Quality"—that meant a noblewoman. Could it be someone I knew? Someone who had been to one of the duke's parties? The duke's ugly friend Flavia had been speaking of the theatre. She was clever, but I didn't think she was noble. I tried to see her as the mysterious author, but I could barely imagine her reading the book, much less writing about it.

Did the Lady of Quality ever come to see her own play onstage? What did she think of the way the actors played their roles? And did she ever go backstage to visit them after?

Teresa drew a harsh breath, and then another. He let her try to find control in the safety of his arms.

"I understand," he said. "It's all right. It's not your fault. You couldn't know."

"I didn't know," she whimpered like a child. "I really didn't know. How could I? No one told me."

She didn't realize how tightly she held the letter in her hand. "Oh, Lucius, he was so beautiful once. He was like a young forest god, all dappled golden. It made it harder to believe what he was capable of. Even when I was all bloody and aching, I'd look at that face, that perfect face, and wonder if I could be mistaken, if somehow I really had done something so terrible that he was perfectly justified in what he did.

"But he never said he was sorry. That's how I knew. The other girls—I knew women married to men who merely drank, or had bad tempers. They never tell you before the wedding— maybe your mother is supposed to know—but theirs must not have, and of course I didn't have one. Afterwards, though, it all comes out. We'd sit together over our sewing and our chocolate, and one would flinch or try to hide a bruise . . . and so we knew. And sometimes, though not often, one or the other would say, *It's all my fault, I know it is. I should try harder. I make him angry. He cries, you know, he cries and tells me how sorry he is, and begs me not to make him so angry. . . .* And she'd show us the jewel he'd bought her, to prove how much he really loved her after all.

"Roderick never said he was sorry. He would just look at me as if I weren't really there, as if my weeping were some pointless annoyance. So maybe I was lucky; at least I knew the truth." She laughed, an old, brittle echo of the drawing room. "I tried to kill him once."

"Why didn't you do it?" Lucius Perry asked harshly.

"I'm not sure." Teresa walked away from him, across the room. If she was going to speak of these things, she did not want to be held or touched by anyone. "I stood over him with the poker while he slept in a chair by the fire. We'd both been reading there, very quiet and companionable, and Roddy fell asleep. I didn't know, when he woke up, whether he would be—agreeable, or the other way. You never knew with him. I stood there with the poker, knowing I had only a few minutes and that I would have to beat his brains out. And it wasn't that I didn't want to spoil his beauty, although I didn't, really. It was just a— a ridiculous moment of clarity, when I realized that putting an end to his life would ruin mine; that it would be simple now and simple afterwards because it would all be over, but that wasn't what I really wanted. I realized I had another choice, which was much less simple but much more attractive."

She put her hand up against the windowpane, looking out at the empty winter garden. "I knew in that moment that I would leave, that it was only a matter of time. It made the waiting bearable as things got worse. I had it all thought out—what I would take, how I would get out—not where I would go, though; there didn't seem to be anything more important than getting out the door, and I was afraid to tell anyone beforehand. So one day I went upstairs, put some things in a bag, and walked out the door and into a great many complications. But at least I had something I wanted. And I have it still."

He stood waiting, listening.

"They never forgave me, the ones who stayed." Her breath misted the glass. "Ladies who'd wept on my bosom, as I wept on theirs—girls I shared secrets with of how to layer powder so the bruises wouldn't show. They are not the ones who buy my work, or send me flowers left over from their parties. They are the ones who castigate me loudly in public for leaving my poor husband when he needed me most. They are the women who won't receive me in their houses, and turn their heads away when they see me on the street."

"I won't let them hurt you anymore."

She shook her head, smiling mirthlessly. "Now you sound like one of my heroes. Maybe that's why I like you so much."

"Love me," he insisted.

"I may. I probably do. But I've tried that word before, and those feelings, and look where it got me."

"Abjuring love? Real people don't do that. Now you're the one who sounds like someone on a stage. That's not the real world. Real people follow their hearts, wherever it takes them. Real people refuse to be put into a little tiny box. You can say you love me or you don't love me, it doesn't matter; I know you have forsworn nothing except an existence you found intolerable."

She really did smile this time. "Now you're making me sound like a heroine. Be honest, Lucius. For all that you go on about the real world with its real people, you don't really want to live in it, either."

"I like," he said in a nobleman's lazy drawl, "to have some choice of which world I inhabit, that's all."

"Yes. And so do I. Which is why I am perfectly content where I am, and as I am." She went to the table, straightened some brushes there. "Really, I don't know why I made such a scene. I must be spending too much time with the theatre. China is so much more restful. All those nice patterns. I'd better get back to it."

"Well, then," he said.

"Well, then." She kissed him, long and hard. "And you have business of your own to attend to." Teresa buttoned up his jacket. "Go to your card party. Come back when you can."

———

I SAW HIM COME OUT THE DOOR IN A HOODED CLOAK, OLD-fashioned and concealing. But I knew who it was. Lord Lucius Perry walked off up the street, and I followed him. He was headed up toward the Hill, and never looked behind him.

The house he stopped at was one of the grand ones, guarded, with a wall. The gates were open, and the house was brightly lit. Not one of his secret visits, then. A party in a noble's house. I thought about following him through the gates, trying to pass as a guest, and then I thought, What for? They wouldn't want me. Nobody did. Alcuin had been right: I was a *thing*, a sword for folk to bet on, a toy for actresses to play with. Even the mysterious Lucius Perry, the duke's pet, the Riverside prostitute, the painter's secret visitor, even Lucius Perry had places he could go, where he could sit and talk and eat and drink like a normal person, but I was nothing.

I stood outside the gate, my velvet cloak drawn tight around me against the cold. It was getting dark. How was I going to get safely back to Riverside? I'd need to hire a torch. It was a long way, through a bad part of town, and I was tired.

"Out of the way, damn you!"

A chaise carried by two burly men nearly ran me down as they turned into the gate. My heart was pounding with shock and rage, now that they were gone by. But as they came out, I saw they bore no crest and might be for hire.

"Stop," I said hoarsely. "Will you carry me to Riverside?"

"'S a long way. You want four men for that."

"To the Bridge, then, will you do that?"

"Maybe. Cost you. Two in silver—and we'll see your money, first."

I dug in my pocket for the theatre change. Eight coppers and five minnows was all I had left. I remembered the weight of the gold chain I'd just carried, and suddenly I felt hot and angry. I wasn't the duke's messenger boy. If my uncle wanted me to do him favors, let him pay for them. The Duke Tremontaine didn't think about these things? Well then, I would.

"To the duke's house in Riverside," I said. "The steward there will pay you—three silver." He could afford it. "And if you won't take it, I'll find others who will."

They were good chair men; it wasn't too bumpy a ride. But even if it had been, I was too tired to mind much. I closed my eyes and saw the stage, the brightly costumed actors trying so hard to be Mangrove and Fabian, Tyrian and Stella for us all, and the men and women crowding around afterwards, with their little swords and roses. I didn't want to think about the crop-haired, trousered Viola, but she was like a sore tooth I just had to poke at. Was I like her? Did I want to be?

The Black Rose had kissed her, and then kissed me. I thought of the way the actress's hair had smelt, how soft it was under my hands, and I felt that warmth again at the cleft of my legs. It wasn't quite as fierce this time, and I remembered that I had, in fact, felt something like it before.

When I was very small, my nurse had caught me sleeping with my blanket ruched up between my legs because it felt nice, the way swinging on a tree branch sometimes did. She said, "Don't you be rubbing yourself there. Do you want to start growing a birdie, like your brothers'?"

When I asked her if she had rubbed their birdies to make them grow, she'd laughed so hard she could barely talk, and then she said, "Indeed I did; and when you're married, you'll rub your husband's to make it grow, oh yes you will."

When I was a little older, the cook's daughter took me to help her feed the fowl in the yard and explained what the rooster was doing to the hens, and how I was to think nothing of it, for every creature on earth did the same. My mother said that wasn't quite true, for men and women weren't like the brute beasts; we had to be married first for it to work.

I'd never thought of all these things at once, never connected each story to the others, and as the chair bumped along, I unraveled and interwove them.

Of course I wasn't growing a birdie now. I shook my head and snorted at my panic in the theatre. I wasn't a baby. Women had pleasure down there. I just hadn't known it could take you so suddenly like that, for no reason.

My grandmother—my mother's mother, and the duke's—had a special chapel in her house. It was because she was Reform, which seemed to mean she believed that everything wrong with the world was because the old kings had been especially evil and done things to displease the gods, and the nobles who overthrew them had been cleansing the land of impurities. She was very pious and always lit candles on the Feast of the Last King's Fall, and told me about our heroic ancestor, who had killed him in a duel. She tried to get me to be Reform, too, but I was very young when she died, and I hadn't met anyone Reform since then. I thought about the things she'd said that had not quite made sense, and realized that what she'd meant about the kings being so awful was not so much that the kings had not always been married, but that they had gone with other men.

No wonder my uncle wasn't speaking to her when she died.

Was I really like him? Did it run in families, after all?

No. There was no way on earth I would ever take up with someone like the horrible Alcuin, let alone start getting drunk and inviting fifteen naked people into my bedroom. Not on this earth. I was not like that, and never would be. I pulled my cloak tight around me—and shivered at the memory that assailed me, the thing I'd almost managed to forget. Last Night, and the firelight at Highcombe, and the sense that my uncle belonged there, in that small room with me and the master. He belonged there as much as I did, because St Vier loved him the way the old kings were not supposed to love people, and whatever my uncle did with the others, he loved the man at Highcombe almost too much to bear.

Well, if I ever loved anyone that much, man or woman, I would never do what he did. I'd been happy at Highcombe; I knew where I was and what I was doing there. And the duke had come and ruined everything, and dragged me back here where I didn't belong. He couldn't stay at Highcombe with the person he loved best in the world, so I couldn't either. He was a selfish crazy pig and I hated him utterly.

I cried then, because it was all so hopeless and I was so lonely and nothing and no one made any sense at all. This city was a terrible place. Look what had happened to Artemisia. When I first came to the city and met her, she had everything I thought I'd wanted, and look where she was now.

I wondered if she had seen the play, and what she would think of it, and what she would think of the Black Rose, and what she would think of me if she knew that Rose had kissed me. In her letters to me, Artemisia signed herself *Lady Stella*. Did she really think of me as Fabian, the peerless and righteous master swordsman? I was glad I had a sword to defend her; I liked being her champion. But what about the kiss that came after?

Would Artemisia kiss me, too, if I wanted her to? What if I killed Mangrove, and then stood over her and said, "Lady Stella, though your enemies sought your destruction, I have made them my own, and made them pay the price for it," what then?

I would definitely kiss Lady Stella. I wasn't sure about Artemisia, though. She was inclined to be a little silly, and not always reliable.

The chaise set down with a bump. I pulled back the curtain and found we were already at the Riverside house. I hadn't even known we'd crossed the Bridge. The house's torches were burning, and my friend Ralph was one of the guards at the door. I got out of the chaise as grandly as I could (considering my feet were so cold I could no longer feel them), gathering my cloak and my sword about me, and, "Ralph," I said, "please see to it that these men are paid. Three silver, not a minnow more. Oh, and make sure they get something hot to drink. It was a long trip."

I went inside the house. I felt as if I had been gone a hundred years, but it was just past dinnertime (the duke dined early and sometimes, when he got hungry, he dined twice). Betty was in the servants' hall. I went and rousted her, and she took my hat and cloak up to my room with me.

"Feather's ruined," she said. "Good show, then, eh, my lady?"

"It was all right."

"Never mind, we'll get you another. Dinner's past; I'll bring you up a tray."

"Take it to Marcus's room, then; I want to go see how he is."

"Sick is how he is," Betty said firmly, "and Cora is nursing him. But I've been wanting to talk about that," she continued ominously. My heart skipped a beat. Was Marcus sicker than we'd thought? Had his throat turned septic?

I grabbed Betty's hand. "What? What is it?"

"Sit down," she said, and I sat. "Don't be in such a twitter, my lady. You know I've got some experience of the world . . ."

"What's that to do with Marcus?"

"I've made some mistakes, we all have, and I don't want to see you making the same ones." She shook out my cloak, and started unbuttoning my jacket. "There, do you see?"

Not Marcus, then; only her usual rambling about her past. "I'm hungry, Betty; just get my dinner, will you?"

"You're growing," she said. "I'm going to have to start corseting you tighter. It's a pity; I could push them up just so to make the most of what you've got . . . But it would ruin the line."

"I don't care about the line. Can I have my dressing gown? I want to go see Marcus."

"Now that," she said, "is what I'm talking about. You haven't got a mother, and your uncle doesn't care, but I'm here to tell you that you shouldn't be visiting that boy alone in his room, let alone half-dressed."

"Don't be ridiculous. Anyhow, Cora's there."

"Cora's there and he's too sick to move. But what about afterwards, I ask you?"

"Afterwards what?"

My maid stood over me, shaking her head. "*You* may be the little innocent, but that boy never was—and he's plenty old now to play the fool with you, my lady."

For a moment I wanted to hit her. But then I looked at her red round little pudding face and remembered it was only Betty, after all.

"Don't worry," I said. "Marcus is not like that, and neither am I. We talk, and we play shesh, and anyhow the duke keeps us too busy to get up to anything." I felt a rush of warmth toward her. She might not be much, but she did care about me, in her way. And so did Marcus, of course. It was funny that, when I'd been so miserable in the chaise, I had forgotten all about him.

chapter IX

THE NEXT TIME IT PLEASED THE DUKE TREMONTAINE TO AT-
tend a meeting of the Council of Lords, he seemed to be the
subject of more than usual interest. Whenever there was a
lull in the proceedings, people would turn to look at him—pretending
to be talking to a neighbor, or checking the procession of the sun out
the window, but their heads turned in his direction.

What have I done now? he thought. It couldn't be Galing or Davenant, that was old business. Were they only just getting wind of the
events of the Rogues' Ball? Surely not. But it was something to do
with Katherine. When they met in the hallway outside, Lord Ferris
himself remarked pleasantly, "A spirited girl, your young niece. The
next time you have business for her in Council, you should bring her
with you, though. She's a bit rough around the edges, particularly for a
Tremontaine lady."

"Like the former duchess," Alec replied, "my niece professes no interest in politics." He said it automatically, because it was an easy dig
at the man who had once been the duchess's lover and political
mouthpiece; the rest of his mind was busy wondering what the Crescent was talking about.

"Teach her, then," said Ferris. "It will keep her off the streets, and
out of other people's business."

"My niece is quite safe on the streets," the duke said frostily. "I've
seen to that."

Y OUR NIECE IS PERFECTLY CHARMING," THE BLACK ROSE TOLD him when she visited him that night in Riverside, in the red velvet chamber. "Is she really your niece?"

"She's really my niece. My sister gave birth to her, a few years back."

"Then you should be more kind to her."

"What?" The duke dropped her leg back on the bed.

"She's very young. The young are hungry, very hungry for all sorts of things, and half the time they don't even know what they are. Do *you* know?"

"I'm perfectly kind to her," he said. "I sent her to the theatre, didn't I?"

"Do you even remember when you were her age?" The actress stroked his back with her foot. "You must have been a perfect horror. All arms and legs and rage and nameless lusts."

"That," he purred, "is precisely my point. I'm not having her go through what I went through, or what my sister did, either."

"You're a funny man." Her foot moved down his body. "You don't get this close to many women, but it would never occur to you to ask me what it is a young girl wants."

"I don't care what she wants. I know what's good for her."

"Heavens." She lay back, arms stretched over her head in the enormous bed. "Is that your mother's or your father's voice I'm hearing?" He reared up, startled. "Are you going to throw me out of bed?" she asked languidly.

"Possibly."

"I may be an actress, my lord, but I'm not stupid." He closed his fingers around her wrists, and she let him stretch his length upon her; allowing him the upper hand, she felt more secure in digging deeper. "What about the boy," she asked, "the shadowy one who follows you? He's not a relative, too, is he?"

"Leave the boy alone," he said sharply. "Nobody touches Marcus."

"Not even you?"

His fingers dug into her wrists. But he made his voice light. "I would be very much surprised if he ever asked me to. Meanwhile, you are not to bother him. Do you understand?"

She said, "When we quarreled, Lord Ferris said that I had played too many Empresses. What he meant was that I thought I was his equal. You would never say that, but you might be under the illusion that I am a creature of huge uncontrollable lusts for everything that moves, including awkward young boys."

"I never—"

"It's all right. I'm just telling you how annoying it is for me when people confuse me with my roles, that's all."

"Believe me, I have no desire to sleep with the Empress."

"Good. Do you know, I don't think you're mad at all."

"Stick around."

"I will."

"And tell me more," he said, "about Lord Ferris."

Sweetest Katherine, my One True Friend—

How long it seems since we were girls together, innocently com-paring beaux at the Tr—— Ball! How I treasure our time together! I still have the feather I wore in my hair that night—some might call it a plume—but its lustre is sadly faded—or perhaps 'tis the dullness of mine eye that makes it seem so. I am sure that if you saw me now, you would not look twice—for my eyes are red with perpetual weep-ing—and yet, such is the virtue of your eyes that I know you would see into my heart as you have always done, and view with kindness the crushed flower hiding there. Oh, when I think of him I feel vile and disgusting! But then I picture your dear face, flushed with righteous wrath, and it is as if your angry tears can wash away my stain.

Like Stella at the races, I see much but say little—and I believe that, like Fabian, you keep faith with me despite appearances. Oh, do let me hear from you! If only to tell me that you are well, and remem-ber your loving—

A F-L

The handwriting was large and loopy and violet, and it just about broke my heart. But what could I do? I'd challenged Lord Ferris, and he'd refused me. Poor Artemisia! I'd hoped at least the challenge would frighten the Crescent into crying off, but it hadn't done even that. Nevertheless, she must be answered. I dashed off a reply.

Lady S—

Know that you and your grievance, though little talked on, are far from forgotten. I watch and wait, and will prevail.

Have you seen the play yet?

Your assured friend,

KT

I sealed it with candlewax and stuffed it in my jacket, and set out to find my delivery boy. But in the hallway I met Marcus, capped and booted and mufflered, a handkerchief in his fist.

"It's the chairs," he snuffled. "He wants to go see the chairs."

"What are you doing out of bed?"

"I'm bored. I want to see them, too."

"What chairs?"

"New ones." He coughed. "New design. It's a fine day. Like spring. We're walking. Want to come?"

"Love to."

So the fine springlike day found the three of us sloshing through the fine Riverside mud on our way to a shop that would have been more than happy to bring the chairs to us if we'd been content to stay indoors. Ever since my trip to the theatre, I'd been taking more care to dress well when I went out; if people saw me, I wanted them to see someone who mattered. Today I wore my green suit, though not my velvet cloak, with an embroidered scabbard and a shirt whose cuffs were trimmed with lace.

My uncle noticed. "Pretty," he said, "but hardly practical. You're my swordsman, not my maid of honor. Steel catches on lace; Richard would never wear it. If it comes to a fight, now, you'll tuck your cuffs under. I know you're a young girl full of nameless lusts involving fashion, but you don't want to die of vanity your next fight. Whenever that may be." He looked around and shrugged. "It's a wonder you've gone unchallenged, after your triumph at Sabina's ball. In the old days, they would have been lined up around the block to try you, the bright new blade in town. No one has any ambition anymore—they just want to sit on their nicely muscled asses drawing nobles' pay to defend the indefensible."

"I'm in your household," I pointed out before he could say any more about swordsmen's anatomy. "They might be afraid a challenge to me is an insult to you."

"Riverside." He sighed gustily, and stepped around an indescribable pile of something that had emerged from the melted snow. "It's not what it was."

"Whose fault is that?" Marcus muttered. We crossed the Bridge, and picked up a couple more guards at the Tremontaine postern.

I had a thought. "But," I asked, "if I *were* to maybe challenge someone, challenge him on my own, I mean, without your authority—would I be able to do that?"

The duke stopped in the middle of the street. Marcus and the guards and I stopped with him and narrowly missed being run over by a carriage that was barreling up behind us. Our retainers and the carriage lackeys had it out while His Grace of Tremontaine regarded me fixedly from above.

"Such as?" he asked. "What sort of hypothetical person were you hypothetically thinking of maybe challenging?" I couldn't say anything. "Not some bravo," the duke hypothesized, "in a tavern brawl or street fight . . . not your style. Those are boys' games."

"Do you think," I asked, momentarily distracted, "they don't even want to fight me? They think, because I'm a girl, I'm not even worth bothering with? Or is it just because I'm related?"

"I don't know," the duke said. Behind us the two factions were close to blows. "Tremontaine makes place for no one!" shouted Ralph, our man. That was certainly true. The duke was placidly ignoring the whole fracas. "But I would very much prefer that you not spill your blood for anything trivial."

"It's not trivial!" I blurted out.

"My Lord of Tremontaine!" a well-bred voice called from the carriage. "If you please! I have a very sick rabbit in here!"

"A rabbit?" said Marcus. "May I see?"

"Bloody Furnival and his stupid pets," the duke growled. "It bites. And he said it's diseased. What are you all doing, standing in the middle of the street—you're supposed to be protecting me, not encouraging nobles with unnatural tastes to run me down!"

But he did not forget.

We went and saw the chairs, and he ordered a dozen, all curvy and strange—very modern, he said approvingly—and we were going to stop at White's for chocolate when he suddenly said, "No, let's go on to Tremontaine House. I want to see the room they'll go in, while it's fresh in my mind. Do you know," he said cheerfully as we trudged on up the Hill, "maybe I should have the whole room redone to match them? Soften the angles of the walls, with molding, maybe, so it's all nothing but curves? That would help take the curse off the place."

We were passing the street that Lucius Perry's sweetheart lived on. I glanced over at Marcus to see if he'd catch my eye, and I didn't like what I saw. My friend's face was pale, his eyes were bleary and his forehead looked damp. I sidled over to him. "Go home," I said.

Marcus coughed. "We're almost there."

"All right, but when we get to Tremontaine House, you're going straight to bed." He didn't have the strength to do anything but nod, and when we hit a steep part, he actually took my arm.

Astonishingly, Tremontaine House was ready to receive us. Marcus went upstairs to collapse on clean sheets. The staff set a table in the pretty room overlooking the garden, and the duke and I sat down there to a small collation of chocolate and biscuits, dried fruit and nuts. Outside the tall windows, the blooming witch hazel and forsythia made streaks of bright color against the general gloom.

"Almost spring," my uncle remarked. "Riverside is turning into a swamp already. We'll bring the household back up here soon."

Just when I'd gotten used to Riverside, he wanted to move me again. It figured. "It's so quiet up here," I said. "Kind of boring, don't you think?"

"I do my best," he drawled, "to enliven it. Tell me, Katherine: does this hypothetical challenge of yours involve one of the neighbors up here?"

I sloshed chocolate all over my saucer. "What challenge?"

"The one everybody in the city appears to know about but me."

"That isn't so! No one knows about it except Lord—" I felt myself flush with the embarrassment of having walked right into his trap. "I was very discreet," I added lamely.

"Discreet is good," my uncle said encouragingly. He was leaning across the table toward me, like a tutor trying to help me with my arithmetic. "Now, then, where does he live?"

"I don't know, exactly."

"You can't fight him if you can't find him, Katherine."

"I can find him."

"I can help—discreetly, of course. This is, as you say, your fight. What's the cause?"

"It's—personal."

His whole body tightened like a string that had been pulled. "How personal? Has someone offered you insult?"

He was so like a father in a book, I couldn't help smiling. "Please," I said as airily as possible, "I can manage."

"Of course you can, I've seen to that. But if anyone has done anything, anything *bad* to you, rest assured that I—"

It was his usual polished hauteur, all drawly and annoying, but I paid attention and saw that his green eyes were glittering and very fierce. I actually reached across the table and touched his hand. "Nothing like that. I'm fine. It's for someone else, a friend."

He looked, if anything, fiercer. "Not your friend Marcus?"

"Marcus? Of course not. Someone else. I can't tell you, though. It's a secret."

The duke nearly choked on his chocolate. "My dear! I've got more secrets than you've got teeth in your mouth. Believe me, I can keep a secret." I didn't say anything. "Never mind," he said, "I can find out.

Will you tell me who it is you're challenging, or do I have to lock you in your room and feed you on bread and water 'til I starve it out of you?"

"It doesn't matter," I said glumly. "He refused me."

My uncle put down his cup. "Hold on. You issued a public challenge to a noble of this city, and he turned you down?"

"It wasn't very public. Just one or two other men there, and then he took me aside and told me not to be silly. I could kill him just for that. He wasn't taking me seriously at all. He kept thinking I'd come from you, even though I told him I hadn't."

My uncle raised his eyebrows, and then his face broke into a slow, delighted grin. "It's Ferris," he said. "You've challenged the Crescent Chancellor. No wonder he never comes to see me anymore."

"He's not—is he a friend of yours?" I hadn't thought of that. I'd never seen Lord Ferris at any of Tremontaine's gatherings, but clearly he didn't have much self-control when it came to the kinds of things the duke didn't either, so maybe . . .

"The ways in which Ferris is no friend to me are beyond counting. That goes for Tremontaine in general: he's got a grudge against the lot of us; he'll kill you if he thinks he can. Fortunately I know some of his secrets, so he's chary of us. Old ones, and new ones, too. What's the latest? What has he done to this friend of yours?"

"I can't tell you," I said miserably. "It's too shameful. And it isn't my secret. It's a question of honor."

My uncle took a deep breath. "Look. Did you tell Ferris what the challenge was about?"

"Of course I did. He did it!—the thing. The thing I'm challenging him about."

"La, la." My uncle shook his head sadly. "She'll tell Lord Ferris what she won't tell me." His eyes met mine. He looked serious all of a sudden. "There are quite a few things Ferris has to be ashamed about. One of them concerns money. One of them concerns the Black Rose." The mention of the actress startled me. My uncle watched me for a moment, and then, satisfied that the challenge did not concern her, went on, "Now, Ferris doesn't know I know about either of those things, not yet. He won't be pleased when he finds out, assuming he ever does. But I can take care of myself; indeed, knowing things about him can be very useful to me. For you, though . . . for you, it's different. If you know something bad about him that no one else knows, he isn't going to feel entirely safe around you. And a worried Ferris can turn very nasty."

My uncle leaned back in his chair; I thought of a tutor again, as he raised his chin to the ceiling. "Think of secrets," he told me, "as being like money. The more you have—of other people's, I mean—the richer you are, and the more likely to be able to afford something you want when you really need it. Now, I'm the head of the family, which means I hold most of the family fortune: houses, land . . . and secrets. You are a junior member, and you hold—one. Give it to me, and you add to the family fortunes. Keep it, and I'm going to set a guard on you. Just in case the Crescent Chancellor decides he'd rather you didn't tell anyone after all."

I stared down at my knuckles. I didn't think he was bluffing. He was really worried.

"If I tell you," I said, "do you promise not to tell anyone else?"

My uncle nodded.

"And if you think it's stupid, you won't lock me in my room and refuse to let me fight?"

He looked at the ceiling. "Good question. Will I? Let's say I won't, this time."

"What you were saying before," I muttered, "when you thought it might be me? It wasn't me; it was someone else."

"Forgive my bluntness, but I need to get this straight: Anthony Deverin, Lord Ferris, raped a girl, and now you want to kill him for it?"

"I'm not sure I'm going to kill him. He has to admit it was wrong, and beg her forgiveness."

"Are you in love with her yourself?"

I could feel myself turning an interesting color. But I wasn't going to give way to him now. I said, "Is that all you can think about?"

"Not all. I just wanted to make sure."

"Well, it's not the point. The point is, he did this awful thing against her will, and he doesn't care, and her family doesn't care—they all want her to get married to him anyway, and she doesn't want to, and nobody's going to do anything about it if I don't!"

"Ahhh." The duke nodded in satisfaction. "The little Fitz-Levi." He shook his head mournfully. "Oh, Ferris. Those years in Arkenvelt have coarsened you, I fear, and given you a trader's soul: tasting the wares before the final sale." He said to me, "You are quite right to call him out. That's no way to behave, with him thinking he can have whatever he wants whenever he wants it. Let him learn some humility first. It's a lesson he's got long a-coming; he's always treated women badly, and only the one time did we make him pay for it." Lost inside a memory, the duke cut a long spiral of apple peel; then he looked up and said, "He's not young, you know. He can't go on like this forever.

Tell your little friend to do her utmost, and maybe he'll drop dead on his wedding night."

I said, "That's disgusting. Aren't you listening? She doesn't want to marry him."

"You're not thinking it through," he said at his most superciliously annoying. "She's damaged goods. Now that she's ruined, marriage to Ferris is the only safe course open to her."

"How can you say that," I hissed, "you of all people? How can you say it's *safe* for her? To live for the rest of her life with someone who could do something like that?" I found that I had risen to my feet and was leaning over the table glaring at him. "Someone *you* don't even like?"

"Oh, thank you," he said dryly. "Sit down, please. I only meant, safe in the eyes of the world. I didn't say I approved. You should know that—you, of all people."

But I did not sit down. "Then *do* something," I said. "Why don't you *do* something, if it matters to you so much? The truth is, you don't care about her. You don't care about any of us, and you're not going to do anything. But I do, and I will."

His knuckles were very white against the table's rim. I was afraid I'd gone too far. But his voice, when he spoke, was measured and calm. "Let me understand you clearly," he said, as though testing a mathematical proof. "You are going to cry challenge against Lord Ferris, not merely to avenge a wrong, but so that this girl need not marry against her will?"

"I'm going to challenge him because you can't treat people that way. No one seems to realize it; no one seems to care. *He* certainly doesn't. He thinks he owns her already, and her parents do, too—and even you. It makes me sick."

My uncle was looking up at me with the strangest expression, as if he were going to cry, if such a thing were possible. What he said next was even more confusing: "Katherine?" There was a curious smile on his face, as if he were telling himself a story that he liked very much. "What do you want for your birthday?"

What did I want? He was the Duke Tremontaine. There was a lot he could give me. There was a lot he had taken from me, too. Why was he asking me this now, all of a sudden? I didn't know what to say. "I'll think about it."

"Good enough. Now sit down. You're right. I'm not going to do anything. I'm going to let you do it." I sat. "So." He was all business now. "You challenged Ferris once, but he did not accept. Neither did you revoke the challenge. So as far as he knows, you could appear any day with a skewer to his gut. He won't like that."

"I told him he could apologize to her."

The duke smiled. "Oh, *that* will definitely happen. When the river boils over. But that's not the point anymore."

"Why not? He's insulted her honor. It isn't as if girls don't have any."

"Have you asked yourself why he doesn't want a fight? And why he's so insistent that the marriage go forward despite your friend's objections?" He held up a hand. "Don't start. I'm not that coarse; I'm sure he had a lovely time wherever he did it with her, but it's not like Ferris to think with his—ah, his privates. He did it to secure the wedding. He did it to secure the funds."

"Isn't he rich already?"

The duke bisected an apple with the paring knife. "Nope. That's his little secret—the one I have, the one he must be afraid is going to come out."

"How do you know?"

"I know it because . . . people tell me things they shouldn't." He took a bite from the apple and grinned. "Sometimes I pay them to. Terrible. Trust no one; or if you do, try not to have any secrets."

"I don't understand."

"Ferris always liked being twisty. Overcomplication has been his downfall in the past. Before you were born, he tried to double-cross your great-grandmother—that's her, there on the wall." He pointed to the glorious lady in grey silk, the portrait with the flamingo mallet I had so admired. "It was my pleasure to ruin him the first time, and get him sent to Arkenvelt. From which he returned about ten years ago, laden with furs which he turned into cash, and so was able to buy his way back into society, a good marriage and back up the rungs of the Council of Lords to his present glorious position. But he never had much land, what he's got is mortgaged to the hilt, and now he's nearly out of cash. He has nothing left to fall back on except what he can create for himself. It's perfectly obvious: every bill he supports, every vote he casts is designed to feather his own nest—taxing the landowners, encouraging trade . . . It makes him look progressive—Karleigh's cronies just hate him, but for all the wrong reasons.

"Politics. I'm boring you. I should start sending you to Council meetings—then you'd know what boredom is. But listen: Ferris needs this marriage. And he needs you not to mess it up. You're lucky he's not taking you too seriously, or he would have had you knifed on the street."

I felt cold. "But that's dishonorable!"

"Ferris has no more real sense of honor than that doorknob. Honor is a tool he uses to manipulate others. Challenge him soon. Do it right; do it in public with everyone watching. Then he can't weasel out. Do you want to rid us all of him forever, or give him time to find a swordsman to take the challenge for him?"

"I don't think I should kill him."

"Probably not. Killing a noble in challenge means it goes to the Court of Honor, and then everything would come out. Either that, or I'd have to step forward and claim the challenge myself, and I'm not really interested in the eternal gratitude of the Fitz-Levis. No, you just fight his champion, and refuse to answer any questions after. Say it was a private affair of honor. People will draw their own conclusions, but with any luck they'll get it wrong, and you'll keep your friend's name out of it. But do it by the book, and do it soon."

"How soon?"

"Because I am your uncle and I have many employees, I will make it my business to learn Lord Ferris's schedule for tomorrow and the next day. That soon."

I nodded.

The duke rose. "Oh, and Katherine . . ."

"Yes, uncle?"

"Where's Marcus?"

"In bed. He's sick again."

"Well, never mind; I'll just write a letter and send it down to Riverside, and then you can ask Marcus where—oh, never mind; I can find the stuff myself."

It was the last time I saw him sober that night.

I went up to make sure Marcus was all right. He was dozing in bed. His room here was smaller than the one in the Riverside house, but it was cozy, with a fire lit and rain beginning to patter against the windows. He opened his eyes when I came in, and I sent for some broth for him and watched him drink it.

It was comforting just to sit with him in silence. There was so much I couldn't tell him now, about Lord Ferris and Artemisia and what the duke had said to me. But Marcus and I had secrets of our own.

"We can't just keep calling her 'Lucius Perry's friend,'" I said aloud.

"Ah." Marcus smiled. "We don't have to. I found out her name."

"How did you . . . ?"

"I do get out occasionally, you know." He sounded like the duke, only with such a bad cough I didn't have the heart to deny him his triumph.

"All right, tell me."

"Her name is Teresa Grey."

"Who told you?"

"No one. I read it on a letter she left lying on a table."

"You went into her studio?!"

"Don't be an idiot. I went over the wall again. She wasn't there, so I went right up to the window and saw it."

 "I can't believe you went without me."

"I would have taken you if I'd been able to find you. But you've been hard to find these days. Anyway, it wasn't for long."

I did not tell him that I had gone there without him, too, the day of the theatre. What was there to tell, really? I hadn't seen any letters, just lurked on the street and followed Lucius Perry up the Hill to a gate I'd been scared to go through. I hadn't told Marcus about the theatre, either, or the Black Rose, or anything. I owed him. And so I said, "All right. You are remarkable. Teresa Grey. I like that name."

Marcus lay back and closed his eyes. "Isn't it lovely, Katie?"

"What?"

"Knowing something *he* doesn't know."

"What if he does know?"

"He doesn't. I'd bet on it."

I giggled. "Maybe we should offer to sell him the information. He likes secrets."

"Not this one. This one's ours."

"Ours and Teresa Grey's." My friend's eyes were shut; he looked as if he were dreaming already. Softly I said, "He'd be furious if he knew we were doing this."

"He doesn't own us. He's the Duke Tremontaine, he's not the king of the entire world."

"What if he finds out?"

"He won't."

"And we won't tell him, will we?"

When Marcus opened his eyes, they were brown and disarming and utterly frank. "I see no reason to. Do you?"

I tucked his blanket back in. "None whatsoever. Good night."

I passed the duke's study. The hall smelt of a peculiar, sweet smoke; I went past quickly. I could hear him crashing around in there, calling for Marcus. I went downstairs and found a footman who could take care of him, and the staff gave me some hot soup and tried to pump me for gossip from the Riverside house, so I went back upstairs through the dark and empty house, and found myself standing in front of the doors with the wet rabbits on them. Funny to think about the first time I'd seen them, with Betty nervous beside me, and me nervous clutching my short cloak to hide my legs. And Master Venturus waiting behind the door, to teach me how not hold sword. And me maybe having already met Marcus, but not knowing really who he was, and still dreaming of sweeping down staircases in a ballgown . . . It was the same day I ran away to see Artemisia. I had not yet picked up a sword. I had not met Richard St Vier.

I went into the dark room; the mirrors gave it what glow there was, but I didn't need to see much. I thought of Highcombe, of the man practicing there with no opponent, who might be practicing now. I ran through the opening moves of a fight, any fight, and then I started thinking about what he would do next, and moved to counter him.

I N THE MORNING, WHEN I WENT TO PUT MY JACKET BACK ON, I found my note to Artemisia still tucked up inside it. I opened it up and sat down and added these words:

> *Sweetest Lady Stella,*
> *A challenge has been issued, and awaits but the turning of the tide to bear a bitter fruit—bitter for some, but sweet, I hope, to your tongue, and a balm to your sad eyes. I told you he'd regret it, and I wasn't joking. Be of good courage—hold fast, and keep faith, for I will meet his champion on the field of battle, and blot out your stain with his blood.*
> *Not Fabian, but True and Faithful*
>
> TYRIAN

I signed it with a flourish, and sealed it with several blobs of the duke's best wax.

Part IV

CHALLENGE

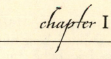

Marcus was better the next day, but the Duke was badly hung over and didn't want anyone near him whom he could hear breathing. I felt jittery about the challenge, jittery about the letter I'd written to Artemisia (which I'd sent by the simple expedient of charging one of the Tremontaine House servants to safely deliver it to her maid). I didn't want Marcus to ask why. To distract us both, I proposed a little stroll down to what I jauntily referred to as "Lucius Perry's Love Nest."

To our silent delight, Perry was there, too. He was sitting on the sofa in a loose dressing gown, drinking chocolate and watching Teresa paint. He must have spent the night: the gown was a flowered print of yellow-gold on a dusky green that looked wonderful with her auburn hair, but didn't do a thing for his complexion. Knowing he was wrapped up in one of her gowns, and that he was slight enough to fit in it, made me feel tremendously tender toward them both.

It was a very domestic scene. We watched as Perry reached for more chocolate, and then he felt in the pocket of the gown and pulled out a folded paper, its seal broken, and looked hard at it.

Teresa Grey had gotten a letter, too.

⟋‾‾‾⟍

Another one?"

"Don't open it," she said swiftly. "It's just more nonsense: ravings and accusations, pleading and boasting. . . . I shouldn't even break the seals anymore. I should just throw them in the fire." Her fingers closed on his, forbidding him the paper.

"Why do they let him?"

"They don't *let* him, Lucius, they force him to write. He doesn't really want me. They egg him on, they keep him in drink until he's all fired up and turns out his pages. I doubt he remembers a day later what he's done."

"But why? Why won't they let you go?"

"Cruelty, I suppose. And oddly enough, I'm still their last best hope for an heir. If the marriage is dissolved, they'd never find anyone else to take him as he is now."

Perry's face contorted with revulsion. "An heir."

"Well, we tried," she said. "Before I left, we tried."

"All right, that's it." He got up from the couch, hitching up his robe. "I'm an idiot. I don't know why I didn't think of this sooner. It's so much simpler, really."

"What is?"

"I'm going to kill him."

"You can't kill Roderick!"

"Yes, I can. It's simple." He put one foot up on the windowsill, looking back over his shoulder. "I know exactly how it's done. Find a swordsman, pay him to challenge poor Roderick to the death without warning, and *poof!* No more letters. No more husband. And you are free to choose . . ." he opened his robe ". . . another." She giggled, and came to his arms. He closed the robe around them both. "Choose me," he murmured, feeling her settle against him.

"No," she murmured. He felt her smile against his neck.

"Or not," he added agreeably. "You'll be free, at any rate."

"But really, Lucius, you mustn't do it. You mustn't think of it."

"Oh?" He drew back, wrapping the robe around himself. "Do you harbor still some tenderness for this forest god of yours?"

"Don't be disgusting. I harbor some desire to keep my privacy intact, and to keep you out of prison."

"Prison? For what?"

"For *this*, Lucius!" she said angrily. "For playing with their property! I married their son; in the eyes of the law, I'm their property yet. Don't you understand that?"

"The laws of challenge—"

"Yes, yes, I know. Your swordsman will slay him and then you'll stand up in the Court of Honor and proudly tell everyone why you killed their son. And the Lords Justiciar will say, 'Well, that's all right, then, never mind; just take her and be happy.' Is that what you're thinking?"

"I'll keep it private. If I must, I'll pay the swordsman to lie."

"And Roddy's family will swoop in with the truth. For all I know they've got spies on me already, and are just saving the juicy facts until they need them—which is to say, in case I ever try anything."

"But—"

"This isn't a game to me: the hiding, the being secret. I'm not doing it for fun, like you. If our liaison became public—and I assure you, if you challenge Roderick and kill him, it will be—then all that still makes my life tolerable will be taken from me in the wake of the ensuing scandal."

"You're a scandal already. You left your husband, you write trash for a living—"

"It isn't trash. And that's a secret. All everyone knows is that I live on the kindness of others, in a house provided by a sympathetic cousin. I make my pin money from friends who buy my china painting. That's the life I live, and the world will put up with it as long as they don't know any other."

"*I* know it," he said quietly.

"Yes. You do know. And I know yours."

He smiled. "Do you think that's why we get along so well?"

"You love your secrets. I merely require mine. It is why I trust you, though."

"You can trust me with anything."

"Can I trust you to be careful? You love danger, you love the sense that you could be caught at any time." In answer, he kissed her hand, bowing low. She touched his hair. "You are my only luxury, Lucius. So far, the cost hasn't been too high. Which is why there will be no challenge. Not from you."

He straightened. "I am a noble of the House of Perry. I have the right to call challenge where honor has been offended."

"Stop playing," she said irritably. "If you won't respect my secrets, have a thought to yours. Challenge him, and they will surely come out. You would hate it, you know you would. But if self-sacrifice is your current dangerous passion, spare a thought for how I'd feel watching them spend my dowry on their petty persecution of us both."

"At least you'd get your dowry back in the end."

"You think so? You've never hired lawyers, have you? And how would the rest of the noble House of Perry feel? Your family would cast you off, Lucius, they'd have to. Even if you're enjoying the image of yourself as my noble champion, this is one role I won't let you try out."

"It doesn't matter," he said softly. "It's not as if I can't support us both."

"Oh, lovely," she said, choking back angry tears. "You'll pay for our room and board by selling your body in Riverside. I'd like that. And when you can't work, I'll support you painting flowers on china and writing drama for whatever theatre will take it as long as they can pretend they don't know who it came from. . . ."

"Intolerable," he growled, "the lot of them. I'll start with him, and then I'll pick them off, one by one, see if I don't."

"You might kill my husband with some justice," she said gently, "for his offenses against me. You cannot kill them all, my Lucius. And you would have to kill them all, to make the world a safe place for the likes of us."

"*He* talks like that, sometimes," Lucius Perry said thoughtfully. "When he talks to me at all."

"*No.*" She seized his wrist in her strong fingers. "Stop thinking what you're thinking. I'm not having it."

"He likes me. He says I'm not a hypocrite. I think he'd like you."

"Lucius, no."

"What's the point of having the Duke Tremontaine as a patron, if he can't do me any real good when I need him?"

"You haven't thought it through," she said, but she didn't sound annoyed. Amused, maybe, and a little sad. "He's not your patron, and he doesn't mean you any good. He has you for the same reason I do; because you're such a lovely secret."

"I'm serious," Lucius Perry said. "I would take on the world for you."

"I believe you." She kissed him. "And I'm not going to let you."

MARCUS SNEEZED. "Let's go home," I said. "I have to practice."

A CHALLENGE HAS BEEN ISSUED." ROBERT FITZ-LEVI FLICKED at the paper with a well-manicured hand. "My dear sister, what does this mean?"

Artemisia glared at her brother across her room, not even rising from the chair she was sunk in, her tangled embroidery on her lap. "It means, my dear brother, that you have been reading my private correspondence without asking."

"Mother read it. She asked me to come and speak with you."

Artemisia sat up straight, her arms on the chair. "What have you to say, then, Robert?"

Robert drew a deep breath, went to the window, and then let it out and turned to her. "Do you know what I really want to say? I want to say that I wish you'd grow up and stop behaving like the queen in some tragedy. You made a stupid error, and now you refuse to admit it and face the consequences. Listen, Artie, do you have any idea how lucky you are?"

"*Lucky?* Lucky to be forced against my will?"

"By your intended, just a few weeks before your wedding night. What's the difference?"

She said, "You make me sick. I thought you'd understand, but you're on *their* side now."

He shouted, "I'm on *your* side, but you're just too stupid to see it!"

"If you really cared for me, you'd fight for me! You'd be out there defending my honor, instead of sucking up to Father so he'll raise your allowance so you and your stupid friends can hire swordsmen to fight over women you—you aren't even related to."

"If you weren't such a romantic bubble-headed idiot, you'd know that your honor isn't compromised unless this gets out."

"Robert," she said. "My honor was compromised the moment that monster laid a hand on me. If you don't see that, there's others who do."

"Enough!" he said, brandishing the letter heavy with blobs of sealing wax. "Who is this *Tyrian*?"

"A friend. A true friend, and willing to fight for me."

"My god," he groaned. "How many of them are there? It's not enough that you drag Ferris off to some sleazy ball for your fun, but now you've got some punk swordsman on your string as well?"

His sister threw the nearest thing to hand, a small table. "How dare you? I'll have her kill you next, see if I don't!"

"You've hired a *woman* to kill Lord Ferris?"

"She's a girl, a girl like me. She's brave and bold and true, and no one could ever make her do a thing that she despises, or harm the innocent. She's not one of your swaggering bullies who fight for money; she's a *real* swordsman. Like Fabian."

"Oh, lord." Her brother looked pale. He put his hand against the wall, oblivious that it covered a frolicking nymph. "Who's Fab—"

"Never mind about Fabian." A tight-lipped Lady Fitz-Levi had entered the room. "That's quite enough nonsense. I don't know where you managed to meet this heroic young lady, but unless you're planning to marry *her*, you'd better tell her to keep her heroics to herself, and leave us all alone. Here, put this on." She held up a gown of soft pink silk, ruffled to perfection.

"I *hate* pink."

"It will give you color, which you sadly lack. Dorrie—" Artemisia's maid appeared. "The hair, please."

"What—"

"Sit still, you'll knot it."

"I don't—"

"Daughter, be still. You will be made presentable, and you will go out. Whether or not you enjoy yourself is entirely up to you, but I urge you to try. (Robert, turn your back.) All the city knows is that you've been ill and fretful, and that Lord Ferris is pining for you. (No, Dorrie, the pearls.) Before we leave, you will write to your heroic friend, telling her she is on no account to make a fuss of any kind."

"It's not a 'fuss,' Mama," Artemisia protested, even as she felt the cool weight of the pearls settle around her neck. "It's a challenge, for my honor."

"Your 'honor' is no one's business but ours, child. More particularly, honor is the business of men."

"But men are supposed to fight for a woman's honor. If Papa and Robert—"

"If your father and brother feel insulted, of course they will fight for you; isn't that so, Robbie?"

"Naturally, Mama. How could I do otherwise?"

"There, you see? (The curls a little higher—where is the butterfly pin?) Your honor is tarnished only if theirs is. And we have all made very sure that there is no breath of scandal, so no tarnish. (Don't tight-lace, Dorrie, she's thin enough as is.) Do you understand, now, dear?"

"Do try, Artie," her brother added encouragingly. "You've always been game. I'm sorry what I said about your champion before—you see, I do take your honor most seriously, on my word I do. I'm your brother, I'm supposed to protect you. I know it's been tough on you, old girl, but you must realize we care a lot for you. While you've been up here soaking your handkerchiefs, we've been making sure there's nothing *to* fight about. Do you see?"

"I think so."

"Of course she does. She knows how much we love her and want what's best for her." Lady Fitz-Levi pinched her daughter's cheeks evenly, to bring out the glow. "Oh, look at her; doesn't she look pretty?"

"A picture, madam."

"Just so. We can all be proud of our little girl, and I know you will never do anything to make us feel otherwise. Now, which slippers do you like, the rosettes with the little heels, or the satin grey?"

"I wore those last year."

"The rose, then. Stand up. Yes, you're quite right about the heels, dear. The line is better so. Turn around. Robert, isn't she a picture? Oh, Dorrie, look at that ruffle, it's uneven—get your sewing kit, quickly. Yes, Kirk, what is it?"

"The carriage, my lady."

"Dear me, already? I'll just go change my gown—no one minds what I look like—and you sit and write that note."

"But Mama—"

Covered in a muslin robe to protect her toilette, Artemisia wrote:

Dearest Fabian,
     All is lost. My ruin is complete. My kind parents and brother
have explained it all to me. There is no hope. Consider me as one dead

and lost to the world. I will always remember you fondly, and will
never forget what you were willing to do to save your—

Artemisia

"Hmph." Lady Fitz-Levi read it over. "That will do. To whom is it addressed? Come, tell me—do not make me pump the servants for information, for I know they have delivered others."

"To—to Lady Katherine Talbert. At Tremontaine House."

"Oh . . . my . . . god," her brother said feelingly.

L ITTLE WAS SAID IN THE CARRIAGE, BUT WHEN ARTEMISIA'S mother was looking out the window, her brother passed her a flask and Lady Fitz-Levi pretended not to notice.

"A little afternoon musicale," said her mother soothingly, "at your friends the Godwins. Your dear Lydia will be there, that will be nice for you. She has written you almost every day, you know."

"I know."

"And there will be no need to say much; just listen to the music, nod and smile, very simple."

"Will—will *he* be there?"

"Oh, lord, child, how do I know? He doesn't send me his comings and goings."

"Don't worry, sis." Her brother squeezed her hand. "If he offends you in public in any way, I'll fight him for sure."

"Will you, Robbie?" she whispered. "Promise? If he's there and he tries to get me alone, you won't let me out of your sight, promise?"

" 'Course I do. You're safe as Nanny's Hedgehog."

She smiled at the childhood memory, and allowed herself to settle back a little.

E VERYONE AT THE GODWIN PARTY WAS CAREFULLY PLEASED TO see her. Lydia practically crushed all her ruffles in a fierce embrace, and whispered, "You look divine! All pale and interesting. I mustn't let Armand catch sight of you; he'll think me a pig by comparison."

Her cousin Lucius was there, too, impeccably dressed as always. He took her hand and bowed and said, "It's good to see you well," but that was all. She saw her old beau Gregory, Lord Talbert, across the room flirting with an older woman, and wondered for a moment what would have happened if she had betrothed herself to him, and wished him well.

She sat on a velvet-covered love seat, wedged between her mother and her brother, and listened to two women playing flute and harp. The sun was coming in the tall windows overlooking the gardens. Lydia and Armand sat between them, a curtain half-pulled across them to disguise the fact that they were holding hands.

When *he* came in, she knew it.

She felt it on the back of her neck, a disturbance of the air, the disturbance of his gaze. The music didn't stop. She gripped the edge of Robert's jacket. She thought she could smell him, over the other people and the hothouse flowers. She found her handkerchief and a vial of geranium scent and applied some and took deep breaths through the linen, although it smelt far too sweet.

She prayed for the music never to end, but then it did. People applauded; she balled her handkerchief in her palm and did so, too. Her mother poked her; she sat up straight, and prepared to greet her promised bridegroom.

Lord Ferris was exactly as she had first met him: well dressed, well groomed, well spoken. He greeted her and her family with just the right degree of civility and warmth. Her mother was flirting like a fool; Robert was trying to be smooth and adult, and sounding prissy instead. Only Lord Ferris was acting normal: charming and considerate, just this side of conspiratorial where she was concerned, as though he shared her opinion of her family, and wanted her to know that he was being good.

"Are you feeling faint?" he asked Artemisia, all intimate concern. He leaned in so close to her that she could see the pores of his face. "Let me get you a glass of something."

Artemisia felt like some actress in a play, and in a sense she was: anyone in the room could be watching her. Whatever she might feel about her family, she would not disgrace *herself*. But her hand was shaking, she couldn't help it. The only way she was going to get through this was to be Stella—Stella at the country house when Mangrove comes to visit . . . Stella, carrying Fabian's child, but to let Mangrove know could mean both their deaths, and so she dances and laughs and flirts with a surprised young cousin, to the disgust of Tyrian, who she doesn't know is there to guard her . . . and in a feat of bravado, she goes to the races and rides her cousin's horse to victory. . . . Fortunately, no dancing would be expected here, or racing either, and Robert made a poor excuse for loyal Tyrian—but she drew in a deep breath, and another, and her hand stopped shaking.

Lord Ferris returned with lemon water. "Are you enjoying the music?" he asked. For once, her mother's tendency to answer for her was a blessing. But then he proposed to sit down next to her, and her mother's skirts rustled as she shifted aside to let him. Artemisia was looking at the floor, thinking, It won't be so bad if I can't see him. . . .

And then the most marvelous thing in the world happened: a pair of shoes appeared. Small shoes, on a girl's small feet, but cut in a boy's pattern, and above them were fine ankles in heavy stockings that met with breeches just below the knee, and the point of a sword hanging by them, surrounded by green velvet with a gold tassel.

"I came as soon as I could," said Katherine Talbert.

"Oh!" Artemisia gasped in admiration. "Don't you look wonderful!"

"Armed, and with a challenge." Lord Ferris sighed. "Lady Godwin may not thank you for interrupting her musicale."

"I am to convey my regrets to Lady Godwin."

"By all means do so," Lord Ferris said. He was still standing. He looked down at her with his good eye. "She is over by the window, the lady in blue."

"I will," Katherine replied, "when we have finished our business, Lord Ferris. Would you like to step outside?"

The girl with her long hair tied back, dressed in a man's suit and carrying a sword, had not joined the Godwins' guests unnoticed. Artemisia could feel the tension in Ferris's stance as the ring of interested onlookers tightened around them. And she watched him make utterly the wrong choice when he replied to Katherine Talbert, "I have no business with you."

"That isn't true," Katherine said clearly. "I challenged you weeks ago, and as far as I know, you have not withdrawn the offense."

On either side of her, Artemisia's mother clutched her hand, and her brother sat poised to do something. Artemisia admired the way Katherine wasn't looking at her, and she enjoyed the preposterous sight the girl made in the music room. If Artemisia had known that she was grinning, she would have hidden it—but it had been so long since she had smiled with all her heart that Artemisia Fitz-Levi only knew that she was happy.

"Oh. So you did. Some time ago." Ferris chuckled. "I imagined, my dear, that *you* had withdrawn, having taken my advice and thought better of it."

"Well, I haven't. So now I must ask you: will you take the fight yourself, or do you have a champion?"

The crowd had been silent. Now Michael, Lord Godwin, resplendent in blue and gold, stepped forward saying, "Ferris, my house swordsman is of course at your disposal."

"You're very kind, Godwin, but I have a man with me, if someone will but send for him."

Lord Godwin looked at the newcomer, and then he looked again. "You are Tremontaine's niece?"

"I'm afraid so. But he's not the challenger, you're not to think he is. I'm—I'm fighting on another's behalf. Someone Lord Ferris has deeply offended."

"I understand," said Michael Godwin gravely.

Lady Godwin put her hand on her husband's arm. "There's to be no fighting in the music room. Out in the courtyard, I think, and people can watch from the steps."

"What about the garden?"

"Too muddy, still, I think, don't you?"

Artemisia's mother tried to hold her back, but she thrust her way to the very front, where the balustrade overlooked the stone courtyard of the Godwin townhouse. Her heart was throbbing not unpleasantly in her chest, and in her throat. She wished Lydia were by her side, but Lydia was back against a pillar with Armand Lindley's protective arm around her.

Ferris's house swordsman was a handsome man, long-limbed and graceful. He bowed to his patron, to the assembled company, and to his opponent. Katherine bowed once to them all, but Artemisia felt the extra flourish of her sword was all for her.

The man standing behind her said, "Good god. Kitty."

"Talbert," his companion drawled, "don't tell me you know the chit. Who is she?"

"It's my sister," said Gregory Talbert. "Or was. I really don't know."

Artemisia wanted to make sharp retort, but the business was going forward. "To the Death," Lord Godwin asked, "or First Blood?"

Ferris was standing in the yard, next to a hitching ring. "Oh, hardly to the Death; it's not that kind of matter. First Blood will more than suffice."

Artemisia hated him all over again. But Katherine nodded assent and saluted her opponent, and then all her care was for her friend. Katherine Talbert was so small and compact next to Ferris's lanky swordsman. How would she even be able to reach him with her blade?

Clearly her opponent thought the same. He circled her lazily, eyeing her stance with a mocking eye, then started twirling the tip of his blade in her direction like a tease, a provocation. She ignored it, though; she followed his movement, but her blade was still. He made a couple of half-passes at her, and her wrist shifted only slightly.

Katherine's face was taut with concentration; his showed disdain. He stamped and thrust, trying to spook her. Someone laughed. She didn't move.

"Five royals on that girl," a man said, but another muttered, "Not here."

Ferris's swordsman made a beautiful move, a twist and turn, darting like a hawk's flight straight to the heart of the stocky little figure. Her frown deepened. She shifted her weight, shifted her blade, and ran a deep gash up her opponent's arm. She looked extremely surprised.

The swordsman yelped inelegantly. His blade flew from his hand. "Blood!" shouted Lord Godwin, and servants ran forward to help the wounded man.

If it had been Katherine's blood, Artemisia thought, I would have bound her wound with my own handkerchief. As it was, she was balling it in her fist, thinking, *I've won. I've won.*

"Lord Ferris?" Michael Godwin nodded to his guest. "Will you withdraw?"

"From this gathering, most certainly, by your leave," the Crescent answered. "But from the city, no."

"Are you sure?"

"The matter was of no great importance. I will take my seat in Council tomorrow, as always."

"Are you sure, my lord? If it is more convenient for you to be elsewhere at this time, we can make other arrangements."

The Crescent Chancellor drew himself up. "Godwin, do you seek to convene the Court of Honor in your stableyard? I said this matter was not such as would dictate my absence. I will be there tomorrow."

"Forgive me." Michael Godwin bowed slightly, and led his lady back indoors.

Although they would have liked to stay, the other guests followed Lord Godwin's example, leaving Katherine Talbert quite alone in the courtyard, cleaning the blood off her sword.

Gregory Talbert lingered for a moment on the stairs, watching his sister as she busied herself with her terrible weapon. Had she seen him? She did not look up. Should he speak to her? It was against the rules. And what would he say? *Well done, Kitty; we are so proud of you?* He should never have said she was his sister. He hurried away.

Artemisia's mother seized her wrist in an iron grip. She made her go through the motions of thanking their hosts and bidding them good-bye, pleading a headache and far too much excitement for a young girl's first day out after a long illness. But when they got in the carriage, she slapped her daughter hard.

"You slut! You fool!" Lady Fitz-Levi burst into tears. "Oh, who's going to marry you now?"

And indeed, the next day Lord Ferris's offer was quietly withdrawn, and the contract dissolved.

chapter III

I RETURNED TO TREMONTAINE HOUSE TO FIND MY UNCLE THE Mad Duke sitting in the library, shredding things. There was a huge pile of ripped-up pages in front of him, and he was fiercely attacking more with a paper knife.

He looked up when I came in. "Old books," he said, "worm-eaten. Theo said it needed doing; I decided to help." The brandy decanter beside him was nearly empty. "How did it go?"

"Well," I told him. I tried to be nonchalant, but it was hard. All the energy from the fight was still with me, converted by my triumph to cheerful bounciness. "Better than I expected. He didn't take me seriously, so he didn't have a chance. It was just like St—just like he taught me: when someone tries a flashy move, look for what they're covering up and take it as an invitation. I got First Blood in about five moves."

"Well, don't get too smug. The next one might take you seriously, and then where will you be?" I lunged at a wall. "Don't you dare hurt my books."

"I'm hungry."

"Didn't they have food, the Godwin musicale?"

"I didn't ask. Nobody offered. I left. Why don't *you* ever have a musicale?"

"I did, once. She bit me."

I laughed.

"And Lord Ferris?"

"He left. I think the wedding is off."

"Good work," he said, and drained the decanter. "Marcus!" My friend appeared. "Get this champion a sandwich."

I started to follow Marcus down to the kitchens, but he turned to me and said, "Don't come down; I'll bring you something. Do you want me to tell Betty you're back? She can draw you a bath."

"Not now," I said, "she'll only fuss. Let's go out to the gardens. It's a lovely day. I want to tell you all about my fight."

"I don't want to hear all about your fight. You hit someone with your sword, and he didn't hit you, that's all I need to know. Fish pond?"

"Meet me there."

Carp flitted amongst the weeds. I took a big bite of the bread and cheese he'd brought. "I like it up here," I said. "The Hill is much nicer than Riverside." Marcus's cold was better, but he still wasn't eating much. He rolled bits of my bread into pellets to chuck at the carp. "The air is healthier, too." I took off my stocking so I could stick one foot in the fish pond. "Why don't you want to hear about my fight?"

"I just don't, that's all. In case you hadn't noticed, I'm not really interested in swordplay."

"I am. Do you think I'm boring, then?"

"Hardly." Marcus rolled onto his stomach so I couldn't see his face.

I flicked my foot at the carp to keep them from the bread. I wondered if I could move without triggering their perfect flight. A swordsman, I thought, should be as quick to sense as a fish. "Who do you think is more interesting, the duke or me?"

"Now that," he drawled languidly, "is just the sort of question *he* would ask."

I nearly pushed him into the fish pond. "And that," I said, "is just the sort of tone of voice he uses when he's trying to get out of answering something."

"Oh re-eally? And what do you suppose I might possibly be avoiding?"

He was doing it on purpose, but I went after him anyway. With one wet foot I flipped him over like a fish on a grill, and pinned his shoulders with my knees. "You tell me," I said. "I don't know what's got into you, but if you think acting like my uncle is going to sweeten me up, you're insane."

"You're the one who's like him, not me."

I gaped at him. "How can you say that?"

"Isn't it obvious?"

I searched his face to see if he was teasing. I didn't know how to read what I saw there. "You're being ridiculous, Marcus."

He pushed against my knees. "You're hurting me."

"I don't care. You're insulting me."

"See what I mean? You don't care about anyone else. You don't even notice what they're feeling, ever. You just care about getting what you want, and how you're feeling. How much more like him do you want to be?"

"You rotten little—" I grabbed a fistful of earth and rubbed it on his face. "You take that back."

Marcus spat dirt out of his mouth. "You're not Tremontaine," he said; "make me." All that training, and I was so mad I just slapped him, hard, across the face.

With a sharp twist he was out from under me, eyes blazing. "You never, ever strike me again, do you hear me?"

"What do you want, then, a sword in the gut?"

He punched me. In the stomach. I doubled over, retching and wheezing in the new grass.

When I looked up, Marcus was sitting in a tree, well out of arm's reach, looking down at me and swinging his legs. "You all right?"

I coughed and wiped my eyes. "You fight like guttertrash."

"There's a reason for that. You fight like a girl."

"There's a reason for that, too."

Marcus stopped swinging his legs. "Peace. Can I come down?"

I looked up at him, successfully treed. My stomach still hurt, and there was a wretched taste in my mouth. "No," I said meanly, lifting my chin. "I don't think so. Not just yet."

"You look like him."

"You act like him," I snapped. "You've got a nerve telling me I do, when you're the one who says mean things like that. I never do; I'm always careful. I don't know what's gotten into you. You can be a total pig, Marcus, and you have been off and on for weeks, now. If I've done something to deserve it, I'll say I'm sorry—but I won't apologize if you won't tell me what it is."

"Don't be silly," he drawled affectedly. "What could you possibly have done? It is I who am to blame, I who annoyed you so much you quite rightly slapped me like a kitchenmaid, and I who consequently punched you most foully in the gut. You should report me to the duke. I should be punished, sacked, turned out of my place—"

"Stop being stupid." Why was he refusing to be serious, all of a sudden? "He doesn't care. You're more like family to him than I am—" I caught my breath. Why hadn't I seen it before? "You're his son, aren't you?"

Marcus hooted. "Oh, not you, too! No, of course I'm not his son.

He bought me off the street, fair and square. You don't pay money for your own flesh and blood, do you? Oh, wait a minute." Marcus paused to consider. "Maybe he does. He bought you, after all." He meant it to hurt, and it did. It felt like I was being stabbed. "You think I don't know all about it? I was there for the meetings with the lawyers. I was there when he came up with the idea for your contract," he taunted mercilessly. "I'm always there, so I hear everything. I heard him dictate all those letters to your mother. I heard how much she needed the money . . ." I picked up a smallish rock, and clutched it hard. "I probably knew the whole deal way before anyone told you about it. The whole household knew; Arthur Ghent was the one who wrote those letters, after all. We all knew about you before you ever came here."

I clenched the rock's edges sharp in my hand, but didn't throw it. "He didn't buy me," I said. "It's not like that."

"Why not? You think because you're his blood he cares more about you? He paid good money for us both, but at least I do useful work around here. You're just a toy to him."

"You're not my friend." The pain was real; I felt it in my throat, and in my chest, so I could barely get the words out. "I thought you were, but I was wrong." I threw the rock in the fish pond. "I don't know what you are, Marcus." I started up the long path back to the house.

"No, wait!" He was out of the tree so fast his jacket tore. "Oh, lord . . . Kit, wait—" He caught up with me, started to touch my shoulder and pulled away as though it burned his hand. I kept on walking. "Will you at least turn around and look at me?"

I ignored him.

"Katie, please listen. I have a temper. It's bad, it's really bad, and I never lose it, but when I do, I just say things. I say things I don't mean—I don't even know what I'm doing, it just comes out, none of it's true—oh, god, Kit, I wish I could cut my tongue out, I really do—please don't walk away from me. Please!"

There was something in his voice—not just pleading, but panic, as though if I didn't turn around he wasn't going to be able to breathe much longer. I stopped walking and turned around and looked at him. He was pulling at his own fingers as if he wanted to tear them off, babbling apologies. "I didn't mean any of it, it was just lies, I swear. I'm all wrong, I know I am. I'm barely a civilized human being. I've read a lot of books, I know a lot of words, but in the end I'm nothing, nothing—I'm nothing but a minnow-a-toss street punk with good clothes and fancy manners."

His desperation cut the knot of shocked rage in me, and I started to sob.

"Don't cry, Katie, please don't cry because of me."

I knuckled tears out of my eyes. "How could you say those things to me?"

"I didn't mean them, please don't hate me—"

"I thought you understood," I whimpered miserably. "I thought we were together here. . . ."

"We are, we are. Look, don't we watch each other's backs? And don't we have secrets together?"

"It doesn't mean anything if you can't be good to me." I sniffled. "How can I trust you?"

"And I let you have your secrets, too, don't I? I'm a good friend, I don't pry. Like, I know you set up that duel without me, and I know you snuck back to Perry's without me, and I didn't say anything because I knew you didn't want me to—"

"Yes, but—"

"And what about Highcombe? Do I ever ask you about whoever it is at Highcombe you still won't tell me about, even though you know I'm dying to and you just love to torment me with it . . ."

Something in his voice made me laugh. He was doing it on purpose; the look on his face was silly and hopeful. "I'll tell you about it someday."

"It's someone you miss. You both do. Is it someone you love more than me?"

"Marcus—are you jealous?"

"You're all I have," he said softly; "you and him." Slowly he unfolded a pristine handkerchief. He reached with it, very carefully, towards the tears on my face, and I stood quite still and let him wipe them away, tender and methodical.

I said, "You know I love you best."

"You do?"

"Better than any of them."

He handed me the white linen. "Blow your nose."

"Especially the duke. You love him, too, don't you? I don't know how you stand him all the time."

"He's interesting."

"So's a bat, or a thunderstorm. I wouldn't choose to live with one."

"He's clever, and he can be kind if he likes you. When he remembers."

I sniffed. "He's not reliable."

Marcus looked at me with steady brown eyes. "I am reliable."

I felt it then, that curious warmth below. It had something to do with wanting to touch his curving mouth and knowing that he wanted me to. He was watching me very carefully. If anything was going to happen, I would have to do it first. I felt the edges of his lips with my fingers, and his breath on them. He was standing very still, his hands at his sides. What would have happened then is hard to say, because it didn't; instead we heard someone running down the path towards us, and it was Betty's voice, calling, "Lady Katherine!"

We broke apart, and just in time, for she took one look at me and started to carry on. "Look at the state you're in! All over mud, and no time to clean your hair; I'll just have to put it up, that's all. And you the duke's own champion, too, I hear, but when we're going to celebrate I do not know, for such a to-do with her coming here I cannot possibly get you all cleaned up in time. Such a fine lady, what will she think of the care that I've been giving you? But if you will go fighting and playing in the garden—"

"Who is it?" I asked. "Who's here?"

"It's your mother."

I felt the whole world shift and drop out from under me.

"My mother?"

What was she doing here? Why had no one told me?

"Don't worry about your hands, we'll just put some cream on them . . ."

But it wasn't my hands I was worried about. "Marcus, I can't!" I gasped. "I can't see her now. I am—I look—I don't have any dresses! Oh, tell her to go away, tell her I'll write to her, I can't, I can't—"

"Katie, stop." He took my clenched hands in his. "Don't be a fool. You can do this. Just go wash up, and put on a clean shirt, and go welcome your mother to Tremontaine House. I'll tell her you're coming."

I held on to his arm. "No! No, I don't want her to see you—"

"She won't." He smiled a funny little smile, and let me watch him transform into a sedate, well-trained servant, perfectly composed. "There, see? Nobody here."

"Don't tell her . . ." I whispered.

He smiled into my eyes. "Don't worry, Lady Katherine. I'm very good at not telling people things. And I'm very reliable."

He bowed, and kissed my hand. He didn't do it very well, but it was adorable. I squared my shoulders, and went off to get cleaned up.

⁓

I HAD FORGOTTEN HOW BEAUTIFUL SHE WAS, AND HOW MUCH SHE looked like the duke. The skin at her temples was thin, and her hair was plainly dressed. She sat in a velvet chair by the window in the mirrored drawing room, looking out over the garden and the river beyond it. I entered very quietly, so that I could look at her first. It was strange how well she fit the room; she didn't look countrified at all, just plain and elegant. She had a book on her lap, but she wasn't reading it; she was turning the pages while staring out the window.

"Hello, Mother," I said.

I saw the shock on her face.

"It's true," she said. "Oh, my god, Katherine, what's he done to you?" She didn't wait for an answer. I felt my swordsman's poise deserting me; suddenly I didn't know what to do with my hands, and I was horribly aware of my legs. "I came as soon as I could. Gregory told me you were just in some kind of fight, and I meant to wait a day, but I came rushing up yesterday because it's been six months, my darling, six long months and I could not wait a moment longer. I wanted to surprise you—"

"I'm surprised," I said. "Truly."

She rushed to me, and took my face in her hands. "Oh, my darling, are you all right?"

I tried not to let her feel me stiffen and draw back. "Of course I'm all right, Mother. It was a short fight. I won."

"Oh, Katherine." Her voice was full of sorrow. "My sweet, brave, good darling. I can only imagine what you have been through. . . ."

I squirmed. "It's all right, Mother, really."

"You don't have to be brave any longer," she said softly. "You've done it, my darling; you've saved us."

I looked down and felt myself flush with pleasure. This was more like it. When she held out her arms this time, I went to her and let her embrace me, and breathed in the scent of lavender from our gardens at home. She guided me back to her chair and I nestled down in the corner of her skirt, my special spot where I always felt safe. "Your hair's gotten thicker," she said, stroking it.

"My maid washes it with special stuff."

"You've got your own maid? Oh, Kitty!"

"And a big room over the river, and a velvet cloak with gold tassels, and—oh, Mother! Are you staying with Gregory? I want you to see my room. You can stay with me, if you like; the bed is huge."

"Now, now, Kitty, we'll talk about all that later. We've got more important things to talk about right now."

"What things?"

She laughed, and patted my back like a puppy's: "Just run upstairs and tell your maid to put you into one of your nice dresses, and you can order us some refreshment, if you like."

"I—shall I order us something now?"

"What's the matter, darling?"

"Nothing, I just—I don't feel like changing right now, that's all."

"I just thought you'd like to show me one of your new dresses."

"Maybe later." I wanted to put the moment off as long as possible, when she would find out what my life in the duke's house was really like. She would not be happy, I knew that. I so wanted her to be happy, now. "Tell me all about you, first. Is your tooth all better? How are the boys? Has Annie married her sailor yet? Did the Oldest Oak survive another winter? What did Seb sow in the south reach this year?"

"You'll see, won't you?" she said mischievously.

"Will I?"

"Well, of course you will, my pet. Not right away, of course: I thought I'd stay in town and do a little shopping—you don't want to be seen with your silly old mother looking like some country frump, do you? And I can still have my own 'Season,' even if it's a little late!" She laughed. "You won't mind that, will you my darling, if we stay a few weeks?"

"Of course not, Mother," I said automatically.

She squeezed my shoulder. "I knew you'd understand, Katherine, you always do. After all, there's no hurry, is there?"

"I don't think so. I mean, if Sebastian's all right at home without you—and you haven't seen Gregory in ages—is he coming to visit me, too?"

"I don't think so, darling; he and your uncle don't really see eye to eye."

"Oh." That didn't surprise me.

"Anyway, it doesn't matter—Greg will put up with me awhile longer, and then, when the town empties out for the summer, we can all go home together."

There was a clutch in my stomach. "Home?"

"Yes, my love."

"But my uncle—the contract—don't I have to stay?"

She flicked her hands in the air, very like the duke. "He's not as clever as he thinks he is, for all his money. I've got new lawyers, much better ones than before. They say there's absolutely nothing to keep you here. We promised him six months, and he's had them."

I had never seen the contract, but I had watched my mother go through lawyers like kindling before, trying to get out of other unwise bargains she had made. I wondered what the truth was this time. I wondered why it had never occurred to me until now simply to ask

Arthur Ghent to take it out and read it with me, so I could understand it myself.

"Just think—you'll see all the dear little ducklings, and the lambs. You always love to give them names and help Fergus with them."

"Of course, Mama." I'd forgotten all about the lambs—the lambs and the linen and the liniments and all that. It seemed like a hundred years ago, or something I'd read in a book. Did I like lambs? I did, of course I did. Lambs were sweet. Then why was my heart pounding as if I were in a fight? I took a deep breath. "Just not quite yet, as you say. You want to see the city, first."

"That's my darling." She hugged me. I had dreamed of her arms, but now I was finding them a little too tight. "I know I can always depend on you." She smiled tenderly at me. "You have no idea how lovely it will all be, now that we've got our money back again. All the funds that were tied up while he picked quarrels about them, returned to me with interest; it's quite a lot, much more than I thought it would be, and I mean to spend it now. I'm going to have a carriage, and I've ordered new hangings for the bedrooms, and all sorts of lovely fabrics and china—"

She was always forgetting the practical things. "What about the roof?"

"Oh, a new roof, of course, and books for poor Sebastian, and more kitchenmaids, so Cook has agreed to stay on after all— It will be lovely, much nicer than before, you'll see! I'd no idea there was so much there. All thanks to you, of course, my brave heroic daughter, who walked right into the ogre's den without a thought for herself, and captured his treasure for us." She hugged me. "I mean to get you the best of everything: pretty clothes, and fine furnishings, and an extra sewing maid so you don't ever have to do that nasty mending again— You can even have a real Season someday, if you want one, with balls and gowns and flowers and everything."

I thought of the Godwins' musicale, the girls in their bright dresses, and me with my sword and breeches standing before Artemisia to challenge Lord Ferris. "Oh, that's all right," I said. "I don't think I'll bother with that after all."

"But don't you want to be like all the other girls here?" she asked anxiously.

"Not really."

"Oh, Katherine." She breathed a sigh of admiration—or maybe it was just relief. "I couldn't do without you."

I took the end of her hair ribbon and twisted it gently, teasing her, but anxious for the answer. "But you've managed a *little* without me, haven't you? Just a little bit, on your own, for six months?"

"Just a *little*. Of course Sebastian has been a great help with the house, once he stopped moping. I think he wished the Mad Duke had sent for *him* instead of you—the duke is a patron of the University, and you know how Seb loves his books."

"Maybe he can come to classes, when we've got everything settled."

The little frown appeared between my mother's brows. "Oh, no. No one else understands farming the way Seb does. I wouldn't know what to plant, or how to tell if the tenants were cheating us."

Sebastian was by far my favorite brother. I wondered if the duke would like him. Perhaps he would be willing to help him find a farm manager and send him to University. "I'm longing to see Seb again. Maybe he can come back with me in the fall, for a visit."

My mother's frown increased. "But why would you want to come back so soon?"

"Back here?" I looked at her blankly. "I—well, I've got things to do here."

"What things, Katherine?"

"Well—friends and things. And my lessons, of course. And, well—things."

"Katherine Samantha," she sighed. "You have not been listening to what I've been telling you. You're coming home with me, so we can put this all behind you."

"What? No. I mean, that's not possible."

"My poor heroic darling. Of course it looks that way to you, locked up here with this madman for so long, and no one to turn to for good counsel. But listen to me." My mother leaned forward. "You can still have a normal life. Nobody blames you. They know my brother is a lunatic; Gregory says no one decent will even visit him anymore, or have him in their homes. It's not your fault if he's sent you out in public like this—" she indicated my jacket and breeches "—And now this awful fight at Lord Godwin's . . ." At least Greg hadn't told her about the Rogues' Ball—maybe he didn't know himself. "Well, they'll forget in time, if we let them. The best thing to do," she explained with elaborate patience, "is to get you settled back home, do you see? Just long enough that people can forget all about it. A year or so should be enough."

"And then?"

"And then . . . well," she said archly, "if you decide someday that you can do without me—for I surely will never be able to do without you—well then, perhaps we can find a nice man for you to marry, and you can have—"

I couldn't say it. Not to her face, not with my heart pounding and my breath catching in my chest. I stood up, crossed the room so I stood under the portrait of the lady in grey, and clutched the marble behind me.

"I can't," I said. "I can't do any of that. I'm sorry, Mother. It's too late."

"But that's just what I'm saying! It isn't too late. We can still save you—"

"I don't need to be saved."

My mother twisted the ends of her hair. I'd seen her do it a hundred times. It used to look sweet, but now it just looked silly to me. "Katherine. Stop it. You're not being very adult. There's a whole world out there you know nothing about. Gregory has been out in Society, and he understands these things far better than you. He agrees with me that the best thing to do is to get you out of this madhouse as quickly as possible. I've got it all worked out. You'll have a quiet summer at home, and then you can start over, as if it had never been."

"But it has b—" I began, but stopped myself. You didn't tell my mother things like that.

"You can't stay in your uncle's house playing at swordfights forever, all dressed up like some booth at a fair." You couldn't argue with her when she got like this. If only she would be quiet and let me think. But her voice rattled on, more and more shrill. "You may be having fun now, but my brother is utterly mad. When he gets tired of you, you'll be out on the street, and then you'll come running home but the damage will have been done. And then what will you do? Answer me that." What kind of damage did she think there was that hadn't been done already? I remembered Marcus saying, "He bought you, too." If my uncle had bought me, my mother had sold me to him. "We must think of your future, Katherine. You know I only want what's best for you."

"You should have thought of that before you sent me here." The words were out of my mouth before I could stop them.

I opened my mouth to apologize, to take them back before I could do any more harm. But my mother was quite still. She stood looking at me as if she were looking at a stranger, at someone she did not love or even like at all.

"You'll do as I say," she told me. "Go get your things. We're leaving."

"No, Mother, please. If you could just—"

"Katherine," she said, her voice musical with suppressed rage. "Don't make a scene." She picked up a silk pillow, thick with embroidery of exotic birds with long tail feathers, and began picking at the threads with her nails. "This nonsense has to stop. We must think of your future."

"I can't," I said miserably, watching the bright threads of silk flying out of her hands, clinging to her skirt, falling to the floor. "I would if I could, honestly, Mother, but I just can't do it now."

Her fingers dug into the cloth of the cushion. "It isn't like you to be so selfish. Do you want to bring disgrace on our entire family? What am I going to do without you? I can't manage alone!"

There was a noise as the door opened. The Duke Tremontaine stood in the doorway, dressed to go out, and only slightly more sober than when I'd seen him last. He looked at me, and looked at his sister, and blinked.

"Hello, Janine," he said. "Welcome to Tremontaine House."

My mother looked her brother in the eyes. He was taller than she was, but her gaze was fierce. "My daughter," she said to him. "You have ruined my daughter."

My uncle looked startled. "Ruined her? I never touched her."

"You didn't have to. Look what you've done to her!"

"She seems all right to me. Are you all right, Katherine?" I pressed my back against the wall, as if I could melt right into it, and didn't answer. I knew what was coming, even if he didn't. He took a step toward my mother. "There's nothing wrong with your daughter. My cushion, on the other hand, you are certainly ruining."

"What do you care?" she said, tearing it further. "You've got plenty more. You've got everything in the world here, haven't you? Look at this house! Look at your suit, for that matter—I can't imagine what that costs."

"Neither can I; that's why they send me the bill."

"Are you trying to make me laugh? You have everything, everything, everything—money, jewels, land, heaven knows what, and it isn't enough for you—you have everything you want and more—and now you try to take my child from me."

I wondered if it was worth darting in and trying to clear things from her path. But that would only make it worse. And she was right; he could buy plenty more.

"That's ridiculous," the duke said weakly.

"Is it?" my mother hissed. "Is that what it is?"

"Janine, stop carrying on like some sort of mad stage witch." She picked up an etched glass bud vase, clutching it in her hand like a dagger. "Janine, listen to me and be reasonable and put that down."

"Why should I be reasonable? Were you reasonable? You didn't think much about being reasonable when you ran away and ruined our chances with Grandmama and left us thinking you were dead, did you? You left me all alone to deal with Mother and you know what she was like—"

"I left you? *I* left you?" Something changed in him, like a fighter who thinks he's playing in a practice bout and suddenly realizes the swords are not tipped. His face was very white, and his hands were no longer elegant. He opened them and closed them on nothing. "You're the one who left, Janine. I was there waiting for you. Don't you remember? You said you would run away before you'd marry that old fool. And I said, Right, then, we'll do it. I said, No one is going to take my sister away like that. I said, Meet me in the orchard—in the *orchard*, Janine, *not in the goddamned chapel!*"

I had never heard him roar like that before. She was staring at him, mesmerized, as white as he was and whiter, down to her lips, as though his story were draining all the blood from her. He stepped toward her, and she didn't move. "What on earth was I doing freezing in the orchard all night with a bag of food and a pair of cloaks, while you were being laced into your wedding dress?"

My mother shook her head, mute. I had my hands pressed to my mouth, listening, listening. The trouble was, I could see it. I could see it all perfectly clearly.

"I missed the main event," he said dryly, a bit more like himself. "I got in trouble for that, for missing my sister's wedding. Mother locked me in the—" for a moment he lost the word, lost his smooth and cruel habit of speech—then he gasped and regained it— "She had them lock me in the storage cell, you remember? Well, of course you do, you'd been there, too, not long before. I wasn't whipped; I was just locked in, to teach me manners. It was very cramped in there, I was getting big for it. But it didn't matter. Nothing did, because you weren't coming back."

She held out a hand to him. "I didn't know. I thought you were angry with me, that's why you weren't there. I wanted to come. But I was so afraid of them."

"I would have helped you!"

"You couldn't." When she said that, he actually flinched as if he had been struck. "You couldn't help me. You couldn't do anything. You couldn't stop them marrying me off any more than you could stop them locking you up, Davey. I knew that then."

She tried to touch him, but he turned away. "It was a long time ago," she said. "But I did the right thing."

"You did what they told you to do. And what did it gain you?"

"I had a husband," she said. "I have my children. I did my duty."

"You should have fought," he growled. "You should have stood and fought."

Oh, stop, I wanted to tell him. *Mother never fights, not the way you mean. Stop before something happens.* But I was afraid to come between them.

"You're being unfair. Our parents meant well. They wanted the best for us."

He looked at her in real surprise. "No, they didn't. We were raised by servants. Don't you remember? All Father cared about was his maps. Mother cared about chapel and about getting back at her own mother, the dread Duchess Tremontaine, who was, let me tell you, a real piece of work."

"I wouldn't know. I never met her. She had no interest in me, Mother said."

"Mother didn't wait to find out, did she? She was in too much of a hurry to marry you off to the highest-bidding country bumpkin. I would have brought you to the city with me—"

"No, Davey. She did try. When Charles first offered for me, Mother wrote to the duchess, to ask if she would bring me out properly and make a better match. But the duchess wrote back to say, no, she wasn't interested. So Mother accepted Charles's suit."

My uncle stared at her. "To *spite* her? She married you off to that idiot just to spite her mother?"

"Charles wasn't an idiot. He was a prosperous landowner, from a fine old family. I was very lucky, really. So were Father and Mother, because I lived nearby so I could look after them—"

"Stop it!" he raged. "Stop *lying*! How can you be saying all these things? You, you who were—oh, god. You, Janine. You were so pure of heart. You saved my life, you held me in your arms and told me stories when things were really bad—you made up whole countries for us to hide in, horses for us to ride there . . . don't you remember Storm Cloud and Flame of the Sea?"

My mother clutched the folds of her skirt, saying nothing. He turned his back to her, poured himself a brandy. "You were strong and true. I wanted to be like you." He knocked back the drink. "I know you fought them. You've forgotten, that's all. I wasn't there. I was in the orchard. But you tried, I know. I remember, if you don't. And afterwards—everything I did, I did to avenge what they did to you. Everything."

"Including trying to ruin me and my family?"

He turned slowly to look at her, his head low. "You could have come to me. You could have written, or you could have come."

She turned to him with that same strange gesture he had made before, hands outstretched, opening and closing on nothing. "You know why I couldn't come."

"I know now," he said harshly. "It's because you've forgotten everything. You've turned it all into comfortable lies. You're just like the rest of them now. Go away. I don't want you in my house."

"No!" I heard my own voice shatter the awful stillness of the room. But I wasn't fast enough this time. I should have been. Had I forgotten? I should have seen her looking back at the glass bud vase. I should have been by her side, I should have taken it out of her hand before she smashed it against the table and held a shard so tightly the blood started seeping between her fingers.

"Oh!" I heard the duke draw in his breath, not shocked, but as if he'd suddenly remembered something.

She dropped the glass to the carpet, showed him her open hand, bleeding. "This is truth," she said. "I know that this is truth, don't you?"

"Oh, yes," he said. "I used to do that, too." He took her palm and examined it. "It's all right." She let him wrap his large white handkerchief lightly around her hand to catch the blood. "But I've got something better, now. Here, I'll show you. Want to see?" She stared at him, spellbound. He crossed the room to a locked cabinet and took out the key.

I knew what he kept in there. "You can't give my mother that!"

"Watch me," he said calmly, taking out the little vials of precious stuff. "Or better yet, don't."

I shouted, "You put that down!"

"Don't speak to your uncle like that," my mother said. "He'll think you weren't brought up properly."

"Run along, Katherine," my uncle said. "Your mother and I have a lot to talk about."

I took the stairs to my room two at a time, and slammed the door and locked it behind me. Maybe Marcus could stop him, but he'd never stopped the duke before, and I didn't want him to see my mother like this. I didn't want to ask Marcus for anything, either, not after what had nearly happened in the garden between us. I got into bed and snapped the curtains on their rings closed around me, and pulled the covers over my head.

I had wanted to know family secrets. Well, now I knew them. My uncle didn't hate my mother after all. And he had always been angry at everyone, not just us. He didn't know that she still told wonderful stories, and snuck off to the orchard to eat apples when she should be counting spoons. He didn't know that my father and mother had planned a garden together, and stayed up all night when I was sick. Maybe she was telling him now. If she was even there. If they could even talk.

The night was coming on. I unwrapped myself, and lay stiffly staring up at the dusky canopy above me.

Today I had wounded a man, and hit my best friend and almost kissed him. I had seen my mother for the first time in half a year and defied her. Three fights in one day, and only one I knew that I had won for certain, the one with rules.

Just that morning, I had been polishing my sword for the duel. I had to remember that whatever else happened, today I had avenged the honor of my friend Artemisia. I had challenged a real swordsman, who was neither stupid nor drunk, and I had bested him. Maybe my family didn't want to hear about my fight, but half the nobility of the city had witnessed it. People would talk about me, and know my name. I had spoken it loudly and clearly, for all to hear. Maybe I would become fashionable; maybe people would invite me to dinner and demand to hear the details. In my head, I played over again all the moves of the duel. It was harder than I thought to remember each one in order, but I wanted to get it right, for when someone finally asked me.

I T WAS DARK WHEN I WOKE UP. BETTY HAD UNLOCKED MY DOOR. I heard the clatter as she warmed milk for me at the hearth.

"Where's the duke?" I asked, and she said, "Out."

"Where is my mother?"

"Gone with him, gone . . . Never you mind all that, my hero, it doesn't matter. You be easy, now."

She poured whiskey into my milk, and stirred, and gave it to me and I drank it. She poured cans of warm water into my tub, and bathed me, and washed and dried and plaited my hair, and crooned, "My champion, my great sword, you are, you are . . ." I smelt the whiskey on her breath, and I didn't care. I just sat in the tub and cried, and let her dry me off and put me back to bed.

I WOKE UP EARLY THE NEXT MORNING. THE HOUSEHOLD WAS barely stirring. The duke would not be up for hours yet. Marcus might be awake, but I wasn't ready to face him. I had to see my uncle, first.

I put on some loose clothes and went to the wet-rabbit room and practiced furiously for a long time. When I heard the commotion that meant the duke was awake and asking for things, I went to change out of my practice clothes, because it would be another hour before he was fit to be spoken to.

At noon I found the Duke Tremontaine eating breakfast in the morning room.

"Where's my mother?" I demanded.

He looked quizzically at me. "Are you going to accuse me of ruining her? Please don't. And don't speak to me in that tone; I'll think you weren't brought up properly."

I didn't laugh. "Where is she?"

"How should I know? She cried a lot. We talked. We devoured eight whole tablets of raw chocolate and the rest of the brandy. We talked until midnight, when it was time for me to be at Blackwoods'. She lost money at cards. She plays very badly, your mother."

I ground my teeth. "Has she gone back home?"

"To your brother's. The respectable one on Lower Patrick Street. I don't know where she's going next; I suspect she doesn't, either. You can write her and ask," he said. "You're free to correspond with any-one you like, now, you know. As she reminded me more than once. The woman has no head for drink, none at all. If I understood her, she will be writing you frequently. I'm sure you'll hear all about it."

He was in that kind of mood.

"And get your things together. We're going back to Riverside until this place is truly habitable."

"I'm staying," I said.

"Here? On the Hill? By yourself?"

"I mean, I'm staying with you."

"Well, of course you are. Pass the jam."

I wanted to throw the toast in his face. "What about me? Were you so busy debauching my mother you lost track of why she came here in the first place? Did you get her drunk just so you wouldn't have to talk about my—my *future?*"

"Your future is entirely up to you." The jam was perfectly within his reach when he bothered to lean up and over for it.

"Well, who is going to provide for me?"

"Please don't shout."

"I'm not shouting. My mother thinks you're going to toss me back out when you're sick of me, you know. She thinks you've made me into an unmarriageable freak." He didn't interrupt; he just kept crunching on his toast. I'd had enough. "Do you even think of me as your kin at all, or am I just some—some minnow-a-toss street kid to you, with good clothes and a sword?"

It got his attention—but not the way I wanted. He put down his toast half-eaten, and gazed at me icily. "Where did you hear that phrase, pray?"

It's what Marcus had called himself yesterday, but I was certainly not going to tell him that. "I dunno."

"Do you know what it means?" he asked.

Cowed, I answered, like a schoolgirl with a lesson: "A minnow's what they call a brass coin in Riverside. A toss—some kind of ball game, I guess."

"Keep guessing," he said dryly. "And don't let me hear you use that phrase again."

I glowered at him. "You're not my mother."

"She doesn't know what it means either. But if you say it around someone who does, they will either slap your face or laugh at you. There—you are warned." He slathered more jam on his half a piece of cold toast. "I suppose, if Janine is going to be unreasonable, that I'm going to have to offer you something or you'll pester me to death. A salary, or a gift of land, or something. You figure it out; it will be good for you, teach you the value of money and how things work. Come to me when you have some idea, and we'll negotiate. You'll learn a lot."

"I'll ask a lot," I said, and he said, "Fine."

"And by the way," I added, "I think I know all your names now."

"What?" he asked, through a mouthful of toast.

"The first day I came here—you don't even remember, do you?"

"Of course I remember the first day you came. Ring for more toast. Have you eaten? Well, in that case, have you seen Marcus yet today? He seemed a little odd."

I had not seen Marcus; I'd wanted to confront my uncle before anything else happened. Now I went upstairs to find him and bring him up to date.

Marcus was extremely odd. He was in his room packing for River-side already. He folded each of his own shirts very carefully, lining up all the seams like folds on a map.

"Your mother's pretty," he said, folding.

"What did she say to you?"

"Nothing. I make a very convincing servant."

"Well . . . well, thank you." It was utterly maddening, the way he fussed over that shirt and wouldn't look at me. "Marcus," I asked, "are you still angry with me?"

"No."

"Then tell me what's wrong or I'm going to rip that shirt right out of your hands!"

He put it down and looked straight at me.

"Are you leaving?" he said. His face was very white—I could see some stubble against his skin. I didn't know he shaved.

"No. She wanted me to, but I said not."

"Oh." He picked up the shirt, and put it down again. "Oh."

"Why are you doing that? I bet Fleming would pack for you, if you asked him."

"I don't like other people touching my things."

"How about me?" I offered. "I bet we could get it done in no time, if you let me help."

Marcus smiled slowly. "Katie. You're up to something."

"I was just thinking . . ." And I was. I needed my friend now; I needed to put yesterday behind us, and take us back to where we were together, bonded in mischief and common cause. "The duke's still in his dressing gown, eating toast," I said. "He'll be hours, yet. If we hurry, we can still nip down the Hill to Teresa Grey's together before we leave for Riverside. That is, if you're still interested in what she might be up to."

"Hand me those brushes," Marcus said.

We left the duke being shaved by his valet and changing his mind about his clothes again, and went off down the hill to the house of Lucius Perry's mysterious lady, together.

L<small>UCIUS</small> P<small>ERRY'S</small> <small>LOVER APPEARED TO HAVE GONE MAD.</small> W<small>E</small> stared, fascinated, from the bushes, as Teresa Grey paced up and down the length of her studio, waving her hands in the air and shouting. We couldn't hear what she was saying, but it was clearly pretty awful. She lunged into space, twisted, fell down, and then jumped up again and dashed to the table where she dipped a pen in ink and started scribbling furiously.

Marcus poked me with his elbow and grinned. Her hair was a mess, and there was an inkblot on her nose where she'd rubbed it without thinking.

"Love letter?" I mouthed, but he shook his head: "Watch."

I watched. She got up and did it all over again, and then went back to her pen, and then she rose and turned her back to us and shouted something.

She must have been calling for Lucius Perry, because he came in then, looking fresh as a daisy and very glad to be summoned. She moved him into place, and did the same movements again, only this time he was talking and gesturing back at her so she didn't look so crazy, and then it all started making sense. They were acting out a scene together, a fight of some kind: first an argument, and then a struggle that ended with Teresa Grey falling to the floor. Lucius helped her up, and then he hung over her shoulder while she wrote. He pointed at the paper, and she changed something and laughed.

Our Lucius looked very young; he wasn't trying to be anything, he was just enjoying himself.

Then she shook sand onto the wet ink, and blew it off and lifted up her page and read. She pitched her voice loud enough that we could hear just the sound of it, but not any of the words. In the bushes, we writhed quietly in frustration—if only we could get close enough to the window to hear! Seeing them through the long double windows, with curtains on either side . . . it was like being at the theatre with wax stuffed in our ears.

"A novel?" Marcus murmured. "One of those things girls like to read?"

Teresa Grey bowed, and Lucius Perry applauded. But I already knew. "It's a play," I said. "She writes plays."

Lucius put his arms around her, and the paper dropped to the ground. This time, she returned his embrace eagerly, warmly. Oh, the way he held her, the way he touched her hair! The way she smiled and stretched out her throat for his kiss. . . . I dug my nails into my palms. The way her fingers clenched in the small of his back, the way he moved to be closer to her.

I snuck a look at Marcus. Did he see what I saw? A way for two people to be together, to touch each other and be happy and be friends without fear? What if he laughed at them, or was disgusted? What if he saw something entirely different?

He was watching them with enormous concentration, as if he were trying to figure something out for the first time: a math problem, maybe, or a series of moves in shesh, and not at all sure he'd got it right.

"If it's a play," he said, "I hope it has a happy ending."

I'd moved a little closer to him without realizing it, but now I moved away. "Come on," I said, "we'd better not be late."

We didn't even bother to be quiet going over the wall; they weren't going to hear us.

A RTEMISIA FITZ-LEVI WAS NOW FREE TO MARRY ANYONE WHO would have her. She was not, however, free to leave the house.

She had taken up fancywork. It gave her something to do with her hands, so that she didn't tear her mother's eyes out, or better yet, her tongue. She plied her tiny hook with a vengeance, creating yards of tatted lace of varying sizes.

"At least Lord Ferris is behaving like a gentleman," Lady Fitz-Levi said again.

Artemisia jabbed the shuttle through another hole. It made a change from yesterday's refrain of *There, miss, are you satisfied?* or the day before, with its shrieks of *Ruined, ruined, this* friend *of yours has ruined you!*

"A real gentleman would have permitted me to break the engagement myself."

"And make you look like a jilt? Oh, no. Lord Ferris is behaving as he should—though I could wish he had waited just a little longer after that odious challenge so people would not be tempted to connect the two. As long as he continues to comport himself with discretion and not let anyone suggest the fault was yours . . ."

"But Mother, I won the duel! That proves it wasn't my fault!"

"Shh, darling. We know that, but you understand that no one else must, now must they? Or they could find out about that—*other* thing, and we don't want that, now, do we? Oh, Artemisia, we must do what we can to get you back on your feet! Perhaps a companion, someone sedate . . . My cousin Lettice married a drunkard, she never had any sense, and now that she's widowed she's short of funds; perhaps she'd be willing to come chaperone you."

"I don't care."

Her mother considered her. "No, Lettice could never handle you. There's only one thing for it. You need a new lover, and quickly."

"*What?*"

"Yes, indeed, my darling. It's the only way to allay suspicion: to make it look as though you fell for someone else and Ferris kindly released you. Now, who among all your beaux did you like second-best?"

"No one." Artemisia twisted her shuttle with a sure hand. "I will never marry."

"Is that what you want to be, a disgraced old maid? It's not a life for you, my dear, indeed it's not." Now her mother softened and seemed to look at her directly. Even sulky and resentful, Artemisia was a pretty picture in the low chair by the window, her dark curls gleaming, her slender neck bent over her work. "You like lively people and nice things. You love Society—and Society will love you once again, once we have you settled. The question is, who is still available who's worth having? Someone nearer your own age, I think, dearest, so you can enjoy a long life together." Artemisia shuddered. "It's a pity Terence Monteith is taken—he was just mad about you, wasn't he?"

"He was a bore."

"Yes, a bit. Still, he is such a *safe* young man. So unexceptionable."

"He wouldn't want me now."

"Do you think so?" Her mother looked archly at her. "I happen to know he'd snap you up in an instant. But he would have to break with Lady Eugenia first, and that would cause scandal, and I think we've had enough of that for one season. What about Gregory Talbert, then?"

"You said he was unsuitable."

"His mother has come to town. She is spending a great deal on clothes for herself and furnishings for their country house. He is not as unsuitable as he once was. And he is still free."

"Dream on, Mama. The fact is, I'm damaged goods."

"Don't be a fool, girl. Nobody knows about that unfortunate incident, and as long as Lord Ferris keeps on being a gentleman, nobody has to, since fortunately there was no . . . untoward result. It is simply a matter of discretion. Discretion, breeding, and . . . well, a reasonable offer on our part, which of course we will make. Your marriage portion will be the same as it was for Lord Ferris; better, even. He can see that and regret it 'til his dying day."

"May it be soon," Artemisia muttered.

Her mother ignored her. "Many of the finest families are overburdened with second, third, even fourth sons whose inheritance is nothing to speak of. Any one of them would be delighted with the match. In fact— Oh!" Her mother smiled. "Why did I not think of this before? It seems so obvious, and you've been such good friends for years, now."

"I can't marry my brother," Artemisia said waspishly.

"No! I was thinking of your cousin Lucius."

"Lucius Perry," Artemisia said softly. Well, of course. He already knew of her condition; he'd brought her home from the Rogues' Ball, after all, and never told a soul. "I thought he'd disgraced himself, somehow."

"Well, dear . . ." Her mother weighed the situation and decided it was time to be frank. "The truth is, when dear Lucius first came to town he was very young, and he fell in with the wrong crowd. He made a bit of a spectacle of himself, and your aunt and uncle were very upset."

Artemisia remembered Lucius sitting in her window seat saying, "It's the old story: boy comes to city, boy disobliges family, family hears about it, ructions ensue." Is this what he'd meant?

"But he's a good boy, you see. As soon as he learned how much harm he might be doing his family and himself, he promised them he'd stop. And I think you'll agree he's behaved admirably ever since. There's not a breath of scandal anyone can attach to Lucius Perry."

"No," Artemisia said thoughtfully, "he's never around for people to notice. He's sleepy, and quiet, and he's always late for things."

"But there's no harm in that. He's a handsome boy with nice manners, very fond of you. I really think I shall write to my sister and see what we can arrange."

"*Then* may I go to the play?" She said it just to annoy, knowing the answer already.

Predictably, her mother launched into: "And don't think I don't know what kind of nonsense That Book's put into your head. 'Fabian,' indeed. When we read it, my friends and I knew that he was a monster, a seducer and a cheat—we all agreed Tyrian was worth two of him—Helena Nevilleson was even planning to name her firstborn Tyrian, but her husband wouldn't permit it. To put such a thing on the stage, and with the Black Rose, of all people . . ."

"All the girls have seen it," she wheedled.

"Well, now," her mother said. "Maybe you should go, at that. We don't want you to disappear, do we? Why don't we all go next week, and invite your cousin Lucius to join us?"

T HE DUKE TREMONTAINE HAD RETURNED TO RIVERSIDE. THE Black Rose did not like visiting him there as well as she liked his house on the Hill, but now that she had accepted a substantial gift from him and severed her ties with her last protector, she hardly felt that she could be too choosy about where to consummate their new arrangement.

"Points to you," she said; "points to you and your little niece."

"What in hell are you talking about?" He sucked a deep breath in on his pipe. "You must forgive me, but I've been enmeshed in family matters. I'm not up on the talk of the town."

"The talk of the town, as you very well know, is that Katherine challenged and defeated Anthony Deverin, though it didn't faze Ferris one little bit. No one is claiming the challenge, so it's anyone's guess what the offense was, and to whom—but all the safe money's on you, of course, on behalf of someone he'd insulted. . . . Oh, Alec," she wrapped herself sinuously around him, "dare I think that it was on my behalf?"

"Think what you like," he said; "it wasn't."

She laughed. "If you weren't so completely useless, I'd be in love with you already. You're the only one who tells me the truth."

"It was Katherine's idea, really. Ask her, if you like. She's around. I thought it best to keep her in Riverside for a while. The Hill is such a . . . busy place right now."

"Yes, you're right. Much safer for her here, if dear Tony tries anything. He's not a forgiving sort, as I know." He offered her the pipe, but she shook her head. "I don't. You shouldn't, either."

"Why not? It relaxes me."

"You want to be on your guard," she said. "You've made a real enemy of Lord Ferris."

"I did that before you were born." He laid a warm hand on her thigh, and she did not contradict his arithmetic. "Kiss me," he drawled, "I can't feel my knees."

chapter V

ANTHONY DEVERIN, LORD FERRIS, WAS PREPARED TO PUT UP with a great deal of inconvenience, even of affront. But he did not readily forgive. In the matter of his stymied marriage, he put the blame where it truly lay: not with the gormless Fitz-Levi clan and their bubble-headed daughter, but with his ancient and annoying enemy, the Duke Tremontaine. Ferris needed to know: had the duel been a mere whim, an opportunity to discomfit him and show off the duke's latest family eccentric, or was it more, the opening salvo in a plan to bring Ferris down altogether? It would not do to wait to find out. He would strike first, to make sure Tremontaine knew he was not without resources.

Ferris made certain inquiries and was not disappointed; if anything, he was a bit surprised at just how many fronts young Campion had left himself exposed on. Going after him would be like shooting arrows at a popinjay tied to a pole. Only the question of St Vier remained open. But it was early days, yet.

It began, innocently enough, with a bit of doggerel and a little art-work, nothing out of the ordinary in a city where printers regularly catered to the tastes of a population that simultaneously gloried in the glamour of its resident nobility and loved seeing them taken down a notch.

On this particular broadsheet, it was His Lordship of Tremontaine being taken down. But instead of the usual willing boy or overen-dowed swordsman, the duke's partner was a grossly fat woman, dressed like a cross between a peasant and a shopkeeper from what one could see, for her skirts were up over her head with His Lordship crawling under them exclaiming: *Behold the motions of the stars!* while she pointed upward, responding: *No, you fool! They're up there still!*

The duke's Riverside household staff, from scullions to secretaries, were far from pleased. What went on between their walls was private business, family business. Those snooty Hill servants might be given to passing on gossip up and down town, but in Riverside things were different. For the duke's ugly Mathematical Girl to be the butt of city jokes was dead wrong. Someone had been talking, and the wrong person had been listening.

"I'll have them put out on the street," the duke told Flavia, "whoever it is."

"You're an idiot," she said mechanically. The Ugly Girl herself was unaware of the rush of sympathy the household felt on her behalf. She'd received little of it in her life, and did not look for it now. "It could be anyone—one of your scholars, drinking in a tavern, making a quip where some apprentice would overhear him, that's all it would take."

"I'll find someone to whip the printer, then. If it distresses you so."

"Don't be an idiot."

The second broadsheet was even more offensive: calculations on a slate being made by a piglike woman with the duke's own tool engulfed in her hammy hand—

"And they're not even *right!*" she wailed, waving the sheet.

He chuckled. "Would you expect them to be?"

She said, "Yes, dammit. They owe me that, at least."

Again he said, "I'll make them stop, if you mind so much."

She looked bleakly at her friend. "*How* will you make them stop? Will you really set bullies on the printer? the artist?"

"Why not?" he said airily; but he knew he was in the wrong. He answered her unspoken accusation himself: "It's not unheard of. Karleigh did it when they targeted his mother. Davenant is known as a man not to mock. In a city where most of the wealth is controlled by a small few, certain things are overlooked, particularly when it comes to the assertion of privilege."

"Don't you dare." She stood rigid, clutching the latest broadsheet in her two hands in front of her.

"Well, it's not as if I can cry challenge on tradesmen, more's the pity."

"You damnable hypocrite, don't you dare."

The duke paced his study once, twice. His back to her, he stopped and said, "Flavia. I'm the Duke of Riverside. I build things here and pretty much keep the peace, and discourage certain behaviors. If you think all that has been achieved through entirely civil and lawful means, you've had your head in a bucket."

"I've enjoyed having my head in a bucket. It's a very nice bucket. I've enjoyed the books and the fire and food and conversation. But you're right to call me on it. You're right." She picked up a couple of books, examined the spines. "These are mine, aren't they? You really did give them to me?"

"Put those down," he said. "Don't be an idiot. Our theories stand. We both see clearly; we know what's right. Even if it's not always possible to act on it, don't you think it matters to be able to call things by their true names?"

"It's not your fault," she said. "I'm not a total idiot. I know you do your best. I was just stupid to think you could—I could—" She shrugged and swiped at her nose with one wrist, her hands being full of books. "I thought I would be safe here."

"You are." For the first time, he touched her, touched her hand. "Safe from everything but paper and ink. Please. Put those down."

"Paper and ink." She clutched the books to her ample chest. "They're not nothing, Alec. They're pretty much everything to me: the embodiment of ideas, of thought—of free and open thought. Of inquiry and supposition. All of it."

"I know," he said. "But—"

"You've got all your other things—your poetry, your drugs, your pretty men and fancy clothes. You don't need just this. I do."

He said with unusual patience, "Do you think, if you leave my house, everything will suddenly slip back into place?" And when she didn't answer right away, he said more heatedly, "And you're going back where? To an unheated room at University and one cooked meal a week, tutoring students too stupid and lazy to attend lectures given by masters with half your brains? You'd leave my house for that?"

"Your patronage," the Ugly Girl said. "I'm leaving your patronage. Don't you understand? I don't like being looked at. I don't like being talked about. I don't really like compromise."

He said, "And I don't like you letting them chase you away. It seems, well, cowardly."

"It is. I have my limits. Clever of them to find them. Who are 'they,' by the way?"

"I don't know," the duke said. "I wonder who I've offended lately?"

"Everyone. You offend everyone."

"Don't leave," he said. "It will give them so much pleasure."

"Almost, for that," she conceded, "but no. I'd better."

"Come to dinner next week," he urged. "Ridley and his gang are going to argue about circulation. Maybe he'll demonstrate on a roast chicken again."

"No," she said. "I'm going to disappear for a while—as much as I can, anyway; nobody really cares about the University. And I never liked those dinners. Didn't you notice? It was always best when you told me about them after."

"Breakfast next morning, then?"

"Don't wait up," she said.

She left the crumpled broadsheets on the floor. And she left an enormous space in the duke's library, in his study, in his days and nights.

But in the end he got back at her, even if he never got her back. Before the year was out, the stuffy old University at the heart of the City boasted the first ever Women's Fellowship in Mathematics, which was taken by the only suitable available candidate, a large and ugly woman of indeterminate age who always wore a voluminous black scholar's robe over her shapeless gowns and lectured with a combination of rigor and dry wit that made her classes, in time, immensely popular.

Artemisia Fitz-Levi witnessed Lord Ferris's second strike against the duke herself.

She witnessed it from a box at the theatre in the company of her mother, her brother, and her cousin Lucius. Lucius Perry had not yet declared himself a formal suitor, despite his parents' indication that they would view the match with favor, but Lady Fitz-Levi still wanted him seen with her daughter, and Artemisia was simply grateful for his company.

The truth was, it took courage for her to go out in public. Despite her friends' assurances that it was nothing, she knew people were still talking about her ruptured betrothal and its possible causes. Although no one who knew them well could seriously entertain the notion that the Fitz-Levi family had hired Tremontaine's wild niece, the proximity of the challenge to Lord Ferris's break with Artemisia was hard to ignore. There was talk of a romance between the two girls, though no one had ever seen them together. Those who believed the challenge lay between Ferris and the Mad Duke were still free to wonder what had caused the Crescent to release Lady Artemisia from her betrothal.

If she had not been the wronged party, then perhaps something else about her had put Lord Ferris off, and her deficiencies were lovingly enumerated, even by her friends.

Thus the Fitz-Levi party arrived early at the theatre, so as to be settled in their box before the crowds started in. Artemisia sat towards the back of the box where she would not easily be seen, wishing she didn't have to. All thought of her own situation vanished, though, when the play began. Candles were lit, and there was Stella's bedroom, with its tall window and canopied bed, exactly as in the book. In walked a beautiful woman—a little old for girlish Stella to Artemisia's critical eye, but she carried herself well. "No, thank you," the actress said, her head turned a little offstage. "I will put myself to bed."

"Let the duke do it!"

A man's voice, crude, from the cheap back seats. There was general *shushing,* and the scene went on. The Black Rose won Artemisia over with her portrayal of Stella's gentle innocence. When Fabian appeared in her chamber, armed and ready to kill her as he was sworn to do, Artemisia clutched her fan so hard she nearly broke it. Stella did not plead for her life; she let her youth and beauty of spirit plead for her. And the swordsman succumbed, as he must. "Lady Stella," he said, "your girlhood ends tonight. Whether by my sword or in my arms, I leave the choice to you."

"It is no choice," she said, trembling. "Either way, my will is forced."

"Is it?" Though the length of his sword was still between them, he looked deep into her eyes. "Know this, then: that you choose for us both. For in taking your life tonight, I end mine as well. The sun cannot rise on the face of a man who has destroyed such a jewel."

"What is your name?"

"If you will it, it is Death. Death for us both."

"And if I will otherwise?"

"Then I will give you joy." He fell on his knees before her, his sword at his side, the distance still between them. "And I am your servant, now, until the moment I draw my final breath."

Artemisia found that she was weeping—not the slow pleasant tears that theatre usually called forth, but wrenching sobs she felt her body could barely contain. She tried to stifle them, to hear what came next, although she knew the words by heart:

"Then rise," bright Stella said. "I choose freely, and I choose you." She held out her hand.

"Save it for Tremontaine!" A different voice, from a different corner of the theatre.

"Shut your face!" a woman shouted back, and others chorused agreement. This was Stella's moment, and no man would take it from them. The theatre was silent as the Black Rose parted the curtains of the huge bed, and silent as the couple embraced within them.

Silent, too, as Viola appeared on the stage above, jacketed and breeched as Tyrian, wondering what had happened to keep Fabian so late.

The two friends met (while the bedroom was made to disappear), and Fabian explained his desperate case and even more desperate remedy. To save Stella's life he must betray a patron, and in so doing betray his honor, a swordsman's most cherished possession, and next to his sword, his most valuable. But one bright, fated woman had turned the world inside out, changed honor to disgrace and death to life. He would leave the city now and send word to his patron that he had found the mark too easy, that his blade rebelled and sought a worthier foe.

"Think you," said Tyrian, "they'll let it go at that? Dream on, my friend. I will watch your beauty, and if she be not worthy of your love, I'll challenge her myself."

Mangrove appeared next. In the book this happened later, but Artemisia could see that it was time to present the villain, who was Stella's evil cousin's swordsman and second in command. Mangrove waited for Stella in a temple, where he knew she was coming to pray, which was not in the book but allowed them to drop some impressive columns from the flies above. He leaned arrogantly against one and said, "Here comes the lady now."

The Black Rose entered, veiled head to toe in midnight blue.

"Is it raining?" Lady Fitz-Levi inquired. It wasn't rain: all around the theatre, people were hissing. The sounds of *shh!* mixed with the hissing, making it worse. The Black Rose said something, but no one could hear her. She stood very still, and so did Mangrove, frozen in his sneer.

Someone began a rhythmic clapping, making it impossible for the actors to be heard. People in the audience started shouting, and the language wasn't pretty.

At last the noise subsided. Stella lifted a hand to her veil, and Mangrove stepped forward. "Gentle lady," he said, a terrible mockery of Fabian's opening lines, "allow me."

But she kept her hands on her veil. "Sir, you are not known to me. My face—" The rest of the speech was lost in a volley of hisses. Every time the Black Rose opened her mouth, it was the same.

"Let's go," said Lucius Perry. "They'll never get through the play."

Her mother was outraged. "Can't they make them stop?"

"You can't control such an audience, Aunt."

"But what's wrong?" Artemisia asked. "I think she's very good."

"Goose," her brother said fondly. "It's a setup. Someone's paid to have her booed. A rival, perhaps—for the part, or for her affections . . ."

"Well, whoever did it, I'd like to slap them," his sister said. "Oh, look, Robert, people are throwing flowers! Quick, rush out and buy me some, I want to throw them, too."

The stage was slowly carpeted in blossoms. When they grew deep enough, the Black Rose scooped up a great armful, and swept offstage.

WORD REACHED RIVERSIDE QUICKLY. THE DUKE TREMONTAINE sent his carriage for her, and it carried the Black Rose unimpeded to the Bridge, where a closed chair waited to bring her to him.

"They *booed* me." Her eyes flashed regally, and she would not sit down, although she accepted a goblet of brandy. "I have never been hissed in a theatre before. Never."

He said, "How lucky for you. Whom have you managed to offend?"

She stopped her pacing long enough to fix him with her startling eyes. She was not a small woman, and the duke was sitting down, teasing at a flower that had fallen from her hair. "Don't you know?" she said. "I heard it clearly, and so did everyone else, I'll be bound. Your name, dear, not mine. I am very popular. You, it seems, are not."

"What a surprise." He dropped petals on the floor. "And what a good thing I don't care."

"How nice for you that you don't have to."

"Meaning," he drawled, "that you do."

"Just so." She leaned down and kissed him long and hard, 'til she felt his breath quicken and his hands grow restless, then she pulled away and said complacently, "It's a good thing you're not stuck on screwing actresses, dearie, or you'd have a very dry time ahead of you."

The duke straightened his jacket. "You weren't by any chance brought up in Riverside, were you?"

She knelt before him in a rustle of skirts, so that her eyes were level with his. "You don't remember me, do you?" He looked dubious. "Well, why should you? I was just a scrawny girl, wiping down the tables and clearing away the beer mugs at Rosalie's."

"Rosalie's?" It was a name he hadn't heard in years: the tavern where he used to drink and wait with his lover, the swordsman St Vier, for a challenge or a fight.

"I thought you were a prince back then," Rose said. "I made up stories about you. You and him, you was—you were like magic, something no one could touch. I wanted people to look at me like that. And the way you talked—oh, lord . . . Rosalie let me bring you a drink, once. You were dicing—"

"Probably losing."

"Oh, yes, losing." She smiled. "When I brought it, you said, *Look, a glass of fresh luck!*" She imitated him perfectly. "You took the drink, but the swordsman paid for it, because you were broke. I remember, he said—"

"No." The duke held up his hand. "That's enough."

"It's all right," Rose said. "I never could do him the way I could do you. I used to make the other girls laugh with it. . . ."

"What a good thing I didn't know! I might have had him kill you."

"Never." The Black Rose smiled. "He didn't do women, everyone knew that."

The duke said, "Last year. I sent you my ring, with that note. . . . When you came here and saw me, you must have been surprised."

"Oh, no, Alec. Not at all." Her arms twined around his neck. "Why do you think I came?"

He ran his lips along her cheek. "Revenge on a crooked lover, I thought. Not that I wasn't grateful. I put what you brought me to good use, I assure you. And I'm grateful yet. I won't let Ferris chase you from the theatre."

"No," she said, "you won't."

Through pride and perversity he strove to keep her with him as long as he could, but in the end she rose from the tangle of clothes and said, "Farewell, my prince. Act heartbroken if you can; curse me if you must. I'd rather one curse from your lips than a hundred *boos* from an annoyéd crowd."

He looked critically at her. "Someone else wrote that."

"Of course. I changed it a little to fit the circumstances, that's all." She busied herself with the hooks of her bodice, and he did not offer to help. "I'll do what I can to let them know we've quarreled. You do the same."

On the stairway she found the duke's niece, that peculiar girl with the sword. Rose straightened herself just a little more and adjusted her glow to become once again the Black Rose. "Katherine," she said brightly. "How wonderful to see you again."

"Oh." The girl looked startled. "Hello, there."

"I salute you," said Rose. "You are the hero of the hour."

"Am I?"

"The duke is very proud of you, and so he should be. Remind him of it, when you can. He's sad," Rose said. "I am a little, too." She put her hand on the girl's soft cheek, and Katherine blushed. "I know," the Black Rose said. "It's all so very difficult, until you get the hang of it." She kissed the girl on her brow, and left the Riverside house.

I T WAS NOT FAIR. THE DUKE ALWAYS GOT WHATEVER HE WANTED. What did he need the Black Rose for? He had the whole city to choose from. She liked me, I knew she did. Hadn't she kissed me in the theatre?

It probably wasn't her fault at all that she'd ended up with him. She was just an actress, and he had money and influence that she probably needed, while I had nothing to offer but my true heart and my sword. Girls were dying all over the city for her. And there she was, patting me on the head and telling me to cheer up my uncle and look after him. Why didn't she tell anyone to look after *me*?

I didn't go down to dinner; I did not want to see the Duke Tremontaine that night. I found some old biscuits in my emergency hunger tin and ate those. But it turned out I'd missed a meal for nothing; the duke, too, was taking his meals in his rooms.

Or so Marcus told me, when he banged on my door to see what had happened to me.

I opened the door a crack. "Go away," I said. "You're not supposed to be in here alone with me. Betty doesn't approve."

Marcus laughed. "Betty," he said, "is making up to Master Osborne, who knew her back in the old days when he wasn't good enough for her. You don't have to worry about Betty for a while. He's got the keys to the wine cellar, after all."

"Well, anyway, I'm busy. I'm thinking."

"So am I," Marcus said insinuatingly. "I've been planning amusements and diversions. Want to know?"

"Tell me," I said.

"I'll tell you when I've got all the bits worked out. Maybe tomorrow, if all goes well. Meanwhile, I'll have a tray sent up. You must keep up your strength. Then you can practice killing someone. It'll do you the world of good."

He was the most provoking boy.

Dᴀᴠɪᴅ Aʟᴇxᴀɴᴅᴇʀ Tɪᴇʟᴍᴀɴ Cᴀᴍᴘɪᴏɴ, Dᴜᴋᴇ Tʀᴇᴍᴏɴᴛᴀɪɴᴇ, knew that he had annoyed a lot of people. It wasn't fair to blame everything on Lord Ferris. He set his network to make inquiries, first through the usual channels: the University and Riverside. Riversiders got around. Some were virtuoso housebreakers and pickpockets, still others had climbed up the social ladder to become house staff of various kinds. Servants, all but the most disciplined, talked. So did scholars—outrageous gossips all, even those who now worked as tutors and secretaries to the nobility, many of whom Tremontaine had helped out in their starving student days. Spread his nets wide enough and something would turn up that he could use—and, as usual, a number of things he hadn't been looking for that could be useful later would come to light as well.

The question was, how serious were these strikes against his friends? Did his enemy wish only to annoy, or was this the prelude to something worse? It was not the first time Tremontaine had been under attack. When he'd inherited the duchy quite a few disgruntled contenders had tried to alter the succession through means foul and fair. And there had been others since then. He was well defended, now, with swordsmen and lawyers and everything in between. But what was he to defend against?

He made a list of possible serious foes. Heading it was Anthony Deverin, Lord Ferris. It wasn't just that Ferris currently had legitimate grudges against both Tremontaine's lover for spying on him (if he'd found out) and his niece for challenging him. It was also a matter of style. The petty cruelty, particularly directed toward vulnerable women, smelt very familiar.

In the old tales, things always came in threes. So who was next? The duke made his best guess and doubled the guard on certain people who, with luck, need never know that it was there at all. And he sent once last time for the Black Rose, to come in secret and speak to him in his Riverside house, and he asked her to go as his messenger to Highcombe.

Aʀᴛᴇᴍɪsɪᴀ ʙᴇɢᴀɴ ɢᴏɪɴɢ ᴏᴜᴛ ᴀɢᴀɪɴ ᴛᴏ sᴇʟᴇᴄᴛᴇᴅ ᴘᴀʀᴛɪᴇs. She held her head high, even when she had to sit out dances without a partner. She refused to flirt with any of her old beaux. If the ones who had once clustered around her begging for a smile now thought themselves too good for her, so much the worse for them. She had won her challenge. She was free and in the right. Lydia Godwin's father always made a point of dancing with her, gracefully and superbly, and so did Armand Lindley. Lydia would take Artemisia's arm and walk around the ballroom with her in open declaration of affection. Jane Hetley often joined them, though Lavinia Perry, now betrothed to Petrus Davenant, was making herself scarce. It was going to be that way, Artemisia realized: they would be friends in future only if their husbands got along.

She found herself hoping more and more to see Lucius Perry at these events. Lucius would always talk with her, easy and amusing. He made her feel like herself. He was a good dancer, too, and he never failed to claim her for a dance and bow deeply when it was over. Even when he was on his way elsewhere, he seemed to make the effort to drop in where he knew she would be. He would stay long enough to dance with her twice—but the third dance, the one that declared him a serious suitor, that Lucius Perry never gave her.

Once, just once, it almost happened. The music being over, Artemisia held on to his hand that little bit longer, and as the next tune started up they nearly merged back into the dance. She saw him pause, and look at her, and realize. He kept her hand, though, as he guided her back in the direction of her seat, and so doing, he slipped his arm around her waist, drew her a little closer to him— She didn't mean to flinch and pull back, she just did it.

"What a clumsy dolt I am!" Lucius said smoothly. "Always stepping on people's toes . . ."

She felt a rush of great warmth for him then. Lucius understood. As she watched his back disappear across the ballroom floor, off to whatever his next engagement was that night, Artemisia realized that she would marry him if he asked her. She would take good care of him. She'd make a beautiful home, and invite his friends to dinner, and she would see to it that there were always plates of his favorite biscuits, the brown crispy cinnamon ones. They would attend the theatre together, and give musical afternoons, and on quiet evenings she would sew and he would read to her. And he would never, never do anything to her if she asked him not to. Surely he never would.

ROSE HAD NEVER KNOWN A CARRIAGE RIDE TO BE SO EXHAUSTING. It was ridiculous, really; here she was in the lap of luxury— the duke hated traveling, he said, so tried to make his carriages as

comfortable as possible, and as far as she was concerned, he'd succeeded. His footmen, in plain dress (as was the carriage, with the
duke's escutcheon covered), were attentive but not presumptuous,
and the basket of provisions abundant. It was the opposite of what she
usually had to put up with on tour, and she should have been luxuriat-
ing in it. But all she wanted to do was sleep.

It was especially annoying because she had lines to learn. Henry
had decided to mount a new production of an old romance, *Lord
Ruthven's Lady*. It was a difficult play, seldom performed, being neither
wholly tragedy nor comedy; but based on the success of *The Swordsman Whose Name Was Not Death*, Henry felt *Lord Ruthven's Lady*
would draw crowds.

Lord Ruthven is a courtier who offends the king's young sister Helena by his callous and predatory conduct toward women. Helena per-
suades the court wizard to turn Ruthven into a woman, cursed to remain so until he can gain a woman's love. As a woman, Ruthven
realizes he loves Helena and must bend all his skills and powers
toward seducing her in his woman's form, or perish of terrible, un-
slakeable desire unlike anything he has ever known. Rose would play
Ruthven once he was transformed. She had seen the play done entirely for laughs, but she had no intention of letting that happen here.
While there were certainly comic moments to work with, her
Ruthven would be troubled and passionate, vulnerable and confused,
and ultimately tragic. By the time Helena finally returned Ruthven's
love, she wanted all the ladies in the audience to be moaning with
need. Her dear friend Jessica Bell was cast as Helena. Jess would give
the princess just the right mix of fragility and backbone, and her slender pallor would play well against Rose's robust stature. Never one to
leave a profitable thing unexploited, Henry had insisted on writing in
a part for Viola Fine: Helena now had a pageboy with a crush on
Ruthven-the-woman, which was gilding the lily with a vengeance, in
Rose's opinion. But Rose did not doubt that once the show opened,
she would have her pick of noble lovers, passionate adoring women
who would make a very nice change from the tortuous intrigues of
Lord Ferris and the Mad Duke Tremontaine.

She would, at least, if she could ever learn her lines. Rose had begun studying the part and was finding it almost impossible. Long
speeches usually gave her no trouble; she loved the rhythm of the
words, but these refused to stick in her head. There was a lot of repar-
tee and wordplay, as well, and she kept jumbling phrases. She had to
be word-perfect or the comedy would be lost, and you needed the
play's wit to balance the poignancy. *From the top, dear*, she told her-

self, and put her hand over her playbook and began the transformation scene:

> What is this heaviness about my chest?
> My arms feel lighter, without strength or power.
> Have I been sleeping? Ill? I cannot tell.
> What, boy! Attend me here!—What is that
>   sound?
> That is not mine—my voice! My voice! My
>   voice!

Oh, she was going to have a good time with this. Triple repeats gave you so much to do. The next line was—was— God, she'd lost it already. She'd lost it, and she was going to puke. She should know better than to read in a moving carriage. But it had never given her trouble in the past. She opened the basket, looking for the wine. There was something in there—something that smelt like—quinces. Quince tart. She loved quince tart, and the duke had remembered, how sweet. But not this quince tart. This one was overwhelming. It was as if she was choking on the very smell of quinces. It sat in her hand, all crispy and golden. She threw it out the window.

The air made her feel better. She took a sip of wine and lay back. Her corsets were too tight. She'd told her dresser to tie them looser, but Emily must not have been paying attention. Her breasts were popping right out of her bodice. Rose lay back and closed her eyes.

She was asleep when the carriage pulled into Highcombe and came to a halt on the sweeping drive before the house's front door, where torches were already lit, expecting her arrival. The duke had insisted that she travel alone, but he had sent an outrider on ahead, and the household's small staff miraculously included women who could take care of her. Muzzy with fatigue, she let them usher her up to a quiet bedroom and unlace her shoes and coo over her elegant dress and petticoats, hang them up and bring her water to wash away the journey. "Put your feet up, my lady," they said in their thick country accents, and she did not correct their assumption—she'd played great ladies often enough, and could certainly do so now—"that'll help they swelling to go down." She had never enjoyed the unlacing of her corsets quite so much. This was the country, and there was no "adoring public" here, no audience except for the mysterious personage she was to meet, for whom the duke had hired her to read the letter she carried. With that duty discharged, she could go with her laces loose for a couple of days; maybe it would ease the ache in her breasts.

Sitting upright in her chair with her feet on a stool, waiting for a soothing tisane, Rose fell asleep again, and was roused by an elderly maid who, unsure of the etiquette for waking nobility, was holding the steaming mug under her nose. The acrid smell of herbs made her flinch. "Take it away," she said; "I don't want it."

The sharpness in her own voice surprised her. These people were trying to be kind. Rose shook her head and laughed. "I'm sorry! I don't know what's wrong with me!"

"That's all right, my lady," the servant said. "It just takes some women that way, is all."

"Oh, no," Rose laughed, "I'm usually quite a hardy traveler."

The older woman chuckled. "Most every woman finds this journey hard, ma'am," and Rose said, "Oh, no," in quite a different tone.

chapter VI

A YEAR AGO, ALEC CAMPION WOULD HAVE TOSSED LORD FER-
ris's brief note of invitation on the fire.

Let us sit and discuss together, it read, *like reasonable men, matters
to our mutual advantage.*

Now the duke's secretary drafted a reply saying that His Lordship of
Tremontaine would call upon Lord Ferris at a particular day and time.
Ferris replied that the day would be perfectly convenient, and as to
the time, he hoped that His Lordship would not be much delayed.

The duke arrived early. Conceding the gesture, Ferris did not make
him wait but had him shown directly into his study and insisted on
sending for refreshments. With his good eye, he surveyed the younger
man. Tremontaine had taken trouble to dress up for the visit: his lace
was very white and there was plenty of it. Instead of his accustomed
black he wore the green of the House of Tremontaine, which also
matched his disturbing eyes. The duke did not lack for jewels: promi-
nent among them was the oblong ring of the Tremontaine ruby, set
with diamonds. Ferris knew it well; his own abuse of the jewel had
helped bring about his humiliation at Tremontaine's hands almost
twenty years back. For the boy to choose to wear it to this meeting was
either provocation or poor judgment—or possibly both.

The duke refused brandy. "Keeping a clear head?" asked Ferris, delicately sipping his. "Good. This needn't take long, and I want you to remember what was said."

"Stop enjoying yourself, Ferris. I'm here and I'm sober, and I want to know what you think you're doing."

"Consider it an invitation," Ferris said cordially. "This is, after all, the first time you have ever bothered to call on me. If it took making a little trouble for some of your friends to get you here, I suppose it was worth it."

"You admit it? All of it?"

"Why not? An invitation, as I said. To come sit down and discuss our situation together, like noble and reasonable men."

"Which involves threatening my friends?"

"I was afraid you wouldn't take me seriously."

"I did. But I am preparing," the duke said, "to revise that opinion. Stop playing and tell me what you want."

"And you'll give it to me?"

"What do you think? If it's reasonable, I'll consider it. If it's not, I have the resources to annoy you very much as you've been annoying me. It's true I have more scruples—but I'm willing to suspend them. I also have more money, you see—lots more money. I wasn't planning to waste any of it on you, but I could be convinced to change my mind."

"Ah." Ferris rolled his glass between his fingertips. "That answers that question. The interference with my wedding plans was just one of your little pot shots, not the launch of a new campaign."

"I never—" The duke began to say something, but then thought better of it. He settled back in his chair—which Ferris was meanly gratified to note was just a bit too small for the duke's long body—and said simply, "No campaign. Your fiancée wanted out, and it was an easy fix."

"Well, that's all right, then," said Ferris smoothly. It was all coming together, in one of the several patterns he'd laid out against this meeting. He felt the almost sexual thrill of being the one in the room with all the power. The words seemed already written for him to speak. "I have now, as you say, an easy fix for both our troubles. You don't really trust me to stop attacking you where you're vulnerable—or you shouldn't, anyway—and I certainly do not trust you not to make such attacks necessary to me. Even with your great supply of scruples, not even you can always be quite sure what you'll do next, can you?"

The duke glared at him, but said nothing. "So," Lord Ferris went on, "you are going to provide me with a very fine token of your goodwill, which will also recompense me for the trouble you've caused already."

"And that is?"

"You are going to contract with me to marry your niece."

The duke turned very pale, right down to his lips. Then his cheeks flushed, making his green eyes appear to glitter.

"Oh, come, Campion, what else were you planning to do with her? It's a generous offer. In one sweep she is reinstated in Society with a position higher than any she might otherwise hope for. Even your crimes against her delicate girlhood—" Tremontaine started to rise; Lord Ferris lifted a manicured hand "—I mean, of course, only the silly masquerade of sword and breeches—are forgotten in the general haze of romance. We'll say I fell in love with her at the Godwin swordfight. It'll delight the entire city, just like a play—like that swordsman one the Rose is doing now, in fact. Lady Katherine likes the theatre, I hear."

The duke said nothing.

"You will provide her with a suitable dowry, of course. I know you are very fond of her. And should the two of us be blessed with issue— well, I would never presume to interfere with the ducal succession (that's not my place, is it?)—but I know you would take them into consideration, being so fond of the Lady Katherine and wanting the best for all of your family."

The duke sat very still, as if he were afraid to move. He wet his lips. "Are you sure," he said, "there isn't some ruling in the books somewhere stating that once you have slept with a woman it's a crime to marry her great-granddaughter?"

"None that I know of."

"Pity. I'll have to put a motion up before the Council to have one passed."

"Oh, no you won't," said the Crescent comfortably. "There's a fine now for frivolous suits."

"I'll pay it," the duke said. "But it might be cheaper for me just to hire a swordsman to settle the matter and put you out of your premarital miseries."

"Well, now." Ferris leaned back, brimming with his own particular kind of happiness. He'd always known he was ten times smarter than this man, but seldom did he get such a good opportunity to display it. "You might want to think that one through. You see, if it turns out that we are not to be wed, I might want to challenge your niece, instead. Having now seen her fight, I admit I misjudged her ability as well as her persistence this last time; but I don't make the same mistake twice. I can find a swordsman with enough superior skill to mop up the floor with her. There are some serious ones left, you know—they can easily skewer a young blade, even one who somehow learned a few of St Vier's tricks."

The duke said, "I could send her away. Back to her mother's house."

"Oh? Do you think the mother would refuse my suit? I don't. There's some bad blood between you, isn't there? Just what did your noble sister do, exactly?"

"She married," the duke said dryly. "Against my will."

"I am sure you have given her ample opportunity to regret it." Lord Ferris rose, and stretched, and pulled on the bell by the hearth. "You act quickly," he told his visitor, "but you don't always think very quickly. So I'll give you a little time to think over my offer and its ramifications."

"How little?"

Ferris cocked his head. "One day should be sufficient. After that, I will expect your answer, or I may well extend another of my invitations. I will go well guarded until then." A footman answered his summons. "His Grace of Tremontaine requires his carriage. Will you pass the word and see him out? I've Council business to attend to. Good night, my lord."

It was a dismissal, and not a very civil one, from one great lord to another. Lord Ferris's footman was therefore very surprised when the Mad Duke not only tipped him handsomely but gave him a schoolboy's wink before getting up into his splendid carriage. He wasn't called the Mad Duke for nothing, then. The footman couldn't see anything to wink about. Neither could the duke, if truth be told, but he was damned if he'd let Ferris know it.

THE BLACK ROSE COUNTED ON HER FINGERS, AND DID NOT LIKE the results. The thing was possible, and it certainly explained a lot. She could play Ruthven to the hilt, now, understanding what it was to feel sudden changes in one's body—transformation unwelcome, undesired, imposed from outside her by another person. . . . But could she get through the rest of the Season before she started to show? Could she keep awake? Could she remember her lines? Her breasts felt huge, now that she knew; they were like someone else's, darker and bigger than her own. *What is this heaviness about my chest,* indeed?

The Rose composed herself for her morning meeting with Highcombe's mysterious resident. She was a professional, after all, and Tremontaine was paying her well just to read a letter to some person here, an aged relative, perhaps, and to answer any questions he might have. Whatever her own situation, she could execute this not particularly demanding role with grace, dignity and ease.

When Richard St Vier walked into the room, she let out something between a squawk and a full-blown shriek.

He was unarmed, but she saw him start to make a move to defend himself, and then to realize, and stop, and smile. "He didn't tell you," he said.

"No." Her hands were shaking. She fumbled in her bodice. "Oh, god—I have a letter—I had no idea—"

"Sit down," he said. "It's all right. He's just being cautious, or theatrical, or something."

Rose grimaced. "Well, why not?"

"Or maybe he's annoyed with you."

"He is, a little." Rose sank into the chair by the window, looking up at the swordsman anxiously. "But he told me he trusted my absolute discretion." She laughed shakily. "He must be desperate."

"Do you think he is?" Richard St Vier asked her.

"Annoyed, or desperate?" She tried to recapture her usual lightness. She was not a Riverside tavern girl anymore. She was the Black Rose, the toast of the city, the honor of the stage.

"They go together sometimes," St Vier said; "especially with him." He pulled up a chair. He sat so close that when he breathed deeply, his knee ruffled her skirts. "What does he want?"

She thought of the Mad Duke's plots, his vices and excesses, his quiet rages and his enemies. "You," she said.

"Ah," St Vier said. "What's in the letter?"

That morning, with defiant panache, she had folded it carefully so that it nestled in the cleft of her bosom, planning to whip it out with two fingers and present it to the mysterious resident. If she hadn't squawked before with so much force, it might not have slipped down that little extra way, causing her to have to fish for it with those same two fingers while her other hand kept her stays in place.

"You don't even know who I am," she said.

"Nor do I. You didn't introduce yourself, and I don't like to pry."

That sobered her up. "I'm an actress. I'm Rose." It reminded her, too, that even the neatest stage business sometimes misfired and costumes misbehaved, and then all it took was a quick hoist and a tug to bring the letter out into the light.

Rose broke the seal, and then she stopped. Shouldn't she just hand it to him? "I'm sorry," she explained; "he said to read it to you."

"Yes, please do."

She looked down at the page. "It's short," she said. "One line: *Will you come for Katherine, if not for me?*"

She cleared her throat. "That's all."

"That's discreet," St Vier said. He did not ask her anything else.

"Katherine's a nice girl," she said.

"Yes. I know." He stood very still in the middle of the room.

"He's made a lot of enemies. He doesn't mind it, but they do. I don't think he'd ask if—if it weren't . . ." Shut up, Rose, she thought.

He looked out the window for a while, and then he looked at her. "Yes," he said. "I will go. He didn't say how soon?"

"He didn't say anything. But I would make it soon."

"I can be ready in a day or two."

"All right." Weariness washed over her, and the kind of sadness she had spent her life trying to keep at bay. She stood up. "Do you mind if I go lie down?" she asked. "The journey was very tiring."

She wanted to make a good exit, but her balance seemed to have deserted her. She staggered against Richard St Vier, and for the first time in her life she felt the swordsman's hand close around her, warm and firm on her elbow, holding her up. "Are you all right?" he asked. And she thought, *No, I'm not all right. I'm stuffed with your sweet Alec's child!*

She said, "I'm fine. Just tired, is all."

"What are you going to do?" he asked, and she thought somehow he knew, he knew with his supernaturally clever body that had kept him alive through so many fights, through his years in the streets and taverns, somehow it saw her and recognized her distress, her condition, and he knew—but then he went on, "Will you wait and ride back with me? or are you in a hurry to go home?"

Rose closed her eyes. "I don't know. I need to think about things. It's been a difficult season. I might stay here awhile; the rest would do me good. After that . . . we'll see. Life in the theatre is so unpredictable."

chapter VII

S ERIOUS SWORD-PRACTICE MADE ME FORGET TO THINK IN words, so that I didn't always understand when people spoke to me. I had been at it for some time, drilling first to a rhythm, and then tricking myself with changes, when Marcus came in and said something.

I shook sweat out of my eyes. "What?"

"I've got some time free. It's nearly dark, you'll have to stop soon anyway."

"Yes, all right." I stretched out around the room, carefully polished the sword and put it away.

"Good, Katie. Now that I have your attention, I thought I'd invite you out for a night on the town. What do you think?"

I'd just begun to get my breath back from practice, but now my heart started beating hard again. Something about his jaunty nonchalance, just a little too studied . . . He was up to something, and he was mighty pleased with himself. "A night out in Riverside?" I did my best to match his tone. "How naughty. How daring. Why not? What's up?"

Marcus negligently kicked the stand so that all the swords rattled back in place. "I'm taking you to Glinley's."

That undid me; I barely managed not to squeak. I had to call on the duke for backup: "Oh, re-eally?" I said, in my best Tremontaine.

"Not just the two of us, of course. Your uncle would never permit it." The look on my face must have been enough. Marcus dropped the pose and grinned at me. "It's Perry. He's here right now, and I happen to know he's working tonight. Want to follow him?"

This was ground I knew; stalking Perry was just something we did. "Why not?" I said, but this time I meant it.

I toweled off in my room and changed into a clean shirt with dark clothes and soft boots, and buckled on a sword; it was, after all, night in Riverside. No one was in the kitchen; we helped ourselves to bread and cheese and our favorite ginger beer, and then went out the side kitchen door to wait for Lucius Perry.

He wasn't long in coming. He wore his old-fashioned hooded cloak, with the hood pulled over his head, and he moved quickly. It was a good time of day to be following someone. Although the sky was still pearly in patches between the roofs, down in the street it was dark. I pretended I was a moving shadow, and Marcus, breathing softly next to me, was another. Only Perry was real, as he passed by other shadows, shadows of women heading for clients, shadows of musicians heading for jobs, shadows of thieves heading for houses, shadows of cats heading for food. We were almost to the Bridge when Perry turned down a side street and stopped in front of a large and rambly house with a deep-roofed portico.

"So," I said softly, "that's Glinley's."

"That's Glinley's." Marcus was smug, as if he'd pulled it out of the air for me.

Like our house, Glinley's had once been many small town houses, now knit together into one. Lucius Perry hesitated at the front door and then turned round the side as people came out to set torches in the holders in front.

We drew back further into the shadows. "Now what?" I asked.

"He takes off his clothes and wallows in depravity, what do you think?"

"No, I mean—now what do we do? Shouldn't we follow him?"

I heard Marcus's clothes rustle as he pulled back sharply. "In *there*? You can't go in there!"

"Why not?" Even at Teresa Grey's we had tried to climb the wall.

"Because—because you're a lady!"

I stared at where I knew he was in the darkness. "Marcus," I said. "That is completely idiotic. The duke has just spent half a year making sure I'm not a lady."

"Katie—"

"I'm not going to *do* anything, Marcus, I just want to see what it looks like inside." I could sense his whole body taut with resistance. "Marcus, have you been in there already without me?"

"No, I haven't. But I know what goes on in places like that."

"Well, so do I. It's just like the duke and all his friends, isn't it?" He was being so protective, it made me want to do something rash just to show him. But I wasn't going in there alone. "You've said it yourself: it's just full of people copulating. It can't be any worse than home. What are you afraid of?"

"I'm not afraid of anything. It's just, you won't like it."

"If I don't like it, or you don't like it, we'll leave."

"Promise?"

"I promise. I only want to see, that's all. Like Teresa Grey's: we'll just look, we won't do anything."

"Good," he said, "because it costs money, and we don't have enough. You're right. It is just a house. A house, and some people doing what people do everywhere. Nothing to worry about. Let's go."

I followed him as he strode across the street into the circle of light and under the dark porch of Glinley's front door. "Now what?" I whispered. "Do we just knock, or what?"

"There's a bell." Marcus turned the plain brass door-pull. After a moment that was just long enough to belie the fact that people were always waiting for it to ring, the door opened. Light from inside nearly blinded us. A stocky, muscular man stood there, plainly dressed, quietly armed. I felt his eyes flicking up and down, sizing up our clothes and our purses.

"Well, hello there," he said to Marcus. "Fancy seeing you here after all this time. What's your pleasure, then?"

Marcus drew himself up. "We're here to see Mistress Glinley," he said haughtily.

That worked. What we were going to tell her, I had no idea, but the man drew back and bowed, and let us in.

The halls were dark and shadowy, well suited to a house of vice. I'm sure brothels uptown are better lit. It was all part of what the duke liked to call the Riverside Flair. We followed the man to a small room hung in red, with a fainting couch prominently placed next to a little round table. He lit the candles. There was a decanter of wine and two glasses on the table. Marcus stood there watching while the man filled both glasses of wine for us. Where did he know Marcus from? Maybe the man had worked for the duke once.

"I'm sure you and your . . . friend will be comfortable here," the man told him, glancing at the couch. I wondered how many women with swords he saw each week. He looked back again at Marcus, and his face shifted in a sly way. He said, "Very comfortable for you, sir. Tremontaine business, is it, sir?"

Marcus turned his back, and took a glass of wine. "I thought," he said, "you were paid not to ask questions here."

"Oh, no, sir, of course, sir." The man bowed his way out of the room, leaving us in sole possession of couch, candles and wine.

"Well, I'm impressed." I plumped myself down, testing the couch. It appeared to be stuffed with goose down. "That was quick thinking, Marcus. You've got him on the run, cheeky villain. I don't know what we'll tell Mistress Glinley, but we'll think of something, won't we?"

"She'll think we're from the duke." Marcus drank. "I hope she doesn't tell him, that's all."

"What do you think this room is used for?" I bounced a few times, keeping my sword nicely out of the way. "Do you think people come here in pairs, or do they send someone in? Would we both fit on this couch?"

"Quit that." He held me still with both hands on my shoulders. "You're not five years old."

"I'll bounce if I want to. That's what it's there for."

He stood looking down at me, his two hands on my shoulders. "You know, Lady Katherine, if you screamed in here, no one would care."

"I know." I stopped bouncing and looked up into his eyes. "I could say the same to you."

"They'd just think we were having fun."

His eyes were dark, the pupils large in the candlelight. "Well, that's what it's here for, isn't it?" I said.

"Of course."

"Do you want to try anything, then?"

"Yes," he said, so suddenly I had only just heard him when his mouth was down on mine. It was hard and warm and exotic and very, very nice. I kept my arms at my sides. His fingers were still; everything was happening with our mouths, which changed shapes and textures to accommodate all sorts of feelings. My eyes were closed. I felt the velvet under my hand, and I wanted to sink down into it while his mouth and mine explored.

A gentle knock on the door made it necessary to stop. No one might care if we screamed, but one of us did have to say, "Come in."

Nan Glinley was everyone's vision of a perfect mother: small, round, placid and pleasant-faced. She was gowned in grey, and her hair was modestly coiffed in the manner of city women. I could tell from the way she looked at me only once that she knew who I was. But she spoke to both of us. "How can I help you?"

"Um," I said, and Marcus said, "We're investigating."

"My house," its mistress asked, "or yourselves?"

Was it that obvious? I guess it was. With the little sense left to me, I realized that if we stayed in there alone, Marcus and I could very well end up naked on the couch, and that was not what I had come to Glinley's for. "I want to see a man," I said imperiously. "A really, really handsome one. Dark haired, not too young—experienced, that is. Classy, though. Not trash."

"I see." She turned to Marcus. "And you?"

"Me, too," he said swiftly, having caught my plan. "We're together."

"Shall I show you what's available?"

I nodded. We would find Lucius Perry in here, actually see him in place in the halls of Glinley's House of You-Know-What. Why waste the chance? After that, we could go.

"You may select a partner first, if you like, and then we can all discuss what sort of setting you'd prefer, and what combination. Or we can sit down together now and decide in advance—"

"Oh, lord!" I exclaimed gauchely as I caught her drift. "I mean—we just want to look—to see—"

"Ah." Nan Glinley nodded. "Hidden observation? We can accommodate that."

I let out a breath of relief, and only hoped she didn't hear. No way on earth was I ending up on a couch with Lucius Perry, and neither was Marcus.

"Discretion, I think, is key here," she said, "given your tender years. We'll let you go masked while you search. Excuse me just a moment."

Nan Glinley left the room. Marcus and I looked at each other and burst out laughing.

"Hidden observation!" That's what we'd been doing all along.

"We'll never get away with this," Marcus chortled nervously.

"What if they throw us out?" I put my hands over my mouth to keep in the laughter.

"Get a grip on yourself and they won't. Start thinking up a story—"

Nan Glinley came back, carrying a bundle. "You might like to disarm," she said. "Your weapon will be safe here. Unless that's part of your personal preference . . . ?"

She knew perfectly well it wasn't. But she was treating us like real clients. I was impressed. If I ever really did want a little experience, this would be the place to get it, with a nice woman like that taking care of me. I took off my sword with a rueful smile to say of course we wouldn't be needing it in this lovely woman's house.

Nothing was forbidden at Glinley's, but privacy was respected. We were encased in silk capes from neck to toe, surmounted by masks with animal faces. I was a cat, and Marcus was an owl. He cut a caper in the corridor, so that his shadow danced wingéd on the wall. "Come," said Mistress Glinley, and we followed her through the halls.

We started by looking through peep holes into bedrooms decorated in various styles. They were also decorated with young men sitting or lying around trying to keep themselves amused. It was too early for them to be busy, but clearly they were expecting to be very busy soon. One was painting his nails, one practicing the guitar. Another was smoothing oil all over his body; I was tempted to stay and see what happened with him next—but it wasn't Perry, after all.

"No?" Nan Glinley asked us at the end of the corridor.

We shook our heads.

"Then let us try the Flower Garden."

The Flower Garden was amazing: an indoor room with a pool surrounded by plants, strewn with a variety of bodies scantily clad. We picked our way amongst them, feeling almost indecently overdressed, and moving strangely because we had to turn our heads to see anything through the eyeholes of the masks. Cloaked as we were, we had no gender. Bodies of both men and women did what they could to entice us: a languid glance, a flutter of fingers, a roll of the hips. Suddenly it all seemed possible—not seemed, but was—to take one by the hand, go off and learn to minister to desire in perfect safety. I licked my lips. That one . . . or that one . . . the golden hair just edging above the trouser line, but how swiftly they'd slip off to reveal the whole . . . the soft breasts floating unconfined beneath the gauze, to be nuzzled, stroked, explored. . . .

"Come on!" hissed Marcus.

"Are you made of stone?" I whispered back.

He said, "They're only whores," as though their very availability rendered them worthless.

We nearly missed Lucius Perry altogether. He was dressed like some nobleman wandered down from the Hill, in black brocade and silver lace. But his face was painted like a mask, skin powdered to white, and his eyes, with blue and gold on the lids, were lined with black, so that they seemed immense. His lips were stained red as old blood. He was sitting solitary by a fountain, staring at the water. He looked very helpless, fragile and alone. It wasn't only his painted face that made him unrecognizable—I'd never seen those qualities in him before. I wondered if he was doing it on purpose, if it was a mask he liked to wear. He did have a choice, after all.

Marcus raised his arm and pointed. Perry's eyes flicked our way, and he rose in one graceful movement. But Nan Glinley came forward and put her hand on his arm and murmured something low to him. He nodded and walked out of the room.

"You like him, do you?" She smiled. "You've made a good choice. And you're in luck; he's got some clients arranged, and he doesn't mind being watched tonight."

Now was the time to tell her, *No, that's all right, we don't want to see any of that, thanks; sorry to bother you, we're just leaving.* . . . Nobody's ever really died from embarrassment, have they? I turned to catch Marcus's gaze so I could pick up his thoughts, but of course the stupid costumes made it impossible. My friend was an owl. And I was amazed to hear his muffled voice saying, "Good," from behind the mask. "I'd like that. I want to see what he does. I want to see how he does it."

Well, if he did, so did I. This was better than anything we'd see at Teresa Grey's—or anything we wanted to see there—wasn't it? The final piece to Perry's puzzle, and practically with his consent.

She led us to a little cupboard of a room. We took off our capes and masks and gave them to her. "I'll be back in an hour," Nan Glinley said. "That should be enough." Well, it should. I could always close my eyes if it got to be too much. I turned my attention to the room.

There was a long slit in the wall, a sort of narrow window covered in mesh through which we could look into a luxurious bed chamber, dimly lit and gloriously appointed. It wasn't very tasteful; it practically screamed wealth and power—or at least, wealth. There wasn't a thing, from firetools to candlesticks to bedposts, that wasn't gilded or carved or ornamented in some way.

In his lace and brocade, Lucius Perry looked like yet another ornament, and not a very tasteful one, either. He sat in a chair next to the bed, as still as he had sat by the fountain in the Flower Garden. Gold candlelight on rich hangings made it look like a scene in a painting.

I wondered what he was thinking. Did he know we were there yet? Probably not, or he'd be doing something more enticing, wouldn't he? Why didn't he have a book to read? When would something happen? Marcus shifted in his seat and I moved away from him; there wasn't much room in there, but we were careful not to touch each other.

We both jumped when a knock on the door to the room broke the stillness. Perry turned slowly. A man came in and threw his coat on a chair.

"Well, hello." Lucius Perry smiled.

I peered at his customer. The man was short and a bit stout; he could have been anyone you'd pass on the street without a second thought. He stood staring at Perry as if he couldn't believe his eyes. "Yes," he said. "Yes. God, you're gorgeous. They were right."

"I'm here for you. Name your desire—or better yet, don't name it, just show me." Perry began advancing on him, but the man held up his hand.

"No, wait. I want to look at you." Perry stopped, obedient. "You are . . . exquisite. But the paint—the eyes, and whatnot—it's a little much. I wonder if you'd mind wiping it off?"

"That," Lucius said, "I cannot do." As the man drew breath to object, he added swiftly, "But why confine yourself to looking, when you can touch?"

"Yes," the man said again. "Yes. Come here, then." He put his hands to either side of Perry's face, and pulled his mouth down, kissing him. He pulled Perry's head back, and traced his eyes, his cheeks . . . the paint was smeared all over his face, making the mask all the more effective, but the way he held his body—I watched Lucius Perry melting, melting in a fluid surrender, as though sinking into a water of anonymity. . . . The man's hands were all over him now, opening his jacket, plunging under his shirt, squeezing and pulling on his body, and Lucius Perry flowed with it all, his head thrown back, his eyes closed. He loved being touched. He loved being admired. Glinley's was made for him.

But the client wasn't really interested in Lucius Perry's pleasure. He was undoing his own breeches now, and guiding Perry's hands down to where his tool sprang out. I shut my eyes for a moment, and heard moaning. I peeked through my lashes. Lucius was kneeling before him, obscuring the worst of the view. It was perfectly obvious what they were doing.

"Hmph," Marcus muttered beside me. "He could have had that on the corner for a whole lot less than he's paying here."

"Hush," I hissed. The man dug his fingers into Lucius's hair, and arced his back, and shouted so loud I thought the whole house would come running. But nothing happened. The man subsided onto the bed, and Lucius handed him a towel. The man wiped himself off and started to get up, though you could tell he didn't really want to move.

"There's no hurry," Perry said. "Can I get you something to drink?"

The man drank a glass of wine. From his face, I guessed it was better wine than he was used to.

"Thank you," he said. He began putting his clothing together. "I wish that I could stay, but . . ." He shrugged. Glinley's was expensive.

Perry nodded. "Come back," he said. "Come back and see me, when you can."

The man smiled. "Don't tempt me. I'll dream of you, first, for a good long time."

He closed the door softly behind him.

So that was it, was it? Did they all do that? A solid hour of this would be the end of me. Our hiding room wasn't very big, and it was dark. I couldn't see Marcus, but I could hear his breathing next to me, shallow and a bit uneven.

"Are you all right?" I whispered. I wondered if we really should have come.

"Fine. Don't fuss."

Lucius Perry was carefully putting himself back together again. Like an actor, he cleaned off his face—and for a moment, I saw the man we knew, his skin pale in the candlelight, his eyes bright. He was staring into the mirror over his dressing table. He turned his face from side to side, examining it as if trying to see what it was that other people saw. He touched his lips, ran his finger down the straight line of his nose, smoothed his eyebrows, stuck out his tongue and laughed. He took out little pots from a drawer and began layering the paint back over his eyes. The colors made him look magical, like a creature in a dream. The last thing he did was his lips, drawing his crimsoned finger across them slowly, savoring the sensation. He rubbed them over and over, until they were saturated with color. If you didn't know about the paint, it was as if he had flushed them with stroking. He picked up a comb and drew it down through his tangled hair, again and again until it lay sleek on his head. Then he peered critically into the mirror and ran a hand through his hair, and looked up.

I had missed the knock. Another man came in. Lucius Perry stood, and bowed to him. The new client was dressed like a merchant, a shopkeeper, perhaps. He looked around the room at the canopied bed, the hearthfire, the tapestry; at one point he even looked straight at us, which gave me a scare, but our peephole must have been part of something like a picture or a hanging, and I suppose he was admiring it. "Well," he said. "A nobleman's bedroom. I've never been in one of these before."

Lucius Perry drawled, "You'll find it's much like any man's." He sounded quite a lot like the duke, actually.

The client's hands were clenching and unclenching. "And are you much like any man?"

Lucius preened. "I'm better. Look at me. Don't you think so?"

"A better man than I? I do not think so."

"Don't you? Maybe you need a better look."

"Anyone looks good with thirty royals' worth of clothing on his back. Take it off."

"How dare you?" Perry said arrogantly. Oh, he was enjoying himself, even I could tell, being just as horrible as the man expected him to be. This was different from the last one. There was a contest here, and a sort of drama. "This coat alone cost fifty."

"I deal in cloth, you slut. I know exactly what that getup's worth. You've probably passed my shop a hundred times and never looked at me. But you'll look at me now. You'll look at me, and like it." He was breathing so hard, I was afraid he was going to hit poor Lucius. But the younger man showed no alarm.

"I'm looking," Perry said.

"Keep looking," the man growled.

"I'm looking." They were both starting to breathe hard.

"What do you see?"

"I see you. I see you, and I like it. You make me want things I shouldn't want."

"Such as?"

"I want to take my clothing off for you. I want you to strip me naked. I want you to see me the way no one's ever seen me before."

"Your noble friends would not approve."

"My noble friends cannot imagine the pleasure. Strip me. Reveal me."

"Strip yourself," the man said thickly. "I want to watch."

Perry lifted a hand to the buttons of his coat and slowly undid them, and his breeches as well, 'til he stood there in his shirt, lovely as ivory, with the silver lace framing his shoulders.

The man watched, entranced. It was like wizardry: Lord Lucius Perry, who wasn't himself but someone else who looked just like him, taking off layers of disguise until he stood revealed as a painted whore, less himself now than when he started fully clothed in noble's garb. That's what I thought, anyway. He wanted to see how far from himself he could go, and this was how he did it. I hoped someday he didn't lose himself entirely.

The cloth merchant lifted Perry's shirt behind, and stroked him. "Lie down," he said. "You're mine, now."

"I'm yours," Perry sighed, and laid himself facedown on the tasteless, gilded bed.

What they did didn't really seem so terrible, because I couldn't see much, just a back and some legs. The noise was the worst of it, especially at the end.

Beside me, I felt Marcus turn to the wall. I reached for his hand in the dark, but caught only the edge of his cloak. He was shaking.

The man was already up and buttoning his clothes. "Get dressed," he said curtly. "I'll see you next week. Wear something different, though."

"As you wish."

When he'd left, and Perry was washing himself, Marcus murmured to me, "Well. Now I know how it looks from the outside."

"Outside what?" I whispered.

He pulled away suddenly. "Sorry," he said, and flung the little door open. I tumbled into the hallway after him, and found him kneeling over a convenient basin, puking his guts into it. There were, I saw, many such basins, large and ornamental, placed strategically along the hall. I guessed they were used fairly often, for one thing and another, at Glinley's.

I tried to hold his shoulders, but he waved me away. Of course he had brought his own clean handkerchief. "You need water," I said. "It'll wash the taste out. Was it the wine, Marcus? Did it make you sick?"

He sat all scrunched up with his arms tight around his knees. "No. I'd like more of it, actually." His teeth were chattering. "C-can you find me some?"

I looked wildly up and down the candlelit corridor. "Not a prayer. But—" There was a bellpull. I pulled it. The man who came was the same one who had first let us into the house.

"My friend is ill," I said. "We need to get our things and go. I'm sorry about the mess—"

"That's normal," he said. "A little too rich for your blood, sir?"

"Stuff it," Marcus growled.

"Quit being so uppity," the man said. "You may be the duke's own bumboy now, but I'm an old friend of Red Jack's, and I know what you was."

Marcus seized the sides of the basin again.

"You lay off him," I said to Red Jack's friend. "He can be uppity if he wants to." I heard Marcus laugh—it was an awful sound, in the midst of his retching, but it gave me heart. "Now show us to our room," I said, "and make yourself scarce."

The man glowered at me, but when Marcus could stand, he led us back to the room with the couch.

"You won't get much good of him here, my lady," the man said rudely. "Too bad—he used to be the sweetest little tosser on the streets."

"*Out*," I said, looking for my sword. He left before I could find it— and without a tip, I need hardly add.

My friend sat shivering on the couch. I put my cloak around him and made him drink some wine. "Never mind," I said. I needed to pace, since Marcus wouldn't let me touch him. "He's just a filthy stupid whoremongering idiot. We'll tell my uncle, and he'll have him thrown out on the street."

"No! Katie, no, you can't ever tell Tremontaine about this, *please*, Katie, swear!"

"Well, all right," I said. "You're right. I guess it was a bad idea. But it's over now, Marcus; you'll feel better soon. I'm sorry it made you sick. You couldn't know."

"Yes, I could," he said fiercely. "I knew exactly. Don't you understand?" He was shaking so hard he could barely hold the wineglass, so he knocked it back in one gulp. "You heard the man. And I told you that day, in the garden, but you still don't really understand, do you?"

I was beginning to; I just wished I didn't have to. "It's not your fault," I said. "You were just a kid. It was in Riverside, and you were just a little kid and you needed the money, right?"

"I didn't get any money. My mother's man sold me to Jack when she died. Jack gave me food and a place to sleep, and I worked for him. When I stopped being little and cute, he didn't have any use for me. Someone told him the Mad Duke liked them older. So he took me to the duke and sold me to him."

It was true, then, about him and my uncle, what people said and what I'd refused to believe. I swallowed bile. I didn't know how I could stand it, but I was going to have to. Fear is enemy to sword. I listened, and I kept very still, but I couldn't look my friend in the face.

"Tremontaine saved my life. He gave me a room, and a door that locked."

I let out breath I hadn't known I'd been holding, and drank some of the wine. "Oh, Marcus." I wanted to put my arms around him, but I saw from the way he was gripping my cloak around himself that he didn't want to be touched; he wasn't done saying things.

"He gave me teachers, and books, and—well, you know, everything. I owe him like nobody's business. He's been protecting me all this time; nobody touches me, and oh god god god, after all that—" Marcus was twisting his fingers together— "If Tremontaine finds out I came here after all that, he'll fucking kill me, Katherine. He will. You mustn't tell him!"

"I won't," I promised.

"I mean, it's been all right for so long, I thought I could do this—I didn't think it mattered, it was all about someone else, like I could test myself—just watching Perry—I don't know how he does it, honestly I don't—"

"He's testing himself," I said. "Like a swordsman. It's some kind of challenge for him."

"Well, he can have it. He's crazier than I thought."

"Is there any wine left?" I poured us each another glass, and drank. It made me feel warmer and braver at once. "Let's just go," I said. "I think I can find the main door." I buckled my sword on, a little unsteadily.

"Right." He was still shaking. He turned his dark eyes wide on me. "Do you hate me now?"

"Hate you? How could I hate you?" I put my arm around him, and this time he let me. "Come on," I said; "we're going home."

Glinley's smelt of sandalwood and beeswax and smoke and drugs and bodies. We wound our way down infinite identical corridors, trying not to be noticed. Once we actually stood like statues in empty niches as customers passed by. The halls started looking familiar. "Have we been here already?" I whispered. A door opened, and since there was no niche, we flattened ourselves against a wall. It was Lucius Perry, leaving the room where he worked. He was brushed and cloaked, on his way out. We followed him through the house, dropping back far enough not to be obvious. Once he looked behind him, so we quickly seized one another in embrace. I buried my head in my friend's shoulder, and Marcus put his face in my hair until we heard his footsteps fade away.

When we got outside, even the Riverside air smelled fresh.

I began to turn toward home, but Marcus held my wrist. He nodded in the direction of Perry's departing back and raised his eyebrows. I shook my head: enough was enough for one night. Besides, Perry was nearly out of the radius of the house's torchlight—he'd be stopping for a linkboy or his own torch soon, and I didn't fancy trailing behind him in the dark. We stood in the shadows of Glinley's, and watched Lucius Perry walk away into the night.

And we watched two men walk after him, faster and faster, and then we heard a loud thump and an even louder shout.

We ran toward the sound, Marcus with his knife and I with my sword. It was one of those little Riverside streets where the houses nearly touch across. We could barely see the shapes of the two men and one more, whaling on one crouching figure who was not quiet as they laid into him.

"Stop!" I shouted, and to my horror I heard one say, "Is that the girl? That's her!"

"Run, Katie!"

With my sword in my hand, I could not run. I just couldn't do it. I knew I could take them on—they didn't have swords, and I did.

"Katie, *please!*"

"Get help," I said to Marcus as they came at me, leaving poor Lucius Perry gasping on the ground—but help was already there.

Men from my uncle's house—a footman and a swordsman, not wearing livery, but I knew them well and had never been so glad to see them. They laid into the three bullies, and they were much better trained and well-armed, besides. I'd like to say I helped, but I didn't—everyone was much bigger than me, and it was street-fighting without any rules—I hung back, and it was over so fast, with two of the bullies running away and the third one kept for questions, hands bound behind him. The swordsman took charge of him and the footman picked up Lucius Perry, because he couldn't walk. We went slowly. I felt much better when the Tremontaine swordsman, Twohey was his name, who was having trouble with his prisoner, said, "Lady Katherine, if you could just give him a good jab in the ribs—with your pommel? Good and hard—that's it, thanks. Come on, you."

My uncle was wearing a bright yellow dressing gown that didn't suit him; I'm not sure it was even his. He stood blinking in the hall at the top of the main house stairs, having been alerted by what I was coming to see was an admirable network that something had happened.

"For once," he drawled, "I try to get to sleep at a reasonable hour, and you bring me—bodies."

"One for questioning and one for bed, my lord," said Twohey cheerfully.

"Not my bed, I hope," the duke said; "that one's a bloody mess—" He saw who it was. "Oh, god. Get him seen to. Now. What the hell do you think you're doing, holding him in the hall like a package?"

"And this one?" My prisoner moaned, so I whacked him in the ribs again.

"Katherine, my dear! I want him for information, not for kickball. Take him down cellar—Finian can work on him. I'll be down later. Marcus, come help me find my—"

"I'd like to go to bed, now, please."

"Re-eally?" the duke drawled, then snapped, "Get up here."

Swaying gently, Marcus met his master on the stairs. I watched them anxiously. Was it all true? Had the duke saved my friend and never really touched him? If he hurt Marcus, I'd kill him.

As if he could hear my thoughts, the duke said coldly, "Katherine. I don't believe this. I leave you alone for one instant, and you debauch my personal attendant."

I felt utterly sick in the pit of my stomach. How did he know? What would he do?

"This boy is drunk," the duke said. "And I suppose that means you are, too. Go to bed, the pair of you. If you wake up in the morning with a bad head, ask Betty for some of that unspeakable green tisane. But don't disturb me; I'll be up all night torturing prisoners."

He stalked off in a blaze of mustard-colored glory. I suppose I was drunk enough to think that it would be a good idea to explain to him that I was not in the least bit drunk—I certainly didn't feel it. Marcus had had much more wine than I; but then, he'd needed it. I watched Marcus go on up the stairs alone. He had very nice shoulders.

"Good night," I said, though there was nobody left to hear me.

LUCIUS PERRY DREAMED HE WAS A TREE, AND THAT WOODSMEN were chopping at the bark that was his face. It hurt like anything. Well, now that he knew that trees felt pain, he'd tell his brother to stop cutting the ones on the estate. He was flying now, way above the forest where the trees were, but something was pulling on his leg, and he was all off balance. He fell into the trees, and branches exploded all over his body as he crashed to the forest floor, a wild goose shot full of arrows. They stung him when he tried to move.

Hold still, a deer said. *Drink this.*

It put him to sleep, the deer's drink. When he woke, he was in his own body, lying in a bed. The Duke Tremontaine was bent over his head. Lucius's mouth was all stuck together, and he could see out of only one eye. It hurt so much to move that all he could manage was a feeble moan of protest. The duke pulled away. "I'm not looking for your favors," Tremontaine said. Someone Lucius couldn't see put a spout between his lips—an invalid's beaker, filled with water that drizzled into his mouth.

He heard Tremontaine's voice. "Perry. I am sorry. I know the man responsible for this, and it is entirely my fault."

What happened? he wanted to ask, but his lips were too stiff to form the words.

"I had one day," the duke said. "I didn't know it ended at midnight. —Never mind. You may stay here while you recover. I promise you'll be safe. Or, when you are a little better, I can send you home." The duke went on, something about messages and assurances, but Lucius closed his eyes so he could see the walls of a little white house with the sun on them, and a bowl of roses, freshly blown, on a table re-flected in a mirror.

Y OUR UNCLE'S BEING A PIG," MARCUS SAID. WE'D BEEN PLAY-ing shesh in his room all morning because we were not allowed to leave the house. Marcus wasn't really concentrating on his game, so for once I was winning. "He's not speaking to me, and he won't tell me what's going on."

"Because of Glinley's? You didn't—you didn't tell him, did you?"

"Are you joking? He'd have to torture it out of me, and he doesn't have time. But he knows we did something. He just won't say."

"Is he drunk?"

"No, then he'd talk. He just glares at me and says not to bother him. No one in the kitchen knows anything, either—all he's eating is bread and cheese. And meeting with secretaries and lawyers and shady characters, and writing letters."

"It's Perry," I said wisely. "He's probably planning revenge on who-ever did it. Do we know who yet?"

"How should I know? He won't talk to me."

"He's got to know. That man in the cellar . . ."

"He's gone; I've already checked."

"Check."

"I did."

"No, I'm *checking* you. Look to your other wizard."

Marcus took one of my peons. "I knew you'd do that." I ignored the gibe. "We're definitely still locked in," he said. "I think he thinks someone's after us, like Perry. After *you*, I should say."

"And you're just locked in with me to keep me company?" He took my queen. "Oh, dammit, Marcus, I didn't even *see* that!"

"I know." My hand was on the board; he put his own hand over it. His skin was warm, and a little damp.

"Marcus?" I asked. "Are you sorry you kissed me?"

"Not really. Unless you are."

"I'm not," I said. "I'd do it again." His hand tightened on mine, but he didn't do anything. "It's men that make you sick, right? Not me?"

"You don't at all."

"Just because I dress like one sometimes . . . If that puts you off, I can—well—"

"Take your clothes off?"

"Because I'm really not a man. I've got—well, developments."

"I'd noticed."

"So do you want to?"

"If you do."

I touched his mouth with my free hand. "I do."

This kissing was very different: more like eating, really, satisfying an appetite you hadn't even known was in you until you found yourself with a big mouthful of pleasure. It was as if the minds that had been playing shesh suddenly flew out through the roof. All I knew was what things felt good, and that I wanted more of them. I had never even imagined Marcus with his clothes off, and now here I was ripping them away to get at more of his skin. I didn't mind when his hands found my breasts—in fact, I encouraged him, and I pushed his head down so I could feel his face and his mouth on them.

We ended up on the rug because we were too embarrassed to get on the bed, and we rolled around on it and stroked each other and knocked over the shesh board (we never could find the black peon, after) and rolled all over each other. Marcus started groaning and saying, "Katie, stop," but I didn't see any reason to, and then he clutched me and cried out hard, and went very still. When he started to weep, I held him, and didn't even mind the mess he'd made all over us.

"Who cares about going out?" I whispered into his hair, and he laughed, then, and I licked his salty ear.

⁓

IN A COZY ARMCHAIR IN HIS STUDY, WHERE HE WAS READING A history of the rise of the Council of Lords after the fall of the decadent kings, Lord Ferris received word that David Alexander Tielman Campion, Duke Tremontaine, had arrived at his front door desiring to speak with him.

Lord Ferris smiled. "I am busy at the moment. He is welcome to wait, if he likes."

"Shall I offer him refreshment, my lord?"

"Of course. Nothing too sweet; I believe His Grace likes salty foods. And plenty of wine. He might want some diversion, as well. Why don't you give him this?" He handed the man his book, *The Triumph of the Crescent*. "It might prove instructive."

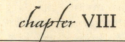

chapter VIII

THE HOUSEHOLD WAS SO TOPSY-TURVY, THERE WAS A chance no one would notice if we lay on the rug all day. But it was a chance we were not quite willing to take. And so we hunted down all our clothes and put them back on. There would be other mornings, when the duke did not rise early to torture prisoners. He never noticed anything in the morning.

Marcus went out to investigate, while I put my hair back into some kind of order. "He's gone out," he said when he came back. "And we're still not allowed to." He'd brought apple tart; we sat on the window seat feeding it to each other.

We wished we could be sure that what had happened to Lucius Perry had nothing to do with us, but we had to consider the possibility that it did. Maybe we'd led those bullies right to him. Maybe they'd been after us to begin with. One of them had recognized me—though, as Marcus pointed out, I was getting to be pretty well known. But why were we locked in the house now, if not for our own protection? If we hadn't followed Lucius Perry, maybe he never would have been attacked. Unless what happened to Perry had just scared the duke into worrying about us.

Then there was the question of those Tremontaine guards. They had been remarkably on the spot, coming to the rescue like that. Possibly the duke had set them to keep a protective eye on Lucius, or on Glinley's, which was part his, after all. He did have people watching all over Riverside . . . but maybe—horrible thought!—they'd been there to keep an eye on us. Maybe they'd been following us all along. In which case, the duke knew perfectly well where we'd been. When he got back from wherever he was, there would be ructions.

To take our minds off it, and because the last thing we wanted was for him to return and find us naked on the rug, we went to check on Perry's progress.

For reasons no one could entirely remember, Lucius Perry's nurse was named Gobber Slighcarp, or if they knew, they wouldn't tell us— I mean about his name. Gobber was a very competent nurse. It was perfectly reasonable for him to take care of Perry. He used to surgeon hurt swordsmen, having been thrown out of the College of Physic for unmentionable crimes that no one remembered either.

To make up for what had happened, we tried to make ourselves useful to Gobber Slighcarp. Marcus fetched things from the kitchens. I gave Betty money to go out and buy flowers and scented candles, which are nice when you're ill.

We weren't really eager to see Perry himself. But Gobber came out of the sickroom to say the nobleman wanted to speak to me, and before I could think of an excuse, I was by the hurt man's bedside.

After what I'd observed through the peephole at Glinley's, I couldn't imagine having a conversation with Lord Lucius. But that fled my mind as soon as I saw him now. He didn't look like the same man at all. His face was purple and green. One eye was swollen shut, and his nose was crooked and large and bandaged. And his mouth, his sensual, elegant mouth—

I said, "Oh! I'm so sorry—"

"Not to," Lucius Perry rasped. "You saved me."

"It's better than it looks," Gobber explained to both of us. "It won't heal pretty, but it'll heal all right. Ribs, too—I've seen worse. And if we're careful with that leg, it won't stiffen up too much."

"Come," said Lucius, gesturing with a scraped-up hand. I realized he couldn't see me unless I was near his good eye. "Cousin Artemi'a friend. You know. Mus' marry her."

"Why?"

"Family."

"The family want you to marry Artemisia?" This was awful. He was all wrong for her. And what about Teresa Grey? "But— does she want to? Have you asked her?"

"Ready now," he sighed. "Safe. All m'fault, w'happened. You write her. Ask her to. I'll sign."

Gobber looked at me and shrugged. He had no idea what this was about. But I did. And I wasn't having it.

"I'll write her," I said, and went to find Marcus. He didn't argue, much. And he liked showing how well he could sneak out of the Riverside house without being caught.

Once he left, I went and wrote a letter to Artemisia telling her she was on no account to agree to marriage with Lucius, whatever her family said. I didn't tell her that he was riddled with vice, or that he already loved someone else; I just reminded her that where there was no love there could be no lasting joy. I added that my heart was with her, and I hoped she'd find someone really nice to marry, but if she didn't, she should not marry at all.

Then I did what I should have done ages ago: I went to the duke's chief personal secretary, Arthur Ghent, and explained that Artemisia's family didn't want me writing to her, and might even be reading her letters, so could he please see to it that she got this one safely? Arthur smiled just short of a grin, and said he'd see to it.

Then, in utter penance, and to keep myself distracted, I went and offered to read aloud to Lucius Perry. He let me choose, and I was well into *The King's Hunt* when Marcus returned with the woman from the Hill, the one Lucius Perry truly loved.

She didn't handle it well. Marcus swore to me he really had told her just how bad Perry looked, and that he would get better, but it didn't seem to matter. When Teresa Grey saw Lucius Perry, she made an unhappy sound and clutched at the wall, and Gobber had to make her sit and put her head down. "Oh, no," she moaned; "oh, no. . . ."

I ran and got lavender water to chafe her wrists with. She had very strong and flexible hands; she could have learned to hold a sword if she'd wanted. "It's all my fault," she said. "Oh, what shall we do? What shall we do? Oh, Lucius . . ."

I held her hands tightly, and got her to look into my eyes. "It wasn't you," I told her. "Truly, it wasn't. I don't know if you know, but Lord Lucius has been working for Tremontaine."

"I know, all right, you curious child," she said to me, which at least was better than moaning.

"Well, then. It was all because of that. He has a lot of enemies, the duke."

"Does he?" she said in that annoying way adults have of humoring children who are telling them things they already know.

"Yes, well, if you know that already, you'll know this has nothing to do with you. It was someone trying to get at our house."

Teresa Grey stood up. Even with her hair all wild and her dress disordered, she managed to look astonishingly beautiful. "Where is the duke?" she said. "Let him see me, and tell me so himself."

Marcus said, "He doesn't know about you yet. We're the only ones who do."

She looked closely at him. "Is that so? And what do you know about me, pray?"

I said, "You are Lucius Perry's one true love. The rest mean nothing to him—especially not the duke. You are a painter, and a writer, and—well, a Lady of Quality."

She stared at me as though I'd lost my mind. "Oh, this is too much!" she cried. "You! You're a girl! Are you some kind of actress, some protégé of his? Am I supposed to be writing a vehicle for you, is that what this is about? Because I'll tell you right now, I'm not doing a thing for him or for anyone until I find out who's responsible for this. Right now, I—I wouldn't piss on the duke if he were on fire."

"Watch it," Marcus said with surprising heat. "Katie's a lady."

She swirled back to Marcus, and then to me, and back to him again. "You. You were the one who delivered those pigments."

He ducked his head.

"Marcus, you rat!" I said. "You did that without me!"

"Were you in on it, too?" she demanded.

There was a strangled noise from the bed. We all jumped and turned to attend to the hurt man. But there was no need. Lucius Perry was laughing.

"Go away," Teresa told us all, even Gobber Slighcarp.

We went. We left them alone together, and it did not even occur to us to try and look in through the keyhole until much later. They were both asleep, his head on her soft breast, and *The King's Hunt* lying open on the floor beside them.

⌒

T HE DUKE TREMONTAINE WAITED IN A YELLOW-AND-BLACK drawing room that was the height of fashion and reminded him of stinging wasps. He was prepared, he told Lord Ferris's man, to wait until tomorrow, if necessary, as long as they would bring him a pillow for the night. He ate only nuts from his pocket, and drank only water, but he opened the book Ferris had sent him and after a few pages took out a pencil nub and started scribbling comments in the margins.

The day was well advanced when Lord Ferris admitted the duke to his study.

He did not bother with preliminaries. "You come unarmed?"

"You know I can't fight."

"That, my lord duke, is becoming increasingly obvious. All the same, if you will empty your pockets, please?"

"You're joking."

"I am not joking. We are alone in this room. Let me see what you carry."

Tremontaine glared at him. "Do you want me to trade my marbles for your string collection and broken top?"

"Do you want me to have you searched? Please don't be offended— or rather, be as offended as you like. We both know you're not going anywhere."

The Duke Tremontaine put three nuts, two handkerchiefs, a penknife and his pencil stub on the table. He fished a little deeper and disgorged a button, two calling cards and half of the Knave of Cups with some calculations scribbled on it.

Ferris looked at them impassively. "And where is my contract?"

"Your what?"

"My marriage contract with your niece."

"She's just a girl," Tremontaine said bluntly. "What possible use can you have for her now? She's much too young."

"Early marriages are a tradition in your family," said Lord Ferris. "She's sixteen now— See? I cared enough to check—older, in fact, than your mother was when you were born, like her mother before her. But you don't respect your own traditions, do you? Your family's, or anyone else's. Do you think the Perrys will be pleased to know you've been employing their son as a Riverside whore? Or the Fitz-Levis, for that matter, who are even now trying to foist him on their not impenetrable daughter? Fussy people, the F-L's."

"You give me too much credit," the duke said. "I didn't find him his trade, I found him already at it."

"They might not believe that."

"They can ask him themselves. I've got him in my house—what's left of him."

Ferris laughed aloud. "If they ask him, he'll blame you, if he's got any sense."

"And say he does? What difference will it make? The Mad Duke debauches another beautiful nobleman—again. All yawn. The question is what they'll say when they learn what you've done to spoil his beauty."

"I?" Lord Ferris cocked his head. "What did I do?"

"Oh, come, my lord." The duke gave a pretty good imitation of the older man. "Hired bravos aren't that hard to bully information out of."

"Or to bribe. Of course you'd pay some Riverside tough to say I hired him. You've got plenty of money, we all know that." The duke glared at him. "Face it. You may have friends, I'm not saying you don't—all sorts of eccentric people adore you. But you've got no allies. No one who counts."

Lord Ferris picked up a paper-knife, a long silver tool ornamented with a lascivious nymph. He rubbed his thumb along her while he talked. "You've brought this on yourself, you know. What do you think I've been doing for the past ten years? Building alliances, creating systems that will hold me. Yes, it's cost me, but I can get more funds, one way or another. People respect me—and they fear me— and well they should, as you now know. Do they fear you . . . Alec? I don't think so. They used to, back in your murderous Riverside days. But you've let that particular power go. You've gotten squeamish. Here I am, the elected leader of the land's most powerful governing council. And you are . . . what, now? An entertainment. A curiosity." He held the nymph up. "For your grandmother's sake, I did try to warn you. Now you're on your own."

"Ferris," said Alec Campion in a curious growl. "You are making me angry."

"Try to control it," Lord Ferris said agreeably, "or you'll never get anywhere in life."

"Very angry," the duke repeated in the same half-musical tone. "It makes me wonder what it would be like to take the battle you've begun to its next logical step. To hire people to attack your people on the streets on no provocation but that they support you. You'd retaliate in kind, of course. I'd need to arm my friends, or have them guarded well. But there are plenty of swords out there, looking for work."

Ferris turned his whole head like a bird, to look straight at the duke with his one good eye. "You would, too, wouldn't you? You'd plunge this city back a hundred years and more, to when liveried houses were fighting each other on the streets, when houses were fortresses, and nobles hired swords to keep from cutting each other down. You'd do all that, rather than capitulate or work out a reasoned, reasonable compromise. You would." Without warning, Ferris slammed his hand against his desk. "*What* was the woman thinking? Making something like you her heir! I admired her, I even loved her for a while, but in the end, she must have been mad."

"They say it runs in the family," the duke said doucely.

"I am hoping that isn't the case."

"Still planning on breeding my niece?"

"We'll merely skip a generation—write you off as a bad egg and then move on. The girl has neither your grandmother's looks nor her charm. Maybe she has brains, though. I trained with the duchess; she passed on to me what she knew of statecraft and the human heart—and believe me, she knew a lot. I've even forgiven her for throwing me over for Michael Godwin; I see now she chose well, he's a capable man." Lord Ferris's nostrils were white, distended. He was breathing rapidly through them. He had lost his temper, but didn't realize it yet. "Or maybe . . ." he went on cruelly, "maybe you had to sleep with her to get the benefits. I did wonder about you for a while, but now I'm quite sure you never did, or you wouldn't be such a fool."

"I'm crushed."

Eventually, people the duke disliked did lose their temper around him. It was a peculiar talent that he had, and he usually enjoyed it. He waited, now, to see what Ferris would say. The Crescent was working himself up to something unforgivable. The duke wondered what it would be.

"Did she think you'd change, I wonder? Or did she merely think St Vier would keep you in line?"

"We didn't discuss it. Her face was all frozen."

"She thought you'd keep him, though, I'll be bound. I would have bet on it myself. He seemed unreasonably attached to you. What on earth did you do to lose him?"

"How do you know he isn't dead?"

"I know," Ferris said. The ruby at the duke's throat jumped wildly against the lace it was pinned to. "Did he, too, come to find you unbearable? What would it take to drive him from your side? Not hissing, like your whore of an actress, or mockery, like your fat friend. St Vier was a reasonable man, and gifted. Not a man to be bought, as I found to my own sorrow. Perhaps, when his love soured on you, you trusted to all that nice money you have to keep him by you, only to find it wasn't enough. Really, you'd do better to give your niece to me, before she, too, finds you unbear—"

There was a bronze figurine in the duke's hand, and he swung it at Ferris's head—from the side with the eyepatch, of course. Ferris groaned, and went down.

It was a small statue of a god leaning on a pedestal. The pedestal had sharp edges; the back of Ferris's head was bleeding heavily. His eyes were closed, but his hands were moving.

The Duke Tremontaine considered the statue. It had little bits of skin and hair on it. Now that he'd relieved his feelings with one blow, he didn't really fancy bashing Ferris's skull in with it.

Nor did he like the idea of what Ferris would do if he survived now.

His eye fell on the nymph, fallen from Ferris's hand. The long knife wasn't silver after all, just a strong alloy plated in silver. He could tell from the weight. He stuffed his neck stock into Ferris's mouth, to discourage breathing as well as noise.

"Listen, if you can hear me," said Alec Campion. "You were right about one thing. The duchess never named me her heir. She believed she was immune to death. Certainly she was very resistant; when it felled her, she stayed breathing for quite some time. They asked her whom she'd chosen, but by then she couldn't answer. They went through a list of names. Maybe yours was even on it; I don't know. But when they got to mine, she made a sign with her hand, and they took it for assent."

Lord Ferris groaned. The duke pulled open the man's jacket; no need to make this any harder than it had to be. Third and fourth ribs, right in between . . . He closed his eyes, pictured an anatomy text. Richard always made it look so easy. One blow, straight to the heart— if he liked you.

How many men had Alec driven onto St Vier's sword? His turn, now. Loser of knives, lover of steel . . . It took more force than he was master of. Ferris grunted and thrashed. I'm going to look like an idiot, he thought, if I don't do this right. He took a deep breath, and then struck home.

The duke did not ring for a servant, simply walked out the door, left the house and started walking back to Riverside. He washed his hands at a public fountain, and if a very tall man in very disheveled, very expensive clothing walking the length of the city was hard to miss, he was, if you knew the proclivities of the nobility, easy to ignore. And there had always been something about Alec Campion at his worst, some air of dangerous negligence, that made even the toughest element give him a wide berth.

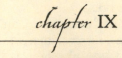

chapter IX

Aᶠᵗᵉʳ ᵈᵃʳᵏ, ᵃ ˢᵐᵃˡˡ, narrow carriage pulled into the courtyard of the duke's great Riverside house, the horses sweating and dusty from the road. The footman knew better by now than to try to help his passenger out of it; he merely opened the door and attended to the baggage, while the man stiffly eased himself out. He stood for a moment in the courtyard, waiting, or looking around. Many of the windows were lit; in others, light passed from window to window as people hurried through the house.

One of the lights came toward him. "Finally," a young man said. "You're here. He's been waiting for you. Please come with—" He put his hand out, and jumped at the newcomer's reaction.

"It's all right," the man said. "I'll follow you."

Iɴ ʜɪs sᴛᴜᴅy, ᴛʜᴇ ᴅᴜᴋᴇ ᴡᴀs ʙᴜʀɴɪɴɢ ᴘᴀᴘᴇʀs. Wʜᴇɴ ᴛʜᴇ ᴘᴀɪʀ came in he looked up but did not rise, just kept feeding things to the fire. "Good," he said, "you're here. I was afraid the Bridge might be closed."

"Not yet. Will it be?"

"Soon, if they've got any sense."

"Alec, what on earth have you been doing?"

"You didn't get here in time, so I had to kill Ferris myself." The duke waited a moment for the full effect.

"Did you?" his friend asked curiously. "How?"

"Eclectically. But conclusively."

"You didn't poison him, did you?"

"Heavens, no. That would be dishonorable. No, I stabbed him with a nymph."

The other man laughed.

"I was in his house, and his whole staff knows it. I expect to be arrested any minute. So I'm leaving."

"Rather than face a Court of Honor? Look, it's not so bad, really. Did you challenge him first?"

"I forgot. There wasn't time. But I can always say I did. There was no one else there."

"You'll get off, then."

"Not necessarily. I had to whack him on the head first. Not very convincing as a challenge, even for a lenient Court, which this one won't be—did I tell you he was also the Crescent Chancellor?"

"Oh, Alec." St Vier shook his head. "Still, you are the Duke Tremontaine. Maybe you can bribe someone. You have supporters, surely."

"The whole thing's too much trouble. And anyway, I'm sick of it here. You were right."

St Vier considered the fire. "I know."

For the first time, the young man spoke. "You mean we're leaving the city, my lord? Why didn't you tell me? I'd better pack—"

"I'm going," said the duke. "You're staying."

"No, I'm not. Not this time."

"Yes, you are, Marcus. Katherine's staying, so you're staying. It's all on the desk over there, signed and sealed. Make sure she opens it as soon as I've gone. That's important. Don't look right now—just find me my penknife—I know I put it down there somewhere, and it's gone."

"You're Marcus?" St Vier said. "Why didn't you say so? I thought you were younger."

"He was," said the duke. "They grow."

"So where are we going, anyway?"

"Somewhere nice. Somewhere with bees, and sun, and lots and lots of thyme."

S HE SAT IN HER WINDOW SEAT, WATCHING THE SHADOWS SHOOT up against the walls of the courtyard as people with torches scurried about with horses and baggage. There was no light in her room. She sat with her knees hugged in her arms, her face pressed to the glass, just tilted so that her breath didn't mist it. It was a play, she thought; it was some kind of play, and when it was over someone would come and tell her what it meant, and what her part would be.

Then she saw him, or thought she did—the man who used to live here and said he'd never come back. He was standing in the court-yard, against a pillar near the well, just standing there looking at it all.

"Master!" Her breath fogged the glass. She struggled with the casement catch. "Master!" He didn't look up. "Master St Vier!" she shouted into the courtyard.

The man turned his head. She couldn't hear what he said. "Wait!" she cried. She bolted down the stairs, around the corridor, around another and out the door.

"It's you!" Katherine called. "Oh my god, it's really you!" She didn't think about whether or not he wanted to be touched; she just flung herself into his arms, and smelt the woodsmoke as he folded her in his cloak.

"Are you all right?" he asked.

"Yes," she gasped. "I'm different, but I'm all right."

"Good." Carefully he unwrapped her from the embrace, and set her before him. "I can't stay," he said. "Your uncle's finally killed someone."

"Oh, no!"

"Oh, yes."

"Are you going to—"

"No. Not this time. I can't stay."

"Please," she said; "I've got things to show you, things to tell you . . . ."

"Let's go inside," he said. "I think that there are things to tell you, too."

———

IN THE HOUR BEFORE DAWN, THERE WAS A GREAT POUNDING ON the doors of Tremontaine's Riverside house. City guard, some adorned with moldy vegetables that had been flung by Riversiders who resented their incursion on their turf, escorted an officer of the Court of Honor of the Noble Council of Lords bearing a warrant heavy with seals that had taken most of the night to get fixed and approved, summoning the Duke Tremontaine before the Court.

A sleepy watchman opened the door. Like most of the household, he'd only just gotten to bed.

"What in the Seven Hells do you want?" he asked.

"By order of the—"

"Do you know what *time* it is?"

"None of your cheek," the officer barked. "Just fetch Tremontaine, and be quick about it."

He wasn't invited in, but he stepped over the threshold anyway, as did as many of his guard as would fit in the tiny old hallway. He wondered if he would find the Mad Duke wild and bloodstained, or in his cups, or draped with boys and unmentionables.

A young girl appeared on the stairs above them. She had wrapped a velvet cloak of green and gold over her nightgown, and her long brown hair was plaited for the night.

"Yes?" she said.

"Young lady, I am here for Tremontaine. If you could just—"

"I am the Duchess Tremontaine," she said. "What is it you want?"

CODA

HAVING DEFEATED HER SWORDMASTER IN A SERIOUS BOUT that morning, and being in the process of acquiring a new dress that afternoon, the young Duchess Tremontaine was in excellent spirits. She stood in a sunny room overlooking the gardens of Tremontaine House encouraging her chief secretary, a balding young man named Arthur Ghent, to read her correspondence to her. The duchess's personal aide was ensconced in the window seat going over her farm books, eating oranges and lobbing bits of orange peel at her when he thought no one was looking, as she simultaneously tried to avoid them and to hold still for the modiste who was fitting the gown, while her maid begged her not to stand there making a half-naked spectacle of herself in front of everyone.

"I'm perfectly covered up, Betty," the duchess said, trying not to tug at the bodice, which pinched. "I've got yards of sarcenet over quite a lot of petticoat and corset, and a very modest fichu—ouch!"

"A thousand pardons, my lady," the modiste said, "but your grace's waist has gotten smaller since our last fitting, and it must be taken in."

"It pinches," Katherine fretted. "And the sleeves—they're so tight, I can hardly move my arms. Can't you open up this seam here?"

"It is not the mode, madam."

"Well, *make* it the mode, why don't you? Attach some ribbons right across here—"

"Very seductive," the duchess's personal aide piped up from the window seat.

"Oh, honestly, Marcus. It's just my arm."

The modiste consulted with her assistant. "If my lady will permit us to remove the upper half of the garment, we will see what can be done."

The duchess sighed. "Close your eyes, Arthur. Betty, hand me my jacket. There, is everyone happy? Now, please! Lydia is coming to take chocolate soon, and then Lord Armand and the Godwins are joining us for dinner before we go to the concert—oh, hush, Marcus, it's very lofty and elevated music, not *tweedle tweedle*, Lydia says so— and then Mother's arriving tomorrow, but who knows when she'll really get here—oh, Betty, make sure they haven't forgotten the flowers for her room—and I promised Arthur I would get this business done before then, so now really is the only time. Go on, Arthur."

Arthur Ghent picked up a stack of colorful butterfly papers. "These are next month's invitations—but as time is short today, they can wait 'til last. Let's start with business." He unfolded a plain note from another pile. "The Duke of Hartsholt says you can have his daughter's mare at the price agreed, but only if you confirm it today."

"Tell him yes, then."

"You'll fall off," said Marcus dourly. "You'll fall and break your neck."

"I certainly won't. I grew up riding all over the countryside. This is nothing. But—it does seem a lot for a single horse. Can we honestly afford it?"

Marcus pretended to consult his calculations. "Hmm. Can we afford it? Only if you give up brandy."

"I don't drink brandy."

"Well, then. Get a horse. Get ten if you like—they don't eat much, do they?"

"Ahem," said Arthur Ghent, shuffling papers. "This should interest you. The Trevelyn divorce. Speaking of things you can afford. The lady has produced a written statement of cause for petition, and the lawyers have found an obscure law protecting it from any public scrutiny until the matter has been privately settled—that ought to give the family pause."

"Excellent. What about Perry's pension?"

Arthur extracted another letter. "Lord Lucius sends a note of thanks. He and Lady—Miss, ah, Grey are resident in Teverington. He writes that he is walking greater distances, and hopes soon to be rid of his cane."

"Oh, good! Put it on the stack for me to read later. What about my play?"

"Now as to that . . ." Arthur Ghent glanced at the door to the room. But the play, if he expected it to materialize, was not there.

"My lady?" The modiste and her assistant eased the duchess back into the top half of her new gown. Ribbons crisscrossed the seam below her upper arm. The duchess flexed her arm, trying a full extend and a riposte, while the modiste stifled a protest that gowns were not made to fight in and she truly hoped the duchess would not so tax her creation—

"This is such lovely fabric," the duchess said. "It moves very nicely, now. Do you think you could do me a pair of summer trousers in it, as well?"

"Oh. My. God." Artemisia Fitz-Levi stood in the doorway, a fat leather-bound tome in the crook of her arm. Her hair fell in perfect ringlets as always, but there was a smudge of dust on her forehead, and her apron, worn to protect a striped silk gown, was dusty, too. Nonetheless, Arthur Ghent straightened his jacket and ran his hand over what was left of his hair and bowed to her. "Katherine." She stared at the gown. "That is—that is beyond— Oh, Katherine, every girl in town is going to want those sleeves!"

The modiste permitted herself a smile of relief. In matters of fashion, Lady Artemisia was seldom mistaken.

"Do you think so?" Katherine said shyly. "I don't want to look silly."

"You won't." Her friend kissed her cheek.

"I'm doing papers with Arthur, and we're almost done." Artemisia stood back against the wall, the image of a useful person staying out of the way. "Go on, Arthur." The secretary handed the duchess two finished letters to approve, which she read standing. "Nothing from my uncle?"

"Nothing new. As far as we know, he and Master St Vier reached the sea and sailed as planned. The next letter may not reach us for some time."

"If he writes at all."

"He'll write," Marcus said. "When he runs out of money. Or books."

"Well, then. Is that it?"

"That's it for now, except for next month's invitations—"

"Invitations?" Artemisia butted in. "For next month? But my dear, no one will be in the city next month! No one who matters. Everyone goes to the country. Here, you'd better give me those." She held out her hand to Arthur Ghent, who delivered the invitations to her with a deep bow. "I'll just see if there's anything worthwhile, though I'm sure there's not." She shoved them in her apron pocket. "You won't want to stay here either, Duchess. Now, I've already gotten a list of your country houses, and I've noted the five most suitable for you to choose from. I can fetch my notes if you'd like."

"Not just yet." Katherine was still a prisoner of laces and pins. "Have you got *History of the Council, Book Four* there? I think we can get a bit more in while they finish my fitting."

Artemisia waved the book in the air, and a wad of paper fell out. "Oops! More invitations—"

But Katherine had seen the plain and heavy sheets. "It is not! It's my play, you wretch—it's the first act, isn't it? She's sent it!"

Artemisia and the secretary exchanged glances; hers was roguish, his helpless. "I was saving it," Artemisia said primly, "until we got to the end of the chapter on jurisdiction reform."

"Are you mad? My first commission? Read it. Now!"

"Yes, Your Grace." With a rustle of skirts, Artemisia seated herself in a sunny spot by the window, aware of all eyes upon her. She carefully unfolded the heavy sheets, thick with writing in a clear black hand, and began:

"*'The Swordswoman's Triumph.* By a Lady of Quality.'"

ACKNOWLEDGMENTS

IT TOOK ME QUITE A FEW YEARS TO WRITE THIS BOOK, WITH STARTS and stops along the way. Many people encouraged me, and all deserve thanks. I hope I will not leave anyone out, but lest I hope in vain: *Thank you, all. You know who you are—even if I don't.*

Careful readers Holly Black, Gavin Grant, Kelly Link, Delia Sherman and Sarah Smith (the Massachusetts All-Stars) gave me the benefit of their whip-smart brains and nuance-sensitive souls this past year. Justine Larbalestier roused Katherine from her sleep in the file drawer and listened to me read for hours as I shuffled through dog-eared manuscript pages until I fell in love again. Eve Sweetser is one of Tremontaine's very oldest friends, and proved true once more with keen insights and wise suggestions. Paula Kate Marmor made me a promise and kept it. The *Rouges' Ball* was Skye Brainard's idea. eluki bes shahar drew pictures. Debbie Notkin championed the Ugly Girl. Christopher Schelling made me do it before the smoke was cleared and Julie Fallowfield undoubtedly wants to know what took us so long? Mimi Panitch is an invaluable Serpent Chancellor and always says the right thing. Patrick J. O'Connor is generous with both love and erudition. Other wise and patient readers included Beth Bernobich, Cassandra Claire, Theodora Goss, Deborah Manning, Helen Pilinovsky, Terri Windling and of course my editor, Anne Groell.

Many people on LiveJournal generously shared their knowledge of trees and ducks and pregnancy. Joshua Kronengold and Lisa Padol did the fact-checking for an imaginary country; any slips or omissions are mine, not theirs—they did try to warn me. Nancy Hanger is one copy editor in a million. Office Archaeologist Davey Snyder dug me out large blocks of uninterrupted time.

Gavin Grant and Kelly Link gave me a country retreat to write in when I needed it most, and so did Leigh and Eleanor Hoagland.

Finally, I owe a huge debt of gratitude to British writer Mary Gentle, who introduced me to Dean Wayland, who introduced me to the true world of the sword. If not for him, I would not really understand how sharp a sword is and how dangerous; how hard it is to get one to hang properly on your hip, and how easy it is to stand perfectly still while a man with no central vision takes a swing at you with one.

This book and the author owe much of their present delightful existence to Delia Sherman, the perfect editor, lover and friend.

The Death of the Duke

T HE DUKE WAS AN OLD MAN, AND HIS YOUNG WIFE HAD never known him when his hair grew dark and heavy, and lay across the breasts of his many lovers like a mantle.

She was a foreigner, and so she did not understand, when he'd come home to his city to die, and the nursing of him through his final illness began to tax her strength, why his relations were so concerned to help her in the choosing of a manservant to attend him.

"Let him be pretty," said gentle Anne with a blush.

"But not *too* pretty." Sharp Katherine flashed her a look.

"By all means," the young wife said, "why not let him be as pretty as may be, if it will please my husband, so long as he is strong and careful?"

And since neither one would answer her, nor even look at her nor at each other, she chose a lovely young man whose name was Anselm. She did not know how badly he had wanted the job.

A NSELM HAD A STEADY HAND AND CLEAR EYES. HE COULD FOLD linen and pour medicine, slip a shirt on and off with a minimum of fuss, and wield a razor quickly and efficiently. The Duke insisted on being presentable at all times, although he was no longer able to go anywhere. In his youth, the Duke's cuffs had foamed with lace, breaking like waves over the backs of his hands. His hands had been thin then, but they were thinner now.

Now the old Duke lay in the bed he had not lain in for twenty years, in the house he had built, furnished and decorated, and then abandoned. In a time when today's young lovers were not yet born, the Duke had left his city and his rights and his duties to follow his lover, the first and oldest and best, to a far island where they might live at last for love, although the word was never spoken.

Sitting by him on the bed, his young wife said to the Duke, "There was an old woman outside, waiting for me in the doorway of your house. She took me by the wrist; quite strong, her fingers. 'Is he in there?' she asked me. 'Is he? They say he's come back home. They say that he is in there dying.' "

The Duke's smile had always been thin as a whip. "I hope you told her they were right."

His wife pressed his hand. She loved him helplessly and entirely. She was to be the last of his loves. Knowing it comforted her only a little; sometimes, not at all.

"Go and dress," he told her. "It will take you longer than you think to dress for the sort of party you are going to tonight."

She hated to leave him. "My maid can lace me up in no time."

"There's still your hair, and the jewels and the shoes. . . . You'll be surprised."

"I want to stay with you." She snuggled into the bony hollow of his shoulder. "Suppose you're hungry, or the pain starts up again?"

"Anselm will bring me what I need." The Duke twined his fingers in her hair, stroking her scalp. "Besides, I want to see if they fitted it properly."

"I don't care. I'm sure it's a beautiful gown; you chose it."

The stroking stilled. "You *must* care. They must learn to know you, and to respect you."

She said, "At home, no one could respect a wife who left her husband to go to a party when he was—when he was ill."

"Well, things are different here. I told you they would be."

It was true. But she would come with him. Five years ago, she had married a stranger, a man wandering her island half-crazed with the loss of his lover, the oldest and the best. In her village, she was past the age of being wed. But it was only that she had been waiting for him: a man who saw her when he looked at her. He surprised her with her own desires, and how they could be satisfied.

That he had once been a duke in a foreign country was a surprise he'd saved for the end. The rings on his hands, which he'd never removed, not even in his grief, he wanted to return to his family himself. She had begged to come with him on this final journey, although they both knew that it would end with him leaving her there alone. She wanted to see his people, to visit the places he had known; to hear him remember them there. She wanted his child to be born in the house of his fathers.

THE LAST JEWEL WAS SET IN PLACE ON HIS WIFE'S GOWN, THE last curl pinned, the last flower arranged to suit the Duke's discerning eye. Exotic and stylish, livid and bright, the Duke's foreign wife went off in the carriage in a clatter of hooves and outriders, a blazon of flambeaux.

Candles were lit by the Duke's bed. Anselm sat quietly in a shadowed corner of the room.

"My wife," the Duke said, his eyes shut, white face against white pillow, "was the daughter of a great physician. He taught her all he knew, passed on to her his philtres and potions. She was justly proud, and healed a king with them. She loved a boy, a nobleman, but he was haughty, and did not return her love, nor could she make him. There are no philtres for that, whatever anyone may tell you." His own laugh made him catch his breath in pain. "Nor for this. It vexes her. And me."

Anselm said, "I wish it could be otherwise."

The Duke said dryly, "You're very kind. So do I. I suppose, being old, I should be graceful about it, and pretend not to mind much. But I have never lived to gratify others."

"No," said the lovely servant, whose loveliness went unnoticed. The Duke's eyelids were thin, almost blue, stretched over his eyes. His mouth was stiff with pain. "You caused some trouble in your time."

The taut face softened for a moment. "I did."

Anselm approached him with a drink poured into a silver cup. The cup was engraved with the Duke's family crest, a swan. There was no telling how old it was.

The Duke was tall, long-boned. There was not much flesh left on him and his skin was dry and parchment-thin. Anselm held him while he took the drink. It was like holding the mirror of a shadow: light instead of dark, edged instead of flat.

"Thank you," said the Duke. "That ought to help, for a while. I will sleep, I think. When she comes home, I want to hear what happened at the party. Something is bound to have, her first time out."

"You want to cause some trouble now, do you?" his servant gently teased.

The thin lips smiled. "Maybe." Then, "No. Not now. What would be the use?"

"What was the use then?"

"I wanted . . . to be amused."

Closer now, the planes of his own face gilded by candlelight, Anselm said, "Men died for you."

"Not for me. For him."

"He killed them for you."

"Yesss . . ." a long breath of satisfaction.

Anselm leaned closer. "And you remember. I know you do. You were there. You saw it all. How they were good, but he was the best." His strong hand was dark against the linen sheet. "There is no swordsman like him now."

"But there never was." The Duke's voice was stretched so thin that Anselm, bending close, must hold his breath to hear. "There never was anyone like him."

"And will not be again, I think." Anselm said as softly, and as much to himself.

"Never."

The Duke lay back, his color gone, and the pillow engulfed him, welcoming him back to his new world, the world of brief strengths and long weaknesses.

STILL GLITTERING WITH FINERY, AND THE KISS OF WINE AND rich company, the Duke's wife returned to him, to find out whether he slept, or whether he waited for her in the darkness.

From the huge bed his thin, dry voice said, "You smell of revelry."

She struck a light, revealing herself in splendor. The flowers were only a little withered at her breast. Despite the scratch of lace and the weight of gold, she settled herself beside him on the bed. "Ah! That's good, now I no longer need to be held up." She sighed as he slowly unlaced her stays. "I pretended—" She stopped, then went on, shyly, determined not to be afraid of him, "I told myself they are your hands, keeping my back straight before them all."

He chuckled. "And were people so hard on you?"

"They *stare* so! It is not polite. And they say things I do not understand. About each other, about you . . ."

"What about me?"

"I don't know. I don't understand it. Empty, pointless things that are supposed to mean more than they say. How you must find the city changed, and old friends gone."

"All true. I hope you were not too bored."

She pinched his shoulder. "Now you sound like them! No, I was not bored. I even got a compliment. An old man with diamonds and bad teeth said I was a great improvement on your first wife. He had very poor color—liver, I should think," she added hurriedly, having spoken of something she had intended not to.

"Yes," her husband said, impervious. "They can forgive me a foreigner better than they can an actress. Or maybe I finally merit pity, not censure, because I am sicker than any of them would like to be. Maybe that's all it is." His ruminations gave way to a story, more disjointed than he intended, a tale of past insult, of revenge. A lover spurned, the Duke's first wife publicly hissed; a young man's anger and the answer of money and steel. Blood and no healing, only scars closing over a dirty wound.

These were not stories that she had heard before, on the sunny island where they had been wed among the bees' hum and the thyme. They did not even describe a man she knew.

Lying undressed in the dark, next to his thin and burning body, she wondered for the first time if they had been right to come here to this place of his past.

His hand moved, half-aware, to her shoulder blade, cupping it like a breast. Her whole body flushed with memory. She desired him suddenly, wanted her strong lover back. But she knew the disease, she knew its course, and clenched her heart around the knowledge that that would not happen. All that had passed between their bodies was done, now, and was growing in her belly. In the future it would comfort her, but not now.

"People do not forget," he said. She'd thought he was asleep, his breathing was so quiet.

"You," she said tenderly. "They do not forget you."

"Not me. Themselves. I was important only for what I made them feel. Remember that." His fingers tightened on her, urgent and unalluring. "And do not trust anyone from my past. They have no cause to love me."

"I love you."

A little later, he sighed in his sleep, and spoke the name of his first wife, while he held her. She felt her heart twist and turn over, close to the child she carried, so that there was room for little inside her but pain and love.

· · ·

PHYSICIANS HOPING TO MAKE THEIR FAME AND FORTUNES CAME to bleed him.

"There isn't enough left of me as is," said the Duke. He sent his wife down to chase them all away, knowing it would give her satisfaction to have someone else to be angry with.

Anselm was shaving him, gently and carefully. "In the old days," Anselm said, "you would have had them skewered."

The Duke did not even smile. "No. He did not kill unarmed men. There was no challenge in it."

"How did you find challenges for him? Did you have a good eye?"

Now the old lips quirked. "You know—I must have. I never thought of it. But there was a certain kind of bully I delighted in provoking: the swaggering cocksure idiot who pushed everyone out of the way, and beat up on the girl who worked to keep him in funds. That sort generally carried a sword."

"And would you know now?" Anselm busied himself with cleaning the brushes. "Would you know a decent swordsman if you saw one— by the swagger, say, or by the stance?"

"Only," said the Duke, "if he was being particularly annoying. May I see that?"

When Anselm offered the brush for inspection, close, so the weak eyes could focus on it, the Duke closed his fingers around the young man's wrist. His touch was paper-dry. Anselm kept his arm steady, although his eyelids trembled, a fringe of dark lashes surrounding blue eyes so dark as to be almost violet.

"You have a good wrist," the Duke observed. "When do you practice?"

"In my room." Anselm swallowed. His skin was burning where the bony fingers barely touched it.

"Have you killed anyone?"

"No—not yet."

"They don't kill much, nowadays, I hear. Demonstration bouts, a little blood on the sleeve."

The Duke's wife came in at the door without knocking, full of her achievement. But the Duke held his servant's wrist for one moment more, and looked at his face, and saw that he was beautiful.

VISITORS SOMETIMES WERE ALLOWED, ALTHOUGH NOT THE ONES who promised a miracle cure. The pain came and went; the Duke took to asking his wife two and three times a day whether there was enough poppy juice in the house laid by. The medicine made his mind wander, so that he talked with ghosts, and she learned more of his past than sometimes she wanted to hear. When visitors came, people who were still alive, she often sat quietly in a corner of the room, willing herself invisible, to learn more. Other old men, more robust than her husband, she still found not half as beautiful. She wondered how he ever could have touched them, and tried to imagine them young and blooming.

Lord Sansome came to gloat, her husband said, or maybe to apologize; either way, it would be amusing to see what time had done with him. She thought admitting such a man unwise, but he made a nice change from the ghosts.

Sansome had bad teeth and a poor color, but he took the glass of wine that Anselm offered. The nobleman approved the young servant up and down. He settled by the bed with his gold-headed stick upright between his knees.

The Duke watched his visitor through half-lidded eyes; he was tired, but wanted no drugs until he'd gone.

Sansome uttered no commonplaces, nor was he offered any. And so there was silence until the Duke said, "Whatever you are thinking is probably true. Thank you for coming. It is prodigious kind."

His foreign wife didn't know what *prodigious* meant. It sounded like an insult; she readied herself for action. But Lord Sansome continued to sit.

The Duke closed his eyes but kept on talking: "I do not think that I am going to die while you sit there. Though I know it would please you greatly."

Across the room, Anselm made a noise that in a less well-bred servant would have been a snort. He busied himself with the brushes, so that all they could hear was their *hush-hush-hush* as he cleaned.

At last, Sansome spoke. "I thought you gone years ago. No one knew where you were. I thought you'd died of a broken heart."

"It mended."

"You told me you didn't have one."

"Wishful thinking. I see that yours beats on."

"Oh, yes." Sansome's thick-veined hands opened and closed on the gold ball of his stick. "Mine does. Though we never know what's around the corner, do we?"

"I believe I do."

"Perhaps something may yet surprise you." Unexpectedly, Lord Sansome smiled warmly at the Duke's manservant. Anselm looked annoyed.

"He's good with a blade," Sansome observed.

"You've had the pleasure?"

"Once or twice. A nice, close shave."

"Oh." The old Duke laughed, and kept on laughing at a joke no one else could see, until his breath drew in pain, and wife and servant shut him off from view while they held and gave him drink to ease him.

When Lord Sansome was gone, "People do not forget," the Duke said dreamily. "I think this pleases me. Or why would I have come back?"

M Y REFERENCES CAME FROM SOMEWHERE." ANSELM WAS CURT with the Duke, who had been goading him with revelations. They were alone together. "I never would have gotten in to you without them. Your family checked; and I do know how to valet. Now tell me again. Tell me about how he held his hands."

"They were never empty. He was always doing something: gripping bars to strengthen his wrists, squeezing balls, tossing a knife . . . and other things." The Duke smiled most annoyingly to himself. Anselm was coming to know that smile, and knew that there was no coaxing out of the Duke whatever memories it hid.

The old man's face clouded, and he began to swear, inelegantly, with pain. Anselm wiped his sweating face with a cold cloth, and kept on this way until the Duke could speak again: "As an adventure, this is beginning to pall. Life grows dull when all I have to wonder about is how long my shirt will stay dry, and whether I am going to swallow soup or vomit it up. I would say, Let's have it over and done with, but my wife will not like that. Of course," he bared his teeth in a painful grin, "she doesn't like me in this condition, either. There really is no pleasing some people."

"You must take comfort in the child that is to come."

"Not really. That was only to please my wife. I do not want posterity. I was a great disappointment to my parents."

Anselm shrugged. "Aren't we all?"

"But when I am dead, it will keep her from doing something stupid. That is important."

Anselm was good at catching hints. "Shall I fetch your lady?"

"No." The Duke's hand was cold on his. "Let us talk."

"I'm not like you," Anselm said hopelessly. "Words are not my tools. All I can do is ask questions. You are the one who knows things, sir, not I. What I want to know, even you cannot show me."

"Annoying for you," the sick man said; "since sometimes I do see him, yet—in the corners of the room. But it's only the drugs, since he never answers when I speak."

"He was the greatest swordsman who ever lived. If taking drugs would let me see him, I'd do it." Anselm paced the room, his measured valet's demeanor given way to an athlete's ardent stride. "I wonder, sometimes, if there is any point even in trying. He took his secrets with him. If only I could have watched how he did what he did!" The sick man made no reply. "You were there. You saw. What did you see? Can't you tell me? What did you see?"

The Duke slowly smiled, his vision turned inward. "It was beautiful; not like this. He killed them quickly, with one blow, straight to the heart."

"How?" Anselm demanded, fists clenched. "No one offers his heart to the sword."

With every one of his fighter's senses, he felt the Duke's regard full upon him, unclouded by dream or pain. It drew him back to the bed, as though to close with an opponent, or a partner.

"No one?" the Duke whispered. Anselm knelt to hear him. "Not no one, boy."

The Duke's hand drifted down into his dark and springy hair.

Anselm said, "You are a terrible man." He seized the fingers, tangled in his hair with his own, and pulled them through his curls down to his mouth.

L YING BY HIM IN THE DARK, THE DUKE'S WIFE SAID, "I HAVE SEEN so many women through childbirth, I should be more afraid. But I am not. I know this will be a good child. I hope that you will see him."

His hand was on her gently rounded belly. "I hope he will not be too unhappy."

"As you were?" she answered sadly. "No, my darling. This one will know that he is loved, I promise you!" She gripped his fragile hand; fading, like the rest of him, even in the dark. "And he will know all about his father, that I promise, too."

"No," the man said; "not if it makes him unhappy."

"He will be happy."

"You promise that, do you?" She heard his smile. "Will you take him back to the island, then, to run with the goats?"

"Certainly not!" Sometimes the things he assumed amazed her. "He will stay here, with his family. He must be raised in your city, among people who know you."

"I think he would be more happy on the island." The Duke sighed.

"I wish I could go back there, after, and rest on a hill above the sea. But I suppose it is impossible."

In a small voice she said, "I suppose it is. Where will you go, then?"

"I shall lie in the Stone City: ranks and ranks of tombs like houses, with all my ancestors, my family—that should please your sense of decorum. They are not the company I would have chosen, but I suppose I will not care then."

"I will bring him there. To visit you."

He pulled his hand away. "By no means. I forbid it."

"But I want him to know you."

"If you insist on telling the child stories about me, do it somewhere nice, with a fire, and bread and milk. . . ." She had given him poppy syrup; soon he would sleep. "I hope he will be beautiful. Not like me. Beautiful as you are. As *he* was."

Some of the time, he spoke of people she did not know. But she knew this one well, this loved ghost from his past, the beautiful, the rare, first love and best. She willed her breath to evenness, her arms to softness. A memory, nothing, against a living child.

"I wanted him to kill me. Years ago. But he never got round to it."

"Hush, love, hush."

"No, but he promised! And so I hold him to it. In the end he failed me, he left me. But he will come for me. Long ago he promised to come for me. He is my death."

She held him tightly to her, hoping he was too far gone to notice her sobbing breath, and the tears that fell on both their skins.

L ORD SANSOME DID NOT COME AGAIN, THOUGH HE SENT THE Duke's bodyservant, Anselm, a gift of money.

"What will you spend it on?" the Duke inquired; "swords or sweethearts?"

His servant frowned. "I feel I should return it. It isn't right for me to take what I do not intend to earn."

"Oh, re-eally?" Weariness drew out the old man's drawl. "But surely my old friend can be nothing but pleased that you care for me so thoroughly? It is his right to tip you if he wishes."

Anselm drew back. "Do you want to be shaved or don't you?"

"Is anyone expected?"

"No one but Her Ladyship, and that not until noon."

"She will not mind. The way I look, I mean. Put that thing down, Anselm. It is the wrong blade for you. Lord Sansome doesn't know it, but I do. I do."

• • •

THE HOURS WHEN HE KNEW HER GREW FARTHER APART. AT last, she was uncovering every thing that he had kept from her—promises to his first wife, quarrels with his lovers, games with his sister—she heard a young man's voice, disputing with a tutor, and murmuring provocation so sweet it could only be to his old lover, the first and best. Did she give him more poppy than she should, to keep the voices coming, and to shield him from the pain? She tried, but in the end she had to fail, as even love could not appease the author of the play that he was in. He did not eat, he barely spoke. The old tart who had known him young came back to the door. His lady would not let her in to see him now, but, seeking her own comfort, went down to sit a moment with this relic of his past.

In the shadowed room, the Duke's patient servant waited.

The old Duke opened his eyes wide and looked at him.

"Oh," he said. "I didn't think it would be now."

"When else?" said the swordsman. "I promised, didn't I?"

"You did. I thought you had forgotten."

"No. Not this."

"I always wanted you to."

"Of course you did. But that wasn't the time."

"How bright it is! Do it quickly. I'm afraid of pain."

The other end of the bright blade laughed. "You can't breathe properly. You can't even feel your feet. This will be quick. Open your arms, now."

"Oh," said the old Duke again; "I knew you'd come."

ABOUT THE AUTHOR

Ellen Kushner is a novelist, performer, and public radio personality. Her work includes the weekly national public radio series *PRI's Sound & Spirit with Ellen Kushner*, the recording *The Golden Dreydl: a Klezmer 'Nutcracker' for Chanukah* (Rykodisc CD) and a live performance piece, *Esther: the Feast of Masks*. Her novels *Swordspoint* and (with Delia Sherman) *The Fall of the Kings* share a setting and quite a few characters with *The Privilege of the Sword*. She is a member of Terri Windling's Endicott Studio for Mythic Arts and co-founder of the Interstitial Arts Foundation. She lives in New York City and travels a lot, giving shows and readings, lecturing, and teaching. You can keep up with her whereabouts and learn more about Riverside and its denizens at *www.EllenKushner.com*.